LOST LOVE
FOUND

LOST LOVE FOUND

Bertrice Small

BALLANTINE BOOKS • NEW YORK

Library of Congress Catalog Card Number: 88-61352

ISBN: 0-345-35275-0

Text design by Debby Jay
Cover design by Richard Aquan
Cover painting by Robert McGinnis

Manufactured in the United States of America

First Edition: February 1989

10   9   8   7   6   5   4   3   2   1

To Louisa Rudeen with love—
from the lady who knew her when . . .

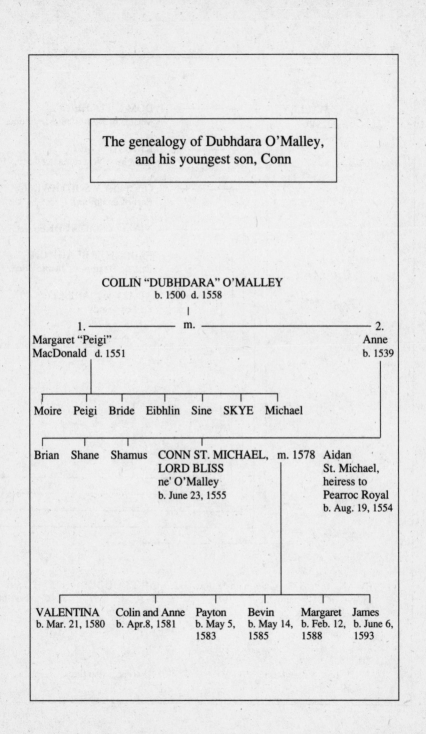

The genealogy of Dubhdara O'Malley,
and his youngest son, Conn

COILIN "DUBHDARA" O'MALLEY
b. 1500 d. 1558

1. ———————— m. ———————————— 2.

Margaret "Peigi"   Anne
MacDonald   d. 1551   b. 1539

Moire   Peigi   Bride   Eibhlin   Sine   SKYE   Michael

Brian   Shane   Shamus   CONN ST. MICHAEL,   m. 1578   Aidan
                         LORD BLISS   St. Michael,
                         ne' O'Malley   heiress to
                         b. June 23, 1555   Pearroc Royal
                                                       b. Aug. 19, 1554

VALENTINA   Colin and Anne   Payton   Bevin   Margaret   James
b. Mar. 21, 1580 b. Apr.8, 1581   b. May 5,   b. May 14,   b. Feb. 12, b. June 6,
                                    1583   1585   1588   1593

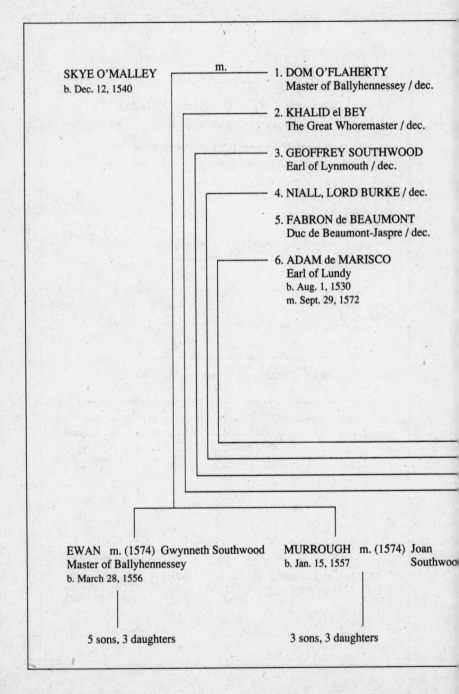

SKYE O'MALLEY
b. Dec. 12, 1540

m.

1. DOM O'FLAHERTY
Master of Ballyhennessey / dec.

2. KHALID el BEY
The Great Whoremaster / dec.

3. GEOFFREY SOUTHWOOD
Earl of Lynmouth / dec.

4. NIALL, LORD BURKE / dec.

5. FABRON de BEAUMONT
Duc de Beaumont-Jaspre / dec.

6. ADAM de MARISCO
Earl of Lundy
b. Aug. 1, 1530
m. Sept. 29, 1572

EWAN   m. (1574) Gwynneth Southwood
Master of Ballyhennessey
b. March 28, 1556

MURROUGH   m. (1574) Joan
b. Jan. 15, 1557   Southwoo

5 sons, 3 daughters

3 sons, 3 daughters

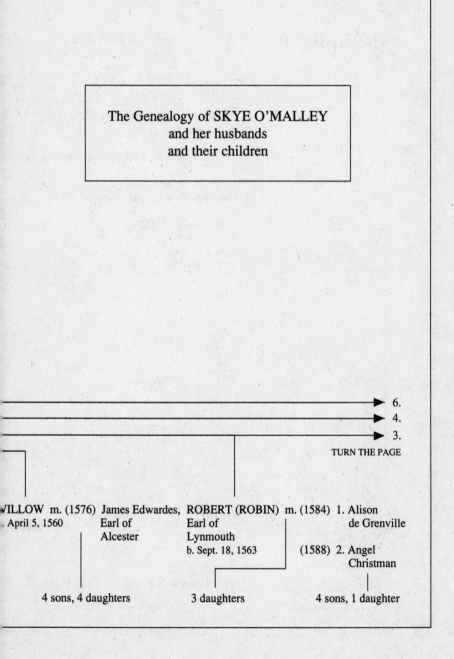

The Genealogy of SKYE O'MALLEY
and her husbands
and their children

6.

4.

3.

TURN THE PAGE

WILLOW m. (1576) James Edwardes,
, April 5, 1560　　Earl of
　　　　　　　　Alcester

ROBERT (ROBIN) m. (1584) 1. Alison
Earl of　　　　　　　　　de Grenville
Lynmouth
b. Sept. 18, 1563　　(1588) 2. Angel
　　　　　　　　　　　　Christman

4 sons, 4 daughters　　3 daughters　　4 sons, 1 daughter

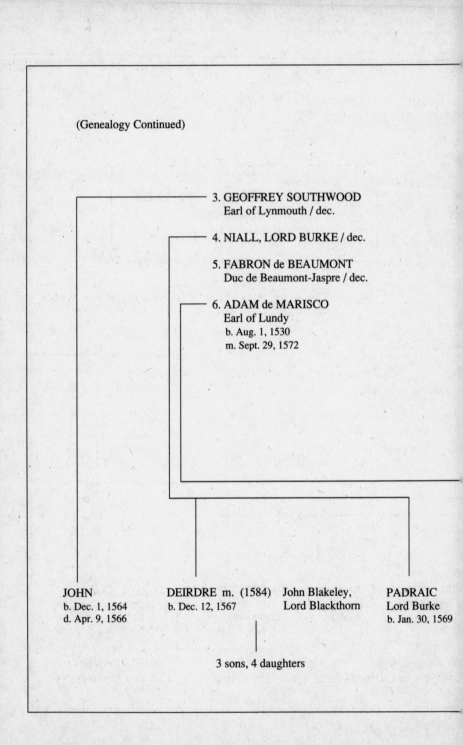

(Genealogy Continued)

3. GEOFFREY SOUTHWOOD
Earl of Lynmouth / dec.

4. NIALL, LORD BURKE / dec.

5. FABRON de BEAUMONT
Duc de Beaumont-Jaspre / dec.

6. ADAM de MARISCO
Earl of Lundy
b. Aug. 1, 1530
m. Sept. 29, 1572

JOHN
b. Dec. 1, 1564
d. Apr. 9, 1566

DEIRDRE m. (1584)   John Blakeley,
b. Dec. 12, 1567   Lord Blackthorn

PADRAIC
Lord Burke
b. Jan. 30, 1569

3 sons, 4 daughters

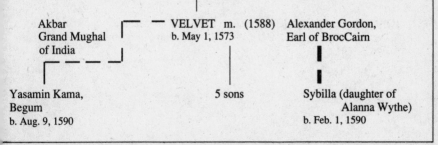

— — — — Velvet's daughter through her Indian
marriage to Akbar

▬ ▬ ▬ ▬ ▬ Alex's daughter by his mistress, Alanna Wythe

Akbar
Grand Mughal
of India

VELVET m. (1588)
b. May 1, 1573

Alexander Gordon,
Earl of BrocCairn

Yasamin Kama,
Begum
b. Aug. 9, 1590

5 sons

Sybilla (daughter of
Alanna Wythe)
b. Feb. 1, 1590

LOST LOVE
FOUND

PROLOGUE

Hill Court

JULY 1, 1600

VALENTINA, LADY BARROWS, KNELT IN PRAYER beside her bridegroom's bier. For all her youth and inexperience in such serious matters, Valentina knew her duty. If in her short tenure as the lady of Hill Court she had not yet had the time to earn her servants' respect, she did so now with this stark act of wifely obligation. She was garbed entirely in black silk, a starched white ruff at her neck the only relief, and she held herself unnaturally still, hardly breathing. Her lustrous dark brown hair with lovely copper highlights was tucked modestly beneath a simple, sheer lawn cap. Her earlobes were bare, for she wore no jewelry except her heavy gold wedding band.

Not once during the long hours of the night did Lady Barrows leave her post, keeping her vigil by her husband's cold body until the first golden rays of dawn began to mark the sky beyond the stained glass chapel windows. In the kitchen the servants of Hill Court mourned far more than their master's death, for the laundress had firmly assured them that Lady Barrows's monthly flow was upon her that very day. There would be no heir from the tragically brief marriage of their late lord and his beautiful bride.

The sound of birdsong caused Valentina to pause in her prayers. The silver and ebony crucifix dangling from her slim white hand by its onyx beads slipped from her fingers to the floor. As she reached down to pick it up, Valentina found her mind traveling back to the morning before this one, when she had stared down in surprise and stark horror at the broken body of her husband. Ned lay so still, so very pale, upon the roughened plank. He had never seemed so quiet. Not even in sleep.

"Wh-what has happened?" she managed to gasp, attempting to focus on the groom who had ridden with Lord Barrows, or on the men who had carried his body home, anywhere but on that poor broken body.

The men all shuffled their feet nervously, looking stricken, leaving Derwin to explain. This was a fine piece of business he found himself in the midst of, thought the groom. But then, he had never had much luck. He had been hired only this past spring to replace the elderly groom who had always ridden with his lordship, the man who had taught Lord Barrows to ride as a child and had been with him his entire life. Now, thought the hapless groom, he would have to find himself another position, and without a reference, 'twas likely.

"*Please.*"

The groom's head snapped up at the tragic note in her ladyship's voice, and he began his explanation. " 'Twere that big briar-rose hedge that divides the pastures, m'lady," he said. Deep in his soul he felt that it was he who had failed, had somehow caused this terrible accident. "His lordship were riding that new stallion he got from yer cousin, Lord Southwood, as a wedding gift." He took a deep breath and continued. "The beast stopped sudden-like, just short of the hedge his lordship wanted him to take. The master were real patient with him, m'lady. Turned him around, he did, talking all gentle and encouraging-like. Took the animal back a-ways and approached the hedge again, he did. The horse hesitated a second, m'lady, but then it took the jump." The groom shook his head. "Off balance he was. Lost his footing coming down on t'other side. Threw his lordship, and then fell on top of him he did.

"They was both caught inside the hedge. Horse broke two of its legs. Had to destroy him, we did, m'lady. Terrible waste it 'twas. His lordship, well, his neck and back was broken in the fall. Dead as a mackerel, he was, when we finally got the big beast off him. Yer pardon, m'lady," he amended as Valentina grew even paler. "The men straightened him out for ye though, m'lady, so he wouldn't look so funny when ye saw him."

The groom was miserable. In his whole life he had never said so much at one time. His throat was extremely dry, and he wished he could go to the kitchen for some cold cider. Nervously he tugged at his ear, and his feet moved restlessly upon the polished wide floorboards of the house's main entrance hall.

Valentina went numb, but her mind still managed to function despite her shock. She was, she considered a bit ruefully, her mother's daughter after all. She had her duty to perform, and she would not fail in it.

"A bier must be set up," she told the men in what she hoped was a calm, authoritative tone. She had never been so closely associated with death before. "Take his lordship's body into the Great Hall," she said, "then wait while I consult with the priest."

The estate laborers, still silent, lifted the plank once again and carried it into the Great Hall.

"I'll run and fetch the priest for ye, m'lady," said the guilt-stricken groom eagerly, anxious to be off. Valentina's calm demeanor made him very nervous. It seemed to him that a woman faced with her husband's dead body ought to be crying and carrying on something fierce. Not be calm and cool like this one was. Enough to give a man the willies. Maybe the news had made her go mad, the groom considered with a superstitious shiver.

Valentina fixed him with a glassy gaze and nodded absently. "Aye," she said. "Go and find Father Peter." She stood perfectly still as the man ran off. I must sort this all out, she thought. But, dear heaven, it all seemed so unreal.

She had not seen Ned since the evening before, when he had come to her bedchamber to make love to her. She had married Edward Barrows just three and a half weeks ago, on the sixth of June. Now, on this first day of July, she suddenly found herself his widow. Poor Mama, who had despaired of ever seeing her wed, would be so very disappointed. Her parents! She must send a messenger to her parents!

The messenger would be but a courtesy, of course, for Edward would have to be buried before her family in Worcestershire had time to get there. It was at least a day and a half's ride to Pearroc Royal, and an equal time to return. As they were having an unusually warm summer, Valentina knew she would not be able to wait for her family to arrive before she buried Ned. In this heat the body would quickly begin to stink.

Tears welled up suddenly and without warning, filling her lovely amethyst-colored eyes to overflowing. She brushed them away impatiently. Poor Ned! He had been a good man. It was not fair that he should lie dead in his own Great Hall on such a beautiful summer morning.

"Mistress Valentina?"

Lady Barrows turned. It was Nan, dear Nan, who had once been her wet nurse and was now her tiring woman. Nan had lost her own husband but six months back, and thus had been free to leave Pearroc Royal with her young mistress when she married Lord Barrows.

"Is it all over the house then?" Valentina asked, suddenly weary.

"Aye." Nan put a strong arm around her mistress. "Come and sit down now, my lamb. 'Tis a great shock this, and no mistaking it, but we'll get through it, you and me." She led Valentina into the small salon that Lord Barrows had had decorated especially for his new bride. It was a cheerful little room with a fireplace and a lovely window seat. On the seat was a brightly woven cushion that Valentina sank into gratefully as Nan fussed. "Now you sit right down here, my lamb." Then the tiring woman hurried to pour a goblet of wine, which she handed to her mistress. "Drink some of this, m'lady. 'Twill ease you."

Valentina gulped the wine down in a single swallow, not even tasting it. Then she said in a sad and hollow voice, "I did not love him, you know."

"Aye, I know" was the quiet reply. Of course she had not loved him, thought Nan. I could see that all along. Why couldn't the rest of them see it? Not that his lordship wasn't the kindest and best of gentlemen, for he was, God assoil his poor soul, but the plain truth of the matter was that Mistress Valentina had not loved him.

Valentina sighed forlornly. "Perhaps I might have learned to love him, Nan. I could have loved him if only we'd had the time."

"Aye, sweeting," Nan said, comforting her. " 'Tis certain that in time you would have come to love him, m'lady. I know it. You've always had a good heart. Better than most." Too good a heart, the loyal servant thought silently, yet Mistress Valentina could be strong-willed, too, when she chose to be.

There came a polite rapping on the salon door. Opening it, Nan found herself facing the head footman, who bowed politely and said, "Will her ladyship be requiring a groom to send any messages today?"

"Of course she will," Nan snapped, taking charge momentarily. "Have the fastest horse in the stables saddled and ready to go, and pick someone with a brain for the messenger. Not one of yer lackwits, all puzzled eyes and slack-mouthed, not knowing east from west. Her ladyship will expect the groom in ten minutes." She closed the door firmly on the head footman, who, with the faintest lift of an eyebrow, hurried away.

Nan brought a small lap desk from a nearby table and set it on Valentina's lap. "There's a quill freshly sharpened," she said. "You had better hurry, for the messenger will be here in a moment, m'lady. Best to be brief."

Valentina nodded numbly, blinking back tears, but the message was ready when the groom arrived.

Nan handed the rolled and sealed parchment to the man and escorted him from the room, saying sharply, "Ride like the devil hisself was after you, and put this message into the hands of Lord Bliss himself. *No one else.* Not even Beal, the majordomo, who was me late husband's dad. Only Lord Bliss, do you understand?"

The groom gave her a cheeky grin. "And if I does you a favor, my pretty Nan, will you come up into the hayloft with me when I gets back?"

"Ain't you no respect?" Nan said huffily. "There's a dead man in the Great Hall, and I'm a respectable widow, I am!"

"Well, the dead man ain't me, my pretty." The groom chuckled.

She swatted at him half-heartedly. "My late husband was a head gamekeeper, I'll have you know! Not some lowlife from the stables."

"I'm the assistant head groom, and me name is Alan. A man needs a good woman to help get him up the ladder of life," the groom replied.

"Get you gone to Pearroc Royal," said Nan, "and when you come back, me boy-o, we'll see. I'm not a woman to go into the hayloft with just anyone, you know."

"I can see that, my pretty." The groom grinned, and giving Nan's ample bottom a quick pat, he hurried off, as Father Peter came slowly shuffling into the hall.

Nan tucked a stray lock beneath her cap and curtsied to the cleric. She hoped the priest hadn't overheard her conversation with Alan. He was a bold devil, that one, but his very look had set her heart to racing as no one had since Harry had died. "Her ladyship's waiting for ye, sir," she said primly to the religious, and ushered him into the little salon.

The ancient priest had spent most of his life here at Hill Court. He had baptized Edward Barrows as an infant. He had buried Lord Barrows's parents and his first wife. He had baptized and buried all of the weak babies that poor Mary Barrows had borne Edward.

Father Peter shook his head sadly. He had had such hopes of his master's second wife, who came from a large and healthy family. He had certainly never thought to bury Lord Barrows, and less than a month after his marriage.

"Dear madam," he said to Valentina. "What comfort can I possibly offer you at such a tragic time?"

Hearing the quaver in his old voice, Valentina managed to pull herself together. "Tell me who I am to notify and who my husband's heir is. Being but newly wed to Ned, I do not yet know his distant relations."

"There is no one, my lady. With Edward's death the Barrows family is now extinct unless you can tell me that you carry your husband's child. If you do not, then you are your husband's heiress, my lady," the priest told the surprised Valentina.

"*No one?*" Valentina was astounded. "Surely there must be someone, Father Peter. Alas, I am not with child, of that I am certain. My lord and I were not wed long."

Father Peter shook his white head. "My lady, there is no one then. Old Lord Henry Barrows and his lady had three surviving children, Lord Edward, Master William, and Mistress Catherine. Master William was killed young in a war, though I cannot recall which one it was. He never wed. Mistress Catherine died in childbirth at the age of sixteen, and her babe with her. Lord Edward's first wife and all of her babes are long gone. There is no one but yourself."

"Perhaps some cousins?" Valentina pressed the priest.

He shook his head again. "Lord Edward had one cousin, the lady Mary. He wed with her when they were sixteen. She was the only child of his father's only sister. There is truly no one. No one at all, m'lady."

Valentina sighed deeply. She did not know which was worse, that Edward had no living relatives to carry on his name or that the only one left to mourn him was the bride who had not loved him. "What shall I do then, Father Peter?" she asked the kindly cleric. "I have never had the responsibility of a death before."

The elderly man took her pretty, soft hand in his old, gnarled one. "You must have the old women come from the village to prepare his lordship for burial. He should lie in state in the Great Hall tonight and tomorrow morning. 'Tis long enough for his few neighbors and his tenants to pay their respects. The mass and the interment in the family vault will take place tomorrow afternoon."

"So quickly, Father Peter?" Valentina looked genuinely distressed.

"Time enough, my lady, for there are few to attend the rites. Besides, the weather will not allow us otherwise, I fear."

Valentina sighed. "You are right," she agreed, feeling even worse. *Poor, poor Ned!* It seemed such an ignoble end for such a good man. She gave herself a little shake. She must not allow herself to give in to a fit of melancholy. She owed her husband the courtesy of seeing that he was buried with whatever ceremony she could arrange.

"Will you ask the appropriate women to come and tend to my lord, Father Peter? I will go now to choose the clothing that he should wear."

The priest patted her hand and, giving her his blessing, hurried off. For a long moment she stood where he had left her. Then, wondering how her mother would behave in this situation, Valentina hastened to her husband's apartment to choose the garments in which he would be buried.

The old women came from the nearby village, keening their grief. Tenderly they prepared Lord Barrows's body for its final journey, weeping copiously over their task. They all claimed to remember in detail the very day Edward Barrows was born, forty-one years ago. They recounted with relish their first sight of him just shortly after his birth, when his father had proudly presented him for all to see. They remembered his days as a mischievous toddler, as a boy who galloped his pony with joyous abandon, as the gangling young bridegroom of his pretty cousin, Mary. There was not one of the women who had not grieved with the Barrowses, beset by so many deaths over the years.

How they had rejoiced in June when Lord Barrows brought home his beautiful new bride. Consequently, when Valentina appeared, carrying her husband's finest garments, the old goodwives went into even greater paroxysms of grief. They realized that, without heirs other than the lovely widow, their own futures were in serious doubt. What would happen to the estate? Who would care for them if they had no master? Without a Barrows who would care for their children and their many grandchildren? There had been Barrowses on this estate for as long as memory served, and the women remembered tales told to them by their grandparents of a king named Richard against whom another Lord Barrows had fought. Life without a Barrows was inconceivable.

When at last Lord Barrows's body had been washed and dressed, he was set gently upon his bier, his limbs straight, his arms crossed over each other upon his chest. On each side of the bier, tall beeswax candles set in carved and footed silver holders burned. By the side of the bier was a blackened oak prie-dieu with a well-worn tapestried cushion on its kneeler. Here good manners and custom required that the widow keep an all-night vigil over the mortal remains of her lord. Valentina performed as she was expected to do, remaining all night beside the bier.

At dawn, the sound of the door to the Great Hall opening star-

tled Valentina. She rose to her feet, her head spinning a little
from exhaustion and shock. Nan's strong arms steadied her
mistress.

"You'll need some food and rest before the funeral, m'lady,"
she said. "Come with me now, dearie, and let Nan take care of
you."

"Aye," Valentina answered. "I must not disgrace Ned's
memory."

In the afternoon, his tenants and few neighbors having all
dutifully paid their respects, Edward, Lord Barrows, the last of
his line, was laid to rest in the family tomb beneath the estate
church next to the body of his first wife, Mary, and their long-
dead children. Father Peter said the mass, which was attended
by Lord Barrows's widow, his household servants, and his neighbors. The day was bright and warm, making the funeral service
even more poignantly sad.

Afterward, Valentina sat alone in the Great Hall of Hill Court
eating with little appetite the supper made for her by her servants.
She thought wryly of their nearest neighbor, one Lady Marshall,
who had blurted out that she was certain dear Ned was happy
to be with his Mary again, and so soon, too! Then, after the words
were out, Lady Marshall realized to whom she was speaking, and
the poor woman turned red, white, and then red again as she
attempted to stammer an apology. A kind woman by nature, she
was horrified by what she'd done. Valentina managed to ease the
unfortunate lady's discomfort, then gratefully accepted Lady
Marshall's excuses as to why she and Lord Marshall could not
stay for the funeral supper. What on earth would they have talked
about, Valentina wondered.

She sighed deeply, wondering why she could not, even now,
have a good cry over poor Ned's untimely death. Admittedly she
had not loved him, but she had certainly liked him, and they had
started to become friends. What kind of an unnatural person was
she? Valentina slept well that night, exhausted after being awake
all the previous night during her vigil.

In the morning she awoke with a headache. For lack of anything to do, she found herself wandering aimlessly about the
house, meandering without purpose through the well-kept gardens, now all abloom. Suddenly she came face-to-face with the
dreadful reality: She did not know what to do with herself. Wed
less than a month, she barely knew her duties as the mistress
of Hill Court. What on earth did a widow do with her time? How

did she behave? All of the servants except her own Nan were looking to her for guidance. What was she to tell them, that they knew more about Hill Court and its late master then she did? She simply had no idea what to do with herself, no idea how to manage Hill Court now that its master was dead.

In the evening, during the most glorious of sunsets, there came the steady *thrum thrum* of horse's hooves on the road leading to the manor. Valentina hurried in from the garden to see who her visitor might be. Her eyes widened and she gasped with relief. The anxiety that had been pinching her features all afternoon drained away when she recognized the rider.

The great black stallion reached the front door of the manor and the big, handsome rider slid easily from its back. Opening his arms he enfolded her in his embrace.

"Papa!" cried Valentina St. Michael Barrows. "Thank God and his blessed Mother you've come!"

Conn O'Malley St. Michael, Lord Bliss, of Pearroc Royal, hugged his eldest child warmly. "And here, lass," he said gently. "we thought we had you all settled."

It was at that exact moment, that Lady Barrows chose to burst into fulsome tears.

PART I

Valentina

SUMMER–AUTUMN 1600

Chapter One

"IT IS ALL YOUR FAULT, Valentina!" Anne Elizabeth St. Michael said, sobbing, her dark green eyes, so very like her father's, now wet and shining with tears. "It is all your fault," she repeated, "that my wedding has been ruined! Oh, I shall never forgive you, Val! Was it not bad enough that Robert and I had to wait so long while you made up your mind which of your many suitors you would choose?" Her lustrous brown hair, as rich with coppery highlights as her sister's was, swung back and forth as she paced the room. "Just because *you* chose to have your wedding be a hole-in-the-wall affair, must I also?"

It was astounding that Aidan St. Michael, Lady Bliss, who was frankly somewhat plain, had produced the seven incredibly handsome young people now gathered together in the little family hall at Pearroc Royal. Aidan's husband, Conn, however, had once been called "The Handsomest Man at Court," and as he had fathered these children, their beauty was placed squarely at his door.

"Anne, I am sorry," Valentina said quietly. "I will accept the responsibility for taking too long to choose a husband, but, my dear, I simply cannot assume the blame for the accident that killed poor Ned! If you must assign blame, then our cousin Robin is responsible, for 'tis Robin who gave Ned the stallion that killed him." The black-garbed Valentina was a study in calm as she sat with her graceful hands holding the embroidery hoop lying in her lap. "How can one affix blame in an accidental death, Anne?" she continued. "As for your wedding, I have interceded as best I can, asking Mama that she not allow my mourning to interfere with your wedding plans. You will be married on July twenty-sixth, I promise you." Valentina reached out to pat her younger sister, but Anne shrugged her off. "My wedding is ruined!" she insisted. "Mama has sent messengers to all of the important guests telling them not to come because although the marriage

17

will take place, it must be a discreet event because of *your* mourning!"

"I cannot bring Ned back from the grave so that you may have a festive wedding celebration, Anne," Valentina said dryly. "I regret that I have inconvenienced you, but I cannot help but wonder which is more important to you—your marriage to Robert or the fuss surrounding the wedding, which makes you the supreme center of attention."

"You are hateful!" Anne St. Michael hissed at her sister.

"I am merely being observant," was the reply. "Besides, Anne, times are hard. England has not had a decent harvest in four years. The government is short of money. Why, the queen has been pawning her heirlooms and jewels in order to support herself! She is so desperate that she allowed Aunt Skye and Uncle Adam to buy Queen's Malvern, and those are not the only crown lands Her Majesty has sold."

"What has that to do with me?" demanded Anne.

"Dearest Anne, you must learn to think of other people besides yourself," Valentina said gently. "This entire family, all of its many branches, has earned its living over the years by trade, but much of England's trade has ceased because of our unending war with Spain. Only Aunt Skye's wisdom and instinct has helped us all to keep our fortunes at a time when most of the great fortunes of the past twenty years have been lost. Look at Papa's brothers. They have lost almost everything they ever gained privateering for England along the Spanish Main. Now their sons have joined with Hugh O'Neill, the Earl of Tyrone, in his rebellion, and Ireland cannot win that war. In the end, the O'Malleys of Innisfana will be worse off than in our grandfather's time."

"And England, too, Anne," put in Anne's twin, Colin. "The Earl of Essex mismanaged the whole bloody affair, lost twelve thousand men and over three thousand pounds!"

"But all of this has nothing to do with me," wailed Anne.

"Yes, it does," Valentina said a bit sharply. "Does it not seem wrong to you, with all the hardship our country is facing, to have a large and ostentatious wedding?"

"Our tenants are not starving," snapped Anne. "Papa's monopolies on nutmeg and cloves have kept the estate solvent, and when the old queen dies, things will be better. Once we have a king again, England will prosper. Robert says so."

"Elizabeth Tudor is the greatest monarch, man or woman, that England has ever had," said Colin St. Michael vehemently. "I only wish I had been old enough to participate in those glorious days that Papa speaks of so fondly. It is the war that weakens our country, not the queen."

"The queen is old," Anne replied staunchly.

"Because she is old does not mean she is unable to govern well," Valentina said.

"None of which has anything to do with the fact that my wedding is ruined!" snapped Anne.

"I am glad *my* wedding is not until autumn," said Bevin St. Michael a touch smugly.

"You will be lucky if you have a wedding at all, as you are marrying an Irishman with Irish lands," Anne said spitefully to her younger sister.

"Henry's father, Lord Glin, is English, and the Glins of Glinshannon are loyal to the queen. Henry says there has been no fighting in or about their lands, and his father said last summer in the thick of it all that nothing would stop his son's marriage to me. So there, Anne!"

"I shall have the grandest wedding of you all," announced twelve-year-old Margaret St. Michael airily.

"How can you be certain of that, little Maggie?" asked Colin, ruffling his littlest sister's copper-colored curls fondly. "Was it not you who swore to me only last year that you intended to be a holy nun like our Aunt Eibhlin?"

"Aunt Eibhlin is of the old church," said Maggie. "The one that gives its allegiance to a foreign power in Rome. We are members of England's own church, and no longer have nuns in convents. Nay, Colin! I shall marry a great man one day and have the best wedding of all. Val has already had her wedding. Anne's is to be a quiet affair. That leaves only Bevin, and whatever Bevin has, I shall have twice as much of, I vow it!" Her green eyes sparkled with malicious triumph. As the youngest daughter she was usually last, but here was one place where being last would give her the advantage, and Maggie was quick to see it.

"But what if Val marries again?" Colin teased, laughing. "She is still young, and the most beautiful of you all."

"And an old maid at heart," Anne sniped. "She married Lord Barrows to escape spinsterhood. Who will have her now?"

"I married so that you and Bevin would not have to wait any longer to wed!" said Valentina spiritedly. "I shall never forgive myself for doing it, either. Had I not *settled* on a husband to please you, Anne, perhaps Edward Barrows would still be alive!

All I have ever wanted is a man to love, one who would love me as Mama and Papa love each other. So many around me have found that kind of love. Why can I not? *Why?*

"How dare you whine at me that your wedding has been spoiled, and by me? Next week you will marry the man you love, Anne. Do you not realize how fortunate you are? I cannot believe you to be so self-centered and so blind. If you cannot see your good fortune, if all you desire is to be important for a day and to wear pretty clothing, then you are a bigger fool than I have believed you to be all these years. A supreme fool!"

"*I? A fool?*" Outraged, Anne St. Michael flushed unbecomingly.

"Aye," Valentina repeated. "A fool! What else would you call a beautiful young girl about to wed a wealthy young man she loves? A man who loves and adores her in return? What else would you call such a girl, Anne, who has all and yet still complains that her life is not perfect? That she cannot have a large wedding? God's foot, Anne, there are people going hungry in England tonight for whom a crust of bread would be heaven, and you dare to cavil over the fact that your wedding will be a small one instead of a large one. Shame on you, sister!"

"Val and Annie are squabbling again! Val and Annie are squabbling again!" sang out seven-year-old James, the youngest of the St. Michaels, as he capered devilishly around his two eldest sisters.

"Jemmie, you little beast!" snapped Anne, striking out at her small tormentor, but he dodged the blow and, grinning, stuck his tongue out at the angry girl as he danced out of her reach.

"Careful there, young 'un," said seventeen-year-old Payton St. Michael, chuckling. "Our Annie does not easily forget an insult." Payton, tall for his age, had not yet filled out, and consequently appeared gangling. He was dark-haired like his father, but he had gray-green eyes whose expression was very like his mother's. Of all the St. Michael children he had the mildest temperament, and among his siblings was usually the peacemaker.

"How many times have I told you not to call me Annie?" shouted his irate sister as she glared furiously at the handsome lad. Payton, however, used to Anne's temper, merely laughed and mischievously thumbed his nose at her.

"Oh, you are all impossible!" cried Anne. "Why can none of you understand my point of view?"

"Because it is a ridiculous one—and Val is right," replied her twin brother. "You are making a mountain out of a mole's hill, Anne, and behaving like a child to boot. How do you dare to carp for plum pudding when all about you the need is for bread?"

Before Anne could speak again, Valentina said calmly, "There is another solution to your problem, Anne."

"And what is that?" demanded Anne irritably.

"Mother has imposed a three-month period of deep mourning on the family during which time we can neither attend nor partake in any festivities. By October, however, we will be out of deep mourning. If you absolutely cannot be happy without a large wedding, why not postpone your wedding until October?"

"*Postpone my wedding*? Are you mad, Val?"

"She cannot be wed in October!" shrieked Bevin. "*My* wedding is in October, and I have no intention of sharing my festivities with anyone but Henry!"

"Anne could be wed on the eleventh and Bevin on the twelfth, as is already planned. The guests would all be here. It seems like the perfect solution to me," said Colin.

"Well, it is not!" said Bevin huffily. "How could you even consider such a thing? I—"

"For once I agree with Bevin," Anne interrupted. "I most certainly will not postpone my wedding."

"And I know why." Bevin giggled, tossing her golden-brown curls. Her blue eyes sparkled maliciously.

Anne shot her a venomous look, which was not missed by the two elder St. Michael siblings.

"Then you have no choice but to have a small wedding now," said Valentina quickly, lest the younger children, particularly the quick-witted Maggie, comprehend Bevin's broad hint. "I am sure that you would not want to embarrass Mama and Papa, Anne," she finished quietly.

"Embarrass them? *How*?" Maggie's green eyes were alight with interest.

"By calling off her wedding because Anne is in one of her famous tearing tempers, lambkin. That would only cause gossip. Does Robert Grayson know how fierce your temper is, Anne?" Valentina deftly steered the subject out of dangerous waters.

Anne glowered at Valentina, causing Bevin and Maggie to break into giggles.

"Payton," Valentina instructed, "you and Bevin take the little ones to the kitchen. I happen to know that Cook has baked a cherry tart, and there is fresh clotted cream to go with it."

Payton St. Michael was still young enough to be unashamed of his appetite for sweets, and he knew that Colin would tell him later about what had transpired after his departure. The two young men were but two years apart in age, and had always been the best of friends. He hurried his younger sisters and little brother away in the direction of the kitchen.

"And why can you not postpone your wedding?" Colin demanded angrily of his twin sister, suspecting the truth.

"I just . . . cannot," Anne said evasively.

"You little fool!" growled her brother. "You are fortunate that Robert Grayson is a gentleman. Old Mag is quite fond of imparting a certain saying to any and all who will listen: Why buy the cow when you can get the cream for free? Did you ever consider that you might be destroying your chances of marriage with Robert when you easily spread your skirts for him? Could you not wait, Anne? God only knows Valentina never behaved in such a flighty fashion. Could you not emulate her good behavior instead of acting like a milkmaid of easy virtue?"

"Ah, Colin, you forget one thing," interjected Valentina, when she saw that Anne was close to tears. "No one ever *asked* me to spread my skirts for him. I very well might have for the right man, you know."

Anne St. Michael's eyes widened at her sister's ribald remark. Unable to help herself, she giggled, then clapped her hand to her mouth in a vain attempt to stifle her laughter.

Colin groaned, defeated, and shook his head in frustration. "You two have spent your lifetime in collusion to drive me mad," he said grumpily. "I do not intend to remain with either of you for another moment while you attempt to convince me that wrong is right and that love excuses wrongdoing. I am going riding. Horses do not talk back to one." He turned toward the door.

"Colin," Valentina called after him. "Not a word to Mama or Papa. Anne has admitted nothing to either of us. You have only your naughty suspicions and imagination to fall back upon. Remember that."

"Hah!" came the reply. But Colin shrugged and, with an agreeable wave, left his two sisters. The twins were thirteen months younger than Valentina. Valentina and Anne had had a love-hate relationship all of their lives.

"Did you see the look on Colin's face when you said that no one had ever asked you to spread your skirts? He was shocked that you, of all people, should say such a thing!" Anne broke into fresh laughter at the memory.

"For a man whose love life is as active as our brother's is," remarked Valentina tartly, "I think he was being a bit self-righteous with you, Anne. A woman is a woman, be she great lady or farmer's daughter. Both Mama and Aunt Skye are agreed on that. For lack of evidence to the contrary, I must agree with them."

Suddenly Anne St. Michael hugged her elder sister. "I am so sorry, Val, that I have been contrary with you about my wedding. You are right, and I know it, even if I am disappointed." She sat beside her sister and asked slowly, "Did you really mean it when you said you'd married Lord Barrows only so that Bevin and I could finally be wed? I would feel terrible if I thought you had made such a sacrifice."

"Yes and no," came the reply. "Oh, Anne! It is so difficult to explain. I *had* to marry. What else is there for a respectable woman to do? I know I must have seemed hard to please in the eyes of the family, but I wanted a love for all time—a love such as our parents have. I like to think that I am a practical woman, like Mama, and yet it may be that I really am not. After all, marriages are not supposed to be arranged for love, but for more important considerations. To better a family's social position. To gain lands and other wealth, or to acquire influence. That is the nature of the world in which we live, Anne. I know that.

"Yet within our own family none have married except for love. Our parents. Our Aunt and Uncle de Marisco. All of our cousins! You, dearest Anne, have found love with Robert Grayson, our childhood friend. Our sister Bevin is so moonstruck by young Henry Sturminster that she can hardly bear the wait before they wed and she can hurry to Glinshannon as his wife. Yet never, *never,* in all my twenty years have I met a man who arouses in me either physical passion or those nebulous feelings called love. All of you seem to encounter those feelings without even trying!"

"Then why did you marry Lord Barrows if you did not love him?" Anne was not quite able to grasp her sister's thoughts.

"I married him for several reasons. Remember, Mama would not let you and Bevin wed until I was wed. Do you have any idea what a burden that was for me? I married him because I grew weary of the look of disappointment in Mama's eyes each time I dismissed a suitor. Dear, sweet, wonderful Mama who took one look at our father and was forever lost to love! No one, Anne, has

ever affected me that way. Perhaps something is wrong with me."
Valentina sighed deeply. "When Ned came courting, there was
nothing to distinguish him from all the others.

"He was kind. He had a great wit. He knew how to laugh. At
that point I decided that perhaps the kind of love that you have
found was not for me. I decided that since I had to marry, I should
do well to pick a man with whom I could live easily. Ned was a
good man. There was nothing I disliked in him. So when he asked
me to marry him, I accepted his offer.

"Now Edward Barrows is dead, and the problem of another
husband for me will begin again, won't it, Anne? At least you
and Bevin will be wed safely and happily to the men you love
before I am considered fair game once more. As for little Maggie,
it will be several years before Mama and Papa will fret about her
future. For now I am safe. And perhaps this time I will find my
own true love."

"Oh, Valentina! I never understood," Anne cried, her green
eyes filling with tears. "I have been such a horrid beast to you
since your return home. I am sorry, truly I am!"

Valentina put her arm around her sister to comfort her. "Do
not feel sad for me, Anne. I am not really unhappy. If anything,
I am slightly stricken with guilt."

"Guilt" Anne looked puzzled.

"Naturally I feel sorrow that Lord Barrows should have met
such an untimely death, but I cannot, it seems, mourn any more
than I could love him. There is something unfeeling in such an
attitude."

"Nonsense!" replied her sibling, with a sudden burst of uncommon good sense. "How could you feel deep sorrow for a man
you hardly knew, Valentina? Do not be foolish, I pray. This is
very unlike the Valentina we all love."

"And I cannot help but feel a trifle guilty," continued Valentina,
"that your long-planned-for wedding should be spoilt by my misfortune. Oh, I know, 'tis but a case of what Mama calls *kismet*,
but still . . ."

"Look on the bright side," Anne urged. "Even though our
guests will be only the family, we will have four earls and their
countesses, two barons and their ladies, and our cousin, Lord
Burke. 'Tis hardly a shabby assemblage, is it?" She chuckled.
"And let us not forget our thirty-two cousins of various sizes,
shapes, and ages who will be parading about on the lawn. I think
we are fortunate that our cousin Ewan O'Flaherty, the Master

of Ballyhennessey, his wife, and their brood of eight will not be here. We are already sore pressed for space to house all of our family, even though the de Mariscos and Cousin Deirdre are taking some.

"Did you know that Velvet and Alex are already here? Velvet *will* have her English summer, and Alex gives her whatever she desires, so besotted is he with her still. Frankly, I am quite amazed that she is here, for I overheard Aunt Skye telling Mama that Velvet is again with child. Four sons, Valentina! God's foot, I hope to prove as good a breeder as she has been," Anne finished a trifle breathlessly.

"You already have, have you not, Anne?" said Valentina softly.

Anne blushed becomingly, then grinned. "But I shall not know until next spring whether it is a son or a daughter that I carry. Oh, Val! Do you think I was wrong in yielding to Robert's pleas? We have waited so long, and he can be most persuasive," she said dreamily. "Oh, I am so happy!"

"What is done is done, Anne. I cannot judge you, for I have not the right to do so," said Valentina. "You will be wed in a few days, and if the baby comes *early*, it will not be the first baby that has come early to a marriage. It will be a welcome child, early or not, for it has been conceived in love. I think, perhaps, that is more important than proprieties."

Anne hugged her sister again. "I do love you, Valentina!" she said, "and it will be a wonderful wedding, won't it? You are, as always, correct, elder sister. The people I love the best, our dear family, will be here to share the happiness of that most joyful of days with Robert and me. Once more I beg your pardon, Valentina, for my unkindness. I am, as you have so wisely pointed out, most fortunate to be marrying the man I love. I can but imagine how dreadful it would be to have to wed someone you did not love!" She shuddered delicately.

Valentina laughed. "No, no, Anne. While I did not love Ned, we were content in our short time together. It was not all that awful, I swear it."

"I hope not! I couldn't bear the thought of you being unhappy, Val," Anne cried.

Unhappy. No, she had not truly been unhappy, Valentina mused during the next few days. Contentment was a good word to describe her marriage to Edward Barrows. She had been content. But nothing more.

It still surprised her to realize that there had been almost nothing between Ned and herself. Directly following his death, she had managed to convince herself that, given time, she might have come to love him. Now with Edward buried for three weeks—the same amount of time they had been married—she knew she would never have loved him. Been fond of him and cared for him, aye. But it would never have amounted to more.

She was grateful that, even in her shock over Ned's death, she had had the presence of mind to instruct the bailiff in the running of the estate during her absence. Later, perhaps, she might send her brother, Payton, to oversee the property for her.

Their vast and scattered family began arriving for Anne's wedding. Their Aunt de Marisco, Skye, would bear most of the guests, for many were her children and grandchildren. Up from Devon came Captain Murrough O'Flaherty with his pretty wife, Joan, and their six children. The family had teased Murrough for years over the size of his family, pretending amazement that he had any children at all, considering that most of his time was spent at sea. Murrough, his skin wind-bronzed, his blue eyes crinkled at the corners from years of squinting into the sun, bore their jibes good-naturedly. He insisted that his brood of three sons and three daughters proved that, when he was at home, he spent his time there to his best advantage.

Willow, the lovely Countess of Alcester and Skye O'Malley de Marisco's eldest daughter, reached Queen's Malvern in a convoy of five coaches, with a dozen outriders. They thundered up the graveled drive with great importance.

"Thank God she is not staying here." Lord Bliss laughed when his sister reported the arrival. "Why must Willow travel with so great and ostentatious a party?"

"She and James will not ride with the children," said Skye, "not that they are all that young any longer, but they are a rambunctious and noisy brood. It astounds me that my prim and proper, oh-so-English daughter should have mothered such offspring."

"Like their grandmother," murmured Lord Bliss.

Ignoring him, Lady de Marisco continued, "Willow and James rode in the first coach. There was a coach for their four daughters, another for their four sons, a coach for the baggage, and another for all of their servants. I will say for Willow that she is a thoughtful guest and does not burden my servants with her family.

"Of course, James and the two oldest boys brought their own horses. Henry and Francis consider themselves quite above the two younger boys and are apt to lose patience with them on a long journey. With the horses, they have the option of riding when the confines of the coach become too close."

From Devon came Lady de Marisco's third son, the Earl of Lynmouth, his countess, and their family. Robert Southwood, called Robin by his intimates, would shortly be celebrating his thirty-seventh birthday. He was the handsome image of his late father, but lacked Geoffrey Southwood's slightly sardonic look, for Robin was a happy man who had led a singularly fortunate life, never knowing serious sorrow until he was left a widower with three tiny daughters, all still in infancy. He had found un-dreamed-of happiness with his second wife, the beautiful, golden-haired Angel Christman, whose three stepdaughters, Elsbeth, Catherine, and Anne, could remember no mother but their gentle and aptly named stepmother.

Her marriage to their father had given them not only a loving mother but eventually a houseful of siblings as well. Nine months after their father's marriage to Angel, she had borne her husband his first son, named Geoffrey after his grandfather. Young Geoff was followed in 1591, 1594, and 1596 by three brothers; and a year ago, to Angel and Robin's delight, baby Laura arrived.

Robin and his wife were to stay with his half sister, Deirdre, Lady Blackthorn, and her husband whose home was nearby. Deirdre and her husband were the parents of seven children, three sons and four daughters. Lord and Lady Blackthorn would also host Deirdre's brother, Padraic, Lord Burke. At thirty-one, Padraic was yet a bachelor. Gentle Deirdre despaired of her brother ever finding a wife, for not only had he turned aside all of her, her sisters' and their mother's attempts at matchmaking, he did not even seem interested in finding a wife.

Arriving first, already comfortably settled at Queen's Malvern by the time her elder sister's entourage thundered importantly up the driveway, were Velvet de Marisco Gordon, the Countess of BrocCairn, and her husband, Alex. Each summer they traveled from their home, Dun Broc, in the Scottish Highlands where the earls of BrocCairn had been settled for several hundred years. Their four sons ranged in age from seven to a set of three-year-old twins. Alex also had a ten-year-old daughter by a long-forgotten mistress. He had seen fit to make the baby legitimate, and although the child, Sybilla, had been in her natural mother's care for the early months of her life, she did not remember her. The only mother she cared to remember was the stepmother who had raised her. She and Velvet were particularly close, for Sibby had winning ways. Skye, however, thought her too pert.

The bride's family was to host the groom's family at Pearroc Royal. Robert Grayson was the only surviving son of Arthur and Margaret Grayson, Baron and Baroness Renton, of Holly Hill. Apart from Robert, his parents had been singularly unfortunate with their offspring, losing the two sons born in the five years following Robert's birth. After that, poor Lady Margaret had suffered a period of infertility until Robert was nine, when his mother birthed his now fourteen-year-old sister, Saxona. Two more miscarriages followed. At last Pamela, now eight, was born. The Graysons, whose small estate bordered on Pearroc Royal to the northeast, had known Anne St. Michael all her life. They were delighted to have such a charming and wealthy young lady for a daughter-in-law, especially in these hard times.

Also attending the wedding were Sir Robert Small, Lady de Marisco's business partner, and his elder sister, Dame Cecily, who was a grandparent to all of Valentina's generation of cousins and the generation that followed as well. The Smalls were very much a part of the family. Outsiders assumed some blood tie, which neither the St. Michaels nor the de Mariscos bothered to deny. Sir Robert and Dame Cecily were in their early eighties and as lively as ever.

Originally from Devon where they had owned an estate called Wren Court, they now lived on a small estate near the de Mariscos called Oak Hall. Wren Court had been turned over to Willow. She had been born there. And because neither of the Smalls had married, Willow was their heiress. Sir Robert, or Robbie as they all called him, had only recently and with great reluctance retired from the sea.

Anne St. Michael's wedding day dawned fair and hot. After an unusually rainy spring the entire month of July had been sunny and hot. The bride, lovely under any circumstances, was proclaimed by all uncommonly beautiful in her wedding gown of creamy satin with a heavily pearled bodice. Atop her flowing dark tresses she wore a delicate wreath of gold-washed silver filigree, pearls, and amethysts. Her bouquet was of pink and white roses. She was attended by her two younger sisters, who were garbed in pale green silk, their bodices embroidered with tiny seed pearls and gold-thread butterflies. They wore wreaths of field flowers in their unbound hair and carried matching bouquets tied with gold ribbons.

The groom, a handsome young man with dark blond hair, was garbed in a suit of pale blue silk. He stammered his vows nervously, to his father's amusement, while his mother dabbed at her eyes with a white lawn handkerchief. The bride blushed becomingly, to her parents' pride and the giggles of her younger cousins and siblings. When they were pronounced man and wife and Robert Grayson kissed his new wife, everyone cheered mightily.

Afterward there was feasting and dancing on the lawn of Pearroc Royal. The tables overflowed with the bounty offered by the bride's family. The feast was shared by the wedding guests and also all of the tenants belonging to Pearroc Royal as well as its servants and the villagers. A caravan of gypsies was seen traveling nearby, and it was invited to join the festivities. In gratitude to their hosts, they told the guests' their fortunes.

Taking Valentina's hand, an old woman who was the tribe's elder stated, "You are newly widowed, but there was no love."

Valentina said nothing. Her gaze did not waver from the gypsy's.

"Soon," the crone continued, "you will learn a secret long kept. You will journey a great distance to seek that which you already have. You will also find that for which you have long sought, that which you believe has eluded you, a lost love found. It has been here all along, but you cannot see it, and you will not see it until you have fulfilled your destiny."

"Tell me what you mean," Valentina begged.

The old woman shook her head. "In time, lady, all will be clear," she said, and moved away to tell another fortune. Valentina looked after the Gypsy, confused. Then, shaking her head, she laughed. Who knew if the woman had really seen anything in her hand? Gypsies could be such frauds, but then the woman *had* known that she was newly widowed, that there had been no love between herself and Edward. For a moment, Valentina felt uncomfortable, but then chiding herself for being a fool, she rejoined her happy family.

Huge barrels of cider and brown ale were emptied and rolled away several times before the moon rose. The guests drank rich, fragrant wines from the vineyards of Archambault, the château belonging to Adam de Marisco's half brother, Alexandre de Saville, the Comte de Cher. Finally, when the barrels and kegs had been emptied a final time, the ceremony of putting the bride and groom to bed was held. The newlyweds were hustled off to be undressed and placed in their nuptial bed with much laughter and teasing. Though surrounded by those who loved them, the couple was rosy with embarrassment. The caudle cup was drunk with hopes for their fertility, and at last the celebrants departed. Anne and Robert were left alone.

The following morning the newly married couple left with the groom's family to make their home at Holly Hill. Slowly, Pearroc Royal returned to normal.

As they sat in the small family hall, working at their embroidery, Valentina and her mother talked. The lead-paned windows of the little room were open wide, allowing the flower-scented breeze to perfume the sun-filled room. The July heat showed no signs of abating, so the fireplace was cold.

"I do not envy my aunt," remarked Valentina as she finished embroidering Bevin's initials onto an elegant linen pillowslip. She nipped off the excess thread and laid the linen aside.

"Why do you say that?" Aidan asked her.

"Her company will remain for several weeks, Mama. Deirdre's also."

"Skye and Adam love their children, Valentina. They are happy to have them under their roof." Aidan was embroidering French knots into the corner of a linen tablecloth.

"It is not my cousins of whom I speak, Mama," said Valentina with a chuckle, "but their many offspring. There are nineteen of them staying at Queen's Malvern and fifteen with Deirdre!"

"I envy Skye her grandchildren, as I once envied her her children, Valentina," replied Aidan quietly.

"But, Mama, you're too young to have grandchildren!"

Aidan St. Michael colored prettily at her daughter's compliment. Her mirror told her that Valentina's compliment was not overly extravagant, for although her waist had thickened a little with childbearing, she was not plump, and her face was as smooth as a young woman's. Nonetheless she replied, "I am closer to fifty than forty, Valentina, and the mother of a twenty-year-old daughter who would herself be a mother had she wed earlier in life. Now, alas, just when I thought to have you settled, you are widowed."

"Robert and Anne will give you grandchildren soon enough, Mama," Valentina said with a smile.

"In about seven months, I suspect" was the mischievous reply. Aidan's gray eyes twinkled.

"*You knew*? Oh, Mama!" Valentina was astounded.

"Of course I knew," said Aidan calmly. "Remember, Valentina, this is my house. Nothing happens here without my knowing. The laundresses report to me, as do all our servants. And very upset was the head laundress when she came to me several weeks ago. You would have thought Anne was *her* daughter, not mine."

"But you said nothing to Anne, Mama."

"My dear, what could I say? The deed was done, and as the marriage was to take place shortly I saw no need to embarrass your sister. Besides, I could see that Anne was enjoying her little secret," Aidan finished with a laugh.

"Does Papa know?"

"Gracious, my dear, of course not! You must never tell him, either. Conn would be horrified that one of *his* girls could behave so rashly. He forgets that his own wife asked the queen for his hand in marriage, and that the women in this family are known to be quite passionate. If I tell him that his first grandchild has simply come early, he will believe it, bless him! Your father, for all his lusty and checkered past, is still an innocent. I love him for it."

"The women in this family are known to be are quite passionate," her mother had said. Valentina thought on her mother's words later that afternoon as she strolled the gardens of her family's home. All but me, she considered sadly. I have yet to feel passion. Certainly I did not feel passion with Edward Barrows, but then, I do not think Ned himself was passionate. He never looked at me the way Papa looks at Mama. Or the way Uncle Adam gazes at Aunt Skye.

I wonder if *they* make love with all their nightclothes on. I never saw my husband naked, nor he me, for he always came to me after the candles were snuffed out. He would come to my bedchamber three nights each week, make love to me once, and then depart without a word. He never stayed with me an entire night except for our wedding night. Yet I know that Papa always sleeps with Mama, and my uncle with my aunt. I wonder if I somehow displeased Ned, and he was unable to tell me.

"You are frowning, cousin." A deep masculine voice broke into her reverie.

Looking up from the graveled path on which she had been concentrating her full attention, Valentina saw her cousin, Lord Burke. "Padraic," she said, smiling at him, "I did not hear you. When did you learn to walk like a cat?"

"I could have brought a troop of mounted horses with me, Val, and you wouldn't have heard. You seem to be pondering something most unpleasant. What makes you look so unhappy, sweet coz? Tell me, and I shall make it all better, as I did when you were a little girl." He took her slender white hand in his, and they walked together down the graveled path. Though he was some years her senior, and a man, there had always been a deep closeness between them. Neither had ever been afraid to be completely frank with the other. They were the best of friends.

She smiled up at him. "I doubt, Padraic, that you would be interested in the musings of a poor widow."

Padraic Burke laughed. "I would hardly call you a poor widow, Val. Your husband was quite comfortably situated, and I am told you have inherited everything. Besides, you do not strike me as an object of pity. Come now. You are my favorite cousin, and I am interested in what troubles you. Tell me."

She shook her head. "It is only silliness, nothing more. I would not trouble you with it."

Lord Burke was four inches taller than his cousin, who, at five feet ten inches, was considered very tall for a woman. Now, pulling himself up to his full six feet two inches, he looked down at her with a piercing gaze. A lock of black hair fell over his forehead. His eyes, a most startling aquamarine blue, gave him a fierce look. "Tell me, sweet coz," he inquired in an innocent tone, "are you still as ticklish as you once were?"

Valentina stepped away from him. "Padraic! You wouldn't dare!"

"Tell me your thoughts, Val," he demanded, reaching for her and grasping her arm. "Are they so deliciously wicked that you are afraid to reveal them to me?" When she blushed, he chuckled. "Ah, wench, your face betrays your guilt! I shall not rest until you divulge all."

She made a valiant effort to break free. "No, no, you devil, I won't! My thoughts are my own, and I will not share them with you!"

Holding her arm firmly, he reached toward her slender rib cage and began tickling her. "Confess, Val, or else this will be but a tiny taste of your punishment," he threatened, waggling his heavy dark eyebrows dramatically.

"*Padraic!* Damn you!" she shrieked, trying to squirm away from him. Realizing finally that she could not, she capitulated, saying, "I was merely wondering if married people always made love with their night garments on."

Taken aback, he released her. "Did your husband?" he demanded, knowing full well he had no right to ask her so personal a question.

"Aye," she returned simply.

"Then he was a bloody fool," he said hotly, "and no connoisseur of feminine beauty. The men I know enjoy being *au naturel* in their beds with their wives or mistresses. Certainly, in this family, the men feel that way."

"I somehow thought so." She sighed. "But, having so little experience, I could not be certain."

"He never saw you as God fashioned you? Or you him?" asked Padraic.

Valentina shook her head.

"He was not unkind to you, was he?" His eyes searched hers.

"Ned?" She laughed. "No. Ned was a kind and good man, Padraic, but he lacked passion. He was even kind on our wedding night when he found my virginity lodged so damned tightly. Determined but kind. And afterwards, always kind. I just somehow thought there should be more between us than we had. Perhaps it was only that we were not wed long enough."

"Did you love him very much, coz?" he asked softly.

She hesitated just a fraction of a second, then said quite candidly, "Padraic, I am ashamed to tell you that I did not love him at all." He looked so shocked that she explained. "Mama had this silly idea that none of my sisters should marry until I married," she began. "No one seemed to suit me. When I turned twenty last spring I knew I had to wed soon. Lord Barrows seemed as good a man as any of my suitors, so I accepted his proposal. I think he was almost as surprised as I was when the decision was made.

"I have never been in love with any man in my whole life. I do not understand it, for Mama tells me that the women in our family are passionate. I, however, am not. Since Ned's money now makes me my own mistress I do not think I shall wed again, for I have found that to marry simply to marry is not a good thing. A woman should love the man she weds, and she should not take a husband for any reason other than love—no matter what others say to persuade her."

"You are the most beautiful woman I have ever known, Val-

entina St. Michael," Padraic told her fervently. "You could have
any man you choose. Even a prince of royal blood!" Oh, Lord,
he thought. I sound like a gushing schoolboy. She did not seem
shocked by his declaration, and in a moment he understood that
she had missed the passion in his voice.

She laughed lightly. "Alas, Padraic Burke, we have no princes
in England who seek wives. Nor in Ireland, either. Oh, cousin,
you have always had the knack of chasing away my deepest dol-
drums. Thank you for such a lovely compliment, but I think your
mother is the most beautiful woman I have ever seen."

"In her generation, perhaps," he declared stoutly, "but in ours
it is you, Val, who are the most beautiful."

"What of your sisters, you disloyal wretch?" she teased him.

"Willow is too sallow, Deirdre too pale, and Velvet's nose is too
long," he answered casually.

"Villain! I shall tell your sisters what you've said about them!
If any of my brothers spoke so scathingly about me I should wreak
my vengence on them even as your sisters are going to revenge
themselves upon you, my lord Burke!"

"Not, madam, while I have ten fingers with which to tickle
you." He raised his hands and wiggled his fingers in the air.
"These digits are my secret weapon, and they will keep you silent
and obedient to my will, Valentina St. Michael," he told her.

"Hah! You will have to catch me first, my fine lord," Valentina
told him. She scampered off through the gardens, her cousin in
hot pursuit.

Valentina headed for the garden's famous boxwood maze, racing toward its protective greenery.

"Foul! Foul!" he cried, thwarted. "Damn it all, Val, you know
I've never been able to find my way out of that bloody maze.
Come out this instant, you wicked wench!"

She had disappeared into the maze and her laughter, taunting
and victorious, floated over the thick hedges. With a smothered
oath Padraic Burke plunged into the maze in search of her. Valentina, hearing him thrashing about, chuckled over his predicament. When she was very certain he was well and thoroughly
lost within the twisting, turning paths of the living green puzzle,
she exited easily and hurried back to the house. It would shortly
dawn upon him that she was no longer there, and that he would
have the difficult if not impossible task of finding his way out of
the maze. She laughed, delighted.

If she was Padraic's favorite cousin, then he was certainly her favorite cousin as well. Although he was eleven years her senior, they had always been close friends. As a little girl, it was Padraic Burke to whom she had always gravitated.

He had been much at court in his youth, having served as a page in the household of the Earl of Lincoln, whose countess was a cousin of Aidan St. Michael's. When he grew too old to be a page, his mother sent him to Oxford. He studied there for two years before spending a year at sea with his elder brother, Murrough. During that year he discovered that, like his late father, Niall Burke, he was a landlubber through and through. Since then, Padraic had spent most of his time on his estates and at court, performing small, discreet services for the queen. He had joined the Earl of Essex's expedition to Cádiz in 1596 when the English captured and sacked that Spanish city.

Valentina had seen her cousin at every family gathering. Now, she wondered why she had never discussed with Padraic her inability to find a husband she could love. He had always helped her to find answers to her problems. Furthermore, Padraic, like her, seemed unable to find true love.

"Valentina," her mother called as Valentina reached the terrace. "Did Padraic find you? He came today especially to see you."

"You had best send someone to help him find the path out of the maze, Mama. It seems Lord Burke has once again lost his way," Valentina laughed.

"Valentina! Will you never grow up?" Aidan scolded, but she could not help laughing. She was relieved that Valentina had not gone into a decline over Lord Barrows's death. "Jemmie," she called to her youngest child, "go and lead your poor cousin Padraic from the maze."

The little boy scampered off, whooping with glee. His cousin's inability to solve the secret of Pearroc Royal's maze was a long-standing family joke. All of the St. Michael children had easily deciphered the riddle of the twisting paths by the time they were four years old, as had their cousins—all except Padraic. To him the maze was still a conundrum, much to his mortification.

"Why on earth did you lure your cousin into the maze, Valentina?" her mother demanded.

"I did not lure him, Mama. I was forced to flee from him. He was tickling me, and you know how ticklish I am. I knew if I could but get him into the maze I could then escape him easily. I certainly could not outrun him. Besides, would it not be undignified for a newly widowed lady wearing deep mourning to be seen fleeing a pursuer across the lawn? I should hope to have a greater care for my reputation than that, Mama."

"I am pleased to see that you have considered the proprieties, my dear, even if your methods are somewhat unorthodox," Aidan murmured.

"I hope you are prepared to protect me, Mama, when Jemmie releases my cousin from his prison," Valentina said mischievously.

Seeing her nephew striding determinedly toward them from the end of the garden, Aidan took her daughter by the arm and hurried her off. "I believe Padraic is less apt to wreak his vengeance upon us if we are safely indoors," she said.

"Ah, Mama, I am relieved to see you are still willing to defend me."

"I have always defended and protected you, Valentina. From your very infancy I have guarded you, even though you were too young to remember it" was the reply.

"I know," said Valentina. "Nan has told me the story of my kidnapping at least a thousand times over. And Wenda, too, for she also shared in the early part of the adventure, didn't she?"

"Aye, she did," said Aidan with a smile, "but it was the faithful Nan who bore your captivity in Ireland and suffered at the hands of my grandfather FitzGerald and his family. It was she who nursed you and kept you alive until I could reach you. Still in all, I did manage to rescue you even before your father could arrive. In doing so, I met Lord Glin who sheltered me from the FitzGeralds and their wrath behind Glinshannon's sturdy walls until Conn could come for us. Now Bevin is to wed young Henry Sturminster, his father's namesake and heir. One day my daughter will be mistress of that magnificent castle. I can hardly believe it."

"You have done well by your daughters, Mama. Anne will one day be mistress of Holly Hill, and Bevin will have her Irish castle. You will one day have to find an earl for Maggie, for she is determined to have the best wedding of us all. Only an earl will justify the expense," Valentina teased her mother.

"But what of you, my dear?" Aidan asked. "You will one day wish to marry again."

"Oh, no, Mama! You will not sing that tune with me again! When will you accept the fact that I am the odd duck in this family? No man has ever touched my heart, and I doubt one ever shall. I do not pretend to understand it, but there it is. I married

Lord Barrows to please you and Papa, and though he was a good man, it was a terrible mistake. I shall not make such a mistake again. If I cannot have the kind of love that you and my father have, I will not settle for a lesser emotion and tell myself I must be happy. Never again!"

Aidan St. Michael said nothing. There really was nothing she could think of with which to refute her daughter's argument.

She had realized, of course, that Valentina was not in love with Edward Barrows. Still, she had found no logical reason to discourage the match once Valentina agreed to it, so Aidan had closed her eyes to the facts and let the wedding take place. At twenty, Valentina was somewhat long in the tooth for a first marriage.

Aidan had not married her husband until she was in her middle twenties. Still, she reasoned, there had been mitigating circumstances in her case, which were not there in her daughter's. It did not occur to Aidan to consider that, while it was true that she'd had the responsibility of her aged father, she might also have simply been a late bloomer. Her eldest child—so like her in many ways—might be a late-blooming rose, as she had been. But the idea had never occurred to Aidan. What was the matter with Valentina, she fretted, that she could not seem to find love?

In the weeks to come, however, Aidan St. Michael, Lady Bliss, gave little thought to her widowed daughter. There would be time to deal with Valentina's problems later. For the present, she was far too busy preparing for her third daughter's wedding. It was to be a very grand one. Aidan seriously doubted that any mother had ever married off three daughters so well in the short space of less than six months.

In the summer of 1596 Conn O'Malley had taken his family to Innisfana Island, the ancestral home of the O'Malleys of mid-Connaught, to see their grandmother, Anne O'Malley. Anne O'Malley was sixty that year, and seeing the deteriorating conditions in which his mother lived, Conn sought to bring her back to England with him, but she would not come. Her warm brown eyes were sympathetic as she had told him, "I was born in Ireland. I have lived my entire life here. I shall die here. And I will say no more about it, Conn."

He accepted her decision, though he was most unhappy about it. His brothers, through stupidity and foolishness, had lost all the wealth they had gained in the years that they had sailed ships for England's sake, harassing the proud dons along the Spanish

Main. Embittered by their losses, blaming everyone but themselves, particularly Elizabeth Tudor and all for which she stood, Brian, Shane, and Shamus O'Malley currently involved themselves in petty piracies along the Irish and Scots-Irish coasts. In the summer of 1596, they were already embroiled with the Earl of Tyrone and his rebellions. It was a lost cause, Conn knew, and his brothers' actions made him fear for his mother's future safety.

It was during that summer of 1596 that Bevin St. Michael, aged eleven, met Lord Glin's eldest son and namesake, Henry Sturminster. The future master of Glinshannon was seventeen and fresh from studying in France. He thought himself quite the traveled sophisticate, but one look at Bevin St. Michael, who had her grandmother FitzGerald's glorious chestnut hair and light blue eyes, and Harry Sturminster had been lost. He told his parents, who had been seriously considering a match with one of his cousins, that he would have no wife but Mistress St. Michael. Seeing his determination, they agreed, so long as no fault could be found with either the girl or her family.

Bevin, however, had not been ready to consider such a serious involvement. She was caught between childhood and womanhood, and Harry's passionate avowals of eternal love frightened her. When he realized his mistake, he had gone more gently with her, and by summer's end, Bevin was half in love. She spent the next two summers at Glinshannon Castle endearing herself to her future in-laws and falling more in love with her Harry.

In the summer of 1599 the Earl of Essex had taken his army of seventeen thousand men into Ireland to put down the Earl of Tyrone, who, with aid from Spain, had mounted the most serious rebellion against the English to occur in many years. The Spanish did not care what happened to the Irish. They merely saw a good chance to harass the English queen. Essex, despite his army and vast resources, was no threat to them, for he hardly ventured beyond the Dublin Pale. Still in all, it had not been a summer for a gently reared English maiden to venture into Ireland, so Lady Glin and her eldest son had came to England on an O'Malley-Small ship so that Harry Sturminster might be formally betrothed to Mistress Bevin St. Michael.

Now, on the twelfth day of October in the year 1600, a huge gathering assembled at Pearroc Royal to witness the nuptials of the young pair. The family was joined this time by all of the neighboring nobility and several of the St. Michaels' friends from court. Once Lord Bliss had been a part of Elizabeth Tudor's circle, but several years ago, prior to Jemmie's birth, they had ceased going to court at all, even for the New Year festivities.

Bevin was radiant with a diadem of diamonds and pearls, her long hair streaming in the warm autumn breeze. Her satin gown was the color of heavy cream and embroidered heavily with diamante, seed pearls, and gold thread. She was attended by her younger sister, Margaret, and several young cousins: Sybilla Gordon, Mary Elizabeth Edwardes, and Thalia and Penelope Blakeley. The bridesmaids wore bright yellow silk gowns and carried bouquets of white damask roses tied with gold ribbons.

The festivities and feasting following the wedding lasted until well past moonrise. The Great Hall at Pearroc Royal rang with laughter and merriment until long after the bride and groom had been put to bed with much ceremony and ribaldry. When, on the following day, the last of the guests finally departed, Aidan turned to her husband and sighed with relief.

"Thank God Maggie is only twelve! I shall not have to go through another wedding for at least three years."

"What of Valentina?" Lord Bliss asked of his wife.

" 'Tis not the same thing when a woman marries for a second time. Besides, our eldest child tells me that she has no intention of marrying again. I don't believe her, of course, but it is enough that *she* believes it. Valentina needs time to come to terms with herself, Conn. We were wrong to rush her into marriage with Lord Barrows. I see that now."

"Was she so unhappy with him?"

"Not unhappy, but not happy, either. She admits to having wed him simply to please us, and that distresses me, Conn." Aidan put her head on her husband's shoulder and sighed deeply. "We are so fortunate in our love, and I would like Valentina to find the same good fortune that I did when I found you, my love."

Lord Bliss agreed with his wife. Like Aidan, Conn did not have the answer to Valentina's current dilemma. Valentina was too old for additional studies, and the responsibilities of running Pearroc Royal belonged to Lady Bliss. There seemed to be no place for her within the household. Conn and Aidan considered their daughter too young to be allowed to return to her late husband's home by herself, and even if she had a proper chaperone, the truth of the matter was that there was even less for Valentina to do at Hill Court than at Pearroc Royal.

"Send her to court," said Skye O'Malley de Marisco when her brother confided his concerns to his elder sister during the families' shared Christmas celebration. "I am surprised that you and Aidan haven't thought of that. Both Anne and Bevin have spent time serving the queen. All of the women in our family have, except for those who are too young and Valentina. Court is the perfect place for her right now."

"You have not been to court in years," said Conn. "It is not like it used to be."

"Because I am still banned from Bess's presence does not mean I do not know what goes on at court." Skye smiled archly. She had just celebrated her sixtieth birthday, yet seen from a distance, many took her for a far younger woman. She stood straight and her lustrous hair was still dark but for a narrow pair of silver wings on either side of her head, just above her ears. Her Kerry-blue eyes had not faded and, as always, her gaze was direct.

"Valentina has never wanted to go to court," Conn replied. "She has always preferred living in the country. She is much like Aidan in temperament."

"With a generous amount of O'Malley stubbornness," was the tart reply. "Listen to me, Conn. Valentina cannot make a judgment without having spent some time at court. Granted, it is not as exciting as it was in our day. Bess is almost seventy, and already the sharks are circling her. Although she will not confirm the succession for fear of being deposed because of her age, James Stewart will eventually be England's king. In the meantime, the glorious days of our youth are long past, brother mine.

"Valentina must, of course, go to court. To live in Bess Tudor's time and not know her would be criminal. My niece is simply shy, as Aidan once was. Had old Lord Bliss not died when he did and left Aidan in the queen's care, it is doubtful she would ever have left her beloved Pearroc Royal at all. Then you would not have found each other, dearest Conn. Think what happiness would have been lost to you. Think on it very carefully. Valentina should think on it, too. Perhaps it is at court that her true love awaits her. Unless she goes, she may never find him."

Lord and Lady Bliss did not wait long to broach the subject with their widowed daughter. To their great surprise she agreed with her Aunt Skye. She had refused a stay at court when she was younger, but her situation was far different now. Remaining at home was gaining her nothing. Marrying Edward Barrows had brought her no happiness. She would journey to court and see if her fortune lay there.

Immediately the house was thrown into an uproar as Lady

Barrows's trunks and boxes were made ready. Aidan's elderly tiring woman, Mag Feeney, took charge of the packing.

"Did I not spend time at court with my lady before she wed himself?" she demanded of the other servants with just the vaguest hint of superiority. "I know what is needed at court."

Lady de Marisco's tiring woman, Daisy Kelly, rode over from Queen's Malvern to help. She was far more experienced in the ways of court than was the elderly Mag, for Skye O'Malley de Marisco spent a great deal of time in the queen's service. Without offending the prickly Mag, she aided her, and her help was much appreciated, for it was rare that old Mag left her bed these days, being greatly crippled in her joints.

Lady Barrows's gowns, underclothing, night garments, furs and cloaks, jewelry, and bedding were all carefully packed. There was a small oak tub for bathing that was packed along with Valentina's down pillows. She would have her own coach and driver, and horses both for the carriage and for riding. She was to be introduced into court by her cousin Willow, the Countess of Alcester, who took great pride in being one of the people the queen trusted.

A place had already been found for Valentina among the queen's ladies, for one of those fortunates had gone home to York for Christmas, caught a severe chill, and died most unexpectedly. Learning of it, Willow quickly importuned the Lady Howard, Countess of Nottingham, to put forward her cousin's name.

"Although my cousin is but twenty, madam, she is a most serious and learned woman," Willow said.

"A widow, you say?"

"Aye, madam. The widow of Lord Barrows of Hill Court in Oxfordshire. They were wed but a short time, and there are no children or other encumbrances to take Lady Barrows away from her duties to Her Majesty." Willow knew that at this stage in her life the queen disliked change, and she sought eagerly to place Valentina in as good a light as possible.

Lady Howard, who had been Catherine Carey, daughter of the queen's late first cousin, Henry Carey, Lord Hunsdon, did not recognize Lord Barrows's name. "Who are your cousin's parents?" she demanded.

"Her father is my mother's brother, born an O'Malley but known these many years as Conn St. Michael, Lord Bliss. Her mother is the only child of the late Payton St. Michael, the former Lord Bliss," replied Willow.

"Conn O'Malley!" A small smile of remembrance touched Lady Howard's lips. " 'The Handsomest Man at Court,' he was called. He caused a most frightful scandal, and the queen married him off to an heiress and sent him from court. He was later allowed back, but I've not seen him in years. He was a charming man!" Then the good woman caught herself and said, "So he settled down, did he?"

"A model husband and father to seven," said Willow with a small smile. Uncle Conn had the most staggering effect on court ladies of a certain age, though she herself could not see it.

"Well," said the countess of Nottingham, "you are not a frivolous woman, Lady Edwardes, and I cannot remember your ever asking for a position for a relative or a friend. You will guarantee your cousin's behavior?"

"Of course, madam, but there is no need. Valentina is a most circumspect woman, as was her mother when she served the queen."

"Aidan St. Michael," mused Lady Howard, and her brow wrinkled in concentration as she searched her memory. "A tall, rather plain girl, was she not?"

"Aye, madam."

"I remember, though vaguely," said the countess. "I also recall that Lincoln's wife was a distant relation, and that when she found out the girl and her wealth had slipped through her fingers, she was most disappointed. Is your cousin as plain as her mother?"

"Nay, madam. She, and in fact all of my uncle's children, tend to favor him," replied Willow.

This conversation took place on the last day of December and, Valentina's place guaranteed, Willow sent a messenger to her mother at Queen's Malvern. On the seventh day of January, 1601, immediately following the family's Twelfth Night festivities, Valentina, Lady Barrows, departed from her childhood home for the second time in six months. The last time she had left a bride. Now she went to seek her fortune.

The servants, most of whom had known Valentina since her childhood, lined up to bid her farewell. Beal, the family butler, was close to seventy now, but was still more capable than most of doing his job. His wife, the housekeeper, still served the family and had lined up the maids in a row. Erwina, the fat cook, and Leoma, the laundress, wept unashamedly and hugged Lady Barrows. It seemed to Valentina that they were more emotional about her going off to court than they had been when she married. Martin, the coachman, gave strict instructions to Tam, his assistant, for it was Tam who would be driving Lady Barrows's coach. Her own coachman had never been to London and was frankly afraid to make the trip. He would remain at Pearroc Royal to assist Martin in Tam's place.

Aidan hugged her daughter. "Now remember, the queen will not like it if you put yourself too forward, my dear. She can be impatient, but she has a kind heart."

"She's a bitch and has a long memory for a fault, an insult, or a slight," said Skye bluntly. "She admires women of intellect, so do not be afraid to let her know that you are intelligent."

"Mind your manners," Aidan admonished Valentina. "Remember to eat with delicacy."

"Beware the gentlemen," continued Skye. "Most will be utterly charming but entirely insincere. They will all attempt to seduce you, be they married or bachelors. The married ones are the worst. A very few bachelors will be worth your time. You will know which ones they are."

"Be sure that your gowns and undergarments are clean and free of stains," Aidan fretted. "A slovenly appearance will gain you the queen's disfavor."

"Guard your reputation," said Skye. "Do not gossip about others, although they will surely gossip about you. If you are careful and give them nothing to talk about, there is little they can say— although they will say something." She laughed. "As for what you hear of others, Valentina, keep your own counsel."

"May we *please* go?" asked Padraic Burke, who was escorting his cousin. "I will be spending the next few months at court, and I promise to watch over this innocent."

The coach and its escort of six armed men rumbled away from the ivy-covered gray-stone house with its peaked roof of Cotswold slates. The day was cold but fair. The estate lake reflected bright sunlight from its frozen surface, but there was little snow on the ground. As she leaned out of the coach window to look back at her beloved home, Valentina could not help but feel nervous.

"Get back inside," Padraic cautioned from atop his horse. "You are going to fall out of the carriage."

Valentina stuck out her tongue at him but obeyed, pulling up the window to fasten it securely by its leather hinges. "Well," she said aloud to the passing landscape as she settled herself back into her seat within the lurching vehicle, "it cannot be any worse."

"What can't be any worse?" demanded Nan, her anxious tiring woman.

"Whatever's in store for me now. The last time I left home I was back within the month, a widow. This journey," she said with relish, "could be the start of a real adventure for us!"

"God forbid it, m'lady!" Nan answered, rolling her eyes in horror. "I'm not an adventurous woman, and I had all the excitement I could take, enough to last me a lifetime, when you was just a wee nursling. I married my Harry Beal, gave him three healthy bairns, two of 'em boys, and then had to bury a good husband when I'd expected to live out our old age together. 'Tis enough excitement for me, m'lady. You just go to London, serve the queen nicely, and find yerself another husband. 'Tis what a woman's meant for, ain't it? A husband and babes."

"Why, Nan," Valentina teased her faithful servant. "Where is your sense of derring-do?"

"I left it behind in Ireland twenty years back, m'lady" came the dour reply.

"Well, you had best find it again, Nan," warned her mistress mischievously. "I have been a little country girl my whole life. I have spent all my time daydreaming about a love that doesn't exist for me, and I never made time for frivolous things. That is why I am going to court, Nan. *For fun!* For the sheer fun of it!" Having announced her intentions to her scandalized tiring woman, Valentina settled back in her seat. There was a smile on her beautiful face such as Nan had never seen.

"God help us both!" the servant said. "If you don't sound just like yer aunt Skye!"

PART II

The Queen's Court

1601

Chapter Two

COURT. IT WAS NOT AT ALL what she had expected. All her life she had heard the many stories told by her aunt and parents of their improbable adventures at Queen Elizabeth's court. Her cousins had spoken glowingly about their own colorful and exciting stays at the social pinnacle of their world. It was strange to try to reconcile those tales of their past to what Valentina found. The court was no longer vibrant. It was a somber, sometimes dreary place of dark mistakes and the ghosts of past triumphs, a haunted place. The air was filled with anxious expectations having to do with the future—a future in which Elizabeth Tudor would have no part.

Most of the famous men who had surrounded Elizabeth, like pearls encircling a precious diamond, were gone. Robert Dudley, the Earl of Leicester, had died in the autumn of 1588, rendering England's great victory over Spain's Armada bitter for Elizabeth Tudor. Sir Francis Walsingham had died in 1590, followed by Sir Christopher Hatton in 1591.

The queen's cousin, Henry Carey, Lord Hunsdon, had passed on in 1596. He was the son of Mary Boleyn, the queen's aunt, and it had been suspected that Henry Carey was actually Henry VIII's son, for Mary Boleyn had been in the king's bed long before her sister Anne came home from France to capture Harry Tudor's heart. Elizabeth had been deeply fond of Henry in spite of all of the rumors, and Lord Hunsdon's loyalty had always been strictly to the queen.

But the death that could still bring tears to her eyes was that of William Cecil, Lord Burghley, on August 4, 1598. Cecil, her beloved friend, her wondrously clever secretary of state who had been with her from the very beginning. Cecil, who first and always worked in the queen's best interest. Lord Burghley had, however, left the queen a most precious legacy, his even cleverer second son, Sir Robert Cecil.

Robert Cecil was a small, hunchbacked man. He was extremely uncomfortable with his appearance, but he was a worthy successor to both his father and Francis Walsingham. Although Robert Cecil had first stood for Parliament when he was only eighteen years old, and had risen rapidly in the queen's government, due not only to nepotism but to his own extraordinary talents, he was equally at home in the witty world of the theater. He was often seen at the Globe attending performances of plays by Master William Shakespeare and Master Christopher Marlowe. Cecil was a man who loved gambling for high stakes and the high society in which he moved. The queen called him Pygmy, a nickname he detested, and one no one but Elizabeth dared use in his presence.

> *Little Cecil trips up and down.*
> *He rules both Court and Crown,*

sang the balladmongers on London's streets. Robert Cecil's crippled appearance made him less than popular with the commoners, who liked their heroes tall, handsome, and gallant, like the Earl of Essex. Yet Cecil effortlessly overcame his appearance with those who took the time to know him, for he was clever and urbane. Like his father, Sir Robert's first loyalty was to the queen and to England. And if he cared a whit for what others thought of him, he did not show it.

As the queen grew older, Robert Cecil saw that his primary duty was to oversee a smooth transition from one monarch to another without making Elizabeth Tudor aware of what he was doing.

It was into this court—a waiting court, a court beneath whose apparently smooth surface there roiled continual intrigue and an eagerness to be done with the past and get on with the future— that the widowed Lady Barrows came, innocently seeking her fortune.

The trip to London was without incident, and upon their arrival Valentina and Padraic went immediately to Greenwood House, which belonged to his mother and was the family's London mansion. The house was located in the village of Chiswick-on-Strand and set like a little jewel atop a swath of lawns bordering the River Thames. There they would have a day to rest before Valentina reported for her new duties.

The queen was in residence at the palace of Whitehall, which, like her beloved Greenwich, was on the banks of the River Thames. Once Whitehall had been known as York Place. Thomas

Wolsey, called "the proudest prelate that ever breathed" by his contemporaries, had, upon his elevation by Henry VIII to the archbishopric of York, taken the two-story house and enlarged it into a grand palace. In late 1529 Wolsey, in an effort to retain his waning favor with the king, gave Henry York Place, which the king renamed Whitehall.

Henry Tudor had acquired more land surrounding Whitehall and designed an expanded palace on the twenty-four-acre site. There were cockpits, a tiltyard, tennis courts, a "ball house" where the nobility played at featherball, a bowling alley, gardens, and several other buildings for pleasure and sport. Unfortunately, the palace grounds were bisected by a main thoroughfare leading from Westminster to Charing Cross. The thoroughfare could not be closed, so although the main buildings belonging to Whitehall lay along the riverbank, it was necessary to cross the road to get to the rest of the palace grounds.

Padriac Burke had wanted to take his cousin to the theater on her first afternoon in London, but Valentina demurred, pleading the exhaustion of the journey.

"Perhaps you are right, coz," Lord Burke agreed. "Best to get some rest while you can, for old Bess will use you fiercely. As the newest lady you will find yourself being called upon for the worst of the tasks. Take my advice, however, and do not allow the maids of honor to order you about, for you are above them in rank."

The queen was served by a huge household of people, among them six unmarried maids of honor and six married or widowed ladies who served as Her Majesty's ladies-in-waiting. It was their job to keep her amused and informed, to calm her, to play cards with her, to flatter her and pamper her. The queen's ladies knew Elizabeth Tudor better than anyone else did—though some would have wished to be spared that dubious honor.

"Will I live in the palace?" Valentina inquired of her more knowledgeable cousin.

"They will find some accommodation for you, I am certain, but do not expect anything grand, Val. You must remember that you are the lowliest of the queen's ladies-in-waiting and only obtained your appointment through an accident of timing and extreme good fortune. You will be taking your place with ladies of rank who are considered the queen's contemporaries and who have known her for years: Lady Dudley, the widowed dowager Count-ess of Warwick; Lady Scrope; Lady Howard, the Countess of

Nottingham, who gained you your place through Willow's good offices. You are very fortunate, coz."

She found his words irritating, yet Padriac had been in and out of court since he was a child. He had to know, so Valentina swallowed her pride to ask him, "What else can you tell me, Padriac?"

"Greenwood will be your home, as it is for all of us except Robin, who has his own great town house next door. Keep most of your clothing here lest it be stolen."

"Stolen?" Valentina was shocked.

"Things are not what they once were at court," came the reply. "Take a change of clothing and keep your jewelry on your person, otherwise you risk having it disappear. Nan cannot stand guard over your things all day. They will be safe here. When the queen travels on her progress, you will have to take more clothing with you, depending on how far from London she goes."

"She is quite old to travel so much," ventured Lady Barrows.

Padriac whooped with laughter. "You had best not mention age, particularly the queen's, if you wish to retain your place, coz. Bess may be old, but age hasn't slowed her down one whit. She walks each day, she even rides, and she tires her maids who are all younger than you, Val. You will have a great deal of fun keeping up with her! There is only one who can stop her—Death. And the queen is not yet ready to surrender to Death, whatever the gossips say."

The following morning, Lord Burke escorted his cousin to Whitehall in his family's barge. Landing at the palace's water stairs, they saw Willow waving to them impatiently from atop the landing.

"Hurry! Hurry!" she called as they mounted the steps to meet her.

"We are not late that I am aware of," Padriac told his sister.

"No, you are not late, but I will need time to check Valentina's dress and brief her on the latest gossip. Are you aware, Padriac, that no one in the family since our mother was Countess of Lynmouth has served the queen as a lady-in-waiting? Oh, we have all had turns as maids of honor, but to be a lady-in-waiting . . . !"

"God's foot, Willow! If you find the position so desirable, why do you not take it yourself?" Padriac demanded.

"Be a lady-in-waiting? Are you mad? I have a family to contend with, brother. Poor James could not get along without me, and have you forgotten my little ones? You bachelors are all alike!

No respect for a woman's responsibilities." Willow sighed, patting a stray wisp of dark hair into place.

She led them into a little antechamber and, ignoring her younger brother, said to Valentina, "Now, cousin, let me see you."

Valentina carefully removed her fur-lined dark gray cloak and handed it to Padraic. She was garbed in a black velvet gown with a bell-shaped skirt that separated in the front to reveal a black taffeta brocade undergown. The undergown was sewn with gold-thread pendant flowers decorated with seed pearls and glittering jet beads. Val's sleeves were of the leg-of-mutton style and covered with many black silk ribbons, each one edged with small pearls. The wristbands turned back to form cuffs with ruffs on them. The neckline was extremely low, causing Lord Burke to draw in a sharp breath, for his cousin had the most beautiful bosom he had ever seen.

"Must the gown be *that* low?" he asked sharply.

"Most women are now exposing practically their entire breasts," rejoined Willow. "Valentina's neckline is just short of dowdy. Besides, she has lovely breasts. Do not be so old-fashioned, Padraic." Willow continued her examination of her cousin, then nodded, pleased.

Beneath her skirts Valentina was wearing a farthingale that gave her gown just the right stiffness of line. Her bodice had a long wasp waist that ended in front in a pronounced downward peak. The bodice was elaborately decorated to match the under-gown. About her waist was a delicate gold chain from which hung a needle case, a small gold watch, and a pomander ball.

Nan had arranged her mistress's hair in the simple but elegant style favored by the women of Val's family. It was parted in the middle, affixed in a chignon at the nape of her neck, and dressed with loops of pearls, a motif carried out in the rest of Valentina's jewelry. There were rings on each of her fingers; a necklace of pearls and jet beads about her slender throat; and fat baroque pearls dangling from her ears. Lady Barrows was the image of a wealthy and respectable widow.

"You are perfect," said Willow. "Your dress shows your breeding, yet you will not overshadow the queen."

"Your mother has told me that that is the one thing I must never do," replied Valentina.

"A pity Mother did not learn that lesson earlier," said Willow tartly.

"Our mother had just cause to quarrel with the queen," Padraic defended Skye. "God's foot, Willow, you sound so *English!*"

"I *am* English," Willow retorted irritably.

"Your mother is Irish and your father was a Spaniard," he returned.

"I was born in England, at Wren Court, brother," Willow reminded him. "I have lived my whole life in England. My husband is English. My children are English, and *I*, damn you, am English as well! As for you, Padraic Burke, you are every bit as English as I am despite the fact that your father was Irish. You have lived here since your infancy, and you own English lands. I see no great passion on your part to go join Tyrone and his rebels. You are far too comfortable an English milord for that!"

"Damn you, Willow! I have half a mind to—"

"Stop!" cried Valentina, interposing herself between the two battling siblings. "I will not have you two fighting! What does it matter if we are English or Irish? We are a family and that is what is important." She turned to Lord Burke. "Now be silent, cousin. Not another word from you." She turned again. "Willow, will you please escort me to the queen? It would not do for me to be late for our initial meeting. I would not have Her Majesty think ill of me."

"The wench has more sense than either of us," muttered Padraic.

Willow ignored him. "Come along, Cousin Valentina," she said. "Lord Burke has business elsewhere, I am certain." And without so much as a backward glance at her younger brother, she shepherded Lady Barrows off to the queen's apartments.

Their entrance was greeted with curious glances by the maids of honor in attendance on the queen. The young women considered their lives at court unutterably boring, save for the trysts they were sometimes able to arrange with gentlemen. During the last several years these young girls from good families who were chosen to serve Elizabeth Tudor had caused several scandals. Less than two years had passed since pretty little Elizabeth Vernon had found herself pregnant with the Earl of Southampton's child. The queen had been furious with her young namesake, although the earl had married the girl. Now, on the very day that Valentina arrived, a new scandal was breaking among the maids of honor.

Lady Dudley, the dowager Countess of Warwick hurried forward to greet them when they entered, saying as she did, "Thank heaven you have come, Lady Edwardes! The queen is in an uproar! Mary Fitton has been discovered to be with child!" Her glance took in Valentina. "This is your cousin?"

"Yes, madam. This is my uncle's eldest child, Valentina, Lady Barrows, a widow." She was dying to ask about the newly brewed scandal, but Lady Dudley was already drawing them across the room toward the queen's privy chamber.

A serving woman opened the door to allow them admittance, and immediately they heard the haranguing of a high, shrill voice.

"There is nothing you can say to me, mistress, save to name the culprit, as if I did not know his name already! 'Tis Will Herbert, is it not?" The queen glowered at the weeping girl, who knelt before her, and Valentina was able to get her first good look at Elizabeth Tudor, who was far more interested in Mary Fitton than she was in her visitors.

The queen was a study in contrasts. Her body was extremely youthful, and her movements—especially those of her beautiful hands—were extraordinarily graceful. But her long, thin face had aged greatly. Her fine dark gray eyes, actually almost black, were still bright and alert, but they were sunken into her head above the once long and prominent nose that had thickened over the years. Her skin was yet very white, or perhaps just seemed so beneath the queen's brilliant red wig.

Elizabeth Tudor was filled with a nervous energy that increased with her anger. She paced as she raged at the helpless Mistress Fitton. "Last summer! Last summer at the wedding of Worcester's son to Lady Anne Russell! Do you remember it? Aye! You remember, you sly jade! 'Twas there that you and the rest of that pack of drabs who call themselves my *maids* invented that silly dance. I asked you what character you represented, did I not? And you simpered at me, 'Affection, madam.' What said I then, mistress? What said I to you then? Can your feather brain recall back that length of time? Can it?"

"You said that affection was false, madam," sobbed Mary Fitton.

"Aye, affection's false, 'tis true, but you would not believe it, would you, mistress? Have I survived this long by being stupid, you dunce? Have I?"

"No, madam," the girl wept.

"Huumph." The queen snorted. "Well, you have learned the truth of my words the hard way, mistress. What a fool you have

been to play the whore when, if you had just waited a while, you
might have had my comptroller, William Knollys, for a husband.
Aye," she told the startled girl. "I know he admires you greatly,
and has looked after you with great care, as your father asked
him. But you would pursue Will Herbert, a man singularly lacking in charm or spirit. Bah! You are a fool!"

"Would you have had me chase after your comptroller, madam,
and William Knollys a married man?" Mary Fitton demanded
with a small show of spirit.

"You are a fool, wench," the queen repeated. "His wife is many
years his senior and expected to die shortly. He would have made
an honest woman of you, not merely taken his pleasure and then
left you to my *dis*pleasure as your lover, Will Herbert, has done.
Oh, I see your motive. My Lord Herbert was to succeed to an
earldom one day, which he now has, and you thought to be his
countess! Well, my girl, he will not have you. Did you know that?
He will not have you!"

Mary Fitton whitened. "He cannot deny the child, madam! It
is his! I swear it by Almighty God! I was a virgin when I went
to him!"

"You are a virgin no more," said the queen fiercely. "Would
you like to know what your lover thinks of you, wench?" The
queen reached into her bosom and pulled forth a folded parchment. Opening it, she read it aloud,

> "To a Lady residing at court:
> Then this advice, fair creature, take from me.
> Let none pluck fruit, unless he pluck the tree.
> For if with one, with thousands thoul't turn whore.
> Break ice in one place and it cracks the more."

The queen glowered at the girl. "Well, mistress? Even as we
speak this shameful verse is being passed about the court. What
think you now of your lover's tender concern for you and for his
child?"

Mary Fitton fainted.

"Huumph," said the queen, looking down at her. "See, ladies?
Look well upon *virtue scorned.* Hah! The jade got no more than
she deserved. Take her away. Place her in the care of Lady Hawkins. As for my lord, the Earl of Pembroke, I should have him
clapped in the Tower, but put him in the Fleet prison to cool his
hot heels for a time. 'Twill do for now." For a moment she stood
gazing with contempt at her maid of honor. Her slender, beringed

hands smoothed the white velvet skirts of her gown with its embroidered silver bodice. Then suddenly she glanced at Valentina. "And who is this?" she demanded.

Lady Dudley curtsied. "Lady Gardiner's replacement, madam, and her cousin, the Countess of Alcester."

"Alcester?" The queen peered sharply, and Willow stepped forward to sweep her a curtsy.

"A happy New Year to you, madam," she said.

The queen beamed with sudden recognition. Several teeth were missing on the left side of her mouth. "Willow, my dear! How happy I am to see you. It has been too long."

"It is the children, madam," replied Willow. "They are hard to leave. I have never allowed servants to bring up my sons and daughters, for if I did they would lack delicacy of manners, as do so many these days. I know that you understand."

"Indeed I do," replied the queen. "The young people today have few, if any, manners, and their morals are worse. 'Tis not like it was, I fear."

"Your Majesty," said Willow with deceptive modesty, "if Mistress Fitton is now dismissed from your service, might I offer you my second daughter, Gabrielle, to serve you? She just had her fourteenth birthday this past December, and like her elder sister, Cecily, who served Your Majesty several years ago, she has been properly trained. She will cause you no scandal, I promise you."

The queen chuckled. "Who would think that Skye O'Malley's granddaughters would be such charming and well-bred young ladies. I am of a mind to grant you your request, my lady countess, first because it pleases me to do so, and second because it will save me the trouble of having to decide from among all the troublesome creatures I shall be beseeched to favor. Sly-eyed wenches, puffed up with their own ignorance and interested in only one thing. Men! Aye! Send me Mistress Gabrielle Edwardes. Now, introduce me to your cousin, who waits so patiently by your side. Who is she? Your family's so damned overgrown now I cannot keep them all straight!"

Those within the queen's privy chamber tittered behind their hands at this royal witticism.

"May I present to you my cousin, Valentina, Lady Barrows, ma'am. The widow of Edward, Lord Barrows, of Hill Court, Oxfordshire," said Willow formally. She was beside herself with excitement at having managed to obtain Gabrielle a position. She had been trying to place the girl for almost two years. It certainly did pay to be in the right place at the right time, she thought a trifle smugly.

Valentina swept the queen a graceful curtsy.

"Who are your parents, my girl?" demanded the queen. "Your cousin's so pleased with her little victory, she's introduced you, but told me nothing."

Willow flushed, embarrassed at having been understood so well.

"I am the eldest child of Lord and Lady Bliss of Pearroc Royal, madam. My father was born Conn O'Malley, although he is now known as Conn St. Michael, having taken my mother, Aidan St. Michael's, surname so that her family would not die out. I have been told that Your Majesty arranged their match yourself," finished Valentina.

"Conn O'Malley." For a moment the queen seemed lost in thought, then she said briskly, "I have not seen your parents in almost ten years, Lady Barrows. Your father was a deliciously wicked rogue! Oh, aye, he was!" She chuckled with remembrance. "He caused such a scandal that I had to find him a wife, and as I spoke on it with my dear Cecil in my privy chamber at Greenwich, bemoaning the fact that there was not the right match for the young devil, your mother—I called her my country mouse, you know, for she was such a plain and retiring creature—spoke boldly, saying she was the perfect match for Conn O'Malley, 'The Handsomest Man at Court.' Hah! Hah!" The queen slapped her knee. "I don't know which of us was more surprised by the declaration. Your mother, Cecil, or me! Of course the wench was perfectly right. She was just the right match for him, and I saw it in an instant. Had them married in my own chapel several days later, I did. How long ago is it now?"

" 'Twill be twenty-three years next month, Your Majesty," replied Valentina.

"And they're still happy?"

"Aye, very!"

"And how many children did your father give your mother?" the queen asked.

"Seven, madam, all told. We are four sisters and three brothers."

"How old are you?" Elizabeth Tudor demanded.

"Twenty-one in March, madam," replied Valentina.

"How long were you married?"

"Less than a month, madam."

"Was he your second husband then?"

"Nay, my first, madam." Valentina looked distinctly uncomfortable.

"You did not wed till you were past twenty? Why is that, my lady Barrows?"

"I could find no one who pleased me, and my parents said I should not have to wed unless the man pleased me" was the reply.

"And did Lord Barrows please you, my lady?" the queen probed nosily.

"He was a good man, madam."

"Hmm," the queen replied. Her eyes were sharp, but she questioned no further. "So you have come to serve me, eh, Lady Barrows? Think you to find a second husband among my gentlemen? They are a poor lot for the most part, I can tell you. Wenching and gambling, 'tis all they are good for these days. There's not a loyal one in the bunch. They sit like vultures awaiting my death, but they will wait a while longer, I think. *Mortua sed non sepulta!* Do you speak Latin, Lady Barrows?"

Valentina nodded. She translated the queen's grim yet humorous words: "Dead, but not yet buried." Then she said, "I do not seek another husband, madam. I seek only to serve my queen in whatever capacity is pleasing to her."

"You have your mother's sweetness of temper, that much I can see," said Elizabeth Tudor, "but I also think you've got your father's proud spirit. I am not certain it is right for such a lovely young woman to cloister herself with a gaggle of old women such as we have become," the queen continued, sweeping her hand about to include Lady Dudley, Lady Howard, and Lady Scrope, all of whom were in the room with her. "Still, I have promised you a place, and you shall have it. The mistress of the maids of honor will be dismissed from her position for this latest scandal. You will take her place, Lady Barrows. It will be your task to keep order among that pack of scatterbrained, wanton jades. I will have no more scandals!"

"God help you," Willow said with heartfelt sympathy when they were alone back at Greenwood later. "The queen has set you a Herculean task. I hope you are equal to it."

"I shall need your help to succeed, Willow," came the reply. "You know the court. I do not. How can I keep order among a group of maids who are far wiser in the ways of the world than I am? I wonder at the queen that she would assign me such a duty."

"Perhaps she feels that being young, you will be quicker to catch on to the little games her maids of honor play. It is usually a much older woman who rules those naughty wenches. At least my Gabrielle will give you no trouble. She may even be of help to you. Oh, I am so pleased at having been with you today just as Mistress Fitton was sent away for her misdemeanors! I do not think I would ever have gotten Gaby settled otherwise. What luck! Just wait until I tell James!"

"Tell James what?" demanded Padraic Burke as he entered the salon.

"I have managed to obtain a place for Gaby with the queen's maids of honor. The Fitton girl has been disgraced. Is that not simply wonderful?"

"That the Fitton girl has disgraced herself?" said Lord Burke. "I do think that is rather uncharitable of you, Willow."

Valentina laughed.

"Of course I am not pleased that the Fitton girl has ruined herself," snapped Willow, outraged. "That would not be very Christian of me, and I hold myself to be a most Christian woman, brother. I am simply pleased that I was in the right place at the right time. I have been trying to get Gaby settled for over two years."

"I thought the purpose of your visit to the queen was to settle Valentina," he remarked dryly. He swung about to face his cousin. "Did you get settled, Val?"

"The queen has appointed me mistress of the maids" came the calm reply.

"God's foot!"

"Padraic, please don't swear! You sound like Mama!" Willow scolded him.

"What the hell was the queen thinking to make a greenhorn like Val the mistress of the maids. Those little wantons will run rings about her!"

"I thank you, my lord, for your great confidence in me," Lady Barrows said tartly.

"Bah!" he said impatiently. "Do not get all feminine and offended, Val. You have lived your entire life in the country. You know nothing about court or the people who live their lives attached to it. You are, my dear, a country bumpkin who has been put in charge of a group of very worldly wise little girls who are going to *make your life hell*. Could you do nothing to prevent this, Willow? Where is your much-vaunted common sense?"

"What was I to do, Padraic? Tell the queen she was wrong? Perhaps you would like to hurry off to Whitehall and tell her yourself. She was verbally flaying the Fitton girl alive when we arrived. After she had been introduced to Valentina and she understood her place within our family, the queen had the idea to make Valentina the mistress of the maids. She fretted about our cousin being incarcerated with a group of old women as she is wont to call herself and her ladies. Despite Valentina's inexperience, I am not certain that it was not a fine idea. Perhaps a younger woman can control the maids of honor better than an older one, being closer to them in age and temperament. I shall be nearby and I will aid our cousin if she needs me. I am not far away."

"I shall stay too," said Lord Burke.

"*You?*" Willow was greatly surprised. "You have spent virtually no time at court since your days as a page in the Earl of Lincoln's household."

"Valentina will need a male friend, for gentlemen are just as apt to gossip as women, dear sister. It cannot hurt to have someone in the enemy camp."

"Men *gossip?*" Willow pretended amazement.

"I cannot believe it myself," added Valentina mockingly.

"Worse than women sometimes," he agreed cheerfully, and they laughed. "When are you due back at court to take up your duties, coz?" he asked.

"The queen has given me two days before I must return to Whitehall," she answered him.

"And I must start for home immediately this very afternoon," said Willow. "Gaby is nowhere near ready to come to court. It will take me at least a week to prepare her, and then not properly, but I dare not delay lest her appointment be rescinded. Once she is safely at court, no one will attempt to remove her." She pulled on her gloves, saying, "You will look after Valentina, Padraic? Have her at court on Thursday." Then she was gone.

"I would not be a bother to you, Padraic," Valentina told him as the door closed behind Willow. "I am certain you have other things to do than watch over me as if I were a small child instead of a grown woman."

"You are indeed a grown woman, Val," he told her, and was

pleased to see her cheeks pink prettily. " 'Tis too late for the theater this afternoon," he continued. "Besides, the weather is growing foul. I shall take you tomorrow if it does not bluster. Alleyne is doing Will Shakespeare's *Richard III*. Let us stay indoors this afternoon and play cards. The queen's ladies are forever playing cards and as I recall, you're a terrible player. You can use the practice. Otherwise you may lose your inheritance from Lord Barrows to the little sharpsters over whom you will be mistress."

"Hah!" she countered. "Just because you were able to beat me at cards when I was fourteen, you must not take the attitude that you can still beat me, for you cannot! Where shall we play, coz?"

"Come," he said, taking her hand, "the library is a cozy place."

A footman set an inlaid wooden card table between the two comfortable chairs on either side of the fireplace, in which a cheerful blaze soon burned. On the round table next to Lord Burke, he placed a decanter of pale golden wine and two goblets. Having helped Lady Barrows into her seat, he withdrew from the room.

"Come, my lord, I am anxious to make you pay for your slur upon my abilities. I assume you can afford to play for honest coin?" Valentina settled her skirts about her and looked across the table at him. Suddenly, as their eyes met, she felt a funny sensation in the pit of her stomach. His eyes were the color of aquamarines. The shade was really most startling, and she wondered why she had never noticed his eyes before. The smile he gave her reached all the way to those eyes, crinkling them at the corners most pleasantly. He was a damnably attractive man, but until this moment she had never thought of him as anything but her cousin. She realized that, for some unfathomable reason, everything was changing.

"I assume that you, madam, can afford the losses you are about to incur," he teased her. "Shall we play Primero?"

She nodded, and the game began. They were evenly matched, it seemed, and he was surprised at how she had improved her skills over the last few years. Then, to his great astonishment, she began to beat him, piling up his coins to her left, all the while chatting away as if she were not in the least interested in their game.

"Why do you never come to court, Padraic?" she asked thoughtfully as she discarded one card and took up another.

"I had a bellyful of it as a youngster," he replied. "I'm not a politician. I find I do not like the city, and 'tis most expensive,

Val. I prefer raising my horses at Clearfields Priory. The queen
sold it to me several years ago, you know, and now 'tis mine. It
is not Burke Castle, which I cannot even remember and, as you
know, was destroyed. Nor is Clearfields Priory on the ancestral
Burke lands. But I have been raised to be a loyal Englishman as
the queen once threatened my mother would be done." There
was sadness in his voice.

"You do not remember your father or Ireland at all, do you?"

He shook his head. "I was but an infant at my mother's breast
when my father left Ireland, never to return. Damn, you have
taken my last coin!"

Her delighted laughter rang out. "Now, my proud lordling,
what will you wager me?" she mocked him.

"A kiss," he said mischievously. "One final hand, Val. My kiss
against all your winnings."

"God's foot, sir, you value yourself most highly," she said. She
knew she was blushing, and her heart was beating erratically.
What on earth was the matter with her? This was Padraic Burke.
She had known him her entire life.

"Well, madam? Has your sporting blood suddenly run thin?"
he goaded her.

"Play your cards, my lord," she said, and when he had laid his
cards before her, she laughed. "You lose, sirrah!" she gloated.

"Nay, madam, I think rather that I have won," he answered.
Standing, he moved toward her and captured her lips with his
own.

Valentina was shocked by the suddenness of his action, but
she could not resist him. Her bones were melting. His mouth!
His mouth on hers was so . . . so . . .

"*Val.*"

He had taken his lips from hers, and she suddenly felt terribly
bereft. Her lovely amethyst eyes mirrored her confusion. She was
utterly at a loss. What was happening to her? She had never felt
this way in her life.

Gently his big hand caressed her, one finger smoothing her
cheekbone and moving down her jaw. "Never let it be said,
madam, that Lord Burke does not pay his debts," he told her, his
voice breaking the tension between them.

Valentina stood, her hands against the card table steadying her
still-trembling body. "Why did you do that?" she demanded of
him.

"I was but paying my debt to you, Val." It was a lie, and both knew it. He had meant it to be a quick kiss, but something had happened to him when his lips met hers. He had not expected to find her mouth so honeyed.

"No," she said.

"I love you." His blue eyes with their hint of silver met hers.

"For how long?" Her upper teeth began to worry her lower lip.

"I cannot remember a time when I did not love you. I cannot even remember when the cousinly affection I had always felt turned to a man's feelings."

"*Yet you let me wed Edward Barrows!*"

"When I learned from my mother that you were to marry him, it was too late," Padraic replied. "God's foot, Val! You are so beautiful! You could have had an earl, and you should be the wife of some great man."

"Indeed, my lord, and was it your place to make that decision for me? I should be the wife of a man who loves me, damn you!"

Lord Burke stood and looked down on Valentina. "I am the son of a displaced Irish lord. What could *I* possibly offer you? You were born to be the wife of a powerful nobleman, not someone like me."

"You are a fool, Padraic Burke! Both of your parents were Irish. My father is Irish, and my mother's mother was a FitzGerald. But as for you and me, though we have Irish blood, we are English by virtue of having lived here our whole lives! You have Clearfields Priory and its lands. You have a full share in the O'Malley-Small trading company, *and* you say that you love me. What kind of a woman did you think I was that I would want more than what you can offer?"

"Then you would marry me if I asked?" He was incredulous.

"I can marry no one until I have completed my year's mourning for Lord Barrows."

"Will you marry me then?"

"I do not know," she said, now infuriatingly calm. "I must love the next man I wed, and I do not know if I love you, my lord. For now, I am angry with you. You say you love me, yet you didn't even attempt to stop me when I planned to marry Ned. I would not have believed you so faint of heart, Padraic. Your father certainly was not. Although he was forced to stand by while your mother was wed to another man, he was bold enough to claim her in spite of it. If you would aspire to winning my hand in marriage, then you must be bolder than you have been. I would love the man I wed, but I would respect him as well."

She turned to leave him, but he caught her and drew her back against his chest. "Perhaps, Val, my fault is that I love you too much, rather than not enough," he said softly, and kissed her again. This was not a gentle kiss. It was filled with dark passion and barely restrained desire.

He forced her lips apart and, plunging his tongue between her teeth, enslaved her tongue with his. Valentina's head swam as sensation pulsed through her body. She sagged against him, half swooning. "Ahh, hinny love," he murmured, releasing her lips. He pressed little kisses across the top of her breasts, inhaling her sweet lily-of-the-valley fragrance.

"Padraic!" she cried weakly. "Cease at once!" She placed her hands against his chest and pushed feebly. Never had she dreamed a kiss could render one so helpless. "I cannot think, my lord!" she protested.

"Perhaps," he teased her, "you think too much, madam." His arms were tightly about her. Had he let go then, she knew she would have fallen to the floor.

At last, as Valentina felt the strength flowing back into her legs, she pulled away from him. "You are bolder than I thought, my lord," she said, "nevertheless I have come to court to serve the queen, and I shall make no decisions about my future now."

"May I court you, Val?" His eyes were laughing.

"Aye, but be warned, I shall not necessarily favor you above others."

"Ho, madam, now 'tis *you* who are bold."

"Perhaps, Padraic, it is time that I became bold," she replied, twinkling.

"You are going to punish me for my sins, then?"

"Aye, my lord, I am, and there is no guarantee that, when I have tired of that game, I will accept your offer. Saying that you love me is not enough, Padraic. You love me, yet you allowed me to wed another even though he was not the man of breeding and power you felt I should have married. Surely you did not believe I loved Ned, for I did not even know him. It frets me that you did not speak up on your own behalf. Had you truly loved me, nothing would have stood in your way. I should, therefore, be very foolish to place all my eggs in one basket. Besides"—she shrugged—"I did vow never to wed again. Perhaps I shall be like the queen and go to my grave without a husband."

He laughed. "I see little chance of that, Val, and I give you fair warning. I intend to have you as my wife. This time I will not be denied. I shall not allow my pride—or any man—to come between us. There is no one for me but you."

"And this time," she warned him, "I shall not be hurried into making a poor decision. Edward Barrows was a good, kind man, but I realize that his sudden death was a blessing for me. I would never have been happy with him. I should have tried my wings at court years ago instead of being a country mouse. I shall not be a fool again. Court me if you will, Padraic, but if there are others who take my fancy, then I will encourage them."

" 'Tis best, I suppose," he said mildly, "that you work the hell out of your system before settling down as my wife and the mother of our children. I fully approve," he said solemnly.

"Indeed, my lord, do you?" Her tone was oversweet.

"Aye, madam," he drawled. He could see her temper rising, and he pulled her back into his arms. "Play your games, Val, as long as you bring no dishonor upon the family." He bent to kiss her, but she twisted out of his grasp, her hand making firm contact with his smooth cheek.

"Do not *ever* dare preach morals to me, Padraic Burke!" she said angrily, enjoying the stinging sensation in her palm and the satisfying smacking noise her hand had made against his handsome face.

"Ouch!" he yelped. "Damn you for a vixen, madam! That hurt."

"It was supposed to, you smug bastard! Loving me, you nonetheless stood aside as I married another man, and now that I am widowed, you have finally gained enough courage to announce that you *will* wed me! Well, my lord Burke of Clearfields Priory, if you want me, you shall have to catch me first . . . and I assure you that I shall lead you a merry chase before you do—*if you do!*"

"What the hell is the matter with you, Valentina?" he shouted as she stormed from the room. *Women!* They were the most maddening creatures! Any sensible woman, told that she was loved, would have reacted with joy. Val was the most impossible baggage, but God help him, he loved her.

Valentina ran up the stairs to her apartment, dashing past a startled Nan into her bedchamber, where she threw herself on the bed.

"Leave me be, Nan," she ordered her servant. "I need to be alone. Go away, and let no one into this room unless I tell you!"

Nan withdrew. She knew Mistress Valentina's tempers. They

came infrequently and rarely lasted long, but she needed to be left alone to recover her equilibrium.

Val did not know whether to shriek or to cry. "*I cannot remember a time when I did not love you.*" He dared say that to her after standing silently by as she wed Edward Barrows? "Damn you, Padraic!" she muttered. "Damn you! Damn you! Damn you!"

Valentina stared hard at the lovely Oriental carpet, all golds and blues. If a kiss could be so unspeakably wonderful, then what might the ultimate act of love really be like? Surely not like what she had experienced with her husband. Poor Ned. He was probably the most passionless man ever created. Even she, inexperienced though she was, had known that.

When he explained to her, on their trip to Hill Court from Pearroc Royal, that he would visit her bed thrice weekly until she conceived, he had instructed her on her behavior. He knew that her family had originally been members of the Roman church but now adhered to the Anglican faith. He, however, maintained a more Calvinistic belief.

"You are a Puritan, then," she'd said, surprised.

"If you will, my dear," he had agreed, explaining that, as a man of pure and stern beliefs, he did not hold with shameless behavior. She was never to appear naked before him, nor was she to make any sound during their coupling. She was to accept his seed like a good and obedient wife, praying fervently as he labored over her that God would allow her to be the instrument of a new life.

When he reached her bedside on those nights on which he visited her, he had smiled his approval to find her awaiting him in her high-necked, long-sleeved white silk nightgown, a matching cap upon her head, its pink silk ribbons her only attempt at frivolity. Drawing back the covers so that he might enter the bed, he had blown out the bedside tapers plunging the room into total darkness. He had insisted that the draperies be drawn lest the moonlight illuminate their shame.

This cannot be how it is between my mother and my father, Valentina had thought each time her husband came to her. She had lain quietly, her arms at her sides as he had bidden her, while Edward Barrows had opened her nightgown to fumble with her breasts. His fingers had kneaded her flesh and, soon, his breathing had grown harsher. He had raised her garment, tucking it neatly about her waist, and his fingers had sought her.

When he was satisfied that she was ready to receive him, he had mounted her, entering with one thrust and riding her, his breathing growing hoarser until finally he had collapsed upon her with a small whimper. When he had recovered himself, he would arise, say "Thank you, my dear," and with unerring accuracy find his way across the pitch-black chamber to the connecting door.

Other than their wedding night, he had never spent an entire night with her. Once she felt impelled to push her hips up at him, but he had immediately ceased his action, saying, "My dear, you are not a whore. Lie quietly beneath me."

Now it terrified Valentina to realize that but for an accident of fate she might have spent her entire life as his wife, never knowing the joyous feelings that Padraic Burke's kisses had given her.

Still, it was those kisses that caused her to consider other men. If Padraic Burke could make her feel so marvelous, perhaps there were other men who would have the same effect. Was that possible?

Valentina rolled over and gazed up at the blue velvet canopy. She must not allow this new knowledge to overrule her good sense. Of all her mother's children she was generally credited with having Aidan's practical nature. This was surely no time to lose her head. She had come to court to serve the queen, not to cause a scandal like poor Mary Fitton.

It surprised her to find that Padraic Burke loved her. Padraic the bachelor. Padraic, whose mother despaired of his ever finding a wife. Aunt Skye thought Padraic was a dreamer. In some ways, Padraic reminded Valentina of her father, and if she was like her mother, then theirs would not be an unhappy match.

"No!" she said aloud. She was not going to allow herself to settle for the first thing that came along just to make everyone happy. Not again! This time *she* was going to be happy!

There was a knock. "Lord Burke wants to know if yer going to have supper with him," came Nan's voice, "or if you're still having a fit of the sulks."

Valentina leaped up off the bed and opened the door. "Did he say that?"

"About the sulks? Nay. He just wants to know if yer eating with him."

Valentina thought a moment, then said, "Tell him I am too tired. I will see him tomorrow. Ask him what time I should be ready for the theater."

"Yer not going to the theater? 'Tis an ungodly place, full of the worst element in all London!" Nan looked horrified.

"You are singularly well-informed for a woman who has spent all of her life in the country, the same as I have," Valentina teased. "What's worse, you sound like a Puritan!"

"I needn't have lived in this stinkhole to have heard that the theater is a dreadful place. Full of cutpurses and whores! Because I'm a servant doesn't mean I am ignorant, *m'lady*."

"Oh, Nan!" Valentina hugged her. "I did not mean to offend you. As I am going to the theater with Lord Burke, I am certain I will be well looked after."

"Humph! He's no more sense than you."

Valentina smiled. "Go and tell Lord Burke that I will see him in the morning, and then please find me some supper. I shall eat in my bedchamber before the fire."

With another "humph!" Nan hurried off.

Valentina closed the chamber door. What would she do without her faithful Nan? Nan, who was her dearest friend as well as her servant. Nan, who was going to have a fit when she saw what Valentina had decided to wear to the theater. M'lady Barrows chuckled mischievously at the thought.

She chuckled again the next day when the put-upon Nan reacted precisely as her mistress had expected.

"You cannot wear that gown in public in the afternoon," Nan argued. "You'll catch yer death of cold for one thing!"

"I'll have my cloak, and 'tis fur-lined. Besides, the day is fair, Nan." Valentina gazed at herself in the long pier glass, admiring the way the amethyst-colored velvet brought out the identical color of her eyes.

"I do not like these overlow necklines, m'lady," said Nan with stern disapproval. "Yer whole chest is open to the elements, and I don't care what you say, yer going to catch a cold! 'Tis bad enough indoors, but standing outdoors at that theater . . . I tell you no good will come of it."

"Nevertheless, dearest Nan, I am dressed most fashionably, and as a member of Her Majesty's court, I cannot be seen any other way. Fetch me the purple lace neck whisk, please. And my jewel box."

Nan went off, grumbling about certain people's willfulness, while Valentina, smiling like a pleased feline, continued to admire her gown. Since Edward had been dead for over six months, she was out of black and allowed to add gray, white, purple, blue, brown, and dark shades of green to her wardrobe. The queen preferred her ladies to wear black and the maids of honor to wear white except for festive occasions, so when in attendance upon Her Majesty, Valentina would have to don more somber garb.

Valentina's gown was of a single amethyst color on the bodice, overskirt, and underskirt. The bodice was decorated with silver threads and pearls in an interlaced design. The panel of the underskirt was sewn with silver threads in a pattern of leaves and vines. The tiniest ruffle of violet lace sprinkled with tiny seed pearls edged the neckline.

Valentina opened a small ivory box and, after carefully studying the contents for a moment, removed two heart-shaped, tiny black patches. She placed one just barely above the right-hand corner of her mouth, the other on the swell of her left breast.

"Scandalous, it is!" fumed Nan, returning with her mistress's jewel case and the required neck whisk. "I just don't know what's gotten into you, m'lady. Your mother would be very upset."

"Patches are in fashion, Nan. There is nothing scandalous about patches. Open the jewel box, and then attach the whisk for me, please." Valentina turned her attention to her jewelry, most of which she had inherited from the Barrows family. She drew forth a triple strand of pink pearls, each strand longer than the one on top of it. A large teardrop baroque pearl surrounded by diamonds hung from the longest strand. When Valentina fastened the necklace around her neck, the great teardrop nestled between her breasts. She next chose fat pearl earbobs and then a variety of pretty, though not spectacular, rings. The pearls were probably the best jewels in her possession.

The neck whisk fastened into place, Nan assured herself that Valentina's elegant chignon had not been disturbed. Then she said, "Since it does no good to reason with you, I suppose I had best get your cloak and gloves. Promise me at least that you will wear the hood, for the wind coming off the river is icy damp."

"I will," Valentina assured Nan, smiling.

As Valentina descended the main staircase of Greenwood House, Padraic was openly admiring. She was garbed in a lovely pale amethyst velvet cloak edged in soft gray rabbit fur and carried a small and decidedly frivolous muff of the same fur, to which she had attached a nosegay of silk Parma violets. She held out a hand encased in a scented pale purple glove. He kissed her hand, his eyes meeting hers.

"Good day, cousin," he said, pleased to see her blush.

"Good morrow, m'lord. Are we ready to leave? Which theater are you taking me to, the Rose or the Globe?" she asked.

"The Globe, and we must hurry if we are to get seats on the stage. I will not allow you to be exposed to the rigors of the pit. On the stage we are safer from the pickpockets and cutpurses, but whatever you do, don't let go of your muff or your cloak, Val."

"Nan is scandalized that you would take me to the theater at all," Valentina admitted as they entered their carriage.

"On reflection, I am not so certain that Nan is wrong. She may have more sense than either of us. The theater crowd is apt to be a rough one. Stay by me at all times, Val," he warned.

"Where is the Globe?" Valentina asked.

"Across the bridge in Southwark," he answered her. "'Tis really the New Globe. The city council and their Puritan allies got the old theater torn down several years ago. The new one was built across the river near the Bear Garden. 'Tis a pretty rough district, but generally safe in the daytime."

"Is it like the mummers, Padraic?"

He smiled. "No, a thousand times better, Val. The mummers act out old plays that go back so far in time that the words have been altered over the centuries. Besides, they are simple stories. A play by Master Shakespeare or poor Christopher Marlowe is a totally different experience. I do not understand how they can form words so that they sound so extraordinary."

"Why 'poor' Christopher Marlowe?"

"He was killed in a tavern brawl several years ago. The man was a genius . . . and a complete madman."

"I remember your sister, Velvet, saying that she had met him during her time at court. She did not like him at all. She said he attempted to take liberties with her."

"Aye, that would have been just like Marlowe. He held himself in great esteem." Padraic chuckled. "I imagine Velvet sent him packing."

It was a beautiful day. The sun shone brightly, and there was almost no wind at all, most unusual for January. They traveled upriver into the city toward the London Bridge. Southwark, with its theaters, Bear Garden, and taverns, was just on the other side of the bridge. The bridge itself was actually more of a street extending itself over the Thames. There were buildings on either side of the bridge containing shops, homes, and elegant whorehouses. River traffic made its way under the bridge except for twice daily during the hours of high tide when "shooting the bridge" became too hazardous except for fools and lovers of danger.

London was a noisy city, and Valentina wondered if she would ever get used to it. There was also the matter of the refuse in the streets, which became muddy during rain or snow. The stink was bad enough in winter, Padraic told her, but worse in summer. As for the rats, she was astounded to see them boldly rifling through the piles of garbage in the streets, neither unimpeded nor fearful of man. The passing crowds paid them little attention, going about their business past the fetid piles without so much as a glance at the red-eyed rodents.

The carriage clattered across the London Bridge. Once in Southwark, it was immediately surrounded by beggars, and Lady Barrows understood why Lord Burke had insisted on their taking along the coachman's assistant and two grooms who rode behind. It was the job of those three men to beat the beggars off and keep the coach free of encumbrance so that John, the coachman, might guide the vehicle safely. When they reached the theater, the four men would guard the carriage so that nothing might be stolen.

"Sit back," Padraic warned Valentina. "When they see a woman, they know there's jewelry — and some are bold enough to leap inside and tear it from you." Although her cape was fastened securely with silver and purple jade frogs, Lady Barrows heeded her companion's advice, drawing the cape even more tightly about her. She pulled the fur-lined hood far forward to hide her face.

The carriage turned down a narrow lane that led directly to the theater, and most of their followers disappeared. A pennant flew above the theater, announcing that there would be a performance that day.

Valentina leaned forward, and to Lord Burke, the lovely face peering from the fur-edged velvet hood was the excited one of a young girl receiving something she had wanted all her life. He longed to kiss her, but he knew this was neither the time nor the appropriate place.

"Remain inside the carriage," Lord Burke told her, "while I see if I can obtain seats for us." He climbed from the coach. The grooms stood guard at each door so that Lady Barrows would not be disturbed.

Fascinated, Valentina watched the street traffic. Gazing up, she could see a cloth-of-gold globe sewn on the bright scarlet silk banner floating from a gilded ash pole atop the tower of the play-house. Outside her coach the playgoers hurried by, common people for the most part, apprentices, shopkeepers and their wives, some foreign visitors who had heard of Master Shakespeare. There were young girls selling fruit from wooden trays; a fat, red-cheeked woman crying, "Buns! Sugar buns! Who'll buy my buns? Two for a hapenny!" There was a water seller and another woman crying her cakes and ale.

The carriage door opened, and Lord Burke handed Valentina out into the street. "I've managed to get us the last two seats on the stage," he said, and led her into the theater. "Keep your cloak tightly about you, Val. Moll Cutpurse is rumored to be here today."

"Who on earth is Moll Cutpurse, Padraic?"

"A most notorious thief. Her name is Mary Frith, and she was born, I've heard, respectable enough. She dresses in men's clothing—itself quite an oddity. She gained quite a reputation over the years and shows no mercy even to her own sex. I hope you haven't worn a great deal of jewelry."

"You cannot expect me to appear in public without adornment," she said sharply, and he grinned.

"Keep your cloak closed, Val," he told her. "I am unarmed and in no mood to get into an altercation over some trifle of yours."

They made their way through the pit, where the common folk sat for a penny apiece. The benches were already filled with a noisy, jostling mob. Sellers who had paid the theater manager a small fee were hawking ale, cider, fruits, nuts, and cakes inside the pit. A group of men were playing cards in a corner of the theater, while in the very center of the pit a hotly contested and vocal game of dice was underway. At the foot of the stairs leading up to the stage they were stopped by an attendant.

"No entry," he said. "This section of the stage is reserved for my lord, the Earl of Pembroke, and his party."

"But I have my threepenny chits," Padraic Burke argued.

"No entry," said the attendant firmly.

"The Earl of Pembroke will not be coming," said Valentina, speaking up boldly.

"Not coming?" The theater attendant looked at her askance. "And why is he not coming, I should like to know?"

"Because he has been in the Fleet on Her Majesty's orders since yesterday. Obviously your ticket seller knew or he would not have sold Lord Burke his tickets. Let us pass, please. I am not accustomed to being forced to stand about a public place waiting to be seated. I am Lady Barrows, one of Her Majesty's ladies-in-waiting."

The attendant made Valentina a leg, then escorted them to their seats. "I apologize, madam. I was not informed. I hope you will not speak ill of the Globe to Her Majesty." He was very impressed by Lady Barrows's air of authority, not to mention her beauty. He had supposed all of the queen's women were dried-up sticks like old Bess herself.

"An understandable mistake," Valentina replied graciously as she was seated. She smiled her thanks at the attendant, then immediately ignored him.

Lord Burke barely managed to contain his glee. "God's foot, what a vixen you are! Another moment, and the poor man would have been begging your forgiveness."

"The Earl of Pembroke is in the Fleet," she said, "so where was the harm in setting the man straight? Would you have stood there and argued with him, my lord? What are those rooms facing the stage?" she asked. "Why do some have their curtains drawn, and others not? Would not one of those rooms been more private?"

"Oh, immensely more private, madam, and entirely damaging to your reputation. You would have been ruined at court the moment you set foot in one of them. Those rooms are where the high-priced whores entertain their customers. You are also apt to find in the audience more than one highborn lady of the court behind jeweled masks offering hospitality to their lovers away from the prying eyes of husbands and friends. During the performance, watch those boxes. The whores will wave and call to the gentlemen from their seats. Those who sit silently behind their masks watching the performance are usually having an illicit rendezvous. As for the curtains, Val, when drawn it generally means that, er, business is being conducted."

She colored. "Gracious! This is certainly a very different world in which I suddenly find myself, Padraic. I think I am very fortunate to have you and Willow to watch over me. I can see that I have a great deal to learn about life in the city and life at court."

"I will indeed watch over you, Val," he said softly into her ear. "You are my most treasured possession, sweet love." God's foot! He loved the freshness of her perfume!

"I am no one's possession, my lord," she said in a low, angry voice. "How dare you say such a thing?"

Before he could reply, a voice called out. "Burke! Padraic Burke! Is it truly you?"

They looked up to see an elegantly garbed gentleman, every bit as tall as Lord Burke, climbing the stairs to the stage and waving at them. Valentina thought him most handsome. His tawny-gold hair reminded her of dark honey. Recognition dawned, and Padraic rose to return the greeting. The two men coming together reminded Valentina of day and night, their coloring was so different.

Taking the seat next to Lady Barrows, the gentleman caught her hand and placed a fervent kiss on it. Misty gray eyes were set above a long, elegant nose beneath which was a beautifully barbered tawny-gold mustache. The stranger stared directly at her, frankly admiring. "Thomas Ashburne, Earl of Kempe, madam, at your service. Tell me that you are not his wife and I shall die a happy man!"

A small smile touched Valentina's mouth. She was feeling a definite stirring of interest. Nonetheless, her voice was cool as she replied, "You are most outrageous, sirrah!"

"But are you his wife, divinity?"

"I am his cousin."

"Then my prayers are answered, madam." He turned to Padraic. "Will you not introduce us, my friend?"

"Tom, behave yourself! This is my cousin, Lady Barrows. She is newly widowed and just up from the country for the very first time in her life. She begins her service to the queen tomorrow. I have made it my personal mission to watch over her."

"I think that rather selfish of you, Padraic. I should very much enjoy watching over Lady Barrows myself." He took up Valentina's hand again and, looking deeply into her eyes, said, "May I also offer my services, madam, as your knight?"

"For God's sake, Tom, are you never going to grow up?" Lord Burke grumbled.

Ignoring him, the earl said, "Well, madam?"

"She doesn't want you hanging about and irritating the queen just as she is about to begin her service," Padraic said.

"I suppose a lady can never have too many charming gentlemen looking after her," replied Valentina with a flirtatious smile. Padraic's possessive remark had rankled her, and now he was attempting to drive off this attractive man when she was absolutely certain that she did not want the Earl of Kempe driven off. "May I have my hand back, my lord?" she asked.

"Only if you insist," he returned with an infectious grin.

Valentina twinkled at him. She could not remember ever flirting with a man. It was fun!

"The play is about to begin," Padraic said pointedly.

Valentina saw that several players were now at center stage. "Lord Burke is correct. We should give the players our attention."

"My voice will be silent then, divinity, but you cannot silence my thoughts or my heart," responded the Earl of Kempe passionately.

"God's foot! What rubbish!" groused Lord Burke, giving his friend a dark look.

Valentina giggled. She realized it was not the sophisticated thing to do, but she simply could not help it. Padraic was jealous, *really* jealous! No one had ever been jealous of her before. She had never had two gentlemen vying for her attention. "I do not think it rubbish at all," she said demurely. "I think it rather charming of you, my lord earl." She favored him with another smile.

Tom Ashburne grinned back, well pleased with himself. Lord Burke sent them both withering looks before turning his attention to the play.

As the play unfolded, both men thought about Valentina. The Earl of Kempe considered how marvelous it would be to make love to her, to kiss that outrageous little heart at the corner of her mouth. Padraic Burke's thoughts were more serious. He had finally faced his love for Valentina, and he had no intention of letting another man near her. You are mine, hinny love, whether you know it or not, he told her silently. You are mine alone!

Chapter Three ·

MARY FITTON HAD BEEN PUT INTO THE CARE of Lady Hawkins. There, she miscarried of a son. Rash and reckless Mary, who had put on a man's great cape and strode boldly through the court to meet with her lover. Mary was in deepest disgrace. Like pretty little Elizabeth Vernon, she had taken a chance, but unlike Elizabeth, she had gambled and lost. The Earl of Southampton had married his lover, Mistress Vernon. The Earl of Pembroke would not. This sudden harsh reality had frightened the five remaining maids of honor into unusually circumspect behavior. They huddled about the fireplace in the Maidens' Chamber, awaiting the arrival of both the girl chosen to take Mary's place and the new mistress of the maids. Their nervousness increased when Lady Scrope entered the room, another woman accompanying her. Who was she?

"Good morning, young ladies," Lady Scrope called to them.

The five young girls rose and curtsied to the two women. Each surreptitiously studied the stranger. She was young, but certainly not as young as they were. Their ages ranged from thirteen to seventeen. Mary Fitton had been close to nineteen, the eldest of them all, and this stranger didn't look much older than Mary.

"This is Lady Barrows, the new mistress of the maids," Lady Scrope told them. "Please come forward one at a time and tell her your name and age."

The five glanced quickly at one another, then the eldest one detached herself from the group and came forward.

"I am Margaret Dudley, and I am seventeen, madam." She curtsied to Valentina, who smiled and nodded. "This is my cousin, Elizabeth Stanley," she said, beckoning the littlest of the girls forward.

"How old are you, Elizabeth Stanley?" Valentina said gently.

"Thirteen, madam" was the piping reply. The child bobbed a curtsy.

The tallest of the girls, a proud-looking blonde whose beauty was marred by a too-long nose, moved into position before Lady Barrows.

"I am Lady Honoria de Bohun," she said, and stepped back.

"You have not curtsied to Lady Barrows, Honoria," admonished Lady Scrope.

"Surely, madam, you do not expect me to do so," the girl said icily. "Certainly a de Bohun takes precedence over someone named Barrows."

"Not knowing Lady Barrows's full pedigree, Honoria de Bohun, I could not say, but her position as mistress of the maids gives her preeminence over you, and unless you make your curtsy, I shall inform the queen of your disobedience. The events of this week have not left Her Majesty with much patience for any of you. She will not hesitate to dismiss you, Honoria de Bohun, for Elizabeth Tudor takes precedence over us all. Do you understand me, child? I would also mention that you have forgotten to tell us your age."

"I am sixteen" was the surly reply. Honoria de Bohun curtsied to Valentina with barely concealed irritation.

"I am Eleanora Clifford, madam," said a rosy-cheeked, dark-haired girl, "and I also am sixteen." She flashed Valentina a merry smile as she accomplished her curtsy.

The last of the maids came forward and curtsied prettily. "My name is Penelope Howard," she said, "and I am fourteen."

"I am pleased to meet you all," said Valentina. "My younger cousin, Lady Gabrielle Edwardes, a daughter of the Earl of Alcester, will be joining you in a few days. I hope that will satisfy your curiosity over the new maid of honor, as I am certain it has been burning brightly."

All of the girls except Honoria giggled, and Lady Scrope said, "Take the afternoon to get to know these hoydens, Lady Barrows. The queen will not need them until this evening, when she is hosting a fête for an ambassador from one or another of those little German states."

"Perhaps the maidens will show me about Whitehall so that I may more quickly get my bearings," said Valentina.

"An excellent idea," Lady Scrope enthused. "I will leave you in their care, Lady Barrows, and good fortune with them. They have driven many a good woman to near madness." So saying, Lady Scrope departed.

A small smile touched Valentina's lips as she settled herself in a chair by the fire. Looking at the five young girls with her unusual amethyst-colored eyes, she said, "Are you really as dreadful as everyone has warned me, or is it perhaps that serving an elderly queen is simply not very exciting? Many of our mothers served the queen in their youth, and they consider it an important part of our social obligation, do they not?"

"Did your mama serve the queen?" asked little Beth Stanley.

"Aye," said Valentina, "she did. The queen called my mother her 'country mouse' as she was very shy and quiet. Because her family was not a great one, no one realized that she was an heiress. This coupled with the fact that she was no beauty, caused people to ignore her."

"Oh, how dreadful for her!" sympathized Penelope Howard.

"Not really," explained Valentina. "My mother, like the queen, is an intelligent woman. She had lived her entire life in the country—as I have. She was not used to court ways, and the one thing she feared was to be liked for her possessions and not her true self. She fell in love with my father on her first day at court, although he did not notice her at all, being far too busy seducing all the beauties. My father was called 'The Handsomest Man at Court.' "

"Ooh!" breathed little Beth, her blue eyes round. "I have heard about him! He is Irish, is he not? All of the ladies adored him, but did he not cause a dreadful scandal of some sort?"

Now all of the maids of honor, including Honoria de Bohun, were gathered around Valentina, sitting on the rug before the blazing fire and looking up at her eagerly. The court thrived on gossip, even ancient gossip.

"Oh, indeed he did," replied Valentina, her eyes twinkling. "What have you been told about it?"

"My mama and aunts would always stop talking about him when I got too close," admitted the youngest maid of honor.

"Perhaps then," considered Valentina, "I should not speak of it."

"Oh, no! No! Do tell! Do!" cried the maids of honor.

Valentina laughed. "Well," she said, "I suppose if you are old enough to be maids of honor, you are old enough to hear about my father. He is indeed Irish born. His name was Conn O'Malley, and his sister, my aunt Skye, also served the queen. It was my aunt who introduced my papa into court. He charmed Her Majesty, and the queen gave him a place in her Gentlemen Pensioners. For several years he remained with the court until he made the mistake of seducing the wife of the ambassador from San Lorenzo, and being caught. If that were not bad enough, a Lady Holden and her twin daughters all claimed that Papa had seduced them as well! Of course, Lord Holden was fit to be tied.

"Under the circumstances, it became necessary for the queen to send my father from court, but old Lord Burghley felt that Papa should also be wed in order to settle him down. The question was, to whom should they marry him? He was Irish, and did not have a great name. On the other hand, he was handsome, charming, and wealthy due to his involvement with the O'Malley-Small trading company.

"As the queen and Lord Burghley pondered their dilemma in the privacy of the queen's closet, my mama, who was Her Majesty's only attendant at that moment, spoke up, suggesting her-

self as the bride! She explained to them that, as she, too, was
half Irish, wealthy, and without a great name, she would be the
perfect bride for Conn O'Malley. She reminded the queen that
Her Majesty had promised my mama's late father that she would
find a husband for Mama. There was but one condition. My mother's bridegroom had to agree to take her family name so that it
would not die out. That is how Conn O'Malley became Conn St.
Michael, Lord Bliss. And that is the story of how my mama and
papa were married," Valentina finished with a smile.

"Is your papa still very handsome?" asked Margaret Dudley.
"The mere mention of his name can make the queen smile, and
she rarely smiles these days."

"Aye," Valentina replied. "He is still as handsome as ever,
though he is graying just slightly at the temples."

"And are they happy, your parents?" Eleanora Clifford asked.

"Aye! They have always been happy and content together, for
they truly love each other."

"Love! Just look where *love* has gotten poor Mary," remarked
Honoria de Bohun bitterly.

"Will Herbert knows naught of love," said Eleanora. "He is a
selfish, ambitious man, and you know it, Honoria. You were an-
gling for him yourself, but Mary caught his fancy. What Will
Herbert wanted from Mary was not love. You were fortunate to
escape his attentions."

"I wonder if there is really such a thing as love," Honoria said,
"or if the queen is right and affection's false."

"Of course there is such a thing as love," Margaret Dudley
replied. "If there were not the hope of love, I do not believe that
any of us would survive. Tell her that love is real, madam," Margaret begged as she turned pleading brown eyes to Valentina.

"Of course love exists," Valentina assured them, "but sometimes it is harder to find than at other times. You must never
give up hope of love, any of you."

"If your father is Lord Bliss," Penelope Howard asked curiously, "then how are you Lady Barrows?"

"I am a widow," Valentina told them.

"Oh," the maids of honor moaned sympathetically.

"Were you married long? Do you have children? What was he
like? Did you love him wildly?" The questions came fast and
furious.

Valentina laughed. What a pack of curious magpies these
young girls were! But then, their life at court was a very unnatural

one, she felt. They were forced to mature far more quickly than she had, safe in her country home. Even Anne had not come to court until she was older, although Bevin had been just fifteen. Of course, Court had not seemed to hurt her sisters any, but Aidan St. Michael's daughters had strong, broad streaks of their mother's practicality in their own natures.

She looked down at the five upturned young faces. Even Honoria de Bohun appeared to be softening toward Lady Barrows. "I was wed less than a month," she told her charges. "Ned was killed in a riding accident. There were, of course, no children. He was a wonderful man." No need to explain further, Valentina considered. The rest was really none of their business.

"Will you mourn him all of your days, madam?" asked Beth.

Valentina forced herself not to laugh. "I think not," she answered the girl. "I know . . . he would not want it so."

"So then, like the rest of us, you have come to court to seek a husband," said Honoria de Bohun bluntly.

"Honoria!" The other girls looked shocked. Of course one came to court to find a husband if one was not already promised, but it was a dreadful lack of delicacy to admit such a thing. Besides, Lady Barrows was their superior.

"Nay, Honoria," said Valentina gently. She wondered why the girl was so hostile.

"Then why have you come to court? No one comes these days without a good reason. The old queen is dying, but she will take a long time doing it, my father says. Tudors are very stubborn."

"I have come to serve the queen as my mother, my aunt, my cousins, and even two of my younger sisters already have done. There is no mystery to it. I am still in mourning for my husband, and quite frankly, my dear, I am not one bit interested in getting married again. Enough, however, of all this chatter about me. You must tell me about yourselves, and then I want you to show me Whitehall. Who will start? Margaret, you are the eldest."

Each girl gave Valentina a description of her family, her connections, and her life prior to coming to court. Two of the five girls, Eleanora Clifford and Penelope Howard, were betrothed before coming to court, and Eleanora was to be married in late summer. Valentina reminded herself to write her mother about that, for Maggie would be thirteen next month, and who knew when another opportunity would arise to place her younger sister among the queen's maids of honor? Who even knew how long the queen would live? When James Stewart inherited England's throne, he would bring his own people with him. The timing was ideal for Maggie St. Michael.

Margaret Dudley had lost her betrothed husband two years ago when he was killed in the New World during a privateering venture. Finding another match for her had not been easy, for though she was a member of the powerful Dudley family, she was part of a distant, less important branch. She had obtained her appointment to the queen's service through the good offices of her distant cousin, the earl of Warwick, who was also a Dudley. Her cousin, Beth Stanley, by contrast, was an extremely wealthy heiress for whom there were numerous suitors. Beth's widowed mother, however, was in no great hurry to turn her only child's fortune over to someone who might not be as kindly disposed toward Beth's mother as little Beth herself was.

Honoria de Bohun, though possessed of an ancient and famous name, had very little money. Her family had scraped together everything they had to send her to court. Their hope was that Honoria's blond beauty and chaste character would bring her a husband, preferably a wealthy one. Though many men had tried, no one had succeeded in seducing the proud girl. Honoria understood the value of her only jewels, her beauty and her virtue. Her initial hostility toward Valentina stemmed from the fact that Honoria viewed every attractive woman at court as a potential rival. Valentina learned this and everything else about Honoria from chatty Eleanora Clifford when Honoria excused herself to go to the necessary in an effort to escape speaking about herself.

When she returned, Valentina said in a kindly tone, "I have learned your history from your companions, Honoria. Is there anything you would like to tell me?"

"I am certain they have told you *all*, madam" was the sour reply.

"Then," said Valentina, standing, "let us take our walk. Please show me Whitehall so that I shall be able to get about without making a fool of myself."

Margaret Dudley took it upon herself to be the spokeswoman and guide. "Whitehall," she said, "is really a jumble of buildings, madam. It is not necessary to go much beyond the Great Court, for the farther away from it you get, the less there is to see. I prefer Richmond, where we shall shortly be going."

"I like Hampton Court best," said Penelope.

"Greenwich is my favorite," Eleanora chimed in.

"That is where my parents met and were married," said Valentina.

"They were wed at Greenwich?" Beth was again wide-eyed.

"In the queen's own chapel by her very own chaplain," replied Lady Barrows. "My aunt Skye and her youngest child, my cousin, Velvet, were also wed at Greenwich, under the queen's good auspices."

"I only wish the queen was as kindly disposed toward romance today as she was in your relations' time," muttered Honoria. "God help any of us to whom a gentleman might attempt to pay court! There is always hell to pay when the queen notices. She is jealous of all of us because we are young and pretty, while she is old and dried-up."

"Honoria!" Margaret Dudley said, genuinely distressed. "You will surely get yourself in trouble if anyone overheard you. You cannot afford to be sent home before you have found a husband. You *must* learn to guard your tongue."

"Well, it is true," Honoria replied defiantly. "None of us has any chance of happiness while the old dragon is watching—and she is *always* watching."

"Margaret is correct, Honoria," Valentina gently remonstrated. "You must guard your speech, for you hold a valued place in the queen's service, and whatever others may think privately about Her Majesty, they would not be above reporting your behavior in order to obtain your place for a relation."

Honoria sighed. "I have been here for almost a year, madam, and I have yet to meet a gentleman whose intentions were serious. It is all so frustrating!"

Valentina smiled. "I have two brothers who will soon be coming to court, and several cousins. I shall have to introduce you to them, Honoria. I cannot vouch for their intentions, but I think you will find them more sympathetic than the usual courtier."

"Are your brothers very handsome?" asked Beth eagerly.

"They like to think so." Valentina chuckled. "Colin will be twenty, and Payton, eighteen come spring."

The palace was inhabited by hundreds of people, from courtiers to lowly servants. There were many paved courts, each with its own name. Valentina found the Preaching Court, where a pulpit had been set in the middle of the garden for summer sermons, a novel idea. There were long hallways and galleries, a profusion of rooms for lodging courtiers and servants, all arranged around the various courts. The courts had been designed in all shapes and sizes, and there were several towers, including the one in which Elizabeth's father, Henry VIII, had wed her mother, Mistress Anne Boleyn.

When Cardinal Wolsey turned over all his possessions to King Henry, the king caused the Privy Gallery from the cardinal's country house, Esher, to be dismantled and rebuilt at Whitehall. It was a chain of connecting galleries with windows on either side that looked out on gardens on one side and the River Thames on the other. The galleries were paneled and wainscoted in fine woods, the carvings of human, animal, and floral figures. The ceilings were fashioned of stone and gold, and there were marvelous tapestries on the walls. Valentina thought this section was the loveliest part of Whitehall.

Margaret Dudley led them at last to the Privy Chamber, where she led Valentina to a portrait hung with honor on a wall near the entrance to the chamber. Henry Tudor's court painter, Hans Holbein, had painted Henry VIII, flanked by his father, Henry VII, his mother, Elizabeth of York, and Queen Jane Seymour, who was the mother of his only legitimate son. Although Queen Jane was dead when Master Holbein painted his portrait, Holbein had known her well, and he painted her into the great portrait from memory.

The maids of honor and their mistress passed through the great Stone Gallery on the ground floor of Whitehall. The queen had once used it to hold entertainments for important foreign visitors. Now, however, the Stone Gallery was divided into three apartments, and there was a temporary banqueting house outside in a courtyard.

A canvas marquee, one hundred yards long, its roof supported by thirty gilded poles each forty feet high, had been designed to appear to be an actual stone building. The outside walls resembled stonework. Inside, the painters had painted the canopy with a sun, stars, and white clouds. Twenty years after being built, the "temporary" hall still stood and was used when the queen entertained at Whitehall.

"She'll be holding tonight's fête here," Margaret Dudley said.

"Is it not cold?" queried Valentina.

"No more so than anywhere else in the palace. Besides, there are braziers of coals and all the bodies to keep the hall warm. And the dancing keeps the blood flowing hotly," said Margaret.

When they returned to the Maidens' Chamber they were informed that the queen would take her supper with only her ladies and young maidens in attendance. She would be wearing a gown of cloth of silver, and her maids of honor were to garb themselves in white and silver. Lady Barrows was free to wear what she liked. Valentina's small private apartment was just off the Maidens' Chamber and there, to her relief, she found Nan waiting.

"This place is no better than a rabbit's warren," grumbled Nan. "I cannot find my way about, and the servants are proper hoity-toity, m'lady. I could get no one to bring bathwater."

"You must tip them a coin for such a duty, Nan. Mother's old Mag told me that. But don't pay them until the water is delivered, for they are likely to take your coin and not bother to bring the water."

"What a place! What a place!" Nan complained. "I wish you would marry Lord Burke, and then we could live in a proper house."

"What is this, Nan? Who told you I was even considering marriage again, let alone marriage to Padraic Burke? I certainly have not said such a thing."

"Well, he loves you, don't he?" asked Nan bluntly.

Valentina stared at her without a word.

"You ain't getting any younger, m'lady, if I just might mention it. Twenty-one this March, isn't it? It ain't easy for an older woman to get herself another husband. Lord Burke is a handsome man with a good fortune. If he's staying at court, and I hear he is, it's because he wants to be near you, I'm thinkin'. Now, ye can't expect the ladies to ignore him, ye know. Ye best beware, m'lady, lest ye lose a good catch."

"Nan, I should not have to tell you that I am still in mourning for Lord Barrows," Valentina scolded. "I cannot begin to consider another marriage until the summer. I am not even certain I *want* to marry again. I am enjoying my freedom."

"Yer enjoying having two gentlemen fight over ye," Nan said huffily. "Lord Burke don't like it that the Earl of Kempe has taken to hanging about ye."

"Lord Burke can go to hell in a handbasket, Nan. He is not my husband, *nor* my betrothed husband, *nor* even my lover! I am my own mistress, and I shall do as I please."

"God bless me if yer gentle lady mother could hear you speaking such words! A lover, indeed! If I ever catch you taking a lover, m'lady, I'll go right home to Pearroc Royal and tell yer father on ye!"

Valentina laughed. "There is little chance of my taking a lover, Nan. For one thing, you are too vigilant a watchdog for me. And I was not, I am afraid, born to dissemble the truth. Now go and see if you can cajole one of the footmen into bringing me some hot water, then find me something to eat."

Valentina ate a light supper of capon, bread, and cheese washed down with her own wine, and was comfortably ensconced in her oak tub when the door to her bedchamber burst open and the five maids of honor burst into the room.

"Here, young ladies, what is this?" demanded Nan, outraged.

"Lady Barrows! Lady Barrows! Honoria has taken my good pearls and will not give them back!" sobbed Beth.

"You have a half-dozen strands more to wear, and I have none," said Honoria, herself close to tears. "You have lent them to me before."

"Who are you setting your cap for tonight, Honoria?" teased Eleanora.

"You need not be so smug just because you are soon to be wed," snapped Honoria. "Not all of us are so lucky!"

"I want my pearls!" wailed Beth.

Valentina closed her eyes. She knew she could not allow these young hoydens to gain the upper hand.

"You have interrupted my bath," she said coldly, and the room went silent as the girls realized the seriousness of their error. "When I have dressed, we will discuss this matter."

The five girls silently backed from the room, closing the door gently behind them.

As the door closed, Valentina said to Nan, "Help me dress so I may go out and settle the argument."

"Which one of those shameless gowns will ye be wanting, m'lady?" said Nan.

"The deep violet with the silver lace," Valentina answered sweetly.

The maids of honor were properly subdued when Lady Barrows entered their room, and they gasped at Valentina's beauty. Earlier, she had been wearing a high-necked black gown, her hair hidden beneath a linen cap. This vision in rich violet velvet stunned them. The gown's underskirt was made of cloth of silver and velvet brocade, and the sleeves dripped with silver lace. The same silver lace coquettishly edged the neckline. The gown was fashionable and wonderfully flattering. Valentina's elegant chignon was dressed with small silver flowers, each sewn with an amethyst center. Pink pearls adorned her ears and throat.

"Are you ready?" she asked them, glad for the impression she was making on them.

"Aye, madam," they chorused, curtsying to her.

"Excellent. We shall go as soon as we have solved the dilemma of the pearls. Honoria and Beth, come over to me." When the two girls stood before her, Valentina said, "Honoria, you were wrong to take Elizabeth's pearls without asking her first. As for you, Beth, the pearls are indeed yours, and if you had wished to wear the strand Honoria chose, you might have offered her another strand in its place. It is difficult for a woman to be without jewelry, you know. Until I married Lord Barrows, I had very little real jewelry.

"I must punish both of you, for you have both been wrong. Neither of you shall wear any jewelry tonight. No ropes of pearls, no earbobs, no rings, no brooches, no bracelets. Tonight your only jewels will be your flashing eyes and sparkling smiles. You will have to depend on your own charm tonight, my fine young ladies."

"'Tis not fair," whimpered Beth, her blue eyes filling.

"Elizabeth Stanley, we have not yet discussed the matter of your rude invasion of my privacy when I was in my bath," Valentina said softly.

"Be quiet, Beth!" Margaret warned her cousin.

Beneath Lady Barrows's stern gaze, the girls removed their jewelry. Then everyone hurried to the queen's apartments, where Elizabeth Tudor was awaiting them.

Her Majesty's sharp eyes swept over the girls, and then she said, "Why are Elizabeth Stanley and Honoria de Bohun not wearing any jewelry, Lady Barrows?"

"A punishment, madam. The sins of selfishness and pride run deep within them," replied Valentina.

"Hah! At last there is a mistress of the maids who knows how to handle those unbridled hoydens! I knew I was correct in choosing you, Lady Barrows. You may have your father's beauty, but you also have your mother's sense."

With a chuckle, the queen departed from her royal apartments, her ladies-in-waiting and her maids of honor following in her wake.

In the queen's banqueting hall, musicians were playing a

spritely tune as the queen entered. Her brown velvet throne,
studded with very large diamonds, rubies, sapphires, and pearls,
had been placed in the most prominent position within the hall.
The queen seated herself, surrounded by her women. She was
most graciously pleased to receive the new ambassador from the
duchy of Cleves. There was a definite edge to the atmosphere,
however, and, listening carefully, Valentina learned the reason
for it.

The Earl of Essex, son of Lettice Knollys, the queen's cousin
and former rival, was once again behaving badly. He had been
the queen's favorite almost from his first day at court, and she
loved him dearly, sometimes as she might have loved a son, at
other times as she might have loved a man. Throughout their
entire relationship, however, the Earl of Essex, Robert Devereaux, had allowed his great pride to rule his head and his heart.
Unlike his wily late stepfather, Robert Dudley, the Earl of Leicester, Essex never learned to put the queen first in their close
relationship.

His ego was monumental, and he was quick to quarrel with
anyone he disliked or anyone he felt had slighted him. There was
not one of the queen's other favorites with whom he did not argue.
For a brief time during the Armada scare, he had healed his
breach with Sir Walter Ralegh, but in the years since there had
been scarcely a civil word between him and the queen's old favorite, "Water." The queen loved Essex, but Essex did not understand that Elizabeth Tudor would not be cut off from others
she also loved.

The Earl of Essex had put himself in direct confrontation with
old Lord Burghley and Lord Burghley's heir apparent and son,
Robert Cecil. After Lord Burghley's death, Robert Cecil had increased his favor with the queen, for he was a shrewd politician
and a loyal servant of Her Majesty, as his father had been. If
Cecil favored a matter, the Earl of Essex was certain to oppose
it.

Essex had shared command of the Cádiz expedition with Admiral Lord Howard, quarreling constantly with the admiral and
irritating him with childish ploys such as placing his signature
so high on a document meant for the queen that there was no
place for the admiral to sign his name above it.

It did not help that the queen raised Lord Admiral Howard of
Effingham to the earldom of Nottingham for his service to England in both the Armada and the Cádiz campaigns, for the Earl

of Nottingham took precedence over the Earl of Essex at official functions, so in an appalling fit of sulks, Robert Devereaux refused to attend the Accession Day Tilt in November of that particular year. The queen missed her young Robin, and, in an effort to attract him back to her side, created him Earl Marshal of England, thus giving him precedence over Nottingham.

The queen had to choose a new lord deputy of Ireland. The Earl of Tyrone had been promised aid by the ever-meddling Spanish, and as the French had signed a peace treaty with Spain, the danger to England was once more very real. Elizabeth wished to appoint her cousin, Sir William Knollys, who was also uncle to the Earl of Essex. Essex, seeking to rid himself of Sir George Carew, one of old Lord Burghley's cronies, suggested Carew for the position. What better place to send an enemy than Ireland?

The queen, wise to Essex's little game, refused his candidate. Childishly, Essex lost his temper, turning his back on the queen in open contempt. The queen boxed Essex's ears. His hand went to his sword, and he loudly declared that he would not have accepted such treatment from Henry VIII himself, let alone a mere woman. Elizabeth Tudor's dark gray eyes narrowed. Seeing her silent rising anger, the Earl of Nottingham wisely placed himself between his sovereign and the earl. The queen, more than a little disenchanted by her favorite's outrageous behavior, walked away without a backward glance. Leicester. Hatton. Ralegh. All had been clever, passionate men whose devotion to her never wavered, though God knew they had all been ambitious. She had given to them gladly, and they had accepted graciously, protecting her and playing at love with sweet, soft words. Not so Robert Devereaux. She did not understand it, and it angered her to realize that for the first time in her life she had erred in her judgment of a man.

The Earl of Essex had insulted the queen, but he could not bring himself to apologize to her. It was at this time that William Cecil, Lord Burghley, chose to die. Elizabeth was lost in grief, for William Cecil had been with her from the beginning of her reign. He had been the father she had never really had. Lord Burghley's death presented a golden opportunity for the Earl of Essex to mend his fences. His mother and sisters told him to do it, but Essex would not heed their advice. He would return to the queen's side in his own good time.

He chose to go to the Accession Day Tilt on November 17 of that year, but his attendance was meant more to spite Sir Walter

Ralegh than to please the queen. Several years prior, Ralegh, without royal permission, had married the queen's favorite maid of honor, Elizabeth Throckmorton. They were in love, and had waited over four years to gain the queen's consent, but she had dismissed the subject each time they attempted to broach it. Finally, Bess and her lover ran off to be wed. When she learned of it, the queen indulged in a great fit of temper over their betrayal. Still, she gave them Sherbourne Castle in Dorset to live in, though they had not been allowed back at court until recently.

Feeling more alone than she had in years, Elizabeth recalled Sir Walter to his place as captain of her guard, and welcomed him and Bess back to court. On Accession Day, Ralegh had dressed his men, at his own great expense, in rich gold and brown velvets with orange-tawny plumes. He wished to honor the queen, on whom his fortunes had always depended. Knowing how much an elegant show delighted Elizabeth, he had arranged to please her with his display.

Essex, however, had learned of Ralegh's plans. Thinking it great sport, he mocked Ralegh by attiring his own great army of retainers in identical garb and plumes and marching them boldly before the queen.

Disgusted by this display of Essex's boorishness, Elizabeth ended the celebration early. She had divined Ralegh's attempt at kindness toward her and appreciated it. She understood Essex's actions just as well, and was hurt that he preferred harming Ralegh to pleasing her.

Essex had returned to court to stay, for he could not allow Sir Walter Ralegh or little Cecil to gain ground over him. For the next few months he made his presence felt by opposing every name brought forth in the council to fill the position of commander-in-chief in Ireland. It became obvious that Essex wanted that position for himself, and finally, the queen acquiesced. She was angry and hurt by the young man to whom she had given so much and who gave her nothing in return except grief. Ireland had been the graveyard of more English reputations, both political and military, than she could remember. But if Essex thought he could succeed where so many others had failed, perhaps it would be to England's good to give him the appointment.

Upon his departure for Ireland in March of 1599, Robert Devereaux said loftily to his retainers, "Methinks 'tis the fairer choice to command armies than humors."

As difficult a personality as he was, the Earl of Essex had the ability to win men to his side, for he could be most charming when he made the effort. Many young courtiers eager to make reputations for themselves, younger sons of the nobility, adventurers, and a host of military veterans from the Cádiz expedition were eager to serve with the earl. Essex therefore departed from England with an enormous army, ample provisions, and the promise of whatever else he might need to secure a victory over Tyrone and his rebels.

Once out of the queen's sight, however, Essex disobeyed every order he had been given, despite the pleading of Sir John Harrington, the queen's favorite godson, and Sir Christopher Blount, Essex's stepfather. The queen had ordered her commander-in-chief to march into Ulster immediately to confront Tyrone. With the element of surprise, there was a good chance of victory. Essex announced his presence to all of Ireland, and remained all during the wet spring and the wetter summer within the safety of the Dublin Pale, that area around Dublin held by the English since Norman times.

The queen's angry letters demanding explanations went unanswered. Finally believing that Robert Cecil and some others were planning his immediate overthrow, Essex dashed north to sign a hasty truce with the Earl of Tyrone that was very much to the queen's disadvantage. Then, flouting the queen's direct order not to return to England, Essex and several close friends did just that.

Arriving on September 24, 1599, at Nonsuch Palace, where the queen was in residence, the Earl of Essex forced his way into the queen's bedchamber before she had arisen. He saw her as no man had ever seen her—without her wig, without her makeup, without her jewelry. Immediately he realized his mistake and, kneeling, kissed the beautiful hand offered him before hurrying off to change his filthy riding clothes. He was certain he could charm his way out of his difficulty.

Later in the morning, to his extreme delight, the queen gave Essex a long, private audience. Those listening at the door heard nothing except a low murmur of voices. Not once did the queen raise her voice to the recalcitrant earl. Elizabeth dined alone in her apartments, however, while Essex commanded center stage in the dining hall. Afterward, she spoke with him again, and this time she could easily be heard demanding explanations for his many acts of disobedience. When Essex could not answer to her satisfaction, attempting to bluster his way out of his predicament by blaming everyone he could think of for his own rash actions, Elizabeth Tudor exploded with a show of her famous temper, sending her favorite of favorites to York House in the custody of Lord Keeper Egerton. There was no hiding the fact now that she was deeply disappointed and very angry with Robert Devereaux.

Essex did what he'd always done when he found himself thwarted and in difficulty. He grew ill, working himself into a deep depression and believing himself dying. When Essex's friends managed to convince him to write a full submission to the queen admitting his wrongdoing and his many faults, plans for his trial were canceled. On Robert Cecil's advice, the queen accepted the earl's long-overdue apology. He was allowed to go home to Essex House, but he remained under house arrest there. Elizabeth was moved by the earl's plight, but she was no longer blind to his flawed character.

Safe inside familiar surroundings, with his retainers and his wife and family, Essex's confidence grew. He wrote to the queen begging that she not ruin him while correcting him. The chief of his monopolies was due to be renewed soon, and he needed the money. The queen ignored his letter. She had forgiven him to the extent of sparing him a public state trial, but Essex was still bound to appear before a royal tribunal of judges at York House to answer for his actions.

He went, and was censured for his outrageous and appalling conduct in Ireland. The judges pointed out to the earl the queen's great mercy in allowing him to go home. Then they pronounced his punishment: He was to remain confined to Essex House until released by the queen's order. He was forbidden from exercising his offices of Earl Marshal, Master of the Horse, and Master of the Ordnance. In the matter of his monopolies, the queen was not yet ready to render judgment.

The fact that she had not confiscated his monopolies gave Essex hope. He became certain that she would not confiscate them. She loved him too much to hurt him, the earl decided smugly.

Indeed Elizabeth did have a soft spot in her heart for her young Robin, and three months later he was released from his captivity. Not having heard from the queen about his monopolies, Essex announced melodramatically that he would retire from public life. His debts were enormous, however, and they grew every day. He desperately needed his chief source of income, the lease of duties on sweet wines that were due to expire at Michaelmas unless the queen renewed them. Essex pleaded with Elizabeth. He needed his leases renewed.

The queen, however, decided to test the earl a final time regarding his loyalty toward her, for even as he groveled for his monopoly on sweet wines, his arrogance was apparent.

"When horses become unmanageable, it is necessary to tame them by stinting them in the quantity of their food," she said thoughtfully. She refused to renew the earl's leases on the duties on sweet wines. "My lord of Essex would do well to remember that England has a queen only, and this queen will teach him that she is indeed the mistress of England—and he but her dutiful subject." The queen confided to her ladies that if the earl would but mend his ways, she would restore his leases, but not just yet. He would wait upon her good nature, which he had sorely tried.

Essex responded true to form, exploding in a fit of blazing temper. The queen's reasons, he declared loudly to all who would listen, were "as crooked as her carcass!" He stormed from court to await an invitation to return that did not come. The queen smiled grimly, saying nothing further about the matter.

The court was heavily peopled these days with young malcontents who, like Essex, had sought to advance themselves as so many before them had advanced themselves. They had come to court to make their fortunes, but times were different now. Twenty years before Conn O'Malley had, to the queen's delight, boldly nicknamed her *Gloriana* even as she nicknamed those for whom she cared; but Elizabeth Tudor was old and tired now. The economy was inflationary, and the rewards of royal service today were much less than they had been in the halcyon days of the past two decades. Still, the queen's reputation was such that many yet came to court, although they were doomed to disappointment for the most part.

It was these eager and arrogant young men, men who had grown up on tales of England's glory under Elizabeth's rule, men who had never known real war or deprivation, who now gravitated to Robert Devereaux. Others joined Essex's ranks as well; his steward had summoned Essex's male tenants from the Welsh borders. There were Roman Catholics who believed that Essex would help them return England to the Roman faith. Essex wrote to Lord Mountjoy in Ireland, bidding him to come and join him. Essex was even in correspondence with King James of Scotland, but the wily James, while he did not refuse Essex aid, also did not send him any of his own. He waited to see what would happen.

Essex grew ill on his own bile. He had obviously fallen from favor, but he would not accept it. He had been kept in close confinement at York House for nearly a year, away from his family and friends. During that time, his megalomania had fed upon itself and now, the renewal of his leases denied, threatened with imminent backruptcy, Essex began to fear he would lose everything. Like a cornered animal, he acted out of desperation. Had he retired from the scene and waited for a change of fortune, perhaps he might have regained the queen's favor, but Robert Devereaux's pride would not allow him to play the chastened penitent. Egged on by his secretary, Henry Cuffe, the earl plotted the queen's overthrow.

Robert Cecil knew, and therefore the queen knew. Elizabeth Tudor waited for Essex to make his final, fatal blunder. This time, she knew, she could show no mercy.

"I have outlived those who were loyal and those who were disloyal. I have outlived those who loved me, and those who wished me ill," said the queen to no one in particular as she paced her chamber on a gray, early February afternoon. "For all his youth, I will outlive Essex as well."

"I cannot believe he really means Your Majesty any harm," said Lady Scrope soothingly.

"His very thoughts, were he discreet enough to keep them to himself, are a threat to the queen," Lady Dudly muttered.

"Aye," seconded the queen's cousin, Lady Howard. "Robert Devereaux is totally out of control. He has been for some time now."

Valentina listened from a corner of the room where she sat supervising the maids of honor as they embroidered pillowslips for the queen's bed. Valentina had great sympathy for the queen and, like Elizabeth's closest companions, had grown protective of the monarch.

A maidservant was placing platters and bowls on the queen's private dining table, and Elizabeth glared at her irritably. "What the hell is this?" she demanded.

"Yer dinner, yer grace," the maid said, curtsying.

The queen looked at the food. There was a joint of beef, a capon in lemon-ginger sauce, a young rabbit baked in pastry, a trout poached in white wine with dill cream, and a bowl of lettuce and mustard greens boiled with red wine and cloves. Steam was rising from the freshly baked bread, and there was a wheel of hard cheese.

"Take it away," the queen said. "I cannot eat it."

"But, Your Majesty, you must eat," Lady Scrope said, fussing.

"Take it away!" the queen shouted, and stamped from the day room into her bedroom, slamming the door behind her.

For a moment everyone was silent, and then the ladies-in-waiting began chattering all at once. Valentina warned her maids to silence with a sharp look. Getting up, she went to Lady Howard.

Catherine Carey Howard was the queen's cousin, and she and Elizabeth were deeply fond of each other. "What is it, Lady Barrows?" Lady Howard asked Valentina.

"If I may speak freely, madam," Valentina said, drawing the other woman aside. Lady Howard nodded. "The queen subsists on barely nothing, madam, and she must eat. Her teeth are the problem, madam. Dame Cecily, my elderly aunt, and Mag, my mother's old tiring woman, have the same problem. They lack the teeth with which to chew their food. The queen's cooks are cooking for her as they have always cooked for her, but the queen cannot chew as she once could. What was it the French ambassador said about Her Majesty? 'She is a lady whom time hath surprised.' The queen is proud. She won't complain, for she considers it a weakness not worthy of a reigning monarch. She will starve to death rather than tell the cooks she can no longer eat joints of beef and lamb."

"My dear, I do believe you're right!" Lady Howard whispered, awed. "How astute of you to realize the problem on such short acquaintance with Her Majesty." Lady Howard smiled warmly.

"I feel as if I have known the queen my whole life," said Valentina, smiling in return.

"What can we do? I am at a loss for a solution."

"I am a simple country woman, madam," said Valentina, "and so I would offer a simple solution if you will permit me." Lady Howard nodded. "The queen needs wholesome, nourishing food that she can easily ingest with her few teeth. If you could introduce me to Her Majesty's cook, I could instruct him and, once he understands the problem, I know he will do what needs to be done."

"Thank God you are 'a simple country, woman', Lady Barrows!" praised Lady Howard.

The queen's head cook was more than startled to see the two

fine ladies standing in his kitchens. Wiping his red face with a towel, he hurried over. He recognized Lady Howard, and bowed awkwardly.

"How may I serve you, m'lady?" he asked politely.

"This is Lady Barrows, the mistress of the queen's maids, and she wishes to discuss a problem with you regarding the queen's meals, Master Browning," said the Countess of Nottingham.

"Is something wrong, m'lady? Was the joint not to Her Majesty's liking?" the chief cook said worriedly.

Valentina gave him a warm, friendly smile. "Your meals are always superb, Master Browning. The problem is the queen's, and it is not a problem she will speak about to anyone, I feel. Therefore, I need your help in a little conspiracy. You see, the queen, like many older people, has lost teeth. Of those remaining, many are loose. She finds it difficult to chew, Master Browning, and so she cannot eat as she once did. Yet you cook for her as you always have."

The cook clapped a hand to his head. "Aye!" he said, "I see it, m'lady! Poor Queen Bess cannot gnaw on a joint as well as she once did!"

"Exactly, Master Browning. I knew you would understand. Still, the queen must eat, and you know she will refuse pap if you tried to serve it to her."

"Aye," he agreed. "She has always enjoyed her food, she has. Then what am I to do, m'lady?"

"Would I offend you if I showed you a country dish or two that you might serve the queen?"

The head cook was flattered. This lady was a noblewoman, yet she was asking his permission to instruct him! "If you would let me put an apron about you, m'lady," Master Browning said. "I wouldn't want you to get yer gown dirty."

"Have you beef stock?" asked Valentina as he tied the apron around her. "And I will need a little piece of raw beef, a carrot, a leek, some sherry wine, and a small pitcher of heavy cream. Have a chopping board, a sharp knife, and a small iron kettle brought to me as well."

As Lady Howard and Master Browning both watched, fascinated, Valentina ladled two spoonsful of beef stock into a small black iron kettle. Quickly she chopped the carrot and the leek, adding them to the stock. With obvious skill she minced the raw beef, adding it, too, and then, looking up, said to Master Browning, "I will need salt, parsley, and fresh peppercorns." These were quickly supplied, and Valentina added a pinch of salt to her brew, chopped the parsley, and added it as well and then handed the kettle to Master Browning. "Bring it to a boil," she said, "and while it cooks I will suggest several other ways of perking up the queen's appetite. She must retain her strength. She is running on pure nerves right now."

Lady Howard was fascinated. Once, she knew, all ladies of the noble class were skilled, as young Lady Barrows was, but that was no longer true. As she watched the young woman work and saw the royal cook's respect for her, Lady Howard thought that perhaps noblewomen had lost something by eschewing this knowledge.

"Meats minced with thinly sliced vegetables and mixed with spices can be put into pies. Capon should be stewed with carrots and baby onions until it is tender. Various fishes minced and mixed with breadcrumbs and spices can be baked in the ovens, then served with a sauce of cheddar cheese and wine. Any meat or poultry or game or fish stock can be made into a rich soup by adding tender bits of vegetable, meat, or poultry. Bring me the kettle now, Master Browning, and I will show you how to finish the soup."

An apprentice cook set the hot kettle on the table and Valentina liberally laced the mixture with sherry wine before adding a full pitcher of thick cream, then mixing it all together. Finally, she ground some pepper into the soup. Dipping a spoon into it, she offered a taste to the queen's head cook. He sipped the hot liquid thoughtfully, and a smile lit his face.

" 'Tis excellent, m'lady! Never have I tasted such a soup!"

"Send it up to the queen's apartments along with a plate of soft rounds of brown bread spread thickly with a good soft cheese and a tart of plum jam with clotted cream. I know Her Majesty loves that," said Valentina. "If in future you will keep in mind the delicate condition of Her Majesty's teeth, I know you can prepare meals for her. But you must say nothing about my little visit, dear Master Browning," Valentina finished.

"White wine for chicken and fish stock," said the head cook. "Good red Burgundy for game!"

"Exactly," replied Valentina with a smile. Then, taking Lady Howard's arm, she bid the cook farewell.

"My dear, you are a lifesaver," said Lady Howard as they walked back to the queen's chambers. "I will not forget this."

"Madam, I love and respect the queen," said Valentina, "and

I know you will not be offended when I say this, but though she is our queen, she is also an elderly lady—even if she will not admit to it. Her spirit is not old, of course. In spirit the queen will always be a vital, vibrant young woman. But her body has grown old, and it must be cared for in a different way than when she was young."

They reached the corridor leading to the queen's apartments, and Lady Howard stopped. Looking up into Valentina's face, she said quietly, "My child, you are a blessing come to us in a trying time. I will not forget your kindness toward my cousin. You have a friend in me, Lady Barrows, and I hope you will not forget it."

"Valentina!"

They turned to see Lord Burke coming toward them. He bowed. After kissing Lady Howard's hand, he kissed Valentina's.

"This is my cousin, Lord Burke." Valentina introduced him to the Countess of Nottingham.

"You are Lady de Marisco's son?" asked Lady Howard.

"Aye, madam, I am."

"I remember your mother. There was always much excitement at court when she was here."

"Indeed, madam, so I have been told," replied Padraic, his eyes twinkling.

Lady Howard chuckled, then said to Valentina, "Take a few moments for yourself, my child. I will see to the maids." She hurried into the queen's apartments.

"You have not been at court, my lord," Valentina told him.

"I have been at Clearfields seeing that everything is snug and safe for the winter months. Did you miss me, hinny love?"

"I have been too busy to miss you, Padraic. Willow's Gaby arrived ten days ago. Unlike the others, your niece is not in the least intimidated by me. Fortunately, she has James's sweet nature, and . . ."

"I missed you," he interrupted, slipping an arm around her slender waist and leaning forward to kiss her earlobe.

"Padraic! Behave yourself! You'll lose me my place," she scolded him.

"In that event, you would have no choice but to marry me, hinny love," he told her.

"I have no intention of marrying anyone!" she said firmly. Twisting out of his grasp, she hurried into the queen's apartments. Damn him! Why was he so sure of her? She was not even sure of herself. He hadn't bothered to tell her that he was going to Clearfields. One day, he had simply not been there, and when she asked Willow, Willow hadn't known where he was, either.

"How very like Padraic," Willow had said. "He always was a will-o'-the-wisp."

That was small comfort, indeed! Oh, why was Padraic being so difficult, changing when she wanted everything to remain the way it had always been? He was her best friend, and she liked that. It confused her when he murmured love talk to her and kissed her ear. She felt . . . funny. As if she were not really Valentina St. Michael but someone else.

"Oh, Lady Barrows!" Beth was calling to her. "There is to be a small fête this evening with dancing! The queen says we may wear our prettiest gowns!"

"And is your prettiest gown all sponged fresh and pressed, Mistress Stanley?" Valentina asked Beth, giving her a hug. "You may put your needles aside, my maids. If Her Majesty does not need us for the present, then you are free to attend to your gowns for this evening."

Indeed the queen did not need them. She was busy eating a large bowl of delicious soup that her cook had sent her and eyeing a plum jam tart on the sideboard with great interest. Her mood jovial now, she waved the maids of honor away.

That evening, her mood still light, Elizabeth Tudor entertained her court playing on her perfumed glass virginals with zest and vigor. Many there had never heard her play, and they were quite surprised by the queen's skill. Afterward, there was dancing, for the queen always loved dancing. There was a time when she would have danced every dance, but she was unable now to spend a whole evening capering. Garbed in white velvet embroidered with gold, pearls, and rubies, wearing a bright red wig, the queen danced the Spanish Panic, a rowdy, vigorous dance with much stomping and hand clapping. Aged, though she was, no one danced it better than Elizabeth Tudor. She danced with Sir Walter Ralegh, silently regretting the loss of Sir Christopher Hatton, who had been such a marvelous dancer and her favorite partner over the years.

A waltz-like lavolta followed. Valentina, who had danced the Spanish Panic with Padraic, suddenly found herself facing Tom Ashburne, the Earl of Kempe. As the music began, the earl made her an elegant leg and she swept him a curtsy. "Divinity," he murmured just loud enough for her to hear. Val could not suppress a smile. To the side, she saw Padraic, successfully cut off from her, dancing with little Beth Stanley, who was gazing up at him with rapt adoration. Lord Burke appeared decidedly annoyed.

When the dance ended, Tom Ashburne tucked Valentina's hand in his and walked her to the picture gallery. "I have been trying for weeks to gain your attention, and get you alone," he said softly. "You are a difficult woman, madam. Do you take no time for yourself?"

"I am here to serve the queen, my lord, not to offer myself as amusement for bored noblemen." How had they arrived at this secluded alcove?

"Madam, you wound me!" His arm around her waist; he drew her close to him. "Has anyone ever told you that your eyes are like amethyst stars?"

"Aye, my lord, many have," she answered smoothly. Her heart was beating wildly.

"Liar," he drawled, and then his mouth closed over hers. "Let me see if your tongue is as sweet as it is sharp, divinity," he murmured.

His lips were warm fire, gently forcing her lips apart as he invaded her mouth with his tongue. Padraic had done that to her, but this wasn't Padraic, she told herself, beginning to panic. This man was a stranger, yet she could feel herself responding to him. Her breasts swelled over the neckline of her black velvet gown, and his hands gripped her waist as she leaned backward. With a low groan, he bent to cover her breasts with hot kisses, but when his mouth closed over a nipple and he tongued it swiftly to a hard point, Valentina cried out.

"No! No! Oh, please, my lord! No!" She pushed him away, drawing up the errant lace to shield her bosom from his passionate glance. Backing away from him and shaking her head, she began to cry. "I am no one's light-o'-love, sir. Forgive me, for I did not mean to lead you onward when I would not go onward."

His misty gray-blue eyes smoldered. His fires were barely banked, by no means cold. "Surely you cannot believe I will be satisfied with such a tiny taste of paradise, divinity?" He did not move toward her, but somehow that made it worse.

"I am a respectable widow in mourning for her husband, my lord Ashburne. I am ashamed that my behavior enabled you to believe otherwise."

"I want you," he said quietly.

Her eyes widened. She had told Padraic that she wanted a bold man. Now that she stood facing one, she was not certain she liked it. "Even if I were not in mourning for Lord Barrows," she continued desperately, "I would not play the wanton. Please, tell me you have not thought otherwise." Her tears mortified her. She felt younger and more foolish than the six silly girls in her charge.

He sighed and, moving toward her, brushed away a tear. "Do not cry, Valentina," he said softly. "Do not cry, my exquisite divinity. Believe me when I tell you that you are the most respectable and proper of widows. But that does not alter the fact that I desire you."

"You should not speak to me so," she admonished him, but her heart was not really in the rebuke.

He knew it. "I want you to know how I feel, divinity, for I intend courting you once you have ceased to mourn your husband."

He almost took her breath away, but drawing on her inner strength, she said coolly, "I do not know if I shall marry again, my lord. Having had one husband, I do not see the necessity for another."

"Who will care for you?" he asked her.

"Ned left me well cared for, my lord."

"You will need a husband if you want children, divinity. That is one thing you cannot get without a husband."

"I am the eldest of seven. I have spent many hours caring for children. Perhaps I am weary of such tasks, my lord." She was feeling a bit stronger now that he was not gazing at her so fiercely.

"You are not an adventurer like your famous aunt Skye, madam. You are meant for home, hearth, and family," he said.

"Indeed, my lord? You have reached this conclusion based on your short acquaintance with me?" He was beginning to sound more like Padraic. *Why* were men so irritating?

"You are a woman, madam, and women are meant for home, hearth, and family," he repeated. "There is no mystery to it."

"I am not," she said with a sigh, "like other women. In fact, sir, all women are as different from one another as are all men. Have you never looked at a rosebush, my lord? Though the flowers are all red, each one is slightly different from the other. So it is with people, male or female."

"What you say must be truth, divinity, for I have known many women, but none has ever made me desirous of courting her. You, however, have."

"You are a bold man, my lord! I do not encourage you in your folly," Valentina exclaimed.

"I do not think it folly to court you, madam." His eyes twinkled. "You do not discourage me from courting you, I think."

"Take me back to the queen," Valentina ordered him. "You have already played havoc with my reputation, my lord."

"One kiss," he said.

"I shall scream," she answered him.

"I think not," he told her, stealing a quick kiss, his mustache tickling her lip.

"My lord!" Valentina stamped her foot. "You presume far too much."

"Nay, divinity, I merely dare to dream," he replied. Taking her arm, he led her back to the dancing without another word.

"It is our dance, I think, Val," Padraic Burke said coolly as she and Thomas entered the hall. Padraic swept her away without acknowledging the Earl of Kempe.

The dance was a long one. When it finally concluded, Padraic managed to maneuver her out the very same door that the earl had taken her through so recently. Valentina almost laughed aloud to find herself in the very same discreet alcove she had shared with Tom Ashburne.

"Padraic, what is this?" she demanded.

"I want to kiss you, Val, and I am scarcely of a mind to do it before the entire court."

"And if I am not of a mind to be kissed, my lord?" It was all too funny, and she was very near to laughter. What was suddenly happening in her life?

"Valentina Elizabeth Rowena St. Michael," intoned Padraic, "I cannot believe you would play favorites—particularly considering that you are such a respectable widow in mourning for her husband."

"You were listening? Oh! Villain!" She blushed even as she hit out at him, but he caught her hand in his and placed a kiss on the upturned palm. The kiss sent a shiver of shock through her.

"Did you believe I would allow Tom Ashburne to beat me, hinny love?" He drew her close, successfully pinioning her arms to her side with his embrace.

"You had no right to spy on me, Padraic Burke!" Outraged, her eyes flashed angrily at him. Damn all men to hell and back!

His aquamarine-blue eyes mesmerized her own eyes, silently saying things he would not at this time give voice or words to; daring her to play the coward and look away. Then slowly, slowly, he lowered his dark head to join his mouth to hers. For the life of her, she could not refuse him. He kissed her deeply, and after a moment, she began to kiss him. She wanted to fight him, to thrust him away from her, but could find no strength to do it. Raising his head, he caught her gaze and then pressed soft little kisses across her quivering mouth. Deliberately, gently, he eased one of her breasts from its confinement and, cupping it in his big hand, gazed at it lovingly.

"Don't! Oh, don't!" she whispered, feeling her cheeks growing warm as before her very eyes, the rosy nipple puckered tightly like some October frosted bud, yet he had not touched it.

"You have no idea," he murmured, "how very beautiful you really are, sweet love. Your mouth is half bruised with my kisses, and your lovely eyes are warm with a passion you do not even understand yet. I will regret to my dying day that I allowed you to wed Edward Barrows when I wanted you for myself. It is not a mistake I will repeat, Val. You belong to me." He kissed the little nipple, and a great shudder tore through her.

"I am my own mistress," she gasped. She was aching with a longing she very clearly recognized.

"As long as you are not Tom Ashburne's mistress, Val. He would seduce you, and you are, as you see, very vulnerable. Edward Barrows may have been a cold fish, God rest him, but when he deflowered you, Val, he let loose a passion that a man like him could not have imagined. It takes a real man to stoke those passions, and you, my beauty, are aflame. Amuse yourself. Flirt with Tom Ashburne if you must, but remember, hinny love, that you are to be my wife when you have finished mourning Ned Barrows," Padraic concluded.

Gently, she extricated herself from his tantalizing grasp, ordering her gown. "Lord Kempe does not wish to seduce me, Padraic," she said. "He, too, wishes to wed me. You would wed me . . . he would wed me . . . and I would not wed at all. It will be interesting to see whose will prevails in this matter," she said wryly.

Padraic Burke grinned at Valentina. "Aye, sweet, it will be. I wish to remind you that we Burkes are used to getting what we want."

"Indeed, my lord? Well, we shall see. I have four more months of mourning for Ned," she reminded him.

"Dark colors become you," he told her. "This gown makes your skin look even more like white rose petals."

"A nicely turned phrase, my lord Burke," the Earl of Kempe called to them as he joined them in the picture gallery. "So we are rivals for the lady's affections, are we? Not unlike the old days, is it, Padraic?" He gave Padraic an amused look.

Valentina was appalled. Had Tom been spying on her and Padraic even as Padraic had spied on her and Tom? To cover her embarrasment, she said, " 'The old days'?"

"Tom and I met on the Spanish Main in our salad days, Val," Lord Burke explained.

"And we were also at Cádiz together with the Earl of Essex," Lord Ashburne told her.

"You are not involved with Essex now, I hope," Lord Burke asked him.

Tom Ashbourne shook his head. "He plays too dangerous a game, Padraic. Adventure is one thing, but Essex flirts with treason. He will not survive it, I fear."

"On that we are in agreement, Tom."

"My lords, you must escort me back to the hall," Valentina said. "If you wish to continue your discussion of the old days, continue it there. I am not certain your behavior has not compromised my good name."

The two men grinned and, bowing to Valentina, each offered her an arm. Together the trio entered the chamber where the queen's fête was reaching its peak.

"May I have this dance, madam?" asked Thomas Ashbourne.

"Nay, Tom, 'tis my dance, I am certain," countered Padraic.

"I will not dance again this evening, my lords," she told them firmly, "and please do not draw any more attention to us than you already have. I will have no scandal."

"There you are, my dear," said Lady Scrope, unwittingly coming to her rescue. "The queen would have you attend her, Lady Barrows."

"My lords," said Valentina, curtsying to her two escorts. She turned quickly and followed Lady Scrope.

"She is mine," Lord Burke said quietly without even turning to look at his opponent.

"Nay, Padraic, she will be mine," said the Earl of Kempe.

"'Tis to be a battle to the altar then, Tom?"

"Aye. No quarter given and none taken," was the reply. "And may the best man win."

"I intend to." Lord Burke chuckled. "Oh, I intend to, Tom. This time 'twill not be like it was in Cádiz."

"When I won the fair Maria-Constanza from you?"

"When you *stole* the fair señorita from me," said Lord Burke. "This time the wench is mine, Tom."

"Only if you win her, Padraic. Only if you win her," said the Earl of Kempe softly.

Chapter Four

THE QUEEN'S COUNCIL WAS TO MEET IN SECRET at Lord Buckhurst's home. Elizabeth Tudor slipped quietly from the palace with only one lady in attendance, for the queen did not wish her absence to be known. She took with her young Lady Barrows.

"You are not well-enough known yet to be missed, my child," said the queen as their coach moved through the city. "And I know you can be discreet and will say nothing of what you hear today."

"I am first and always Your Majesty's loyal servant," replied Valentina.

"So I have discovered," the queen answered graciously. "My cousin, Kate Carey, tells me 'twas you who suggested that my menus be changed. She says you worried that I was not getting enough to eat and that you feared my strength would be sapped at a time when I need it most. Like your mother, you have eyes that actually *see*. Yet you are not a gossip."

"I merely wished to aid Your Majesty," said Valentina, choosing her words carefully, for the queen would not tolerate any reference to her age.

"Humph." The queen, chuckled saying nothing further but reading Valentina's thoughts accurately.

They were ushered into Lord Buckhurst's large and comfortable library. The queen was seated in a chair by a blazing fire and Valentina was offered a stool by her side. The council was already present.

Robert Cecil drew in a breath, exhaled it, and then began. "I have only just learned that Lord Mounteagle and several others, whose names will for now remain unspoken, went across the river into Southwark to the Globe Theatre, where they bribed the Lord Chamberlain's Players to stage, this afternoon, a special performance of *Richard II.*

"For weeks Essex has been in correspondence with James of Scotland, and although the wily royal Stewart has apparently not offered our rebellious earl any direct aid, James's continued correspondence with Essex may be taken as encouragement of Essex's plot. Of that plot, I now have full details."

The queen nodded. "Say on, Pygmy. I would know the worst now rather than later."

Cecil nodded, then went on. "Essex's stepfather, Lord Blount, and Lord Charles Danvers are to be here within Whitehall, strategically placed. Several gentlemen are to be placed at the Royal Mint and others at the Tower. When all is in readiness, the Earl of Essex plans to enter Your Majesty's privy chamber and secure your person."

"Does he, indeed?" Elizabeth cried. There was the slightest touch of her old humor.

Robert Cecil continued, the eyes of all the council upon him. "The earl believes that once Your Majesty is in his keeping, London will declare for him."

"The fool!" said the queen. "London has been my city since the beginning. It will never turn on me."

The others murmured firm agreement.

"To what purpose does Essex attempt this rebellion, Pygmy?" Elizabeth asked of Robert Cecil.

Robert Cecil allowed himself a rare dry chuckle. "To rid himself of me . . . and anyone else on whom Your Majesty depends who is at odds with the earl. He intends to declare a protectorship over Your Majesty with himself as lord protector until such time as . . ." Cecil hesitated.

"He seeks to rule in my name until I am dead and my successor takes the throne," said the queen bluntly.

Sir Robert nodded.

Elizabeth shook her head. "Gentlemen," she asked, "where did I fail with young Robin? Others have served me well, but young Robin seems incapable of serving anyone but himself. I have warned him often enough that there is but one ruler of England." She sighed so deeply and sadly that Valentina took the queen's hand in hers and placed it against her cheek in a silent effort to comfort her.

Elizabeth Tudor gave the hand in hers a little squeeze. "So," she said, "he would have Master Shakespeare's play staged, questioning the divine right of kings and showing the deposing of a monarch, so he might whet the public's appetite and gain support for his little treason. Oh, Essex! You great fool! I was queen of this land long before you were a glint in your mother's eye. That she-wolf! 'Tis Lettice he takes after, y'know! She is probably in this, too, as her young husband is. The bitch! First she would have Dudley from me, and now her son must have my throne!"

"Do not distress yourself, dear madam," Robert Cecil comforted his mistress. "There is yet a small chance that the Earl of Essex may be brought to repentance."

Tension rose, filling the room, for there was not a man there who believed such a thing was possible.

"What would you do?" the queen demanded.

"Let us send a summons to the earl asking him to wait on the council. Perhaps he can explain his actions."

"More than likely he cannot," muttered Lord Buckhurst, the royal treasurer.

"Do it!" The queen's words were sharp and staccato.

A summons was sent to Essex House requesting the earl's immediate attendance on the Privy Council, but the courier was jeered by Essex's friends, newly returned from the theater where they had just seen a spirited performance of *Richard II*. The courier was not even allowed to see the earl, who begged to be excused.

The courier returned to Lord Buckhurst's house and explained his failure.

"Repentant? Hah!" The queen snorted.

"Patience, dear madam," Cecil soothed her. "The earl has climbed the scaffold steps. Let us allow him at least the opportunity to put his own head in the noose before we pull it tight." He ordered the guard around the palace doubled.

Master John Herbert, the council's chief secretary, was sent to Essex House with the same summons to appear before the Privy Council. At first the earl tried to avoid receiving him, but John Herbert was no mere courier. He was a member of the Earl of Pembroke's family. The Earl of Essex could not see him now? John Herbert would wait until Essex could see him. Here was a quandary, and Essex knew it. With much bad grace he allowed John Herbert into his presence, where he received the summons to appear before the Privy Council.

"Tell them I cannot come now," the earl said.

"'Tis not that simple, my lord Essex," replied John Herbert quietly. "Why can you not come? If you refuse the summons, I must know the reason. Otherwise your actions may be, well, misunderstood. Misinterpreted, even."

"I fear for my life," was the reply. "Lord Grey attacked me in the Strand tonight. I fear to leave the safety of my house lest I be murdered. The council must understand this. I will not come because I dare not!"

"Enough," said Elizabeth Tudor, when Master Herbert reported all of this. "It is almost midnight. We will meet in the palace council chamber at dawn to decide what to do about my lord of Essex."

The queen was silent as the coach returned to Whitehall. She had not, in all the hours they had been at Lord Buckhurst's, let go of Valentina's hand. Now as they reached the queen's apartments, she did so, saying simply, "Thank you, Lady Barrows, for your help."

Valentina curtsied to the queen and hurried off to her own apartment.

"Where have you been?" Nan demanded. "Both Lord Burke and the Earl of Kempe have been here asking for you twenty times over."

"I was with the queen, and ask me no more," Valentina told her, knowing better than to say more.

There came a knock at the door, and a grumbling Nan admitted Lord Burke. Before he could speak, Valentina said, "I was with the queen, and I do not wish to be interrogated."

"Have you eaten?" he asked.

"No," she said, suddenly realizing how hungry she was.

"Go to the kitchen, Nan. They will give you something for your mistress. I will keep her company while you are gone."

With a broad grin, Nan bobbed him a curtsy and hurried off.

Without warning, Lord Burke picked Valentina up. Walking

over to the blazing fireplace, he settled himself in a tapestried wing chair, cradling her. "You look exhausted," he said.

"I have been with the queen since early afternoon," replied Val.

"You are not used to this life. She is, and she sometimes forgets that others don't have her stamina. Why did she not take one of her own ladies with her? Why you, Val?"

"She wanted someone who would not be missed, although with you and Tom Ashburne both knocking at my door all evening, it was obvious that I was not here," Valentina said wryly.

He massaged the back of her neck. "You are not used to such long hours," he repeated, and she said, "Stop cosseting me, Padraic. Though I admit to never having lived this way before, I find court life stimulating."

He leaned over and kissed her soundly.

"I cannot think when you do things like that," she protested, pulling her head away.

"I do not want you to think, Val." He laughed, cradling her closer. "You think far too much, hinny love. I want you to stop thinking, to stop considering everything you do so carefully. I want to sweep you off your feet, my practical country girl. How can I do that if you deliberate about everything so?"

"Oh, Padraic." She sighed. "I am so tired. But even tired, I will not be cajoled into making a hasty decision regarding my life. The last time I made such a decision, I made it for my mother, who worried, and for my sisters. The next time I wed it must be because I really want to wed. Can you not understand?"

"Aye," he answered, "but you must understand that I lost you once, Val. Had I for one moment suspected that you did not love Edward Barrows, I'd have claimed you for my own. I cannot, *will not*, lose you a second time. I love you, Val. Do you not love me just a little?"

"I do not know, Padraic. I honestly do not know. You are Padraic Burke, my cousin and my best friend. I have loved you my whole life—but I am not certain that the love I feel for you is the kind of love you seek."

He kissed her again, slowly and passionately this time, moving his lips over hers softly. "I think you love me, Val, even if you are not ready to admit it."

"All I know," she murmured, "is that you turn my bones to water each time you kiss me. But is that love? Tom Ashburne has a similar effect upon me."

He sighed. She would not be easy to win. He had waited for her his whole life, and now having finally admitted that to himself, he could not lose her.

Valentina grew silent, and soon he realized she had fallen asleep. He carried her into her little bedchamber and laid her gently on her bed, drawing the coverlet over her.

Leaving the room, he found Nan returning with a tray.

"She has fallen asleep," he told the tiring woman.

"She cannot sleep in her clothes," Nan said, fussing.

"I will be most happy to help you undress her, Nan," teased Lord Burke.

"Oh, m'lord! Yer a terror, ye surely are." Nan chuckled. "I'll need no help, thank you!"

Padraic returned to his mother's house, Greenwood, on the Strand.

"What do ye hear of the earl of Essex and the queen, me lord?" asked the werryman who ferried him along the river from Whitehall to Greenwood.

"You probably know more than I do," said Padraic, "but the gossip at the palace is that Essex is near to treason."

"Aye, and that's a fact," the werryman agreed. "He's an eager young fellow, but he ain't Queen Bess for all she's naught but an old lady now."

He had difficulty falling asleep, for his mind was far too full of Valentina. She claimed to want a bold suitor, but he wondered how bold a man she actually desired. He could have had her tonight, he thought pensively. She might be facing her twenty-first birthday, and she might be a widow, but she knew nothing of passion. He had not needed her admission that his kisses turned her bones to water, he had known it. The way in which her lush young body moved against his told him that. She was a powder keg only awaiting a match, and he wanted to be that match, but then there was the matter of Tom Ashburne. Lord Burke found himself in a quandary. His family was not one to force a marriage upon any of its children so that road was closed to him. He would really have to win her to him.

He dozed toward dawn, to be rudely awakened by his sister and brother-in-law in the late morning. He was deep in a dream in which he was making passionate love to Valentina when the voice of his body servant, Plumgutt, intruded.

"Wake up, m'lord! Wake up! The Earl and Countess of Alcester are here to see you!"

"Tell them to go away!" he muttered, trying to fight his way back to paradise.

"Padraic! Wake up this instant!" Willow's voice demanded, and she yanked his thick, dark hair.

Reluctantly, Padraic rolled over and opened his eyes.

"I may kill you with my bare hands, sister mine, if this is not important," he threatened.

"Essex has attempted a rebellion!" Willow said. "Is that important enough?"

Lord Burke was awake instantly. "What happened?" he asked, sitting up.

"You tell him, James," Willow instructed her husband. "James was there," she told Padraic.

"The council met at dawn," James Edwardes began. "Essex had been summoned to appear before them last night but he refused to come, claiming that Lord Grey had made an attempt on his life. This morning the queen sent Lord Keeper Egerton, the Earl of Worcester, Sir William Knollys, and several others, including me, to Essex House to bring Robert Devereaux before the Privy Council. The courtyard of Essex House was swarming with armed men, and although the earl came out to greet us pleasantly enough, when the lord keeper told him that we had come to escort him to the council, Essex behaved in a perfidious and rash fashion, claiming that he had been badly dealt with and that we actually sought his life. His men cried out that we were abusing him and would betray him. They began to shout for our lives. Essex brought us into the safety of his house. And then, to our complete surprise, he locked us in his library! He called through the door that he would return and free us after he'd made order of the disorder.

"Fortunately, the mob in the courtyard followed him out into the street, and opening the windows in the library, we could hear Essex shouting, 'For the queen! A plot is laid for my life! For the queen!' Ralegh had come with us to try to talk his cousin, Sir Fernando Gorges, out of following Essex, but he could not dissuade him. Ralegh escaped before we were brought into the house."

"James was so brave," Willow said proudly.

"What happened next?" Padraic demanded.

"'Tis Willow's part of the story," said the Earl of Alcester.

"Do not tell me that you were in the midst of all this?" Lord Burke said incredulously.

Willow laughed. "I know, I know! 'Ever proper Willow.' But aye, I was. Even though it is Sunday, I had gone to my dressmaker on Fenchurch Street. I simply must have a new gown for the queen's Shrove Tuesday fête, and Mistress Jones is so very busy. Well, Mistress Jones lives right next door to Sheriff Smith's house, and Essex, it seems, had been given to understand that the London sheriff would have a thousand trained men for him. He never even spoke to Sheriff Smith, yet he believed *that*!" She shook her head.

"How do you know he did not speak to the sheriff?" asked her brother.

"I'll get to that in a moment," Willow said, and picked up the thread of her story.

"We were very surprised," I can tell you, "to hear a great shrieking mob turning from Poultry and Lombard streets into Fenchurch. They were crying things like, 'England is sold to Spain by Cecil!' Did you ever hear of anything so completely ridiculous? How they pick on that poor little man simply because of his appearance! There were shouts of 'They will give the crown to the Infanta!' and 'Citizens of London, arm for England and the queen!' I have never in my life heard such folderol. Everyone was hanging out of their windows gaping at this nonsense.

"Poor Sheriff Smith ran out the back door of his house in his nightshirt into Mistress Jones's establishment so that he should not even have to see the Earl of Essex much less speak with him. The dressmaker sent her son to the sheriff's house to get his clothes so he might hie himself to the Lord Mayor which, I can assure you, he quickly did. The poor man was dreadfully upset when the dressmaker's boy returned with his clothing, saying that the Earl of Essex was sitting in his house claiming that Sheriff Smith had promised him a thousand armed men! The poor man was absolutely green around the gills, I tell you. He ran to the lord mayor to proclaim his innocence. He kept saying, 'But I don't even know his lordship! Oh, aye! I know him by sight, but who in London does not? I have never met him!'

"As soon as I safely could," Willow continued, "I departed from Mistress Jones's house and hurried here to Greenwood. Near St. Paul's a chain had been drawn across the street, and there were soldiers with pikes and muskets, so I was forced to go around. Sir Thomas Cecil, the new Lord Burghley, the Earl of Cumberland, and about a dozen others came down the street preceded by royal heralds proclaiming that the Earl of Essex and his followers were all traitors whose actions were against the queen, not in her behalf. Poor Essex. I fear he has overstepped his bounds at long last."

"Poor Essex?" Padraic Burke echoed. "Surely you do not sympathize with the man? He has been so puffed up with his own importance these many years, it's a wonder he didn't burst long ago!"

"Do not be a fool, Padraic, Of course I am not seriously in sympathy with Essex, but I cannot help but feel sorry for him. He had so much and he has wantonly thrown everything away."

"What is happening now?" Lord Burke demanded.

"Essex finally returned to his house," said the Earl of Alcester, taking up the tale. "He released us from the library. He had, it seemed, attempted to gain passage through St. Paul's but had been refused. Sir Christopher Blount, who was with Essex, attacked one of the queen's officers with his sword. He was wounded and taken prisoner. In the uproar that followed, several others were wounded and one was killed, or so we have heard. Essex fled down to the river and commanded a startled werryman to take him home.

"After entering the library, he paid scant attention to us, and we watched in amazement as he consigned many of his papers to the fire, including a little bag around his neck. The entire household was in an uproar, with Essex's wife, mother, and one of his sisters—Lady Rich, I believe—all shrieking and wailing. We simply walked down the lawns to Essex's water gate, hailed werries, and hurried back to Whitehall."

"God's foot!" Padraic leaped from his bed, forgetting that he was nude.

"Padraic!" Willow shrieked, blushing.

Realizing his state, Lord Burke dragged a sheet about his loins, muttering an apology.

James Edwardes laughed. "Your wife, should you ever decide to take one, will certainly be a lucky girl."

"James!"

The Earl of Alcester laughed again. "Come along, my dear. I believe your brother wishes to dress."

"I want to get to the palace," Padraic said. "The queen will need her loyal friends about her. And what of Valentina? This is not over yet, I fear."

"I will go with you," said his brother-in-law. "I would not miss this for all the world."

"Well, you are certainly not leaving me behind!" Willow declared. "Besides, Gaby will probably be terrified and need her mother."

At Whitehall, the palace was in an uproar. Barricades of coaches had been drawn across the streets leading to the palace, and the lord admiral had collected a small, impromptu army. The citizens of Westminster were arming themselves against Essex, and the little nearby village of Chelsea rallied to defend their queen. Elizabeth Tudor, however, was not one bit nonplussed by the turmoil going on about her. Master Browning, her cook, had presented her with a magnificent Sunday dinner, and she was looking forward to eating all of it.

There was a rich, clear broth of game bird, fragrant with burgundy wine, with tender bits of pheasant floating in it. There was a carrot pudding sweetened with clover honey and a platter of hot pastries filled with either minced chicken, beef, or lamb, seasoned impeccably. There was a covered dish filled with delicate bits of seafood in a sauce of heavy cream and sherry. There was fresh bread, sweet butter, and soft Normandy cheese. On the sideboard in the queen's private dining room were an egg custard and a plate of small sweet cakes soaked in malmsey.

She bowed her head and said grace. "God hath preserved me since my birth. He hath placed me in the seat of kings. God will preserve me in my seat until he sees fit to call me home. Amen." She then set about to enjoy her meal, which she very much did. And when she had finished, she said to her ladies, "I will now go and see what these rebels dare to do against me."

The Countess of Nottingham, the lord admiral's wife, said to her, "Nay, cousin. For your safety's sake, you must remain indoors until this is over."

"Bosh! Did I remain indoors during the Armada crisis? I did not! I went to Tilbury and rode among my soldiers to address them personally. I do not fear Essex and his rabble!"

"I think Lady Howard is suggesting that the sight of Your Majesty would rouse your Londoners to violence against the earl and his followers. Your Majesty could unwittingly be harmed in such a melee," Valentina put in, feeling braver about speaking up.

"Lady Barrows speaks with uncommon good sense for so young a woman," agreed Robert Cecil as he entered the queen's apartments. "I must add my voice to hers. No one questions your bravery, madam, but this is a trying time."

"Oh, very well," grumbled the queen, helping herself to another wine-soaked cake. "So London stands firm for me, does it? I knew it! Did I not say so, ladies? London has ever been my city, as it was my father's city."

The Earl of Nottingham and a small army surrounded Essex House. Lady Essex, Lady Blount, Lady Rich, and the other women in the household of Lord Essex were allowed to go forth. Essex was then told that if he did not surrender, a cannon would be used to demolish him, his followers, and his home.

" 'Tis more honorable to die fighting than by the hands of the executioner!" the Earl of Essex shouted defiantly, but his followers were not of the same mind, and they prevailed on him to surrender.

On that February night, in a cold, misty, sleeting rain, the Earl of Essex and his followers exited Essex House and surrendered their swords to the Earl of Nottingham. Essex and the Earl of Southamptom were housed at Lambeth Palace rather than in the Tower. There was no doubt as to Essex's guilt, but whether or not the queen would sign a death warrant in his name was a moot point.

Elizabeth Tudor was once more placed in the kind of difficult position she had always attempted to avoid. The French ambassador came to call, wishing to ascertain the queen's condition under such trying circumstances. If he had hoped to pass on to his master a report of a broken Elizabeth Tudor, he was doomed to disappointment. The queen, every bit her elegant self, greeted him warmly.

"I grieve with Your Majesty over the sad fall of my lord of Essex," he said politely.

"My lord Essex is a senseless ingrate who has at last revealed what has long been in his mind. Good riddance!" the queen answered.

Privately she grieved, but she would not show her grief to all of Europe, to people only too ready to laugh at a foolish old woman's fancy.

Elizabeth's women comforted her, and because of their afternoon at Lord Buckhurst's, the queen now sought out Valentina.

"You remind me of your mother," the queen said to Lady Barrows. "Not in appearance, of course, for Aidan St. Michael was a plain girl for all her lovely hair and eyes. It is your manner, Valentina. Your heart is good, and I need a kind heart now."

"I will not leave you, dear madam," Valentina vowed.

"His trial begins in a few days," the queen said softly.

"It will be over quickly, and then there will be nothing to distress you, dear madam," Valentina told her.

"Only my memories, Valentina. Only my memories."

The ladies nearest to the queen were amazed by this sudden fondness for young Lady Barrows, but they all liked her greatly, so there was no animosity. Valentina had gained their respect by turning the queen's maids of honor from a group of wanton, bad-mannered hoydens into a cheerful band of well-mannered and delightful girls. Valentina's gentleness soothed the queen who wanted her more in her company, thus relieving the overworked ladies in waiting.

Valentina had her own reasons for such devoted service to Elizabeth Tudor. It meant that she had less free time, and was thus able to avoid her two passionate suitors, for both Padraic Burke and Tom Ashburne refused to be denied. The maids had begun to notice and very much enjoyed teasing her, particularly as Gabrielle Edwardes was happy to good-naturedly supply her companions with little family details and tidbits of gossip.

"Fancy Uncle Padraic falling in love with cousin Valentina," she said brightly. "We have all thought that Uncle Padraic would remain a bachelor.

Even the queen, who more often than not disapproved of romance amongst her ladies, found herself amused by Valentina's situation. She had little enough to amuse her now.

Eleven days after the Earl of Essex's act of treason, he and the Earl of Southampton were brought to trial in Westminster Hall. The others would face trial later. Lord Buckhurst presided over the court, which was arranged in a square directly in the center of the hall. The great room buzzed with clerks and judges as twenty-six peers of the realm prepared to judge the traitors.

Both men pleaded not guilty. Outside, the February wind howled mournfully. Essex declared himself a loyal subject of the queen. He claimed that what he had done had been done only in self-defense, that any reasonable man would have done the same. The attorney general, Sir Edward Coke, rebutted the earl's statement, recounting the details of the uprising and claiming that any Parliament called by Essex would have been a bloody Parliament.

"A bloody Parliament would that have been where my Lord of

Essex, that now stands all in black, would have worn a bloody robe! But now in God's last judgement, he of his Earldom shall be Robert the Last, that of a Kingdom thought to be Robert the First!" Sir Edward finished.

Witnesses and depositions followed one after another as the day wore on. There were confessions from the Earl of Rutland; Lords Cromwell, Sandys, Mounteagle, and Danvers; and Essex's stepfather, Lord Blount. Like an onion, the layers of the Earl of Essex's treachery were peeled away. Essex, finally beginning to realize that he would not this time escape retribution, accused Robert Cecil of favoring the claim of the Infanta of Spain to England's throne. Cecil, listening to the trial from a nearby room, dashed into the hall. Kneeling, he begged Lord Buckhurst's permission to defend himself against the earl's slander.

"There is not a man here who would believe such a thing of you, Master Cecil," Lord Buckhurst assured Cecil.

Little Cecil, hunchbacked and fragile, his face white with fury, insisted. "My lord of Essex," he began in a surprisingly strong voice, "the difference between you and me is great. For wit I give you the preeminence, you have it abundantly. For nobility, I give you place. I am not noble, yet a gentleman. I am no swordsman, there you also have the odds. But I have innocence, conscience, truth, and honesty to defend me against the scandal and sting of slanderous tongues. And in this court, I stand as an upright man, and your lordship as a delinquent."

There was a low murmur of assent. The Earl of Essex could not look at Sir Robert, who continued, "I protest before God I have loved your person and justified your virtues, and I appeal to God and the queen that I told Her Majesty your afflictions would make you a fit servant for her, attending but a fit time to move Her Majesty to call you to court again. I would have willingly gone down on my knees in your lordship's behalf before the queen, but now that you have showed us your wolf's head in a sheep's garment, I wash my hands of you! God be thanked, we now know you! I defy you, sir, to name the councillor to whom I ever said that the Infanta's claim took precedence over others. Such slander is just that. 'Tis but an invented fiction!"

Essex was silent, but the Earl of Southampton leaped to his feet and cried out, " 'Twas Sir William Knollys himself, my lords! I swear it on my mother's honor!"

Essex's uncle was immediately sent for to clear up the dispute. He arrived, extremely surprised at having been called. He was sworn in and the testimony was repeated to him. He thought for a moment and then said, "I have been seriously misquoted, my lords. Mr. Secretary, Cecil and I were speaking some time back regarding a book in which the titles to the throne were set down. He said he found it strange impudence that the Infanta's claim to England's throne was given the same right to the succession of the crown as any other. He said he believed her claim to lack true validity. Never, my lords, did he favor such a claim, nor ever did I claim such words of Robert Cecil."

As a vast sigh of relief echoed about the hall, the Earl of Essex insisted, "Sir Robert's words were reported to me in another sense, else I should not have accused him."

"No, my lord. Your lordship, out of malice toward me, desires to make me odious, having no other true ground," Cecil replied spiritedly. "I beseech God to forgive you for this open wrong done to me."

A recess was called so that the peers and judges could make their decision. After refreshing themselves with beer and smoking their pipes, they returned to the courtroom to pronounce sentence. Each peer stood in his turn to answer the question put to him. "My Lord, is Robert, Earl of Essex, guilty of treason? Is the Earl of Southampton guilty of treason?"

"Guilty," answered every voice.

Both earls were brought back to hear the verdict. Essex, to everyone's surprise, accepted his fate with good grace, even begging that young Southampton be spared. The sentence was pronounced on both men. Death by hanging, drawing, and quartering. As peers of the realm, however, they would suffer a more merciful beheading. Even so, it was a traitor's death.

The two men were escorted through the streets of London, the blade of an axe turned toward them to announce the verdict to the watching crowds. It was past six o'clock, and snow had begun to fall.

Robert Devereaux faced death the way he had always approached everything. With enthusiasm. Guided by the Reverend Adby Ashton, he cleansed his soul and wrote a four-page complete confession indicting his stepfather, Christopher Blount; his sister, Lady Rich; his secretary, Mr. Cuffe; and Lords Mountjoy and Danvers as foremost among the conspirators urging him toward his folly. He never thought to write to his grieving mother or his neglected wife. He had finished with earthly cares and wanted nothing more than to devote his remaining hours to the salvation of his soul. Few would have recognized in the contrite young man the overproud and ambitious Earl of Essex except for his total self-absorption.

Valentina understood how hard a time this was for Elizabeth. Upon the queen's desk lay Essex's death warrant. It was necessary for the queen to sign it, but oh, so difficult. Captain Tom Lee was arrested at the door to the queen's privy chamber, attempting a mad scheme to force Elizabeth to pardon the earl. For his effort, he would forfeit his head. Valentina wondered if the plotting would ever end.

The queen's cousin, Lettice Knollys, Lady Blount, managed to accost Elizabeth as the queen went to her private chapel on the morning after the sentencing. Lettice, once the queen's *bête noire,* now groveled at her cousin's feet, begging for the lives of her son and her third husband.

"Leave Robin to cool his heels in the Tower, Bess, but spare his life, I beg of you!"

"What?" the queen countered. "Are you mad, Lettice? Or do you wish that viper you spawned to have another opportunity to destroy me? Did he not himself admit that England was not large enough to contain us both? Leave me be! The heart I did not believe I had has been broken a thousand times over by your ungrateful offspring!"

"But what of Christopher, Bess? He cannot harm you. He is a follower, not a leader. I have never been happier since becoming his wife. Do not take him from me also, I beg you!" Tears poured down her face, making dirty tracks in her cheeks.

She is getting old, too, thought the queen with a small measure of satisfaction, and then she boxed Lettice's ears. "How dare you plead for Lord Blount's life in such a manner, you she-wolf? So you have been happier with him than with anyone else, have you? What of Dudley? What of my Robert, whom you slyly stole from me? You will learn to live with unhappiness, I have no doubt, Lettice, and you will survive it—even as I have survived it. No, I will spare neither your traitorous husband nor your perfidious offspring! Get you gone from my sight, cousin! I never wish to lay eyes on you again. I give you permission to remain in London until after the executions. After that, you are banned from London and from court!" The queen swept by the sobbing, kneeling woman and entered her chapel.

It was Shrove Tuesday, but because of the attempted rebellion and the coming executions, the queen's usual pre-Lenten fête had been canceled. In the late afternoon after the Shrovetide play, the queen returned to her privy chamber, walked directly to her desk, and signed the warrant. She handed it to Robert Cecil without a word. Then she withdrew to her bedchamber, refusing all company but Lady Barrows's.

"If only he had asked, perhaps I might have spared his life," she whispered brokenly to Valentina.

"By not asking," said Valentina, "he has done you a kindness, dear madam. You could not have commuted the sentence. You know that to be true, and so does the Earl of Essex."

"I loved him," the queen said sadly.

"And this final act of the earl's proves his love for you, dear madam. You cannot spare him, so he spares you by refraining from asking it of you."

" 'Twas ambition, you know," Elizabeth Tudor observed.

"Ambition and love are at opposite ends of the world, dear madam. The earl could not help himself. He was driven. He allowed ambition to overwhelm his love, and that was his downfall," Valentina replied. "You cannot blame yourself, for you gave the earl all you might give."

The queen sighed deeply and went to sit in a chair by the window to watch the river. In the early evening she dozed off where she sat.

When she awoke, Valentina coaxed her to eat a little soup and toasted cheese. The queen then went to her salon and played cards with her ladies until several hours after midnight. She then retired to her bed.

The bed was a marvelous, fanciful creation that enchanted Valentina, carved with gilded beasts, hung with rich royal purple velvet, and topped with multicolored ostrich plumes spangled with gold.

The queen slept for three hours. Arising, she dressed and, with her ladies and maids of honor in attendance, went to chapel to receive communion and Ash Wednesday ashes. Then, returning to her apartments, she drank a cup of mulled wine and broke her fast with eggs poached in cream and marsala wine. Then she sat down to play her virginals, a regal figure in gold-encrusted white satin, with pearls and rubies about her neck, in her earlobes, and adorning the beautiful, graceful hands that teased such exquisite music from the virginals. As she played, her bright red wig with its wonderful dressing of pearls and gold bobbed merrily. A stranger seeing her thusly would have thought her cold and uncaring, but those who loved and knew her knew better.

Sir Robert Cecil had suggested that the Tower cannon be muffled so that the queen would not hear it, and so it was done. At a little after nine o'clock in the morning the news was brought to her that the Earl of Essex had paid the price for treason. Elizabeth stopped playing the virginals to receive the message. There was an unnatural hush within the room, and then Elizabeth began playing again as if nothing out of the ordinary had happened. Her grief was great, but she was England's queen and could not show that grief. Her mourning would be terrible, and she would live through it alone.

Hearing the story several days later in Paris, the French king Henry IV cried passionately, "She, only, is a king! She, only, knows how to rule!" All of Europe respected Elizabeth Tudor's courage in this matter.

To none of the maids of honor's surprise, both Lord Burke and the earl of Kempe came calling upon Valentina now that the crisis was past. She wanted to send them away, but the maidens protested loudly.

"It has been the most gloomy of winters," complained the usually contented Margaret Dudley, "and now it is Lententide with no plays or the Bear Garden! Please, Lady Barrows! Please let the gentlemen stay at least for a game of cards."

"Very well, but you must be quiet. There can be no high spirits or noisy romps, for though the queen says naught, she mourns the earl of Essex deeply."

"If I cannot have you for myself, divinity, then I am content to share you with such delightful and charming company," said Tom Ashburne.

The maids of honor giggled, and Honoria de Bohun said most flirtatiously, "It is a pity that we cannot dance in the Maiden's Chamber of an evening as we used to in days past."

"There will be no dancing, Honoria," Valentina said firmly.

"Is she a very stern taskmistress, my ladies?" teased the earl.

"Oh, no, my lord!" little Beth Stanley said earnestly. "Lady Barrows is the kindest of ladies. We have never been happier since she came."

"Ahh," sighed the earl, "how fortunate you all are, for Lady Barrows is not kind to me at all."

"Tom, behave yourself." Valentina laughed in spite of herself.

"I cannot tell you how vastly relieved I am to hear that Val does not encourage your feeble attempts at courting," said Lord Burke.

"I neither encourage him, nor discourage him, even as I do with you, my lord," replied Valentina tartly.

"Is there anything sharper than a woman's tongue?" demanded Tom Ashburne.

"Nothing, I vow!" agreed Lord Burke, and again the maids giggled.

"Are we to play cards, gentlemen, or not?"

"Are you so anxious to be beaten by me once again," teased Padraic, "that you can scarce contain your eagerness to play?"

"Hah, sirrah! The last time we sat down to a game of Primero, you lost to me as I recall it," Valentina countered.

"And you never gave me a chance to regain my honor, as I remember," he said.

"'Twas my honor that was at stake, for you accused me before we began of being a poor player," Valentina rejoined.

"Your honor will never be a stake where I am concerned, madam," he returned, and she blushed to the maids surprise and wonder.

"I, on the other hand," said the earl, "am a terrible player. I shall need Lady Barrows instruction to aid me. Will you sit by me, Valentina, and teach me all I would know."

Again Valentina felt her cheeks growing pink, for the earl's words held a far different meaning to her than it appeared to the maids of honor. "Let Mistress Stanley help you, my lord. She is an excellent player of Primero," Valentina decided. She would not fall into Tom Ashburne's sly trap.

He smiled at her, and blowing a kiss in her direction with his fingertips, he acknowledged his temporary defeat at her hands.

Winter passed, and spring came filled with brighter promise than springs of recent years. The queen dictated that they move to Greenwich for a time, and so the court moved itself, bag and baggage. Greenwich had always been a happy place for Elizabeth, but this year, looking around her, all the queen could see were the missing faces of those she had loved. Her grief for Essex was deep and relentless.

"Bring me a hand mirror!" the queen commanded her women one afternoon, and there was a moment of shocked silence. For years the queen had not looked at herself closely, declaring narcissism was prideful.

Lady Barrows found a heavy silver handmirror and passed it to little Beth Stanley, the youngest maid. Timidly, the young girl crossed the room and, curtsying to the queen, handed her the mirror. There was not a sound as Elizabeth looked hard at herself for the first time. Quietly, she handed the mirror back to the little girl.

Sighing deeply, she said, "How often have I been abused by flatterers whom I have held in too great estimation, and who have taken delight in informing me to the contrary with regard to my appearance."

Essex, Christopher Blount, Charles Danvers, Sir Gilly Merrick, and Henry Cuffe had paid with their lives for their rebellion. Now, in the late spring of 1601, Elizabeth put an end to the blood-letting. The Earl of Southampton remained in the Tower under threat of execution, but it was understood that, although the queen would not issue him a pardon, neither would she sign his death warrant. The other young nobles involved in the aborted uprising were all fined heavily, putting many in debt for the rest of their lives. To Essex's neglected widow, however, the queen was kind, aiding her financially until she married again.

The queen moved to Richmond. "We shall go a-Maying in the forest at Lewisham," she announced without any enthusiasm.

"This is the first May Day I have not been at home in my whole life," Valentina said to Tom Ashburne. "We have a custom in our family. We always ride to the top of the highest hill near Pearroc Royal to see the sunrise. I will miss that."

"Come with me," Tom said. "I will take you to a place where we may see the sun rise on May morn."

"Where is your home?" Valentina asked, suddenly realizing that she knew nothing of this handsome man beyond that he was persistent.

"My home is in Warwickshire just southwest of the Avon River on the Worcestershire border. It's a small estate, but a fertile one. My family have lived there since the time of Henry II. The manor house is called Swan Court, for there is a lake before the house that has always been home to a large family of swans, both black and white. It is a happy house, Valentina, and you would grace it magnificently."

She ignored the extravagant compliment, asking, "Do you have brothers and sisters, my lord?"

He smiled, understanding her better than she realized. She

had meant it when she had told him she would not be rushed into a second marriage, and he admired her honesty. Too many women were coy, saying one thing, meaning another. "I have a younger brother, Robert, who is a churchman, and three younger sisters, all married. My father died when I was with Essex at Cádiz. My mother is alive. I was thirty-three years old on April first, and I have all my teeth and other moving parts, madam. Now, what of you—other than your extravagant beauty?"

She laughed. "I became twenty-one on the March twenty-first just past. You know I am widowed. My husband left no heirs beside me. I have three sisters and three brothers, all younger. I was born and bred in Worcestershire. I am afraid, my lord, that I am not an interesting woman at all."

They were walking in the gardens at Richmond, and he drew her off the main path into a little arbor. "I find you most interesting, madam, indeed fascinating. You tell me everything about yourself, yet you tell me nothing." He pulled her into his arms and looked down at her. "Does your heart not beat a little faster when you are with me? Mine does when I am with you, Valentina. Do you know how very much I want to make love to you, divinity? To kiss that luscious mouth that tempts me so very much?" He brushed his lips across hers lightly.

Valentina felt her heart leap at the touch of his lips upon hers. She was genuinely curious to see how she would feel should she let him go further, but she knew she was not ready at this time to play such games. She was not even certain she knew how to play such games. She wanted him to kiss her, perhaps to even touch her again as he once had, but she was not certain she would have it go further than that. Better to hide behind her mourning until she knew what she was doing, but who could tell her?

"My lord, enough," she said coolly. "It is not proper that you behave in this fashion toward me while I am in mourning."

"Did you love him so very much then, divinity?" he asked.

"Whether I loved him or not is neither here nor there, Tom. Edward Barrows was my husband. He is deserving of my respect, and I will give it to him in full measure."

"What a woman you are," he said admiringly. "I understand, and I really do try to behave myself when I am near you, divinity, but it is difficult."

"I think you attempt to wheedle me, Tom Ashburne, but heaven help me, you have such charm I admit to being unable to resist it."

"Then you will go a-Maying with me?" he persisted.

"I go a-Maying with the queen, my lord, and you, of course, are welcome to join us," she told him.

"You are a hard woman," he grumbled.

Valentina laughed. "And you, sirrah, are far too used to getting your way, I think. Well, you shall not have your way with me, I vow."

"Not now, perhaps," he teased, "but we have many tomorrows before us, divinity, and I intend to make the most of all of them!"

Chapter Five

ON MAY DAY THE QUEEN AND HER LADIES went a-Maying in the cool, green forest of Lewisham near Richmond Palace. They cut branches of flowering hawthorn and hazel, gathered daisies, poppies and rock rose from the fields, and long stalks of foxglove from the forest's edge, to which they added leafy ferns. The spring had been early and was pleasantly warm. The beech trees with their new green leaves allowed the sun to dapple the forest floor. The day was delightful, with only the faintest hint of a breeze.

They ate in a clearing surrounded by pine trees that bordered a swiftly flowing stream. After a light luncheon of meat pastries, hard-boiled eggs, sweet cakes, and early strawberries, the ladies and gentlemen of the court rested on the grass or strolled nearby. With the queen's permission, the maids of honor were allowed to remove their shoes and stockings and went wading in the icy waters of the little stream. Several young gentlemen, including Valentina's two brothers, Colin and Payton, who had recently come to court, joined the young maids. There was much shrieking and giggling, but the queen, who ordinarily might have been cranky about the unseemly behavior, seemed not to care.

"They come and they go," she said. "The years are passing too swiftly for me. Once there was not a face I couldn't put a name to, Valentina, and oh, how many gallants there were to play at love with me! Now"—she shrugged—"there are few I love, and fewer still who love me in return."

"I love you, dear madam," said Valentina honestly and with open feeling.

Elizabeth Tudor looked closely at the young woman, and what she saw brought tears to her eyes. "Why, bless me, my sweet Valentina, I believe you do, and I am right glad for it!" The queen lowered her voice. "I am an old woman now, my girl, though I have never admitted it before. Nor am I apt to again, but you will not tell on me, I know." Her eyes twinkled then as Valentina had never seen them twinkle before.

Impetuously, Valentina kissed the queen's cheek. "Age, dear madam, is but the passing of years, and the years cannot change what is in one's heart and soul."

"But they can, alas, change one's face." The queen chuckled. "We will not think of it again, however. Now, my good mistress of the maids, I need your advice. Eleanora Clifford's parents have written to me that they would have her home as soon as possible to prepare for her wedding in August. I face the tiresome task of choosing another silly chit for my service. Would you advise me in this matter?"

"I would choose a little girl, madam," said Valentina.

"Why?" demanded Elizabeth.

"A younger girl is easier to control. It is likely to be her first experience away from home, and she will be in awe of the court and of Your Majesty. A younger girl is less apt to become prey to those randy young lordlings who consider it their duty to attempt the seduction of Your Majesty's maids as a rite of manhood."

"Hmm," the queen considered. "You are a practical young woman, Valentina, and I believe you are correct. The question remains: Who shall I pick? There are none whom I would care to honor at this time who have young daughters." She thought for a moment, then asked, "Do you not have a younger sister, Valentina?"

"I do, dear madam. Her name is Margaret. We call her Maggie. She was just thirteen this past winter. My other two sisters are married and have already served Your Majesty. I have several young cousins who might suit as well as my little sister. Johanna Edwardes is eleven, as is my cousin Velvet's stepdaughter, Sybilla."

"Too young," said the queen. "They are apt to miss their mothers when they are too young. I shall write to your parents to send Mistress Maggie and to Lord Clifford telling him he may have his daughter back as soon as Mistress St. Michael arrives. There! That is settled, and I feel the better for it. Tonight I shall dance as I have not danced in some time. I only wish your handsome father were here, for next to Hatton no one partnered me as well as Conn O'Malley."

"What's this, Your Majesty?" asked Sir Walter Ralegh as he approached them. "Do I not partner you with grace and verve?"

"With enthusiasm, perhaps, my Wat-er, but you've two left feet, and we both know it." The queen chuckled.

"I am wounded!" Sir Walter cried.

"The truth is always apt to wound one, Wat-er. 'Tis something I learned early in life," the queen replied sadly. With Valentina's help she struggled to her feet. "This grass is damp," she complained. "Let us begin our walk back to the palace."

That night Elizabeth Tudor held a great ball at Richmond for the visiting Duc de Nevers. Together they opened the ball, dancing a graceful galliard, and the queen moved with all the lilting grace of a girl of seventeen. She wore a magnificent gown of scarlet silk lavishly trimmed with lace. The sleeves were embroidered with rubies, pearls, and jet beads in the pattern of a writhing dragon. It was rare that the queen forsook her favorite white. A huge starched, sheer linen ruff edged with elegant lace fanned out behind Elizabeth's head. Her jewelry was ropes of great pearls, a ruby necklace, and bracelets and earbobs of more pearls. On her hands she wore but a single large ruby. She had not looked so well in years.

Valentina wore a beautiful gown of dark green silk with an underskirt of iridescent green-blue. The bodice was sewn with pearls and silver threads, as were the sleeves. Both her neckline and cuffs were lavish with lace. About her neck she wore her fine pearls, and in her hair there were cloth-of-silver roses. Though there were a number of women more magnificently garbed, there was no woman as lovely as Valentina St. Michael.

The French duke danced twice with Valentina. Lord Burke and the Earl of Kempe could not, of course, keep the Duc de Nevers from his choice of a dance partner, but they could dissuade other gentlemen of the court from pursuing Lady Barrows, which they did with vehemence. The queen was much amused. Valentina was not.

"They presume far too much," she said irritably.

"Will they come to blows over you, I wonder?" the queen asked.

"God's foot, madam, I hope not!" Valentina looked genuinely shocked.

The queen laughed, and for the first time since Essex's execution, her laughter held real mirth. "You will give them both a fine time of it, I can see, before you finally decide which one you will wed," she told Valentina.

"I am not at all certain that I will wed again, dear madam," Valentina replied.

"My dear," the queen told her, "you must wed again. It is your duty to do so. England will always need strong sons and daughters, and the way in which you care for the maids and fuss over me tells me that your instinct for mothering is strong. A woman needs a husband. I am certain that your own mother has told you that, and even that impossible creature, your aunt, Skye O'Malley, knows it to be true."

"I would be my own mistress. Like you, dear madam," Valentina said.

"My dear child." And here the queen lowered her voice so that no one else could hear her. "I have lived an unnatural life, and that is the truth. Had my brother Edward lived, married, and had children, had my poor sister Mary really been capable of giving England an heir, I should have remained simply the Princess Elizabeth. I would have been matched with the proper prince or king or reigning duke and been a wife and mother. But God did not ordain that I survive my youth to be a woman like other women. It was God's plan for me that I be England's queen, a reigning queen in her own right. As such, I could not take a husband. What lord would bow a knee to his wife? Such a thing is intolerable. I did not survive my youth to turn the destiny of this land over to someone not born to rule it as I was born to rule it. I sacrificed my womanhood to be England's queen, but no such sacrifice is demanded of you, my dear. Your future is with a husband and the children you will have together. Oh, happy future, my dear Valentina!"

Deeply touched, Valentina said, "Do you really think it so, dear madam?"

"I do," said the queen, "and how fortunate you are to have two such fine young men courting you."

"Perhaps I am," Valentina replied thoughtfully, "but for now, dear madam, let me stay with you. I would rather be with you than with a husband."

"I am not unhappy with that decision," the queen told her. "We will both know when the time is right for you to make your choice and leave me. For now, my dear, enjoy the spirited competition between Lord Burke and the earl. In my lifetime I have had many contending for my favors. 'Tis most flattering to have the gentlemen vying for you."

"I am enjoying it," Valentina admitted. "Perhaps that is why I am so loath to make a choice. I have never before had gentlemen vying for me. In my youth I preferred staying home with my parents."

"Gracious, my dear," said the queen, laughing, "you are still quite *in* your youth!"

The court moved on. To Windsor Castle, where the queen had a special bathing room whose walls and ceilings were all mirrors. To Hampton Court, where the throne room was so beautiful that it was called the "Paradise Chamber." To the Earl of Nottingham's country home, where the queen was much taken with a set of tapestries depicting the Armada victory. The countess had commissioned them to commemorate the fifth anniversary of the occasion. The earl was extremely proud of the tapestries, for he had played an important role in that great victory. The queen hinted, none too subtly, that she would enjoy possessing the earl's fine tapestries. The earl, just as pointedly, ignored her hint. Kinship went only so far.

The French king, Henri IV, was at Calais. When she learned of his visit to that channel port, Elizabeth hurried to Dover and sent him a message to cross the short distance separating them to see her. Henri had been greatly aided financially by the English during his troubled reign. He owed Elizabeth the courtesy of accepting her invitation, but he did not. The queen was deeply hurt by his refusal.

Eleanora Clifford had departed for her home in Kent in late May and was replaced by Mistress Maggie St. Michael. Margaret Dudley, facing her eighteenth birthday, had been made a suitable offer by Penelope Howard's second brother. With the queen's permission, she accepted, and the wedding was scheduled for Christmastide. Payton St. Michael was secretly courting the prickly Honoria de Bohun. Valentina had warned him that the queen was in no mood to lose another maid of honor so soon.

"Are you mad?" Lady Barrows scolded her brother. "You are

a younger son, so your success in life depends on your success at court. Why do you invite the queen's wrath? She is more difficult about changes than she has ever been."

Payton St. Michael looked abashed, but his jaw, so like his father's, tightened in a show of stubbornness that Valentina quickly recognized. "What makes you think I intend to spend my life in this cesspool?" he demanded. "I love Honoria, and if she can overcome her foolish pride, she will admit to loving me. I am not a rich man, but I am comfortable and have more than enough to share with a wife and children."

Valentina shook her head at him, but she gently patted his cheek. "Be cautious," she said softly. "If your intentions are truly honorable, then I would see neither you nor Honoria in disgrace."

By September, the queen was feeling poorly, for her summer had been a busy one, but she would not admit her failing health to anyone, least of all to herself. She carried on as she had always carried on, going full-tilt, wearing out those half her age. She attended all council meetings, continued to ride and hunt, and when she did not feel up to dancing—only, she would complain, because she had not the wonderful partners of the past—she sat during the evening and watched the dancing, clapping her hands and keeping time with her feet.

The good news from Ireland, for Lord Mountjoy had been successful in beating the Earl of Tyrone and propping up the English governor in Dublin, cheered the queen. Valentina looked forward to the opening of Parliament, for in all of Elizabeth Tudor's long reign, there had been only fourteen Parliaments called.

In early October, Lord Bliss arrived at court without warning to take his sons and daughters home to Pearroc Royal. His visit was a joy for the queen, who had not seen him in nearly ten years.

Valentina and her little sister, Maggie, looked up, startled, as their father was announced and he entered the queen's salon.

"Papa!" they cried in unison.

His smile acknowledged them, but he walked directly to the queen and, kneeling, raised her hand to his lips. "It has been a long time, Gloriana," he said. "The years have not been overly unkind to either of us, I see."

Elizabeth's gaze softened as she looked down upon the dark head, now sprinkled with silver. The eyes that looked up at her were as direct and honest as they had always been. "You have put on flesh, my lord, since we last met," she noted as he rose.

" 'Tis all that good country food and country air, Gloriana. I am a contented man, thanks to you, and my Aidan is a contented woman, thanks to me. All that I have is due to you, so it pains me that I must ask for the temporary loan of my daughters who serve you."

"Is all well with your lady wife and your other children, my lord?" The queen could see that Valentina and Maggie were looking worried.

"My family is well, madam, but an elderly family retainer, my wife's old tiring woman, Mag Feeney, is near death and wishes to see all the children before she dies. It is for that purpose that I have come. The physician says her time is short, no more than a month or two at most. Mag helped to raise Aidan, and has helped to birth and raise all our children. Our little Maggie is named for Mag, for Aidan loves her dearly. We all do."

The queen nodded. "I know how you feel, my lord, for I felt the same way about my dear Kate Ashley. Of course Valentina and Maggie must go home, but you must promise me that they will return after the old lady has been buried. You see, I cannot do without either of them, particularly my dear Valentina." The queen smiled. "As for Mistress Maggie, my lord, she is most obviously your daughter. She has a silver tongue and a mischievous way about her that has given us all fits of laughter. I have not laughed so much in years. Since your little lass has joined us, my sides ache constantly. I will miss them both. Go now. Take them with you, my Conn. But send them back."

As Valentina and Maggie curtsied to the queen, Elizabeth said in a low voice, "Promise me you will return, Valentina."

Valentina's lovely eyes were damp with emotion. "I will come back, dear madam. You may rely on me. I will not fail you." Then she caught the queen's hand and kissed it. Elizabeth Tudor gave her a warm smile.

"And you must come back, too, Maggie, my little scamp," the queen said to Maggie.

"Oh, I will, Your Majesty," the young girl said, "for being at home is ever so dull, and court is so exciting!"

Conn smiled tenderly at his youngest daughter, and then the three backed from the room. Conn's eyes met the queen's, and Elizabeth said, "You are still the handsomest man at court, my lord Bliss. Farewell and Godspeed!"

"I will be back, Bess," Conn said softly. "That I promise you."

She nodded, and then the door closed between them.

"Is Mag very bad, Papa?" Valentina asked her father.

"She was having a good day when I left, but there are more bad days now, my love. She will not last out the year. She has been lonely since Cluny died two years back. I think she will be glad to be with him again."

"I must tell my girls that I am leaving. Nan, of course, will be delighted to be going home, even for a short time."

"Then you are happy at court?" her father asked her.

"Aye, I am! I know eventually I must choose another husband—even the queen tells me I must—but for now I am content to serve her. She is so very lonely, Papa. It is not like the days when you and Mama and Aunt Skye were at court. They all wait for her to die. All of them. Even little Cecil, loyal as he is, makes preparations for turning the government over to King James."

"Then she has named James Stewart her heir?"

"Not formally," Valentina replied, "but we know that she will. She drops broad hints about what she would like to have happen after she is gone. All she has left is her power, and even that is hollow. Of all the men who loved and served her, only Sir Walter Ralegh is left. This terrible business with Essex broke her heart, Papa. The queen needs her friends now, poor lady."

Lord Bliss nodded. "She has always needed her friends, Valentina. It is not easy to be a reigning queen, but by God, Bess has done it better than anyone, even her father."

They reached the Maidens' Chamber, and Maggie St. Michael hurried in, eager to be first with the news that she and Valentina would be leaving court. Conn drew Valentina aside.

"Have Nan follow us on the morrow with your things. We will leave as soon as you and your sister can be ready. Your mother is anxious and will not rest until I get you home."

"Aye, papa, I understand. I shall hurry Maggie, I promise." Her entry into the Maiden's Chamber was greeted with cries of distress.

"Lady Barrows! Lady Barrows! Oh, say it is not so! Please say you are not leaving us!"

"I am, but Maggie and I will be back as quickly as we can, my maids," Valentina told them. "Our old servant is dying, and we cannot refuse her plea that we come home so she may bid us a final farewell. While I am gone, however, you must all be on your best behavior. I would be very distressed and disappointed to have you slide back to your old slothful and wanton ways. Serve the queen with diligence and courtesy while I am away, and I shall be proud of you," Lady Barrows finished.

Maggie had hurried to her elder sister's private apartment off the Maidens' Chamber to tell Nan the news, and the tiring woman was beside herself with delight. "Poor old Mag," she said when her mistress entered and began changing into her traveling clothes. "I don't wish her ill, and that's a fact," said Nan, "but I can't help being pleased that we are forced to go home."

Valentina smiled and pulled on her riding boots. "See that the coachman and his assistant are fed, Nan, and do not pack everything now, for we *are* coming back."

"I know what to pack, m'lady," Nan said sharply, then chuckled. "I'm so anxious to get home that even though I shall start the day after you, you may arrive at Pearroc Royal to find me already there!"

As they departed from the Maidens' Chamber, they found the Earl of Kempe talking with Lord Bliss. "So, divinity," he said, turning to look at her with admiring eyes, "you think to creep away without telling me, do you? I shall not let you do it."

"Tom Ashburne, you are a most impossible man!" Valentina laughed. "Do the walls of this palace have ears, and have those ears wings that you know of my plans only minutes after I do? You have, I may assume, introduced yourself to my father, Lord Bliss?"

"Indeed, madam, I have."

"Then we will bid you farewell, for we must hasten," said Valentina.

Making her an elegant leg, he caught her hand and kissed it passionately. "Farewell, divinity! We will meet again, and sooner than you think. Mistress Maggie. My lord." Turning, he was gone.

"You have a suitor." Lord Bliss nodded thoughtfully.

"She has two, Papa!" Maggie said gleefully.

"Maggie!" Her elder sister sighed. "Please."

"Two suitors? Indeed, my lass, do you? Who is the other?" their father inquired.

"Cousin Padraic, Papa!" Maggie cried before Valentina could speak for herself. "He and the earl are forever in competition for Val's favors, but she tells them she will not marry again—which only makes them try harder. I do not understand men at all!"

Conn and his elder daughter laughed at the observation, and

Conn told his young daughter, "I would just as soon, my Maggie, that you did *not* understand men. At least not right yet."

Lord Bliss, his two daughters, and two sons were protected during the journey by a half-dozen men-at-arms from the St. Michael estate. Leaving the city, they rode into the countryside at noon through golden autumnal forests, past small farms, through orchards whose heavy-boughed trees perfumed the warm air with the scent of ripe apples, by fields purple with Michaelmas daisies. Shortly before dusk fell, they arrived at a cheerful country inn, The White Rose, where they would put up for the night.

It was a small establishment and had but four guest chambers. The men-at-arms would have to make do in the stable loft after their supper. The innkeeper's wife was an excellent hostess, and the meal set before them was pleasing. There was a large country ham, several juicy capons all roasted and golden, a platter with a large salmon set amid a bed of cress, a rabbit pie, and a wonderful-smelling dish filled with chunks of lamb and vegetables in a sherried cream sauce. There was a dish of boiled carrots and one of braised lettuce. There was bread in abundance, crocks of sweet country butter and a wheel of sharp, hard cheese. Upon the sideboard sat a bowl of polished red apples and russet pears; a custard with cherry preserves; an apple cake with its own bowl of clotted cream. There was ale and cider in frosted jugs upon the tables.

The St. Michaels family ate with a good appetite. They were a family who enjoyed being together, and when the meal had been cleared away, they all gathered about the fireplace to talk.

"I want to leave just before dawn," Conn told his children. They groaned, and he laughed, teasing, "All your high living at court has made you soft."

"Serving the queen day and night is hardly easy living, Papa, and you well know it," Valentina said. "As for Colin and Payton, however, they have been sporting with the ladies and frolicking at the theaters and in the Bear Garden. 'Tis a wonder they have not grown old before their time."

"Young men at court are supposed to frolic," Payton St. Michael protested.

"But you are frolicking with Mistress Honoria de Bohun, and if the queen catches you, you will be out of favor with her quickly, even if you are Papa's son." Maggie giggled.

Payton shot his little sister a black look. "I like Mistress de Bohun," he said.

"You are the only one at court who does, for she is such a crab apple," Maggie replied. "All those airs and fine manners and la di da ways of hers. What does she have to be so proud about, I ask you? She is as poor as a church mouse. Had her family not been owed a favor by a very important person at court, she would never have become a maid of honor."

"Maggie, you are being uncharitable," Valentina said. "I like Honoria. She just takes a little getting used to, for she is very sensitive about her family's poverty, and she never forgets that her family sent her to court to find a husband. All she has to recommend her is her prettiness, her virtue, and an old name. It is hard on a woman to have nothing when she lives in a world that judges one by material possessions. I hope, Pay, that you will treat her kindly and not attempt to seduce her, for she is a good girl."

Maggie pouted at her elder sister's gentle rebuke while Payton shot Valentina a grateful look, glad for her support.

How like her mother she is in temperament and kindness of heart, thought Lord Bliss of his eldest child.

They soon heard the bustle of another guest's arrival, and in a moment the Earl of Kempe entered the inn. He bowed elegantly to Lord Bliss and his sons and kissed the ladies' hands. "Did I not tell you, divinity, that you would see me sooner than you expected? I made my honorable intentions known to your father earlier, so you cannot object to my accompanying you home to Pearroc Royal." He grinned at her wickedly.

"To what purpose do you follow me, my lord?" Valentina demanded of him.

"You can no longer hide behind the wall of mourning, divinity. Lord Barrows has been dead and gone fifteen months. To what purpose have I followed you? Why, I have come courting, my dear. I have come courting."

"I have no wish to be courted," she said emphatically.

"Then I must convince you otherwise. And how can I do that if we are not together?"

"Good night, my lord," Valentina said, and turned to go up the stairs.

"She is not an easy woman," said Tom Ashburne, shaking his head ruefully.

"Nay," agreed Lord Bliss, "she is not, but if you win her, my lord, she will be worth the trouble."

"You approve my suit, sir?" the earl said.

"I do not disapprove it, my lord, but understand that the final decision rests with Valentina. I have never forced my daughters to the altar, and I will not do so now."

"You are liberal with your offspring," remarked the earl.

"As a father of seven I can say that I believe children thrive beneath a firm but gentle hand. Valentina is my daughter, not my possession, sir."

In the hour before dawn, they came downstairs to discover that Lord Burke had arrived during the night. The innkeeper's wife had spread a pallet before the fire for him to sleep on. Seeing the Earl of Kempe, Lord Burke said, "Did you think to steal a march on me, Tom?" His eyes were merry.

"Indeed I did, Padraic. I believe I underestimated you."

"As always, Tom, you have once again allowed your ego to overrule good sense," Lord Burke replied.

"Peace, man!" The earl laughed.

"Good morrow, Val," Lord Burke said to his cousin.

"Good morning, Padraic. You are as big a fool as Tom, I see," Valentina said sharply. She had not slept well, not being used to getting so much sleeping time any more. She had very much enjoyed yesterday with her family despite the reason for their trip home. The arrival of both Tom Ashburne and Padraic Burke was an intrusion she did not appreciate. They behaved more like two young boys squabbling over the last piece of jellycake than like two grown men.

As if reading her mind, Lord Burke said, "I apologize, Val, for this invasion of your privacy and your sadness, but you will understand that because I love you, I would share your sadness with you."

"Oh, Padraic," she said contrite, "it is I who should apologize for greeting you so harshly. I am saddened by Mag's approaching death."

While everyone's attention was on the morning meal, Lord Bliss watched his daughter and nephew talking, the two dark heads close together. So little Maggie had not exaggerated the situation. Perhaps, one of these men would be the one to make her happy. She had not been happy in her first marriage, Lord Bliss knew that now. They had all pushed her to the altar, so that Anne and Bevin might wed their sweethearts without further delay, and he must not allow her to be hurried again. This time, he would see Valentina as happy as he and Aidan were happy.

Several days later, they reached Pearroc Royal under gray skies. Aidan St. Michael hurried outside to greet her husband and children. Her joy in seeing them dampened by the reason for their return.

She had been used to a houseful of children, and with Anne and Bevin wed and the others at court, she'd had only her youngest child, Jamie, now seven, to keep her company. Until this moment, she had not admitted to herself how lonely she was.

Hugging her sons and youngest daughter, she then turned to her eldest child, holding out her arms. Valentina stepped into her mother's embrace and, kissing her soft cheek, looking lovingly into the beloved gray eyes. "Dear child!" Aidan sighed, hugging Valentina tightly.

"Mama! It is so good to be home!"

Together, mother and daughter entered into the house, Aidan not noticing for a moment her guests, so involved was she with her daughter. "Are you happy at court? Does the queen treat you well? Have you met any gentlemen, perhaps?"

"I am happy at court, Mama. I love the queen dearly, and how is Mag?" was Valentina's reply.

"Not good these last two days, but now that you are all home," said Lady Bliss looking about her, "I think she will rally some. Padraic! I did not see you for a moment, and who is this other gentleman who is with you?"

"They are both Valentina's suitors, Mama!" burst out Maggie. "Padraic and Lord Ashburne want to marry her! Isn't that wonderful?"

Everyone laughed, and Conn said to his wife, "My dear, I would present to you, Thomas, Lord Ashburne, the earl of Kempe. Both he and Padraic are valiantly attempting to court our eldest child, but to no avail, I fear, although I suspect that eventually she will succumb to one of them and their charms."

"What charms?" demanded Valentina mischievously.

They both made a great show of ignoring her, and the earl raised Aidan's hand to his lips to kiss it. "I hope you will forgive my intrusion, madam, at such a sorrowful time, but I simply cannot allow Padraic the advantage over me. After all, he has known Val her entire life. I, to my great regret, have not."

"You are most welcome to Pearroc Royal, my lord," came the gracious reply.

"Can I see Mag now, Mama?" Valentina said, bringing back to them the reason for this visit home.

"Of course, my dear, go right up. I must make these two gentlemen comfortable if they are to bide with us awhile," her mother said.

Valentina hurried to old Mag's bedchamber, which was located on the same floor of the house as were the family sleeping quarters. The old lady had been with the St. Michael family for nearly fifty years, and was considered family. She was well over eighty years old. Before her arrival in England, she had been a nursemaid, and then she had become the tiring woman to Lady Bliss's mother, Bevin FitzGerald. She held a place of honor in many hearts. Valentina opened the door to Mag's room and slipped inside. Maide, a young maidservant, sat watching by the bed where the old lady was dozing. She arose and curtsied as Lady Barrows entered.

"She ain't been as restless these last few hours, m'lady, and right glad she'll be to see ye home," the girl whispered.

"I'll sit with her awhile, Maide," Valentina whispered back. "You go and get something to eat."

"Thank ye, m'lady." The door closed quietly behind Maide.

Valentina bent down and kissed Mag's forehead. The old woman opened her eyes. As recognition dawned, she smiled. "God bless ye, child, coming all the way from London to see me on my deathbed. 'Twill not be long now. Master Cluny's waiting for me, ye know. Right impatient he is, too, the old fool!" Cluny had been Lord Bliss's manservant and had come with him from Ireland. He and Mag had been the closest of friends and the greatest of antagonists; and it always surprised the family that they never married. Cluny had died two years prior, and Mag had silently mourned him.

"Colly came back with me, and Pay and Maggie, too, Mag," Valentina told her with a smile.

"Yer sister Anne has come, and she's brought the baby with her," Mag said. "A lovely boy he is, too. Looks just like his da, he does, and Master Robert is ever so proud. Produced him just six and a half months after the wedding, she did, yet he was healthy for an early bairn." The old lady struggled to sit up. "Prop my pillows behind me, child, so I can get a better look at ye." When Valentina had complied, she asked sharply, "Are ye happy at court? 'Tis a hurly-burly place. I remember it."

" 'Twas that way last winter with the earl's rebellion," said Valentina, "but mostly they wait for the queen to die."

"She's good to ye?"

Valentina nodded. "I am very fond of her, Mag. She has so few about her now whom she can trust. It is tragic. But we have talked long enough, Mag. Mama says you have been poorly these past few days, and you need to rest."

"Nonsense, child! I'll soon have all the rest I could ever want. Eternal rest! Now, do not look low, my dearie. I am a very old woman, and I am not sad to be going, though it pains me to leave those I love behind. Still, there is Master Cluny, and he will have his way in this as he ever did. Ye'll not leave me until I've gone, will ye, child? The queen will let ye stay with me?"

"Aye, Mag, she will. She is a good mistress," said Valentina, close to tears.

"Mistress Bevin's bairn is near to being born now, ye know," the old woman confided. "How I wish I might see her and the babe before I die, but 'tis not to be, I know that."

Over the next few days, Valentina spent a great deal of time with old Mag, nursing her, talking with her. Mag loved her and thrived on the attention. She was delighted to learn that Valentina was the object of a rivalry between Lord Burke and Lord Kempe.

"Yer a late bloomer like yer mother," she said, "though I did not see it at first. Which one will ye choose, my dearie?"

"I do not know them well enough to make a choice, Mag," Valentina said.

"Not know yer cousin, Padraic? Why ye've known him yer entire life, child!"

"I've known him as my cousin, Mag, but until recently, I have never thought of him as a husband. Padraic has always been my friend, for all the difference in our ages."

"And this earl? What of him?"

"Tom? I do not know what to make of him, Mag. I am never certain if he is really serious or not. He outrageously handsome, and he has great charm, but for all his persistence, I do not know if he is the man I seek," said Valentina thoughtfully.

"Bring them both to see me," said old Mag. "Ye know I've always had an instinct for people."

"It would not tire you to receive visitors?"

"No, child. It cheers me to see people."

"I shall bring them tomorrow then," Valentina promised, and she did.

Mag was delighted. "Let me look at ye, Master Padraic," she said. "Lord bless me but yer a handsome fellow! So ye love my pretty girlie, do ye?"

"Aye, Mag, I do," he said as he kissed her withered cheek.

"Ye might have spoken up sooner, and saved us all a pack of trouble," she grumbled.

"I wish I had."

"Mag, dearest, this is Lord Ashburne," said Valentina, drawing the earl forward.

Mag looked him up and down boldly, then nodded. "He looks presentable enough," she said.

Tom Ashburne laughed. "My old nurse used to say that a handsome face could hide a multitude of wickedness," he teased her gently.

"But it doesn't with yer lordship. That much I can see. Ye've gotten all the hell out of yerself by now," said Mag. Then she looked at Valentina. "Well, dearie, ye've a hard choice here. I'm sorry I'll not be here to dance at yer wedding."

Mag rallied in those first few days that Valentina and the others were home. One warm, late October day she asked to be carried to the window so that she could gaze out across the estate fields. Her eyes took in all the autumn beauty of the landscape. When Val opened the window, she smiled, hearing the birdsong and sniffing eagerly at the air, and waved weakly to Lord Burke and Lord Ashburne who were riding in from a morning's hunting. That night, however, Mag took a bad turn, slipping into a delirium.

"I will sit with her," Valentina volunteered.

"But you were with her most of the day," Aidan protested. "You will exhaust yourself, my child. I will sit with her. I have, after all, known her longer than any of you."

"I will relieve you at midnight, Mama," Valentina said, and Aidan agreed.

"Is it the end?" Padraic asked Valentina before she left the hall to sleep.

"Perhaps," said Valentina softly. "Poor Mama! Mag has been with her for Mama's entire life. She'll miss her terribly."

At midnight Lady Barrows slipped into the invalid's room and Aidan departed for her own chamber. The old woman tossed restlessly, her brow wet with sweat. Valentina wiped the dampness from Mag's forehead and then seated herself by the bedside. She read by the light of a large candle. Occasionally the old woman muttered unintelligibly. There was a clock upon the mantel that slowly ticked away the hours and Valentina began to nod. She put her book aside and went to the window, drawing the curtains back to look out at the moon-silvered landscape. The moon rode high on a bank of dark-edged clouds, and the night scene so enraptured Valentina that she started when she heard old Mag speaking. Her voice was clear, and Val thought she might be awake, but she was not. Valentina wiped the fevered brow again, but this time Mag would not be soothed.

"I should not have listened," Mag's voice rasped, her breathing harsh. "I should not have listened at Mistress Aidan's door when his lordship went in to her." Her head rolled from side to side as her breathing quickened. "France. Mistress Aidan's in France. God forgive me. Should not have listened."

"Mag! Mag! 'Tis all right," Valentina said gently.

"Not in France! My mistress is not in France! There's a prince, and a wicked king . . . Oh, Cluny! She is not sure the bairn is his lordship's child! God forgive me! I should not have listened! Mistress Aidan does not know who the father of her bairn is!"

At first Valentina did not comprehend what she was hearing. "She is not sure the bairn is his lordship's child." What child was Mag speaking of?

"They'll never know," muttered Mag. "They'll never know, for his lordship's accepted the bairn, praise God! He loves little Mistress Valentina, but she doesn't look like either of them. Still, who is ever to know? Oh, I should not have listened! God forgive me!"

A cold hand clutched Valentina's heart as the words sank in. Was she not her father's child? What prince and what wicked king, and what did they have to do with this? What secrets had been kept from her? What had Mag listened to?

For all the rest of that night, Valentina sat in agony. Who am I, she wondered, if I am not who I think I am?

In the hour before dawn, old Mag opened her eyes, smiled sweetly at Valentina, and said, "I must go now, dearie. Cluny will not wait another minute." Then the life fled from her eyes, and she was gone.

Bending, Val kissed Mag's brow. "Farewell, my dear friend, and Godspeed. I wish, however, that you had not left before you explained yourself." Walking to the window, Valentina pulled back the draperies and opened the casements wide. The sky beyond the hills was rich gold with the impending sunrise, and the air was crisp and fresh. How many autumn mornings had been exactly like this. It was as always, and yet everything had changed for her. She knew that her mother held the key to the mystery that the dying Mag had revealed, but Valentina also knew that until the old servant was buried, it would not be kind to burden her mother. She left the room to inform her parents of Mag's death.

Margaret Feeney, known all her life as Mag, born in the village of Ballycoille in Ireland on the first of January in 1517, was laid to rest on the twenty-fifth of October, 1601. Mag was buried in the cemetery of Pearroc Royal's church. She was buried next to Peter Cluny.

The following morning, Aidan and her eldest daughter entered Mag's room to sort through the old woman's things and give away what was useable to those who were in need.

"Oh, look!" Aidan cried softly. " 'Tis a lock of your hair, and your very first cap! How tiny that little cap is. You were such a beautiful baby, my dear."

"My hair was copper-colored like yours when I was born?"

"Aye, it was, but it fell out when you were about six months old. When it grew back, 'twas dark brown, but it still has copper lights." She reached out and stroked her daughter's head. "Such beautiful hair, my dear."

Valentina could not bear it any longer. "Who is my father?" she demanded bluntly.

Aidan St. Michael paled and, staggering slightly, grasped a chair to keep her balance. "What on earth do you mean?" she managed to gasp.

"Mama," Valentina said clearly, "I want to know who my father is." Valentina could feel the iron entering her soul. She knew she would need it, for she saw her mother's distress.

"You are my daughter, Valentina, and your father is Conn O'Malley St. Michael."

"Who are the prince and the wicked king?"

"Who has mentioned the prince and the sultan to you? Who has told you these things, Valentina?" Aidan shrieked "Oh, God! *Why now*?"

"Mag spoke in her delirium, Mama. It appears that she listened outside a door once and learned that you were not certain of the paternity of your eldest child. There were three men involved. Papa, a prince, and a wicked king. That child was me, Mama! I want to know why you were not certain of your child's lineage! How could you keep such a secret from me? It is my right to know!" Valentina raged at her mother, who began to weep.

Aidan fled from the room, but her daughter followed. Lady Bliss ran down the stairs to her husband's library and flung herself into his arms, sobbing, "She knows! She knows!"

Conn's arms closed about his distraught wife. Over her shoulder his eyes met the angry eyes of his eldest child. "What is this about, Valentina?"

"I wish to know who my father is, my lord," was the cold reply.

"I am your father," Conn said evenly, his expression giving away nothing.

"Then what of the prince and the sultan?" Valentina demanded fiercely.

He nodded understanding. How the hell had she found out? It didn't matter. She knew, and she must be told the truth. His arms tightened about his wife as he said, "It is obvious, my darling, that Valentina must hear the tale of your adventures. We must clear this matter up."

"I cannot!" Aidan wept. "Oh, Conn, do not make me live that time again. I have put it from my mind all these years. I cannot go back!"

Conn gently settled his wife in a comfortable chair and put a glass of wine in her hand. Then he turned to his daughter. "What brought this about, Valentina? What do you know, and who has told you?"

"I know little except there is doubt as to my paternity. That there is a prince and a wicked king involved. That there is a secret to do with me. Mag spoke quite clearly during her final night, when she was asleep."

"How the hell did Mag know?" Conn wondered. "Only your aunt and uncle de Marisco and I knew of the difficulties. *I* have never accepted that there was a problem, Val. I am your father. You are my eldest daughter. Of that I am certain."

"Mag, it seems, listened at a door once," said Valentina. "It weighed on her conscience when she was dying, for she kept saying, 'God forgive me.' " Valentina hesitated, then said, "Please, sir, tell me the truth, I beg you."

"Do not call me 'sir,' " he said.

"Please, my lord."

"Nor 'my lord' either," he said harshly.

"Then *what*?" she cried.

"Papa."

"But until I know the truth, I cannot be certain you *are* my father," Valentina said, her voice trembling.

"I *am* your father, my dear. Believe me." Lord Bliss turned to his wife. "Tell her all of it, Aidan. Never in all the years we have been wed have I commanded you to do anything that displeased you, but now I must. *Tell her!* Sit opposite your mother, Valentina, so that she may see you as she speaks."

Aidan St. Michael, a tall and big-boned woman, had never in her entire life looked more fragile. Her copper-colored hair was threaded with strands of silver gilt, for she was forty-seven, and her eyes were anguished as she began to speak.

"How do I begin?" she wondered aloud. She looked so helpless that Valentina nearly stopped her.

"Begin at the beginning, Mama," she said kindly.

Conn stood behind his wife, his hand resting lightly on her shoulder, a comfort and an encouragement.

"I had a cousin, Cavan FitzGerald, born a bastard. The Spanish king wished to discredit the O'Malleys of Innisfana and your Aunt Skye in the eyes of the queen and her government. Your uncles were then raiding and pillaging, under England's protection, along the Spanish Main. They were successful enough so that King Philip's income was greatly reduced through the O'Malleys. In the East Indies, your aunt's ships were beginning to make a tiny dent in the riches offered there, and the Portuguese, who were controlled by the Spanish, resented it.

"My grandfather and my cousin were recruited by the Spanish. They were to make it appear as if your father were involved in a plot against the queen's life. He would be executed, your aunt's trading company would be confiscated and discredited, and the O'Malleys—their fine Irish tempers ablaze—would turn on England. I, and the wealth my father left me, were to be their reward. Cavan was to marry me. My grandfather believed my riches would be turned over to him for his futile war against England. Cavan, however, planned on gaining respectability through our marriage, and intended keeping my wealth for himself.

"The plot went awry. How? It does not matter now, but old Lord Burghley needed one final piece of evidence against my cousin and his Spanish accomplice, who did not realize they were close to arrest. I was to go to Cavan at his London inn and tell him that my wealth had been confiscated. I was so convincing that my cousin's confederate decided that they must escape from London that very night. The ship they were to sail on belonged to a renegade Spaniard who sailed for the Dey of Algiers as a merchant. His secret cargo was always fair young women. The Spaniard suggested that Cavan bring me along. He said I would fetch a high price in the slave markets of Algiers. That way, my cousin would make a profit from me."

"That is loathsome!" Valentina was deeply shocked.

"That, my child, is the way of the East. A woman's worth is judged by the number of horses or camels or sheep or goats she will fetch. Human life is cheap, a woman's life particularly so. So I was rendered unconscious and taken aboard this vessel, where, in the course of the voyage to Algiers, I lost the child I was expecting." A tear rolled down Aidan's soft cheek, and Valentina reached out to squeeze her mother's hand.

"In Algiers, I was stripped naked to be examined by the purchasers. The Dey of Algiers himself decided to purchase me as a gift for the sultan of the Ottoman Empire, Murad. I was shipped to Istanbul. On the very day of my arrival there, I was presented as a gift to the new ambassador from the khanate of the Crimea, Prince Javid Khan. I was no longer Aidan St. Michael, Valentina. I was renamed Marjallah, I was told over and over that I must forget Aidan St. Michael.

"The prince and I were happy together. He had come to Istanbul to forget a terrible tragedy. His twin brother, Temur Khan, as different from him as night is from day, had murdered Javid Khan's entire family. It was believed that Temur Khan was mad from birth, for he had always had an unreasonable jealousy of his brother. The Great Khan, their father, sent Javid away to ease his pain. I, too, was in great pain. I had lost my child, lost my whole identity. I had been torn from the husband I loved. I had learned enough Turkish to communicate, but this was not my real life. Yet I was told there was no hope of my ever returning to England.

"Javid Khan fell in love with me, and after a time, I loved him. He freed me from slavery and married me in the faith of Islam. We began to build a life together in our little palace on the Bosporus. Because the prince was so pleased with me, his happiness reflected well on the sultan. The sultan's mother and his wife, usually at odds with one another, were pleased with me as well and offered me their friendship. They were the two most powerful women in that land, Valentina, allowed privileges other women never even dreamed of.

"There was another woman who offered me friendship, and in the end she helped save my life. Her name is Esther Kira. She is the matriarch—the founder, in fact—of the great banking house of Kira. The Kiras are Jews. Esther is well over one hundred now, yet she lives on still directing her family and ruling over them all. I know this because your aunt's trading company does business with the Kiras." Aidan smiled a little at the memory of Esther Kira. "I can still see her sitting opposite me in my caïque as we were rowed on the water.

"On that terrible morning, I arose early and went to the city to fetch Esther. I wanted to show her the perfection of our tulip gardens. While I was away, Temur Khan attacked our home. His Tatars killed everyone they could find. They carried off my serving woman, Marta. Esther and I returned while the fighting was still going on. My caïque fled back to the city so that we might seek help from the sultan." After a silence, she said softly, "Javid Khan was killed. Marta saw his body by the stables as the Tatars carried her off.

"The sultan's mother and his favorite wife were so kind to me. They understood the horrors I had lived through. But at that time, despite what everyone had said to me about not being able to return home, I was determined to do exactly that. My beloved prince was dead, and surely no one else would treat me so well. Also, I was a free woman, no longer a slave. Eventually there was bound to be an O'Malley-Small trading vessel in the harbor.

"What I did not know was that the sultan lusted after me. Having seen me with Javid Khan, he had regretted his generous gift. He did not intend to part with me again. So he claimed that I was not free. As the prince was dead, his possessions reverted to the sultan, and I was one of those possessions. I was forced into carnal bondage by Sultan Murad and made to do such things for his pleasure that you, my sweet daughter, cannot even begin to imagine. Finally, I could bear no more. I attempted to kill him. Alas, I failed. I was sentenced to death. I was to be sewn into a weighted lavender silk sack and taken to a place off an island in the Marmara, where I would be drowned.

"By that time, your father had traced me to Istanbul, thank God. Or, I should say, thanks to Esther Kira, who was an intimate of the royal ladies.

"I was drugged and sewn into my sack with Tulip."

"Tulip?" exclaimed Valentina. "Our old cat?" Her mother nodded. "But Tulip died only three years ago," said Valentina. "The same Tulip, who fathered at least ten generations of cats on this estate?"

"The very same," replied Aidan. "Tulip was born in the sultan's palace in Istanbul. Tulip was the only living creature, human or animal, to survive the slaughter of the prince's palace. He escaped because the Tartars were there early that morning, and Tulip had not yet returned from his nightly roamings."

"But how did you escape drowning, Mama?" Valentina was nearly overwhelmed by then.

"One family had, for three generations, been in charge of rowing the death boat of the Ottoman sultans. They were Jews. No Moslem would take the task, believing it was bad luck. This family was in debt to the Kiras. Esther offered them money to save me from drowning.

"The boatman rowed out to the island as if doing his duty. But a large ship sailed by him, which blocked him from view of the shore. Your father was aboard that ship, and it was he and his friends who, with the Kiras' help, arranged my rescue. As the great ship and the little death boat passed each other, a boy in a bosun's chair was lowered from the deck to lift my sack and hoist me safely aboard the ship. Another sack filled with ballast was substituted for mine. None of this could be seen from the city. I, of course, was unconscious, and knew none of this until afterward, for which I thank God!"

Aidan became silent for a minute, and then resumed her story. "Later, when we had reached land, I discovered that I was with child. I was terrified. For a few weeks, I kept the knowledge to myself." Here she blushed a deep red. "In a short period of time, I had been with three men. Javid Khan, the sultan, and my dear Conn—the day of my rescue. Which man was the father of my child? How could I know? Fear overcame me, and I locked myself in our bedchamber, refusing to speak to anyone but your aunt Skye. Learning of my doubts, she soothed me, and she made me see that the father of my child was undoubtedly her brother, my husband. Then I told your father of my fears, and he, too, accepted paternity."

Aidan gave her daughter a searching look and said, "Mag probably listened at the bedchamber door when your father came in to reassure herself that everything was all right. You see, she had not known of my captivity in Turkey. Only your father knew, and he feared the shock of knowing what had happened to me might kill her. Mag was told that I was in France and that Conn had joined me there later, that we were being punished by the queen, but would be permitted to return home soon.

"I believe that Conn is your father, Valentina," Aidan declared. "He believes it, too. I am so sorry that poor Mag's delirious mutterings distressed you, my child," Aidan finished.

"Why did you never tell me all of this?" Valentina asked her mother.

"Because it was not necessary, and because I wished to forget all of it. What happened to me almost twenty-three years ago is a painful memory that I have, until today, managed to put from my thoughts.

"You cannot know the agonies I suffered, Valentina! To lose my first child while imprisoned aboard a slave ship! To be paraded naked before strangers! To be told that I should never see my beloved husband again. To be given to another man! Had not Javid Khan been the kind and gentle man he was, had he been like Sultan Murad, I would have died in captivity, I am sure."

"If you questioned the paternity of your child, Mama, what made you certain suddenly that Papa was indeed my father?" Valentina demanded.

"He was the last of the three to possess me," Aidan said.

"Perhaps you were with child before Father rescued you," her daughter countered. "You cannot be sure, can you? Therefore, neither can I!"

"Javid Khan and I made love the night before he was killed," Aidan told her. "I had just renewed my link with the moon. My cycles were irregular, and had been since I lost my first child. I was in the sultan's possession only a few weeks, not even a month, and then I was with your father. My link with the moon was not broken in that time, Valentina, but I know that Conn is your father. *I know it.* It can be no other!" Aidan insisted.

"It can be a prince or a sultan, Mama, and you are a fool to believe otherwise!" Valentina lashed out. "God's foot, but you delude yourself!"

"*Valentina!*" Conn's voice was sharp. "You will not speak to your mother like that ever again!" Calming his anger, he said, "I believe myself to be your father. Your mother believes it. You bear our name. I have loved you from the moment I knew of your coming. I held you in my arms only minutes after you were born. When I looked into your face and you looked back at me with those wonderful eyes, Valentina, I knew you were my daughter. I gave you my finger and your tiny fist wrapped around it, but it was not only my finger you captured, Valentina, it was my heart. *You are my child.*

"I have loved you. I raised you. Your triumphs have been my triumphs, your sorrows mine. If by some perverse quirk of fate the blood flowing in your veins at your birth was not mine, then it is mine now. You must never doubt it!"

Valentina's beautiful eyes were filled with tears that overflowed and slid down her pale cheeks. "I love you," she said, "but I must know who I really am before I will ever know peace again."

"How can you find out?" Conn asked her gently.

"I must go to Turkey," replied Valentina, surprising herself, for she had not known she would say such a thing.

"*No*," moaned Aidan. "Oh, God, no, my dear. Do not even think of it."

"Sultan Murad is dead, Valentina," her father told her. "And as Javid Khan is also dead . . ."

"There must be someone who can help me to know," Valentina insisted.

"I will die if you go there." Aidan sobbed.

"I will die if I cannot find out who I really am," replied her daughter firmly. "Tell me more, Mama. Tell me about Prince Javid Khan and his family. About the sultan. Help me unravel this puzzle, Mama, I beg of you! Look at me! I favor neither you nor Papa, yet all my siblings do. Do I look like any relation that you remember? Tell me, I beg you!" Valentina paused for a moment, and then, taking a deep breath, said, "Do I look like either the prince or the sultan, Mama? Tell me. Surely you remember them well enough to know if there is any resemblance."

"No! I will tell you nothing more! Conn O'Malley is your father. No other. I will tell you nothing more," Aidan cried.

"What do you wish to hide from me, Mama? Why can you not speak about these men?" Valentina shouted back. "You tell me I must not go, but you will tell me nothing else. It will not do, Mama. It is not enough. I must know, I must!"

For the next hour, mother and daughter raged back and forth. Their voices carried throughout the house until finally family and servants were gathered in alarm outside Lord Bliss's library door. It was Padraic Burke who finally had the courage to knock loudly.

Lord Bliss went to the door, roaring at his wife and daughter as he went, "Be silent!" The two women stopped their noise.

"Uncle," Padraic addressed Conn, "we cannot help but hear. The servants are frightened, and I, frankly, am curious."

"There is nothing to fear," Lord Bliss told his servants. "Go about your business now." He glared at his children, who were standing in the hallway. "Have you nothing better to do than listen at doors?"

"No," Valentina cried. "Let them come in. Padraic and Tom as well. This matter concerns them, as they both court me. Come in! Come in!" She waved them into the library. The servants went about their business.

"Valentina, do not do this," her father warned. "Your mother may not—"

"No, Conn. There has been too much hidden. The truth must be known," Aidan said softly. "It is time my family knew."

Lord Bliss's library was filled with his family, his son-in-law, Robert Grayson, his nephew, Lord Burke, and the Earl of Kempe. They looked from Aidan, who sat with her head in her hands, exhausted, to the stony-eyed Valentina.

"Padraic, Tom, this affects you both. Before you learn the story, however, I want to say that you are both freed from any obligation you may believe you have toward me. You are better off seeking wives elsewhere, for Lord Bliss's eldest daughter may not be his daughter at all."

For a long moment, they all stared at her, uncomprehending. Finally Valentina's sister Anne St. Michael Grayson cried, "Valentina! What can you possibly mean?"

Valentina gave her mother a probing look. It was not her story to reveal, but Aidan's. Would she tell it? Aidan nodded. Gazing at the floor, she told them her history. When she had finished, the room was so silent that the floating of a feather might have been heard as it drifted to the floor.

Then the Earl of Kempe knelt before Aidan and lifted her hand to his lips. "Madam, I salute you," he said gently. "No Englishman under fire at Cádiz could have been as brave as you were during your trials in Barbary. Be assured that I will not withdraw my suit for your daughter's hand. The daughter of such a gallant lady is just the kind of wife I want. The kind of mother I desire for my children. If you believe that your husband is her true sire, madam, then I accept your word in the matter. To do anything else would render me less than a gentleman."

Looking gratefully into Tom Ashburne's eyes, Aidan said softly, "Thank you, my lord. You are indeed a gentleman, a very fine one, I think."

"It is you I love, Val," said Lord Burke, going directly to Lady Barrows, "and, whatever the truth in this matter, it is you I will have. Like Tom, I am content to accept my aunt's judgment. And besides, Val, you are too stubborn to be anything except an O'Malley, so you must surely be one."

There was laughter at the remark, and Valentina's sisters and brothers gathered about her, reassuring her, but she would not be satisfied. "I must go to Turkey," she said. "Only there can I learn the truth."

"But," Aidan put in, "there is no assurance that going there will yield the truth. With both men dead and—"

"It is a chance I must take," her daughter interrupted.

There was no dissuading her. Conn sent for his elder sister, Skye O'Malley de Marisco, the family matriarch. She came at once, disdaining her coach, and riding across the autumn fields that separated her home, Queen's Malvern, from Pearroc Royal. Her husband Adam rode beside her.

Skye had always been a beautiful woman, and though she was shortly to celebrate her sixty-first birthday, time had not dimmed her beauty. Neither her face nor her body had aged appreciably after her fortieth year. Her wonderful blue-green eyes, the same color as the water off the Kerry coast, were as alert as ever, and she missed nothing. Her hair was still a silky black but for two silver wings at her temples.

Settling herself comfortably in her brother's library later that day, she listened as he explained what had happened between Aidan and Valentina. Her gaze went to her beautiful niece and Skye said, "You are determined to go?"

"Aye," replied Valentina. "I am."

"Then she must go, of course," said Skye.

"God's foot!" shouted Aidan. "Are you mad? You have been in the East, Skye! You know what it's like!"

"Valentina is of age, Aidan. She is a wealthy widow and has the means to do precisely as she pleases. Oh, you can stop her. You could, for example, lock her in her room until she dies. Or you could force her to the altar and let her husband handle the problem. But she will hate you for it and you know it. If she cannot be content until she goes, then go she must."

"Thank you, Aunt Skye," said Valentina gratefully.

"Don't be too quick with your gratitude, my girl," said Skye. "There are conditions attached to my acquiescence. As your mother said, I have been in the East. Twice. I know the East only too well. You must heed what I tell you."

"I am not unreasonable, Aunt. Tell me what to do to ensure my safety. I will do what you say. I am not anxious to end up in some Turk's harem," Valentina said.

Skye nodded. "You are Aidan's daughter for all your O'Malley temper, my girl. Very well, listen to me. You will travel in an O'Malley-Small trading vessel that will be outfitted solely for your expedition. You will bear the cost of that outfitting, Valentina, and for the two ships that travel with it for your protection." Valentina winced but said nothing. "While at sea, you will obey its captain's orders. Is that understood?"

"Aye, Aunt."

"I must speak with the Kira bankers in London. They will be your contacts in Istanbul. But I do not know about the Crimean khanate. I must investigate that," Skye murmured thoughtfully.

Adam de Marisco smiled at his wife. Since their last voyage to India ten years ago, Skye had remained at home involving herself in their estate, the horses they raised, and their grandchildren. She had been happy, of that Adam was sure, but he had not seen her so interested in a project for a long while. There was a sparkle in her blue-green eyes, and he suspected that she missed all the high adventure and intrigue of her youth, although she never said so.

Suddenly, his stepson spoke.

"Valentina cannot travel alone to such a distant and dangerous place without a protector. I am going with her."

"An excellent idea, Padraic!" his mother approved. "I had intended mentioning some sort of chaperon, considering where your cousin is going."

"Ho, my lord! Think you to get ahead of me?" said the earl. "If you go, then I will go also. Another good sword is always welcome when one goes adventuring."

Skye looked curiously at her son, and then at Tom Ashburne, and then at Valentina, then back to her son. She grinned. "So that's how it is," She chuckled. "Well, you are right, my lord. Another good sword is always welcome on such a dangerous venture, but be certain that you and my son remember this: Your common enemy is not each other. Also remember that your reason for accompanying Valentina is to protect her."

"Madam," said the earl with a rakish smile, "I have been offering her my protection for months now, but she will not accept it."

"Ah," said Skye, chuckling, "if I were twenty years younger, my lord!"

"Madam, 'tis not the twenty years that discourages me," Tom Ashburne teased. " 'Tis your husband, who even now is glowering at me."

"Behave yourself, little girl," growled Adam, "and remember that you are a grandmother."

"A grandmother I may be, my lord," she rejoined with pungent humor, "but I am not yet a corpse!"

They all laughed, and the tension began to lift.

In the next few weeks, careful plans were made for Valentina's voyage, to begin shortly after the new year. Anne, her husband, and infant son departed for their home. Colin, Payton, and Maggie returned to court, bearing with them a message from Valentina to the queen explaining that there were difficulties that made her immediate return impossible. Valentina promised to see the queen before Twelfth Night.

Aidan was still not happy with her daughter's decision to go to Turkey. "Why can you not accept my word in this matter?" she asked her daughter. "Why must you deliberately put your life in danger on a whim? You have no assurance of learning anything."

Valentina tried to reassure her mother. "In our entire family, I do not see my face. Not among my siblings, nor in the family portraits that hang in the picture gallery. I must make every effort to learn what I can."

Her mother shook her head.

"Tell me of Javid Khan, Mama. What did he look like? And Sultan Murad? I know it is painful, Mama, but help me!"

"If I tell you, will you cease this foolishness?" Aidan asked her daughter desperately.

"I must go!" Valentina said firmly, "even if I return home without learning the truth. I must try. I must find out who my father is if I can."

Aidan sighed. "Javid Khan was a handsome man. His hair was a tawny blond, perhaps a little lighter than Bevin's. His eyes were light blue and so compassionate."

"I thought Tatars were a dark-haired people, Mama."

"Originally they were," Aidan replied, "but they have intermarried with others over the centuries. Then, too, Javid Khan's mother was a Frenchwoman. She had been on her way to marry a duke or a prince in one of those countries far to the east of France. I do not remember which one, Val, for it is a very long time since I've thought about this. She was captured by a raiding party of Tatars led by Javid's father. He took her for a wife, and eventually they were happy."

"Eventually?" Valentina echoed.

"The Frenchwoman was fortunate to find love with her Tatar lord, my child. Many women are forced into harems. They hate their daily existence and the man who owns them. Listen to me, Valentina. You must understand where you are going. In the East, women are for pleasure and for breeding *only*. No one is interested in their intelligence or whether they can read or speak another language or even work in the family business. Women are . . . things. They are for a man's amusement. Creatures for bearing healthy sons. Daughters do not count.

"I thank God that your hair is dark, but even so, you are in danger, Valentina. You are a fair-skinned Christian English-woman. The rules of fairness that apply in Islam will not apply to you, a foreigner. You will be fair game, I warn you. Your aunt Skye's dark hair did not prevent her from twice being caught in that beautiful and violent world of sensuality that Islam is. Do not go, Valentina! I beg you!" Aidan pleaded with her daughter.

"Tell me of the sultan," Valentina said, not meeting her mother's soft gray eyes.

Aidan sighed again. "His hair was red-gold. His eyes were dark. He was a sensualist through and through. He was interested in clocks and the acquisition of gold and women for himself. In his time, the price of beautiful women was driven up in the slave markets of Istanbul, for Murad wanted them all for himself. His sexual appetite was prodigious, and he was cruel beyond all men. Ask me no more, Valentina, for I cannot bear to remember!"

Valentina could not bear to think of what her gentle mother had suffered. "Tell me of Murad's favorite wife and his mother," she requested, hoping to steer the conversation into less turbulent waters.

"Nur-U-Banu is dead now. I have learned the news of Istanbul over the years. Nur-U-Banu was the sultan's mother, and her only interest was power. She ruled through her son, who was vulnerable to her whims. Murad was happy with his favorite, Safiye. They had a son, the sultan who now rules. Mehmed is his name. Nur-U-Banu believed that Safiye had gained too much influence with Murad and so she worried her son about his favorite's inability to produce more children. She tempted him with the most exquisite beauties and eventually Murad succumbed to the beautiful temptations that she dangled before him. He strayed from Safiye's side, and her only consolation was that one day her son would rule and she would possess Nur-U-Banu's power. Now she does."

"So," said Valentina, "in the end, everything worked out all right despite Nur-U-Banu's meddling."

Aidan laughed harshly. "When Mehmed became sultan, he practiced an old Ottoman custom. He had all nineteen of his brothers—little boys actually, ranging in age from eleven to infancy—strangled. Those of his father's women who were with child suffered the fate meant for me. They were sewn into silken sacks and drowned. This is the place you are going to, Valentina. It is a beautiful yet terrifying world. You will be in danger there. You *are* your father's daughter. Why can you not simply believe me?"

"I do, Mama. And yet . . . I cannot. Mag's words torture me night and day. I must go."

Tom Ashburne had gone home to Swan Court to set his affairs in order. Lord Burke, however, remained at Pearroc Royal in an attempt to comfort Valentina, for the knowledge she possessed had made her restless and unhappy. She had written to the queen explaining her dilemma and begging Her Majesty's permission to leave her service so that she might follow her fate to Turkey. The queen had reluctantly allowed Lady Barrows a temporary leave on the condition that Valentina stop in London before departing for the East.

There was nothing for Valentina to do but wait at Pearroc Royal, for the provisioning of the ships was not her affair. All that was required of her was that she provide her Aunt Skye with the monies required to outfit her expedition.

They would be ready to leave in early January. Skye had arranged through the Kiras and her own factors in Istanbul for Valentina's ships to pay a visit to the khanate of the Crimea, pretending to be on a trading mission. Once Valentina was there, it would be up to the Great Khan to see her or not, as he chose. Aidan did not even know whether the Great Khan was Javid Khan's father, still living, or some other relative. They would not find out who possessed the throne until they reached the Crimea.

They would stop in Istanbul first so that Valentina could make arrangements to see the Valideh Safiye Kadin on her return from the Crimea. The protocol involved would take that much time.

The waiting was hard on Valentina. She could not speak to her mother without upsetting her greatly, and Conn's concerns were for Aidan, who was positive that Valentina was walking into terrible danger. Val's siblings were all gone but for Jamie, and the little boy could not possibly comprehend his sister's distress. That left only Padraic. She was grateful that he had stayed at Pearroc Royal to be with her.

"What of Clearfields?" She worried for him. They were talking in the upstairs hallway.

"I've a good bailiff, and Adam has promised to oversee any problems. My horses will be brought to Mother at Queen's Malvern with their grooms, so only the farms will need supervision."

"What of the house?" she asked.

"I've lived alone in it these last years and have only needed two servants to oversee the place. They will see to things while I am gone. I have already spoken with the workmen who will be refurbishing the house. Later, it will be up to you to see to the decor, for I want you to be happy in your home," he finished calmly.

"I have never said I would marry you, Padraic. What of Tom Ashburne?" Valentina found herself slightly giddy.

"Tom will have to find his own true love, Val, for I have found mine" was Padraic's calm reply. He was behaving as if everything were settled between them!

"But I have not said yes, you ass!" she shouted.

"You will," he answered, grinning.

"I won't!" she snapped, infuriated by his proprietary attitude.

He chuckled with infuriating confidence. "Aye, hinny love, you will. But I'll give you the time to come to your own conclusion."

"You are the most impossible man!" she fumed. "You have always been such a gentle man, with a sense of deference. What has happened to you, Padraic Burke?"

"Gentle deference, Valentina, has not won you. Perhaps it is time I became more like my long-departed father, who took what he wanted without a care for the consequences." With that, he swept her into his embrace and, carrying her a few quick paces, kicked open the door to his bedchamber. He carried her inside and booted the door closed behind him.

"Padraic!" she shrieked, shocked by his behavior.

"Padraic what?" he demanded, dumping her on the bed and flinging himself on top of her.

His body was hard against hers, and she felt a thrill of hot excitement run through her. "Padraic," she whispered, her voice trembling, "what are you doing?"

"What I should have done months ago, Val! I am going to make love to you," he said smoothly.

"No!" Her amethyst eyes were wide with shock.

"Yes!" he said through gritted teeth, and then his mouth was on hers, bruising it with a fierce kiss. He raised himself slightly off her and, hooking his hand into her bodice, tore it to the waist, baring her lovely breasts to his fiery gaze. His smoldering glance almost scorched her flesh.

She attempted to cover her bosom, but he imprisoned her wrist in a tight grasp. Valentina's heart was hammering. She was not afraid of him, for she knew that Padraic Burke would never hurt her, yet there was something wild in his behavior, something she had never guessed existed within him. This passionate man was not the Padraic Burke she knew, and she wondered if she might not be a little afraid of him. She could not, however, seem to find her voice.

He rolled onto his side, still holding her one hand. His other hand reverently caressed her breast, the long fingers following the swell of her warm flesh, cupping her lovely breast in his big hand. His thumb began a slow and beguiling encircling of her nipple. Fascinated, she watched him. For the life of her, she could not move. His touch mesmerized her, and she was aware that a new and most decidedly delicious sensation was permeating her entire being.

He lowered his dark head to take the bud of her nipple into his mouth, to tease it with his warm, satiny tongue. It was wonderful. Into her benumbed brain came the thought that her husband had never touched her like this. If he had, surely she would have enjoyed his attentions more. With that thought a second followed. Padraic was not her husband, and therefore it must be wrong for them to be together like this. "Padraic," she said softly, "you must not do these things to me."

He lifted his gaze to hers. His aquamarine-blue eyes had a fevered look, almost a drugged look. "Why?" he demanded.

"Because . . . because . . ." She could not think of a good reason, and she gasped as his teeth gently scored her other nipple. "Because it is not proper!" she finally said.

He laughed low. "Tell me to cease, Val, and I will," he promised as his hand slid beneath her skirts and up her leg to caress her soft inner thighs.

She made a helpless little noise, but no words came.

"You cannot, hinny love!" he growled, triumphant. "I know from the discreet bits of information you so innocently disclosed that your husband was a cold man. He possessed you, yet he knew not the treasure he had! You, the most exquisite of creatures, and he knew nothing of how to stoke the sweet fires that burn within you!" Lord Burke leaped from the bed. So swiftly that he astounded her, he pulled her skirts and underthings from her, leaving her naked but for her black silk stockings with their gold ribbon garters.

Valentina was absolutely frozen by what was happening, although one part of her brain kept anxiously urging her to flee. What was it about him that everytime he kissed and caressed her, she could not function normally. She felt like such a fool. It seem to grow worse with each instance, and now she watched with startled eyes as he roughly stripped off his own garments, exposing his long, hard body to her curious gaze. Valentina had never seen a grown man completely nude, and the sight was a fascinating, but powerful one.

"You are beautiful," she murmured without meaning to speak.

"So are you, my sweet hinny love," he purred, lying down again and drawing her into his arms. "I love you, Val, and I will do nothing to hurt you," Lord Burke reassured her. His hand slipped between her thighs, the fingers seeking, finding, stroking. "He never touched you like this, did he, Val? He never gave you pleasure or teased the sweetness from you!" His mouth closed over hers, and Valentina's senses whirled. "A woman is meant to be loved with gentleness and fire, Val, as I am now loving you!" he whispered between kisses.

Why wasn't it like this with Edward, the sane part of her brain demanded, but she already knew the answer. Ned had certainly never put his hands on her as Padraic was now doing. Never had they lay together like this as God had created them. *Why*? What Padraic was doing to her could not be wrong. Nothing that wonderful could be wrong! This had to be what had made her mother, her aunt, and her cousins so happy in their marriages, for what woman could not be happy being loved so passionately.

There was a part of her that felt near to bursting with pleasure, the delicate flesh with which he even now toyed. She gasped with disbelief as rapture, hot and sweet as boiling jam, filled her with a bliss that was totally foreign, but altogether delightful. "Oh, Padraic!" she heard herself sighing.

"Ah, hinny love, you are so ready to be loved," he told her. His kisses covered her face, his mouth moving to the wildly beating pulse that leaped at the base of her throat. His mouth scorched a path across her swollen, aching breasts down her torso. Beneath him, Valentina's flesh quivered with desire. As he eased himself on top of her, Valentina made one last effort.

"This cannot be right, Padraic," and her eyes pleaded with him to take the initiative and cease this marvelous torture.

His hand smoothed her face and he said gently, "You're no virgin, Val, and I mean you to be my wife. This cannot be wrong." Tenderly, he spread her legs with a knee and pressed forward.

"This changes nothing between us, Padraic, for I will not be forced to the altar!" she half sobbed, realizing even as she spoke her desperate and newly awakened need for him.

His laughter was gently mocking. "*This,*" he said, thrusting into her, "changes everything, my hinny love!"

Her eyes closed as she experienced the fullness of him, amazed at the sensation he caused in her, for she had not remembered it this way. He grasped her hips and pulled her to him, driving back and forth within her until Valentina was whimpering with pleasure she had never before experienced. Her arms closed about him for the first time, and she clasped him to her, her aching breasts pushing against his furred chest, her nails digging cruelly into the flesh of his back. Her teeth sank into his shoulder, and he grunted. Her heart was hammering wildly, and she began to feel as if her body were separating from her mind.

"Padraic!" she cried out. "I am going to die!" To her amazement, she realized that she didn't care. If this was all that there was to be of life for her, it mattered not.

"Nay, hinny love," he groaned, " 'tis just the loving, and I'll not let you fall!"

The words were reassuring, but it made no difference. She was whirling, drawn down into a dark vortex of pure passion, and only the hot, full hardness of him was real. Her bones were melting, her flesh was dissolving, and there was nothing left but sweetness. When at last she could draw a breath again, she realized that she was still alive. Padraic lay sprawled across her, panting, his hands tangled in her dark hair, which had come undone during their melee. He rolled off her, but caught her hand tightly in his.

For a long time there was only silence between them. Then Padriac said softly, "Did you mean what you said?"

Valentina sighed, knowing what he referred to, and felt almost guilty. "Aye, I did," she finally answered.

"Bitch, you will drive me mad," he said. "I hope I've put my bairn in your belly so that you've no choice!"

"Do not say so, my lord, for the child will be nameless. I have warned you that I will not be forced to the altar by any man. I did not seek this interlude with you, Padraic—for all I do not regret it. You have used your experience in these matters to cajole me, and 'tis not fair!"

He laughed ruefully. "I will do what I have to, madam, to make you mine. Only tell me what you desire of me."

"What I desire at this moment, my lord, is to return to my own chamber *unnoticed*. Have you destroyed my gown?"

Again he laughed. "The bodice, perhaps, in my enthusiasm, but I only loosened your skirt and petticoat tapes. You will find them in good repair, madam," he said, "for I am expert in the art of disrobing a woman."

"Is that something you should brag about, Padraic?" she teased, rising shyly from the bed to dress herself. She drew her lower garments on and fastened them carefully about her slender waist, feeling horribly self-conscious.

He chuckled at her look, and rising from the bed, walked across the room to pick up his cloak. He draped it about her shoulders. "Here, Val. This should get you to your room in a state of decency, but what Nan will say when she sees the condition of your bodice, I do not know."

"Nan, thank God, is in bed with a toothache," Valentina said with some humor, "else I should refer her to you, my lord." Suddenly she realized that she was feeling better than she had ever felt in her entire life. Boldly, she let her eyes slide over him. His body was slender, but he was tall and beautifully formed. She reached out and touched his shoulder, rubbing her fingers over the marks her teeth had left in his skin. She had not expected a man to have such soft skin. "I did not mean to hurt you," she apologized. "I do not know why I bit you."

"Your passion overcame you, Val. I will treasure the mark, hinny love. May it be the first of many such marks you make upon my helpless body." He caught her hand and placed a warm kiss in her palm.

Color flooded her cheeks, and Valentina fled from his bed-chamber to her own. She was grateful for the lateness of the hour, and the fact that all her siblings but Jamie were away. She was in no mood for chatter or to explain her disheveled appearance.

She slept badly that night, the memory of her passionate interlude with Padraic half haunting, half pleasing her. His remark about putting a child into her belly frightened her. Remembering vaguely some gossip about her aunt, she rode out at dawn for Queen's Malvern.

"God's foot!" Lady de Marisco exclaimed. "You are an early riser, my girl. What brings you out at such an hour on this cold morning?"

"I believe you have a potion . . ." Valentina began, then burst into tears.

"God's foot!" Skye exclaimed again, and sat Valentina down by the warm fire. "What has happened? I want the whole truth, my girl!" she growled.

Between sobs, Valentina told her aunt the entire story. Her pathetic, unhappy marriage. The competition between Tom Ashburne and Lord Burke. Lord Burke's seduction of her. His wish that she bear his child. "I will not be forced to the altar this time, Aunt Skye. I will not!"

"But you admit that making love with Padraic is totally different from making love with Lord Barrows," Skye reasoned.

"Aye!" Valentina sighed. "As different as night and day, but 'tis not the point. I would make up my own mind this time, free of encumbrances of any kind. I cannot be happy unless I make my own life."

Skye nodded. "I understand, Valentina. I truly do, and if Padraic has not already impregnated you, then I will see that you have my special elixir."

"Is it different with different men, Aunt Skye?" Valentina asked Lady de Marisco shyly.

Skye chuckled. "Aye, for each man is different. Your late husband, for instance, seems to have been a good and decent man, but passionless. My first husband was a pig", Skye said bluntly. "I hated him. He was filled with a dark passion that he could not control. He gained pleasure, not just from making love, but from having the power of life and death over his lover. My fifth husband was a sensual, tortured man, who, until I taught him better, could gain pleasure only through pain. As for my other four husbands and various lovers, they were tender and passionate men, but for one. Men are indeed different, Valentina, but so are women. Why did you marry Edward Barrows, if I may ask?"

"I did not think the love that exists for others would exist for me. I was facing my twentieth birthday. Anne and Bevin were desperate to wed their own lovers, and Mother kept insisting that I wed first." Valentina shrugged. "He seemed a good man with whom I might live in peace."

"Do you love my son?" Skye asked her bluntly, eyeing her shrewdly.

Valentina thought for a moment. "I am not certain, Aunt. Padraic is my friend. Now, of course, I am forced to think of him differently."

Skye nodded. "You're honest, my girl, and I am glad for it. I would not have Padraic hurt. I can see you're not the kind of woman to hurt a man, not purposely any way. Do you love Tom Ashburne, perhaps?"

"Nay, I think not, but then I do not know him well enough to make that judgment, do I?" Valentina smiled. "He is most handsome, is he not?"

"And even now you're wondering whether or not he can make you feel like Padraic can—or even better," Skye observed mischievously.

"*Aunt!*" Valentina looked shocked.

Skye laughed aloud. " 'Tis no crime to be curious about such things, my girl. 'Tis honest curiosity. Do you not think men wonder such things about women? Well, I can tell you that they do!"

Valentina allowed herself a small chuckle. "I did suspect it," she admitted. "Do not tell Mama and Papa the purpose of my visit, Aunt, please. I would not distress them, nor raise their hopes about another son-in-law, either. Mother is terribly worried about my coming venture, and I cannot calm her fears."

"Her time in Turkey was a frightening one, except for the little interlude with her prince," said Skye. "The sultan's treatment of her was brutal and it has colored her memories more sharply than anything else."

"Was your time in the East a terrible one, too?" Valentina inquired, genuinely interested. She had never felt, before now, that she should ask.

Skye's blue-green eyes grew misty with her memories. "The

first time I spent in Algiers, I had lost my memory. I knew nothing of myself but my first name. Your cousin Willow's father was a most wonderful man, and my life with him was a happy one. The second time I was in the East, I went to try to rescue Padraic and Deirdre's father, Niall, from captivity. To do so, it was necessary that I pose as a slave. My old friend, Osman the Astrologer, helped me. The man who was my master was a terrible sensualist. He was killed. I escaped and helped Niall to escape, too. But he died aboard my ship of the excesses that had been forced on him during his captivity.

"Your mother has explained to you that the East is a dangerous place where women are valued as possessions and nothing else. Knowing that, you are far better prepared to deal with whatever may arise than either of us was. You go of your own free will, and you will be protected by your own ships and by two men who love you. But be warned! All that may not be enough. Life offers many surprises we cannot even begin to anticipate.

"Still, if you are prudent, you will return from your venture unharmed. You are less innocent than Aidan was when she was taken to Turkey. I do not fear for you, my girl." Skye stood up and stretched. "Go home now, Valentina, and tell my son I want him to come to Queen's Malvern to visit with me until it is time for you to leave for the East." She smiled. "Unless, of course, you would rather have him remain at Pearroc Royal."

Valentina shook her head. "Another night like last night, Aunt, and I shall be helpless in the face of Padraic's will. Your son has the most amazing effect on me!"

Skye chuckled, nodding. "A man can do that to a woman. But let me tell you something, Valentina. *You* can do the same thing to *him*."

"I can?" Valentina was shocked. What did her aunt mean?

"Aye, you can." Skye smiled, amused by her niece. "You have been allowing him to kiss you, but I will wager you have not made a serious effort to kiss him back. You have been taking, not giving. Do so, and you will be amazed to learn of the power you possess, my girl! Now go home, and if there are no 'difficulties' from your adventure last night, then I will see that you have not only a supply of my special potion but the recipe for it as well."

While Lady Barrows rode back across the brown-and-beige late-autumn fields for her home, Lady de Marisco returned to her bed to find her husband awake and curious.

"Who dragged you from our bed at such an early hour?" he demanded, drawing her into his arms and nuzzling her neck lovingly.

"Valentina. Padraic seduced her last night, and she wants my elixir."

Adam de Marisco's deep chuckle rumbled through the room. "He took his time finding a woman to love, our Padraic, but now he desires to waste no more time. Good for him, I say!"

"Just like a man!" Skye punched her husband on his big shoulder. "Valentina had an unhappy first marriage, it seems. She married to please everyone but herself, so this time she wants to be certain. I have worried about Padraic for years and, God only knows, his cousin would make him a perfect wife. But I'll not have her forced to it by him or by circumstances created by him. They must both be content to wed, and if they are not both content, then it must not be, Adam. Not just for Valentina's sake but for Padraic's as well. I want them happy, as we are happy."

"All right, all right, little girl. I have not a doubt that you'll get your way in this as you do in everything you set your mind to," her husband said. "For now, however, I would have *my* way with *you*." His hand slid up beneath her green silk robe.

"You're a randy old man," Skye said softly, kissing his mouth.

"You're a randy old woman," he said, chuckling, "and glad I am of it!"

Lord Burke could not have imagined such a scene between his mother and his stepfather of twenty-nine years. When he faced them later in the day, they seemed most formidable to him, and he felt like a boy again, not like a grown man of thirty-two.

His mother wasted no time in coming to the point. "Could you not have kept your cock in your breeches a bit longer, Padraic?" she demanded tartly. "Sometimes you are just like your father! Careless of others! Heedless of the consequences! If you understood Valentina at all you would know that she *must* unravel the mystery of her birth before she can make a new life for herself with another husband! But, no, all you could think of was that, having finally decided that you love her, you must have her! Damn you for a fool, my son! I thought I had taught you better than that," said Skye.

"Are your ears so big, Mama, that they stretch to Pearroc Royal?" Padraic demanded hotly, flushing. "How the hell did you find out about last night? I am still not quite certain that what happened between Valentina and me was not a dream."

Skye snorted. "You seduced your cousin most boldly last night, my son, and she came to me this morning for reassurance and aid. A man is hardly likely to forget a thing like that, unless, of course, Valentina was so unmemorable a lover."

"She is magnificent!" he defended his cousin. Then, seeing the amused look in his mother's eyes, Lord Burke flushed again. His stepfather grinned, though Adam attempted to check himself.

"You will remain here with us at Queen's Malvern until you sail, Padraic. There will be no repeat of last night," his mother told him firmly.

"Damn, Mother, I am not a child!" Lord Burke exploded. "You cannot force me to your will as if I were. I love Val, and I want to be with her."

"You will be with her soon enough and in very close quarters for several months, which should give you more than enough time to plead your case, Padraic," Skye said calmly.

"Aye, and so will Tom Ashburne!" Lord Burke replied irritably.

"Surely you are not afraid of a little competition? If you press her, you will drive her right into his arms," Skye warned her son. "Do not be a fool, Padraic. You're behaving like the child you claim not to be. You see something and want it. Not tomorrow, but now! You cannot have Valentina now, Padraic. She must resolve the mystery of her birth before she can decide whether she will have you or the Earl of Kempe, or neither. Do you remember the last time you acted in haste? I do. Your rash action sent your sister Velvet running off to India and into the Grand Mughal's arms."

"No harm came of it," he replied sullenly. "Velvet was returned to us unscathed."

"*Unscathed?* Nay, Padraic, my son, she was not returned to us unscathed," Skye said quietly.

"Skye!" Adam warned. "You cannot tell him."

"I must if he is to understand, Adam. It will not go beyond this room, for Padraic would not hurt his sister willingly." Skye looked at the youngest of her four sons and said quietly, "Velvet had a child by the Grand Mughal, Padraic. A daughter whom she was forced to leave behind. The little girl is now eleven. Though Velvet never speaks of the child, I know she has never forgotten her. No woman forgets her own child, whether she raises that child or not. That is what your actions cost your sister, my son. Do you understand now why I caution you to be more careful?"

Lord Burke was pale. "My God, Mother. How could she leave her child? What have I done?"

"There is no need to feel useless guilt, Padraic," Skye told him. "What is done is done and over, and has been for years. As for Velvet's daughter, neither the mughal nor your Uncle Michael believed it wise to bring the child to England where she would have been an outcast. In India she is a royal princess and honored as such. She is the child of a legitimate marriage according to the laws of that land."

Padraic Burke nodded, beginning to comprehend what had happened to Velvet. "It will not be easy," he said, "being patient with Val, especially now, but I promise you, Mother, that I will be. And I will not speak of this to Velvet."

Lady de Marisco smiled warmly at her son. "Good!" she said. "Make no mistake about it, I want Valentina as a daughter-in-law, Padraic. I have asked little of you in your lifetime, but this I demand of you. Do not fail me, my son."

"Fail you, Mother?" he teased her. "I would sooner fail the queen than fail you."

She grinned back at him. " 'Tis a wise son who knows his own mother, my boy," she told him, and the two men laughed heartily. Skye O'Malley de Marisco, for all her sixty-one years, still had the ability to both fascinate and command.

PART III

The Quest

WINTER–SPRING 1602

Chapter Six

THE DOOR TO THE QUEEN'S PRIVY CHAMBER opened and Lady Scrope announced, " 'Tis Lady Barrows here to see you, madam."

Elizabeth Tudor looked up eagerly. She had been feeling despondent, for it was now eleven months since the Earl of Essex's rebellion and his subsequent execution. She could not forget Essex, though publicly she appeared unmoved by his death. "So, child, you have returned to me after all," she cried as Valentina hurried into the room and sank into a graceful curtsy.

"I could not go off without seeing you, dearest madam," Lady Barrows replied.

"And you must go?" the queen inquired, grieved to be losing her.

Valentina nodded. "I have no other choice, dearest madam, as I told you in my letter. When old Mag spoke those fateful words, she set my course for Turkey as surely as if she had led me there by the hand."

"And what of your two swains?" asked the queen. "Will they be content to wait for your return?"

"They go with me, dear madam." Valentina laughed, and her lovely eyes twinkled.

"Both of them?" The queen's eyes widened, first with surprise, then with amusement. "Why, bless me, my dear, you're a sly one!"

"I would as lief they both stayed at home," Valentina told the queen, "but my family was in an uproar over my going, so Padraic volunteered to escort me. That calmed them a trifle. Then the Earl of Kempe insisted that he go also so that Padraic could not gain an advantage with me. I have accused them of behaving like children squabbling over the last slice of jellycake, but I cannot shame either of them into behaving. They will carry on their rivalry for me despite my objections!"

The queen laughed heartily. "My dear child, I know just what you are going through," she said. "Once, gentlemen fought over

167

me in such a fashion. 'Tis flattering, but 'tis annoying as well. You'll be in close quarters on your vessel, and there will be no escaping them, I fear."

Valentina laughed herself. "Perhaps, if they prove too randy for me to control, I shall have the captain clap them in irons," she said. The queen cackled appreciatively.

A bit later, when her women had joined them, the queen lowered her voice so that only Valentina could hear her.

"I am dying, my child. I sense it. Oh, not yet, not yet. I've a good year. Perhaps two. But no more. Had I wed and had a daughter, you are what I would have wanted in my own child. Hurry about your business, Valentina, and then come home to me. I do not want to take my final journey without knowing the end of your story. I would see you happy, my child." Elizabeth Tudor shook her head. "I have become the old fool they accuse me of being behind my back, have I not?"

"May I be such a fool one day, dear madam," Valentina said passionately. "If you are weak now, you are yet stronger by far than any of them."

"I will miss you, child," the queen said wistfully. "You're good for me. But I will tell you, your little sister keeps me well amused these days. What a naughty minx she is!"

"The maids are my one regret, dear madam. Who have you chosen to look after them in my place?"

"No one," the queen said emphatically. "I have told my ladies that we must all be responsible for the maids, and I have taken other measures as well. I have taken your advice about bringing in biddable young maids. Margaret Dudley's marriage is set for the end of this month, and she will be replaced by your cousin, Anne Blakeley, who is only thirteen. Penelope Howard leaves after Easter to be married. Gabrielle Edwardes's younger sister, Joanna, who is twelve, will replace her. I do not expect Honoria de Bohun to be with me much longer, for your brother courts her slyly when he thinks I am not watching. I know he will not seduce her, however. He is Conn's son, and a true gentleman."

"Nay, he will not seduce her," Valentina said. "I know he means to make her an honorable offer. With Your Majesty's permission, of course."

"I thought as much," said the queen. "Well, when that happens, I shall replace mistress de Bohun with another little girl. You were correct, my dear child, when you suggested I take only very young girls as my maids of honor. The gentlemen do not seem interested in unripe fruit." The queen chuckled. "I have also told the families of the girls who serve me that I will hold them personally responsible for any wanton behavior on the part of their daughters. Such behavior will cost them dearly in fines to the crown. Also, I have assigned two sharp-eyed gentlewomen to sleep in the Maidens' Chamber each night. The maids of honor are well-chaperoned and, I think, safe from seduction.

"Personally, I do not think much of the young men who come to court these days," she went on. "Perfumed fops, all of them, and, God's foot, their blood runs thin. 'Tis true that one can live too long, my dear. I remember the fathers and grandfathers of these mincing creatures. They would not have tolerated such offspring in earlier times."

" 'Tis a new century, dearest madam, and with the years come changes, some pleasant, some not so, but we cannot stop change, can we?" Valentina observed.

"When I was young, there were moments so wonderful that I thought I wanted to stop time," the queen told her quietly, "but my years have given me the advantage of retrospect. I know now that, as the Bible says, there is a time for everything." She held out her arms to Valentina, who hugged the queen. "Now," said Elizabeth Tudor, "it is time for you to go, dear child. It seems to be the fate of women in your family to go adventuring, beginning with that impossible aunt of yours. She, her daughter, your own mother all have come home safe. I know you will, too." The queen kissed Valentina on both her cheeks. "Goodspeed, my dear! God bless you! I shall miss you, my dear!"

Lady Barrows curtsied low to the queen and backed from the room. There were tears prickling behind her eyelids as the door to the queen's privy chamber closed and she had her last glimpse of Elizabeth Tudor in her white velvet gown, with her flaming red wig and her sunken bright pink cheeks. The queen did not look well at all, and Valentina wondered if she would have a year or two, as Elizabeth believed. Outside the royal apartments her two gallants awaited her.

"Come, divinity!" The earl took her by the arm.

"Aye," Padraic said. "You took your time with the queen, Val. Our captain wants to sail with the early tide, and we shall just make it." He grasped her other arm.

Lady Barrows stopped dead. Shaking them both off, she said, "I am capable of walking by myself, my lords. You must stop this rivalry between you. We shall have no peace, any of us, if you do not! Listen to me, both of you. You have each made it clear that you would have me to wife. Today, this fifteenth day of January, in the year of our Lord 1602, we set off on an adventure together. I will make no decision regarding either of you until we return to England. If, knowing that, you still wish to accompany me, you may do so—provided that you will cease this constant competition between you. If you cannot do that, then do not come. If you come and still cannot cease this behavior, I will have you either put off at the nearest port or thrown overboard— whichever is more convenient for the captain!" So saying, Valentina hurried off toward the palace water stairs. Her two suitors followed meekly behind her, glancing at each other.

It seemed a good omen to Valentina that her ship was called *Archangel* and that the two accompanying it were *The Royal Bess* and *Homeward Bound*. *Archangel* was captained by Padraic's older brother, Murrough O'Flaherty. Of all of Lady de Marisco's children, Murrough was the only one with a taste for the sea. *The Royal Bess* was captained by Michael Small, a foundling who had been rescued as a child by Sir Robert Small, the de Marisco's trading partner. Sir Robert had raised him. *Homeward Bound* was captained by Rory McGuire, a great-nephew of Lady de Marisco's first senior captain, Sean McGuire, long dead. Skye was taking no chances with the safety of her niece and son. The ships were all as sound as possible, very modern, eminently seaworthy. Their crews were the most experienced men in the O'Malley-Small trading fleet.

At the foot of the water stairs, the Greenwood barge was awaiting them. It quickly whisked them downriver to the London Pool, where their vessel lay at anchor. The tide was rising fast, and they just had time to "shoot the bridge" before it would become impossible to do so for several hours. Climbing up the sturdy rope ladder from her barge to the ship's deck, Valentina realized for the first time that she was truly off on an adventure, the kind that ladies of her station rarely saw. For the briefest moment, she wondered if she was doing the right thing.

"Just in time, lass!" Murrough O'Flaherty said as he lifted his cousin onto the deck. He was a handsome man, who, of all his mother's children, looked the most like her. His eyes were the same Kerry blue, and his thick, wavy dark hair and well-cut, short beard were the same blue-black as Skye's hair. "We've but five minutes to spare. Welcome aboard! Ye also, my lord, Padraic! Young Geoff will show ye to the main cabin while I get us underway." Captain O'Flaherty turned away from them and began shouting orders to his first mate, Peter Whyte.

Geoff O'Flaherty, Murrough's fifteen-year-old third son, bowed politely to the passengers and led them away from the scene of activity. "Yer servant has already settled ye, Cousin Valentina," he said shyly.

"You didn't tell me anyone was coming with you," Padraic said. "Tom and I were both told by Mother that we could not bring our servants with us because it would shorten the crew by two."

"You are both quite capable of taking care of yourselves," Valentina said. "Have you not campaigned with Essex and Ralegh? Surely you did not travel with servants then, my lords. I, on the other hand, am but a helpless woman. As such, I need a servant of my own sex, not simply to aid me but for company as well."

"Ho, madam, you toy with us!" the earl teased her.

"Indeed, sir, do I?" Valentina said.

Geoff escorted them into a large cabin with a huge window that filled the entire rear of the vessel. A pretty young girl with bright black eyes and dark hair in two neat plaits came forward and curtsied.

"Welcome aboard, m'lady. I have unpacked everything as Mother instructed me. I hope it will meet with your satisfaction."

"Thank you, Nelda," Valentina said. "This is Lord Burke, Nelda, and this gentleman is the Earl of Kempe."

Nelda curtsied.

"Where is Nan?" demanded Padraic. "And who is this pretty wench?"

"Nan fears the sea and does not have the stomach for it. This is her youngest child, Nelda, who is to serve me in Nan's place," replied Valentina. She shed her fur-lined cape and handed it to the girl. "Be sure to brush it well," she said as the girl hurried off with the garment.

Young Geoff's eyes followed Nelda admiringly. Then, suddenly aware of his position, he swallowed hard and said, "This is the ship's day room. Usually it is the captain's domain, and he and his officers dine here. The captain says ye are to consider it yers while you are aboard *Archangel,* though he and his officers must, of necessity, continue to take their meals here. Ye are, of course, invited to join them each evening for dinner." Stopping to catch his breath, Geoff flushed slightly, for he had never before felt so important. "*Archangel* is a very special ship," he continued. "She has been built to carry passengers as well as cargo. Consequently, yer accommodations will be quite comfortable. Cousin Valentina . . . my lady . . . yer sleeping cabin is through that door. Yer servant will sleep on a trundle beneath yer bed. My father's cabin is next to yers. My lord earl, ye will have the cabin on the other side of this room, and Uncle Padraic, ye will be next to the earl. My father, the captain, hopes ye will be quite comfortable." He bowed politely. "I must be about my other duties now. Ye will be out of the way here until we clear the pool." He strode briskly through the door.

The day was bright for January, the sky clear blue, the sun almost warm. There was a good breeze coming up that rattled ever so faintly at the small panes of glass in the great bow window. The gentlemen went topside immediately, but Valentina preferred to remain snugly ensconced in the window seat of the bow window, a fur rug about her for warmth. She watched London disappear behind her and the river begin to widen as they passed Greenwich. She was leaving England and everything she knew, all that was familiar. Suddenly, she was blindingly aware of the incredible chance she was taking. Javid Khan and Sultan Murad were both dead. Who was left who could tell her if she was the daughter of either of those men unless, perhaps, she looked like one of them or one of their relatives? How could they know? Would she ever learn the truth? Aye! She would. There had to be *someone* who could help her unravel the mystery that haunted her.

At least one worry had been lifted from her shoulders. She had twice suffered her flux since that wonderful night with Padraic. Now each day she took a carefully measured dose of her aunt's special potion. She had a good supply, and Nelda had both the recipe and the herbs necessary to make it. Valentina did not intend to be caught again! True, Padraic's behavior had been most circumspect afterwards, but still. She smiled to herself. Bless him! Though she would never tell him! Had he not made love to her that night, she would have never known just how very sweet love could be.

What a fool she had been, Valentina thought. She had been so distressed that she could not find love within her that she had really believed that such love did not exist for her. Why had she not stopped to consider that she had never been attracted to a man enough to pursue a relationship with him. What a revelation she had faced in the arms of both Padraic Burke and Tom Ashburne.

Suddenly she felt the *Archangel* dip and swoop, and her heart leaped. She looked out the window again. The sea! They had reached the sea! They had sailed through the mouth of the Thames, the ship cutting neatly through the waves. There would be no turning back.

The weather held for the three ships as they made their way down the English Channel and out into the Atlantic. The Bay of Biscay, usually rough and stormy, was pleasant, the air hinting of balminess as they sailed across it. Occasionally they saw other ships, though never closely enough to identify any. The O'Malley-Small ships flew, from their topmost masts, flags that guaranteed them safe passage through the waters controlled by the Ottoman Empire and the Dey of Algiers. Ships without these pennants ran the risk of being captured by Ottoman ships. Capture meant confiscation of the cargo and, worse, slavery for the crew and passengers.

They passed through the Strait of Gibraltar, past its great mountain and into the azure Mediterranean Sea. It had been arranged that they would stop at the duchy of San Lorenzo where they would take on fresh water and food.

"There is but one town in San Lorenzo, its capital, Arcobaleno," said Murrough O'Flaherty. "It's a charming place, and we will anchor there for a few days to provision the ships."

"Arcobaleno," said Valentina. "That means *rainbow* in Italian, doesn't it?"

"Aye, it does," her cousin the captain replied.

"Why is it called rainbow?" Valentina wondered aloud.

"Wait and see," he told her with a chuckle.

The explanation was immediately obvious from the harbor of Arcobaleno. The town was built on a group of small, steep hills, and the buildings were painted every imaginable color. Red lay next to purple, which was on top of green, followed by blue, pink, orange, yellow, violet, rose, turquoise, and peach. The hills were olive with their winter cover and the brown vineyards lay dormant, although they would soon begin to show new growth. Atop the highest point in the town was the white marble palace of the duke, Sebastian di San Lorenzo III.

"It's wonderful!" said Valentina, laughing, as *Archangel* and her sister ships were made fast to the quays. "May we go ashore, Murrough? What language do the people speak?"

She was looking particularly lovely today, he thought. Her silk gown was dusky rose and very flattering. Her eyes were sparkling with anticipation. It was obvious that the voyage agreed with Valentina.

"Of course you may go ashore, Val. The language spoken here is Italian, but they understand French as well. The late duchessa was French-speaking. There is a wonderful marketplace at the top of the first hill that you will enjoy very much. Tonight I suspect we will be invited to the palace. The duke is a friend of mine."

The day was invitingly warm and Valentina, her servant, and her two gallants walked from the quay up the hill to the marketplace of Arcobaleno. Although it was winter, there were flowers tumbling from all of the boxes in all of the windows, and the town's inhabitants were friendly, smiling at the beautiful *signora* and her two handsome cavaliers.

In the marketplace they found close to a hundred merchants and farmers selling a large variety of merchandise beneath gaily striped awnings. Valentina could not return to the ship without purchasing an armful of fluffy mimosa.

Nelda was positively wide-eyed, for the girl had never before been more than five miles from Pearroc Royal. She gaped open-mouthed at an entertainer who was amusing the crowd with his troupe of six dogs and had to be pulled away by her laughing mistress, for Nelda would have been content to spend the day watching the man.

When they returned to the ship, an invitation had indeed been delivered from the palace requesting their presence that night at dinner. Valentina chased the gentlemen from the large day room and had a tub of warm, fresh water set up so that she might bathe. She luxuriated in the soft, fragrant water. Nelda, carefully instructed by her mother, washed her lady's hair using a special mixture of soft soap scented with Valentina's favorite fragrance, lily of the valley.

"This is wonderful!" Valentina sighed as she sat back in the tub. "Wouldn't you like to bathe with fresh water, too, Nelda?"

"Tonight when yer ladyship's at the palace, I'll do so," Nelda told her. "My old granny said too much bathing wasn't good for ye, but it don't seem to hurt ye."

Valentina laughed. "The gentlemen like it when a lady smells sweet," she noted.

Bathed, dried, and powdered, Valentina rested in her cabin,

drowsily hearing the sounds of the tub being emptied and stored away. A soft breeze came through the cabin's porthole, lulling her into a restful sleep. When Nelda finally woke her, Valentina stretched and yawned lazily as she rose from her bed to be dressed.

Her gown was of apple-green silk, the brocade underskirt sewn with a design of seashells in gold thread and small pearls. The sleeves were loose and hanging, showing undersleeves made of very sheer, creamy silk edged in lace. The low, square neckline was edged with matching lace and displayed Lady Barrows's magnificent bosom perfectly. Her jewelry was simple, pearls about her neck and pear-shaped pearls dangling from her ears. A pretty fan of white feathers dangled from the gold ribbon she wore about her slender waist. Her rich dark hair was dressed with gold ribbons and white silk roses.

The gentlemen had chosen to affect the elegant black costume so favored by the Venetians. Both were most appreciative of Valentina's gown, and as Padraic and Tom leaped forward to offer her their arms, Valentina brushed past them and slipped her hand through Murrough's arm. Murrough grinned delightedly, his blue eyes laughing.

The sun was setting in a blaze of red and gold as they set off into the hills in the duke's carriage to the palace. Quickly, so quickly that it surprised the visitors, the Mediterranean night fell, velvet black with thousands of crystal stars. Valentina had never known a night like this, the air seductive with the scent of night-blooming flowers mixed with the pungent, sharp tang of the salt air.

"Did you not take the opportunity to bathe, gentlemen?" she questioned them, trying to take her mind off her body, which seemed unusually sensitive in this climate. The silk of her gown rubbed against her nipples with each breath. "I had a magnificent tub of fresh water this afternoon."

"Murrough took us to a Turkish bath here in Arcobaleno," Lord Burke said. "Mother had told me about such places, but I have never been in one before. 'Twas most refreshing, was it not, Tom?"

"Aye," agreed the earl. "I cannot remember ever having been so clean in my life. They begin by wetting you down and then they scrape the dirt off with a little tool, rinse it away, put you in an incredibly hot room filled with steam, where you—forgive me, Val—sweat. Then they rinse you again, soap you all over, and rinse you a final time before massaging your body with sweet oils. I think I liked that part the best," he concluded with a grin.

"I should have liked it better if the women massaging us had been younger and prettier." Murrough chuckled.

The duke's carriage reached its destination. Awaiting them on the palace steps was the duke himself. Murrough leaped from the vehicle before it had stopped, then wrapped the ruler of San Lorenzo in a bear hug.

"Sebastian! How are ye? Have ye found a new wife yet?"

The duke laughed. He was a tall, handsome man with night-dark hair and amber eyes. "There is time enough for me to marry again, old friend! My boys are both healthy, praise God! For now I far prefer to imitate nature and, like the honeybee, buzz from one sweet flower to another."

Murrough laughed heartily, his blue eyes twinkling. Turning back to the open coach, he helped his beautiful cousin from the vehicle. "Highness, may I present my cousin Valentina, Lady Barrows," he said.

"She is much better looking than you have ever been, old friend," the duke observed wryly.

Valentina held out her hand to the duke. To her surprise, and she hoped it did not show, his touch was unsettling.

The duke kissed the slender white hand warmly, perhaps a trifle too warmly. And his golden-brown eyes never left her. "Madonna, you grace my small kingdom. It is suddenly a thousand times more beautiful!" he avowed passionately in a low, seductive voice.

"I do not see how that is possible, Highness," Valentina replied, her cheeks growing warm with his extravagant compliment. "What I have seen of San Lorenzo is pure perfection."

"Then it is only fair that perfect beauty be here in my palace tonight, is it not, madonna?" the duke murmured, his eyes openly caressing her décolletage admiringly.

"If you can tear yer eyes away from Valentina's bosom a moment, Sebastian," Murrough teased the duke, "I will present ye to my younger brother Padraic, Lord Burke, and our friend, Thomas Ashburne, the Earl of Kempe, who is traveling with us." Murrough O'Flaherty waggled his eyebrows warningly at the two young men, who were glowering fiercely at the handsome duke. Murrough was having a very difficult time keeping his composure, for it was a delicious situation, one that his mother would particularly appreciate.

The duke turned to greet his guests with warm, sincere words of welcome. The two gentlemen found themselves liking the duke in spite of themselves, even when, with amazing finesse, Sebastian di San Lorenzo turned once again and, tucking Valentina's hand through his arm, led them into his palace.

They dined outdoors on a large, wide marble terrace that seemed to hang suspended over the sea. There were fragrant white rose trees in great yellow porcelain tubs set on the black-and-white-tiled floor. On a small raised dais a quartet of musicians played a virginal, a harp, and strings. Tall, footed lamps cast a subtle golden light over the scene.

The meal was magnificent, lavish, a marvelous change after the simple ship's fare. There was a whole fresh fish, a Mediterranean mullet, dressed with lemon, white wine, and tarragon. On another platter were dainty ortolans, small game birds, roasted to a golden hue, each stuffed with half an apricot rolled around an almond and sitting on a bed of risotto, bright with bits of green onions. There was a whole baby lamb, flavored with rosemary and garlic; a small pig roasted until its skin was black; goose with plum sauce; and a turkey stuffed with oysters and chestnuts. Artichokes swam in delicate olive oil and red wine vinegar.

When the main course had finally been cleared away, the servants came to each diner bearing a silver basin of scented water and a towel so that they might wash away all evidence of their gluttony. Afterward, desserts were placed on the table, and Valentina's sweet tooth was tempted with apricot cakes soaked in sweet wine; creamy custards with cherry sauce; marzipan confections dipped in honey; candied angelica, violets, and rose petals; and delicate sugar wafers.

Throughout the meal, a liveried servant assigned to each diner kept the silver goblet filled with a pale golden wine that was the most delicious Valentina had ever tasted. The duke told her that it came from his own vineyards, and that San Lorenzo was famous for these particular wines.

"My uncle's half brother is the master of Archambault in the Loire, and we have always obtained our wines from him," Valentina said. "When I have my own home again, Highness, I shall want some of your fine wines in my cellar."

"Your *own* home, madonna? I do not understand," the duke replied.

"I am a widow, Highness. My family did not think it proper that I remain alone in my husband's house. We were wed only a short time and I have no children," Valentina told him.

"A widow? How curious, madonna. I am a widower. But I am fortunate in that my wife left me with two fine sons. Twins! Georgio, after my father, and Nicolo, after Madelaine's father, who is the Duc de Beaumont de Jaspre."

"Nicholas St. Adrian?" Padraic Burke exclaimed.

"Why, yes," said the duke. "Do you know him?"

"My mother was once the Duchesse de Beaumont de Jaspre," said Padraic. "She was wed to Duc Fabron. When he died and Nicholas inherited the kingdom, he sought to marry my mother, but she wed an old friend instead," Padraic finished. There was no need to attempt to explain the Byzantine events surrounding his mother's passionate love affair with Duc Nicholas, his own father's sudden reappearance, his mother's desperate attempt to save him, her failure, and her eventual marriage to Adam de Marisco. It was much too complex. Padraic turned away from his cousin and the duc in order to help himself to a dish of small quail being offered by a servant.

"Nicholas St. Adrian was wed to Madelaine de Monaco," Sebastian di San Lorenzo explained. "His son, Nicholas, was born in 1571, but it was not until twelve years later that his wife produced further offspring, twin daughters, Louise and Madelaine. That birth killed her. My father-in-law has never married again. Louise married into a Venetian ducal family whose eldest daughter, Giovanna, is now married to my brother-in-law, Nicholas the younger. My lovely Madelaine died birthing our sons.

"How sad that you do not have the comfort of children, madonna," Sebastian finished, turning his full attention to Valentina once again.

"Edward and I were wed less than a month when he was thrown from a horse," Valentina replied.

"You were no more than a bride, madonna," cried the duke. "You had not even time to learn about love, did you? How I envy your bridegroom even the few lessons he taught you."

Valentina felt her cheeks grow warm once more. "Highness! You are too bold, and you make me blush!"

"You are adorable when you blush, madonna," he told her.

"You are wicked," she told him. "My cousins and the earl will hear."

"Have you never wanted to be even just a little wicked, madonna?" he teased her.

"Please, monseigneur," she warned him.

He laughed softly. "They are far too involved in their conversation with my Jesuit to notice what we are saying."

Valentina turned her gaze to the others for a moment and discovered that the duke spoke the truth. Murrough, Padraic, and Tom were all heatedly debating England's breach with Rome of over fifty years before with the duc's personal confessor, who had joined them for supper. They were not one bit concerned with her.

The duke took her by the hand and pulled her up, drawing her away from the table and into the shadows of the balustrade. "You are so beautiful, madonna, but then I am certainly not the first man to tell you that," he said, and nuzzled the softness of her cheek. "We have only met, yet I find myself inexplicably drawn to you. I long to steal you away from here and make love to you."

Valentina gasped. She had certainly never met a man like this one!

"You are shy," the duc said. He smiled, pleased. "You were a virgin when you wed, weren't you?"

"Monseigneur! What do you take me for?" Valentina said, outraged.

His answer was to draw her into his arms and press his lips to hers. Her instinct was to struggle, but somehow after the first shock, Valentina found she did not want to struggle against the duc's warm mouth. He kissed very well, though her toes did not curl, as they did when Padraic kissed her.

She closed her eyes and enjoyed the embrace, allowing him to part her lips and permitting his tongue to play hide-and-seek with hers.

"Ah, madonna," he murmured against her ear. "Now I *know* I must make love to you," and he bent her backward and pressed hot kisses over her throat and bosom.

Too late, Valentina realized that the duke was most serious. Her arms were pinioned against her sides by his embrace, and she could no longer struggle. Frightened, she gasped, "Monseigneur! Please, no! You must not!"

Sebastian de San Lorenzo was an experienced lover. He could easily recognize when a woman was being coy and when she was being truthful. Valentina was genuinely afraid. He ceased his sweet assault immediately. "Madonna, forgive me," he told her gently, loosening his hold on her. "You are too beautiful and my passion for you is an honest one, but I see I must go slowly with you, for you are not a lady of great experience. I do mean to pursue you, but for now, let us join the others."

"Ye have had a little adventure," Murrough teased her softly when she took her place at the table.

"Is he so passionate with all the ladies?" Valentina whispered. "He quite took my breath away, Murrough."

"He is considered a great lover by those who believe themselves knowledgeable in such matters, sweet coz," Murrough replied. Then he said thoughtfully, keeping his voice low, "He *is* in the market for a wife, Val. 'Twould not be such a bad catch for ye."

"It was not marriage he had on his mind, Murrough." She laughed. "'Twas seduction, pure and simple. Even I am competent to recognize seduction. Besides, do you not think two suitors enough for an old widow of twenty-one?"

The captain chuckled. "When a woman lacks the lure of virginity to entice a lover," he said, "a small taste of well-aged honey is a fine inducement to elicit a proposal! Ye would make a lovely Duchesse di San Lorenzo."

"Murrough! You sound like more and more your mother. Perhaps the duc would be an eligible suitor for your Gwyneth."

"Her blood is not noble enough for such a match," Murrough answered his cousin.

"And mine is? Nonsense, cousin! We are shoots from the same tree, our grandfather's, Dubhdara O'Malley's, tree."

"But ye have great beauty to recommend ye, Val. Beauty such as yours is a great asset. My daughters, bless them, are just like their mother, sweet-natured and passably pretty. Ye have wit and intellect to go with your beauty. Ye are more like my mother than ye realize."

"Sebastian di San Lorenzo could not enjoy a wife like that," Valentina whispered, taking care that their host not hear. "He is a man who must be dominant. Eventually he will marry a sweet, docile little Catholic princess or duc's daughter who will defer to him in everything and bear him many children as she grows plump with his loving and too many sweets."

Murrough burst out laughing at her astute observation, and

the eyes of the others at their table went to him questioningly. "A family joke," he said, chuckling.

"Will you share it with us, Murrough?" the duke called from the head of the table.

"'Twould not be understood without much background, Sebastian," Murrough excused himself. "Val was naughty to bring it up at all."

"Were you naughty, madonna?" the duke inquired. "I should like you to be naughty with me." His amber eyes glittered.

Lord Burke's fists tightened beneath the table, and the earl's jaw grew taut. The young men had not failed to note the duke's interest in Valentina. It went far beyond the bounds of mere good manners. The duke was obviously taken with Valentina, which pleased neither of them.

"I have a surprise for you all," the duc said expansively. "You will be here for several days while your ships are supplied with food and fresh water is brought aboard for the next phase of your journey. I thought you would enjoy living ashore during that time rather than in the cramped quarters of the ship.

"Do you see the charming little pink villa just below this terrace? I have had all your luggage taken there. Your servant as well, madonna. You will remain there in comfort for the length of your stay in San Lorenzo."

"'Tis uncommonly kind of ye, Sebastian," Murrough said gratefully. "We shall all enjoy your villa, and Valentina may indulge herself in daily baths, which she cannot do aboard ship."

"What a lovely little villa!" Valentina said, delighted. "I shall enjoy staying there. Thank you."

"The villa has a romantic but sad history," the duke told them. "In the time of my great-great-great-great-grandfather, Sebastian II, the pink villa was home to the Scottish ambassador. The ambassador's daughter was a beautiful maiden who was betrothed to my great-great-great-grandfather, who became Rudolpho V.

"The young couple were very much in love, but the ambassador would not allow his daughter to marry until she was fifteen, so the young people were forced to wait. The young woman, whose name in Italian was Gianetta, was somewhat eccentric in that she loved swimming in the sea and sailing a small boat about the numerous coves and bays of our coastline. She could not be dissuaded from this pursuit, and 'twas this very passion that was responsible for her unspeakable fate.

"One afternoon in winter—it was, in fact, just this time of

year—Donna Gianetta left the pink villa with her African slave
to go to a favorite beach, two miles down the coast, out of sight
of Arcobaleno. That beach and its cove have ever since been
called Gianetta's Folly, for there the young girl was captured and
kidnapped by slave traders. Her slave, a gelded male who had
been a gift from the young Rudolpho, escaped to return to Arcobaleno. It was believed that he was involved in the kidnap. He
was tortured, and he admitted his culpability before he died.

"Gianetta was taken to the great slave market in Candia on the
island of Crete, where a representative of my ancestor, attempted
to purchase the lovely Gianetta's freedom. Alas, she was purchased by an agent of the Ottoman sultan and disappeared into
his harem. Heartbroken, her father and family left San Lorenzo,
never to return.

"The next ambassador from Scotland would not live in the villa,
for his wife said it was unlucky. Since it belonged to my family,
we housed the ambassador elsewhere and used our property
ourselves."

"Poor girl," Valentina said sympathetically, "but tell me, Highness, what happened to the young bridegroom, Rudolpho? Did
he mourn her loss greatly?"

The duke smiled. What a charmingly romantic creature she
was! "I am afraid not, madonna. It was necessary that Rudolpho
marry and sire sons. Three months after Gianetta's fate was determined, Rudolpho di San Lorenzo married my great-great-
great-grandmother, the Princess Marie-Hélène of Toulouse."

Valentina sighed. "Was Gianetta happy in San Lorenzo?"

"It is said that she loved my country very much."

"Then, although your tale has an unhappy ending, the villa
was a happy house," Valentina reasoned.

He reached out and took her hand. Turning it over, he placed
a warm kiss upon the sensitive flesh of her wrist. "How wise and
kind you are, madonna. You have a *simpatico* heart and soul.
That is a rare and precious gift."

Murrough could see that his brother's temper was close to
exploding. "This has been a long day for us, Sebastian," he said.
"I think we had best retire."

"Of course, my friend," the duc replied graciously. "A carriage
will convey you to the villa, but there is a path that leads from
this very terrace down to the pink villa's gardens, and I claim the
privilege of escorting Donna Valentina there myself." Smiling at

the gentlemen in parting, he offered his arm to Lady Barrows.
"Madonna?"

There was no gainsaying him. Valentina took the proffered
arm. In a way it was amusing, for there was nothing subtle in
the duke's manner. Most of her life she had lived in relative
obscurity at Pearroc Royal, and few gentlemen had courted her
seriously despite her beauty, for she had an aloofness that frightened them away. Now she was suddenly the object of desire to
three very attractive men. She did not understand why. Was there
something different about her now?

The duke led her from the terrace down a flight of marble steps
to a gravel path below. Valentina wondered why she had not
noticed the path before, but then she realized her eyes had been
on the moonlit sea and, of course, on the duke. Bordering the
path were tall silver torches burning scented oil, casting a flick-
ering golden light over the path. Along their route, marble niches
were fitted into the hillside. Within each niche was a marble
statue draped in the classical manner. Valentina raised an eyebrow. "Do you always keep this path lit so well, Highness?"

"Only when I have need of it, and you will call me Sebastian,
madonna," he answered her. He stopped suddenly. Putting an
arm about her waist, he turned her toward him. "I must hear
you say my name, madonna!" he murmured urgently. His amber
eyes were glowing with an almost savage gleam.

She could feel the fingers of his hand splaying over her rib
cage and she found it difficult to breathe. Her amethyst eyes
widened slowly with the shocked realization that her body was
responding in a frightening fashion!

He brushed her lips with his own. "Say my name, madonna!"
he begged her huskily. "Say it!"

"Se-Se-Sebastian!" she whispered.

"*Dio*, you intoxicate me!" he cried softly, and his mouth covered hers in a torrid kiss.

I am going to faint, she thought, but she did not. His mouth
worked insistently against hers until she parted her lips and his
tongue shot within the cave of her mouth. Again she thought, I
am going to faint, but she did not. The invading tongue insin-
uated itself about hers, teasing, stroking, playing with it, and
Valentina's arms wound around the duke's neck, but it was for
support, not in passion, for her legs were shaking.

"Sebastian! You must stop!"

"I want to make love to you," he said frankly. "I know you are virtuous, Valentina. I suspect you have known no man but your late husband, but I must have you! From the moment I saw you this morning, I knew that I must have you! You enchant and bewitch me with your beauty and your strange innocence. I cannot remember the last time I felt this way about a woman."

"The others . . ." She attempted to draw him away from the subject. "The others will be wondering what has happened to us, Sebastian."

He laughed. "You will not deter me, madonna, but very well, I shall yield to your good sense this time."

They moved down the side of the hill toward the pink villa and its gardens, which were also lit with silver torches. "Are you always so bold, so very determined in your desires, monseigneur?" Valentina asked.

"Are you not determined in your desires, madonna?" he returned.

"I have been very sheltered, and I have never known a man like you," she told him truthfully.

"Nor I a woman like you, madonna. You look a man in the eye. You do not simper. You do not hide your intelligence. You quite fascinate me, and I am not ashamed to admit it," he told her.

They were nearing the villa's gardens, and to Valentina's amusement, both Padraic and Tom were coming to meet them.

"They are very protective of you, your two cavaliers," the duke noted with just the barest hint of humor in his deep, musical voice.

"You have paid me extravagant attention this evening, and they are quite jealous, I fear," she told him.

"They have cause to be jealous, madonna," he told her, and kissed her hand. "I will leave you here. Until tomorrow." With a courtly bow, he turned and went up the hillside to his home.

"How kind of you to bring me the rest of the way," Valentina said with false sweetness as her two suitors reached her.

"You look flushed, divinity," said the earl, his voice strained.

"Did he kiss you?" demanded Lord Burke angrily. "He has no right!"

"You have no right, either of you, to interrogate me or comment on either my appearance or my behavior," Valentina told them sharply. She swept by them and hurried into the villa.

Nelda, awaiting her, chattered brightly as she showed her mistress to her apartment. "Isn't this just lovely, m'lady? 'Tis so nice to be in a room that don't rock! Isn't this the dearest little house? The gardens are ever so nice, and so are the servants, even if I can't understand a word they're saying! It sounds like so much jibber-jabber. But they never stop smiling."

Valentina's rooms were beautiful, airy, and spacious, looking out over the gardens and the sea, which was silvered with moonlight. The salon held gracefully carved furniture and the marble floors were covered with magnificent carpets of blues and golds. The bedchamber was equally lovely, and the bed was hung with coral-colored silks.

"And look here, m'lady! I've never seen anything like it!" Nelda opened a small door set almost invisibly into the bedchamber wall. "The captain says 'tis a bathing chamber! Imagine! A whole room just for washing yerself! Me mum won't believe it, will she, m'lady?"

Valentina laughed. "I promise to back your word, Nelda. After all, the queen's godson, Sir John Harrington, built Her Majesty a water closet inside the palace. A bathing room seems little different, though nicer." Valentina's gaze swept the little bathing room. Its walls were of pale green marble, as was the round pool set directly in the center of the room and sunk into the green marble floor. Above the bathing pool was a round glass window through which Valentina could see the night sky.

"The water's nice and warm," Nelda said, breaking into her mistress's thoughts. "I stuck my hand in it. Now, how do you suppose they do that?"

"If I remember my history lessons," Valentina mused, "there is a water tank beneath the room that rests just above an open coal stove. They had baths like this in ancient times. And remember, this land was part of that ancient world, Nelda."

"A coal stove to heat the water! If that don't beat all!" the saucy servant exclaimed.

Valentina laughed again. Nelda was such a cheerful little thing. "It is assuredly easier than hauling buckets of hot water, which sometimes cool off while they're being hauled," she told Nelda.

"But how do they get the water into the pool, m'lady?"

"It is piped in, Nelda. See the gold spigots on the side of the bathing pool? The ones shaped like swans?"

"Well, if that don't beat all!" Nelda repeated. "Ma ain't gonna believe a word of this! I don't care what you say, she just ain't!"

San Lorenzo offered a peaceful and charming interlude. The

duc redeemed himself somewhat with Lord Burke and Lord Ashburne by taking them hunting in the mountains behind Arcobaleno. They were gone for three days, during which time Valentina explored the town thoroughly, indulged her passion for bathing in the fragrant warm waters of the bathing pool, and rested. She saw Murrough only in the evening, for his days were taken up with supervising the provisioning of their little flotilla.

The Royal Bess had sprung a small leak when the anchor crashed into the ship just beneath the water line, where there was a bit of rotted wood. Murrough insisted that the leak be repaired and the ship inspected for any additional rot. He would not sail until that was done, for even a minor leak could cause serious trouble in a storm. Murrough was too good a captain to endanger either a crew or a ship. The repair meant a slight delay, which the visitors to San Lorenzo found no great hardship.

Two days before their scheduled departure, just after the hunting party returned to Arcobaleno from their mountain retreat, a winter storm bore down fiercely on the duchy of San Lorenzo. It rained so hard that night that they could not join the duc for supper, and when a jagged streak of lightning tore across the sky followed by a rumble of thunder, Valentina reminded the others, "Thunder in winter is the devil's thunder, it is said. I am grateful we're not out at sea."

"I've ridden out worse storms," said Murrough casually.

The wind rose as the evening lengthened and was howling noisily about the pink villa by the time they were ready to retire. At every crack of thunder and its accompanying flash of lightning, Nelda crossed herself.

"Do you not like storms, Nelda?" teased the earl in an effort to relax the girl.

"Not good, honest English storms, m'lord, but this foreign storm, well, I guess I'm a mite edgy," she replied bravely.

"There is no need to worry," Lord Burke assured the servant. "We are safe within a marble building. Come, Nelda. Look out the window. The storm over the sea is very beautiful viewed safely from our elegant shelter."

With some coaxing from her mistress, Nelda stood with the others, gazing out, fascinated by the lightning. She had never considered that one might actually stand and watch a storm. Everyone sheltered from a storm until it was over, didn't they?

Suddenly, a great flash of lightning hurled itself from the black sky and, for a moment, the world was as bright as day. There was a loud crack as the lightning found a target, and even from where they were, they could hear the sound of splintering wood.

"Jesu! Mary!" Murrough swore ferociously. " 'Tis one of the ships! I know it! Nelda, lass, get my cloak! Hurry!"

"You cannot go out in this, cousin," Valentina protested.

"Do you not understand, Val? 'Tis one of our ships that has been damaged!" Murrough said impatiently.

"*Has,* Murrough, *has* been damaged. The injury is already done, whatever it may be, and you can do nothing to prevent it now. Your first mate is in command. If he needs you, he will send for you. Wait at least until you hear from him, or until the storm is over."

"She's right, Murrough," Padraic said. " 'Tis what Mother would do."

"Hah! Mother would rush out into the storm just as I would like to do," Murrough replied. "But given your good advice, Mother just might listen to reason, and so shall I."

The storm blew itself out in the early hours of the morning, and the day dawned clear and warm. After hurrying down to the harbor before the sun rose, Murrough discovered that *Archangel* had been hit. One of her masts had been split in two by the lightning. It was not, fortunately, the main mast, but a smaller one that could be replaced with material available on San Lorenzo, though it would take two to three weeks to do so.

The voyagers were not happy. Murrough, like Valentina, was anxious to continue on their odyssey. Both Padraic Burke and Tom Ashburne were concerned by the attention paid Valentina by the duke. Why, the wench even seemed to be enjoying herself despite her protestations of wanting to get underway as quickly as possible. They could not complain to the duke about his actions, for the man was their host.

There had been hot caresses in the duke's gardens within a rose arbor. Twice he had managed to fondle her plump, wonderful breasts, to bring soft cries of pleasure to her lips, even as she protested his bold hands with her own hands and pleading amethyst eyes. His own hunger rose wildly on each occasion, pressing hotly against his clothing.

The days had slipped by. One week. Two weeks, and now the day of their departure had been set for two days hence. *Archangel* was fully repaired and being provisioned once again. Valentina was relieved. It had grown increasingly hard to put the duke off, for he was incredibly persistent in his pursuit of her. She had been perilously near, she frankly admitted to herself, to succumbing to him on several occasions, for she could not help but be curious about his attributes as a lover. She was not a wanton by nature, but Valentina's brief encounter with Padraic had opened a Pandora's box of curiosity for her.

"I think it a good thing that we leave in two days," Valentina told Padraic. "You have come perilously close to insulting the duke, and we cannot go on like this."

"Do you not wish your virtue protected?" demanded Lord Burke.

"I am quite capable of defending my own virtue, Padraic," Valentina answered irritably.

"I am not so certain of that, divinity," Lord Ashburne told her. "For once I must agree with Padraic. Our host presumes too much. Without a doubt, the fellow is a scoundrel."

Overhearing them, Murrough, who had just returned to the villa from the waterfront, spoke up. "Not really, Tom. You must understand that Sebastian is used to getting his way, for he is a ruler. Then, too, he is, by reputation, quite a lover. I can imagine the rebuff to his pride that my fair cousin has caused him."

"You are ridiculous, all of you," Valentina said. "The duke has been a perfect gentleman. He has asked for nothing, and I have given him nothing. I am quite able to look after myself, and I very much resent being spied on by two buffoons with the manners of schoolboys!"

"You little fool!" raged Lord Burke. "Do you think your short stay at court, cloistered as you were with the queen's ladies, has given you the wisdom of the world? The duke would seduce you in a minute if only he believed he could get away with it! It is the constant presence of these two *buffoons* that has saved you, Val. What a pity you are not wise enough to see that."

"Aye, divinity!" put in the earl. "If Padraic and I joust with one another over you, at least you may be certain that our intentions are honorable. We each love you, and we each hope to make you our wife, though one of us will, of necessity, fall by the wayside. The duke's intentions are of a different nature. As a man well schooled in the art of seduction, I can assure you that what I say is true."

Murrough could see that Valentina was prepared to give battle, so he said quickly, "Let us not argue among ourselves. In two days we will once again be at sea, and 'twould be a shame to be angry with one another over such a trifle as the duke." His blue eyes twinkled at his cousin. "I know you are competent to handle Sebastian, Val. Do not be angry with these two. They are jealous and fretful at the thought that another man might engage your heart."

"I suppose I should be flattered," grumbled Valentina. Then she laughed. "Very well, Murrough, I shall not be angry. I shall instead indulge myself once again in my bathing pool, for it is one of the things I shall miss when we leave San Lorenzo."

"And what are the other things, divinity?" demanded Tom Ashburne.

"What, indeed, my lord?" she answered, and, with a mischievous smile, sauntered off toward her apartment, humming.

Lord Burke's visage was thunderous, and only his older brother's warning look kept him from going after her. "She is the most irritating vixen," he growled angrily.

"If she so arouses your ire, Padraic, then perhaps you should leave her to me," teased the earl with a wicked grin.

"Go to hell, my lord!" was the furious reply.

Murrough burst into laughter at the antics of the two, and his sibling sent him a dark scowl.

"Do you think," Padraic asked Murrough, "that our mother aroused her gentlemen to such heights?"

"I cannot remember my father," said Murrough, "but I do remember yours. Niall had a tendency to react when Mother irritated him in very much the same way you do when Val irritates you,"

"Hmm," said Lord Burke thoughtfully. "I find it interesting that none of our mother's daughters is very much like Mother, even our headstrong Velvet. Yet Valentina's behavior bears striking similarities to our mother's."

Murrough chuckled. "Aye," he concurred, "I've noticed."

"I remember my father speaking of your mother," said Tom. "She cut quite a swath through court in her heyday, didn't she?"

"Aye!" the brothers agreed, each smiling with his own particular memory of Skye O'Malley. "She did, indeed!"

The visitors were invited to dine that night at the palace. The skies above the balustraded terrace were like black silk sewn with sparkling gemstones, for the waning moon had not yet risen. The meal was delicious, and afterward a troupe of Gypsies entertained them. Valentina had never seen Gypsies like these before, for the tinkers who came to her parents' estate were very English. This group was very different in appearance and manner: dark-haired and swarthy with strong, handsome features and bold ways.

The men, in their bright red pantaloons, white shirts, and leather vests, played pipes and stringed instruments as three very exotic young women danced in a haze of twirling skirts that allowed daring glimpses of bare legs and long, swirling dark hair. The dances, which at first seemed peasantlike and cheerful, soon grew sensual. The dancers whirled and dipped, allowing quick views of full breasts as the light of the torches gilded their smooth bare shoulders. The three Englishmen did not restrain their admiration. They leaned forward for a better look, which the three Gypsy girls were happy to give them. Happy milords meant more coins in their pockets.

Valentina suddenly became aware that the duke was trailing his fingers up and down her arm. He leaned forward and daringly kissed her bared shoulder, rubbing his cheek provocatively against the scarlet silk of her gown as he inhaled her floral fragrance.

"Do you find the dancers exciting, madonna?" he asked her.

"Perhaps a bit too obvious, Highness," she noted coolly.

He hid a smile. She was jealous because her two usually attentive cavaliers were otherwise engrossed. Soon, madonna, he silently promised her. Soon you will have all the attention you could ever crave.

He signaled to Giacomo, who came forward bearing a Venetian crystal decanter of rose-colored liqueur. "Will you taste a small goblet of this special liqueur I distill? It is made from a very rare and ancient grapevine that I treasure, and then mixed with just the tiniest bit of angelica and other special herbs that I cannot divulge to you, for it is a family secret."

Valentina smiled and nodded assent. "Will you not offer the others some, monseigneur?" she inquired.

"Do you think they would enjoy it, madonna? They are far too intoxicated by the dancers to appreciate my prized liqueur. I think they would not thank me for interrupting them now. Only you and I shall partake of this nectar of the gods," he said softly.

She glanced over at the others and saw that it was as he said. They were spellbound by the Gypsy dancers and noticed nothing else. "You are absolutely correct, monseigneur, and I agree with you. 'Twould be a pity to waste your fine cordial."

Giacomo poured out two small goblets of his master's special liqueur. The duke took his goblet and, touching hers, murmured, "To you, madonna, and to all the beautiful things that could be between us if you would only say yes." His golden eyes ignited as he spoke, and her heart raced at his passionate, suggestive declaration.

Valentina felt a blush suffusing her face and neck. I cannot allow him to think I am responding positively to such a toast, she thought. Swallowing hard, she said, "Monseigneur, I toast you, your kind and lavish hospitality and San Lorenzo itself, surely one of the loveliest countries in the world." Then with a small smile, she sipped at her liqueur.

The duke returned her smile and drank from his own goblet. Why was it, he considered, that the women a man might choose from to wed were so dull, while the women a man desired were so damned interesting? It was, he decided, one of the ancient mysteries of the world.

Valentina could see that her companions were enjoying the dancers, and not being mean-spirited, she decided she did not wish to distract them. But she was feeling tired and desired nothing more than to retire. Leaning over, she whispered her dilemma to the duke, who told her, "My servant, Giacomo, will escort you to the villa. I would do so myself, but I cannot leave my guests. I understand," he went on, "that you enjoy my fine golden wine each night before retiring. I am gratified, and I have ordered several casks placed aboard your vessel so that when you leave San Lorenzo, you will remember us. When you drink your wine tonight, think of me, fair Valentina. Perhaps, at least in your dreams, we can be more to each other than just friends. Surely there can be no harm in dreaming."

"Monseigneur! You are wicked," she scolded. She laughed softly. "Perhaps if I were a different kind of woman . . . You are a devilishly attractive man. I will admit that to you, now that I am to leave."

He nodded slowly. "Then I will forgive you a little, madonna, for breaking my heart."

She smiled. "My conscience is quite clear, Highness, and you flatter me outrageously. I have not broken your heart at all. You must keep it intact for the lady you will wed one day." She rose from the table. "I will bid you good night," she said, and moved quietly away lest she disturb the others.

* * *

Murrough O'Flaherty had never been more surprised in his entire life than he was the next morning when the duc visited him. It was true that he had teased Val about the duke being very eligible, but he had not taken seriously the duke's interest in his cousin. Yet there was his old friend, Sebastian, royal duke of San Lorenzo, offering for Valentina!

"You're jesting!" The words were out of Murrough's mouth before he could restrain them.

The duke smiled. "No, I am not. I have fallen in love with your cousin, and I would wed her, make her my duchesse. Oh, I know what you are thinking, Murrough. That her breeding is not the equal of mine. That is so, but it is time for some new blood in San Lorenzo. For centuries my family has confined their bridal searches to Monaco, Beaumont de Jaspre, Toulouse, Genoa, and Firenze. There has been an occasional Roman contessa for variety. I want new blood, strong Northern blood! I want Valentina."

Murrough was astounded. "I'll have to ask her," he said, stunned.

"Ask her? Not ask her father?" Now it was the duke who was astounded.

"My Uncle Conn adores Valentina," Murrough said. "She is his eldest child. He has always doted on his daughters and has allowed them free choice of husbands. If Valentina will not agree, then it is no use speaking with my uncle, for he will not force any of his daughters to marry against her will," Murrough said, then quickly added, "Even when the marriage proposal is as magnificent as yours, Sebastian."

The duke had not considered such a thing. Would Valentina refuse him? Surely not. In her wildest dreams she could not aspire to a match as good as he offered. No, she would not refuse his offer.

He smiled at his old friend. "You must ask her then, Murrough," he said confidently. "I shall return a bit after noon."

At twelve-thirty, the duke returned to the ship and met with Murrough, who had been to the pink villa and spoken with Valentina.

"No," she had told her cousin emphatically. "The duke is making me an honorable offer and I am grateful for his high opinion of me, but I do not love him, and that is all that matters to me. I married once for expediency's sake. I will not do it again. I must love the man I wed so greatly that I have no doubts about the wisdom of our marriage."

Murrough had listened with complete understanding, having known she would refuse the duke. "I will tell my friend Sebastian what I need to tell him in order to assuage his disappointment." He had grinned and confided, "I expect this to be a shock, for women never refuse him, or so I am told."

"She refuses my suit?" The duke could not believe he had heard Murrough correctly.

Murrough nodded sympathetically. "Aye, Sebastian, she does, but you must not think of it as a rebuff. Valentina was tremendously honored by your offer, but she could not bear the thought of living so far from her family and from England. She's not an ambitious woman at all, you see."

"But . . . I have offered her a duchesse's crown!" the duke exploded.

"My cousin will not be parted from her mother," Murrough told him. "We are a very close family, Sebastian, and Valentina, having been widowed, is skittish. There is no accounting for female vagaries, is there?

"You will not be embarrassed by her refusal," he told the duc, "for your association with Valentina has not been a public one." He clapped the duc on the shoulder. "I am flattered that you think enough of Valentina to offer her your name. One good thing has come of this, Sebastian. You have learned that you are ready to marry again."

"Aye," grumbled the duke, "I am. And the woman I choose breaks my heart. It is not to be borne!"

"Nonsense, my old friend." Murrough chuckled. "You've never allowed a mere woman to upset you before this, and you are not going to now. You must announce that you are seeking a bride. Then settle back to enjoy the flurry your announcement causes while you relish all the fun of picking and choosing, eh?"

"Well," Sebastian di San Lorenzo considered, somewhat mollified, "perhaps you are right, Murrough."

The two gentlemen drank a toast to the duke's search for a new wife, and then Murrough returned to the pink villa.

Valentina suggested they sail as soon as they could, and Murrough agreed. He told her, "The duc, in an effort to avoid you and to save face, has said he cannot dine with us tonight. I think, under the circumstances, we might sail with the late-afternoon tide, Val. Would you like that?"

"Aye," she said, "but what of Padraic and Tom? They have not yet risen and 'tis nearly noon. I somehow suspect they will not be well," she remarked dryly. "I am frankly amazed at *your* excellent condition, my dear Murrough."

"Hah! Hah! Hah!" He chortled. "Very little misses you, Val, I can see that. Here we thought you were so involved with Sebastian last evening that you would not notice our little peccadillo. I hope you are not angry with Padraic and Tom."

"No," she said, smiling. "They are men, and men, your mama tells me, are prone to temptation. They are still asleep, however, while you have been up for hours. How do you do it, Murrough?"

"I simply wore the wench out before midnight so that I might get a good night's rest, cousin," he told her mischievously. "I am older and wiser than my brother and Tom. I have learned to temper my passions. They will learn the same wisdom, one day.

"As we are nearly packed and ready, I shall send our luggage to the ships as soon as I waken Tom and Padraic. We will sail at two o'clock."

As they cleared the harbor of Arcobaleno several hours later, Valentina said gaily to her two companions, "What a glorious day! I can almost smell spring in the air, and 'tis not even March."

"The sun is too bright," said Lord Burke testily. His eyes were dry and felt as if they might pop from their sockets at any minute.

"The sun is warm and lovely," she returned innocently, "and for some reason, being at sea again gives me a feeling of great freedom. The wind is simply perfect! Feel how the *Archangel* sweeps grandly along over the waves, like a great bird swooping and soaring!"

Tom Ashburne groaned. He looked decidedly green about the gills. "Woman," he snarled, "cease your chatter about sweeping, swooping, and soaring!"

"Do you not feel well?" she inquired of him sweetly.

The two men glowered at her.

"I am not surprised," said Valentina. "Not surprised in the least. Tsk, tsk! All the wine you consumed last night, and then those exotic Gypsy girls! They looked as if they could drain the life from any man. Judging by your appearance, they obviously did."

Both men looked very chagrined. So she was fully aware of how they had spent their evening? They flushed, almost in unison, and she laughed.

"What is that biblical verse? 'As ye sow, so shall ye reap.' Ah, yes, I do believe that is it." With a wicked grin she moved away from them down the deck, her silk skirts blowing in the wind.

"I am going to kill her," growled Lord Burke.

"I would like to help you, but I myself died several hours ago," muttered Lord Ashburne.

At that moment the ship dipped sharply, and both gentlemen were forced to avail themselves of the rail. It did not help to hear Valentina return, moving past them as she hummed a merry tune.

Chapter Seven

THE *ARCHANGEL* AND HER TWO GUARDIAN SHIPS swept down the Tyrrhenian Sea through the Strait of Messina and around the boot of Italy into the Ionian Sea. There they were hailed by a great merchantman of the Venetian Levant, the *San Marco e Santa Maria,* out of Venice, bound for London. Its captain came aboard the *Archangel* and closeted himself alone with Murrough for an hour before leaving to return to his own vessel.

"What was that all about?" Padraic asked his elder brother.

Murrough smiled. "Fortune is smiling directly on your venture, Val," he said to her. "That was Enrico-Carlo Baffo, younger brother to the Sultan Valide herself! He has asked us to carry a message to his sister. Their father, who was near death, has recovered despite his vast age."

"What difference does that make to us or to Val?" Padraic said.

"When we reach Istanbul," said Murrough, "and we speak with Esther Kira, we will give her this message to pass on to the Valide along with our request for Valentina's audience with her. The sultan's mother will not, under the circumstances, refuse Valentina. I was not certain before now how we were going to arrange to see that lady. This, however, is our entry to her."

The little three-ship convoy moved on past the Grecian Peloponnesus and up into the Aegean Sea, sailing among the Cyclades; Andros; Khíos, the birthplace of the famed Greek poet, Homer; past Lésbos, the island that had, seven centuries before

Christ, been the very center of the civilized world. The ancient
woman poet, Sappho, had been born on Lésbos.

March had brought spring to the region, and each day was
lovely with clear blue skies and bright sun. Just before they entered the Dardanelles, they stopped at a small island to replenish
their supply of fresh water.

"Who lives on the island?" Valentina asked Murrough.

"The island is deserted, although it is fertile," he replied. "The
Turks captured the Cyclades almost forty years ago. There is a
temple, I am told, or what is left of an ancient temple, on the
island's crest. The people believe that the island was dedicated
to Aphrodite, the goddess of love. After her priesthood died away,
the island remained uninhabited, and a legend grew that the
goddess actually lived there. The island was therfore forbidden
as a habitation for mere mortals. Aphrodite, however, is hospitable to travelers. She offers us her sweet water, provided that
we respect her. It is the custom to leave some small offering on
her altar."

"And will you?"

"Aye, Val, I will. We sailors are a superstitious lot." Murrough
smiled.

"May we go ashore?" she said.

"Of course! Tomorrow we enter the Dardanelles, and with luck
two days after that we will be in Istanbul. If you would like, we
can spend the day here. It will allow the men to let off a little
excess energy. We will all have to be on our best behavior after
today, for what has thus far been a pleasant and amusing journey,
tomorrow becomes serious business, Valentina, for the crew as
well as for us. The Ottoman and Tatar people are fierce, as volatile
as a field afire, and as unpredictable. There will be no margin
for mistakes."

There were goats on the island, and the crew slaughtered several to roast. Lord Burke fell and badly twisted his ankle while
trying to capture one of the beasts. He was returned, under protest, to *Archangel* so that the ship's physician could be certain
the ankle wasn't broken.

"Aphrodite has answered my prayers," murmured Lord Ashburne as the dory containing Lord Burke pulled away from the
island. "I will have to make her a most generous offering, divinity.
Will you come with me?"

"Oh, Tom! Shame! You are wicked to say such a thing. Poor
Padraic!" Valentina cried sympathetically.

The earl thought how lovely she looked in her simple white silk shirt and dark green linen skirt. The shirt, with bared shoulders, affected a peasant look. Valentina's long dark hair was drawn back off her face held by a single white silk ribbon embroidered with tiny seed pearls.

"But Lord Burke's misfortune is my good fortune, divinity. I have not had a single opportunity to be alone with you in weeks, and damn it, Val, I am not sorry that my rival has been removed from the picture. I would be a hypocrite to say so. Padraic is not seriously injured, so do not waste time in sympathy for him that might be spent in sweet contemplation of my adoration of you." He slipped an arm about her waist and drew her close. "Walk with me, Val. Let us find flowers to gather that we shall lay together upon the altar of Aphrodite, that magnificent bitch goddess whose mere whim can change a mortal's life for the better. Or the worse."

"You have a poet's soul, Tom," she said, looking up at him and smiling.

" 'Tis only the babble of a man in love, Val," he answered, his gray eyes scanning her face for some sign of encouragement. He was pleased to note that his words brought a faint flush to her cheeks.

They walked together up a narrow path from the beach to the top of the island. There they found spread out before them a field abloom with scarlet, purple, and white poppies swaying gently in the soft breeze. Directly in the middle of the field was a white marble building. It was not a ruin at all. It was a square, porticoed structure open on all four sides to allow the sunlight into its sanctuary.

Directly in the center of the temple stood an enormous statue of the naked goddess herself rising from the sea, as legend had depicted her birth. The statue, in excellent condition, was of polished white marble with just the faintest hint of pink. It was surely as beautiful as it had been the day it was placed there. Within the porticoed shelter it was safe from the ravages of sun and rain. The statue was set on a raised dais of white marble shot through with veins of dark red, and the goddess stood on a huge scalloped shell of the same marble that served as her altar. Upon it were the remnants of some previous visitors' offerings.

Valentina spread the armful of flowers she had gathered on the altar. Then she turned to the earl with a smile. "Do you think that will satisfy the goddess, my lord?"

"Nay," he answered softly, "but perhaps this will." Drawing her into his arms, he kissed her, and as his lips moved tenderly over hers, Valentina sighed. Emboldened, he placed little kisses all over her face, on her flushed pink cheeks, her quivering eyelids, the corners of her mouth, the tip of her nose. "Ah, divinity," he said, his hands cupping her face, "you ravish me with your sweetness. I adore you, Valentina. Can you not love me just a little?"

She opened her eyes to look into his, and for the briefest second, his vulnerability was evident. "Tom," she whispered, for to speak loudly in this place seemed wrong somehow. "Oh, Tom, I do not know how I feel! Do not press me, I beg you, for I can make no decisions now."

"Let me love you a little, divinity," he pleaded. "Let me love you here, in this perfect place that is dedicated to love!" He slipped to his knees, drawing her down with him. He kissed her once again, but this time his kisses were more demanding.

She murmured a faint protest as he drew her silk blouse down to bare her breasts to the warm air. His kisses scorched across her perfumed skin, his mouth finally fastening on a pert pink nipple. She sighed, knowing she ought to stop him, but unable, somehow, to gather the energy she needed to push him away.

He suckled her nipple for several minutes before moving on to the other. His arm slipped beneath her buttocks to brace her as he drew her down to the temple floor. Gently, he pushed her skirts up, baring her long legs in their black leather boots, plain white silk stockings, and green ribbon garters. His big hand moved softly over the flesh of her thigh, stroking her with a circular motion while his mouth continued suckling at her nipple.

She should stop him! She knew she must stop him, yet his mouth on her breast, the tender fingers stroking her thigh were all so pleasurable that she couldn't gather her thoughts together. "Tom!" she finally managed.

He lifted passion-glazed eyes from her wet, aching nipple and gazed down into her face. "I love you," he groaned. "Do not forbid me, divinity!"

Her eyes filled with sudden tears. "But you must cease, she said, "for I have not the strength to fight you."

"Tell me that you do not feel the passion, Val, and I will stop. *Tell me!*" he demanded cruelly of her.

"I cannot lie to you," she sobbed. "I *do* feel the passion, but passion is not necessarily love. I must love a man for reasons other than passion before I can give myself totally. Oh, Tom! You must understand that!"

A spasm crossed his handsome face and he said, "Let me at least give you what pleasure I can without completing the act, for that will give me some pleasure also."

She wanted to say yes. Dear God, how she wanted to say yes! Instead she whispered shakily, "Tom, please!"

"I am not a lad, unable to control his desire, Val. I can give you the pleasure you need now to ease your own suffering!" His supple fingers slipped between her nether lips to explore for just a second and then he said, triumphant, "You cannot deny your longings, divinity, for you are already honeyed." Fumbling with his breeches, he unbuttoned the slit and slipped his manhood out. Catching one of her hands, he placed it on the throbbing organ.

Valentina gasped and tried to draw away. "Tom, you must not!"

"Just caress him, divinity," the earl pleaded. "That is all I will ask of you, I swear it! The poor fellow has been in desperate need of soothing these last months. Surely you would not be so unkind, now that he has felt your tender touch."

"Oh, Tom, you are very bad, and I am afraid," she said.

"I swear I will not take you, Valentina, even though I long to," he promised her. "You are right in that passion for passion's sake is not a good thing. I will respect your view, for I agree with it. But let us at least have the joy of easing each other's longings."

Her conscience was not entirely placated, but she thought that she would have had to be a saint in order to refuse him now, for even if she would not admit it to him, she was willing to admit to herself that her own desires were high. Her slim fingers swept up and down the smooth column of hot, hard flesh. He groaned softly when, with surprising audacity, she cupped and fondled the sensitive pouch beneath his manhood. "Does this really give you pleasure?" she said.

"Aye," he gasped, "it does, but now I want you to stop so that I can reciprocate."

"Nay, 'tis all right," she protested shyly, but he would not listen to her obviously faint-hearted protests which had only been brought on by a new attack of conscience.

Firmly he pressed her back upon the marble floor, placing little kisses across her face before moving down to her swollen breasts. A thrill ran through him when she held him against her bosom, for it was her first voluntary act of passion. God's foot, how he loved those marvelous globes of hers, exuding their faint aura of lily of the valley. She truly had the most perfect breasts he had ever seen, and he would have been content to spend hours adoring them.

Passion gripped Valentina now, for the games he wanted to play with her were potent, indeed. Whimpering, she boldly caught his hand and drew it down to her pretty pink Venus mont.

Tom Ashburne smiled softly. What a marvelous bed partner she was going to be when he won her for his wife! All that fire beneath that cool surface . . . and it would eventually be his!

Twisting himself away from her breasts, he slipped down between her legs. He had sworn not to couple with her, but he would show her a sweet trick he would wager Lord Barrows had never shown her.

She knew! The moment his head moved between her thighs, she knew! He intended touching her in the most shockingly intimate way, and she realized intuitively that, if he did, she would lose control of herself completely. But before she could squirm away or speak to stop him, his fingers spread her and his tongue touched her in a warm, dizzying way that made her gasp aloud. Valentina arched her back in an effort to be closer to the mouth that was bringing her such unbelievable pleasure. This was bliss beyond bearing! This was . . . wonderful! As her crisis neared, she cried out with rapture, then wept sweet tears. He gently kissed them away as her elation faded.

Afterward, he held her in his arms as the goddess looked down on them with a benign, approving gaze. He stroked her hair and rocked her until her tears had stopped and she sighed deeply. "Better now?" he inquired softly.

"Worse, I think," she said. "This sweet soothing of yours is for little girls with no knowledge of what is to come. I yearn now more than before, Tom, and I am certain that you knew I would."

"Nay, divinity, I truly only sought to give you pleasure. Had I known how you would feel, I should not have made my small offering to Aphrodite." He pointed to the base of the goddess's altar where he had spilled his golden seed. "Had I but known, Val, I'd have held back so that you might be fully satisfied, my darling, for despite all your protestations, I believe you would have enjoyed our union even if your conscience did prick you afterward."

She blushed, then laughed weakly. "Nay, we were wise to abstain from fully satisfying our passion. I am not a wanton, to couple with every man who takes my fancy." Valentina pulled her blouse up and, standing, smoothed her skirts down. She reeled, dizzy for the briefest moment.

He leaped to his feet to steady her, murmuring jealously in her ear as he did so, "And just how many men have taken your fancy, divinity?"

"Button yourself up, my lord," she said, gently easing herself from his embrace. "We must return to the beach lest Murrough send someone after us and we are caught in our dalliance. The walk back will cool our passions."

"Having tasted of your sweetness, Val, I am not certain that the memory of this moment will not but increase my passion for you. A mere walk is not apt to bank my fires, divinity," he concluded, laughing weakly.

"The goddess," said Valentina, "has shown us both of her faces, Tom. We have been pleasured, yet neither of us is truly satisfied. I wonder if there is meaning in that." Then her mood lightened. "Let us gather flowers on our way back and use them as an excuse for our long absence."

"No one," he said, "will dare to question us."

"Not even Murrough? I think he will tease us," she said with a laugh.

Murrough, surprisingly, said nothing. This business between his cousin, his younger brother, and the Earl of Kempe would eventually sort itself out. He hoped that Valentina would choose to wed Padraic, for he suspected that if she did not, Padraic would never marry at all. He was such an intense young man and had surely not lost his heart easily.

Murrough was glad that the match his mother had arranged long ago for him with his stepsister, Joan Southwood, had turned into a love match and a happy marriage. Murrough was not a man for high passion and wild romance.

"Did ye place an offering on the goddess's altar?" he asked Val and the earl when they returned to the shore. The goats had been roasted, their cavities stuffed with wild thyme the crew had found growing on the sandy hillside.

"Aye," Valentina replied. "We offered an armful, just like these. We picked these for Padraic. How is he?"

"This ship's physician says 'tis just a light sprain. Padraic should be fit and walking by the time we reach Istanbul, if he will stay off the damned thing until then. 'Twill be your job, Val, to make him behave."

The moon was already silvering the placid sea when they arrived back at the ship after feasting on savory kid. Padraic was awaiting them, sitting on the deck, his leg propped up, looking grim.

Valentina ran to his side with the flowers. "Look, Padraic! We brought them for you. Are they not lovely?"

"Did you visit the temple?" he asked gruffly.

"Aye," she answered. "'Tis a little jewel of a building, white marble, with pillars all about it, open on all sides. Inside is a marvelous great statue of Aphrodite herself and the altar is a shell at her feet! Oh, I wish you could have seen it! The top of the island is a large field, and it was filled with poppies, all scarlet, purple, and white. The temple sits amid all that splendor. Tom and I gathered poppies and laid them on the goddess's altar. Then we gathered these for you."

She was speaking too quickly. Too brightly. A sign that she had something to hide, he thought. His glance flicked to Thomas Ashburne, and the earl's gray eyes met Padraic Burke's calmly, telling him nothing yet saying everything. Damn the bastard! Damn him!

"You might have brought me some of that fresh meat I can smell even from here," Lord Burke lashed out.

"We did, little brother," replied Murrough, calmly taking it all in. These three on his peaceful ship were a storm waiting to break.

Valentina glared at Padraic, her anger rising. How dared he behave like this? Even if she had made love with Tom, it was none of Padraic's business! Did he seek her approval when he had taken that Gypsy slut to his bed in San Lorenzo? He had not!

"Let me escort you to your cabin, divinity," the earl said.

"Don't you mean her *bed*?" growled Lord Burke.

"No, he does not!" Valentina raged, "and how dare you even suggest such a thing?" Furiously she flung her armful of flowers at him as she stormed off.

He almost fell over backwards onto the deck, and covered in brightly colored poppies Lord Burke made a most comical sight. His two companions began to laugh.

Struggling to his feet, Padraic exploded, "Damn her! She's driving me mad!" He winced at the pain in his ankle, and seeing it, the two other men slipped on either side of him, and helped him to his cabin.

"If it will make you feel any better," said Tom Ashburne, "I did indeed attempt to make love to Val, but she would not have it."

"*She wouldn't?*" The lilt in his brother's voice was almost pitiful thought Murrough.

"She said passion without love was not something with which she was comfortable. That she would make no decision on our suits until after this quest of hers is over. I would not tell you this but that you are injured, and I do not want you doing something foolish, my friend. You are, God help you, like me. A man in love! Now, I will bid you good night," said the earl, and he withdrew.

Having helped his younger brother to disrobe, Murrough said quietly to Padraic, "You don't own her, Padraic, and you're going to lose her if you don't begin behaving like a man. For God's sake, you're past thirty! If you had spoken up in the first place you might have had her to wife long ago. But you did not, so now you will simply have to play out your combined fates."

"I made love to her once," Lord Burke said softly to his sibling.

"What?" Murrough was surprised.

"Aye, I did. 'Twas last autumn. I couldn't help myself. I thought perhaps if I did she would send Tom away, and forget this mad quest of hers. Marry me. Even as I took her she told me that it made no difference, that she would not be forced to the altar." Padraic ran an impatient hand through his dark hair. "God, Murrough, I love her! The thought that she might choose Tom drives me mad!" He sighed deeply. "Are all men such fools over the women they love?"

Murrough thought for a long moment on Padraic's question. He and his elder brother, Ewan, were separated in age by barely ten months. Their mother had betrothed them when they were little boys to her third husband's twin daughters from his first marriage. Murrough and Ewan had wed their wives when they were seventeen and eighteen respectively, in the same ceremony. There had never been anyone else for Murrough but Joan, nor had there been anyone else for Joan but Murrough. Sweet Joan, his little English wren with her pretty golden-brown hair. If he were in the same position as Padraic and Joan were the lady in question, would he be making a fool of himself? Aye, he decided, he would, for he loved his Joan as his younger brother loved Valentina.

"I suppose," he said to Padraic, "that we are all fools when it comes to love. But that does not change matters. Valentina is no child. She's a grown woman, and like all the females born into this family, she has a strong will. She will have her way, brother, and ye'll have to learn to bend before her breeze, or ye'll not survive this sickness called love that afflicts you so badly." Murrough put a hand on his sibling's shoulder. "Good night, Padraic," he said. "God grant ye the woman ye love." He departed.

Padraic Burke lay restless in his bed. The port was open, and through it he could see the moon glowing brightly. The air was warm, and there was a faint elusive perfume upon the gentle winds that filled *Archangel's* sails. He could feel the smooth, deep swell of the sea beneath the ship as it glided along over the waves. Suddenly the door to his cabin opened and closed. "Who's there?" he demanded of the shadow that had glided so quickly inside.

" 'Tis I," Valentina said crossing the little room to seat herself on the edge of his bed. "Has your temper cooled yet, Padraic?"

"Aye," he chuckled feeling a sudden warmth at her presence.

"Then if you are all right, I shall seek my own bed," she said quietly rising to go.

"Val!" His hand caught at her night rail. "Tom told me that nothing happened."

"I told you that nothing happened, Padraic," she said, and her voice was cool.

"I cannot help myself, hinny love! I desire you so greatly!"

"You *desire* me, Padraic?" There was a dangerous edge to her tone. "If all you seek of me is *that*, then have me!" She pushed the night rail over her shoulders, and it slid with a silken sound to the floor to puddle around her ankles.

There she stood, naked before him, the moon silvering her lush form, looking for all the world like some primitive goddess. He could feel his body reacting to the sight as any man would react to such a sight. "*Val!*" His voice was ragged.

"What, sir? You no longer *desire* me?" she mocked him.

"Cloth yourself, damnit! This instant, madam! You shame us both with your behavior," he hissed.

Valentina stretched slowly, raising her arms above her head so he might gain a fuller view of her magnificent breasts. Then with a taunting smile, she bent and drew her night rail back up, slipping her arms into the full, long sleeves, and tying it shut at the neck with its pink ribbons. "I am my own mistress, Padraic Burke," she said. "Even should I consent one day to be your wife, I will not be any man's possession. Remember that!" The door opened and shut once again, and he was alone.

Archangel plowed on through the moonlit night, gliding smoothly across the satin seas to enter the Dardanelles just as, to their starboard, the skies beyond the dark hills of Asia Minor began to glow with the crimson stain of dawn. By late afternoon they had entered the Sea of Marmara, and along either side of the dark blue waters, on both shores, Turkish forts were visible. The following day Valentina sat on the deck of the ship beneath a canvas awning that protected her fair skin from the bright sunlight. She watched with amazement the many ships moving up and down the Marmara. There were great vessels of the royal Ottoman navy and ships belonging to their vassals, the corsairs of the Barbary Coast. Merchantmen from London, Marseilles, Genoa, Amalfi, Malta, Toulon, Algiers, Tangier, Alexandria, and the Venetian Levant swept by in a never-ending procession. It was a very busy waterway.

Valentina awoke before dawn the following morning. She had slept restlessly all night long and could no longer bear to be cooped up in her cabin. Quietly she dressed in green split-legged skirt and silk cream shirt, pulling her stockings and boots on quickly and clasping a wide leather belt around her waist. Impatiently she brushed the tangles from her long hair and braided it into a single braid, wrapping a rose-colored ribbon around it to hold it. She crept softly from the cabin so as not to wake Nelda.

She found Murrough on deck. "Do you never sleep?" she demanded.

"Of course I sleep," he said, chuckling, "but a ship's master must by virtue of his great responsibility sleep the least of all aboard his ship. Actually I've gotten more sleep these past two nights than in quite some time."

"How near are we to Istanbul?"

"In a few minutes it will be dawn," he told her, "and you will see the towers and walls of the city. Wait here for me and I shall identify for you some of the more interesting places, but first I must give my mate his orders."

She peered into the gray mists of early morning until he returned. "Will the mist lift?" she asked.

"There is usually a wind at dawn that blows the mists away. To have your first glimpse of Istanbul in this way is very exciting. I have been here many times, but it always thrills me to see the city at dawn."

As Murrough had predicted, a breeze sprang up, tearing the silken mist to tatters and filling their sails with new life. The city appeared suddenly on their port side, rising from behind the ancient walls that surrounded it on the sea side, to climb its seven hills in an unending procession of splendor. As gold and scarlet light reached out to gild the domes and soaring minarets, the call of the city's many muezzins rose as one voice over Istanbul.

"It is wonderful!" cried Valentina. "It is like nothing I have ever seen before!"

Murrough nodded. "Aye," he agreed. "It *is* like nothing you have ever seen."

"What are all those buildings over there?" Valentina pointed.

"That, cousin, is the Yeni Serai, the new palace, where your mother was once imprisoned. It is quite a gilded cage, I am told, with various palaces, treasuries, mosques, and gardens. The sultan and his family live there, and 'tis where you will meet his mother, the Sultan Valide. You will have more to tell me once that has happened than I can tell you now," Murrough said.

"Will we be docked near it?"

"No, we will be docked in the Golden Horn below the Jewish quarter of the city which is called Balata. Most merchantmen have sought their dockage there since the days of Constantine despite the fact that, even in ancient times, there were many other harbors around the city."

"May I leave the ship?" Valentina inquired.

"Only, cousin, under certain restrictions. This is Islam, Val, and you are a Christian woman. Unless you obey the laws of Islam, you could be vulnerable to public ridicule or insults at the very least, bodily harm at the worst. If you leave the ship, you must be accompanied by Nelda and several men who will be your bodyguards. You must travel in a closed litter. No respectable woman of the upper classes would do otherwise. And you must wear a yashmak. Nelda, too. Only with these precautions will you be able to move about the city in safety."

"What is a yashmak?" Valentina demanded.

"It is an outdoor garment that will cover you from your head to your feet, and you must be veiled as well."

"Veiled? Am I some harem girl to be veiled?" Valentina said irritably. "Really, Murrough, are these precautions necessary?"

"And," continued her cousin, "you will keep your eyes lowered modestly at all times. No decent woman looks a man in the eye when she is out in the streets."

"God's foot!" Valentina swore. "It is ridiculous! It is demeaning! I am an Englishwoman, not some downtrodden slave girl!"

"You will not go ashore, Val, unless you obey my instructions absolutely. My mother has charged me with your safety, and knowing what you do of Islam from both our mothers, you would be wise to heed me," Murrough said severely. "You gave my mother your word that you would obey my orders."

Valentina was anxious to meet with the elderly matriarch of the Kira family, the venerable Esther. The old lady had been unable to leave her home for several years, which was not surprising, considering her vast age. But if her body was failing her, Esther Kira's mind was as sharp and quick as it had ever been.

"When can we see Esther Kira?" Valentina demanded of her cousin at midmorning.

"This is Istanbul, Val, and things are done according to a set protocol here, even among those who are not royal." Murrough chuckled. "You must be patient."

At noon word came that Esther Kira would be pleased to receive them at two o'clock that afternoon.

In her cabin Valentina tried on the yashmak that Murrough had presented her with, grumbling, "It was not made to fit over a gown like mine. I will die of the heat! Nelda, call my cousin, the captain, and tell him it is impossible!" She had spent over an hour dressing in her finest gown in order to honor Esther Kira, and now she couldn't wear it!

Nelda disappeared, returning a few moments later with Geoff, who was carrying a small leather-bound trunk. "The captain's compliments, Cousin Valentina," said Geoff. "He apologizes for not giving ye this sooner, but he forgot. My grandmother ordered it put aboard for you. If ye will open it, ye will find the solution to all yer problems."

Valentina lifted the lid. Within were a half dozen garments in various lovely colors, all carefully packed. Drawing one forth, she asked, "What are these?"

"They are caftans, Cousin Valentina, the proper garb of Istanbul. Yer yashmak will fit quite nicely over them. My father says ye'll be cooler." The boy bowed, then hurried from the cabin.

"Lord, m'lady, they're lovely!" Nelda told her, moving closer for a better look. "Oh, do wear the rose-pink gown. 'Tis ever so flattering to your coloring!"

"This silk is magnificent," Valentina murmured, "and look at the embroidery and beading on this, Nelda. Why, I believe these must have once belonged to my Aunt Skye!" She removed her gown and peeled her petticoats away.

The young servant lowered the caftan over her mistress's head, and it slipped down to fall gracefully at Valentina's shoulders, flowing to her ankles. The V neckline was embroidered in pink-gold metallic threads and mauve crystal beads, as were the caftan's wide cuffs. With a chortle of delight, Nelda drew forth matching slippers. They fit Valentina's feet perfectly. The tiring woman brushed out her mistress's long dark hair and, braiding it again, fastened the single braid with a rose-colored ribbon embroidered with tiny white pearls.

"There, m'lady. You look beautiful—even if the clothes is foreign," Nelda observed.

By the time they were ready leave, Nelda had changed into a pretty blue caftan of her own, for at the bottom of the trunk were several plain but lovely garments and resting on them a piece of parchment with the words "For Nelda" written on it.

Murrough was awaiting them on deck, and he nodded with approval at the women's garb. Each was clad in an all-covering yashmak of dark blue silk. With a grin he affixed a veil across his cousin's face. It, too, was of dark blue silk, and when he had finished, nothing could be seen of Valentina except her mutinous amethyst eyes. Nelda, however, found her garb exciting.

"'Tis just like being in a fairy tale, m'lady," she said, giggling.

"I do not think I can breathe in this thing," Lady Barrows grumbled.

There were three well-mounted horses on the dock for Murrough, Padraic, and Tom. Beside them was an elegant litter, gilded and studded with precious jewels and hung with coral silk curtains. Valentina and Nelda were helped inside, where they found the litter awash in turquoise and coral velvet cushions. Eight black slaves, matched perfectly in height and build, all garbed in turquoise pantaloons with magnificent jewel-studded collars around their necks, lifted the litter as if it were weightless. Quickly they moved through the crowded docks.

Valentina longed to peek out from between the curtains and see what she could, up close, but Murrough's warnings about Islam prevailed. She did, however, loosen her veil on one side so that she might breathe more easily. She was amazed by the ease with which the litter bearers padded along in the afternoon heat, through streets that wound up a hill to Balata, the Jewish quarter. Throughout the journey, Nelda sat, her eyes wide with half-fright. For once, to her mistress's enormous relief, she was silent.

The bearers stopped, gently setting the litter down. They drew the curtains back, and Valentina quickly attached her veil again.

She accepted the hand that was offered her and stepped from the litter into a yellow-tiled courtyard. A tall, bearded young man in a long, striped robe, a small round cap on the back of his head, greeted Murrough, Padraic, and Tom. Then he came forward to greet Valentina.

"Lady Barrows, I am Simon Kira. I welcome you to our house."

"You speak English!"

"Indeed, my lady, I do, for I spent three years in London with the English Kiras, a year with the French Kiras in Paris, a year with the Hamburg branch of the family, and another year in Moscow. God willing, I will one day be head of the House of Kira, so it was necessary that I learn all I could of our more important banking centers."

"Is your grandmother not in good health, then, sir?" Valentina asked.

Simon Kira's warm brown eyes twinkled with good humor. "Esther Kira is my great-grandmother, Lady Barrows, and she is, as always, in excellent health. When Yahweh has taken her to his bosom, my father, Eli, will head the House of Kira. My grandfather, Solomon, died four years ago. No, it will be many years, God willing, before I must shoulder the responsibilities of this family. But come! I shall not live to see that day if I do not bring you to Esther at once. I can, even from here, hear her foot tapping with impatience."

"What language will I speak with her, Simon Kira?" Valentina politely inquired. "Murrough taught me Turkish during our voyage."

"Esther is fluent in French, Lady Barrows," he answered. "Gentlemen, you must come with us, for Esther's quarters are separate from the women's quarters. She does not like being denied access to visitors."

They followed Simon Kira from the lovely courtyard with its blue-and-yellow-tiled fountain. The house was shut off from the street by a windowless outer wall and two sturdy, iron-bound oak gates. The Kira home rose three stories from the main level and, unlike the majority of houses in Istanbul, which were built of wood, the Kira house was made of white-washed brick. Esther Kira's quarters were on the main floor, overlooking the gardens that in turn overlooked the city. The Kira house sat upon the highest point of Balata, and because it was so clearly visible, had been cleverly designed to appear a bit more modest than it was. The large wall blocked the gardens and many windows from view. The Kiras knew better than to flaunt their wealth. Still, the house was imposing. And the interior was splendid. The double oak doors into Esther Kira's apartments were overlaid with gold leaf, and the inside of the matriarch's salon was a testament to luxury. A tiled fountain poured forth scented water. The conical hood over the fireplace was of silver, as were the six ruby-glass lamps. The windows facing the gardens were actually glass doors extending from floor to ceiling, which gave Esther access to her beloved gardens. The carpets on the polished wooden floors were so thick that feet sank into them. The furniture was of ebony and other precious woods, inlaid with mother-of-pearl and semiprecious stones.

In the center of all this splendor sat a small woman with snow-white hair and lively black eyes. She was dressed in a heavily embroidered gown of peacock-blue silk, and decked in rich gold jewelry except for her hands. She wore no rings other than an enormous diamond that sparkled with red and blue fires.

"So," she addressed them in a surprisingly strong voice, "you have finally managed to bring our visitors to me, Simon. Well, well, do not stand there! Introduce them to me!" Her dark eyes darted from face to face.

Simon Kira smiled lovingly at the old woman. It was obvious that he adored her. He introduced the three men, and Esther greeted them cordially, but her gaze kept moving to the two veiled women.

"Take your yashmaks off," she finally commanded impatiently, and when they had laid the garments aside and turned back to her, she studied them both carefully. Finally, her eyes on Valentina's face, she said, "You are far more beautiful than your mother ever was, daughter of Marjallah."

For a long moment, Valentina said nothing. At last she stepped forward and knelt before Esther Kira. Taking the old woman's hands in hers, she kissed them both. "Thank you, Esther Kira," she said quietly. "Thank you for saving my mother's life so many years ago."

"Get up, child, and sit by me." Esther Kira smiled at her. She waved the others to seats.

"Marjallah. I know that was what my mother was called here," Valentina said. "What does it mean?"

"It means a gift from the sea, and as your mother was brought over the sea from Algiers to the sultan's seraglio, that is what she was named. But tell me, child, what is it you seek? Why have you made the long journey from your home to Istanbul?"

"I have come to learn the truth of my paternal parentage, Esther Kira," Valentina responded nervously, then plunged into an explanation of her plight.

Esther Kira listened carefully, and when Valentina had finally finished speaking, she said, "Child, child! You seek the impossible! Only Yahweh himself knows the answer to your question."

"I cannot be satisfied until I have learned the truth, Esther Kira, and I pray I will be able to learn the truth some how, some way," Valentina replied firmly. "I know that the wicked sultan who enslaved my mother is long dead, and his mother as well, but I also know that his favorite, the current Sultan Valide is living. I would speak with Safiye, Esther Kira. She knew Sultan Murad best, and I believe she may be able to tell me if I am his daughter. When I decided to make this journey, I knew I might return home without being certain who my father was, but I must try."

The old woman shook her head. "It will not be easy, child," she said. "Safiye was always a high-strung creature. Only the Valide Nur-U-Banu's firm hand kept her in check, and that clever lady died nineteen years ago. Since then Safiye's power has grown and grown. She is not the woman your mother knew. She is greedy and venal and lives for two things only—gold and power.

"When Nur-U-Banu died, Safiye hoped that she could regain Murad's complete attention, but the sultan, having developed a taste for other women, was not of a mind to change his ways. Why should he, when the empire and all the surrounding lands were continually combed for the fairest and most nubile of virgins for his pleasure alone? Safiye grew older, but Murad forgot the years, for he was constantly surrounded by youth. Mind you, the sultan always gave Safiye the respect due the mother of his heir, but it was not enough. Safiye grew terribly embittered.

"Other sons were born to Murad, nineteen in addition to Safiye's son, Mehmed, and eighty-three daughters, twenty-seven of whom are living. Prince Mehmed, the heir, was indulged and spoiled dreadfully by his mother, who had no one else to love but her son. When he was denied anything, the boy's temper was terrible, dreadful in its intensity. He reminded me then of his great-grandmother, Khurrem. Prince Mehmed was sent away from Istanbul to govern a province. When Sultan Murad died, the boy, by then a man, was quickly brought back to the city and proclaimed sultan. With that, Safiye Kadin became the Sultan Valide Safiye, the most powerful woman in the empire. Can you guess what her first act was?"

Valentina shook her head.

"She advised her son to murder his nineteen half brothers. Mehmed obeyed her. He sent for his siblings, who ranged in age from eleven to infancy. He assured them that they had nothing to fear from him. He said he wished them to be circumcised, for they had not yet been. After each boy was circumcised, he was led into a room for what was supposed to be a ritual bath. Instead, the executioners awaited. Every one of those innocents was strangled!

"Her bloodlust not sated, Safiye instructed her son to dispose of the seven of his father's women who were pregnant and so those poor girls were sewn into silken sacks and drowned in the Marmara off the Prince's island.

"Her son's position secured, Safiye then secured her own. Murad's entire harem was sent to the Eski Serai, the old palace. Safiye began to populate the seraglio with her own creatures. Sultan Mehmed is completely under her control, for she understands and feeds his lusts, even as Nur-U-Banu fed Murad's. Mehmed is a strange man, given to great kindnesses and even greater cruelties. He not only murdered his brothers but he had his own eldest son, Prince Mahmud, and Mahmud's mother and her favorite companions all killed as well.

"Are you certain now that you wish to meet the woman who produced such a son? Besides, Safiye does not know that your mother survived her execution. Though it happened twenty-three years ago and in another reign, I cannot be certain how she will react when she learns the truth. She was your mother's friend, so she may be glad. For some reason, your mother never made Safiye jealous, as others did. Perhaps, just perhaps, if you truly desire it, it can be arranged."

"I must go to Kaffa first," replied Valentina. "I would speak with the family of Javid Khan in regard to this matter. That will give you time, Esther Kira, for I will be gone for two or three months. Perhaps after I go to Kaffa, it will not even be necessary for me to discuss this with the valide. Although I must leave for Kaffa almost immediately, when I return I should appreciate the opportunity to pay my respects to Safiye. We have brought a message from Safiye's brother that their father has recovered from his illness. Our message can be my excuse to gain an audience with her.

"If it is necessary for me to speak with her about my parentage, can I not claim that you knew nothing of my mother's rescue or who I am? After all, I do not look like my mother. I shall tell the valide that an English ship was passing by as the executioner dropped the sack into the sea and the sailors aboard the ship, being familiar with that form of execution, dove in and and rescued my mother, whom they then returned home. After all, my mother's husband is part of an important trading family. Learning her identity, the captain anticipated a reward! It is not necessary that your role in the rescue be revealed, Esther Kira."

"Aiiii! You may not look like your mother, but you have her quick wit, child! That is just the sort of story Safiye would believe. Accidental rescue, and no one to blame! Her dear friend safe, praise Yahweh. Or Allah. Or whoever. A wonderfully romantic tale, and for all her wickedness, Safiye is a fool for a fairy tale! Aye, it will be just the thing, but for one alteration. Safiye must be told that I know who you are because you came to me today and told me. This will ensure that she will agree to see you. She is like a child that way. She will be intrigued and fascinated by it all. Do not, however, tell her that I helped in your mother's rescue. No, let all of that seem a wonderful accident of fate."

"But how will you see her, Esther?" asked her great-grandson. "You have not left this house in three years. Your body is far too frail, and Sarai will have my head if I even suggest that you have called for your litter."

"Heh, heh!" the old lady cackled. "Do not fear, Simon, I shall not endanger you with Sarai. The valide will come to me if I invite her. I have remained her friend in spite of it all, for when one commits to a friendship in this life, one accepts one's friend, warts and all, for do our friends not accept us the same way? Heh! Heh!" She chuckled to herself.

"Then I shall go on to Kaffa, safe in the knowledge that the valide will invite me into her presence when I return," said Valentina.

"As God wills it, child," came the reply. "Now, our business over with, you must tell me of your mother's good fortunes these many years. Simon, take the gentlemen away and discuss your business with Captain O'Flaherty. After they have had refreshment, you may return."

When the men had gone, Esther Kira instructed her servants to bring fruit sherbets, mint tea, and an assortment of honey cakes. As they sat indulging their appetites, Valentina related to Esther Kira the path her mother's life had taken during the past twenty-three years.

"Seven children," said Esther approvingly. "Your mother did well by your father. And now she is to be a grandmother. It is hard for me to believe."

"It is hard for me to believe also, Esther Kira, for my mother has not changed very much over the years. She has always seemed so sensible and . . . and peaceful. Can you imagine my shock when I learned of her adventures in Istanbul!" exclaimed Valentina.

The old lady cackled with dry humor. "Children never believe that their parents could have had any life before them, let alone an exciting life. Look at me! All you can see is a wizened old woman, but once I was as fresh and young as you are, and oh, what times I had! Now I sit, my limbs crippled so that I can barely walk, like an ancient old spider right in the midst of this web that I have woven. Do you know, I enjoy it. I have liked every moment that God has given me, for each age has its compensations as well as its difficulties. I have even outlived my children. I have seen many about me grow old and never cease to complain about it. It is their constant carping that has really made them old. Age is but another step in the natural cycle of life. We are growing old from the moment of our birth. My mind has always been the most active part of me, daughter of Marjallah. And now, even if my body refuses to cooperate, I still have my wits about me! Heh! Heh! Heh!"

"Just how old are you, Esther Kira?" Valentina demanded.

"I will be one hundred and twelve years of age on the first day of April, my child. How old are you?"

"I will be twenty-two on the twenty-first of March, Esther Kira" was the awed reply.

"Today is the twenty-first of March, child," Esther Kira said softly. "How strange that you should arrive in Istanbul on this day of all days. I wish you felicitations on your natal day."

There was a sudden knocking at the door connecting Esther's apartment to the rest of the Kira house. A servant opened it to admit a richly dressed Turk. "Esther Kira!" he said in a deep, mellow voice as he entered the room. "I had business with your grandson, Eli, and could not leave the house without stopping to see you." His eyes flickered to Valentina, then back to the old woman.

"My lord vizier, you honor me with your presence. Sit! Sit! How is your princess wife?" Esther Kira spoke to him in French so that Valentina could be part of the conversation.

"Quite well, Esther Kira," replied the vizier in the same language, understanding the reason for his hostess' choice. "Will you introduce me to your beautiful visitor? She does not look like a Jewess of your family." He turned his blue-gray eyes on Valentina with frank curiosity.

"My lord vizier, I would present to you Lady Valentina Barrows, an Englishwoman. She is the daughter of an old friend of mine whose family does business with my family. You are correct. She is no Jewess. Valentina, my child," she continued, turning her gaze to Lady Barrows, "I would present to you Cicalazade Pasha, Grand Vizier to his Imperial Majesty, Sultan Mehmed, may Yahweh grant him a thousand years!"

"You are English! My second wife was a Scot," the vizier said. "The women of your race have independent spirits, which I find very exciting." His gaze locked with hers, and he leaned forward. "You have magnificent eyes, lady. They are like jewels."

"You are gracious to say so, my lord vizier," Valentina said, discomfited by his look and his bold words. "I have never met a man with two wives," she finished, very much at a loss for words and uncertain as to whether it was polite to speak of such things. Esther Kira did not seem distressed, however, so she concentrated on seeming relaxed.

The vizier laughed, showing perfect, strong white teeth against his tanned skin. "I *had* two wives," he said. "My second wife died several years ago. It was most unfortunate. She was very beautiful, and she delighted me greatly. Her name was Incili, which means Perfect Pearl."

"I had heard that the men of Islam were entitled to four wives," Valentina said. "It would appear that you are a most conservative man where women are concerned, my lord vizier."

"Because I have only one wife?" His eyes were dancing with merriment. "My first wife is Lateefa Sultan, an Ottoman princess, lady. I can take additional wives only with her permission, for that is a perogative of royal Ottoman females. I do not, however, need her permission to maintain a harem, and I believe I have well over one hundred women in my harem at present. Men of Islam do not believe that a woman must be a wife in order to pleasure a man."

"My lord Cicalazade, for shame!" scolded Esther Kira. "You will shock Lady Barrows with such talk."

The vizier laughed. "Do I shock you, lady?" he asked her, his blue-gray eyes mocking her silently.

"If I were to apply my country's morals to your behavior, my lord vizier, then perhaps I should be shocked," Valentina replied coolly, refusing to be intimidated. "But I am well aware that, in Islam, things are different. I can see certain advantages to a harem."

"Indeed, lady? What advantages do you see?" He was mocking her openly now, and enjoying his game very much.

"To a man, the advantages are obvious, my lord vizier, for like a honeybee, he can flit from flower to flower, never wanting for variety. For a woman, however, there is the advantage that if she detests her lord and master, she does not have to bear his company very often, not in a large harem, at any rate. If she is clever, he need never know of her dislike, and her jewelry case would be well filled by her grateful, unsuspecting lord. 'Tis most practical, I think," Valentina concluded.

Brief anger sprang into the vizier's eyes, but it was quickly masked and he said softly, "If you were my slave, lady, I should quite enjoy taming that wild spirit of yours. Such beautiful lips were made for kissing, not releasing unseemly thoughts into harsh words."

This is dangerous, thought Esther Kira. I have not seen such interest in Cicalazade Pasha's eyes since Incili. He is a ruthless man, and Yahweh only knows what would happen if Marjallah's daughter were to remain in Istanbul.

"My thoughts, my lord vizier," said Valentina sweetly, heaping fuel on the fire, "are but those of my independent spirit."

Cicalazade Pasha laughed once more with genuine amusement. "Lady, you do, indeed, have an independent spirit. Tell me, is it this spirit that sends you so far from your homeland? Where is your husband?"

"I travel with members of my own family, my lord vizier. I am a widow, and my parents believed I should ease my mourning better away from England. We travel to Kaffa on business, then we will return home."

"Will you come back again to Istanbul, lady?" he asked with a smile.

"I am attempting to obtain an audience with the valide for Lady Barrows," said Esther Kira. "Valentina has been kind enough to bring a message to Safiye from her brother in Venice."

"If I may be of any help to you, Esther Kira, do ask—though you have far more influence with the royal Ottoman family than I do, despite my being married to one of its members." The vizier chuckled.

"You flatter me, my lord vizier," the old woman said.

"Hah, you wily old female, I speak the truth! It is you who seek to flatter me," the vizier said with a smile. He rose. "Now I will take my leave of you, having satisfied myself that you are alive and as wicked as ever."

"Heh! Heh! Heh!" Esther Kira chortled, and she wagged a finger at him. "Do not forget to bring my love to your lady wife. Tell her if she should decide to set her foot in Balata, I would welcome a visit from her. I have not been able to get about a great deal on my own since I broke my hipbone."

Cicalazade Pasha turned to Lady Barrows. "Valentina," he mused. "From the Latin, *valentis,* meaning strong. Aye, you are indeed, strong. We will meet again, lady. That I promise you." His white cape swirled about him as he left the apartment.

"That," said Esther Kira, "is a dangerous man."

"You told me he is the sultan's grand vizier, Esther Kira, but who is he, really? He has a most commanding air about him."

"His mother was the daughter of Ferhad Bey of Morea. Her name was Fatima. She was captured by Christian knights when she was a girl. After converting to Christianity, she wed her captor, Giovanni Antonio di Cicala, an Italian count. She bore him three children, two sons and a daughter. The elder of her sons went off to fight the infidel at the age of eighteen and was captured by the Turks. Following his mother's instructions for such an emergency, he proclaimed his noble birth and his Turkish mother. He was converted immediately to Islam. His actions saved him from the mines. His intelligence noted, he was sent to Istanbul to the Prince's School, where the empire's public servants are educated.

"He moved slowly up the ladder of success by virtue of his intellect and hard work. He stands very high with Sultan Mehmed, for he saved the sultan's honor in battle years ago by turning a rout of Ottoman forces into a great victory. Mehmed will not forget that. His wife is Lateefa Sultan, the sultan's cousin. She is a kind and lovely woman who has given him three sons and two daughters. They are good friends, and he respects her greatly, even asking her advice on rare occasions. She, in turn, does not complain about the size of his harem, for Cicalazade Pasha has a huge appetite for women. His harem is famed for its variety of beauties. He prizes intelligence as well as beauty."

"What of his second wife, the one who died? The Scotswoman?" Valentina was quite curious.

"Ah, Incili!" The old woman's eyes clouded. "Ah, yes! The vizier was away on business for the sultan. Incili loved a little island that the vizier owned in the Bosporus. She begged to be allowed time to herself on the Island of a Thousand Flowers while her lord and master was away. No one really knows what happened to her, but she died, and the eunuchs guarding her attempted to cover it up and claimed to have executed her servant girl for her negligence in caring for her mistress. The vizier's head eunuch, Hammid, executed the eunuchs even before the master returned. Although Cicalazade Pasha was inconsolable for many months, he did forgive Hammid in the end. The creature is, unfortunately, irreplaceable, and he had, after all, done his best. Incili had gone to the island many times before her death, and there had never been any difficulty. It has remained a mystery."

"What do you think happened to her, Esther Kira?" Valentina was intrigued. Listening to the old lady was like hearing the most wonderful fairy stories. The usually voluble Nelda hadn't uttered one word since they had arrived; her large dark eyes had simply stared all about the room, taking it all in so as to report everything to her mother, who would doubtless refuse to believe a word of it.

"What happened? What happened? Perhaps Incili fell from the top of the cliffs where the vizier's little palace was. Perhaps she drowned in the pool or choked on a bone. Who knows? All that is certain is that the eunuchs guarding her panicked and behaved badly."

"Poor girl!" Valentina said sympathetically. "Was she very beautiful?"

The old lady nodded. "Aye, child, she was. She was very beautiful, indeed, but more important, her heart was brave and good."

There was a knock once more on the door to the salon, and the gentlemen came in. "It is time for Lady Barrows to leave now,

Esther," said Simon Kira. "They must get back to the harbor and be underway before the Sabbath begins, else they cannot go for another day."

"Aiiii!" the old lady exclaimed. "You are right, Simon. Such a place we live in! Such a place! The men of Islam celebrate their Sabbath on Friday, we Jews on Saturday, and the Christians on Sunday! There are but four days of the week during which we can all do business, but at least here in Istanbul we recognize the right of the other faiths to exist."

Valentina rose from the marvelously comfortable pillows and, bending, kissed Esther Kira's soft, wrinkled old face. The elderly woman smelled of spring flowers, a contrast with Esther Kira's most practical nature. It was the fragrance of a young girl.

"Farewell, dear friend," Valentina said softly. "I will be back in several months. Perhaps Safiye will be ready to see me by then. Thank you for all you have done! Not just today, but for the many yesterdays."

"Travel safely, child, and may Yahweh be with you," Esther Kira answered. "Beware the Tatars, for they are a fierce, cruel people. Do not run recklessly into danger."

"I will not, Esther Kira. I seek only to speak with the mother of Javid Khan, as one woman to another."

Esther Kira shook her head. "I do not know what she can tell you, child, but go. Your spirit will not rest unless you do. I will look for your return by the end of spring."

They departed from the Kira house, traveling down the narrow, winding streets from Balata. The late-afternoon heat was fierce. As they approached the waterfront, Valentina and Nelda heard the hum of fierce activity as those sailors anxious to be on their way hurried to leave the Golden Horn before sunset and the restrictions of the Islamic Sabbath.

Their papers were in order, and the harbor master stamped them. The ships' lines were loosened from the quay and *Archangel* and her sister vessels slipped down the Golden Horn into the Bosporus straits.

Leaning against the ship's rail, free of her yashmak and veil, Valentina watched the city as she sailed away from it. It was hard to believe that just this morning they had arrived in Istanbul, and the wheels were now in motion for her audience with the sultan's mother. Perhaps, however, she reminded herself, she would not need that audience. Perhaps she would learn in Kaffa that it was Javid Khan who was her real father. Did she want a

Tatar prince for her father? But did she want a half-mad Turkish
sultan for her father either? Conn's face rose up before her, and
her eyes filled with tears.

"Oh, Papa," she whispered, "how I wish Mag had never opened
this Pandora's box!" Then his words came back to her.

"I *am* your father, my dear. Believe me. . . . I have loved you
from the moment I knew of your coming. . . . *You are my child.*"

"Oh, I want to believe you, Papa," she sobbed, the tears flowing
freely.

"Hinny love, what is it?" Padraic was at her side. Turning her
to face him, he said, "Sweetheart, don't cry! What is it?"

How could she tell him now after having dragged them all so
far from England? How could she tell them that she wished she
had never begun this quest, that she wished they were home?
She couldn't. They were so close to the Khanate of the Crimea.
What was the harm in seeking just a little bit farther? "It is my
birthday," she said, sobbing, "and no one has remembered! Not
even me! Not until Esther Kira reminded me."

"I remembered," he said softly. Reaching into his doublet, he
drew out a delicate gold chain from which hung a heart-shaped
pink diamond surrounded by pearls. "Happy Birthday, Val," he
said, slipping it about her neck. Tipping her face up to his, he
kissed her.

"Oh, Padraic!" Her arms went about his neck, and she kissed
him back.

"Oh, Valentina!" he answered, and his lips found hers once
again. Smiling down into her face, he said, "There is nothing
about you that I will ever forget. Remember that when you make
your decision, hinny love. Remember it!"

Chapter Eight

THE VOYAGE ACROSS THE BLACK SEA to Kaffa, capital city of
the Crimean khanate, was as pleasant as the rest of their trip had
been. The original inhabitants of the peninsula had been the
Tauri, descendants of the Cimmerians. The Tauri were followed

over the next thousand years by Greeks, Romans, Goths, Huns, Khazars, Byzantine Greeks, Mongols, and Genoese. The Tatars had entered the peninsula a hundred and twenty-five years earlier with the help of the Turks, whom they accepted as overlords in this area.

Kaffa had always been a merchant city. Once it had been a terminus of the overland route to China, and the city was a polyglot of races and religions. It had reached its zenith under the Genoese, but the rich minority merchant class of Kaffa had been cruel masters of the majority of poor. There had been, therefore, at least five serious uprisings in the last years of Genoese rule, which had ended on June 6, 1475.

The merchants of the city acted as middlemen to traders whose caravans arrived daily. They brokered everything from plain goods, such as grain, wax, fish, salt, wood, leather, honey, and cooking oil, to more exotic items like furs from Muscovy, wines from Greece, ivory from Africa, precious gemstones from Asia and India, fine cloth from Italy, caviar, and Asian musk. Kaffa was also the most important slave trade center for the entire khanate of the Crimea. Tens of thousands of captives passed through Kaffa's slave markets on their way to Turkey and other Mediterranean and Black Sea destinations.

Valentina had expected a savage backwater. Instead she found Kaffa a bustling, beautiful city of busy streets and magnificent Italian architecture as seen in the towers, walls, and palaces of the city.

"It is not as prosperous as it once was," Murrough told his cousin. "Since its fall to the Tatars and the Turks in 1475, Kaffa is but a shadow of its former self. Neither the Turks nor the Tatars have a knack for business. Conquest is their strength. Kaffa's small continuing prosperity is due to the Jewish community, some remaining Genoese, and a few Venetians."

They had no sooner docked when a gentleman hurried aboard. By the small skullcap on the back of his head, Valentina knew him for a Jew.

Murrough, smiling broadly, bowed to their visitor. "Levi Kira, I thought you might be here to greet us," he said in Turkish.

The gentleman, very tall and thin with a most ascetic face, smiled broadly. It was a kind smile, wholly out of keeping with his solemn appearance, and it brought a warm light to his dark eyes. "Welcome again to Kaffa, Murrough O'Flaherty. My grandmother informed me of your coming. I am to tell you that the

Turkish governor, Arslan Bey, awaits you as soon as you are able
to come to the governor's palace."

"Does Javid Khan's mother still live, Levi Kira? Will it be possible to see her?" Murrough asked.

"Borte Khatun is alive. She is not in the city, however. The
Geray Tatars left two weeks ago for their summer trek. You will
have to either wait until the autumn, when they return, or go
after them—which could prove most dangerous. The renegade,
Temur Khan, has been raiding this spring. We thought we had
seen the last of him, for he disappeared several years ago, going
toward the east. But he has returned like a bad dream to haunt
us. Temur Khan seems to have more lives than a cat," Levi Kira
finished.

"I thought Temur Khan was dead!" Valentina burst out.

"My cousin, Lady Barrows," Murrough said dryly.

Levi Kira nodded politely to Valentina. "Dead, my lady? Where
did you hear such a thing? Would that it were true, for Temur
Khan has cost every merchant in this city dearly with his pillaging
of caravans. He steals our goods, which he then boldly sells back
to us at inflated prices. He and his men rape and destroy valuable
slaves without a thought. He is a violent, vicious man. Temur
Khan dead? May it be from your mouth to Yahweh's ear, my
lady!"

"I understood, that he was killed years ago by the sultan's janissaries after he murdered his brother, Prince Javid Khan, at the
prince's home outside Istanbul. Is that not so?" Valentina asked,
thanking God and Murrough that she was able to speak Turkish
so well.

"Alas, no, my lady. I remember hearing of that incident. The
self-important janissaries believed they had killed Temur Khan,
but they were so anxious to return to Istanbul with the story of
their great victory that they neglected to decapitate their victims.
After they had gone, Temur Khan and three of his men who also
survived returned to the Crimea. He quickly built a new force,
for there are always malcontents who are anxious to join with a
man such as Temur Khan."

"But why, if he is so cruel?" Valentina wondered aloud.

"Once, my lady, the Tatars were the roamers of the steppes.
They did not live in cities as they do today. It was not that long
ago, either. Now, the old Tatars tell their tales of a winter's night,
and the Tatar youths listen to those tales of their glorious past.
Some, the restless, the discontented, cannot reconcile them-

selves to their present condition. It is not enough for them to raid Russia for slaves. They want more, and Temur Khan appeals to them. He gives no fealty to the Turks or any other. He does as he pleases, plundering and murdering, and there are young men who admire him for it and follow him. He professes to follow the old ways of the Tatar," Levi Kira explained. "But he is a dangerous and evil man."

"I *must* get to Javid Khan's mother," Valentina said to Murrough. "Let us go and see the Turkish governor now! Then we can start immediately. Today!"

Levi Kira looked at Murrough, amused. "Your cousin is an impatient lady," he observed.

"Aye," Murrough answered. "She is." He turned his attention to Valentina. "You are *not* going to see the Turkish governor. Arslan Bey would be insulted if a mere woman demanded an audience with him," he said. *"And,"* he continued, raising his hand to forestall protests, "we are not starting today. I am not easy in my mind about exposing you to the dangers of a journey on the steppes, particularly in light of the fact that Temur Khan is thereabouts. I must think on it. If I allow you to accompany us, it will only be because we have a goodly party to travel with, Val."

Valentina knew she could not dispute Murrough's judgment. "Then go and see the Ottoman governor," she said. "I will await your return. But hurry, Murrough!"

Arslan Bey was known to Murrough O'Flaherty, for the captain had traveled the Black Sea trade lanes for many years, and Arslan Bey, a loyal civil servant of the sultan, had represented his master in Kaffa for fifteen years. He was a mild-mannered man with a taste for comfortable living and an open-minded practical nature. The two men greeted each other as old friends, and Murrough explained that his widowed cousin had a message that only she could deliver to the Great Khan's mother. They had not realized, Murrough explained, that the Geray Tatars might not be in Kaffa.

"They persist in roaming the steppes every summer," said Arslan Bey with a bemused expression. "I do not understand. In the winter, the steppes are bitter cold and extremely windy. In the summer they are no more hospitable, being arid and hot. Here in Kaffa the climate is mild and healthful, but nevertheless, between the second and third moons of spring, the Geray Tatars depart from Kaffa, their own capital, and we do not see them back here until the first and second moons of autumn."

"Do you know where they go?" Murrough asked.

"Oh, yes," the sultan's governor replied. "I am always in touch with them."

"Then perhaps you would help us. I will have to put a party together and travel to their camp with my cousin."

"You would allow a woman to travel with you?" Arslan Bey was horrified. "Oh, no, no, no, my friend! It is much too dangerous for a helpless woman to travel to the camp of the Geray Tatars. Temur Khan is raiding this year!"

"I had thought to disguise my cousin as a young man," Murrough said, "and she is quite competent at riding astride. Would it not be possible under those conditions to get to the Geray Tatars? We would be an armed party of men, no caravan of goods ripe for pillaging."

"Aye, under those circumstances, it might be possible. Unless, of course, Temur Khan is spoiling for a fight at the time you choose to travel," the governor noted. "I have a better idea, built upon your idea."

"I am listening, Arslan Bey," Murrough told him.

"Each week I send a party of six men to the encampment of the Geray Tatars, who move only about three times each season. I am always kept informed as to their whereabouts. The Great Khan and I conduct our business in this way, through my men, while he is away. I keep him informed about everything he needs to know, and he is able to communicate with me."

"Temur Khan never bothers my men, for they carry nothing of value to him. Even the information they bear with them is easily obtainable elsewhere should Temur Khan desire it. My messengers depart tomorrow. What if you, your cousin, and one other take the place of three of my men and travel with them? I can offer you only three places. You would reach the Great Khan quickly and safely."

Murrough thought a moment, then said, "Would there not be gossip regarding the replacement of three of your men by three strangers, Arslan Bey?"

"Not if no one knows," the governor replied. "My men must report to me before they leave. You and your people will be brought into the palace secretly. You will replace three of the men who will be quietly concealed in the palace for the length of time it will take you to conclude your business with Borte

Khatun and return. My own personal body slave, who is mute, will see to the comfort of those detained. He could not speak of the matter even if he desired to. The captain of this group will be told, just before he sets off for the steppes, to pick his two most trustworthy men. There will be no time for any gossip to escape into the city regarding this matter. I will supply you and your party with the proper clothing."

"The sultan does not misplace his judgment in trusting you, Arslan Bey. You are an extremely clever man," Murrough noted. "Let it be as you have said. I thank you kindly for your help. Instruct me as to how we are to enter the palace without being seen, and we shall be here at the appointed hour."

The governor smiled, pleased at the flattery, and then said, "Give me today to make my arrangements. You must tell me, however, whether your cousin is large or small, tall or short, if I am to have the proper garb for her." His tone indicated that he did not think a great deal of a woman who could be disguised as a man, let alone one able to ride astride. "And what of your other companion? Who will he be?"

"I shall choose one of my people when I return to the ship," Murrough answered. "I have one of two men in mind, but I am not certain yet which one to choose. Both, however, are big men. As for my cousin, she is tall for a woman, about your height, I should say, and slender as well."

"Look for my servant tomorrow. He will bring you what you will need as well as a message from me telling you how to enter the palace."

The two men took their leave of each other, and Murrough returned to the ship to report on the interview. Valentina was delighted, but neither Padraic nor the earl looked pleased.

"Which of us is to go?" Lord Kempe demanded.

"You would both like to go, of course," noted Murrough.

"Aye!" They said in unison.

"I, of course, must go," Murrough said, "and so I will need one of you to remain behind to be the authority in command aboard the *Archangel*. Does one of you prefer that task?"

They glowered at him.

Murrough laughed. "I thought not. You will have to dice for it. The highest throw will win."

"Why not simply choose one of them?" Valentina said.

"Because," Murrough replied, "if I choose Padraic, then Tom will think I have favored him because he is my sibling. If I choose

Tom, then Padraic will think that I am treating him like my 'little' brother instead of the man he is. By leaving it to chance, neither of your eager suitors has anyone to blame but fate."

Valentina smiled. Her cousin was wise.

"Get the dice!" Padraic ordered Geoff, and the lad instantly complied.

"Give them to me," Valentina said. Taking the ivories, she hid them behind her back, switching them from hand to hand until she was sure that neither man knew for certain in which hand the dice were. Holding out her tightly closed fists, she said, "Choose."

"Right!" said the earl.

Valentina opened her hands to reveal the dice nestling within the palm of her left hand. "You have the first toss," she told Padraic, who grinned broadly, extremely pleased.

He threw a three and glowered furiously. The earl barely attempted to hide his glee as he took the dice, but his triumph was short-lived. He threw a two.

Murrough allowed his brother no time to gloat. Neither would he allow the earl any time for regrets. "It is settled," he said bluntly. "Tom, I know you have had some experience with ships, having sailed with Her Majesty's privateers in your youth. And you certainly have the experience of command, having been with Essex at Cádiz and in Ireland. I shall have no fears for *Archangel* knowing that she is in your hands."

"Should Valentina not remain behind with Temur Khan about?" the earl inquired hopefully.

"Valentina will be disguised as a young man." Murrough chuckled. "There is, I am assured by Arslan Bey, no danger involved."

"*Valentina, a boy*? Impossible!" the earl said. "She is the most perfect woman I know. You could hide her hair, and put her in pants, but how the hell are you going to disguise her. . . . . ah, her. . . . . her bosom damnit! Her chest will surely give her away, Murrough."

"There are ways, Tom"—Murrough chuckled—"of even hiding such bounteous charms as my cousin possesses. Wait and see."

Although Lord Burke said nothing, his look was as skeptical as was the earl's. It disturbed him that Valentina could be exposed to danger, even death.

"How long will you be away from me, divinity?" Tom Ashburne

asked Valentina that evening as they strolled the deck. "I think fate a most unkind bitch to have given the toss of the dice to Padraic." His arm stole about her waist.

"Perhaps ten days or more," Valentina said. "Murrough tells me it is several days' ride from Kaffa to the Tatar encampment." She removed his arm, for she was in no mood for romance now.

"Damn it, Val, I shall not see you for a good two weeks! Will you not let me press my suit tonight?"

She gave him a stony look, and he said, "Will you at least kiss me before you go?"

Valentina laughed softly. "Your singlemindedness does you credit, my lord. Very well. One kiss, but no more. I will not have my brain befuddled by passion at a time when I need my wits about me."

"You are so practical, divinity, and yet I have known you to be otherwise," he teased her.

"The art of practicality is something I learned at my mother's knee, sir, and if I am in doubt as to my paternal parentage, I have no doubts as to my mater," she teased him back. Then with a small smile, she raised her face to his, and he kissed her.

It was a tender kiss, for he had been warned and did not wish to get into her bad books. "You are becoming a hard woman," he complained, reluctantly drawing his mouth away.

"Only sensible, my lord. I must be, and so should you. I did not invite either you or Padraic along on this journey, Tom. 'Twas each of you who invited yourself. Until I have unriddled this riddle, I shall not be satisfied."

"I do not know how you can unriddle it, Valentina," he replied. "Unless you are the mirror image of either the prince or the late sultan, I do not know how you can be certain either of those men fathered you. I think your family mad to have allowed you this journey!"

"My lord, it is obvious that you do not understand me at all," said Valentina, "and so I shall bid you good night."

She left him, and he stood at the rail, looking up at the star-brilliant sky. He loved her. He did not understand why Lord and Lady Bliss had not simply accepted either him or Lord Burke as a son-in-law and pushed Valentina to the altar once her mourning was up. She should be married now and preparing for her children, not traveling about the world in a futile pursuit to a question that could probably never be answered! He loved her. He adored her, and the truth of her paternal heritage meant nothing to him.

He wanted her for his wife, yet he absolutely did not understand her.

In the late hours of the night, while the Earl of Kempe tossed restlessly, four muffled figures departed from the ship and disappeared into the darkness of the city. They moved swiftly through the deserted streets in total silence until at last their leader brought them to a wall with a small locked door, which he unlocked and locked again behind them. They continued down a flight of steps into a well-lit tunnel.

"My friend!" the governor welcomed Murrough as they exited the tunnel into a small, windowless room.

The two men clasped hands in greeting, then Murrough said, "My lord governor, may I present my younger brother, Lord Padraic Burke, and my cousin, Lady Valentina Barrows. You may speak directly to my cousin, my lord governor, for she understands your tongue."

The governor and Lord Burke clasped hands, and then Arslan Bey salaamed to Valentina. "As you are such a handsome gentleman, my lady, I can but imagine what a beautiful woman you must be. I hesitate to allow you to depart on such a journey as you are proposing to make. Is it really necessary for you to speak with Borte Khatun now? Can you not wait until she returns to Kaffa in the autumn?"

Valentina smiled at the governor, and he suddenly realized that she was, indeed, a beautiful woman. "You are most kind, my lord, to distress yourself so about my safety, but I must seek out Borte Khatun as soon as possible. I am expected back in Istanbul by the end of May for an audience with the Sultan Valide. It would not do, I am told, to offend that lady. I am certain that I shall be safe traveling with my cousins and your men."

Arslan Bey shook his head ruefully. "There is no arguing with a determined woman, and I should know it. I have three wives and seven daughters, all of whom have a strong streak of stubbornness. Go if you must, lady, and Allah be with you, for you will surely need his protection if you come to the attention of Temur Khan." The govenor turned again to Murrough. "She is, indeed, tall for a woman," he said, "but her height may help to disguise her." He eyed Valentina critically. "If I did not know better, I should be convinced she was a pretty young man. One thing, however, if I may." He signaled to his servant, who came forward with a little tray. Arslan Bey lifted a counterfeit mustache from the tray. "I think, if you will wear this, my lady, your disguise will be perfect. Baba will affix it for you, showing you how, and he will supply you with a tiny pot of glue to carry along with you so that you may repair your mustache daily."

The mute slave led Valentina to a mirror, then carefully showed her precisely how to place the mustache below her nose, above her upper lip. It was a small mustache, dark, with little pointed ends. The transformation was miraculous. The pretty young man disappeared, and Valentina became a very handsome male. Even she was astounded as she gazed wide-eyed into the mirror.

"I do not," she decided, "look like any of my brothers."

"None of your brothers has a mustache," Padraic noted, and ducked the friendly blow she aimed at him.

The governor smiled at them. He found Lady Barrows's easy way with the gentlemen encouraging. She did not behave like any woman he knew or that Temur Khan would know. There was nothing meek or helpless about her to attract Temur Khan's suspicions. "I do not suppose," he ventured, "that you are adept with any weapon, my lady?" It was a ridiculous question, of course, but he was curious about her.

"I am competent with both sword and dagger, my lord governor," she answered him. "My father did not believe a woman should be defenseless."

"Astounding!" The words were out of Arslan Bey's mouth before he realized it.

Valentina laughed. "The differences in our cultures are indeed astounding, my lord, as much so to me as to you," she told him. "Yet, despite our differences, the world continues to spin through the heavens as it has done since the beginning of time. I think the Diety we all worship—the one you call Allah, the Jews, Yahweh, and we Christians, God—must possess a great sense of humor."

The governor began to chuckle, and the chuckle grew into a chortle of laughter. Finally he said, "Wisdom in one so young, my lady, is a great gift. I can but envy the man you will one day marry."

When Ali Pasha, the governor's captain, had been summoned, the governor introduced him to the English visitors. "This is my old friend, Captain O'Flaherty, his brother, Lord Burke, and their cousin, the gracious Lady Barrows. They will travel with you, as I have already explained to you, to the camp of the Geray Tatars and then return with you to Kaffa." Ali Pasha greeted the gentlemen and bowed, his brown eyes twinkling, to the mustached

Valentina. "This lady," the governor continued, "stands very high in the favor of the Sultan Valide. Protect her life at all costs."

"As Allah wills it, my lord," Ali Pasha replied, striking his chest with a fist and his forearm as he bowed to his master.

Standing in his palace courtyard, the governor watched them go, six figures identically garbed in dark blue baggy pants, long-sleeved white shirts, dark blue silk vests embroidered with red and silver threads, long, dark capes, which spread over the flanks of their horses, dark boots that reached their calves, and small turbans. They departed at a trot, looking no different from any other party of messengers traveling from his palace. The men-at-arms on the palace walls did not even bother to look down at them. Arslan Bey sighed with relief.

They moved off to the north and west of the city, Ali Pasha leading them, Murrough at his side. Valentina and Padraic rode in the middle, and the rear was brought up by the captain's two men. To the southeast there were several parallel ranges of mountains. They traveled away from the mountains, heading toward the flat plains of the steppes.

The coastal area of the Crimea was lovely and fertile. The road wound between flowering orchards of cherry, peach, apricot, apple, and pear. There were fields of wheat and barley, the new growth laying a carpet of green across the landscape. There were vineyards just beginning to exhibit life and meadows in which cattle grazed in the spring sunshine and lambs played exuberantly near their more placid mothers. The English riders would have enjoyed it more if they had ridden at a more leisurely pace, but they rode hard. They were the governor's weekly couriers to the Great Khan, and they rode with their usual strong sense of mission.

They stopped at a small caravanserai just before dusk. By good fortune, they were the innkeeper's only guests. Murrough had carefully instructed his cousin that a Moslem man squatted when he made water and relieved himself, his back modestly to others of like intent. Positioning herself in a corner her two cousins shielding her as she obeyed nature's call, Valentina wished she were anywhere but where she was. Murrough looked very solemn, his eyes carefully averted from her as he attended to his own business, but Padraic caught her gaze in his and, insufferable beast that he was, grinned at her when her face grew pink with embarrassment.

Their supper was a rich, spicy lamb stew, filled with small onions and chunks of tender meat. There were no utensils. They

ate with the three fingers of their left hand, dipping their hands
into the hot stew from a communal pot or using wedges of flat
pita bread to scoop up portions. They drank water from a nearby
stream to ease their thirst, for the innkeeper was a devout man
and served no wine.

They slept on the floor before the fireplace, wrapped in their
heavy cloaks. Before dawn they arose and ate a thick wheat por-
ridge sweetened with honey before starting off again. At dawn
they stopped for prayers, unrolling the prayer rugs slung across
the rear of their saddles, kneeling on them, and bowing toward
the holy city of Mecca. Anyone spying on the governor's couriers
would observe nothing unusual.

At noon they stopped to rest their horses while they attended
to nature's call and then ate a lunch of bread and goat's cheese.
They had reached the edge of the steppes. The great plain
stretched out endlessly before them, fuzzed in a spring green of
new growth. A wind still edged with winter blew at them from
the north despite the bright spring sun. Mounted once more,
they set off, traveling at a smooth and steady pace across the vast
openness until the glorious sunset faded away into a smudge of
charcoal red against the night sky. Here they would find no car-
avanserais, and when they finally stopped in the shelter of some
lone rocks, they built a campfire, filled a small open kettle with
water from their goat skin canteens, and tossed in several hands-
ful of dried grain, boiling up a wheaten cereal very much like
the one they had eaten that morning. There was no honey to
sweeten it, but a pinch of salt made the glutinous mess more
palatable.

"How much longer to the Geray Tatars?" Valentina asked Ali
Pasha.

"Perhaps by tomorrow night, my lady, or perhaps early the
following day. It depends on how quickly we move tomorrow."

"There is a moon tonight," she replied. "Could we not ride for
a few more hours?"

"I admire your spirit, my lady," Ali Pasha said, "but here on
the steppes a party traveling at night is usually a party of raiders.
They are liable to be attacked by others who cannot identify them
in the dark as friend or foe. If you are anxious, however, to reach
our destination, then you will not mind if we leave an hour or
two before dawn."

"Aye, let us, for I am, indeed, anxious to reach the Geray Tatars," she said. Murrough and Padraic agreed.

They slept before their campfire that was kept burning

throughout the night to ward off animals. Each of the five men took a turn at watch, dividing the night into two-hour segments, so that all might have a decent sleep. Long before dawn, even as the moon was setting, they started off once again, fortified by cold chunks of the wheaten cereal and boiling tea sweetened with a small loaf of sugar and sipped from a communal mug.

The day dawned overcast. By noon, a driving rain was falling, mixed with sleet and large, wet flakes of snow. Shivering, Valentina hunched down into her cloak as did her silent companions, chilled to the bone. The icy dampness seeped through their clothing. It didn't help that all Valentina could think of was a large, hot tub of fragrant water.

Murrough fell back a moment and, riding next to her, said, "Ali Pasha says that if you need to stop, we will, but if we are to reach the Geray Tatars by evening we must push on. Unfortunately, this rain has slowed us."

"I want to get there," she answered him. "This weather may not change by nightfall, and I do not relish sleeping in the rain."

Murrough nodded and spurred back to join Ali Pasha.

"Ever practical," said Padraic. "Not that I don't agree!"

She laughed. "What a tale we'll have to tell the queen, Padraic! I wonder how she is."

"Do you miss the court?" he asked.

"Nay, I miss the queen," she replied. "The court is a sad place."

"It won't be when James Stewart inherits," he noted.

"Perhaps not, but 'twill all be strangers then, Padraic. Those who come after the queen is gone will be a different sort. 'Twill not be like the old days."

"Hinny love, what do you know of the old days? We have not been a part of that Golden Age," he told her.

"I know, but our families have. Growing up hearing all those tales, it seemed as if we were a part of it all. Even you as a child served as a page in the Earl and Countess of Lincoln's household during the time the earl was high in favor with the queen."

"Yet, like my brothers, I did not care for the life," he admitted. "I am not a man of politics. I have no patience with those who dissemble the truth or seek great power. Perhaps I have simply seen too much of that in my life."

They grew silent as they rode on, heads huddled within the hoods of their capes, seeking respite from the driving wet wind. When hunger assailed them, they chewed on the leftover pita bread in their pouches.

Near sunset—although they could not see the sun—they spied

ahead of them three structures. Murrough signaled Valentina to come forward and ride with Ali Pasha.

"The Tatars," said the captan, "bring their herds of sheep and goats to the steppes each year to graze them, but as the pastureland is limited they do not gather all together in one place. Rather, one or two families camp together. Several miles away, another small group will be found. This will be the case until we come to the best grazing area in this region, where the Great Khan and his immediate family will be camped. Even they will have to move one or more times during the season, and each move generally means the loss of some livestock."

"Then we are not far from our destination, Ali Pasha?"

"Another ten to twelve miles, my lady, a few hours at the most. If I may say so, my lady, you are a brave and strong woman."

"Thank you, Ali Pasha," Valentina replied.

"My lady?"

"Yes, captain?"

"Do all women of your race and tribe ride horses?"

"No, Ali Pasha. But some do."

"Such strong women must make strong sons," he considered. "I do not think I should like it if your country and mine warred against each another!"

"Then let us thank Allah for seeing that there is peace between us, Ali Pasha."

"I would be honored if you would ride with me the rest of our journey, my lady," the captain said shyly.

"I am honored that you would ask me, a mere woman," Valentina said with great tact and diplomacy.

"You are beginning to sound like a Turk," he said, chuckling.

His words pleased her. Valentina had learned the Turkish language from Murrough during the entire voyage, and it had not been easy. In Istanbul she had been astounded to find that she could understand the gossip of the porters on the docks. Listening to the chatter on the streets as they traveled to and from the Kira house, she was delighted that she could comprehend most of what was being said. Murrough had proved to be a good teacher. They had spoken only Turkish since leaving *Archangel*, for they did not wish to draw attention to themselves by speaking English. Besides, the practice was important. Val told herself how fortunate she was that her family seemed to have a facility for learning languages. Padraic and Murrough had learned several languages because of their mother's international business.

They reached the little group of buildings, and immediately a

man came out to greet them. Seeing Ali Pasha, the Tatar broke
into a smile.

"You pick a poor day to seek the khan, Ali Pasha. You and your
men look as bedraggled as wet sparrows. Come in! Come in!
There is hot tea and a good fire to warm yourselves by. My family
and I would be honored to have you join us."

"Thank you, Ibak, but as the rain has slowed us down we must
continue onward in order to reach the Great Khan tonight. How
far ahead is he?"

"Eight miles, captain, no farther."

"Bid your family good day in our behalf, Ibak. We appreciate
your offer of hospitality. Would that we might accept it!"

"May there be some nice girl willing to warm your back tonight,
Ali Pasha!" the Tatar said with a chuckle.

They moved on, the rain heavier now, soaking through their
woolen cloaks and weighing them down.

"Ibak must have moved his yurts since last week," said the
captain. "I am relieved we are closer to the khan than I had
thought. We will all be lucky not to catch an ague from this
weather."

"What are yurts?" Valentina asked.

"Those buildings we just passed are yurts. They are tents of
a sort, in which the people of the steppes live. They have a frame
that includes a roof and crown of naturally shaped willow rods
and green saplings. These frames are covered with layers of wool
felt, which, in warm weather, is rolled up to allow air to circulate
within the yurt. Inside the yurt the frame is covered with reed
mats in the summer. Layers of felt are added in cool weather.
The yurt can be assembled or disassembled in an hour or less.
No Tatar maiden goes to her husband without bringing him a
yurt. They are amazingly sturdy and never blow over in a storm.
A good yurt frame can last forty years or more."

"I noticed a wooden door," Valentina said.

"Aye." The captain chuckled. "Ibak is very proud of that door,
for it shows he has come up in the world. A wooden door in a
yurt is a very modern thing. Originally all yurt doors were felt.
The Tatars use brown felt appliquè over white felt for their doors.
Many still do, for there are those who value tradition more than
modern ways."

"What is the inside of a yurt like, Ali Pasha?"

"Very comfortable, my lady. Opposite the door on the far side
of the yurt is the family altar. There is a hearth in the middle of

the yurt that keeps it nicely warm. The men's side, with all of
their belongings, is on the left side; the women's side, with all
of their things, is on the right. There are places for visitors, children, servants, and a place of honor. We will be welcomed and
well fed, I assure you."

"I hope so!" Valentina said fervently. She couldn't ever remember having been so cold and so wet. What had happened to
spring?

The rain eased for a time, and they cantered forward, taking
advantage of the respite. Finally they could see, directly ahead,
an encampment of six or more yurts. The rain began to beat down
heavily again.

"There are no guards to keep watch?" Valentina was surprised.

"The Tatars know we are coming, my lady. You simply cannot
see their men. They, however, can see us" was the answer.

They galloped the last mile through the driving rain. Valentina
was beginning to feel dreadful. Although she was shivering
within her sodden cloak, she suddenly felt feverish. Following
the captain's lead, they made directly for the yurt of the Great
Khan, which sat dead center within the camp. Even had it not
been in the center, there would have been no mistaking it, for
the yurt was easily thirty feet in diameter and had an elaborately
paneled door, hinged, not in rope, as were the others, but in brass.

The door was flung open, and servants came out to take the
steaming, sweating horses. Dismounting, Valentina felt her legs
going out from beneath her, and she cried out in alarm. She was
quickly lifted up by Ali Pasha and carried into the yurt. But once
inside, the captain hesitated, for he did not know whether to place
her on the women's side of the yurt or on the men's side.

Two people came forward. One was a tall man with light brown
hair and hazel eyes. The other was a small, elegant woman with
silver-gilt hair piled high on her head to give her height. Her
bright blue eyes were interested as they quickly scanned the
captain's burden.

"Put him down here, Ali Pasha," the man said. "Has he been
injured? We hope you did not meet with Temur Khan."

"No, my son. The captain will bring the lady to me," said the
sweet but firm voice.

"The lady, Mother?

"The lady, my son. Where are your eyes?" She laughed softly.
"I am correct, am I not, Ali Pasha?"

"Aye, Borte Khatun, you are indeed correct," the captain said, and he gently set Valentina on her feet, which seemed steadier once the soaking cloak had been removed.

Valentina removed the small turban and, drawing away several tortoiseshell hairpins, allowed her long braid to fall free.

"By Allah! It is a woman! What mischief is this, Ali Pasha? Why is this woman dressed as a man? Why have you brought her here? Who is she?"

"So many questions, Devlet." Borte Khatun laughed. "Our visitors are cold and wet, my son. Can we not first offer them some refreshment and the warmth of our hearth? I feel certain that, whatever the lady's reasons for being here, she does not constitute a threat to the Tatar nation."

Borte Khatun turned to the captain again. "And who are these two gentlemen who are not Turks, Ali Pasha? They have not the look of Ottoman officials at all, but rather European travelers."

"I will allow them to introduce themselves, Borte Khatun." The captain looked at Murrough.

"I am Captain Murrough O'Flaherty, madam, a member of the O'Malley-Small trading company. I sailed from London several months ago. This is my younger brother, Lord Padraic Burke. The lady who accompanies us is Lady Valentina Barrows, our cousin. It is my cousin who has come to see you, madam, but why is her tale to tell, not mine."

Borte Khatun nodded, understanding perfectly. "Then," she said, "we will wait."

A young lamb was killed and roasted for the visitors, and finally the inhabitants of the Great Khan's yurt and the visitors settled down for the night, wrapped snugly in down and bedding and lying by the hearth.

Borte Khatun instructed her servants to carry the sleeping foreign woman to a private place and to remove Valentina's garments. They sponged her with warm, scented water, placed a silk robe about her, and put her to bed. Not once during all the ministrations did Valentina awaken. Safe behind her curtained alcove, a small charcoal brazier burning to keep the space warm, she slept soundly despite the ferocity of the storm that had increased in intensity and howled about the yurt.

She awakened in the morning to find Padraic sitting by her side looking somewhat haggard. "Where are we?" she asked sleepily.

"In the yurt of the Great Khan, Val. How do you feel?"

"Ah, yes, I remember! I made a rather dramatic entrance into

the camp of the Geray Tatars, didn't I, Padraic?" Her eyes were
twinkling now, and she emitted a throaty chuckle.

"Aye, you did, but how do you feel? I'm not supposed to be
over here on the women's side of the yurt, Val, and but for the
kindness of Borte Khatun, I wouldn't be."

"I feel better, Padraic," she told him. "I was just tired, wet, and
so damned cold. The wetter I got, the more I thought of a hot
bath."

He smiled. "I was worried, Val."

She reached out and patted his big hand. "I know," she said,
"but you need not have been. At least half of me is of good, sturdy
English stock, my love."

My love! She had called him her love! Did she realize it? Had
she meant it? Or had it been used casually? He did not dare ask,
for he knew how much she hated being cornered.

"Padraic?"

He started. "Aye, hinny love?"

"When will Borte Khatun grant me an audience, do you suppose? Have you told her why I am here?"

"Murrough told her last night that it was your story to tell, Val.
They are content to wait. Can you walk, hinny? There is hot tea,
that wheaten cereal we've grown accustomed to, bread, and
goat's cheese by the hearth."

"I am starving!" she cried, and rose to her feet. "What am I
wearing? Who took my clothes?"

"Borte Khatun had her servants undress you last night. They
even bathed you, but you were not awakened even by that," he
teased her. "You just snored on, Val!"

"I do not snore!" she protested.

He laughed. Taking her hand, he led her into the central portion of the yurt, where the others were already breakfasting. All
eyes swung toward her and anxious questions were asked of her.
She was able to reassure them that she was perfectly all right,
having had a good night's sleep. She admitted to being hungry.
Quickly they filled a plate for her with chunks of leftover lamb,
bread, and cheese, as well as a bowl of steaming cereal and a
small honeycomb. Her hosts watched admiringly as Val consumed it all.

"A woman who enjoys her food without coyness is an honest
woman," the said Great Khan. "A woman who can travel from
Kaffa in three days' time and survive is a strong woman. I can
always use another wife, and strong women breed strong sons."

Devlet Khan looked at his beautiful guest with frank admiration and undisguised interest. He hadn't been able to tell it last night, but now, with her long dark hair flowing past her shoulders and her female curves obvious, he had to admit that she was one of the loveliest women he had ever seen.

As the Great Khan's words penetrated her suddenly awake mind, Valentina choked on her hot tea.

"My cousin is already promised to my brother, my lord Khan," Murrough said quickly. "They have not wed before now because they have been waiting out her term of mourning for her first husband. You honor us greatly with your offer, however."

The Great Khan smiled, disappointed but nonetheless cordial. "Of course a beauty such as your cousin would already be promised. Still, it does not hurt to ask, does it?" He sighed.

"Has the rain stopped?" Valentina asked, unable to think of anything else to say.

"Between first light and dawn," the Great Khan replied. "It is a fine day for hunting. Will you gentlemen join us?"

The brothers looked at Valentina. "Go," she said. "I must have my talk with Borte Khatun."

The Great Khan, Murrough, Padraic, and Ali Pasha scrambled to their feet. Collecting weapons from the weapons box, the men took up their cloaks and left the yurt. The servants cleared away all evidence of the morning meal, leaving the two women with their tea. Then they discreetly departed.

"You have rested well, I can see," the Great Khan's mother said to Valentina. "You are, indeed, a strong girl, for you did not catch an ague as I feared you might. Your clothing was absolutely soaking. Your disguise will be restored to you when you are ready to return to Kaffa. In the meantime, I assume you will not object to wearing the clothing of my people."

"Your people? But you are French, madam," Valentina said.

Borte Khatun looked surprised. "And how, my child, did you know that? It has been so long that I have almost forgotten that once I was a Frenchwoman. It has been sixty years since I saw France. I have lived all that time as a Tatar."

"My mother told me you were French, madam."

"Indeed, child." Borte Khatun lifted a delicate eyebrow. "And how did your English mother, whom I do not know, know of my heritage? Who am I that a stranger should know of me?"

"It is a lengthy tale, madam, but I will try and be as brief as possible . . . if I may have your permission to speak," Valentina said.

"Say on, my child! I love a good tale, and you have whetted my appetite with your arrival and your air of mystery," Borte Khatun replied, her blue eyes twinkling.

"Long ago," began Valentina, "my mother, an Englishwoman, was kidnapped from her homeland and brought to Algiers. There the Dey of Algiers claimed her as his portion of the booty brought in by the Barbary pirates who had stolen her. The Dey sent my mother to Sultan Murad as part of his yearly tribute. On the very same day that my mother arrived at the seraglio, she was chosen by the Sultan Valide Nur-U-Banu to be the sultan's gift to the newly arrived ambassador from the khanate of the Crimea, Prince Javid Khan."

Borte Khatun gasped, her hand flying to her mouth. Suddenly, for just a moment, she looked every day of her seventy-five years. As quickly as she had reacted, the Great Khan's mother recovered. Taking a deep breath, she ordered Valentina to continue. The color slowly returned to her face and she sat perfectly still, her blue eyes intent on her visitor's face.

"My mother was, of course, terrified of what had happened to her. She longed for England. She longed for her husband. The sultan's mother and his favorite wife managed to convince her that she would never again see either her homeland or her husband, that she must accept her fate. They urged her to begin life anew with the prince to whom she was being given. They gave her a new name, Marjallah.

"Prince Javid Khan accepted the sultan's gift graciously, but although he was kind to my mother, he seemed distant. My mother soon learned that the prince had only recently suffered the great and tragic loss of his wives and children through the insanity of his jealous twin brother, a man as different from Javid Khan as day is from night. The fact that Javid Khan, too, had known terrible bereavement encouraged my mother to reach out to him. They fell in love, and the prince made my mother his new wife, formally freeing her from her slavery when they wed."

Valentina paused a moment to catch her breath. She wanted to blurt out her question, but knew it was necessary to tell the whole story first. She was surprised to see that Borte Khatun's eyes were filled with tears. "Are you all right, madam? Would you prefer that I stop for a while?" she asked the older woman.

"No, child, I must learn all of this now" was the answer.

Valentina took a sip of tea, then began again. "My mother's great passion that autumn was the creation of a bulb garden at her little palace that was called the Jewel Serai. There were a great many Portuguese slaves that year due to their great defeat by the Turks at Alcazarquivir, and Mother had a great contingent of them as gardeners. She worked very hard herself on the gardens, for we English are a people of the soil. When spring came and the gardens burst into bloom, my mother decided to invite the donor of the bulbs to view all of that splendor. With her husband's permission, she arose very early one morning and went into the city by means of her caïque to fetch a guest. It was almost dawn when they returned, and drawing near to the Prince's palace they saw that it was in flames.

"My mother ordered her slaves to the shore, but her elderly guest wisely counseled their return to the city, to seek help. There was nothing, she told Mother, that two women could do to help.

"Upon hearing my mother's story, the sultan sent a troup of his janissaries to the prince's palace. His mother and his favorite wife cared for my mother who was in deep shock. My mother was later told that Prince Javid Khan had been killed. The janissaries who chased after the raiders were said to have slain them all, but now I know that not to be true, for Temur Khan lives.

"My mother mourned Javid Khan greatly, but as she was widowed, she decided to return to England, to her first husband, and hope that he would accept her back. She was, after all, a free woman. The sultan, however, lusted after my mother and played a duplicitous game with her. He insisted that she was not a free woman, but still a slave. Since she had originally been his slave, he would claim her for himself. Mother argued violently, but Sultan Murad mocked her, demanding to see her papers of manumission, which she could not, of course, produce, for they had been burned in the fire at the Jewel Serai.

"Nur-U-Banu and Safiye Kadin both pleaded the sultan's cause to my mother, but she resisted them. There was no choice however, and mother was brought to the sultan the Friday following the prince's death. Murad forced himself upon her, raping her, using her in vile ways, driving her to the brink of madness. She quickly came to realize that her only escape from the sultan would be death, but she knew that Murad would not willingly release her, even to death if the choice was his. She attempted to kill him, and when she failed there was no other choice open to Murad but to execute her."

Valentina then went on to explain how her mother was rescued by her husband, and had been saved from drowning. "And that" Valentina finally finished "is how my mother escaped from Turkey, my lady,"

Borte Khatun's eyes were shining with delight. "What an absolutely wonderful tale, my child! It is as exciting as the stories of Haroun al Rashid's beloved Scheherazade, but I still do not understand why you have come seeking me."

"I have come, madam, because there is a chance that I . . . I may be the daughter of your late son, Javid Khan." Borte Khatun gasped, and Valentina said, "Several months ago, I sat by the bedside of my mother's aged servant, keeping the death watch. Through her ramblings, I learned that there was doubt regarding my paternity.

"When I questioned my mother and father, I learned that my mother had lain with Javid Khan, Sultan Murad, and her English husband within a short time. Although my parents admitted that old Mag's ravings had substance, both declared that they believe me to be the child of my mother's husband.

"The damage has been done, however. I could not wipe the old woman's words from my memory. My mother is a sweet woman, but she does not have the beauty that I possess. Her husband is an extraordinarily handsome man, yet I do not look like him. I do not look like anyone in my family.

"Suddenly I could not be content until I had sought the truth of the matter. Everyone keeps telling me that only God can give me the answer to my question, and I know that is so. Still, I believe that, if I could see you, perhaps you would see your son in me, or see my resemblance to someone else in your family. If you do not, then I must seek out the Valide Safiye. Perhaps she will see something familiar in me, something that reminds her of Sultan Murad—although I hope not! You see, madam, I cannot rest until I know who my father really is," Valentina concluded.

"My poor child," Borte Khatun said quietly. She shook her head despairingly. Then she reached out and touched Valentina's cheek gently. "I wish I could give you the assurances you seek, but I must tell you honestly that I see nothing of my son in you. Still, that does not mean Javid might not have fathered you. There is one way, one means only by which I can tell if you are my grandchild.

"Do you," she asked, "have upon your body a small birthmark in the shape of a quarter moon? It can be anywhere on your body. If you do, then I may claim you as my kin. I bear that mark on my left shoulder. My mother and sisters all bore that mark. My daughters bear it, as do all my female descendants. Do you have that mark, Valentina?"

"I do not believe so, madam," Valentina said slowly, "but then, I have never examined myself closely for such a mark."

"Disrobe for me now then," said Borte Khatun, "and I will inspect you for my family's birthmark."

For a moment Valentina hesitated, feeling shy, but then she drew off the quilted silk garment and laid it across the low table where they had breakfasted. Borte Khatun carefully perused the young woman, ordering her to turn slowly as she inspected Valentina's creamy skin. There was no quarter-moon birthmark.

The elegant old woman sighed. "You are not my grandchild, my dear. I am sorry, for I should be proud to have such a granddaughter as you. Cloth yourself now, lest you catch another chill."

Valentina pulled the robe on, saying, "You are certain, madam? You are positive that I am not your son's child?" She lifted each of her feet in turn, looking to see if the mark might be on the soles of her feet, but they, too, were clear.

Borte Khatun shook her head reluctantly. "Nothing would please me more, child, but I cannot lie to you."

"Then I must return to Istanbul and speak with the Valide Safiye," Valentina said sadly. "Oh, how I pray I am not Murad's daughter! To know that the blood of that monster flowed in my veins would be too dreadful to bear!" She shuddered.

"Yes," the older woman said, "I can understand how you feel, child. I bore my husband five sons and four daughters. My daughters have been all a mother could wish for, but one of my sons is a monster beyond belief. You know of whom I speak, although his name has not passed my lips these past twenty-five years. When he so brutally destroyed Javid's family and household, my husband would have retaliated in kind, but Javid would not let him. He pleaded that his brother's wives, women, and children were innocents. When, however, my eldest son followed his twin brother and once again wrought destruction upon Javid, my husband could not be stopped. Because they were his kin, however, he was merciful. He poisoned our eldest son's women and their offspring upon learning what had happened to Javid. He could not bear the thought of such bad blood continuing, tainting our family tree with its shame."

"Yet surely," said Valentina. "Temur Khan has not been celibate all these years. Certainly he has had other children."

"No," Borte Khatun replied. "His seed was never potent, strange to say, for the men of this family produce many male offspring, yet my eldest son had but one boy, a feeble child who would not have lived to manhood anyway, even if he had been allowed to do so. In the ensuing years, my eldest has taken many women to his bed, I am told, but he has never sired another child. Allah is indeed merciful!"

Valentina took Borte Khatun's hand and kissed it. "You have been so kind to me, madam," she said quietly. "I am sorry if I have revived sad memories."

"Not at all, child," the Great Khan's mother reassured her. "I must face the fact of my eldest son's evil, and I always have. Strangely, it is easier than denying it, and facing it has enabled me to live in peace with myself, for neither my husband nor I can be blamed. When Javid and his brother were born, the elder came squalling into this world, clutching tightly in his hand the umbilical cord of the other, which was wrapped about Javid's neck. Had they not been born so quickly I might have lost Javid, who was always the better half of the pair." The old woman forced a smile. "The day is very fair after such a nasty storm, child. Such fine days are rare here upon the steppes. It is usually either too hot or too cold. My servants will find you some fleece-lined boots and then you must go out and walk about the camp. Our people are very curious to see the girl who rode all the way from Kaffa dressed as one of the Ottoman governor's soldiers. It is a feat worthy of a Tatar, and they are most admiring of you. Do not stray from the camp, however. The weather here can turn quickly, and you might easily get lost. My son and the hunting party will not return until tonight."

Valentina thanked Borte Khatun again for her kindness before she prepared to leave the yurt.

"Be sure and stop at the yurt with the bright red door," Borte Khatun told her as she pulled on the boots. "It belongs to my sister, Tulunbay, and she is anxious to meet you. We occasionally speak our native tongue, but Tulunbay says we have forgotten much over the years and she enjoys the opportunity to speak French with a European. I am sure you speak French."

Valentina nodded that she did, asking, "Were you born in France, madam?"

"I was, indeed, born in France," Borte Khatun replied. "My family and I were traveling in Hungary on our way to my wedding when we were attacked. Our parents were killed. Our brother escaped. My sister and I were taken as wives by the men who captured us. Tulunbay is my youngest sister. Our middle sister had planned to be a nun, and she killed herself several months after we were kidnapped, preferring death to what she believed was dishonor. It was, I feel, a foolish choice, but that is all in the distant past. Run along now, child, and enjoy yourself."

With a smile and a wave, Valentina left the yurt.

Borte Khatun watched her go. Then she moved across the great structure toward a heavy curtain. Behind it was another yurt, cleverly hidden within the main structure. Lifting the heavy curtain, Borte Khatun pushed past the traditional felt doorway and stepped through. "Good morning, my son," she said quietly to the man seated in a padded, thronelike chair.

The man's stern features softened at the sight of her. "Good morning, Mother," he replied.

"Did you hear and see everything?" she asked him.

"Everything," he affirmed. "I would not have recognized her as Marjallah's daughter, for my sweet jewel was hardly the beauty this girl is. Yet, when she disrobed! Ah, Mother, how the memories flooded back! Marjallah had the most perfect body I have ever seen on any woman, and her daughter's body is the image of hers. I regret that she is not my daughter," he said sighing, "for I should be proud to have such a daughter. As I listened to her speak, I could hear Marjallah's voice. I thought the pain long done with, Mother, but it is not. I loved Marjallah as I have never loved any woman! Even my sweet Zoe and my wild Aisha. I have never forgotten her." He had a faraway look in his eyes. "I shall speak with her daughter."

"My son, is that wise? Your brother, Devlet, the faithful Orda, Konchak, and I are the only ones who know you are alive. We have kept you safe for twenty-three years. Do not, I beg you, take any chances. Do not let that devil I spawned have the final victory! Think of our people! Devlet is capable enough to lead them in battle, but he does not have your administrative abilities. To all the world, Devlet Khan is a great ruler, but without your secret counsel he would be nothing, for it is you who are the true Great Khan."

"There is no danger, Mother. The girl will leave in a day or two. I wish to know how the years have treated my precious jewel, and only she can tell me that. Humor me, Mother. There is no risk involved. Marjallah's daughter would not betray me. It is so little I ask. To have word of my Marjallah after all these years."

Suddenly the felt door was pushed aside and a Tatar of indeterminate years ran inside. "Temur Khan is within the camp, Borte Khatun! He has heard of the foreign girl. *He has heard that she is Javid Khan's daughter!* Hurry! The girl is in danger!"

Borte Khatun paled, staggering just slightly. "Allah! Allah! Will it never end? Will his hate never be sated?"

"Not until he is dead, Mother," was the quiet reply. "He has always been driven by a thousand devils, and none could help him. Go! Help Marjallah's daughter!"

It had happened so suddenly that Valentina was not certain how it happened. She was exploring the camp, a place filled with friendly, smiling people who spoke to her rapidly. She could just barely understand what they said. They were curious about her and about England, interested in the country that produced such brave Tatarlike women. Were all Englishwomen so brave? Suddenly, without warning, thundering hoofbeats heralded the arrival of a large pack of horsemen. The women in the encampment shooed their children indoors, and everyone disappeared into their yurts. All of the men, save the very elderly, had gone off with the Great Khan, for it was unthinkable that anyone would attack his camp.

Finding herself suddenly alone, Valentina realized that she, too, should seek shelter. But it was too late.

She was surrounded by horsemen. A more scraggly, filthy bunch could hardly be imagined. Their tough little steppe ponies seemed to be no more than muscle and sinew, and she was frankly amazed that they could support the weight of their riders. The men wore baggy pants, shirts, and vests of an indeterminate color. All wore square fur hats, and all were mustachioed.

One of the men kicked his felt-booted heel into his pony's side and moved directly in front of Valentina. He was no taller than she was and lean to the point of emaciation. His mustache was dark and graying and hung in two long, narrow strands. His narrow, slanted eyes were the most alive thing about him, for they blazed black and were filled with hate. He looked down at her from his mount's back.

"You are the daughter of Javid Khan," he said without preamble.

"I am not the daughter of Javid Khan, to my regret," she replied.

"I am your uncle, Temur Khan, and you lie, you half-breed bitch!"

"I am Valentina St. Michael, Lady Barrows, an English-woman," she told him. "It is not my habit to lie, Temur Khan. Now tell your men to get out of my way and allow me to pass!" A sudden trickle of perspiration slid down her back and her heart began to hammer wildly. She was amazed that she hadn't soiled herself in her fright, that she could still stand, for her legs felt like jelly. Her bearing however, gave none of her fright.

Temur Khan glared fiercely. "I am going to kill you, bitch," he announced coldly.

"Why would you kill me?" she demanded. "What have I done to you? Why would you murder a complete stranger?" In another minute she was going to collapse, Valentina felt certain of it, but she stood tall and proud. If she was to die, then it would be as a brave Englishwoman.

"You are the daughter of Javid Khan, and I can allow nothing of my brother to remain on this earth. I believed that I had wiped his memory from the world years ago! Nothing of Javid Khan may remain alive, for then he remains living, and I will not permit him immortality! Your father—may his soul be damned—took everything from me. He stole my birthright, my place in my parents' hearts as their beloved eldest son! My position as the Great Khan of the Geray Tatars!"

"*I am not the daughter of Javid Khan!*" Valentina shouted at him.

"And I say you are!" he countered, and with that Temur Khan reached down and clamped a strong arm around Valentina's waist, pulling her up and throwing her facedown across the front of his saddle. "I will destroy you, my beautiful niece, but first I will enjoy you. And when I have had my incestuous fill of your body, my men will have their pleasure of you."

"*No!*" Borte Khatun approached the ring of horsemen and they let her through. "Put the woman down. She speaks the truth. I have personally examined her for the birthmark, and she does not bear it. Your informant did not wait long enough to learn the *whole* truth."

"Of course you would protect the child of Javid Khan, would

you not, my mother?" Temur Khan spoke scornfully, bitterly. "What a pity you did not protect *my* children as well. Do their innocent little ghosts not haunt you at all?"

"Oh, you have not changed, have you?" she said fiercely. "You were never, even as a child, able to accept responsibility for your own actions. It was always someone else's fault, wasn't it? Your children are dead these many years because of your actions, not because of anyone else's."

"*No!*" He howled the word as if in pain.

"Yes!" countered his mother angrily. "You have never listened to the truth, for you are a coward! Stand and hear me now, if you dare! Neither your father nor I ever showed any preference between you and your twin. We saw the devils that tormented you from your birth and, if anything, we made allowances for your cruel and rash behavior. All of us did! Javid, your younger brothers and sisters, *all of us!* When you so wantonly destroyed Javid's home and family, your father wanted to take revenge on your family, but Javid prevented it."

"Because he was weak," sneered Temur Khan.

"Because he had compassion," Borte Khatun shouted at her son. "Because he did not believe your family should suffer the consequences of your brutal actions! He left the Crimea hoping it would ease your torment, but you could not be satisfied. You sought him out and destroyed once again! I will never forgive you for that!"

"The young woman you have flung across your saddle is not your brother's daughter. But she is a friend of the sultan's mother. She is a widow. She came to Kaffa on her family's ship in the company of her cousins in an effort to assuage the grief of her mourning. The Valide Safiye entrusted her with a message for me, and that is why she sought me out."

"Yet," replied Temur Khan, "she was overheard to say that she believed herself to be a daughter of Javid Khan. Why would she say such a thing, my mother, if it were not so?"

"Her mother was your brother's wife in Istanbul. The woman's name was Marjallah. She was in the city the morning you attacked your brother's palace. Afterward, she returned home to England. Because she bore her English husband a child within a year of her return to her homeland, the woman Marjallah was uncertain as to that child's paternity. That is why this young woman came to me, but I have most carefully examined her for the birthmark of my family and she does not bear it. She cannot be Javid Khan's daughter. You know that. Each of your own daughters bore the birthmark, as do all my female descendants, yet none of your father's children by his other wives bore that birthmark. Without it, there is no possibility of her being my grandchild. Release her at once!"

"No, I will take her to my own encampment and examine her myself. I believe that you lie, my mother, in order to protect the half-breed bitch! I have heard of her journey from Kaffa with the Ottoman governor's soldiers. No foreign woman would be capable of such a feat unless she had Tatar blood in her veins. Such an exploit exhibits the daring of a Tatar woman!"

"She is an Englishwoman!" Borte Khatun said, and there was now a desperate note in her voice.

He heard it and smiled cruelly, enjoying his triumph.

Borte Khatun saw the pleasure in her eldest son's eyes and she steeled herself once again against hurt. How could this creature hate her so? "Release the woman. We will take her to my yurt where you may examine her for the mark yourself," she urged him.

"No," he said emphatically. "But perhaps I will return her to you after I have taken her to my camp and sought the mark you claim is not upon her skin. Tell Devlet not to approach my encampment unless he first sends a messenger to request my permission. Otherwise I will kill the woman without another thought, even if she is not Javid's daughter. Do you understand me, my mother?"

Borte Khatun nodded. Turning away, she passed through the circle of horsemen and, shoulders straight, walked back to her own dwelling. She never once looked back.

Valentina, lying stunned and frightened across Temur Khan's saddle, the blood rushing to her head, began to lose consciousness. She struggled to rise. A brutal hand shoved her back down.

"Lie still, bitch. Save your strength! I'll want you fierce and defiant later on when you pleasure me. I don't like a woman who just lies there like a docile animal, but you won't, will you?" He chuckled. "You'll be full of fight till the very end, I can see that!" He kicked his pony into a gallop, and Valentina lost her battle, her body relaxing completely as she fainted.

Temur Khan laughed to himself. "Niece or no, I mean to have you, bitch," he growled. "What sons I could get on a strong woman like you! Without sons, my existence will be as mean-

ingless as my brother's was. There will be nothing of me left
behind, no sons to make me immortal."

Temur Khan's encampment, which consisted of ten yurts, was
only five miles from the camp of the Great Khan. He lived on
the steppes the year round, scorning the civilized, city life that
the other Geray Tatars embraced for half the year.

He defied his immediate family and clan by deliberately camp-
ing near them in the warm months. The Great Khan, on the
advice of his mother, ignored him. The outcast found being ignored far more irritating than warfare would have been.

On rare occasions, Temur Khan raided an outlying camp belonging to his clan, but swift retaliation from Devlet Khan kept
his misbehavior toward his own people at a minimum. He usually
concentrated on less troublesome victims, ones with little ability
to retaliate.

Only his deep and abiding hatred of Javid Khan, his twin
brother, had brought Temur Khan to the camp of the Great Khan
today. Javid, dead these many years . . . yet now possibly alive
in a daughter. Temur Khan's informant in the Great Khan's camp
was a misshapen, ugly girl whose squinting left eye was generally
considered an evil eye. Consequently, no one would have anything to do with the creature, and she remained in her father's
yurt, little more than a servant to her aging and querulous grandparents, who had been cousins of Temur Khan's father. Temur
Khan had caught her alone on the steppes one day two years
ago, and it had amused him to rape her with particular violence.
Having taken the maidenhead of her vagina, he forced the girl
onto her hands and knees and sodomized her sadistically, but,
to his amazement, her screams were cries of joy instead of the
pain he had meant to inflict. Afterward, she clung to his legs and
begged to be his slave. Her name was Oelun.

Temur Khan had never met a woman like Oelun. At first she
frightened him, for her capacity for depravity seemed as great as
his. Then he had realized that it was just her loneliness that
made her seem to enjoy the pain he inflicted. In reality, Oelun
only desired to please him so that he would fuck her again. He
realized the treasure he had in her: she would be his eyes and
ears within the camp of the Great Khan.

He supplied Oelun with two pigeons that, when released, returned to him with the message she had scrawled in a cramped
hand and stuffed into a message capsule on the bird's leg. He

was amazed that the creature could write. She had, it seemed, taught herself one winter in Kaffa, out of boredom. In return for her spying, he met her occasionally and used her eager cunt to relieve himself. Sometimes it amused him to give Oelun to other men and watch. She complied, for she loved him, and desired nothing more than to please him. He suspected that Oelun secretly believed he might one day make her his wife. He did not discourage her dream, for it kept her willing and obedient. One day, of course, he would have to kill her.

Reaching his camp, he dismounted and pulled his captive off the pony. Carrying her into his yurt, he commanded the woman within, "Bring water, Esugen! I want this bitch awake!"

The woman, her long hair lank, her face worn with years of hardship, shot him a bleak look but hurried to obey.

Valentina's first realization of returning consciousness was the awareness that her head was no longer swimming. Still, she kept her eyes closed. She struggled to remember what had happened, and the dawning knowledge brought a groan. Her eyes flew open. She found herself staring directly into the face of Temur Khan. She shuddered. He was the most evil-looking man she had ever seen. From his shaven head hung a braid, and his long French nose was somehow at odds with his yellowed skin, high cheekbones, and fathomless, slanted dark eyes.

The narrow mouth stretched itself into a slash of a grin, showing sharp, ivory-colored teeth. "You're very beautiful," he said. "I am sorry you are not a virgin, but I will enjoy bending you to my will anyhow. By nightfall I will have you as cowed as any well-trained bitch, and by tomorrow's dawn, I will have you begging for my cock!" He ground his mouth cruelly onto hers.

Not quite as helpless as he had anticipated, Valentina was able to turn away, and she bit his lower lip with all her might, relishing the taste of his blood in her mouth and his howl of pain. "Never!" she said, her voice no more than a fierce whisper.

Temur Khan's eyes glittered with fury. Pinning Valentina down with his hard body, he slapped her viciously several times, causing her head to snap back and forth.

Valentina, however, was yet defiant, and she spat full in his face a mixture of her spittle and his blood. "Never!" she repeated hoarsely.

The woman ran to wipe Temur Khan's face, and Valentina saw in her eyes a mixture of admiration and pity. The look quickly disappeared as she murmured sympathetically to her lord, her cloth gently wiping his face.

Temur Khan leaped furiously to his feet and shoved the woman aside. "Get out of my way, Esugen!" He yanked Valentina up by her hair, his hand wrapping the silken length about his fist. "You will pay for that insult, bitch! Oh, you will pay!" He dragged her outside the yurt.

She blinked, startled by the bright sunlight, for the yurt had been dim. Temur Khan pulled her along, struggling, to the center of the encampment to where two heavy posts had been driven into the ground. Hide manacles hung from the posts and Temur Khan forced her wrists through the loops, drawing them closed tightly, but not so tightly that the flow of blood was constricted.

"Now, bitch, you will learn what it is to defy me!" he growled. "Tatars! Bring your whips!"

She hung suspended between the two posts, the tips of her toes grazing the ground. At his command the woman, Esugen, ran from the yurt carrying a whip that she handed to Temur Khan with a bow. He fussed with the tip, then spoke to the men now gathered about him, each carrying his own whip.

"Ply the tips. I want her clothes removed, but I do not want her marked."

Horrified, Valentina watched as the men about her began to flick their whips in her direction. Although the blows stung, they did not cause her any great pain. But slowly her clothing was shredded until it was no longer the lovely quilted red satin gown that Borte Khatun had given her. When nothing but fluttering rags of cloth clung to her body, Temur Khan ordered Esugen to strip them away, and she hurried to obey.

Her back to her master, the woman said softly to Valentina, "You are a very brave woman, but foolish. He will have his way in the end."

Valentina shook her head. "No," she said softly. "I will kill myself first."

Esugen's dark eyes filled with pity. "He will never give you the chance," she said. "You will live until he decides that it is time for you to die." She stepped back from Valentina. "She is naked now, my lord Temur."

Temur Khan strode over to where Valentina hung. With careful eyes and hands, he examined her for the quarter-moon birthmark. Finally he nodded, satisfied. "So my mother spoke the truth. It is good, for I prefer taking you for a wife to killing you, and I would have killed you, had you proved to be the daughter of Javid Khan. Now, however, I intend punishing you for your insult to me. Esugen! Secure her legs!"

The woman knelt and fastened Valentina's legs with the hide manacles so that she was now spread-eagled between the two posts. Temur Khan surveyed his victim, walking slowly around her. Valentina stiffened her spine as she heard the crack of the whip.

He knew precisely what he was doing, and he rained stinging blows on her back and buttocks, which soon burned with the repetition of the lash. She made no outcry. He moved to face her once more, and lifting his arm, he raised a pattern of thin red welts across her breasts and belly. She glared at him mutely. He nodded slowly, and then moved behind her once again. The whip cracked once more.

A half-dozen more cruelly painful blows found her, and Valentina writhed against the taut bonds. She had no idea how sensual her movements were to the watching men, some of whom licked their lips with longing.

Then, having made his point, Temur Khan ceased the torture. He addressed his men.

"She's to hang here the rest of the day as punishment," he said. "Her cunt, her ass, and her mouth are for my cock alone. Other than that, amuse yourselves with her, but remember, if she pleases me and if I can get her with child, I will take her to wife." He walked back into his yurt, followed by Esugen.

Valentina didn't know whether to weep with her pain or give in to her fright. All about here were Tatars, staring at her naked, helpless form. They were like wolves contemplating prey. Finally, a young man approached her and, smiling into her eyes, fondled one of her breasts. She watched his face, afraid to close her eyes for fear of what he might do next. Another grinning man joined him and grasped her other breast in his dirty hand. They cradled and squeezed the flesh, crushing it, rolling the nipples between thumb and forefinger, pinching them.

"What tits, Boal!" the first man said. "What absolutely magnificent tits!"

"Tits fit for a king, Guyuk," agreed the other, nodding.

Guyuk bent his head and licked at the nipple with his tongue. His lips closed over the flesh and he sucked on it, hard. "Umm," he murmured, finally raising his eyes to his grinning companion. "Her flesh is sweet, Boal. Try it!"

He returned to his pleasant pursuit while the other man slurped loudly at her other breast.

Silent tears rolled down Valentina's face. There was absolutely nothing she could do to escape these men. I can bear it if I do not become frightened, she told herself. At least I am not being raped. Still, there was no escape from these men, and Padraic would never want her now that she had been so horribly soiled.

The two men at her breasts suckled greedily, their teeth scoring her sensitive skin. Suddenly she gasped and tried to arch away from hands that were grasping her buttocks. Cruel fingers dug into her soft skin, and a garlic-laden breath assaulted her nose as a voice whispered the most dreadful obscenities in her ear. Her Turkish was not perfect, but she understood the man all too well. Other men were approaching her now, fumbling with their breeches, releasing their swollen male organs and rubbing them against her hungrily.

"Allah, I'd like to fuck her," one man moaned.

"No woman is worth getting yourself killed over," replied an older, wiser man as he pressed himself against Valentina's hip.

"He can't kill us all, Juchi."

Juchi laughed. "Yes, he can. And the death you would suffer for a moment's passion would be terrible. Better you put your cock into one of our camp whores, Kusala. That way, you'll live to see tomorrow."

Valentina moaned with the horror of what was happening to her, struggling to keep hold of her sanity. They misunderstood. Grinning at each other, they began to mock her.

"Hey, she *likes* all this nice attention we're giving her, eh, bitch?"

"Nooo!" she whimpered.

They laughed, and one cried out, "That pretty pink cunt of hers must want some nice attention, too. I know just how to soothe it!" Kneeling, the Tatar parted Valentina's nether lips and, peeling the delicate pink flesh aside, began to tongue her with his large, wet tongue.

Valentina opened her mouth and screamed. The muscles in her straining throat bulged, but there was no sound. Between her outspread legs the man slurped and sighed, commenting lewdly to his friends, "She's just like wild honey."

"Don't be greedy, Urus!"

Urus was dragged aside, and his place taken by another Tatar, whose mouth feasted at Valentina's flesh.

She could no longer quite comprehend the depravity that was happening to her. Her body felt suddenly icy cold in the hot sun and her eyes rolled back in their sockets as her head fell forward onto her chest.

It was several minutes before her captors realized that she had fainted. Disappointed that their victim was no longer able to enjoy their attentions, they ceased their fun and wandered away.

She hung there, unconscious, until Esugen came and forced water between her lips. Valentina pretended she was still unconscious for she feared that, if she gave any sign of life, the men would come at her again. She knew she could not bear them any longer. Her fair skin ached from the whip and was burned red from the spring sun. There were bruises all over her body, and her nipples were hurt and bloodied with teeth marks.

"Your breathing gives you away, foreign woman. Take the water. No one is around to see," Esugen murmured sympathetically.

Valentina swallowed the brackish water eagerly as it slid down her parched throat.

"Not too much at first," Esugen warned, pulling the waterskin away from Valentina's mouth.

"Who . . . are you?" Valentina gasped.

"I am the unfortunate slave to Temur Khan," Esugen replied. "Had I been fortunate enough to give him children, I might have been his wife. Now that opportunity will be yours. I pray for your sake that you will give him the sons he desires, else you will end up like me. Life on the steppes is hard for everyone who lives here, but hardest for slaves." Fearing to rouse suspicion with an overlong stay, Esugen returned to the yurt.

Valentina slipped into a semiconscious state for a time, only to be brought back to reality by Temur Khan. As the afternoon waned, he came from his yurt and stood gazing at her. His fingers grasped her hair from behind and cruelly brought her to consciousness. Valentina opened her eyes to find herself staring into Temur Khan's face.

"Eyes like jewels," he commented softly. "You have a face and form fit for a sultan's seraglio, bitch. I could get a fortune for you in the slave markets of Kaffa, and twice as much if I made the trip to Istanbul. Instead, it pleases me to keep you for myself."

He fumbled with his clothing, drawing forth his rampant male-ness, which he proceeded to rub against her slit. "You have, I think, learned your lesson, my beautiful panther cat. Imagine what it would have been like, had I allowed my men to have you completely. Every orifice of your body would have been stuffed full of their lust.

"Shortly I will have Esugen release you. You will be bathed, then you will yield yourself to me. I will be your master, bitch. I will pour my seed into your womb, and there it will take root. You will give me sons, and I will be immortal—as the dead Javid Khan can never be!" His hand caressed her hair almost gently now. "Strong sons," he murmured. "You will give me strong sons!" A half-mad light glittered in his eyes.

"Never!" Her hatred leaped forth and nearly scalded him. Temur Khan stepped back involuntarily.

He laughed. "Good! you are not beaten down, nor do I want you to be. Once you have accepted me as your master, once you have given me my sons, I will make you a queen. I will lay the world at your feet." Then without another word, he turned and walked away.

Her whole body was one huge ache, though her arms and legs felt numb from their hide constraints. The sun had sunken con-siderably from its midday zenith and no longer scorched her fair skin. The camp had quieted, for the Tatars were all inside their yurts. Suddenly a hand clamped over her mouth from behind her and a rag was stuffed between her startled lips. Hands were pulling the twin moons of her bottom apart and she felt a thick, hard spear of flesh roughly probing her.

"I'm going to fuck your pretty ass, woman," growled her un-known assailant. "There's no one to see us, and I've made certain you can't—uhhh!"

As unexpectedly as he had been there, her assailant was gone, his attempted violation stopped as quickly as it had begun. The rag was pulled from her mouth, and Valentina gratefully gulped the clean air as a rough voice grated in her ear.

"Say nothing, lady. Your deliverance is at hand!"

Then she was alone again. As her terrible fear eased, she began to make out shadowy shapes dashing among the yurts. Night had fallen and the myriad stars gave off a little light, so that she could see quite well.

All of a sudden, a large party of horsemen made their way into the main clearing of the camp. Her heart hammered wildly.

"Temur Khan! Come forth and face your judgment!" bellowed the Great Khan to his elder brother.

For a moment there was silence, then the doors of all of the yurts were flung open and men burst forth, weapons in hand, screaming terrifying battle cries. A shout, sounding to Valentina like a shout of great joy, went up from the mounted men. Spurring their ponies forward, they attacked Temur Khan's men with great vigor. Soon it was difficult to make out anything but a roiling, rumbling mass of battle.

The women and children watched from the doors of the yurts. From her place between the two posts Valentina watched, wincing at the clang of sword meeting shield, as the smell of sweat and blood and fear began to permeate the camp. Horses screamed as they were injured, but the horsemen clearly had the advantage. They pressed their animals forward, slowly but inexorably driving their enemies into the center of the clearing, almost directly in front of Valentina.

A moment later, the men having been conquered, the women and children were driven from their yurts by the Great Khan's foot soldiers. The woman were keening eerily. Their men were beaten and their half-fear turned to total fear. They were all outcasts, renegades from their own people for one reason or another, and the Great Khan was bound to show them no mercy.

Clutching their children to them, the women sobbed all the louder as, before their eyes, their men were methodically killed until only one man remained standing. It was Temur Khan, beaten to his knees, but still defiant.

"Kill me with your own hand, if you dare, my brother," he challenged Devlet Khan.

"Would that I could, Temur, but that honor belongs to another," the Great Khan told him.

A horseman emerged from the shadows. His features were shrouded. Slowly he made his way across the camp, the Great Khan's ranks parting to allow him forward. At last he towered over Temur Khan, a long spear in his hand.

"Am I to die at the hand of a faceless coward?" snarled Temur Kahn. "Surely I may see the face of my executioner."

The warrior lifted a hand. Loosening the fabric shrouding his face, he revealed his visage to the condemned man. Valentina could not see his features.

Temur Khan emitted a strangled cry, and his eyes widened in shock. "*You!*" he hissed. "*It cannot be! It cannot!*"

Without a word the horseman raised his spear and drove it downward into Temur Khan's chest.

"No! Not you! *Not you!*" Temur Khan whispered, and then he tumbled backward, dead, his hands gripping at the spear in a futile attempt to remove it.

The mounted man replaced his mask, then departed as mysteriously as he had come.

Valentina stared, shocked. Who had Temur Khan's executioner been? The condemned man had recognized him. She was living in a nightmare.

Then her bonds were being cut. Before she could fall, for her legs were far too weak to sustain her, she was swept into strong, familiar arms. As she looked down, she saw the Tatar, Kusala, lying dead on the ground, a knife protruding from his back. Even as she looked, one of Devlet Khan's men bent over the body and, casually retrieved his knife, wiping it on the dead man's clothing before replacing it in his belt.

Lord Burke winced at the sight of his beloved's bruised and beaten body. He and Murrough had been terrified for her. " 'Twill be all right now, sweet love," he assured her, kissing her brow. He carried her across the encampment to where a group of horses were tethered. Wrapping his heavy cloak securely about her nakedness, he placed her on the mount as gently as he could. "We must await the Great Khan's judgment on those remaining, Val," he explained. Mounting behind her, he guided their horse into the center of the camp.

From the ranks of women and children, Esugen pushed forward. Falling to her knees, she wailed forlornly, clutching the body of her master as his crimson blood covered her.

Devlet Kahn nodded to one of his lieutenants, who leaped quickly forward and, pulling a garrote from his belt, strangled the unfortunate slave woman. "Her first reaction was grief," said the Great Khan dryly. "Her second would have been revenge, for she loved him."

He turned to another of his men. "Take my brother's head. This time Temur Khan will not escape his just retribution, nor will I allow any legends to grow up about him. Quarter his body. Give each quarter to one of my soldiers. Each warrior will ride ten leagues in the direction of a compass point and dispose of his section of the body. Each part must go to a different compass point. The body must be left in the open for the wolves and the carrion birds, if they will have it.

"Bury the woman and raise a cairn of stones over her grave so that the beasts do not dig her up. She was a loyal woman and she deserves that much honor."

The Great Khan gazed at the huddled group of women and children. "You will be divided among my men, but no woman may be separated from her children. Girls over the age of twelve will be considered women. Boys seven and over will be given to families within my camp to be raised as loyal warriors of our people. Let all be done now as I have ordered!" He signaled to his men and they rode back to their own camp.

Mounted behind Valentina, his arms about her to keep her from falling, Padraic felt her shudder, and his heart contracted. "It's all right now, Val," he said softly.

She turned her beautiful face toward him, looking at him directly for the first time since her rescue. Her eyes were haunted, filled with emotions he did not recognize. "I am not certain that it will ever be all right again, Padraic," she said to him in a curiously hollow voice, then turned away from him.

Temur Khan's encampment was burned to the ground, for the Great Khan wanted nothing of his brother's property. A black silk night covered them as the Great Khan's party rode back across the steppes to their camp. A blindingly white quarter moon had risen, casting more than enough light for them to see their way easily. Behind them, the last evidence of Temur Khan's existence blazed scarlet and gold against the darkness. Ahead of them, heralding their advance, the head of the half-mad renegade rode upon a pike.

For the Geray Tatars it was both an ending and a new beginning.

Chapter Nine

BORTE KHATUN DID NOT WEEP for her eldest son. Her tears for Temur Khan had been shed long ago. The sight of his head upon its pike was a relief. He could no longer threaten them with his evil.

Her main concern was for Valentina, and she was shocked at the cruelties inflicted on the beautiful young woman during the few hours in which she had been in Temur Khan's power.

At the first sight of the Englishwoman's face, Borte Khatun saw that she was in shock. "Bring her into the yurt," she directed Lord Burke. "My women and I will care for her."

Padraic carried Valentina inside, laying her gently on a pile of pillows. She turned her face away from him.

Borte Khatun sent him away firmly but kindly, letting fall a heavy brocade curtain that shut off the women's section of the yurt from the men's. Pulling the heavy cloak away, she gasped at Valentina's body. The fair white body she had examined only that morning for her family's birthmark, that exquisite blemish-free skin, was now crisscrossed with whip marks, painfully scorched by the sun, and covered with bruises and teeth marks.

"My child, you must tell me," she said quietly. "Were you raped? Do not be falsely modest with me, for if you were, I can prevent further complications from destroying your life. Do you understand?"

Valentian nodded. "No," she whispered. "They did not rape me. Temur Khan intended to this night, but what they did to me was just as terrible. The memory will be with me for the rest of my life!" Then, haltingly, she told Borte Khatun of her nightmare.

When she had finished, Borte Khatun, said, "Tatars can be cruel, my child. I know it. When my sister and I were captured, so many years ago, we were forced to watch as our mother was raped by my husband's men. We were to observe this, we were told, so that we would understand our own fate. When they finished with Mama, she was barely alive, for they had savaged her cruelly, so they cut her throat. Our father, driven to insanity by what he had been forced to observe, was beheaded in front of us.

"That night, my sisters and I were raped by the men who were to become our husbands. We were raped publicly, together, before the other men, so we would not think that any of us was being singled out for favor or for abuse."

"H-how could you come to love a man who would do such things to you, madam?" Valentina sobbed.

"I was fifteen, child. My sisters were thirteen and twelve. When you are young, you want to live. Indeed, you believe you will live forever! At first I hated my husband. My memories of what had happened to my family, of what had happened to me, of my home in France, were strong. When I became *enceinte* I denied the existence of my child until one day I felt life quicken within me. The child was innocent of its father's sin, and so from that time I hated my husband a little less. I have often wondered, though, if my hate toward my husband was responsible for my eldest son's behavior.

"When hate no longer became my reason for being, I suddenly looked around me. I quickly saw that the Tatar way was indeed different from the French way. They had not mistreated and murdered my parents for any reason other than it was their way of life. In all my years as a Tatar woman, I have never come to accept that kind of cruelty, but at least I understand it. And believe me, my child, the Tatars have softened over the years. All except my eldest child, at whose hands you suffered such abuse. For that I am sorry, but you will survive. Now, let me tend your wounds lest they become infected."

"You came to love your husband," Valentina said. It was a statement.

"Aye, I did. Cruelty is but one side of the coin. The Tatars can be kind as well. It was our children that brought my husband and me together. He adored his children, and did not take another wife for several years after Javid and his brother were born. First we became friends. Later I came to love him. This was not the civilized world of France. Here, one needed to be strong to survive, and, believe me, my child, here, only the strong do survive. Much of what I first took as cruelty, I soon learned was only a means of survival. Yes, I came to love my husband, and he came to love me, even giving me the name of the beloved wife of his famous ancestor, Temuchin, who, in the West, was known as Chingis Khan."

She fell silent, and Valentina remained silent as well. Slowly, with great care, Borte Khatun bathed the younger woman's battered body. Valentina blushed shyly as the Great Khan's mother delicately cleansed her most private parts using a bag made from the skin of an unborn kid. Attached to the bag was a cured length of the animal's intestine to which had been attached a narrow, hollowed piece of polished ivory filled with tiny holes. Borte Khatun inserted the ivory length within her patient and began to knead the bag.

"Within this bag is a mixture of warm water, medicinal herbs, and powdered alum. The herbs will ensure that no evil humors harm you, and the alum will make your passage as tight as a virgin's once more. Your betrothed husband is obviously very much in love with you and will gain much pleasure from you when you are wed," Borte Khatun said with a smile.

Valentina said nothing, embarrassed by this very intimate cleaning and the old woman's words. She remained silent until it was all finished. A young serving girl brushed and brushed Valentina's hair until it was free of all dust. Then her long dark tresses were washed in perfumed water, brushed again, and toweled dry. Borte Khatun spread clean-smelling salve over Valentina's wounds.

"I want you to sleep without a garment tonight, my dear," the Great Khan's mother said. "You will be quite comfortable beneath the down coverlet. Are you hungry?"

"No, madam, only thirsty." Though Valentina had not eaten since morning, her appetite was gone.

Borte Khatun ordered a cup of flavored water brought to her patient. "I'm going to put herbs in the cup to help you sleep," she said. "A good night's rest will be the best healer of all. I know you are anxious to return to Kaffa, but you will have to remain here for several days in order to heal and regain your strength. At least you know there will be no danger from Temur Khan on your return trip. For that, I am thankful."

Valentina took the cup and drained it. Then she lay back on her bed of pillows.

Borte Khatun drew the coverlet over her and withdrew from the small, curtained chamber. "Sleep well, my child," she said.

Valentina lay staring up at the willow staves that formed the roof of the yurt. Despite her newly bathed body, her freshly washed hair, she would never be clean again. How could she be? They might cleanse her skin, but they could never cleanse her memory of the foul and degrading ways in which she had been used, the hands and mouths that had manipulated her helpless body. Her mother had been right. The East was a dangerous place, but she had never imagined in her wildest dreams that a woman could be violated so brutally without actually being violated. She shuddered with the too recent remembrance. Tears rolled down her face even as Borte Khatun's herbs took effect. Finally she slipped into a dreamless sleep.

She slept until the following evening, waking slowly, her body aching. The alcove in which she lay was comfortably warm thanks to the small charcoal brazier near her bed. A little bronze lamp burned from its place on a flat-topped chest. Its light cast

a pale gold light over the little space. Turning, Valentina saw a
man seated near her bed. Her heart leaped.

"Wh-who are y-you?" she whispered.

"My name is Javid Khan," the man replied quietly.

"Am I dead?" Valentina asked. She didn't feel dead. Indeed,
she felt warm, and she hurt horribly.

The man's stern features softened and he smiled at her. His
hair was snow-white, his eyes a clear light blue. "No, Valentina,
you are not dead. You are very much alive, as am I. How do you
feel?"

"Awful," she admitted. "I thought you were dead. My mother
was told you were dead. If you were alive, why then did you leave
my mother to the *tender* mercies of Sultan Murad? My mother
loved you!"

"And I loved her, Valentina! Do not, I beg you, believe otherwise. I only thank Allah that she was not there the morning my
brother attacked the Jewel Serai. She would have been killed."

"But you were not, my lord." She sounded bewildered. "Yet
the sultan's janissaries said you were dead. I do not understand
at all."

"Why should you, my innocent English lady? This world of
mine is far different from yours, or so I have been told. Let me
explain so you will not think Javid Khan a cruel and unfeeling
Tatar prince who deserted your sweet mother, and left her to a
cruel fate in the arms of the sultan.

"That morning your mother awakened me to kiss me farewell.
I wanted to make love to her, but she laughingly chided me that
there was no time. Thank God I heeded her, or she would have
died at my brother's hands. I remember telling her I would have
my revenge on her that evening. With a smile, she departed. It
was the last time I ever saw Marjallah.

"I arose, dressed, and went to the stables, for it was my habit
to ride each dawn. At the stables I was struck down. I never saw
my assailant, and my wound was so severe that he assumed me
dead and hurried on to continue his carnage. I never really lost
consciousness, for I knew instinctively who my enemy was. It
was my twin brother.

"Temur and his men destroyed everything they could and fired
the buildings. They took heads in the ancient manner of our
people and piled them by my estate gate. I was allowed to keep
my head because my brother wanted me to be found intact, so
there would be no question about my being dead.

"They had no sooner gone than a young groom who had been

preparing my horse for me crept from the burning stables. He had hidden beneath a pile of straw and been overlooked. He saw me lying on the ground and he stopped to examine me. When he saw that I was alive, though grievously injured, he helped me escape. My brother, in his mad frenzy, had not even bothered to gather up the horses! Orda rescued them from the stables, for at that point only the roof was ablaze. He freed all, keeping two for us. He placed me on one of the animals and we began our long journey home.

"I was unconscious or semiconscious for those several weeks. Orda took care of me. He made our way to an undistinguished seacoast town on the Black Sea and, selling the horses, purchased us passage to the Crimea.

"I don't even remember the voyage. When we reached Kaffa, Orda hid me until he could seek out my parents. We had to be very careful lest we run into my brother. It was my mother's wise decision that my survival from Temur's latest murderous attack be kept a secret until my twin could be captured and dealt with in Tatar fashion.

"When it became obvious that capturing him was not going to be an easy matter, an emissary was sent to Sultan Murad asking for news about Prince Javid Khan's wife, the princess Marjallah. Our people were told that the princess had died of her grief and that the sultan's janissaries had killed Temur Khan. Fortunately, I remained in hiding until the statement about Temur Khan's death was proven false. My brother, with the devil's luck, had escaped.

"It was decided that I would remain in hiding. Our people would believe I was dead. My father believed it only a matter of time before Temur was captured, but while my brother was violent and cruel, he was never stupid. The weeks stretched into months, and the months into years. Temur continued to roam the steppes freely, drawing to him all manner of malcontents and young adventurers.

"Only a few knew that I was alive. My parents, my younger brother, Devlet, who is now the Great Khan, Orda, the one who saved me, and his wife, Konchak. They have cared for me over the years. I have lived hidden within this yurt, rarely seeing the day lest I be seen. Only at night have I been free to face the wind and the rain. I am packed secretly into a cart when we travel the steppes each year. In Kaffa, my quarters are a tower in the palace, believed to be abandoned.

"At first, I did not care whether I lived or died. I had lost your mother, the woman I loved above all others on this earth. To learn that she had died of grief was almost more than I could bear. It seemed to me that once again my brother had destroyed all that was good and true. Without ever having seen Marjallah, he had murdered her, as surely as he had killed my first two wives, Zoe and Aisha.

"But as great as my pain was, the will to live burned like a bright flame within my soul. I did not die. Instead I have lived for twenty-three years in a twilight world, never really knowing if Temur would learn that I had survived, half fearful that he would, yet longing for him to know the truth so that I might have my revenge. Today when my brother stole you away, and I feared so greatly for you, I finally remembered that I was a Tatar. It was I who slew Temur Khan. Now, at last, I am free!"

"I think," said Valentina slowly, "that you have suffered as my mother suffered at the hands of Sultan Murad."

"Tell me about your mother," he said eagerly, leaning forward, his light blue eyes warm with memory.

"Perhaps she has grown older, my lord," Valentina began, "but it seems to me that she has never changed, at least not during my life. She has been the best of mothers. We all love her very much."

"And your father never held it against her that she was my wife?"

"Never! He adores her, and always has. He was so relieved to find her and bring her home again," replied Valentina. Then she said, "I am not certain that Lord Bliss is my father, my lord. Did your mother tell you why I came here?"

"Indeed she did, but I am not your father, Valentina, much to my regret. It would have pleased me greatly to leave one child behind when I die, and you would be a daughter to be proud of, my dear. However, I would never have known you for Marjallah's daughter had you not removed your clothing so that my mother could examine you."

"You saw me!" Valentina blushed furiously, catching her lower lip between her teeth.

He laughed softly. "I saw you, and believe me when I tell you that your body is the image of Marjallah's. Marjallah had the most perfect body I have ever seen, and seeing you brought back very painful memories. Marjallah used to catch her lower lip between her teeth when vexed, as you do."

"You really did love her, didn't you?" Valentina asked quietly.

"I really did love her," he answered.

"What will happen to you now, my lord? With Temur Khan dead, will you take your rightful place as your father's eldest son. Will you become the Great Khan?"

"Eldest sons do not always inherit that position, Valentina," he said. "The position of Great Khan goes to the male member of the family deemed most worthy. It is true that, had I not been forced into a life of hiding, my father would undoubtedly have chosen me to follow in his footsteps, but the Great Khan of the Geray Tatars must not only be a man capable of governing, but a man capable of leading his people into war if war becomes necessary. No man with a physical impairment is permitted to rule our people. My twin's death changes nothing in that regard."

"I do not understand," she said, bewildered.

"I am very flattered, my dear, that you have not noticed it, but I am a cripple. I cannot walk, nor have I been able to since that terrible morning at the Jewel Serai. The lower portion of my body is quite useless, though I am fortunate to have movement above my waist. Had I been left a whole man, Temur Khan would have been dead years ago, for I should have hunted my brother down like the mad dog he was! Once my heart was filled with compassion for him, with understanding of the devils that tortured him, but after the horror of the Jewel Serai, I no longer made excuses for him. Had I been left the full use of my body, I should have killed Temur Khan for the cruelties he inflicted upon me! Today, when I rode with my brother Devlet, I was tied tightly to my saddle that I might not fall, and I rode between my brother and Orda. I had forgotten how good the wind felt upon my face, for it was the first time in years that my body had not been confined to my couch or to my chair."

"The chair," she said wonderingly as she studied it. "Your chair has wheels!"

He nodded.

"Oh, my lord, I am so sorry!" Honest tears filled her lovely amethyst eyes, and Javid Khan reached out and cupped her face in his hand, his thumb smoothing her cheeks and lips. "How lovely you are, daughter of Marjallah," he said, deftly turning the subject aside from his own misery. "Lord Burke is a most fortunate man."

Her eyes grew troubled. "I cannot marry Padraic," she said. "I cannot marry anyone now." The tears spilled down her cheeks.

He released her face and took her hand in his. "What is it, my child? Tell me. Perhaps I can ease your troubles. After all, but for an accident of nature, I might have been your father."

She looked at him unhappily and said, "How can I marry any decent man after what your brother and his men did to me?"

"My mother tells me that you were not raped," Javid Khan said.

"But I was violated in other ways!" she wailed, bursting into tears again.

He leaned forward and, with amazingly strong arms, pulled her into his arms, wrapping the coverlet about her nude body. She sobbed hysterically against his shoulder for some minutes while he stroked her soft dark hair and made gentle, soothing noises to comfort her.

When her weeping had subsided to sniffles, he spoke. "My brother, may his name be cursed, and his men visited upon you the kind of depravity that injures the mind more than the body. Your bruises will heal, Valentina. Your visible scars will fade. But unless you yourself will it to be so, the invisible wounds you bear will only fester and grow until you can no longer bear the pain of them. Did you gain any pleasure from what was done to you?"

"No!"

"Then all those men did was touch your body, they did not touch your soul! Do you understand? You gave nothing of yourself, and therefore they gained nothing of you but a moment's passing pleasure! You have washed your body clean of their touch and their scent. Now free your mind as well, Valentina. Put this horrible experience from you. You are no less a woman now than you were before this incident. If anything, you are more of a woman by virtue of having survived it. I do not believe that your Lord Burke would, for even a minute, consider putting you aside. Indeed, he has been most worried, and even sat with you through all of last night."

"He did?" She look up at him, surprised.

"He did," replied Javid Khan, amused. Allah, how he wished she were his child! His and his beloved, long-lost Marjallah's! "I am a man who knows the signs of love, my dear, and your Lord Burke is very much in love with you, Valentina."

"But he does not know . . ."

"He knows everything, my dear. Do you think he would allow us *not* to tell him? You were no sooner asleep then he went to my mother to learn of your condition." He patted her cheek. "Do not be foolish, Valentina. Do not throw away your happiness. You love this man. I see it in your face, hear it in your voice. Am I not right?"

She nodded. "Yes, I love him, though I have been slow to admit to it, my lord."

Javid Khan chuckled. "You are more like your sweet mother than you can know, Valentina." The strong arms set her back on her couch of pillows. "I will leave you now, my child, but we will speak again before you begin your return to Kaffa. I suspect that, outside this alcove, there is a young man anxious to see for himself that you are well. I will send him in."

She considered protesting, but as she was considering, Javid Khan maneuvered his wheelchair from her curtained alcove and departed. She heard the murmur of voices, and there were sounds and smells of food being prepared. She suddenly realized that she was hungry.

"Val?" Lord Burke entered the alcove and knelt by her side. She suddenly felt unaccountably shy. "Hinny love, look at me," he pleaded. "Do not turn away from me, my darling!"

"Padraic, please!" She had been dirtied. Javid Khan's words did not matter. How could she accept the purity of Padraic's love under such dark circumstances? If only he would go away and leave her to her misery. "Don't you understand?" she whispered. "I have been *used*. By other men! I am no longer fit to be your wife!"

"You were not raped," he replied.

"It was worse than rape!" she cried. "Did Borte Khatun not tell you what they did to me? Then I will tell you! I was stripped and spread open, tied between two posts. They used me with their hands and their mouths! They rubbed their male parts against me and sprayed their lust over my body! There was no part of me that they did not touch!"

"I know," he said quietly. "It must have been terrifying, hinny love, but it is over now. I love you, Val, and I do not intend to allow this misfortune to spoil the lifetime of happiness that I see ahead for us."

"Misfortune!" Her voice rose. "And when did I ever say I would marry you, Padraic Burke?"

"Will you?" he answered softly. His lips brushed her brow. "Will you marry me, my hinny love, my dearly beloved Valentina, whom I have always loved and adored? Will you marry me and make me the happiest of men, or will you continue to persist in this silly charade involving poor Tom Ashburne?"

"Charade?" she said indignantly.

"Aye, charade! Do you love the man, Valentina?"

She glowered at him, but was unable to answer.

"Humph," he said scornfully. "At least you are not a liar, my love. No, you do not love poor Tom. You love me, don't you?" He pushed her down and leaned over her, his lips dangerously near hers.

Her amethyst gaze was held, a half-willing prisoner of his passionate look. She felt herself saying, in spite of herself, "Aye, my lord," and the movement of her mouth, so close to his, teased innocently at his mouth.

Padraic Burke was a man driven. For months he had held himself in check. She was the most tantalizing, tempting, desirable woman he had ever known, and he wanted her! His lips crushed fiercely down upon hers.

She had known it would happen. How could it not happen when the truth of the matter was that they desired each other so incredibly? Her arms slipped about his neck and she drew him to her, her mouth working against his, tasting the texture of him, breathing the special maleness of him.

For a moment her conscience arose to assail her and she drew away. "What of my misfortune, Padraic?"

He stood then, and as she watched, her heart hammering wildly with joy and fear, he pulled his clothing from his body. "Have we not all had misfortunes?" he said softly, his eyes filled with love for her.

"The others!" she gasped. "What if the others should come in?"

"No one will disturb us, Val," he said quietly as he stood before her in his wonderful masculine nudity.

He is beautiful, she thought, seeing him as she had first seen him those long months ago. I thought so then and I think it now. I love the long, lean length of him! Her gaze swept over him, bold and unashamed, and he stood quietly, allowing her to drink her fill of his male beauty. His chest was but lightly furred with dark curls that were repeated in the triangle between his thighs, those beautifully muscled thighs that she knew would soon hold her in an embrace. His manhood hung white and limp, yet she could sense the power in it. It stirred, interested, even as she held it with her fascinated gaze. Soft color flooded her cheeks, and he laughed softly.

"Enough, hinny love," he teased her gently. "You have looked your fill, and now I intend wiping from your memory all the cruelties done you yesterday by Temur Khan and his minions. Trust me, Val, for I love you!"

He unrolled her from the coverlet that had been wrapped about her body and drew her to her feet. For several long moments he let his eyes enjoy her loveliness, his eyes darkening at the narrow weals crisscrossing her body. Then slowly he pulled her against him so that the nipples of her breasts brushed against his chest. He cupped her buttocks in his palms and drew her even closer. He held her captive thusly while his lips pressed tiny kisses on her face for what seemed the longest time. Valentina began to quiver deep within her being.

He sensed her rising emotions rather than felt any physical manifestation of them. Slowly, he slid his hands up the silken length of her back and over her shoulders until they were tangled in the dark night of her hair. His strong fingers kneaded her scalp, tipping her head back so that she was forced to look up into his ruggedly handsome face. The rising passion he saw in her jewellike eyes matched his own.

She could hear her heart thudding rhythmically within her ears. The turbulence churning within her belly was wholly at odds with the tightness in her chest. She didn't think she was breathing. His lips began to kiss her, and she eagerly opened her mouth to him. The kiss turned into kisses, one after the other, each deeper in intensity than the one before. They seemed to be devouring each other with their kisses. Boldly, she sought his tongue with her own and was rewarded to find a willing playmate. Their tongues twined and intertwined warmly and wetly as the power of their kisses grew in potency until, gasping, Valentina pulled her head away, frightened by the feelings his love was generating within her.

He bent, quickly scooped her up, and laid her gently upon her bed of pillows. Joining her, his big body covered her and he once again began to kiss her. Tenderly he pinioned her beneath him, imprisoning her not only by the weight of his body but with his hands, which held her hands captive on either side of her head. His desire for total possession of her grew with each moment.

The touch of his body on hers was explosive. She felt every nuance of him: the dark down upon his legs and chest; the beat of his heart against hers; the softness of his skin; the very masculine, particularly Padraic scent of him; the wiry curls that pushed against her mont; the hardness of his manhood pressing into her thigh. His very being sent her senses reeling, soaring with delight.

"Val! Oh, Val!" he whispered hotly in her ear, kissing it, teasing it with the tip of his tongue. He released her hands and, slipping down her body, sought her breasts.

Suddenly the fright and the memories rolled over her like a wave of terror. For one horrifying moment she was once again hanging between the two wooden posts outside Temur Khan's yurt while, Boal and Guyuk performed their violation on her breasts. Bile, bitter and hot, rose in her throat. She whimpered in fear.

Padraic's head snapped up. Looking into her face, he saw her anguish and realized its cause. "Nay, hinny love, do not be afraid. 'Tis your Padraic, and I only want to love you!"

Valentina shivered. "I do not know if I can bear to have you touch my breasts," she admitted. "I keep remembering, Padraic. I keep remembering!"

"The memories will not fade until they are replaced by new ones, Val," he replied. Gently he let his fingers brush across a soft nipple, encircling the flesh again and again until he felt her begin to relax beneath his touch. "You have the loveliest breasts, Val. I cannot resist them!" His head dipped swiftly, and he nuzzled her with his face. Then his tongue began to tease her, encouraging the nipple to stand bravely at attention beneath his loving. Soon his lips were closing about the nipple, his tongue playing with it, his mouth unable to resist suckling.

At the first tug upon her nipple, Valentina felt the bile rise again in her throat. She fought it down, willing the fear away. This was Padraic. *Her* Padraic! Padraic, who loved her and wished to be her husband. With each pull upon her flesh, her memory of the Tatar violators eased and she allowed herself to concentrate on the pleasure her lover was giving her. Yesterday there had been no pleasure. Now there was. Her hands moved to caress his dark head, her fingers tangling in his hair. Her breasts had become hard and swollen, and a sweet ache permeated her whole being. A low moan escaped from Valentina.

He raised his head from her breasts and kissed her deeply. "You are so sweet, my hinny love," he murmured, and slid down her torso, leaving a trail of warm kisses behind. He tongued her navel, and she moaned again as he rubbed his face against her satiny skin. He moved lower, and suddenly she stiffened.

"No!" A fierce shudder wracked her. "Not there! Not after yesterday, Padraic, I beg you!"

He met her eyes with his. "Yes, Val, I will love you there, too.

You cannot deny me, sweetheart! How can I take the sting of your pain away if you do not let me replace that pain with plea- sure?" His fingers gently teased her and a small sob escaped her. "Oh, my love, let me! Let me wipe your shame away." Bending, he found her tiny jewel and loved it with his mouth.

The touch of his tongue on that most intimate spot did not, to her great surprise, bring back the horrors of yesterday. Indeed, his tongue only aroused her passions. They were passions that she had hitherto kept locked carefully away from him lest he have any advantage over her. Now those passions exploded, and she arched her body to meet his mouth. The time for restraint was past. Her honeyed love nectar flowed most copiously as he drank greedily of her.

She soared like a swallow beneath his fiery tutelage, scaling one height after another until she believed there were no more mountains left to climb, but he surprised her. "Padraic! Padraic!" she whispered his name again and again like some sacred litany.

He could wait no more. That her fears were now gone was obvious. Pulling himself up from between her silken thighs, he thrust deeply between those thighs, his hard, hot manhood driv- ing true. For a long moment he lay gasping above her, throbbing within her passage, which was so wonderfully tight and clasped him so fiercely. With a groan, he drew himself forth and then, buttocks clenching and unclenching, he began the love rhythm.

Her soft arms enclosed him, drawing him down to crush him against her breasts. If she had flown with the birds previously, now she rose to sit among the gods themselves. She had found paradise! Her head rolled back and forth amid the pillows. She stuffed her fingers into her mouth to prevent her cries from being heard, but even so, a low moan escaped her.

"Open your eyes, Val," he growled softly. "I want to see your soul!" His muscled thighs were clasping her firmly.

She heard his command, but her eyelids felt so heavy. Still she tried and, to her great surprise, her eyes opened.

Valentina stared into his face and saw there naked passion for the very first time in her life. It frightened her. Had it not been Padraic above her, she would have been genuinely terrified. "Kiss me, my love," she whispered to him, hiding her thoughts from him, and he complied with her request. Shortly, their kisses were once again out of control, for they could not, it seemed, have enough of each other. At no time did Padraic cease the sensual rhythm of love, and together, at last, they found their pleasure. Padraic sighed so deeply with his fulfillment that Valentina was roused from her stupor and laughed softly.

"I need not," she said, "ask if you were pleasured, my lord, need I?" She reached up and brushed an errant lock of hair back from his high forehead.

He caught her hand and kissed the palm passionately as he rolled away from her. "You are perfection, Val," he said admiringly. "Did I merely dream it in my ecstasy or did you indeed promise to be my wife, madam?"

"I intend to redecorate Clearfields completely," she said by way of an answer.

"When will you marry me?" he demanded, delighted.

"Not until we return home, my love," she said. "We cannot, after all, deprive our mothers of a wedding, can we?" She turned onto her side and shifted her elbow so that she might look down into his face. "Oh, Padraic, you do understand, don't you? I love our family. It would not seem a real marriage unless they were all present!"

He smiled. "I think the thing I have loved about you since your childhood is your deep and abiding loyalty to the family, Val. Like me, you seek no glory other than that which reflects favorably upon the family."

"Together, my lord"—she smiled down into his eyes—"I hope we shall, through our children, add to that familial glory."

His gaze grew troubled. "Val," he said. "What if you should . . . should become *enceinte* before we wed?"

"You need not worry, my lord," she replied.

"Val," he answered seriously, "my seed is most potent." Then he blushed and said, "I had best tell you before the gossips get to you, but in the village belonging to Clearfields, there are several children I have fathered."

"How *many* children?" she demanded, her eyes dancing with amusement.

"Six, eight, I am not certain. It is considered permissible for an otherwise *good* girl to bear my child," he said, chagrined by her reasonable attitude, his blush deepening.

"You certainly have your share of bastards, my lord," Valentina noted, "and your villagers are most tolerant, But now, of course, there will be no more bastards." She rubbed her breasts provocatively against his chest. "You will no longer need other women, my lord, will you?"

"Nay, hinny love," he agreed, his eyes beginning to smolder with renewed interest, "but that still does not solve our problem."

Valentina laughed. "Your mother solved our problem months ago, Padraic. There will be no bairns until we want them, and certainly not before our wedding."

"That damned potion!" he exploded. "Madam, I will not have it!"

She laughed again, this time down into his face. "Nay, my lord, you *need* not have it, but I will!" She kissed him fiercely. Time lost all meaning for them, and Lord Burke forgot entirely whatever it was that had angered him.

They spent the night together enraptured by their passion, wrapped in each other's arms. By morning, Valentina could not recall why she had been so stubborn about agreeing to marry Padraic Burke. As for Lord Burke, he could not ever remember having been so totally and completely happy.

When the morning came, Valentina, though still bruised, felt well enough to travel. Borte Khatun and Javid Khan, however, prevailed on her to wait one more day. "Love is a magnificent physician," said Javid Kahn, smiling, "but you are still not healed enough to undertake such a rigorous journey." They were seated together outside the yurt in the spring sunshine. The Geray Tatars had rejoiced at the miraculous return of Javid Khan, for he had always been a favorite among his clan. His survival was considered an incredible testament to his mother's love and as great an adventure as any his family had undertaken in the past. The prince reveled in being able, once again, to enjoy his siblings, their children, and their children's children.

"My mother will be so happy to know of your survival and your victory over Temur Khan," Valentina told him happily.

"No, Valentina, my dear, your mother must never know that I survived the massacre at the Jewel Serai. For her, Javid Khan died long ago on that fresh spring morning. Let it remain that way. If she knew otherwise, it would only open old wounds, bringing forth old memories that are best left undisturbed. When you return home, tell her only that you visited Borte Khatun and learned that you did not bear the quarter-moon birthmark necessary to prove you were the child of Javid Khan. It was decided that you are not his daughter, for all of Borte Khatun's female descendants have that mark."

"Am I Sultan Murad's daughter, then, I wonder?" Valentina mused unhappily.

"Of course you must see the Valide Safiye," he told her, "but I knew Murad and I see nothing of him in you. I believe that you are your father's daughter, but go to Istanbul, for I know you will not be satisfied until you do." He smiled at her. "Your mother was never one to be satisfied until she had had her own way, either."

"How strange, my lord Javid, for I have never seen her that way. She has always deferred to her husband and family," Valentina told him.

"But," he said, "I suspect that what her husband and family wanted was what Marjallah wanted, eh?"

Valentina thought for a moment, then laughed. "I think you are right, my lord Javid," she admitted.

"Your mother was always a very clever woman," he said, remembering. "I thank Allah that she was able to escape from the clutches of the sultan those many years ago. Your father's love is a strong love that it brought him success in saving your mother in the face of all odds."

"You are certain," Valentina said, "that you do not want her to know of your own happy ending?"

He shook his head. "Such knowledge would serve no purpose, and it might bring her pain. I love your mother too much to inflict even the slightest hurt upon her."

"I love your mother," he had said. Not loved, but love. He still loved Aidan, Valentina thought, amazed, suddenly seeing her mother as other than just Conn's wife. Seeing Aidan as a desirable woman, a woman capable of rousing the deepest passions in an attractive man, a man other than Lord Bliss. It was a startling revelation.

The prince saw her thoughts on her face as clearly as if she had spoken them and again he thought of the woman he had called Marjallah. She, too, had revealed her thoughts easily. He said nothing.

"I think," Valentina finally told him, "that my mother has been very fortunate in the men who loved her."

"We have been fortunate as well," he replied. "Your father and I, Valentina." Then he patted her slender hand. "Go to Istanbul, my dear, and set your mind at rest once and for all. Then go back to England and marry your Lord Burke. From the sounds we could hear last night, he is a most vigorous and satisfying lover. Surely children will soon come of such passion."

Valentina blushed bright pink, much to Javid Khan's amusement. "My lord!" she protested. "I thought we were being discreet."

He chuckled. "Do not be embarrassed, Valentina. We Tatars fully approve of passion."

Valentina giggled. Standing, she kissed Javid Khan on the forehead. "My lord, I should have been proud to be your daughter, and in the short time we have known each other, I have come to love you as a second father. I will always think of you as such." Then she turned away and went into the yurt.

He sat frozen, his heart filled to overflowing with deep and turbulent emotions. Her words had pricked him to the quick, and he felt tears coming. Impatiently, he blinked them away. If she thought of him as another father, then he thought of her as the daughter he would never have. He remembered his own children and sighed. Dead, all dead. Dead by his brother's hand. Only this lovely young woman who was not even his remained to remind him of what might have been.

"Great-uncle!"

Javid Khan looked down to see an almond-eyed girl of about four standing by his chair. "Who are you?" he asked her.

"I am Aisha, daughter of Mangu Khan by his third wife, granddaughter of the Great Khan Devlet. Will you tell me a story, Great-uncle?"

Javid Khan lifted the child to his lap and settled her there. "What kind of a story would you like to hear, Aisha, my greatniece?" he asked her, warmed by her attention. He was enchanted by this little child who bore the name of his long-dead second wife.

"Tell me a story of love, Great-uncle!" the child answered.

"A story of love," he repeated, and thought for a long moment.

"Great-uncle!" Aisha tugged impatiently at his robe, her small, round baby's face eager.

"A love story, is it? Well, my jewel, how shall I begin? Once upon a time, long, long ago in a land far to the west, and over the stormy seas, there lived a beautiful princess—"

"A princess?" said Aisha excitedly. "What was the princess's name, Great-uncle? What was her name?"

"Her name, my child, was Marjallah," replied Javid Khan, and his light blue eyes were filled with sadness.

"And was there a handsome prince who loved her?" the little girl demanded, all impatience.

"Aye, my jewel." He nodded. "There was a prince who loved her."

"What was his name, Great-uncle?" The child's face was alight with curiosity.

"His name, little one, was Javid Khan," replied the prince, "and he loved the Princess Marjallah so very much that for his whole life there was never another. But you are getting ahead of me. I must begin again. Once upon a time, long, long ago in a land far to the west, and over the stormy seas, there lived a beautiful princess, and her name was Marjallah. . . ."

PART IV

Istanbul

SUMMER–AUTUMN 1602

Chapter Ten

"I HAVE LOST YOU!" cried the Earl of Kempe, on seeing Valentina for the first time in three weeks. "I knew I should not have remained here while you made your journey!"

They stood—Valentina, Padraic, Murrough, Tom Ashburne, and the open-mouthed Nelda—within the privacy of the ship's main cabin.

Valentina caught his hands in hers and looked up into his handsome face. His misty-gray eyes were smoky with pain, and she was deeply sorry that she should have to inflict this hurt on him. "Tom, dearest Tom! You never had me, so you cannot have lost me," she said. She sighed. "I think that I have loved Padraic my whole life. As a child, I adored him as my favorite big cousin, but somewhere my feelings changed. I could not admit to those feelings, however. So stubborn was I in facing the truth that I was not able to decide on a husband for myself. How could I when I warred within myself? I found fault with all of my suitors. Perhaps that was my way of remaining unwed until I could face the truth in my heart. But when Anne and Bevin desired so desperately to wed the men they loved and Mama would not allow them their happiness until I had made up my mind, I pushed my confused emotions away and made a practical choice."

"Edward Barrows," Tom said dully.

"Aye, poor Ned! I often wonder, if his fate had not become intwined with mine, might he be alive today? That frets me, Tom, for he was a good man."

"Then there is no chance at all for me, divinity?" he asked, hopeful but knowing the answer.

"I have promised to wed Padraic as soon as we can return to our families in England, Tom. It is the right choice for me. I know that in my heart! I love him! See?" She smiled happily. "I can say it out loud now! *I love Padraic Burke!* I always have, and I always will." She loosed her hands from Tom's and touched his face gently. "Somewhere, dear Tom, there is the right girl for you. I know it to be so! You have just not found her yet, but you will."

He looked at her glumly. "Divinity, I am certain you have broken my heart irreparably, but because I want you to be happy, I will wish both you and Padraic well." He was silent for a moment, then continued, "I have never lost at love before, divinity. I find it a unique, though thoroughly unpleasant, experience!"

Valentina laughed. "Your heart will mend, Tom," she told him.

"But I will never find a woman like you!" he replied.

"Naturally, my lord, for each woman is different, even as flowers are different, even flowers of the same kind. Each one is separate from the other in some way. Somewhere, Tom, there is an English rose for you."

He looked completely downhearted despite her cheerful words.

The next day, as they sailed across the Black Sea for Istanbul, Valentina scolded Padraic, who could not seem to keep his hands off her despite the presence of others. "My lord!" she said huffily. "I will not have you making poor Tom any more miserable than he already is. You seem to delight in flaunting your victory, and 'tis not kind—nor is it like you, Padraic."

"I cannot help myself, Val. I adore you! I keep remembering our magnificent night in the camp of the Great Kahn, and when I remember it, I want you again." He reached out and pulled her against him, her back to his front. His arm was tight about her waist while his other hand slipped into her bodice. "Val! Val!" he murmured, his soft, hot breath in her ear. "I love you!"

She felt his hand cupping her breast. His thumb rubbed seductively against her nipple, teasing it to attention. She leaned back against him for a moment, her eyes closing as she enjoyed his fondling. She wanted to go past the fondling, to lie with him as they had lain together in the yurt of the Great Khan. The creak of the sails as they filled before the wind brought her back to herself.

"Padraic!"

Laughing, he kissed her ear. "I cannot resist, you know," he said sheepishly, withdrawing his hand.

"You must!" She turned to face him and stamped her foot. "Am I some doxy that you think you can tumble at will, my lord? I am your betrothed, and I will be treated as such, else I change my mind!" Valentina exclaimed.

"Divinity! Divinity!" She heard Tom's amused voice as he

joined them at the ship's rail. "You are a hard woman, asking a man to refrain from loving you. I know that were Padraic's and my positions reversed, I certainly could not ignore your obvious charms and play the Puritan."

"I do it for your sake," she protested.

"My sake?" He asked, stunned.

"Aye, your sake, you blond buffoon! For months you have both been courting me. Now I have made my decision. Padraic is happy, and you claim to have a broken heart. I would not flaunt our happiness beneath your nose, my lord. If I have rejected your suit, Tom, I have not rejected your friendship. A friend is caring of another friend's feelings."

"Why, divinity, how kind you are," he said, "but you must not put Padraic off on my account. Seeing you together thusly helps me to accept what I might not otherwise accept."

"I should have felt the same way myself," Padraic said righteously.

Valentina looked from one to the other, outraged. "Oh, men!" she said furiously. "I want nothing to do with *either* of you *ever* again!"

As Valentina stormed off down the deck, Padraic said, "She doesn't really mean it, Tom."

"Aye, I know" was the reply, and the Earl of Kempe grinned conspiratorially at Lord Burke.

The two men understood each other perfectly. Already, without a single word being said, they had made their peace. Valentina was to be Padraic's wife, and Tom would be their good friend. It was all quite simple.

Murrough, from his quarterdeck, watched the trio, his blue eyes alight with amusement. His mother was going to be quite pleased by the results of this voyage. Whatever happened in Istanbul, it would not change Padraic's great love for Valentina or the plans they had made for their wedding. A marriage between cousins merely strengthened a family. He expected that, with luck, they would be home before the autumn gales began to blow, and that the marriage would take place before the year's end.

Archangel and her escort ships plowed gracefully through the deep, dark swells of the Black Sea. It had been Valentina's responsibility to accept the expenses the voyage entailed, but the holds of all three ships were filled with beautiful furs, musk, amber, and precious gems from Asia, so Valentina would find, when the books were balanced, that she had made a fine profit from her trip. The English market would be eager for her cargo.

As the sea voyage to Kaffa had been pleasant, so was their return to Istanbul. They moved easily through the tidal currents at the mouth of the Bosporus and down that waterway to the city, once again docking in the Golden Horn late in the afternoon as the sun stained the waters molten gold. They could see for themselves how the harbor had gotten its name.

It had been two months since they had seen Istanbul, and spring was well advanced. Even from the harbor they could see the city's many gardens and parks, filled with thousands of tulips in full bloom.

How the Kira family had known that the O'Malley-Small ships were returning that day, Valentina did not know. But awaiting them on the dock were horses for the men and the Kira litter for Valentina. A well-dressed Kira servant was shown into the main cabin, and he bowed politely to the assembled passengers.

"I am Yakob, the personal servant of the lady Esther. My lady bids you welcome again to Istanbul and invites you to dwell with her during your stay here. She thought you would enjoy staying ashore, instead of remaining aboard your vessel."

"Oh, how wonderful!" Valentina cried. "I can have a bath!"

The gentlemen laughed, and even the prim Yakob allowed a small smile to touch momentarily the corners of his mouth.

"We would be most delighted to accept the lady Esther's kind and gracious invitation," replied Murrough.

Yakob bowed again. "I have brought the conveyance for the lady and her servant. Bring nothing. All will be supplied."

Once again, Valentina found herself within the confines of a curtained litter. The bearers made their way up the hill from the harbor area to the ghetto of Balata. This time, however, the place did not seem so strange.

"How long will we be here, m'lady?" Nelda asked curiously. "Geoff says his father hopes to get home to England by autumn."

"I imagine that we will, Nelda. I am certain that the sultan's mother will see me within a few days. In the meanwhile, I intend to enjoy our stay in such a beautiful city."

"Home" Nelda sighed dreamily. "I love the autumn, m'lady! I love the colors that the trees turn, and all the little feast days like All Hallows', All Souls', Saint Martin's, and Michaelmas! Oh, m'lady! Do you think we will be home for Michaelmas?"

"Heavens, yes, Nelda! Michaelmas is at the end of September, and 'tis only late May now. We should be long home by Michaelmas." Valentina smiled at her young tiring woman. "Are you not enjoying our travels?"

"Oh, yes, m'lady, I am, but I won't be sorry to go home neither. Besides, we've got a wedding to get ready for, don't we?"

"You do not think Lord Burke and I should wait until next spring, Nelda?" Valentina teased.

"M'lady!" Nelda was outraged. "You will be widowed two years in July, and that is long enough! Poor Lord Burke has waited forever for you."

Valentina laughed. "You sound just like your mother," she said. Then, "You need not fear, Nelda. As soon as Mama and Aunt Skye learn of our impending nuptials, there will be a wedding at Pearroc Royal before any of us can say another word, as quickly as the family can be summoned. Mama will not let Padraic slip away, and I suspect she will be aided and abetted by Aunt Skye, who has long sought to see my Lord Burke wed."

They were so involved in their chatter that they were surprised to find they had arrived at the Kira house. They were greeted by Simon Kira's wife, Sarai. If Simon's mother had still been alive, that honor would have been hers.

"Welcome, my lady Valentina. Esther has demanded to see you immediately. I hope that you are not too fatigued by your long journey." Sarai Kira was a lovely woman with great dark eyes and dark hair that was discreetly covered by a veil. She had a perfect oval face, with smooth olive skin and a serene expression.

"Of course I want to see the lady Esther right away," Valentina replied.

"Thank you for indulging her," Sarai said softly. "She is not always easy, and she has been impatiently awaiting your return for several days now. I will leave you with her and escort your servant to your quarters."

"It is so kind of you to have us," Valentina replied.

"You do not mind staying in the ghetto?" Sarai asked.

"I did not really think about it," Valentina said, "but now that you have brought it to my attention, no. Why would I?"

"We are Jews" was the answer.

"And I am a Christian," Valentina noted.

Sarai smiled at her answer. "You are either very innocent, my lady Valentina, or very enlightened," she said.

"I have been taught to accept people for their individual worth, my lady Sarai, and not for any other reason," Valentina answered. "My aunt is fond of reminding those whose hearts are closed that the Lord Jesus was a Jew. There was no Christianity or Islam then, was there?"

"I wish all people were like your aunt and you, my lady Valentina. Then perhaps we Jews would not have to live in walled ghettos whose gates are locked each sunset and unlocked each dawn," Sarai Kira responded quietly. "Ah, here we are at Esther's apartments. Please enter, my lady Valentina."

"So! You finally returned" was the greeting Valentina received from Esther Kira, who sat ensconced upon a pillow-bedecked couch, a gossamer-thin blue wool shawl wrapped about her legs.

"I have indeed returned, Esther Kira," replied Valentina, going to the old lady and kissing her cheek. "You are well?"

"As well as an ancient crone can be, dear child, but do not keep me in suspense any longer! Tell me what happened in Kaffa. I am quivering with excitement."

"Prince Javid Khan is not my father," began Valentina, then she went on to explain about their trek to the encampment of the Geray Tatars, her meeting with Borte Khatun, her kidnapping by Temur Khan, and the astonishing survival all those years of the crippled Javid Khan.

"Amazing! Amazing!" Esther Kira cried, clapping her hands together excitedly. "Prince Javid Khan's escape is every bit as miraculous as your mother's! Fate meant them to live out their lives, but not together. And you are certain that Temur Khan is dead? He has escaped so many times before."

"He is dead. His head was taken and put on a pike for public display. He is dead without a doubt, and Javid Khan was able to be united again within his family and among his people. Although Devlet Khan is a good military leader, it is Javid Khan who administers," Valentina finished telling all she knew.

"Yes," Esther Kira replied. "He was always an intelligent man." Then she asked. "Will you tell your mother of his survival?"

Valentina shook her head. "He would not have her know, for he says that no good will come of stirring her old memories. I will respect his opinion and do as he says."

"He is as wise as he always was," Esther Kira noted. "Your mother loved him in spite of herself and grieved greatly over his death. Sultan Murad's treatment of her was barbaric, and your mother's mind, made fragile by all that had happened to her, snapped. Javid Khan is right. The knowledge you hold could hurt your mother."

"Tell me, Esther Kira, will the Sultan Valide see me?"

"Aye! She insisted that I inform her as soon as you arrived back in Istanbul, and a messenger has already been dispatched to the palace."

"What was her reaction to our fabrication regarding how my mother escaped drowning?" Valentina wanted to know.

"She said that your mother was the only true friend she ever had and that she was pleased Allah had spared her life. She said that, obviously, it had been your mother's Kismet, her fate, to return to her home and her English husband."

"Did you explain to her why I really needed to see her?"

"No, child. That must be your responsibility," Esther Kira said.

Valentina nodded. "I know it."

"You look happier, child, than you looked when you were here last," Esther Kira observed. "My old eyes are not so weakened that they cannot tell a woman in love."

"I am in love!" Valentina said happily. "I will marry my cousin, Lord Burke, when we return to England. That is why I am so anxious to conclude this business."

"And the question that brought you here is still important to you?"

"Aye, Esther Kira, it is. Javid Khan is not my father, of that there is no doubt. But until I learn whether Sultan Murad was, I cannot rest," Valentina said.

"Then so be it, child," replied Esther Kira. "If it is meant for you to know, then you will know."

Her initial interview with the elderly matriarch concluded, Valentina was shown to her rooms in the women's quarters. She found Nelda practically dancing with excitement.

"Oh, m'lady! Have you ever seen such a beautiful view as this?" she cried, dragging Valentina by the hand to the tall, lead-paned windows that stretched across almost an entire wall of the room.

Valentina gasped. The Kira house sat atop the highest point in Balata, at the peak of one of Istanbul's hills. Beyond Valentina's windows lay a small garden filled with flowering almond trees and carefully plotted beds of tulips. There was a tiled fountain in the middle of the garden that bubbled crystal-clear water. At the far end of the garden, the land tumbled away down a steep cliff side. Below lay the harbor of the Golden Horn, and across it, the twin towns of Pera and Galata, where many of the Christian community lived.

"Nelda, it is beautiful!" Valentina said.

"If I couldn't live in England," said Nelda, "I wouldn't mind waking up to that view every morning! But come, m'lady, and see the rest of this apartment. 'Tis most luxurious."

Valentina looked about the little salon. The walls were paneled in a warm fruitwood, polished to a soft glow. The moldings were decorated with gold leaf and also with a narrow design of red, blue, and gold in a floral pattern that extended from the paneled ceilings nearly to the floors. The floors were of dark planks of wood. Two silk tapestries with a design of fruits and flowers were hung from the ceiling molding on opposite walls. In a corner of the room was a tiled fireplace with a conical copper hood, and in the room's center was a small marble fountain of perfumed water.

There were several area rugs of thick wool woven in deep blue-and-red designs. The furniture consisted of a red silk divan, piled high with multicolored silk pillows, several tables of ebony inlaid with mother-of-pearl and brass and polished to a bright golden hue, and brass lamps set with ruby glass.

Within the smaller bedchamber was a large bed hung with red silk draperies that fluttered in the breeze. The open windows offered the same breathtaking view as the salon. There were chests bound in brass and leather, filled with all manner of exotic clothing.

"To whom does all of this belong?" Valentina wondered aloud.

" 'Tis for you, m'lady," Nelda replied. "The lady Sarai showed it to me when she brought me here. She says the old woman thought you might enjoy wearing the clothing of the land while you are here. These garments will allow you to go out into the city—properly escorted, of course. There are even garments for me! Oh! The lady Sarai said that the baths are just down the corridor, at the end, and that a bath attendant is always there."

"Where are the gentlemen?" Valentina asked.

"They are in the men's quarters on the other side of the house, the lady Sarai told me. Seems very funny to me, m'lady, but that seems to be the custom here."

Valentina laughed. "I agree with you, Nelda," she said, "but if that is the way here, we will accept it for the short time we are in Istanbul. Now, I should like a bath, and you must have one, too. Let us go and find the bathing chamber."

At the end of the hall a smiling servant opened the double doors that led into the marble-walled baths. The two young women were greeted by cheerful, scantily clad servants who helped them disrobe, much to Nelda's embarrassment.

"They don't mean to take off *all* my clothes, m'lady, do they?"

"Aye, Nelda, they do. You cannot be bathed properly unless you remove your clothes," her mistress replied.

"But I ain't never been all naked!" Nelda wailed. "We bathe in our shifts at home! Oh, I know you don't, m'lady, but in our house we're more modest-like."

"You cannot wash in a shift," Valentina said sternly. "Besides, it is the custom here to bathe naked, and have we not agreed to follow the local customs, Nelda?"

Nelda cast her mistress an unhappy look, but she allowed the Kira bath attendants to remove the last of her clothing. Unfortunately, one of the household servants, a young girl, took one look at the triangle of light brown curls at the junction of Nelda's tightly shut thighs and, pointing, giggled. Nelda flushed bright red and sought to cover herself with her hand.

"Why does your servant have hair on her Venus mont?" another of the bath servants asked Valentina. "You do not."

"In my land," Valentina explained politely, "only ladies of rank and wealth pluck the hair from their monts. Most women do not."

The servant nodded. "Your customs are very strange, m'lady," she said, and Valentina was hard-pressed not to giggle at the woman's words, which she then translated to Nelda, whose Turkish was not very good.

Nelda's embarrassment turned to outrage. "English customs, strange?" she said. "Well, I never, m'lady! Taking a bath naked in front of a lot of other people, now that's what I call strange!"

Valentina's laughter rippled through the bath. "Your mum will never believe it, I know!" she said, forestalling Nelda's certain next words.

They were sluiced with warm water and the dirt scraped carefully from their skins before they were rinsed. The two women stood in large, separate marble basins that were attached to the marble floors. Each basin was fitted with a gold drain. The bath attendants began to wash them with a floral-scented, soft soap, rubbing them all over with cloths and sea sponges until they were a mass of suds. Another warm rinse followed.

"Please go through into the bath now and join the others," said the head bath attendant.

"I thought we was in the bath," Nelda said when her mistress explained.

"This outer room is where we are washed and made clean so that we may then go into the bathing pool to soak."

Nelda shook her head. "Well, I never!"

Valentina smiled. She decided not to tell Nelda that the bath attendants had offered to denude her of her body hair. Valentina's firm assurances that Nelda would be considered odd by her own kind had satisfied them. They entered the main portion of the bath and Nelda was faced with another shock, for the room was filled with women and children.

"Come join us!" Sarai called to Valentina. "The other ladies are most anxious to meet you." She waved Valentina into the pool.

"Lord bless me!" muttered Nelda. "All this nakedness is surely a sinful thing!"

Valentina fixed her servant with a stern glance, then stepped down into the warm, scented water to mingle with the others. Nelda, afraid of water, stayed put in a corner of the bathing pool. Valentina moved over to Sarai Kira and a group of women.

"It is the custom for our families here to live together, lady Valentina," offered Sarai. "In the early days of this family's success, the sons left Istanbul to spread themselves throughout Europe so that we might do business with as many countries as possible. Only Esther's eldest son, Solomon, stayed in Istanbul. His sons, excepting my Simon's father, Eli, also departed for distant places in order that the family might command even greater influence. In my husband's generation, the sons of the family have all remained here in Istanbul doing business together, for our family is now well established in the West. We all live here in this house with our children.

"I wish to introduce you to the wives of my husband's brothers. This is Ruth, the wife of Asher; Shohannah, the wife of Cain; Haghar, the wife of David; and Sabra, the wife of Lev."

The group exchanged greetings. Valentina was fascinated by this bevy of lovely young women. She soon learned that Sarai was two years her senior, whereas Ruth, who had light brown hair and amber eyes, was Valentina's age. Shohannah was eighteen and had skin like a lily, which contrasted with her jet-black hair and black eyes. Haghar and Sabra, who were sisters, were auburn-haired girls of fifteen and fourteen whose blue eyes twinkled with mischief. Sabra had been married for only three months.

There were several small children in the baths. Sarai's two eldest sons were considered too old, at eight and five, to join the women in their bath, as was Ruth's seven-year-old son. But Sarai's daughter, who was three, and Ruth's daughters, who were five, three, and fifteen months, and Shohannah's twin sons, who were two, played beneath the watchful eyes of several nursemaids while their mothers gossiped with their English guest.

"Do you have children?" Serai asked Valentina.

"I wed late, and my husband was killed in an accident less than a month after our marriage," Valentina explained. "There was no time for children."

"You have not married again?" Shohannah questioned.

"I am bethrothed to my cousin, Lord Burke, who travels with me, and we will be wed when we return to England," Valentina replied.

"Ah! Then there will be children, for they are God's blessing upon a man and a woman. The Bible says so," Shohannah replied. "I am with child once more, as is Sarai and also Haghar."

"And maybe me, too!" the fourteen-year-old Sabra said excitedly. "My link with the moon is now five weeks broken. My Lev is a splendid lover."

"Your Lev is a noisy lover!" teased Shohannah. "We can usually hear him all over the house when he mounts you."

The other women giggled. Sabra spoke up spiritedly, "It is to be hoped then that he encourages his brothers by his own good example," she said.

"All but Asher, who is too busy in his countinghouse." Haghar laughed.

"Asher has done well by me." Ruth chuckled. "I have no complaints. But, of course, another baby would please me."

"I did not know that you were expecting a child," Valentina said shyly to Sarai.

"I carry low"—the young woman smiled—"and then, too, the voluminous clothes we wear disguises the condition well. My child is due toward the end of June."

"Is it another son or a daughter you desire?"

"A healthy child, may it be Yahweh's will," came the reply. "A man can never have too many sons, yet another daughter would be nice. Dov and Aaron have each other despite the three years between them, but my Tamar has no one."

"What will you call your child?" Valentina was genuinely interested.

"If Yahweh honors us with another son, he will be called

Ruben. If it is a daughter, then she will be named Raphaela. I would name my child in honor of Simon's aunt Rachael. She never married, but stayed home and looked after Esther. She died two years ago, trying to save Simon's mother from some mysterious illness that she then caught and perished from herself.

"Simon's mother, Maryam, was never strong. She gave her husband five sons and three daughters, but she was always considered delicate. Several years ago, the vizier, Cicalazade Pasha, took a second wife, with the permission of his first wife, the princess Lateefa. The woman disappeared under mysterious circumstances, and the vizier's head eunuch, a bestial slug of a creature, ran whining to his best friend, the sultan's Aga Kisler, in an attempt to absolve himself of his own negligence. He took it into his head that the woman had escaped and that Esther was involved. It was quite terrifying to have our peaceful home suddenly invaded by the sultan's janissaries.

"They herded the family into a room, then they began to threaten us. Esther, of course, stood firm, for she was innocent of any wrongdoing and she would not be bullied. But Maryam was frightened beyond all reason and began babbling that Simon's father, Eli, should confess and tell all. There was, of course, nothing to tell, but those two powerful eunuchs pounced on poor Maryam like ducks on a hapless waterbug. First they pretended to be taking David and Lev away for service in the corps of janissaries, despite the fact that Father Eli had paid the head tax exempting them. Then they threatened in the most explicit of terms to take our husbands' eldest sister, Debra, who was on the eve of her wedding to Mortecai ben Levi, our cousin, and present Debra to the sultan for his harem. Maryam was almost prostrate at this point, and even Father Eli had begun to shout.

"Then suddenly, Esther demanded that the room be cleared but for the aga and the vizier's head eunuch. That strange trio remained together for almost an hour, then the aga and the head eunuch and the janissaries left our house, never to return. What happened during that hour, Esther would never say. All she would tell us was that the matter had been taken care of to the satisfaction of the aga, Ali Ziya, and Hammid, the vizier's eunuch. We suspect she paid a huge bribe to those two manless men. After that, however, Maryam was never the same. She died a year later, taking poor Rachael with her."

Valentina was fascinated by the story. "It is like a legend or a myth," she said, "and Esther Kira is the heroine."

Her companions laughed at the thought of their elderly matriarch being a heroine, and all of the women departed from the baths in good humor.

"You will dine with us, of course," said Sarai as she left Valentina in her apartment. "Leah, my servant, will come for you."

The children dined by themselves, as did the men. The women of the household and their favored servants ate together in their own dining room in the women's quarters. The meal was simple but tasty, and there was a generous amount of food. There was a lamb that had been roasted with small green onions; a whole red-eyed mullet poached in white wine; small game birds stuffed with fruit and roasted golden; a large bowl of saffron rice; and flat, unleavened bread. There were olives in brine, tiny pickled onions and cucumbers, spicy hot radishes. A rich, heavy, sweet wine was served with the meal.

The dishes were cleared away, the main course having been almost entirely consumed, and a second course was served. This consisted of plates of delicate gazelle horns: tiny, hollow curved pastries stuffed with a mixture of chopped almonds and dates and soaked in honey. There were flaky pastries filled with peaches and apricots that had been glazed with egg and honey. There were green figs that had been stewed in a mixture of honey and white wine. There were sugared almonds and dates, and a large bowl of apricots, cherries, oranges, and peaches. Turkish coffee was served, the elderly female coffee maker grinding beans for each cup individually. Valentina had never tasted coffee, and she wrinkled her nose at her first taste of the boiling-hot, bitter brew.

The easy chatter that had filled the baths now filled the dining room. Old Esther presided pridefully over her brood of women, her great- and great-great-grandchildren. Looking about the room, Valentina was very much reminded of her own family, so far away.

"Valentina is to see the Valide in three days' time," Esther announced suddenly, smiling at her guest's look of surprise.

"Your messenger has returned?"

"Yes, Valentina, he returned from the Yeni Serai only just before the evening meal. Safiye is pleased to receive you." Esther clapped her hands and told the attending servant, "Go to my quarters and request of Yakob the gift the Valide has sent to our guest."

"The Valide has sent me a gift?" Valentina was astonished.

Esther Kira smiled knowingly. "Safiye has exquisite manners,

my child. You are the daughter of her old friend. She desires to
be remembered kindly by both you and your mother. Then, too,
your family's trading company, though small, is wealthy and has
a certain amount of power, which Safiye admires. Remember, I
did tell you that Safiye loves both gold and power."

Valentina nodded slowly. "You also said she is wicked and
venal, yet you remain her friend, Esther Kira. Why?"

The old woman smiled wisely. "Because I remember her when
she was not that way and because she needs my friendship. My
continuing friendship with the powerful women of the Ottoman
family helps in the continuation of my own family's good fortune.
As long as Yahweh wills that I remain upon this earth, then I
would be of value to my family. Soon, however, I think I will
leave them. I have never known anyone who lived as long as I
have lived."

The women laughed softly at Esther's remark, but Sarai said,
"The Angel of Death has forgotten all about you, Esther, and
when his anxious assistant brings it to his attention, the Angel
of Death declares it is an error on his assistant's part, that you
could not possibly still remain on this earth. Until the angel is
willing to admit his mistake, you will remain with us, Esther."

"No, child, it is not so. The Angel of Death never forgets about
anyone. My time is soon. I feel it in my bones."

A chill settled on the room suddenly, and in an attempt to
dispell it, Valentina said, "Tell me more about the Valide, Esther."

"Safiye," the old lady began. "Her name means purity. She is
of the Baffo family of Venice. When she was but twelve, she was
on her way from Venice to join her parents on the island of Corfu,
where her father was governor. Her ship was captured by Turkish
pirates, and Safiye was brought to Istanbul to be sold in the
women's slave market. The sultan's Aga Kisler saw her there
and purchased her for the harem. She was trained to catch the
sultan's eye. Indeed, when her time came, she did. Murad
fell in love with her to the exclusion of all others, and she with
him.

"She was an innocent then. Sweet and trusting and giving.
She bore Sultan Murad his first son, Mehmed, who is the current
sultan. She had no other sons after that, yet Murad continued
to adore her, much to his mother, Nur-U-Banu's annoyance. The
Valide Nur-U-Banu feared that Safiye's influence would outstrip
hers, which she would not tolerate. In those days, Safiye looked
on Nur-U-Banu as a mother and relied on her to protect her

relationship with Murad. She soon learned that, in the harem, to place one's faith in another woman is to invite disaster.

"Nur-U-Banu worried, rightly, that the succession was endangered by Murad's having only one male heir. She plotted with the Aga Kisler, and together the two of them combed the slave markets of Istanbul seeking the most perfect, the most exquisite virgins that they might present to Murad in order to tempt him away from Safiye's bed. They subtly placed within his mind the idea that one son was simply not enough, that Safiye was being selfish in attempting to hold Murad's entire love when, after twelve years, she had given him but one male heir.

"Their clever ploys worked, for, by that time, Murad's full Ottoman nature was beginning to assert itself. He found it impossible to resist the bevy of beauties being dangled before him. Safiye was no longer a fresh, young girl of thirteen. She was a woman in her late twenties and the lure of nubile, perfumed flesh proved too hard for Murad to resist. He succumbed with vigor and open delight to the variety of pleasures being paraded before him, and the more he tasted of this variety, the more he craved. He was a most sensual man. Perhaps overly so. At first, Safiye was heartbroken. Then, upon learning the extent of Nur-U-Banu's involvement in this plot to remove Murad from her bed, she became enraged.

"There was nothing poor Safiye could really do to avenge herself on Murad's mother. Nur-U-Banu had the power, and in order to retain her position as Murad's absolute favorite, Safiye was forced to swallow her pride and accept her lord's other women. Though she rarely allowed Murad to see that side of her nature, Safiye became an embittered woman. She is not a stupid woman, and she very quickly realized that if she lost Murad's favor, her son might lose his father's favor as well. For Mehmed's sake, she accepted what she had to, knowing that one day when her son became the sultan, it would be Safiye who would be the Valide, the most powerful woman in the empire.

"If Safiye has any regrets, I think it is that Nur-U-Banu did not live to have her position usurped. Safiye has often said she would have enjoyed sending Murad's mother to the Eski Serai to live out a lonely, powerless old age.

"Nur-U-Banu died four years after your mother escaped drowning. It was sudden and quite unexpected, for she had not been ill. There were rumors of poison, but Murad did not believe them, and neither did I. There was no truth to the rumors.

Though Safiye fought with Nur-U-Banu continually, with occasional truces, they both quite frankly enjoyed the rivalry between them. It was exciting. It gave them something to live for,
which is important for women in a harem, without men.

"With Nur-U-Banu gone, Safiye, as Bas Kadin, the mother of
the heir, became the most important and powerful woman in the
empire. There were other sons born to Murad, but Mehmed was
almost a man at that point and only his death could prevent Safiye
from reaching her goal. She became ruthless in her desire to see
her son the sultan. The boy's violent temper had gotten him into
many difficulties and only his position as heir had absolved him.
Murad, in an attempt to cure his son of that temper, sent him
to govern a distant province in the hope that the rigors of running
a government would give the boy a better outlet for his energies
and a focus for his intellect. Safiye, of course, objected, fearing
that, away from her influence, the boy would become independent. She also feared that he might be assassinated. She sent
along an army of food-tasters and bodyguards to protect Mehmed.

"Mehmed, for all his strangeness, loves his mother deeply. Safiye wrote to him regularly, keeping him abreast of all the gossip
and passing on to him advice and information. He answered every
one of his mother's letters with news of his own life. He asked
her questions and solicited her opinions on everything. The bond
forged between them was not broken by their separation, and
Safiye began to look forward to Murad's death, that her son might
rule.

"The younger women of the harem were becoming bolder in
their defiance of Safiye. They believed that, having the sultan's
favor and his children was enough to allow serious consideration
of their sons ruling instead of Mehmed. Safiye, who, in younger
days, might have become publicly enraged by this, remained as
silent as a cat waiting to pounce and bided her time patiently.
Murad was still her best friend. He valued and respected her
publicly and privately. She knew that Murad was not well.
Though few had seen it, the sultan was subject to fainting fits
during the last two years of his life. He was also finding it increasingly difficult to pass his water. He died in January of 1595,
seven and a half years ago."

Here, Esther Kira paused for a few moments and sipped at her
wine thirstily. Her audience was spellbound, even the members
of the household for whom the story was an old, familiar one.
The matriarch knew how to weave a tale.

"Murad's death was kept secret for seven days," she began again, "while Safiye's messengers hurried to fetch Mehmed back to Istanbul. All of Murad's servants who had been with him when he died were quietly and quickly strangled. The other servants were sent secretly to the Eski Serai without explanation. If they knew why they were leaving, they were wise enough to remain silent in order to preserve their lives. Safiye, with a steath I would not have believed possible, waited patiently, behaving as if nothing unusual had happened, as if it were just a normal week. The business of the empire was temporarily suspended while Sultan Murad 'recovered' from a bad winter's cold. No one suspected that Murad was dead, not even the unfortunate mothers of his other sons.

"Seven days later, an admiral's galley brought Mehmed home. It was a gray, drizzily winter's morning. Although the wind was light, it was the kind of damp cold that cuts into a person's bones." She sighed. "The new sultan disembarked from his vessel and, in gratitude for his safe arrival, freed all of the galley slaves aboard the ship. Then he ordered messengers to go to Aleppo to obtain a half-million hyacinth bulbs to be planted at the very spot where he had landed.

"At the first sighting of the new sultan's galley, word of Murad's death was publicly announced throughout the city. In the seraglio, Murad's favorites were already wailing. The historians will call it mourning, but it was really fear of what was to come. They knew, those poor creatures, even if they did not dare voice their fright.

"Mehmed dressed in royal purple before leaving his ship. He followed his father's cypresswood coffin, which was entirely covered with cloth of gold, atop which sat a great belt of diamonds. The procession made its way through the entire city. Mehmed did not ride. He walked, the captains of his personal guard surrounding him; holding palm leaves over him. All of the men of the court followed, dressed in black mourning. As a sign of respect, they wore unusually small turbans on their heads.

"The streets were packed with onlookers, for Istanbul has always been a social city and a sultan's funeral is a great event. The procession ended at the Great Mosque, which, before the conquest, was the Christian church of St. Sophia.

"After Murad was properly buried, Mehmed hurried to see his mother. They had not seen each other in twelve years! Mehmed had been seventeen, still a boy, when he left Istanbul. Now he was a fully grown man of twenty-nine. There was no one else party to that meeting, but when it was over, Mehmed immediately saw to the execution of his nineteen younger brothers. There are those who said he wept at having to invoke the law of Zānan-nāmeh, but invoke it he did, telling those innocent little boys—the eldest was only eleven—that they had nothing to fear from him. He embraced each of them, then saw that they were, in accordance with the laws of Islam, circumcised. After that, they were taken one by one into an adjoining room and bowstrung.

"Safiye was behind it all. She wanted no rival to her son's throne! She wanted her revenge on those young women who had taken her place in Murad's bed, and oh, what a revenge it was! What a terrible and exact retribution Safiye took against those women who had taken Murad's total love and attention from her.

"Mehmed, to give him credit, inspected those sad little corpses in their coffins before they were taken to be buried with their father. When he was officially notified of his brothers' deaths, the notification written in white ink on black paper, he wept genuine tears of grief and ordered a full state funeral to which all persons of high rank were ordered to attend. I have heard him say many times that he hated disposing of those poor little boys, but what else was he to do with them? Nineteen living threats to his reign was too many threats, and by then he already had sons of his own.

"The following day, Safiye, whose son had officially proclaimed her Sultan Valide, sent all of Murad's women to live out the long and lonely days of their lives at the Eski Serai, the old palace, where my dear friend, the valide Cyra Hafise of blessed memory, lived. All but the seven unfortunates who were with child by Murad. These poor girls were sewn into silken sacks and drowned. Free now of those she believed were her enemies and those who had offended her over the years, Safiye set about to corrupt her own son in precisely the same manner as Nur-U-Banu had corrupted Murad. She intended to gain full power for herself.

"Mehmed had a single kadin, Sa'adet, which means felicity in your language. She was the mother of his eldest son, Mamud. Mehmed had sworn to remain true to her alone, even as Murad had been monogamous with Safiye for all those years. Safiye, however, like Nur-U-Banu before her, did not want any rivals, particularly her son's only kadin. Safiye knew better than most the influence that might be wielded by Sa'adet, had the kadin chosen to wield it. Sa'adet was not an ambitious woman, however. Her entire world revolved about Mehmed and their son. So, while Safiye had her carefully watched, she left her in peace for a time."

"Tell Valentina about Chiarezza," said the lovely Shohannah. "She is part of Safiye's story, too."

"Chiarezza!" Esther Kira spat the name scornfully. "She claims to be a Jewess, yet she does not live in the ghetto, and she has neither husband nor father nor brothers nor sons to protect her. She is a spy for the Venetian ambassador, and for Catherine de' Medici as well! The only way she can obtain entry to the harem to gather her information and to talk with Safiye is by pretending to be one of the women who bring their goods to the harem to sell to the ladies of the sultan's household, as I once brought in goods."

"Esther is angry because she can no longer go to the Yeni Serai to conduct her business and to gossip," whispered Sarai to Valentina.

"I hear you, Sarai!" the old lady snapped. "My ears, at least, have not failed me. I am angry that my uncooperative body prevents me from going to the palace. I may lose my influence with Safiye by not being visible to her. If that happens, where will this family be? I have lived through the reigns of Sultan Bajazet, son of the conqueror of Constantinople, this city we now call Istanbul. I have lived through the reigns of his descendants, Selim I; of Suleiman, whom you in the West called the Magnificent but we called the Lawgiver; of his son, Selim II; of Murad III; and now of Mehmed III!

"In the reign of the first Selim, we Kiras were exempted from paying taxes to the state forever. That, in large part, has been responsible for helping us amass our great wealth, and has allowed us to extend our banking empire throughout all of western Europe. There is a Kira doing business in every important country and every important city. During all that time, I have been in evidence, making friends of the Ottomen women, aiding them when they needed it, keeping them in our debt in order that the promise made us by Selim I be kept.

"How long will a promise made us so long ago, by a sultan whose memory has long faded, be kept? What will happen when I am no longer here to see that it is kept? When my influence cannot be counted on and when I am forgotten? I know that you all go to the palace with your wares, even though you do not have to do such things. Yet none of you has managed to make friends with Safiye, for you are all too young and too pretty. This homely Chiarezza creature has wormed her way into the Valide's confidence."

"Only because she carries the Valide's messages to the Venetian ambassador" Sarai said soothingly, "and her secret letters to Catherine de' Medici, dear Esther. Did not Safiye herself come to see you two months ago after Valentina had departed for the Crimea? Did she not agree to see Valentina on your request? The Valide has not forgotten you. You fret too much."

"If I fret, it is with good cause," Esther Kira replied sharply to Sarai. "I have known Safiye practically her entire life. With her, it is out of sight, out of mind. She has no loyalties to anyone except herself, Sarai, and if she came to visit me when I asked her, it was because it suited her to do so, and for no other reason. Never forget that, child. And never trust the Valide, else you live to regret it. She is a very dangerous woman. Gold is her god and power her lover!"

"You make her sound quite frightening, Esther Kira," Valentina said.

The matriarch nodded slowly. "She is dangerous, my child, yet if you saw her, you would not believe it. She has not allowed herself to go to ruin like so many harem beauties. Her hair, once a lovely red-gold, is faded to the color of pale apricot. She stands straight and is still slender. Her manners are flawless, and she has great charm. You will like her, but do not trust her, and guard your tongue when you speak with her."

"I will heed your advice, Esther Kira," Valentina replied.

"Then you will have no regrets, my child. Ah, here is the gift the Valide has sent you," the old lady said, taking the pearl-edged, pale blue silk handkerchief from the waiting servant and handing it to Valentina.

The handkerchief was tied with a pearl-embroidered cloth-of-gold ribbon, which, in itself, had value. Valentina undid the ribbon, giving it to the servant as a gift. Then she opened the handkerchief. Within the silk was an exquisitely carved mother-of-pearl box with a gold lock held shut by means of a diamond-studded golden pin. Valentina admired the box for a moment, then drew the pin through its loop. Lifting the lock, she opened the box.

"God's foot!" she swore softly, using Elizabeth Tudor's favorite oath.

"Ah!" There was a soft exclamation from the other women, who had crowded about her in order to see.

"Oh, m'lady! Is that for you?" Nelda was goggle-eyed.

"Yes, girl, it is a gift for your mistress, and a very fine one," Esther Kira said when she had seen the gift. "Even I am impressed, Safiye, indeed, courts your goodwill, child."

Valentina was too surprised even to touch the gift that rested on a bed of dark velvet inside the carved box. It was probably the most beautiful necklace she had ever seen. The chain was an exquisite filigree of pink gold, and caught within the filigree were glittering diamonds, sapphires, emeralds, amethysts, golden beryls, rubies, pale green peridots, and light blue tourmalines. Three large diamonds hung from the base of the necklace. Each had been cut in an unusual shape: a clear white diamond was shaped like a crescent moon; a diamond with a decidedly blue cast was fashioned like a star; the center stone was a pink diamond in the shape of a heart.

"I have never seen anything like it in my entire life," Valentina finally said. "It is magnificent, almost barbaric in its splendor. It must be worth a king's ransom! I have never owned anything like it, nor did I ever imagine I would."

"You must wear it when you visit the valide," said Sarai emphatically. "It will please her, as will your open gratitude."

"But what will I give her?" Valentina said. "How can I possibly match such a gift?"

"You must not match it, child," said Esther. "Not if you wish to please Safiye. Your gift must be of suitable magnificence to do her honor, but not quite as magnificent as this necklace. Tell me. What cargo did you bring back from the Crimea?"

"Uncut gemstones, musk, spices, furs." Valentina cudgeled her brain to remember. "We have a great deal of sable, I recall."

"Perfect!" the old lady said. "We will have a sable cape made for Safiye with a jeweled closure. That will please her very much!"

"But who will do the work?" Valentina wailed. "We have only three days!"

Esther Kira chuckled. "You will leave it in my hands, child, and it will be done, I guarantee you."

If anyone could arrange the miracle, Esther Kira could, and so Valentina left the matter of the valide's gift in her capable hands.

She slept better that night than she had in weeks, but in the

morning after she had broken her fast, she decided to find Padraic
and the others. A servant was dispatched to fetch them, but after
Valentina had waited for a long time, Sarai appeared.

"I understand that you wish to see your betrothed, but he and
the other Englishmen are not here. They have gone across the
Golden Horn to Pera to pay their respects to the English ambassador. I do not know when they will be back, but I thought
perhaps you would enjoy seeing Balata today. Then perhaps tomorrow you can arrange with your betrothed to visit some points
of interest in Istanbul."

Padraic gone? Without telling her? Valentina was angry, but
there was no help for it, and so she agreed to go with the kindly
Sarai. She fumed to herself, nonetheless, over the situation.
Istanbul was a fascinating city, but she did not like the structure
of Eastern society. She had learned that every house, no matter
how humble, had its women's quarters. Here in the Kira household, the house was, like many, divided into three sections, with
the women's quarters on one side, the men's quarters on the
opposite side, and a public area in the middle of the house. It
was there that the Kiras did their banking business on all but
two days of the week, their own and the Islamic Sabbath.

The male and female facilities were separate, though equal in
their furnishings. The sections came together in only once place;
the kitchens served the entire household. There were doors from
the kitchens leading into the women's quarters, but there were
no doors from the kitchens into the men's quarters. Instead, there
was a sliding panel through which dishes were pushed into the
men's dining room and through which the dirty dishes were
passed back. There were separate baths for men and women.
The entire family shared the gardens. A man might visit his wife's
bed, but she never defiled his sleeping quarters. The sons of the
house were removed from the women's care at the age of seven
and went to live in the men's quarters. Although women were
respected for their roles as lifegivers, mothers, nurturers, and
finally, wise elders, they were still considered simple creatures
who needed the total care and complete protection of their men.
Most responded positively to such treatment, but there were unusual women, like Esther, who could not be satisfied in such
passive roles.

"I could not live this way," Valentina admitted to Sarai as they
prepared to leave the house.

"It is our way, Valentina," Sarai responded. "We are happy,

and we know no other way of life. At least we Jewesses have more freedom than the women of Islam."

"How is that?" Valentina demanded.

"Here in Balata we are free to walk in the streets in order to shop and to visit our friends. It is only necessary that we be respectably garbed. The veil is not required. However, when we venture into the city, we prefer wearing a plain, black yashmak so that we appear like all of the other women of Istanbul. There are those who do not like Jews and would not hesitate to accost us and insult us publicly.

"Wealthy women of Islam spend practically their entire lives in some harem or another. Occasionally, a woman with power, like Safiye, ventures out, but most well-to-do women of Istanbul remain at home. Women of more modest means, wearing their black yashmaks, which leave only the eyes visible, do their own shopping. They even go regularly to the public baths, particularly if there is no bath in their home. Cleanliness is of great importance to us here in Istanbul.

"Sometimes even the women of important households visit the great covered market, for it is a wondrous place, Valentina, with everything you could possibly imagine for sale. We will go there before you return to England."

The ghetto of Balata was like no place Valentina had ever been before. Enclosed within her litter when she had come and gone from the harbor, she had not seen much of Balata. On foot, however, it was a different matter. Balata was a bright, noisy place where the houses were jammed next to each other, their balconies overflowing with brilliantly colored blooms and flowering vines. The houses, like most of those in Istanbul, were of wood. Fire was always a danger, particularly in the winter when the charcoal braziers used for heat were apt to tumble over. Some of the buildings were private houses, but most were divided into apartments that families shared.

There were fountains everywhere, for water was important to the city. It poured through state-built aqueducts into central holding tanks, then into the neighborhood fountains, where its flow seemed unceasing. For the wealthy, such as the Kiras, waterpipes went directly into their homes. In Balata, there were three fine public baths, one for men, one for women, and a ritual bath that was attached to Balata's temple.

There were several open-air markets. In one, Valentina saw an astonishing array of fresh fruits and vegetables spread out on mats on the ground so that the buyer might see for herself that nothing was hidden. There were fresh fish from the harbor and live poultry ready to be slaughtered. The manner of their slaughter was a very particular thing, Valentina learned.

"For all our meats," Sarai explained, "there must be no blood spilled, else the food be defiled. Everything must be in accordance with our dietary laws. We do not mix meat, for instance, with dairy products, and the meat of pigs and certain sea creatures that scavenge are forbidden to us, being considered unclean by our religious laws."

"Why?" Valentina asked, puzzled.

"I do not know," Sarai replied. "You would have to ask one of our rabbis that, but they do not speak to women, for women are considered unclean because of our monthly flow of blood. All I can tell you is that it is our law. It is not necessary for me to know anything beyond that. It has been our people's way for centuries."

If it were me, I should want to know, Valentina thought. How can you simply accept rules without knowing the reasons for them? I could not live here in the East. I just couldn't!

In another market there were marvelous fabrics—silks, brocades, and fine cottons of every possible color and hue—as well as thick, heavy wool carpets. There were stalls filled with beautiful leather goods, displays of Venetian glass, North African brass, and furniture made of ebony and inlaid with mother-of-pearl. There was one merchant who sold nothing but lamps and a cobbler who worked on a pair of shoes or slippers for you while you waited.

A third market sold only live animals: goats, sheep, and horses. Valentina was fascinated by the fine-boned Arab horses the Turks were breeding. She could see the speed that would be possible with these horses, and she began to wonder if it would be possible to transport a few of them back to England.

"I want to buy some horses," she told Sarai, who looked at her blankly.

"Horses?" she echoed. "But why, Valentina?"

"Well, for one thing, I think I should enjoy riding such fine horses as these," Valentina replied.

"You ride horses?" Sarai laughed weakly. "You are teasing me, aren't you, Valentina? And I am so silly that for a moment I believed you! Women do not ride horses."

"In my country they do," Valentina said firmly. "Our family

raises horses, Sarai. These are fine animals, the like of which I have never seen. Yes, particularly fine. I believe introducing such a strain of animal into our own herds might prove beneficial." She smiled at the woman. "I want six mares and a good stallion. You will have to bargain for me, however, as I do not believe my Turkish is good enough."

Sarai looked horrified. "I cannot bargain for horses," she whispered. "I have not the faintest idea how!"

"I imagine it is like bargaining for anything else," replied Valentina, her eye on a handsome white stallion with a black mane and tail. The dealer had several stallions, all carefully separated. The white one seemed the best. Unless, of course, he had some hidden flaw. "Go about it as if you were going to purchase a fine jewel or a rug," Valentina suggested to her startled friend. "Ask the horse trader how much for the white stallion over there," she said, pointing at the horse.

Sarai swallowed hard. She approached the dealer. "My friend," she said, "is a foreigner whose family raises horses. She wishes to know the price of the white stallion with the dark mane and tail."

"Lady", the dealer replied, "I do not have time for pranks. I do not sell horses to women."

Valentina understood that clearly. "Why?" she asked. "Is it against the law in Istanbul to sell horses to women?"

"It is not against any law I know of," he muttered in a surly manner, "but it should be."

Valentina drew an obviously heavy purse from her robes and hefted it meaningfully from one hand to the other. The clink of gold coins was audible as she asked, "My money is not good enough for you?"

The man licked his lips. The coins were surely gold, for only gold made that particular sound. Business had been slow of late, and if he was going to build his wife that house he kept promising her so that they would not have to live forever with his in-laws, he could not afford to say no to this foreign woman.

"How many horses do you want?" he asked her.

"Is this all you have?" she demanded. "Where did you get them?"

"I live outside the city, lady, and I raise the animals myself. These are my yearlings, and a better crop I have never had, may Yahweh strike me dead if I am lying to you!"

"I want a stallion and six mares for breeding," Valentina said.

"They must all be healthy, for they have to be able to withstand a sea voyage to England."

"If you really know horses," said the dealer, "then you will know that these are excellent animals, lady."

"Name me a price for the white stallion," she answered him, and he did.

Sarai gasped. "Thief!" she raged at him. "Even I know a horse should not cost that much. Come, Valentina! This man is a robber. I cannot allow you to do business with him, lest my family be blamed for your being cheated. The Kiras do not cheat anyone."

The horse dealer looked from one woman to the other, then paled. "You are a member of the Kira family, lady?"

"I am," Sarai replied haughtily.

The dealer thought quickly. He could make himself a handsome profit and possibly also gain the goodwill of the most important Jewish family in the entire city of Istanbul. So this foreign woman was eccentric. Was not the matriarch of the Kira family herself—a woman who had lived longer than was decent—eccentric?

"Lady, I apologize," he said to Sarai. "I do not know what possessed me to name such a figure. If you will half the figure, you will have the true price of the animal."

Sarai found that she was in her element. Valentina had been right. It *was* just like purchasing a fine gemstone or a carpet from the bazaars. She began to bargain with the horse dealer in earnest, haranguing him lustily until they finally reached a price for the stallion which they could agree on. Then, while Valentina inspected the mares in the trader's herd and chose the six she wanted, Sarai began her bargaining all over again. Finally, the entire bargain was struck.

"Bring the beasts to the Kira family stables," she commanded the dealer regally. "Tell them they have been purchased by the family's English guests." She took Valentina's purse from her and carefully counted out the coins, then handed them to the dealer. "Do not attempt to switch horses on us, sir," she warned. "The animals will be thoroughly hosed down when they arrive."

"You are too suspicious, Sarai," Valentina said smoothly, extracting another coin from the purse and pressing it into the dealer's hand. "For your trouble, sir," she said, and then the two women walked away.

"I did it! I actually bargained for seven horses!" Sarai said excitedly. "I cannot believe it, and neither will anyone else. I really did it!"

They stopped to buy two fruit sherbets to refresh themselves after their business transaction, then the two women walked back up the winding streets of the ghetto to the great house at the top of Balata. There, to Valentina's annoyance, she learned that Padraic, Tom, and Murrough had decided to remain across the Horn in Pera for another day or two so that they might go hunting with the ambassador in the hills behind the city.

"Does he think he is some sultan and I his slave that he can leave me alone and treat me so?" Valentina fumed to Nelda. "He has certainly taken on the ways of the country quickly enough."

"'Tis just like a man, my mum says," Nelda replied. "Once he's sure of you, he forgets you."

"He will not forget me," Valentina said softly. "Oh, no, Nelda! He cannot forget me! I am wrapped about his heart and I have captured his soul, even if he is not aware of it yet." She laughed. "We will go home as soon as I have seen the Valide, and once in England, my lord and master will find that he cannot bear to have me out of his sight for a moment. Let him play with the other little boys now, Nelda. My time will come soon enough!"

"Oh, m'lady! You're a wild one for all your innocent looks! I hope I may continue to serve you when we get home again. 'Twould be very boring to go back to my old life, or to have to marry just yet. I'd rather serve you!"

"Why, so you shall, Nelda, for you suit me. Your mother, bless her, persists in treating me like the child I am not."

"Then give her a nursery full of bairns to watch over, m'lady, and she'll be content," Nelda replied mischievously.

Valentina laughed again. "Why, Nelda," she replied. "I may do just that!"

Chapter Eleven

THE ENTIRE WOMEN'S QUARTERS of the Kira household marshaled itself to prepare Valentina for her audience with the Sultan
Valide Safiye. In the morning, she was bathed as she had never
been bathed before. Every crevice of her body, every inch of her
skin was soaped and rinsed thoroughly. Her hair was washed
and rinsed, then washed and rinsed again. Her fingernails and
toenails were pared neatly. She was massaged with creams. She
was perfumed.

Her clothing was selected by Esther herself, for whatever favor
Valentina found with Safiye would reflect upon the Kira family
as well.

"There is no hiding your beauty," Esther said, "and so we will
not even attempt to do so. Instead, we will enhance it, and if
Safiye feels a prick of jealousy, she will at least be soothed by
the knowledge that you can be no rival to her in any way."

"I wish Padraic and the others were back to see me in my
finery," said Valentina.

The old woman chuckled. "You are like me," she said. "You
do not like waiting on a man, and you are perhaps a little angry
that your betrothed husband has left you to go hunting with his
friends."

"Aye, I am irritated by it," Valentina admitted, "but probably
because women in this society are so closeted, Esther Kira, and
I am not used to it. In England, I would have been invited to join
the gentlemen at hunting instead of being left behind."

"I have heard that the women in your land do such things, and
although it amazes me, I fully approve. I only wish there were
such independent women among my descendants, but alas! It
is not our way, as Sarai would so fatalistically say."

Valentina giggled. "It does seem to be her favorite expression,"
she noted, "but I did get her to bargain for my horses the other
day and she was quite proud of herself."

"Heh! Heh! Heh!" Esther Kira cackled. "I should have liked to have seen Sarai arguing with a horse dealer!"

The clothing the old woman chose for Valentina was exquisite. There were wide-legged pantaloons of mauve silk, with a pattern of small gold and silver stars woven into the fabric. Seed pearls were sewn at the ankles to give the pantaloons three-inch cuffs. A blouse of the sheerest, palest pink gauze was topped by a sleeve-less bolero of cloth of gold over mauve silk, embroidered with pearls and pink crystals and edged with pearls. Tied about her hips was a wide sash of alternating stripes of cloth of gold and cloth of silver. Gold kid slippers were slipped on her slender feet.

Nelda watched curiously as one of the Kira servants brushed her mistress's hair back and wove pearls into the single braid that she expertly fashioned. Valentina's eyes were then carefully outlined with kohl and her lashes darkened so that her amethyst eyes appeared quite large. The valide's gift necklace was slipped over her head. And then, to Valentina's surprise, the matriarch herself fitted large diamond teardrops into Valentina's ears.

"My gift to you, dear child, to commemorate your visit to Istanbul," Esther Kira said quietly.

Valentina's eyes filled with quick tears. "Thank you," she said simply as the servant mopped at her eyes before she could spoil her makeup.

The other women of the Kira family had gifts for her, too. They presented her with a lovely selection of gold and silver bangle bracelets. Some were plain and others were studded with seed pearls or semiprecious gems.

A feridje, the elegant outdoor garment of the wealthy, was brought. Of lavender silk outside, the feridje was lined with pink silk and had a closure of purple jade.

Valentina donned the garment and found that its hood extended over her eyebrows, like a yashmak. A veil of mauve silk was affixed to the hood, leaving only her marvelous eyes visible. Esther warned Valentina to keep her eyes lowered, as was proper for a respectable woman, and not to look any male, whole or eunuch, directly in the face lest she be considered bold or a whore.

In the courtyard Val was helped into the Kira litter, where Sarai, who would go with her, was waiting.

"Remember what I have said," Esther warned her guest. "Guard your tongue, for as charming as Safiye may appear, she is as dangerous as a scorpion. May Yahweh go with you, child."

"Thank you, Esther, for *everything*," Valentina replied sincerely.

The old woman nodded, then drew the litter curtains closed. Valentina felt the vehicle being lifted, then they were off through the courtyard gates and down the hill to travel from the ghetto across the city to the Yeni Serai, the Imperial Palace of the Ottoman sultans.

"I do not care if the sultan is your ruler," Valentina told Sarai, "his palace cannot have a more beautiful view than your family has from your home. Nelda says if she could not go home to England, she would not mind waking up every morning to the panorama of the Golden Horn with Pera and Galata beyond. You are fortunate to own such a house and grounds."

"The house is relatively new, by Istanbul standards," said Sarai, smiling. "Balata is, of course, a very ancient quarter of the city, but until fifty years ago, the Kira family lived in a brick house on a side street. The brick alone was enough to distinguish the Kiras as a family of wealth, and the house had belonged to the Kiras for centuries. Esther's son, Solomon, received the property upon which our current home now sits as part of his wife's dowry. For years he dreamed of building a home for the family there, but until his uncle and father died, he could do nothing. Once he became head of the family, however, he set about building the house. Esther did not approve, for she said to place our house in such a conspicuous location would only draw attention to us. But Solomon would have his way, and the house was built. My husband Simon was born there, as were all of his brothers and sisters, and the new generation also."

"My home in England has been in my family for several generations, too," Valentina replied. "It is called Pearroc Royal, which is Old English for Park Royal, for it was once a deer-hunting preserve reserved exclusively for the king and his guests. Our house was originally a hunting lodge, although today you would not believe it, for it has been expanded and added to over the years, particularly after my parents were married. There simply wasn't enough space for all of the children, and we have a large family who think nothing of coming to visit on a moment's notice. My father's eldest sister and her family live on the neighboring estate, and there are always birthdays, saint's days, betrothal feasts, marriages, and new babies, occasions calling for a celebration by the entire family who gather from all over England!"

"We are separated by different cultures and religions," Sarai said slowly, "yet we are very much alike, Valentina. It is true that Englishwomen are more independent than we are, but our lives seem to revolve about our families nonetheless, and those families are remarkably similar, are they not? I think, perhaps, if people knew more about each other, there would be fewer wars and misunderstandings among the different races and cultures of mankind. Perhaps that is why Yahweh created us differently, so that we might learn to get along with each other." She stopped. It was an incredibly deep thought for a woman so cloistered and bound by tradition. "You have made me consider things as I have never considered them before," Sarai said wonderingly, and then she grew silent.

My father. Valentina realized that in her previous speech, she had called Conn her father. Javid Khan was not her father. Was Conn indeed her true sire? Or was it the late and wicked Sultan Murad? She had almost forgotten the reason for her visit to the Valide, but now she was sharply reminded. She, too, grew pensive.

The litter bearers moved with assurance through the city, the hardened soles of their feet making sharp *slap-slap* sounds on the sun-baked streets that, in some places, still showed the ancient paving stones that dated back to the Roman or to the Byzantine empires. In other places, the stones had long ago been carted away for other purposes, and the streets were of hard-packed dirt, dusty in the dryest seasons, mud sloughs in the wet times. The city was unbelievably noisy. Many people used the streets to conduct business in, and others gathered to gossip. The Kira servants skillfully wove their way through the crowds. As they neared the palace grounds, the mass of people began to thin until it was suddenly possible to hear the sound of birdsong once again.

The litter came to a stop. Suddenly, one of the curtains was drawn aside and a janissary's head was inside the litter. "Your business?"

"This lady is expected by the valide," Sarai Kira said.

The janissary withdrew, and their litter was allowed through the first of several gates.

"We are now in the First Court of the palace," said Sarai.

"How many courts are there?" Valentina asked.

"Four" came the reply.

Once again their litter was halted and a head poked through the curtain.

"We are expected by the valide," Sarai said without waiting for the question. The curtains were closed again. "We are passing through the Middle Gate into the Second Court now," she continued. After a moment, she drew back one of the litter's fluttering draperies and said to Valentina, "Peek out and you will see some of the gardens."

The enormous court was a magnificent garden. There were carefully tended beds of late-spring bulbs; flowering almond, peach, and apricot trees, graceful olive trees with silvery foliage; and several fountains—all transversed by neatly raked paths of fine white marble chips. Many gardeners were engaged in maintaining the landscape.

"The gardeners are also the sultan's executioners, and quite expert in the art of the bowstring," Sarai informed her companion.

Valentina shivered. "How macabre," she said, "that men who can so easily kill are also responsible for such great beauty." She grew silent again as she realized that the very sights she was seeing now had once been seen by her mother.

"We are coming up to the Carriage Gate, which is one of five entries into the Haremlik. Once inside, we will leave our litter and continue on foot. We must pass through the domain of the Black Eunuchs and the Aga Kisler before we reach the Valide. There is a chance that we will see the aga himself. His name is Ali Ziya, and he is a most evil man. He hates our family with a strange passion, but Esther's influence, even now, is too great for him to overcome."

"Why does he hate the Kiras?" asked Valentina, curious.

"I think it is because Esther is a living link to a time when the Ottoman sultans were strong and ruled without the influence of their favorite women and eunuchs. As long as Esther lives, she is a reminder to Ali Ziya that those times could come again, which would not suit him and his ilk at all. There has been no really strong sultan since Selim I. His son, the great and magnificent Suleiman, was a fine man, and his reign was a long and prosperous one for Turkey, but he was strongly influenced by his mother and his favorite kadin, Khurrem, the Laughing One. His descendants have grown increasingly more dependent on the advice of others," Sarai finished in a low voice just as the litter was stopped for the third time. "We are at the Carriage Gate now," she said softly.

The curtains of the litter were drawn aside by two young pages who reached in to help the women out. A young eunuch stood nearby. "You are the Kira woman and the Englishwoman?" he demanded in a high voice.

Sarai nodded, her eyes lowered.

"You will follow me," the eunuch said, leading them through the gate, which opened into a small, domed room lined on either side with closets.

"Those closets are said to have magical powers," Sarai whispered to Valentina. "Twice, people have gone into them never to be seen again. Once it was a eunuch escaping the wrath of a sultan, and the other time it was a slave girl engaged in a game of hide-and-seek."

Suddenly, so suddenly in fact that Valentina jumped, a tall, ostentatiously dressed gentleman appeared out of the shadows. Their guide, the young eunuch fell to his knees, his head touching the floor. Sarai bowed to him from her waist.

"My lord Aga," she murmured politely.

"Lady Sarai," the man murmured, and then waited for Sarai to introduce her companion.

"This is Lady Barrows, who has come to visit the Valide," Sarai said simply. She offered the Aga Kislar no further information, which she knew annoyed him.

Ali Ziya reached out and loosened Valentina's veil so that it fell away from her face, revealing her features. Her eyes remained modestly lowered as she had been instructed, while he scanned her features with the eye of a connoisseur. "Raise your eyes, woman," he commanded sharply. "I would see their color."

Valentina lifted her gaze to him, and it took every ounce of her willpower not to pull away from the Aga Kisler, whose talonlike fingers were grasping her chin. She had heard that eunuchs were obese, but Ali Ziya was not. He was a big man, but there was no fat on his body. His narrow brown face possessed high cheekbones, a sharp chin, an aquiline nose, narrow lips, and hooded eyelids over narrow, dark eyes that had a decidedly reptilian cast to them.

"Magnificent," he said in his high, whispery voice that was very like a snake's hiss. "You are a most beautiful woman and would grace my master's harem. A pity you are not a slave, for I should enrich your owner beyond his wildest dreams in order to possess you for the sultan."

"Lady Barrows is a woman of wealth and power in England. She has even served her queen," Sarai said quickly, goaded into revealing more than she had intended to.

"Is this so?" Ali Ziya demanded. "You are in favor with the great Virgin Queen who is in correspondence with the Valide?"

"It is so," Valentina replied. "I have the privilege to be in charge of Her Majesty's maids of honor, who are the virgin daughters of the great families who serve my queen."

"A pity." The Aga sighed. "A great pity that I cannot have such a woman as you for my master." Catching himself, he said, "The Valide is most pleased with your gift, lady, and has asked me to escort you into her presence personally. Please follow me." He led the two women from the Dome Room to the outer courtyard, across the Courtyard of the Black Eunuchs, and through the main door of the Haremlik.

Valentina cast Sarai a glance as she fastened her veil and found the young woman's eyes laughing at her in response. She stifled a giggle and hurried along after the long-legged, pompous Ali Ziya, whose opulent fur-edged velvet coat was swinging about his long frame.

When they entered the harem's main door, they turned left down a long corridor.

"This is the corridor where the food is brought in from the kitchens," Sarai whispered. As they turned sharply right, she whispered, "This is the Corridor of the Women Slaves." They exited into an open courtyard with magnificent gardens filled with rosebushes just coming into bloom. "This is the valide's own private court," Sarai informed her.

Ali Ziya ushered the two women into the Valide's Reception Room, then hurried into the next room to inform the Valide that her guests had arrived. Valentina's gaze swept the room. The walls were tiled in blue and white. Beneath Valentina's feet was the thickest, softest carpet she had ever stood upon. Two slave women appeared and took their outdoor garments, removing their veils as well.

Sarai slipped two gossamer head veils from a pocket hidden within her voluminous cherry-red robe and handed to Valentina a mauve one edged in gold and seed pearls. "It is the custom to keep one's head covered except in intimate or special circumstances," she said softly, covering her own dark head with a red veil shot through with gold.

Valentina had just covered her dark hair when Ali Ziya returned and said to Sarai, "My gracious lady, the Valide, bids you to wait here, or, if you choose, you may enter the harem to conduct your usual business." Turning his reptilian gaze to Valentina, he said, "My gracious lady, the Valide, bids you, daughter of Marjallah, to enter her salon."

Valentina felt a shiver ripple through her when he addressed her as "daughter of Marjallah." Her mother was Aidan St. Michael, a good Englishwoman, not some exotic creature who lived in a palace like this. Yet her mother had once lived in this very palace. Lived here as the desperate slave of a now-dead sultan who just might be Valentina's father.

As she followed the Aga Kislar into the valide's salon, Valentina did not know where to look first. The room was one of the most beautiful she had ever seen. Long lead-paned glass windows looked out onto the valide's private court. The walls were paneled with a pale golden fruitwood, and tiles were inlaid every few feet to make a design of flowers. The tiles were all cream, rose, and pink, and were surrounded with gilt moldings.

On the wide floorboards were lush carpets of cream, dark blue, and rose. The furniture was of ebony inlaid with mother-of-pearl and of gilt set with semiprecious stones. On the tables were bowls of flowers whose perfume scented the air. The lamps were of gold inlaid with rubies. In a corner of the room was a tiled fireplace with a conical hood of beaten silver, and in the center of the chamber a blue-and-cream-tiled fountain was filled with pale pink waterlilies and large goldfish. There were several long-haired cats around the room, and Valentina was reminded of her beloved Tulip.

"Come over to me, my child," a musical voice called to her from the end of the room, and Valentina turned to see a petite, beautiful woman who lounged with a regal air on a rose velvet divan.

Standing before the Sultan Valide, Valentina made a proper curtsy.

"You do that quite nicely," Safiye said approvingly. "I can see that the Kiras have instructed you well. Your mother once curtsied to me in such garments. You have her skin, her bearing, her form, but you are far more beautiful than Marjallah. Were I a younger woman, my child, I think I should be quite envious of you," she finished ingenuously.

"You are most gracious to compliment me in such extravagant terms, my lady Valide," Valentina replied, not for a moment fooled by Safiye's charm, "but what small beauty I have cannot begin to compare with that of Sultan Mehmed's beautiful mother, who I must now thank for her magnificent gift to me."

"You also have your mother's tact, my child," Safiye said, "as well as her exquisite taste in gifts.

"I cannot tell you how surprised I was when Esther Kira told me of her miraculous escape those long years ago when she was condemned to drowning for her attempt on the life of my dear husband. Esther's tale was but a brief one, for she said the story was yours to tell. Will you tell me now, my child?" She waved Valentina to an upholstered stool placed directly before her divan.

Valentina settled herself, noting as she did that the room was now empty but for the two of them. Looking up at Safiye, she began the story that she had decided would be the most believable. "This tale, dear madam, is the partial recollection of my mother, blended with what was told to her by the others involved. The last thing she remembers of the palace is being given some draught by the Valide Nur-U-Banu, which rendered her unconscious. She supposed that Sultan Murad's mother was being merciful to her because she had not stopped the sultan from forcing my mother into his harem after the death of Prince Javid Khan. My mother always believed that Nur-U-Banu might have prevented her enslavement if she had desired to do so."

"Indeed she could have," murmured Safiye, easily casting the entire blame on the late Nur-U-Banu, "but she was always attempting to lessen my small influence with my husband. After Prince Javid Khan's tragic demise, your poor mother desired only to return to her homeland, but Nur-U-Banu sought to use her against me. She was unsuccessful, of course, because Murad loved me alone. As for your mother, she was like a sister to me. She never sought to steal my lord's affections from me. Unfortunately, Murad always enjoyed that which was not easily obtained. Had your mother pretended acquiescence to the sultan, he would quickly have grown tired of her and then she would have been safe. It was not in her nature, however, to pretend. I think part of her charm was her unique honesty, but please continue, my dear."

"The next thing my mother remembers," Valentina said, "was awakening in a ship's cabin, its captain and officers anxiously looking down at her. The ship was an English one, and they had seen the royal executioner drop the sack with my mother inside it into the sea. The sack, however, was not tied tightly and my mother's body floated out. Seeing her, two sailors dived from the ship and swam to her. Finding her alive, though unconscious, they brought her aboard. If the executioner saw anything, he made no sign and kept rowing back to shore.

"Several hours later my mother awoke, and after her shock subsided, she told the captain who she was. The captain was astounded. We English are not used to such things. What was even more astounding was that almost immediately thereafter an O'Malley-Small trading vessel was sighted bound for Istanbul. The English captain hailed it, and then the most miraculous happening occurred. My mother's husband was aboard that other ship. He was on his way to Istanbul to find her. It had taken him months to trace her to Istanbul, but he had never given up hope of being reunited with her."

"How wonderfully romantic!" Safiye sighed, genuinely moved. "Your mother always insisted that he would have her back, no matter what, but we never believed her. Tell me more, dear child!"

"Mother was transferred from her rescuers' ship to the O'Malley-Small ship, which turned immediately for home. The English captain and his men were promised a great reward when they returned to England, and indeed they were given a large sum. Special attention and a large sum was paid to the two who had spotted Mother and who dived in to rescue her.

"Within a year of Mother's return home, I was born, but Mother's happiness was marred by a nagging doubt. Several months ago, I learned of that doubt. You see, Mother is not certain who my father was. It might have been Prince Javid Khan or her husband, with whom she had united physically on the day following her rescue. Or"—she paused—"my father could be the late Sultan Murad."

Safiye paled, her beringed hand flying to her heart.

"If I resembled either of my parents, there would be no problem," Valentina said, "but alas, I do not look at all like my mother or her husband. I have visited Borte Khatun, the mother of Prince Javid Khan, but all of her female descendants bear a particular birthmark that I do not possess, and we have concluded that I am not the daughter of Javid Khan. Dear madam, look at me, I beg of you! Is there anything you see in me to make you believe I am the daughter of Sultan Murad? Anything at all?"

Safiye peered intently into Valentina's face. She ordered the young woman to show her her profile, first the left side and then the right. She looked hard at Valentina, then shook her head. "Your features are foreign to me, my dear, but if that were not enough, there is this for you to think on. My husband fathered twenty sons and eighty-three daughters. Of all his children, only one, my son, Sultan Mehmed, has dark hair. My lord Murad had golden-red hair and a passion for blondes and women with red hair. His father, Sultan Selim II, had dark blond hair. Although my hair was a glorious shade of red in my youth, as was my mother's, my father had dark hair, which I remember as similar to my son's. And there is a further element in all this to make me absolutely certain my lord Murad could not have fathered you. I will tell you, dear child, for the sake of your sweet mother who was the only true friend I ever had.

"When I saw, those long years ago, that my lord was weakening and ready to succumb to his mother's blandishments, I was frantic. I had lived in the harem long enough to know how vicious the rivalry between the mothers of a sultan's sons can become. Then one day my servants, in an effort to cheer me, brought me a small casket that had belonged to my husband's grandmother, Khurrem Kadin. Inside were a few amusing trinkets of no great value, but there was also a recipe for a potion that was said to render a man's seed lifeless within a woman's womb. A notation on the parchment stated that the receipe had been obtained from Sultan Suleiman's mother, Cyra Hafise, who, along with her husband's other kadins, had conspired to prevent any more sons being born to Sultan Selim I.

"I can remember even now how excited I became at this discovery. I brewed the concoction in secret. With the help of my most trusted women, I saw that it was introduced into the food and drink of my rivals. Indeed, none conceived by my lord Murad.

"Somehow, Nur-U-Banu found out. She said nothing, but the three women who had helped me were found dead in their beds. Nur-U-Banu's warning to me was heeded. But when my lord Murad decided he would possess your mother, I knew I must chance the use of the potion again. Nur-U-Banu would have used any sons of your mother's to set my son aside."

"Would he have set your son aside?" Valentina asked.

"He was not a weak man, but he loved his mother, and he truly believed in the saying from the Holy Koran, 'Paradise lies at a mother's feet,' " Safiye explained. "Your mother's resistance was fascinating to him. Women who share a sultan's bed are considered honored and they accept their fate with joy. Your mother did not accept her fate happily and consequently made herself, without desiring to, the most intriguing woman my lord Murad had ever known. So you see, a son of your mother's would have been a most serious rival to my son, Mehmed. Had it been any other woman, I should not have cared. Indeed, I did not care when, in later years, other sons were born to my lord Murad. Your mother, however, was my true friend. I did not want to lose her friendship.

"So when it became apparent that my lord Murad would have your mother in his bed, I brewed the potion in secret once more and it was introduced into your mother's food. The potion prevented your mother from conceiving as long as she took it. She was not aware that she was taking it, but I am certain that she took it every day. That, my dear, is why I am absolutely certain that you cannot be Sultan Murad's daughter. So as you are not Javid Khan's daughter, then you are truly the child of your English father."

A huge weight was suddenly lifted from Valentina's shoulders. She really was her father's daughter! The fears that had assailed her these many months were all magically gone. She did not believe there was any reason for Safiye to lie to her, and her intuition told her that the Sultan Valide was telling the truth. With tears in her eyes, Valentina fell to her knees and kissed Safiye's hands.

"Thank you, dear madam!" she sobbed. "Thank you!"

A strangely tender light entered Safiye's eyes, and for the briefest moment, her beautiful face was gentle and unguarded. She caressed Valentina's dark head beneath its gossamer veil, sighing so softly that Valentina was not certain she had really heard the sound. "You must love your father very much, dear child, that you would brave such a dangerous odyssey in order to seek the truth—a truth that might not have been to your liking. Allah has surely looked over you and marked you as one of his own," the Sultan Valide said. "But come, my dear, sit by me and we will have refreshments, now that our serious business is concluded. Tell me of my dear friend, Marjallah, of how the years have treated her. Have you brothers and sisters?"

"Oh, yes, madam!" Valentina said as she settled herself by the Sultan Valide. She began a history of her mother's life in England, and of her own.

After a while, Safiye clapped her hands and her slave women appeared, bringing trays of delicate cakes, bowls of sugared almonds and pistachio nuts, and delicate crystal goblets of fruit sherbets. There were porcelain cups from which they might sip pale green tea if they wished. Valentina found herself quite hungry, and Safiye noted the young woman's appetite.

"Your mother always ate with enthusiasm," she said with a smile. "Would you like to meet someone who served your mother in the house of Prince Javid Khan and also here at the Yeni Serai?"

"I thought my mother's serving women were freed," Valentina said.

"Indeed they were, for Nur-U-Banu promised that to your mother. But there was one servant who remained, your mother's eunuch, Jinji. I took him into my own household, and when my personal eunuch, Tahsin, died suddenly, I elevated Jinji to his rank. He has always been anxious to please, is that not so, Jinji?" she asked of the eunuch who had entered and positioned himself at her side.

"I am always ready to serve my lady Valide" was the reply.

"What do you think of Marjallah's daughter, Jinji?" Safiye questioned him.

"She is as beautiful as the sun, the moon, and a thousand shining stars, my lady Valide, unlike her plain-faced mother, who, nonetheless, possessed a kind and true heart," was the answer.

Safiye laughed. "As always, your tongue is quick to speak the right words, Jinji. May it ever be so, for your sake."

Suddenly, the doors to the Valide's salon flew open and a magnificently garbed man entered the room, striding across it to kneel briefly at Safiye's feet. When he rose, he towered over the two women. "Mother, I was informed that you had company and I came to meet our foreign visitor," he said.

Sultan Mehmed III was a tall man, large and beginning to run to fat. His fair skin was sallow, and beneath his deep brown eyes were pouches that spoke of too many cups of wine, despite the Islamic ban on fermented beverages. He had a large, long nose beneath which bristled fierce twin mustaches. His beard was jet black. He was dressed in a wonderful cloth-of-gold robe trimmed in sable, and there were several long ropes of huge diamonds and pearls about his neck. He wore a large turban with a diamond as big as a man's fist set dead center in its front. The magnificent turban made the sultan appear even bigger than he was.

Boldly, the sultan gripped Valentina's face between his thumb and forefinger and his dark eyes scanned her face, lighting with pleasure at what he saw. "She has eyes like jewels and skin as fine as Bursa silk," he commented to his mother. "Is she for me, Mother? You have outdone yourself this time!"

Safiye, who had worked so hard to impress Valentina favorably, was furious. Her eyes narrowed, and she said in a cold, stinging voice, "My lord! Have I not taught you better manners than this? To behave like a greedy schoolboy at the sight of a sweet! This lady is my guest, not some slave girl!"

"Having seen her, I desire her," the sultan replied. "Am I, the ruler of a mighty empire, the Shadow of Allah upon this earth, to be denied what I desire? It is unthinkable, Mother!"

"Then you must live with the unthinkable, Mehmed, for this woman is your half sister, the daughter of Marjallah, who was once your father's favorite. Do you remember? I recently reminded you of how, long ago, Marjallah attempted to stab your father. She was condemned, but miraculously escaped death, I have learned. After she returned home, her daughter was born— your father's child, your half sister. Greet her properly, my lord, and restrain your unseemly lust," Safiye said sharply.

"My *sister*? How unfortunate," the sultan said dispiritedly. He turned his gaze from his mother to Valentina. The lust had gone from his eyes. "Greetings, sister," he said.

"My lord," Valentina replied.

"Her voice is so musical," mourned Mehmed. "I cannot bear it, Mother! I must leave you now, that I may find some way of assuaging my disillusionment."

Safiye reached out and patted her son's fat hand. "There are a half dozen new Circassian virgins just arrived in the harem, Ali Ziya tells me. Why not go and inspect them? Perhaps you can lift your melancholy that way."

With a sigh, the sultan withdrew from his mother's suite. Safiye turned to Valentina. "You are aware of why it was necessary to tell him you were his half sister? It is not so, of course, but had I not said it, he would not have been satisfied until you shared his bed. Such a thing is not your desire, I know. Esther Kira tells me that you are betrothed."

"I am indeed betrothed, madam, and my intended husband is with me here in Istanbul," Valentina replied.

"When will you leave us, my child?"

"Within the next day or two, madam. There is no further need for me to stay, and we would be home before the autumn gales attack the seas. My mother will be anxious to learn of my adventures, and I wish to tell my father how very much I love him! In my darkest hour, he swore he believed himself to be my true sire. If he was not, he told me, it mattered not, for he loved me anyway. Now that I am free of the terrible doubt, I want to go home as quickly as possible!"

"Of course you do," said Safiye sympathetically. "I am going to ask a favor of you, my dear Valentina. Tomorrow morning, a messenger will deliver to you a parchment from me that I would have you carry to your mother. Will you do that for me?"

"Gladly, my lady Valide!" Valentina replied.

The visit had reached its natural conclusion, so Valentina politely took leave of her hostess. She and Sarai were escorted to the Kira litter, which was waiting at the Gate of Felicity opposite the Throne Room.

The young French-speaking eunuch who accompanied the women was pleased to identify the various sights as they went along. Valentina was so interested in what the eunuch was saying that she did not observe, near the gate of Felicity, the sultan standing with another man in the shadow of a large tree.

"My half sister," the sultan grumbled to Cicalazade Pasha. "I would have paid a king's ransom to possess her, but even I draw the line at incest."

"Your half sister?" The vizier was fascinated.

"Yes," the sultan answered irritably. "She is the daughter of a long-ago favorite of my father's, Marjallah. Unfortunately, my father was not a favorite of Marjallah's." The sultan chuckled. Seeing that Cicalazade Pasha did not understand, the sultan explained about the attempt on his father's life and the subsequent sentence of drowning.

"I met the Englishwoman some months ago at Esther Kira's house," the vizier told the sultan. "I desired her myself, my lord."

The sultan's eyes narrowed contemplatively. "It seems a pity, Cica, that we should both be doomed to disappointment. Well, doesn't it?"

"My lord?" The vizier wanted to be certain the sultan was suggesting what the vizier believed he was.

"If my beautiful half sister were to disappear before she leaves Istanbul, little could be done to find her. Of course, I would insist that all of the slave markets and brothels be thoroughly searched, and I would condemn such an outrage, but I do not believe she would be found *anywhere*," the sultan murmured. "Of course, you would tell me all about your victory, Cica, would you not?"

"Perhaps, my lord, you would enjoy watching me win that victory," the vizier said softly.

"You would not mind?" The sultan's voice had a boyish excitement to it.

"It would give me great pleasure to offer such exquisite entertainment to you, my lord," Cicalazade Pasha said. "I have not been so taken with a woman since my ravishing Incili died. She quite spoiled me for others. I now dislike complacent harem beauties quite heartily. Love, I believe, should be a battle, hard fought and honestly won. These creatures with their soft words and soft bodies quite bore me. I do not believe that the beauteous lady Valentina—which means the valorous one—shall bore me. And you, my lord, will be well entertained by my taming of that marvelous creature with her amethyst eyes and creamy skin."

"How will you capture her?" the sultan demanded eagerly.

"I do not know yet, my lord," said the vizier. "I must first learn her plans for the next day or two. I do not believe I have much time."

"I cannot be involved in the capture," the sultan said. "I must be able to say honestly I know nothing. My mother's eyes are so very keen that she always knows when I am lying," Mehmed finished in an annoyed tone. "The Kiras will come to my mother when the girl disappears, you may be certain of that. They pride themselves on their connection with us—though why they should have that connection I have never known, nor does anyone else. It appears to be a tradition lost in time and tied to that wretched old woman who is their matriarch. I will have to play my part convincingly, Cica, if I am to deceive them successfully."

"Tell me," he asked eagerly, "will you make her beg for your favors?"

The vizier smiled. "She will beg," he said with dark certainty.

The sultan let his gaze drift toward the Gate of Felicity, through which the Kira litter had so recently departed from the palace. "If only she were not my sister," he repeated sadly.

Valentina laughed, relating the story to Sarai. "The Valide told him I was his half sister. You should have seen the look of disappointment on his fat face! I cannot tell you how relieved I was that she protected me from him. I would kill myself before I allowed such a creature to touch me."

"He is said to be like his father," Sarai said, her voice barely a whisper. "Absolutely insatiable and wickedly lustful. During his father's reign and his, the price of beautiful women has doubled and tripled in the slave markets."

"You and your family have been so kind to us," Valentina said, "but now that I have solved the mystery of my paternity, I shall be glad to go home. If the queen is still alive, I intend asking Padraic to allow me to serve her until her death. She is so very lonely."

"She has no family?" Sarai was puzzled.

"No. Her siblings all died without issue, and she never wed. There are cousins, but no one who is close to her. The heir to the throne is the son of her greatest rival, her cousin."

"Poor lady," Sarai said. "I see now how very fortunate Esther is, and why she does not want to leave us."

"Esther will live forever." Valentina laughed. "She is so full of life."

"Ah, but she has slowed since her legs became unreliable," Sarai said.

"It is not her legs that make Esther so alive," Valentina said. "It is her wonderful spirit."

Sarai nodded, then said, "What did you think of Ali Ziya?"

"A snake of a creature," Valentina said. "What happened to Ilban Bey, who was the aga when my mother was in Istanbul? My mother told me of him. She did not say he was an old man."

"He wasn't," replied Sarai, "and he treated Safiye with great respect, anticipating her eventual rise to the position of Sultan Valide. When Nur-U-Banu died in 1583, he continued on in his duties, even though he had been Nur-U-Banu's choice when she became Valide. Tahsin, Safiye's eunuch, was not well. He could not accept so much responsibility. Then he died and Safiye elevated your mother's old Jinji to the position of personal eunuch, but Jinji was too inexperienced to become Aga. So Safiye was content to allow Ilban Bey to remain.

"Then Ilban Bey was found at the foot of a flight of stairs, his neck broken. Ali Ziya was his assistant. There was no one else, so Safiye chose him to be the Aga Kisler. He is a very dangerous man."

"I felt that," Valentina admitted. "How fortunate the valide was willing to protect me from the sultan. I am appalled by the way women are viewed in this land. I do not understand how my mother tolerated it for one moment, let alone a year!"

"She chose to survive," Sarai said quietly, "and in order to survive here, you must accept the culture. It is either that or, as your mother finally chose, death."

Valentina shook her head. "I will be glad to go home to England," she replied. "When Padraic and the others return from Pera, we will make plans to leave as soon as we can!"

"But before you go," Sarai said, "you must let me take you to the Covered Bazaar. Let us go tomorrow, for even if the gentlemen return tonight, it will take several days to provision your ships for your departure. You will not be leaving Istanbul for at least another few days. Surely you want to bring presents to your family? There is no better place in the entire empire to buy gifts than the great Covered Bazaar of Istanbul!"

They returned to the Kira house late in the afternoon to find that the gentlemen had returned from their hunting expedition. Valentina met her cousins and the earl in the only place in the Kira house that they could gather together, the gardens.

"There can be no doubt," she told them happily. "I am my father's daughter!" She related the story of her audience with Safiye, telling them of Safiye's protecting Valentina from the sultan.

Murrough smiled at her. "Your trip has been successful. We may return home soon, then?"

"Aye!" she answered, "as soon as possible."

"Home for our wedding?" Padraic demanded.

"Aye!" She kissed him quickly.

"Home to my lonely life," grumbled Tom.

"No," Valentina said, refusing to allow him to feel sorry for himself. "Home to find you a wife to love, even as Padraic and I have found each other." She kissed Tom on the cheek and he could not prevent a smile from touching his lips.

"And now," she said ominously, "I have a bone to pick with you gentlemen. How could you go blithely off to Pera without even telling me you were leaving?"

"It was quite a momentary decision," Murrough defended himself and the others. "The ambassador heard that we were at the Kiras', and he sent his barge for us. You were sleeping when the messenger came. We did not wish to awaken you, for we knew how exhausted you were, just barely over your ordeal."

"How thoughtful," Valentina murmured sweetly, but they could see that she was not placated.

"What can we do to reinstate ourselves in your good graces, divinity?" demanded the earl.

"Tomorrow, while Murrough prepares the ships for our return to England, you two will take me shopping in the Covered Bazaar. Sarai says there is no place like it anywhere on earth!"

"I can see," said Padraic, laughing, "that our folly will cost us dearly."

"Indeed, sir," replied Valentina, insinuating herself into the curve of his arm, "and should it not? Besides, you have not yet given me a betrothal gift. Because I am a widow and not a maid, do not think to get off lightly!"

"No more than *you* shall get off lightly," Padraic murmured softly against her hair.

Valentina's eyes closed as she leaned against him, and the look on her beautiful face told Thomas Ashburne that Valentina was most certainly in love with Lord Burke. There was no hope for him at all. He sighed softly, wondering if he would ever find that much love, and when. At a touch on his arm, he looked into the sympathetic gaze of Murrough O'Flaherty, and the earl flushed guiltily at having worn his heart on his sleeve for all to see.

"Let us leave them," Murrough said softly, and drew the earl away.

"Do I look as big a fool as I feel?" Tom Ashburne asked his companion.

"You're not a fool for falling in love, Tom" was the quiet reply.

"Were you ever in love, Murrough?"

Murrough chuckled. "I was betrothed as a lad to my stepsister, and from the first time I laid eyes on my Joan, I was lost. When I was a boy at court, there was many a lady who would have made a pet of me, but all I could see was Joan's sweet face, and I would have none of it. Aye, I've been in love, Tom, and I've never stopped being in love. That will come for you with the right woman. Valentina was not the right woman."

Padraic and Valentina stood facing each other. She gazed up at him adoringly, and he said, "If you look at me that way, Val, I shall be incapable of ever leaving you again."

" 'Tis precisely what I had in mind," she returned pertly, then she pressed herself against him. "I do not like this society where men are so strictly separated from women. I want to lie with you,

Padraic. I want to feel your hands on me, for it seems so long since we laid together in the Great Khan's yurt."

"Ohh, vixen!" he groaned. Then his mouth found hers in a fierce, passionate kiss. They kissed seemingly without end until finally he pulled reluctantly away from her. "We cannot do this to each other, Val," he said. "There is no place in this house that we can go to to satisfy our longings, and we are too old to play at courting games."

"Aye," she agreed with a deep sigh. "My lord, we know only too well where such games can lead. Oh, I want to go home this very day!"

Lord Burke laughed. He had never seen her quite like this. "Why, sweetheart," he teased, "I am flattered that your passion for me is so great."

"And would have been satisfied long ago," she grumbled, "had you not been so slow to speak up, Padraic!"

"I wanted only what was best for you, Val," he said quietly.

"*You* are what is best for me, my lord, and I shall be certain that our sons are not so lackadaisical about speaking up!"

He kissed her tenderly, her scolding lips, her beautiful eyelids, the tip of her nose. "I love you, Val, and we are together now and forever. That is what is important. You are my lost love found, and I shall never desert you, my darling, never!"

Chapter Twelve

THE CITY OF ISTANBUL was utterly and breathtakingly beautiful. The Ottoman Turks, in comparison with their predecessors, the Byzantines, had done little to contribute to that beauty, but the Byzantines had built for the ages. There were no street names. Residents of the city referred to streets by some identifying characteristic, such as the Street of the Gemcutters. Like Rome, Istanbul was built on seven hills, so the streets meandered

up and down and all around the city. The majority of houses
were of wood, though the wealthy and upper-middle-class merchants had taken to tearing down their old wood houses and
building new ones of brick or stone. The Sea of Marmara, the
great harbor of the Golden Horn, and the straits of the Bosporus
could be seen from many vantage points.

Water. It was all about them, not simply by nature's design
but because it was an important part of the religion of Islam.
There were fountains everywhere, filled by underground waterpipes that stemmed from cisterns and water tanks that took the
life-giving liquid from ancient aqueducts outside the city. The
public baths were magnificent and open to all. There were even
specific times set aside for the women, who, even if they had the
luxury of baths within their houses, nevertheless enjoyed going
to the public baths so that they might meet with their friends
and gossip.

Peeking from her enclosed litter, Valentina took it all in as she
was carried down the steep hillside streets from the ghetto of
Balata into the city proper. She shared her litter with Sarai and
with Cain Kira's outspoken young wife, Shohannah. Beside the
litter, mounted on fine horses, rode Lord Burke and the earl,
suitably attired in Turkish garments so as not to attract the scornful cry, "*giaour*," foreigner. The crowds gave way before the im-
portant-looking litter and its mounted escort as it moved toward
its destination, the Grand Bazaar. The bazaar was a section of
the city unto itself, comprising sixty-seven streets and enclosed
by a wall with eighteen gates. There were four thousand shops
within the wall, all under one huge roof.

"There is nothing that one cannot buy in the Grand Bazaar,"
Shohannah declared emphatically.

"Nothing?" echoed Valentina, teasing her.

"Nothing!" Shohannah swore. "Slaves, jewels, carpets, cloth,
camels, rose-petal jam, spices, pots, litters! There is nothing in
the world like it!"

"Have you ever been anyplace else in the world?" Valentina
asked the girl.

Shohannah shook her head. "I have lived my entire life in
Istanbul," she replied.

"Then you cannot know for certain that the Grand Bazaar is
unique," Valentina answered. "London merchants sell everything under the sun, too."

"Not under one roof!" Shohannah declared.

"The Grand Bazaar is unlike anything you have ever seen, Valentina, I promise you," Sarai said confidently.

Simon Kira's wife was right. As soon as they entered the Grand Bazaar, they stopped at a small shop that made and sold copper lamps and vases. Everyone walked, for it was easier to see the shops on foot. The litter followed along behind them. Padraic and Tom left their horses in the charge of a small boy who earned his living at the gates of the Grand Bazaar by holding the horses of the rich.

Like all of the women shopping, Valentina and the Kira women were muffled in outdoor cloaks and heavily veiled. Not so much as a strip of forehead was visible on any of them. Valentina was amazed, not only by the profusion of shops, but by the huge building itself. It had high, great-domed and tiled ceilings. Small windows set high in the wall all along the streets let in light.

The cacophony of the many shoppers and the screeching merchants bargaining with them was indescribable. The smells of the animals, of their droppings, of leather being tanned, of perfumes wafted about to attract buyers, of cooking food, of furs being prepared, and of the body odors of all the people combined to create an odor that was unbelievable.

"I must have those carpets!" Valentina declared as they stood in the shop of a jewelry maker. They had visited a rug merchant shortly before, and Valentina had been unable to make up her mind. Now she decided. "They will add to the beauty of the main rooms at Clearfields. And knowing you, my lord, the master chamber will have to be entirely refurbished to suit my taste! I do not relish cold floors on frosty winter mornings. I am going back to purchase those rugs."

"Wait but a few moments, Val, and I will go with you," Lord Burke said.

"'Tis but two shops away, Padraic. Besides, I wish to be surprised by your gift to me. I cannot be surprised if I am standing here while you choose it." She turned to Sarai. "Is it safe for me to go back alone as long as I am well muffled?"

"It is safe," replied Sarai Kira. "Istanbul is the safest city in the world. Ottoman law is harsh on miscreants. We will join you in a few moments. Your Turkish is quite good now, so remember to bargain hotly with the rug merchant or else he will cheat you. I will come as quickly as I can, but I must finish my business here."

"Tell Padraic I favor the rubies," Valentina whispered to Sarai with a grin. Checking to be sure that her outdoor clothing was secured, then waving to her companions, she stepped from the jeweler's shop and out into the bustling street. She had barely gone a few steps when she suddenly realized that she was closely surrounded by a party of six or more men, all of whom wore white robes and turbans and were as muffled about the face as she was. They closed in about her, jostling her as she tried to reach the rug merchant's place of business. The press of their bodies against hers swept her past her destination. Then she felt hands beneath her elbows, lifting her off her feet. She had no time to cry out as she was rushed around the corner and into an alley where a closed litter was waiting.

She was set back down on her feet for a moment, and Valentina opened her mouth to scream, but before she could, a silk scarf was tied about her veiled face, successfully stifling her cries. A robed man knelt to secure her ankles, then she was swiftly lifted into the litter, where her wrists were quickly bound above her head. The thick litter curtains were yanked tightly shut, and in a moment the litter was lifted and the bearers left the alley, melting into the noisy main streets of the Great Bazaar.

Valentina's head was whirling and her heart was pounding with shock and outrage. She forced herself to lie perfectly still, for panic made her want to scream. With a supreme effort of will, she drew several deep, calming breaths. Panic was not the solution, nor would it answer the many questions her frightened mind was now asking. *Who were these men? Where were they taking her? Why had they taken her? Was it a mistake? And if it was, what would they do to her when they discovered their error?*

It was extremely difficult not to give way to fear. She was so busy trying not to be overcome by terror that she lost track of time and was surprised to realize that the litter was no longer moving. The curtains were opened a little and a dark-skinned man leaned in and removed her gag. Her veil was pulled aside and a cup put to her lips.

"Drink, woman!" he commanded.

Valentina turned her head away. "What is it?" she demanded.

The dark man gripped the back of her head with strong fingers and forced the cup against her mouth. "A simple potion to calm your fears," he replied. "Drink!"

"I am not afraid!" Valentina lied.

The dark man looked straight at her, saying, "You prevaricate, woman, but I admire your bravery. Now drink, or I shall be forced to deal harshly with you."

It was a small defeat. She accepted it gracefully, drinking the fruit-flavored liquid. The last thing she saw was the dark man smiling and praising her obedience. She had known that the liquid was drugged, yet it came as a surprise to have to struggled to stay awake. She lost the struggle.

When she awoke, it was from a deep and peaceful sleep. She was lying on a large square bed that sat upon a carpeted dais directly in the center of a large room. In front of her was a wall of lead-paned windows that looked across a garden to the night-dark sea, now silvered by the waxing moon. She stared through those windows until, slowly, her brain began to function. She stretched gingerly and groaned softly.

Immediately, a pretty young woman with large brown eyes and rich golden hair was standing by her bed.

"I am Gülfem," she said in a sweet, clear voice. Two young women appeared by Gülfem's side. One had pale gold eyes and silver-gilt hair, the other red-gold hair and black eyes. "These are my companions, Säh and Hazade," Gülfem continued. "We have been told that you are to be called Naksh, which means the beautiful one. Indeed, you are very, very beautiful. How do you feel? Are you hungry or thirsty?"

"My name is Valentina St. Michael Barrows, Lady Barrows, and I shall answer to no other name," Valentina said angrily.

"You must not distress yourself, Naksh," Gülfem said gently. "It is always difficult at first for a new slave to adjust herself, but in a few days everything will seem quite normal to you."

"I am not a slave!" Valentina was outraged. With difficulty, she struggled to a sitting position. Her head whirled, then cleared. She suddenly realized that she and the other three young women were totally naked but for delicate gold filigreed chains that sat atop their hipbones. "Where are my clothes?" she demanded of them.

Gülfem smiled. "It is not permitted that we wear clothing within the Starlight Kiosk. When we walk outdoors in the gardens, however, or travel to and from our lord's palace, we are suitably garbed."

"And who is your lord? Who is this man who has dared to kidnap me off the streets of Istanbul in defiance of the law?" Valentina demanded.

"It is not permitted that we reveal our lord's name to you," Gülfem said meekly. "You are not yet worthy to know it."

Valentina felt unbridled rage race through her. Her first instinct was to claw at the serene pretty faces that looked at her so anxiously, but then she understood that the three girls were mindless slaves. They were not responsible for her plight. She forced her anger aside. "Where am I?" she asked them. "Is it at least permitted that I know where I am?" If I know where I am, she thought, I can plan my escape.

"You are on the Island of a Thousand Flowers, Naksh," a male voice replied, and Valentina turned to see the dark man who had given her the potion.

"Who are you?" she asked curtly. She disliked him on instinct, having seen the enjoyment he derived from having power over her.

"I am Shakir. I have been chosen to be your personal eunuch. I am in charge here at the Starlight Kiosk. There are three other eunuchs here to aid me. Their names, however, are no concern of yours."

"Why have you kidnapped me, Shakir? I am a wealthy and powerful woman in my own land, and I stand high in my queen's favor. Are you aware that I am friends with the Sultan Valide Safiye? I am also an honored guest of the Kira family, who will certainly inform the valide and the sultan about my disappearance. You must know how much power and influence the Kiras have. You have done a terrible thing, but if you will return me to the Kira household immediately, I will forgive you. Nothing will be said of your foolish crime." Valentina attempted to look as brave as her words sounded.

A small smile touched Shakir's mouth. He was a tall, slender man with a long, straight nose and almond-shaped black eyes. His large lips and polished mahogany skin gave evidence of his African origin. His clothing was extremely rich: a brocaded velvet robe of scarlet and silver and a cloth-of-silver turban with a large black pearl in its center. "Unlike these frivolous butterflies who are to be your companions, Naksh"—he indicated the three other women—"you are a woman of intelligence. You have caught my master's eye, and as he is high in the sultan's favor, his behavior will be overlooked—*should* it be found out, which it won't. You were merely one of many veiled women who shopped in the Great Bazaar today. My master's servants worked so quickly that you did not have time to attract attention. Therefore, nothing unusual

occurred within the Great Bazaar today that would cause anyone
to remember seeing you. You have disappeared off the face of
the earth. Your friends will attempt to seek your whereabouts,
Naksh, but where will they look and to whom will they go for
assistance?"

"The Kiras will go to the Sultan Valide!" Valentina snapped.

"What can she do, protest to the sultan that the streets are no
longer safe? What will the sultan do? He will instruct my master
to send his janissaries to find you. Strange as it may seem, they
will not." Shakir laughed. "Accept your fate, Naksh. You will
never again know any life but this one."

"Go to hell!" Valentina shouted.

The three beautiful girls were scandalized, if not by her words,
then certainly by her tone. One never dared speak in such a
fashion to a senior eunuch.

"Naksh, you must not insult Shakir," Gülfem gently admonished her. "He stands high in the Grand Eunuch Hammid's favor.
He is to be respected. He seeks only to be your friend. With his
help, you can easily become one of our master's favorites. Without
his help, you might be sold in the bazaar and end up in some
terrible place."

"I do not choose to become one of your master's favorites,"
snapped Valentina angrily. "I am Valentina St. Michael, an Englishwoman of rank and breeding. I am betrothed to Lord Burke.
I am a free woman, and I will yield myself to no man other than
my betrothed. Do you understand that, Shakir? Never will I yield
myself to any man except my betrothed husband!"

"You are overwrought, Naksh," was the smug reply. "Hazade,
prepare a sherbet for Naksh. Säh, see to her supper, for she has
not eaten all day."

Valentina leaped at the eunuch, nails poised to claw, but he
caught her wrists and hurled her onto the great bed.

"Attempt that again, Naksh, and you will be restrained," he
said calmly. "Do you understand me? I hold the power of life and
death over you."

She glowered at him in a test of wills, finally deciding to look
away. Let the eunuch believe he had won. She must not let him
know how strong she really was.

The red-haired Hazade handed her a cup. Nodding her thanks,
Valentina drank the too-sweet peach sherbet down. Säh brought
her a plate with slices of lamb, fresh bread, olives, and apricots.
There were no utensils, so Valentina ate with her fingers. When

she had finished, Gülfem removed the plate and drew her up from the bed.

"Let us bathe now," she said in her sweet voice. All four women went to the pretty blue-and-white-tiled bath of the kiosk with its bathing pool of warm, perfumed water. "Although we are members of our master's harem," continued Gülfem, "we have been instructed to serve you, Naksh." She unclasped the dainty golden chain about Valentina.

"I am quite capable of bathing myself," Valentina said curtly.

"A great lady does not perform menial tasks, even for herself," Gülfem chided Valentina. "Besides," she continued, lowering her voice so that only Valentina could hear her, "if you do not allow us to do our duty as we have been ordered, Shakir will report us and we will be beaten. Our master's instructions are quite explicit, and our master must be obeyed at all times. Disobedience can sometimes mean death."

"They would punish you because of my actions?" Valentina said disbelievingly. The three girls nodded earnestly. The more Valentina knew of the East, the less she liked it.

"You must understand, Naksh," said the usually quiet Säh. "We are only slaves."

"I am not a slave!" Valentina exploded.

"You *are* a slave, as we are," Gülfem said patiently. "The only difference between us is that you are now favored in our master's eyes."

Valentina felt the anger boiling in her once again, but she fought it back. Gülfem and her companions could not help being what they were, nor had they kidnapped her. Indeed, they were striving to make her comfortable, and it would be less than gracious if she caused them further difficulties. "Very well," she agreed, "you may bathe me."

With twittering little cries, they bustled about with soaps and sponges. Valentina endured their busy ministrations. Even their nudity was becoming slightly more bearable. She needed a good night's rest. It had been a frightening day. On the morrow, she would explore the island and assess the various means of escape. Still, she was outraged by this kidnapping.

"Come, come!" Hazade beckoned to her. "You must be massaged with rose cream if your skin is to be kept like silk."

"Your master will have no pleasure from me," Valentina muttered beneath her breath, but they did not hear. She was shocked, a moment later, to find that the eunuch, Shakir, was to massage her.

He looked at her mockingly, daring her to protest, his dark eyes reading her very thoughts. "Lie on your belly," he commanded, and without a word, she obeyed. She must not, she knew, waste her strength in fighting hopeless battles.

His hands on her back and shoulders was tolerable, but when Shakir began to knead her buttocks strongly, Valentina swallowed back her nervousness. His touch was impersonal, however, and she relaxed. The three young women sat cross-legged on cushions, playing softly on musical instruments and singing in high, little voices about a garden of love. The eunuch's hands moved down her legs and finally her feet. Then he ordered her to lie on her back and his hands began the return voyage up her body.

It was difficult, on her back, to hide her repugance from Shakir. Sternly, she forced a impassive expression and, closing her eyes, concentrated on her breathing. As his thumbs swirled over her Venus mont, she nearly cried out. But there was no lewdness in the eunuch's touch. Massaging a woman was for him only one of many everyday tasks.

"You have beautiful breasts," he remarked matter-of-factly as he began to massage them. "The master will be very pleased."

She wanted to cry, but Valentina bravely held back her tears. Not since the camp of Temur Khan had she felt so humiliated.

Then it was over, and Shakir was ordering them to bed. All four young women were to sleep on the large bed. Gülfem, Hazade, and Säh placed Valentina in the center, then curled about her. Two eunuchs entered and put out the lamps, plunging the room into darkness. Though it was only a few hours since she had awakened from her drug-induced state, Valentina found herself quickly falling asleep.

In the morning, her intention to explore the island for a means of escape was thwarted. Shakir would not allow any of them the freedom of the gardens. The master, he pompously announced, was not yet ready to grant them that privilege. They were forced to remain indoors, where their day, and the two days that followed, were spent in the baths, on the massage table, eating, and talking. Valentina's body seemed of paramount interest to her companions. They creamed it, oiled it, and caressed it until Valentina thought she would go mad.

When she protested their oversolicitous attention, the three airily brushed aside her complaints. The master, they patiently explained to her, as if dealing with a backward child, must not be disappointed in her after all the trouble he had endured in order to obtain her. It was like trying to reason with a trio of kittens, Valentina decided. She was bored with her companions, who, though sweet-natured, seemed to have no interest in life other than their master, his desires, his pleasures.

Valentina hated all of it, the nudity, the endless preparing of her body as though she was a bird to be dressed for roasting, and the rose odor of the lip balm they painted her lips with. Beneath the makeup and trappings she felt that she was no longer Valentina St. Michael, Lady Barrows. She was not anyone real.

A week passed. Two weeks. Shakir could see that Valentina was near to violence with her close confinement. Weary of dull conversation with Gülfem, Säh, and Hazade, she spent a good deal of time pacing the kiosk for exercise. This confused the others, who preferred being indolent.

"I am going into the city today," Shakir announced one morning. "I shall attempt to obtain permission for you to walk in the gardens, Naksh. You are like a caged tigress and must, I see, have the freedom and fresh air of the outdoors. Do not attempt to bully my eunuchs in my absence. They will report your behavior to me, and I will punish you if you have disobeyed me. You are intelligent enough to understand that I mean what I say." Then he left her.

The Island of a Thousand Flowers was no more than a tall rock in the Bosporus. It rose straight from the dark waters of the straits, and was inhabitable only at its top, where the Starlight Kiosk was set amid its gardens. Shakir hurried down the flight of stone steps cut into the side of the island to the stone quay at its foot. There a caïque awaited him, for he had signaled his master's palace that morning for the vessel. The eunuch stepped into the boat and, seating himself, signaled the rowers.

It was not easy, he contemplated as they sped across the misty morning sea, to bear authority. Naksh was extremely difficult to manage, and he must tell the grand eunuch that. Still, he had acquitted himself quite well so far. The woman's spirit was not broken, for he had been carefully instructed that such was not what their master wanted. She was, however, beginning to bend to their will, even if she was not yet aware of it. With a smile, he meditated on his possible elevation to the position of grand eunuch when the current holder of that title retired. He was, he suspected, that worthy's choice for a successor.

The caïque bumped against the palace quay, and Skakir shook off his daydream. Then he leaped from the boat and hurried up the steps to the palace. He was as anxious to be away from the island as the women were, for the days were long and tedious. Still, the rewards for good service were not to be overlooked.

"Sit down, Shakir, sit down," said Grand Eunuch Hammid in his high, fluting voice. Affably, he waved the younger man to a divan opposite his own. The grand eunuch was a coal-black man whose shortness of stature made his corpulence seem even greater than it was. He was dressed in flowing robes of emerald-green silk trimmed in dark sable. His cloth-of-gold turban bore a large diamond in its center.

"Thank you, my lord Hammid," said Shakir, and seated himself. Pretty prepubescent slave girls passed dainty pastries, sticky-sweet Turkish-paste candies, little bowls of sugared almonds, and, finally, delicate cups of thick, boiling-hot Turkish coffee. Shakir helped himself to several chips of ice, which he dropped into his coffee, then gulped the bitter brew before it could scald his throat.

The grand eunuch watched him from beneath hooded lids. He was much amused by his subordinate, who was obviously anxious to make his report but dared not broach the subject until invited to do so. Patience was a virtue greatly to be admired and slow to cultivation, Hammid considered. He sipped his own coffee, prolonging the silence. Then suddenly his gaze focused on the younger man and he said sharply, "Make your report, Shakir!"

Shakir almost dropped his eggshell-thin porcelain cup, but recovered quickly and began, "The woman to be called Naksh is a very stubborn creature, my lord Hammid! Although she is gentle with her three companions, for she harbors no ill will toward them, she has a fierce temper that she exposes to the other servants. I have kept her indoors these past two weeks, for I feared that allowing her the gardens would encourage thoughts of escape. Nonetheless, she harbors such thoughts, I can tell. She is the sort of woman who might attempt suicide, not from despair but simply to escape what she considers an untenable situation. She is not a weak creature, given to depression or melancholy."

"Have you been preparing her food exactly as I instructed

you?" the grand eunuch demanded. "It is imperative that you be precise."

"Yes, my lord Hammid, I have been most careful! I have added to each portion she eats the precise amount of herbs, spices, and aphrodisiacs you ordered. Moreover, her diet has been carefully planned. She is given only foods conducive to passion. But she is a very strong woman, able to resist us without even knowing she is resisting us."

"Yes," Hammid considered, "these English women are strong. I have dealt with them before and they are not easy. Their wills must be bent, but *never* broken. It is not a simple task. No. It is not simple," he mused thoughtfully. "Still, I have done it before, and I can do it again. I must do it again! In two years, the master has shown no serious interest in his harem. Oh, he has indulged himself with his women, but he has not been the same since Incili. He, whose harem is legendary, has allowed that harem to practically die away. I have done my best to cull those who have grown too fat or too idle. I have replaced them with exquisite creatures like Gülfem, Hazade, and Säh, but to what purpose? He uses them merely to ease his bodily longings. He shows no real interest. I had begun to fear Incili had spoiled him for other women.

"This female is the first to intrigue him since Incili. He is in a fever to possess her, and it is not just her body he desires. He desires her love, her very soul!"

Shakir shrugged. "The woman is in his possession. He may have her at any time."

"No, no, foolish one!" Hammid chided. "If all he desired of the woman was her body, he could certainly take her. It is her heart and soul he seeks, do you not understand the subtleties of that, Shakir? First she must be made to desire him. Then, when he has caught her in his web of lust, she will give him everything he wants of her. *Everything!*"

"Will he not become bored with her then?" Shakir asked.

"Possibly," answered the grand eunuch, "but possibly not. Not if she is as clever as she is beautiful. It makes no real difference, however. What matters is that he is once again showing a serious interest in his harem. Remember that our power within this house comes from the harem. If it is of no importance to him, then we, my friend, are of no importance to him, either. Think on that, my dear Shakir."

"It is a terrifying thought, my lord Hammid," Shakir said with a delicate shudder. "Tell me what I may do to bring Naksh to a more amenable state of mind, for I cannot abide the thought of failure."

"Return to the Island of a Thousand Flowers," Hammid said. "Allow the women their freedom to walk in the gardens this afternoon. The fresh air and the exercise will do them good. Serve them supper before sunset and see that Naksh is given a double dose of my very special elixir in a fruit sherbet. The women are to bathe then, and Naksh particularly ministered to.

"The master will arrive on the island two hours after moonrise tonight. He will sport with the three, but not with Naksh. She is to watch. Under restraint, Shakir, for these women tend to be prudish at first about such matters.

"Make absolutely certain that she does watch, Shakir. It is most important to my plan that she be taunted by the master and his other women. If you have followed my instructions perfectly during these past two weeks, then Naksh has been pampered and cajoled in mind and body. I have never known a woman to resist quite so long as she, but it is, I think, because she was taken from her own people only recently. We must break her grip on her past, for the master grows more eager for her each day. She has become his obsession. I only hope the reality is as pleasurable as the anticipation.

"Tonight we begin our campaign, for indeed, Shakir, love is always a battle. This woman is no virgin, so she knows the delights of passion. She will observe the master tonight and she will be unable to help remembering the passion she has known. Soon, she will begin to long for the passions she once enjoyed. Her will, finally, will be bent to our purpose, and she will have no choice but to yield herself to our lord and master," Hammid concluded.

Shakir threw himself at the grand eunuch's feet. "You are so wise, my lord Hammid," he said with genuine feeling.

A small smile of amusement passed over Hammid's face. "And you are so painfully ambitious, Shakir," he said in an indulgent tone, "but one day you will be competent to fill my slippers. First, however, you must learn, and when dealing with women, you will find there is always something new for you to know. They are unendingly inventive, for all their weakness. Now, get up and return to the island!"

Shakir scrambled to his feet. Bowing repeatedly, he backed from the salon of the grand eunuch. His heart was hammering excitedly, for it seemed the lord Hammid was pleased with him.

Hammid watched him go, smiling. Shakir was a most excellent pupil and would one day make a fine grand eunuch. Not like the puffed-up and stupid Osman who had allowed Incili to escape from the Island of a Thousand Flowers several years ago. It was fortunate that Osman had been killed then. Hammid could have killed him himself with his bare hands. His master believed Incili dead, else they all would have lost their heads. This time there would be no mistakes. The master wanted this woman and by Allah, he would have her! Have her as long as it pleased him to have her, though Hammid did not think his lord's fascination would last as long as his fascination for Incili had lasted. Incili had been an extremely rare creature. Hammid did not believe Naksh had the ability to fascinate his master for a long time.

Now he must go and report Shakir's visit to his master and instruct his master in the finer points of strategy for the battle to come. He arose from his divan with surprising agility for a man of his bulk and walked to the windows from where he could watch Shakir's caïque skimming across the Bosporus to the island. Tonight there would be a new moon. Grand Eunuch Hammid considered that an excellent portent. Shakir would do his part and he would surely do it well. Their success was certain.

Shakir was brimming over with excitement and his own importance as he quickly climbed the last few steps up the side of the island and entered the garden. Hammid had been pleased with him! His star was in the ascendancy! Oh, it was true that Hammid would probably last for years, but he, Shakir, was a young man. He could afford to bide his time as long as he might bask in the constant approval of the grand eunuch. He hurried along the white gravel path to the kiosk, speaking even as he entered it.

"I have come from our master's palace. Grand Eunuch Hammid has given his permission for you to walk in the gardens this afternoon. Your outdoor clothing will be fetched immediately."

The outdoor clothing, Valentina was amused to note, consisted of sheer silk gauze pantaloons and an equally sheer silk blouse. There were slippers, for her feet must not develop calluses. She strove carefully to hide her excitement at finally being allowed the freedom of the gardens. Now she could get the lay of the island! She could consider how to escape. There had to be a boat of some kind on the island, for how else could Shakir come and go?

She was annoyed to have the eunuchs, Halim and Hamza, accompanying them, but again she hid her feelings. She was very surprised to see no vessel at the quay, and she asked casually, "How does Shakir get to the master's palace?"

"He signals the palace and a caïque is sent for him," answered Halim.

Her heart sank. There was no boat on the island, then. How could she possibly get off the island without one? She could swim reasonably well, but the distance to either of the opposite shores was much too great. From her position at the top of the island, she could see that the straits were crisscrossed with nasty rippling currents. How would she ever get back to Istanbul, which she could just barely see in the distance?

For a moment she was very afraid. Not escape? Never see Padraic again? Never go home to England? It was too terrible to contemplate, and in an effort to calm herself, she concentrated on her surroundings.

The gardens were beautiful. The marble kiosk sat directly dead center in the middle of the gardens. The kiosk was surrounded on all four sides by an artificial pool. Fine white gravel paths fanned out from the pools in several directions. There was a small orchard of trees that she easily recognized as pear and peach, their small green fruits already visible. Some of the white paths were lined with stately cypress or fragrant pine trees. There were several small fountains in the gardens containing goldfish and water lilies. The fountains bubbled water from pretty stone statues.

The flowers were wonderful. Never had she seen such a profusion of roses. There were great bushes of damask roses in full and perfect bloom, and their heavy, heady fragrance filled the air. There were spicily scented Gold of Ophir roses as well, and bright beds of Sultan's Balsam. There were beds of red, pink, gold, and white lilies just coming into bloom, an arbor of purple bougainvillea, and an arbor of night-blooming white moonflowers. There were beds of night-blooming nicotiana to complement the moonflowers.

"The master designed the gardens himself," Gülfem informed her proudly as they were herded back toward the kiosk with its reflecting pools. "He is a most talented gardener. It is customary for high-born gentlemen to have a trade, for what Allah gives, He may just as easily take away. Nothing, it is written, is forever."

They crossed the lattice-work bridge over the pool, stepped onto the pillared porch, and entered the kiosk.

They were shooed into the baths and Valentina was forced to endure yet again the ministrations of Gülfem, Säh, and Hazade, whose hands had, of late, taken to lingering too long upon her breasts and thighs. This afternoon, they were extremely intent upon their task, as if they had never before done it.

An early supper was served, and Shakir insisted that Valentina finish everything on her plate, drink every drop from her cup. The fresh air had taken its toll, and she fell into an easy sleep.

"Naksh! Naksh!" She heard the name being whispered urgently and opened her eyes. "Naksh! Wake up! The master is arriving this very minute! Shakir has gone to greet him!"

The master! She sat up, rubbing the sleep from her eyes. That arrogant monster who had kidnapped her and imprisoned her in this boring silken prison. At last she would meet him!

Valentina leaped from the great bed as her companions flung themselves to the floor in a gesture of supreme obeisance.

The man in the doorway stood in the shadows for a long moment. Then he moved into the room with the lithe grace of a large, sleek cat. The lesser eunuchs hurried to take his long, white wool cloak and white turban. They knelt, drawing his boots off so that he would cast no stain on the enormous Medallion rug. They removed his cloth-of-silver vest and cream silk shirt. His white pantaloons rode low over slim hips, contrasting starkly against the rugged tan of his skin. He was fair, however, for just above the edge of his pantaloons was a thin line of pale ivory.

"You!" Valentina hissed venomously.

The light gray-blue eyes mocked her, and a very white smile flashed beneath the clipped and tailored dark mustache. He assessed her boldly, his eyes moving from her face to her beautiful breasts, where they lingered, and then down the length of her. "Superb," said Cicalazade Pasha softly.

Valentina flushed, for she had suddenly remembered that she was naked, a state to which she was now accustomed. Her long, unbound dark hair whirled about her as Valentina reached for the nearest thing, a small vase, and flung it at the vizier with all her might.

Laughing, he ducked the missile, then said to Shakir, "Restrain

her." Then he addressed the others. "You may rise, my little
flowers, and greet me."

With welcoming cries of delight, Gülfem, Hazade, and Säh
sprang up and embraced their lord and master, covering his face
with kisses, entwining their slender arms about him, pulling the
pantaloons from him, drawing him to the great bed. Valentina
stared at them in surprise. Then the eunuchs were holding her
and Shakir was placing velvet-covered manacles on her wrists.
There were short gold chains attached to each manacle. She was
led to the wall to the left of the door to the bath. On one side of
that door was a silk hanging showing a pair of lovers seated in
a garden. On the other side of the door was a width of marble
wall four feet across. Imbedded in that wall were two iron loops
that had been gilded with gold paint. As Shakir affixed her chains
to them, Valentina wondered why she had never noticed those
loops before.

Shakir stood to her right, and his voice was low and menacing.
"I know a thousand different ways to inflict the most excruciating
pain, Naksh, and never leave a mark, except in the mind where
the memory of pain lingers. It is our master's wish that you observe him at play, so that you may learn how to please him.
Should you turn your eyes from the bed without permission, I
have been instructed to punish you, which would give me great
pleasure. Do you understand?"

She turned her head so that she might look at him, and he
brutally pinched her nipple.

"You will keep your eyes on the master at all times, Naksh,
even when answering me," Shakir said.

"You toad!" she whispered angrily. "When I am free, I shall
scratch your eyes out!" But she kept her eyes on the bed.

Cicalazade Pasha was sprawled on his back on the huge bed,
surrounded by his three pretty concubines. Valentina had to
admit that he was an extremely attractive man. His shoulders
and chest were broad, his belly flat, his legs long. She had heard
that some Islamic men denuded themselves of their body hair,
but this was not so with the vizier. His chest was covered with
dark hair, as was the groin where his manhood lay quiet.

Even as Valentina's eyes reached that part of his anatomy, Säh
crawled between her master's legs. Taking his manhood in her
mouth, she began to minister to it eagerly. There was no doubt
that she was enjoying herself. Gülfem and Hazade, on either side
of their master, took turns kissing him on his sensual mouth

while he played with their round, little breasts, cupping and fondling them, teasing the nipples. Then his fingers strayed between their thighs, caressing their sensitive soft skin. When the vizier's manhood had attained its full growth, Säh raised her head and looked at her master questioningly. With a warm smile, he nodded at her. The girl scrambled to impale herself on the great blue-veined ivory shaft, moaning with undisguised pleasure as her body devoured its length. Cicalazade Pasha murmured something low that Valentina could not hear, and immediately Gülfem and Hazade rose from their places and, pressing themselves close to him on either side, they squatted so that he could entertain their sheaths with the thickness of several fingers from each hand. Soon the air was filled with the sensual cries of the trio's pleasure.

Suddenly the vizier's eyes met Valentina's boldly, and he smiled a slow, knowing smile at her, causing hot color to suffuse her beautiful features. She was shocked by what she was seeing, unable to believe that one man could use three different women at once. He read her thoughts.

"The Mughal emperor in India is said to be able to entertain six women at one time and fully satisfy them, my beautiful one. A maiden rides him as Säh now rides me. Two are satisfied in the manner that Gülfem and Hazade are now being pleasured. Two more are entertained with the big toe on each of the emperor's feet. The last by his skillful mouth."

"You are vile!" she managed to gasp. "How can you do this to me? My betrothed husband will find me, and when he does, he will kill you, my lord vizier! If he does not, the sultan will give me justice! I myself would wield the sword that lops off your arrogant head!"

The vizier laughed loudly, with genuine amusement. Unlike the three little sweetmeats now laboring to please him, she was vinegar and spice. And, he suspected, fire and ice as well. Like all women, she would eventually yield to passion, and when she did, it would be he who triumphed in her total submission.

The three young women had worked themselves into a frenzy, and with moans of satisfaction, they fell away from Cicalazade Pasha. The vizier smiled toothily, replete with his own pleasure.

"Your betrothed husband has turned Istanbul upside-down, my beautiful one, and even now vents his frustration in the outer courts of the Yeni Sarai," the vizier told her mockingly. "The Valide has complained bitterly to the Sultan about the *incident*, but alas, the beauteous Lady Barrows has disappeared without a trace, and no one has been found who even witnessed her apparent abduction. It makes it all very difficult. There are rumors that you were swept away by a jinn, who, spying your beauty, coveted you." He chuckled.

Valentina was quite shaken, but she said bravely, "They will find me! *They will!* And then I hope the sultan lets me separate your head from your body!"

Cicalazade Pasha laughed again with great amusement. His three concubines were hurrying to bathe his large genitals and his hands in perfumed water. They cast shocked and disapproving looks at Valentina. When they finished bathing him, the vizier rose from the huge bed and strode across the floor to stand directly before his captive. He fondled the orbs of her breasts in a leisurely fashion as his eyes met hers in a fierce battle of wills.

"You are even lovelier than I anticipated," he said quietly as if they were alone. "You set my heart afire with a deep longing the like of which I have not experienced in years. The blood boils within my veins and I hunger to possess you, Naksh." His lips brushed lightly against her cheek.

"*Never!*" she spat, unable to escape his possessive hands, though she struggled against her chains.

He smiled, and she could have sworn that his smile was sympathetic. "Do not say foolish things, for you are not a foolish woman," he gently chided her. "I saw you and I desired you. I am a man used to getting what he desires. I know that you understand such things, for you are not vapid or witless like the three sweet maidens who serve me." His thumbs rubbed insistently against her nipples. "I can be patient, Naksh. I want you to desire me before I take you. Our mutual pleasure will be the greater for it." He kissed her mouth.

"Desire you? I will never desire you!" she hissed, yanking her head away from him. "You are mad to even consider such a thing!" She did not know how much longer she could bear his hands on her, for she was confused by conflicting feelings. She detested him, yet his hands were exciting her.

"You already desire me. You are simply not experienced enough to know it," he mocked her, a hand releasing her breast to reach down between her thighs and cup her Venus mont. A finger easily found its way between her nether lips, and she squirmed desperately to escape his invasion. "Already your love juices flow," he murmured, leaning forward to whisper the words against her mouth. "You are honeyed with a longing you do not even recognize. Were your mind in tune with your exquisite body, you would be ready to receive me at this very moment."

He stepped away from her and slipped the finger that had been taunting her into his mouth, sucking on it meaningfully, his eyes holding hers prisoner. "You are sweet like the sea," he told her. And then abruptly he turned his back on her and returned to the three girls who awaited him on the great bed.

A deep shudder tore through Valentina. She was suddenly and inexplicably terrified. The truth of his words burst through her like fire scorching a dry field. She rejected him with every fiber of her very strong willpower, but her body, it appeared, had a mind of its own. That body was beginning to respond to this terrible man, to his lustful desires. How could that *be*? She could understand her body responding to a man she desired, but how could her body react so openly to someone she hated?

Cicalazade Pasha pulled the lovely Gülfem beneath him. Facing Valentina, he rode the girl. With slow, deep thrusts of his powerful manhood, he pumped the concubine. The other two girls sitting on their heels on each side of the bed, watched their master and his chosen avidly. The vizier's silvery eyes never left Valentina's as he worked the woman in his possession, and to Valentina's horror she read his thoughts. It was she he wished beneath him, and he was pretending it was so!

"It could be you beneath our lord and master, Naksh," whispered Shakir, compounding her discomfort. "Yield to him, and he will make you the happiest of mortals."

"Leave me be," moaned Valentina. Dear God, the sight of Cicalazade Pasha possessing Gülfem was wickedly exciting!

"He is like a bull, the master! Inexhaustible and skillful in the use of his great lance," whispered Shakir knowingly. "You, who have had a husband and a betrothed husband, are knowledgeable of men. Our master is far larger in his male parts than mere mortal men, Naksh. You see it! You know it! Think of him driving himself into your sweet, aching depths!"

"*Noooooo!*" Valentina sobbed, struggling in earnest against her bonds.

"Filling you beyond anything you have ever experienced," the eunuch continued, his hot breath against her ear. "Bringing you a sweet fulfillment such as you have never known! You are his slave, Naksh! Yield to him and find paradise!"

Cicalazade Pasha's clear gray-blue eyes bore into Valentina's eyes as Shakir whispered his litany of lust. She could see how much the vizier desired her even as he took another woman. The power of his hunger almost took her breath away. With a sob of helplessness, Valentina fainted. Her head fell forward onto her chest.

"She has swooned, my lord," the eunuch said, stating the obvious. "What would you have me do with her?"

"Release her from her bonds and bring her to the bed," the vizier instructed his servant.

With help from one of the under-eunuchs who was waiting in the shadows, Shakir freed Valentina and laid her on the great bed. Then he retired to the side of the room with the lesser eunuch. The two sat on their haunches, alert.

"Poor Naksh," said the sweet Gülfem. "She very much needs the sort of soothing only you, my lord, can give her. Why must she fight her fate? To belong to you, my dear lord, is heaven on earth. Can she not understand?"

Hazade and Säh nodded agreement.

Cicalazade Pasha smiled at his three gentle and docile concubines. "She does need to be soothed, my flowers, but not quite yet," he told them. "Naksh is stubborn and overproud. She must learn, as you have learned, that her duty in life is to please me. Nothing more. Am I not the reason for your being?" he demanded of them.

"Oh, yes, my lord!" Gülfem said, speaking for them all. She flung herself down to cover his feet with kisses.

"Then you will help me to teach Naksh what seems to be a very difficult lesson for her to learn," the vizier replied. He turned his attention to the beautiful woman in the center of the bed. Not since Incili had he been so ravished by a woman. She looked nothing like Incili, who had had tawny-gold hair and leaf-green eyes. So what was it about this woman that attracted him? No, fascinated him beyond reason!

Valentina opened her violet-colored eyes. For a moment, she looked startled. Then the look changed to frustrated anger and defiance. Of course, the vizier thought to himself, excited. It was not only her beauty—though her beauty was extraordinary, as Incili's had been. It was that air of open rebellion that excited him. She was just like Incili in that way. He had known no other such women, for women were meant to be gentle, not savage. But the wildness that Incili and Naksh possessed excited him, arousing his sensibilities beyond anything else.

He stroked her entire length with a gentle hand, and his eyes silently commanded the others. Two of them caught Valentina's hands.

"Let me go!" she snarled at them, her tone so fierce that they quailed. But loyalty to their master overcame fear, and they pinioned her firmly.

"Do not struggle, dear Naksh," Gülfem begged. "How can you object to our lord Cicalazade's touch? He is the most proficient and magnificent of lovers."

"What can you know of lovers, Gülfem?" Valentina said scornfully, lashing out at the girl. "How many lovers have you had in your little life?"

Gülfem was mortally shocked. "I was a pure virgin when I came to my lord," she said with a small show of spirit. "No man but my beloved lord has ever known me."

"Then you can know nothing of lovers, having no basis for comparison! You speak with a fool's voice," Valentina shot back, attempting unsuccessfully to squirm away from the vizier's marauding hands. "I have had a husband *and* my betrothed husband is my lover! I am experienced in the ways of men. No one, not even your master, can make love to me as my Padraic does! *No one!*"

The three concubines gasped with outrage. This woman was obviously quite mad.

Cicalazade Pasha bent down, his lips dangerously near hers, and said softly, "You have an evil tongue, Naksh. You must not shock my three innocent flowers. You will shortly come to accept their judgment in the matter of lovemaking, despite your vast experience. No one, my beauty, will make love to you as I will!" His mouth came down on hers, but to her surprise—for she had expected him to be harsh with her—the kiss was gentle. His mouth moved lightly over hers, exploring its shape, its texture, its sweetness. She was deeply shaken.

"I detest you!" she managed to declare when he lifted his head. She was furious with herself because she had almost enjoyed the kiss.

"Perhaps now," he agreed, "but the time will come when you will love me, Naksh." He lowered his head again. This time his lips targeted a nipple. For several long, agonizing moments, he drew deeply on the tender flesh, sending unwanted jolts of feeling through her. Then his tongue began to trace delicate patterns upon her body, moving ever downward while her heart began hammering with terror, for she realized his inevitable destination.

"No!" she pleaded with him. "Please! No!"

If he heard her, he gave no sign, and their three companions restrained her, Gülfem murmuring softly to her, "Do not resist, dear Naksh. Let the power of passion lead you to the pleasure world. You know that world well. Why do you resist it now?"

Valentina felt his thumbs gently opening her to his skillful tongue. Protest was useless, for he ignored her. She would not give him the satisfaction of knowing how he tortured her.

Why, she wondered, why was she so acutely aware of his touch, more so than she had been with anyone else in her experience? She could not seem to shut out that probing tongue. First it dipped like a bee's straight into her passage, and when she whimpered with desperation, it moved to tease at her little jewel. Frantic, Valentina tried to deny her body's reactions, but even her strong will could not prevail against Cicalazade Pasha's skillful lovemaking. He would not be denied, and faced with his determination and skill, Valentina lost control of her very being.

He sensed that loss even before he heard her moaning, a sound of half pleasure, half sorrow. He raised his head to look upon her face, which had taken on a sweetly wanton expression. Smiling, he lowered his head again so that he might draw her just to the brink. When he had, he stopped, leaving her cruelly suspended between heaven and hell. Her beautiful body was racked with pain.

"Your behavior is quite unacceptable for the woman I have chosen to be my favorite," he said in silky tones. "When you learn to be more amenable, Naksh, then, *and only then*, will I reward you with sweet fulfillment. Until that time, you will serve me only as a plaything, a secondary creature with which I whet my appetite for softer, more willing flesh." Pushing her away, he drew Hazade to him and mounted the eager concubine, who wrapped her arms about his neck in eager welcome.

Valentina curled into a ball, shuddering with pain. Tears coursed silently down her face. She had never imagined that anyone could be so totally cruel. He had forced her against her will to yield a part of herself that she never thought to give to any other man but Padraic. Then, having gained his desire, he had rebuffed her. She hated him!

Suddenly, as the anger coursed through her, the physical agony began to recede. She wanted to taunt him with her victory, as he had taunted her, but she wisely hid her small triumph. She had become aware this night of how innocent she really was despite her marriage to Edward and her love affair with Padriac. Cicalazade Pasha had shown her a dangerous and sensual world she had not known existed.

The vizier was insatiable. His appetite for women was as great as the sultan's, and as justly celebrated. For the rest of the night, he amused himself tormenting Valentina, then satisfying his desires on the willing bodies of his other three. With every assault, Valentina found it possible to ease away the effects of his attack, but she cleverly hid it.

She was greatly relieved when, in the hour before dawn, Cicalazade Pasha and his three nubile playmates finally fell asleep. The eunuchs also slipped into slumber, sliding down to sleep on the floor. Drawing away from the others, Valentina allowed herself the luxury of rest at long last.

The days that followed blurred into one by virtue of their sameness. There were walks in the garden and baths and massages until her skin was so sensitive that even the slightest touch hurt. Delicate and delicious meals were fed to her, and several nights each week Cicalazade Pasha visited the Starlight Kiosk to amuse himself and to continue his attempt to break her spirit.

Although Valentina was able to resist him with her mind, her body responded more and more readily to his very passionate touch. The battle between them was never-ending; there seemed to be no victory in sight for either of them.

She thought of Padraic constantly. Was he still in Istanbul? Was he still trying to find her? Was he any closer to success than three months ago when she was taken?

After his first visit, the vizier had said nothing more about Lord Burke and Valentina would not ask, lest she give him the satisfaction of seeing how desperate she was, for Cicalazade Pasha was likely to use anything to his own advantage.

Escape from the Island of a Thousand Flowers seemed impossible. The distance between either shore was too great, the currents too dangerous. There was no vessel available except by prearranged signals, one signal for the daylight hours, another signal for the night. To her disappointment, Valentina could not learn what the signals were. Had she been able to learn them, she would have attempted escape. Night would be best, of course. She was not afraid of the eunuchs. They could be dispatched easily, for she had learned where Shakir kept his supply of herbs and drugs. She doubted that Gülfem, Hazade, and Säh would give her any trouble, but she would leave while they slept.

Her only hope seemed to be in wearing Cicalazade Pasha down. He had not yet taken her completely. He needed her total submission before he would enjoy her. So she prayed that, when he finally realized he would never achieve her submission, he would free her. Surely that would be soon. Autumn was coming, and Valentina wanted desperately to go home.

Chapter Thirteen

"IT IS IMPOSSIBLE FOR ANYONE simply to disappear without a trace," Lord Burke said firmly. "There is something strange about all of this. It has been three months since Val was taken, and no one can be found who will even admit to having seen her abduction. How can that be, Simon Kira?"

Simon Kira and his father, Eli, both looked uncomfortable.

"My lord," began the younger man, "we have done everything possible to find Lady Barrows."

"It is not enough!" shouted Padraic Burke, anger and frustration boiling over.

"Easy, lad," Murrough O'Flaherty cautioned. He was as frustrated as Padraic, but he knew that in the East, the wheels ground slowly.

"Padraic is right," Tom Ashburne said. "It is not enough. If it were, we should have *some* idea of what happened to Lady Barrows. But as it is, we have made no progress in three months."

"The Valide is very distressed by what happened, and her aid to us has been invaluable," Simon Kira said hopefully.

"Yet, for all her help, we do not have Valentina back," Lord Burke said bluntly.

"The sultan was outraged that such a crime could be committed in broad daylight on the heretofore safe streets of his city," Simon continued. "He has even appointed his chief vizier, Cicalazade Pasha, to investigate. I do not know what more can be done."

"What is this?" Esther Kira's black eyes were suddenly alert. She had been sitting silently, allowing the men to argue, as men were wont to do. "When did the sultan tell Cicalazade Pasha to investigate?"

"He has been involved from the very beginning, Grandmother," replied Eli Kira. His elegant fingers worried at his long beard. "As soon as we brought our complaint to Sultan Mehmed, he delegated authority for the investigation to his chief vizier."

To the amazement of all, Esther Kira began to laugh, wheezing with great amusement. They wondered if she had gone mad. When her humor finally subsided, she pierced them all with a fierce gaze and said, "Asking Cicalazade Pasha to seek the truth in this matter is tantamount to setting the cat among the canaries. Whether the sultan is involved in this, I do not know. But I would stake my life on the certainty that our good friend the vizier has possession of Valentina."

"Grandmother! Beware of what you say! Such an accusation is the sort of slander that could endanger our very lives," Eli Kira blustered.

"Be silent!" she ordered him. "It is I who built the fortunes of our family—long before you saw the light of day, I might add! Were it not for your sons, Eli, I should truly despair for the future of the Kiras. I have not prospered all these years, nor our family either, by relying solely upon logic. One must rely upon one's instincts, too. It is something you have never learned, to your detriment.

"I do not speak idly. Last spring when Lady Barrows first visited me, we were interrupted by the sudden arrival of Cicalazade Pasha, who was in this house discussing business with you, Eli. He was most taken by Valentina and made no secret of his interest. Had she been one of our slaves, I tell you he would not have left the house that day without her in his possession! I remember thinking at the time that I was glad my young English guest was leaving for the Crimea. He is a very carnal man who would, indeed, dare to kidnap a woman off the streets, if that woman appealed to him. Somehow, he must have learned of her return to Istanbul.

"Think! No one saw Valentina kidnapped, or no one will admit to having seen it. Every slave market and every brothel in Istanbul has been thoroughly searched thrice over! Yet there is no trace of her. Why? That is the question I have asked myself over and over again. *Why?* Why is there no trace of her?"

"Perhaps she was taken from the city immediately and sold in some foreign slave market," Eli ventured.

Esther Kira snorted with impatience. "Who," she demanded scathingly, "would kidnap a veiled, anonymous woman who might easily have been the Valide herself? The way the women of Istanbul look in public, one cannot be certain if they are young or old, fair, pockmarked, or ugly. No. This was a planned act by someone who knew Valentina, and knew precisely where she was at all times."

"Why not the sultan, Esther?" Simon Kira asked. "You said that he was intrigued by Lady Barrows."

"Aye," the old lady agreed, "he was, but the valide protected Valentina by telling the sultan that Valentina was his sister by Marjallah, although of course, she is not. Although the sultan was not loathe, for his own sake, to destroy his younger brothers, he has always been most protective and caring of his sisters and his other female relations. He would not stoop to incest. And he had no reason to doubt Safiye's word. As far as Sultan Mehmed is concerned, Valentina is his sibling.

"It is his vizier who is the culprit in this matter, I am certain of it."

"Grandmother, we cannot accuse Cicalazade Pasha of kidnapping Lady Barrows without proof," Eli Kira said nervously.

"Am I a fool? Do you think me a witless old woman that I do not know that, my overcautious grandson?"

"I was not so cautious in the matter of Incili," he reminded her, "and that little escapade almost cost me two sons and a daughter."

"You were younger then, Eli," Esther Kira said dryly, "but like most, you have grown less daring with age. I, however, have not."

A sound, not unlike a muffled laugh, escaped from Simon Kira, who attempted to cover his breach of etiquette by coughing.

Esther Kira's eyes twinkled, but she did not even deign to gaze at her great-grandson. "It has been some time since I saw Lateefa Sultan," she said. "I will invite her to visit me, at her convenience. She will know what is happening in the house of the vizier, and she will tell me."

"Who is Lateefa Sultan?" asked Lord Burke.

"She is the wife, the only wife, of Cicalazade Pasha," the old lady replied. "She is an Ottoman princess, a great-granddaughter of Sultan Selim I. Her great-grandmother was that sultan's second wife, Firousi Kadin, and she descends from one of Firousi's daughters, Guzel Sultan, who was her grandmother. Her father was Guzel's son. As an Ottoman princess, Lateefa Sultan has the privilege of allowing or refusing her husband other wives. Only once did Cicalazade Pasha request her permission for a second wife. She gave her consent, for she is a kind woman with a great heart.

"The woman involved was a beautiful Scots noblewoman who had been kidnapped and sent to the vizier as a gift. Cicalazade Pasha fell madly in love with the woman, Incili. Incili, however, wanted only to return to her husband and family."

"Did she?" Lord Burke said.

"She mysteriously disappeared from the vizier's private island, which sits in the center of the Bosporus," Esther Kira said. "The vizier believes she is dead."

"Is she?" Lord Burke persisted.

Esther Kira smiled, showing partially toothless gums. "No" was all she said. Padraic smiled with understanding.

"I will leave the matter of Valentina's disappearance in your more than capable hands," he said quietly. Esther Kira was obviously more powerful than any of her English guests had thought.

"Leave me," Esther Kira said. "All but Lord Burke."

The others filed from the room dutifully, but Simon Kira stopped to give the old woman a kiss. She patted his hand, nodding in an understanding manner.

Then she and Padraic were alone.

"Valentina has been gone for over three months now, my lord. It is unlikely she has escaped the vizier's attentions. You will, of course, wish to regain custody of her. But you must understand that she will be a different woman. Perhaps, under the circumstances, you will wish to seek another wife."

"If I understand you, Esther Kira, you are telling me that Cicalazade Pasha has used Valentina as a man uses a woman."

Esther Kira nodded.

"I have loved Valentina her whole life, Esther Kira," Padraic Burke said. "I foolishly allowed her to wed someone else in the mistaken belief that someone so beautiful deserved a greater name and fortune than I have to give. Instead, Valentina married a man of no greater importance than I, and not for love of him, but for love of her two younger sisters whose parents would not let them wed until Valentina was wed."

He fixed her with his gaze and declared, "I have vowed not to let her escape me a second time." Lord Burke took Esther Kira's wrinkled hand in his, looking into her dark, sympathetic eyes. "I do not care if Cicalazade Pasha has possessed her body, for she will never really be his. She is mine. I want her back, Esther Kira. I know my Val. Whatever he has done to her, she has not yielded herself to him. He can possess her flesh, but he cannot possess her heart. She put that into my keeping when she accepted my love. Did Incili's husband take her back willingly? I think he did, for he must have loved her greatly to arrange for her rescue, even as I love Val."

"Aye, Incili's husband loved her deeply, and they resumed their lives happily," Esther Kira said quietly, "but those first few months after her return were harrowing ones for them both. A woman used unwillingly must come to terms with herself. Understand that this is what you face, my lord."

"I understand, Esther Kira," Lord Burke told her. "Once, long ago, when I was a very little child, my mother was in a similar position to Valentina's. Although I was too young to remember my mother's anguish, both she and my stepfather have spoken of the situation over the years. You see, my father was involved." Then Padraic, knowing Esther Kira's love of a good story, went on to reveal the adventure his mother, Skye, had had in Algiers.

When he had finished, the old lady said quietly, "Your mother must be a very unique and brave woman to have survived such a dangerous undertaking. I have known three women from your part of the world, and now you tell me of your mother who I see as being as daring as the others. The women of your land are most unusual, yet I understand them, for I have never been a meek creature myself—to the distress of the men of my family who have, nonetheless, profited royally through my eccentricities."

Padraic chuckled. "Perhaps they find your behavior odd, Esther Kira, but I grew up in a country ruled by a woman who very much reminds me of you. I find nothing strange about you. Indeed, I understand you quite well—as does your great-grandson, Simon."

"Ah, Simon!" she said with a warm smile. "He is my hope for a bright future for this family. His brothers are good men and hardworking, but they are too much like my son, Solomon, and my grandson, Eli. Pious men. Righteous men. Dull men, bound by five thousand years of tradition. Men of narrow vision who can see only yesterday and today, but not tomorrow and all the tomorrows that follow."

She chuckled. "They say I am a foolish old woman, but when our parents died and my brother Joseph and I were taken into our uncle's house, the Kiras lived in a simple wooden house on a nondescript lower street in Balata. Joseph and I were poor relations, for our father had been the younger son. He had left the family circle and attempted to start his own business in Adrianople. It was just beginning to flourish when a prominent Jew of Adrianople was accused of a particularly heinous crime, and riots broke out in the city. The ghetto there was burned to the ground and many of our people were killed. Fortunately, these things do not happen today in our more enlightened times. The worst part of it was that it need not have happened at all.

"The Jew who was the cause of it all had a beautiful daughter. One day, while at the public baths, she was glimpsed by the governor of Adrianople, who had a hidden spyhole to the women's baths. The governor sent a message to the Jew, offering to take the girl into his harem. The Jew, however, was a pompous fellow, and he publicly denounced the governor, embarrassing him by scornfully refusing his offer. Suddenly, a pile of bones was discovered in the Jew's cellar, and he was accused of stealing and murdering innocent children for some ritual having to do with the black arts.

"No one had reported any children missing, of course, yet the mindless, panicked populace of the city was driven into a frenzy by daily rumors that grew in intensity until finally the riots began.

"My father, a man of vision, saw what was coming and sent my brother and me to his elder brother in Istanbul. He and my mother were killed in those riots, and everything they had was either stolen or destroyed. As for the Jew's beautiful daughter, she was taken into the governor's harem where she remained for three days before being scorned and given to the governor's soldiers, who killed her with their tender attentions," said Esther Kira.

"That is barbaric!" Lord Burke exclaimed.

"That, my lord," came the fatalistic reply, "is the East.

"Because of my father's vision, Joseph and I survived. I began my career selling wares in the sultan's harem when I was seventeen. I brought only the finest and most unique merchandise to the women, which I sold to them at fair prices. I became an intimate friend of Sultan Selim's favorite wife. Eventually she became Sultan Valide when her son, Suleiman, became sultan. My family's fortunes stem from that good, long friendship."

"Yet you helped Val's mother escape an Ottoman sultan," Padraic said, having been curious about this for some time.

"Only after she was condemned to die, my lord. My own personal ethics will not allow me to betray those who have been as loyal to me as I have been to them. But Marjallah was condemned to drown. And the case of Lady Barrows is also a unique one. What the vizier has done is immoral."

"You are certain the vizier's wife will help you?" For the first time, Esther noticed how drawn and anxious he looked.

"I will not compromise Lateefa Sultan's position with her husband, my lord, but rest assured, she will do what she can when she learns what has happened to Lady Barrows," Esther Kira said with assurance.

A messenger from the Kira household was dispatched to the palace of Cicalazade Pasha, and Esther's invitation was accepted. On the following afternoon, Lateefa Sultan arrived at the Kira home.

She was an exquisitely beautiful woman with magnificent hair the color of silver gilt and turquoise-blue eyes. She was the very image of her great-grandmother, Firousi Kadin, and each time Esther Kira saw Lateefa Sultan it took her back to another time, making her feel almost young again.

Lateefa Sultan wore her silvery hair in a coronet of braids woven around her head, and she was garbed in a slash-skirted dress of turquoise and silver brocade, beneath which showed silver-gilt pantaloons.

A servant hurried to take the pale pink feridje from her and then escorted her into Esther Kira's salon.

The old matriarch sat ensconced amid her pillows on a divan.

"Esther Kira! Do you never change?" Lateefa Sultan demanded imperiously as she came across the room to kiss the old lady's cheek. Then she settled herself on a low chair. "It has been a year since you last invited me, and I am most put out by it. You are, I am relieved to see, looking well."

"When you are my age, Lateefa Sultan," came the wise reply, "the days go by so quickly that a year is gone in the time it once took a month to pass by."

"Your body may have grown old, Esther Kira," said the princess, "but your wit is as sharp as ever."

Esther Kira cackled. "Heh! Heh! Indeed, Lateefa Sultan, my great-grandson, Simon, claims that my body will be dead long before my mind is willing to acknowledge it. He says that my brain and tongue may live on for several years after my passing. But enough! You will have coffee? Cakes?"

The women went about the rituals of politeness until, at last, the time was propitious for Esther Kira to broach her subject.

"I need your help, Lateefa Sultan," she said bluntly.

"You know I always stand ready to help you, Esther Kira" came the quiet reply.

"This is a matter involving your husband, my princess."

"Continue, Esther," the princess said, very curious now.

"Has your husband recently introduced any new women into his harem, Lateefa Sultan?"

"Not to my knowledge, Esther Kira. Yet, for several months, there has been something strange going on regarding his harem," the princess said thoughtfully. "You know, however, that I avoid the harem unless I am needed. All those nubile young creatures depress me."

"Can you tell me anything?" Esther asked, her voice calm.

"Cica has not been on the Island of a Thousand Flowers since Incili's time," Lateefa Sultan began. "Suddenly, several months ago, slaves were sent to refurbish the kiosk and to tend its gardens, which, of course, were overgrown. Soon after, three of my husband's favorite women, Gülfem, Säh, and Hazade, were sent to the island along with four eunuchs."

"*Four* eunuchs? Why four?" Esther Kira demanded.

"I do not know. I was afraid to ask, for it really has nothing to do with me, and although he never dared to accuse me, I sense that my husband's grand eunuch, Hammid, always suspected my part in Incili's escape."

"Hammid dared not accuse you, for then he would have implicated himself," Esther Kira said. "He will never tell the vizier, my princess, for to admit his own culpability would destroy him, particularly so because your husband forgave him his *negligence* in the matter. Indeed, you are more of a threat to Hammid than he is to you, so you need not fear him.

"But tell me more. Three of your husband's favorites and four eunuchs, eh? Are they still there?"

"Aye, they are," Lateefa Sultan said.

"Other than the women, who are important to your husband, are the eunuchs upon the island of any import?"

"One is," the princess replied. "Shakir is Hammid's special pet. I think Hammid grooms him for the day he is too old to do his duties, although I suspect he will not relinquish his power until he is on his deathbed. Hammid lifted Shakir from virtual obscurity, and Shakir adores him."

"Does the vizier go to the island, my princess?"

"He did not go when the others did, but now he goes three and four times a week, remaining all night. In the beginning, my lord Cica returned in quite a good mood, but of late I notice he returns more angry than content."

"It must be!" Esther Kira said with certainty. "She is there, I know it!"

"What is it, Esther? Who is there? I do not understand."

"Forgive me, my princess. I have been oblique with you. How can you understand what I have not yet explained? I will begin." Esther then told Lateefa Sultan about Lady Valentina Barrows, and explained the circumstances of her kidnapping. She concluded by saying, "The sultan has appointed your husband to find Lady Barrows, yet there has been no trace of the Englishwoman. Forgive me, my princess, but I suspect that the reason there has been no trace of Lady Barrows is that she is in the hands of the vizier. The afternoon that he met her here with me, her rebuff of him was absolute, and you know how much Cicalazade Pasha has always loved a challenge. It is said that since Incili, no woman has held his interest, that the women of his harem grow fat with boredom and neglect."

Lateefa Sultan pondered for several minutes. Finally she said, "I have never known your instinct to fail you, Esther, and certainly another woman on the island would account for the fourth eunuch, for my husband's moodiness, for a good deal."

"It would also explain why no trace has been found of Lady Barrows," replied the matriarch. "Lateefa, my child, I *must* know! You love your husband and you would not betray him. I do not ask you to do so. I ask you to save him from his folly, for if he has kidnapped Lady Barrows, he is risking everything he has worked so hard to build over the years.

"This woman is no slave, nor even a woman captured and sold into slavery. She is a visitor in our city, and she has great favor with the Valide Safiye and with her own queen. The wives of my great-grandsons ply our trade within the royal harem, my princess, and they have heard talk on several occasions over the last months of the Valide berating the sultan over this scandalous matter.

"Valentina is not simply an Englishwoman of high birth. I am told the old queen quite dotes on Lady Barrows.

"You know how important the friendship of that queen is to the Valide Safiye, my princess. I myself was in the Yeni Serai the day the English queen's gifts to the Valide Safiye were presented by the English ambassador. Such gifts! A golden picture frame set with rubies and diamonds! A portrait of the English queen! Three silver-gilt chargers, ten garments of cloth of gold, a rosewood case with Venetian crystal bottles set in silver and gilt, two pieces of fine Holland! Then there is the magnificent organ sent to the sultan by the English queen, and set up by her own organ master, who personally taught the sultan to play.

"You have visited the Valide and seen those gifts displayed proudly for all to see. There is not a visitor who comes for the first time to visit with the sultan's mother that Safiye does not parade the gifts before them. The Valide is mortified that one of the English queen's subjects has been snatched from our streets. I must learn, dear child, if your husband has been the culprit in this matter. If his passions have overruled his common sense, will you help?"

"If Cica is guilty of this dreadful indiscretion, Esther Kira, will not the sultan and the Valide wreak their vengeance upon him for embarrassing them? How can I do such a thing to my husband?" The princess was torn between her sense of decency and her deep love for her husband.

"We want Lady Barrows back, dear child, and that is all. We seek no retribution," the old woman reassured the younger woman. She lowered her voice and spoke in a conspiratorial fashion. "You know these Christian women, Lateefa Sultan. Lady Barrows would sooner die than admit to having spent several months in carnal bondage to an *infidel*. Her betrothed husband is a fine man who is willing to overlook her misadventure. He and her party are ready to sail from Istanbul the moment she is safely returned. All the Valide Safiye need know is that Lady Barrows has been found and is on her way home."

"You speak with great certainty, Esther Kira, but what if Lady Barrows complains to her queen despite her personal embarrassment? What if the English queen complains to the Valide Safiye?" Lateefa Sultan asked. "I love my husband, as you well know, and he both loves and respects me. There are our children and grandchildren to think about. If Cicalazade Pasha is disgraced, what will happen to us all?"

Lateefa Sultan could be very stubborn when she chose to be, and Esther Kira was well aware of that. Although it had been many years since she and the vizier had had any sort of physical relationship, the princess did love her husband and was very loyal to him and to their family. Once before, Lateefa Sultan had secretly aided Esther Kira in obtaining the release of a captive from her husband's harem. The princess had done it because she truly understood the nature of love. Then, too, there had been the inescapable fact that the woman captive was her distant cousin. She and Incili had shared a heritage that could not be denied, and for the sake of that heritage, as well as Incili's love for her husband, Lateefa Sultan had helped her escape from the harem of Cicalazade Pasha.

Esther Kira knew that she would need an additional weapon to break through Lateefa Sultan's wall of loyalty to her husband. Asking Yahweh for his forgiveness, the old woman lied, saying, "You were just a girl when this happened, dear child, but almost twenty-three years ago, Sultan Murad took into his harem the widow of the Tatar prince, Javid Khan. The woman did not wish it. Indeed, she wished nothing more than to return to her own homeland. Perhaps because of that, Safiye became her friend, and although Sultan Murad favored the woman Marjallah greatly, Safiye remained loyal to her. Marjallah was equally loyal to Safiye.

"Marjallah continued to brood, and the overwrought woman attempted to stab Sultan Murad. The Sultan Valide, Nur-U-Banu, immediately ordered Marjallah's execution, and she was sewn into a sack and tossed into the sea. She was, however, rescued, and Marjallah was returned to her homeland, where she was welcome by her family and married to a man of good name.

"Marjallah took with her, however, a most priceless gift from Sultan Murad. Unbeknownst to anyone at the time—even Marjallah—she was carrying the sultan's child. *His* daughter, whom she named Valentina. *His* daughter, who disappeared off the streets of the Great Bazaar several months ago. *His* daughter, who is Sultan Mehmed's sister.

"Now do you understand, Lateefa Sultan, why you must help me before it is known that the sultan's dearest friend and confidant has stolen the sultan's sister and made her his love slave?

"My own loyalty to the royal family will not allow me to keep silent in this matter unless I can solve the problem in another way. My love for you brings me to you as a supplicant. I beg you to help me before what has been a quiet scandal becomes an open one. Ambassador Lello, the English queen's representative, has this day been to the Yeni Sarai once again to protest the lack of progress in this matter!"

After thinking all of this through carefully, Lateefa Sultan said, "I will help you, Esther Kira. But you must promise me that you will not let Cica be harmed."

"If Lady Barrows is returned, my princess, what is there to say?" the matriarch answered, smiling.

"It will take me several days to learn what we need to know, Esther Kira. You know how difficult Cica can be, and it may be that I shall not approach him directly. Be patient and I will contact you when I am certain that your instincts have once again proved infallible." She rose to leave. "I have come to love peace in my middle years, but being your friend brings an excitement into my life that I almost believe I enjoy. Farewell, Esther Kira, my old friend. We will meet again soon, I have no doubt." There was a mischievous smile on her face as she left.

When the door to the matriarch's apartments had closed behind the princess, Esther Kira said quietly, "You may come out now, Lord Burke." Padraic emerged from behind a painted screen.

"Is she reliable?" he asked.

"Quite," came the reply. "She loves her husband above all people, even her children. She will do whatever is necessary to protect him. As you see, it became necessary for me to lie to her about Valentina's parentage, though I was but taking a leaf from Safiye's book in order to protect Valentina. Do not be fooled by the princess's look of fragile beauty, my lord. Lateefa Sultan is a strong woman. More important, she is very clever."

Esther Kira knew her ally well. The following day, the vizier received an invitation from his wife to join her that afternoon in her garden for refreshments. Lateefa Sultan knew that if her husband had been having difficulties of any sort, he would eventually confide them to her.

The garden of the vizier's wife was a place of peace and elegance. Everything about it was calm and orderly, from the quiet rectangular reflecting pool to the neat, raked paths of fine white gravel, each of which was lined, every ten feet, with white marble benches. Behind each bench grew a row of perfectly pruned cypress trees. In late September, the square flower beds blushed with the last blooming of pale pink damask roses. At the end of the garden was a charming kiosk that looked out over the Bosporus. It was here that Lateefa Sultan led her husband for their afternoon visit.

After making him comfortable, she offered him a plate of his favorite pastries, delicate ones filled with finely chopped almonds, raisins, cinnamon, and honey. His blue-gray eyes were filled with appreciation. Lateefa Sultan accepted a delicate porcelain cup from the coffee maker, whom she then dismissed, then sugared the brew precisely as she knew her husband liked it and dropped two fat chips of ice into the cup before she handed it to him.

"If you were any other woman," he said admiringly, "I would wonder what you wanted."

"A little of your time only, my lord," she answered with a warm smile. "When did I ever have to cajole you for anything, Cica? You have always anticipated my every wish. But it has been weeks since you have been able to take the time to be with me like this. My cousin, the sultan, has an excellent vizier in you, but you work far too hard, Cica! Even the women of your harem have been complaining of neglect these past few months. That is not like you, my lord," she said, flattering him.

"So they have come to you with their little complaints, my sweet Lateefa?" His voice had a slight edge to it.

Lateefa Sultan pouted prettily, causing the vizier to recall their younger days. "To whom would they come if not to me, Cica? I am your wife, the mother of your children, the head of your women as long as you will have me be. I should not be a good wife if I did not listen and attempt to soothe their silly fears."

"They are right to be fearful," he said irritably. "Most of them bore me to death. With a few exceptions, I should have Hammid sell off the lot of them."

"It might be kinder," she agreed, her voice pleasantly soothing, "to sell them where they will be held in higher regard than to let them linger here, unwanted and unloved." She put her hand on his and said gently, "Come, my lord, what has distressed you so? It is not like you to be like this."

"Like what?" he grumbled, helping himself to another pastry and popping it into his mouth. Lateefa was the one constant in his life, and though he did not make love to her any longer, he loved her dearly. To his surprise, he suddenly realized they were best friends.

"Distracted," she said softly. "Perhaps a bit despondent, and even just a little bit short of temper when no one has done you injury." Lateefa Sultan chose her words carefully, for her husband was not loathe to punish physically a woman who irritated him.

The vizier sighed deeply, then looked into her beautiful eyes. "Ah, Lateefa, my dove, how well you know me! Aye, I am all of those things. Can you guess why?"

A smile played about the corners of her mouth. "A woman, my lord?" she said lightly, teasing.

"A woman," he agreed. "A beautiful, irritating woman, who, for three months, has driven me mad with her refusal to yield to me!"

"I was not aware of any new woman in the harem," Lateefa Sultan said innocently. "But tell me who she is, my lord, and I shall lecture her on her duty to you. She must be a foreigner, that she does not know how to conduct herself in the presence of her lord and master. With your permission, I shall train her in the rules of our etiquette. You should never have let such a thing go on for so long, my dear lord! Have you lost confidence in me, that you would not tell me of her behavior until you had spent a long summer suffering? Oh, Cica! It should not be!"

Her wounded tone, the open distress on her beautiful face, touched him. He caught her hands in his and kissed them. "My sweet Lateefa, I have not lost my well-placed confidence in you. I simply did not believe the girl would resist me for so long and cause me such irritation.

"She is not in the harem, however. When I obtained Naksh, I took her to the Island of a Thousand Flowers. I installed Gülfem, Hazade, and Säh there, hoping that their good example would encourage her to proper behavior. I intended to have a summer's delight on the island." He sighed.

"Summer is not over, my lord. Those sweet, witless little ewes of yours have not aided your cause in the least. Bring the women back to our palace, my lord. I will train this new woman to perfection, and she will soon give you the pleasure you seek. I am not surprised that she has refused to yield to you. She is from the West, is she not? You will have to court her in order to seduce her successfully, my lord."

"How do you know she is from the West?" he demanded suspiciously.

"She must be," the princess replied airily. "A girl born and raised in the East would know her duty toward you, my lord. Western women are different."

"Lateefa, my dove, you are perfect in every way," the vizier said affectionately. "And you are absolutely correct. The woman is from the West. I had forgotten that those women need very special handling. I will arrange to have the Starlight Kiosk closed for the winter, and I will bring the women back to the palace within the next few days!" He rose. "As always, you have not failed me. Indeed, you have solved a very thorny problem for me!" Then he was off, striding purposefully across his wife's gardens.

On the following morning, Lateefa Sultan received a small casket of delicately carved ivory fitted with solid gold fittings. Within, the velvet–lined casket was filled with loose pearls, all large, all flawless. They were, said the eunuch who delivered them, a small token of her husband's esteem. The vizier's wife smiled, pleased with her husband's public show of affection for her.

On the Island of a Thousand Flowers, preparations were being made for the inhabitants' departure.

"What can there be to pack?" Valentina said wryly. "We wear no clothing."

Her three companions giggled. They were now quite used to Naksh's sharp tongue, and they were not surprised by her bitter mood. She would not yield to the sweetness that only their lord and master could provide for a woman. A sweetness that was necessary to a woman's well-being and even her survival. Naksh would grow old before her time without such sweetness. Everyone knew that.

Shakir bustled about, his arms filled with filmy garments that he parceled out to Gülfem, Hazade, and Säh. *"You,"* he said to Valentina with scornful emphasis, "are to stay a day longer than the others—though why our lord would choose to be alone with such a viper of a woman is beyond my understanding."

"Toad!" she hissed. "I will claw your ugly heart out if you speak to me again without my permission!"

Shakir shook his head despairingly. He had failed the trust that Hammid had placed in him. But perhaps, once they returned to the vizier's palace, things would change. "Drink this!" he ordered her, handing her the goblet of fruit sherbet that Halim had brought him.

Valentina did not bother to ask what was in the cup. By now she knew that the eunuch would not poison her. She quaffed the cherry–flavored beverage, asking as she handed him the cup, "Will I sleep from this drug, or merely feel unassuagable passion?" Her voice was mocking, for she knew what they were feeding her. She had fought being influenced by their drugs as she had fought everything else.

The faintest smile touched Shakir's lips. There were times when he wished her as mindless as the rest, particularly when she denied the master so stubbornly, for her impossible behavior reflected badly on his performance. But there were other times when her implacable will and her open intelligence intrigued and amused him. If he could only bring her willingly to the vizier's bed, Shakir knew that his fortunes would be assured.

"You will need your rest for what is to come tonight, Naksh," he answered. "Sleep while you can."

Valentina opened her mouth to scald him once more with her tongue, but the sleeping draught had been strong, and she suddenly felt all the strength ebbing from her. She tumbled down into a soft darkness.

Later, looking at her lying on the silk-covered bed, Cicalazade Pasha felt his lust rising. The rich violet fabric beneath her ivory skin made her body seem even lusher than he remembered. She was sprawled on her back, her torso curved slightly, one leg bent, the other straight. One arm rested across her middle, the other flung gracefully above her head. Her hair, normally braided in a neat plait, was loose and fanned out over the silk in luxuriant dark waves. She was a sumptuous feast.

Seeing her in sleep, he seemed to be seeing her for the first time. Those wonderful breasts, so like Incili's magnificent orbs. Those long, supple legs. Incili had had a small heart-shaped beauty mark atop the cleft of her mont, unlike anything he had ever seen. Naksh's mont was wonderfully plump and pink, and as smooth and perfect as polished marble. There was nothing to distract from that marvelous deep cleft of hers. Tonight he would pierce the walls of that cleft and plunder the sweetness within.

He had waited patiently for three long months for her to yield to him. He had installed her on this exquisite little island, in this beautiful little kiosk. He had given her pleasant companions and excellent servants. Everything had been done to encourage her acquiescence, yet she had stubbornly resisted him.

Lateefa, of course, had given him the answer. Naksh was a woman of the West. Where the women he knew would have been thrilled by the treatment given Naksh, that treatment had encouraged her, not to docility, but to resistance. It had been, he now saw, the wrong approach.

He could not keep her on the island forever. By late autumn, with the winds sweeping down the straits from the Black Sea, the island would be uninhabitable.

He had sent the others away, and there was no one on the island except himself and Naksh. Tonight he would take her. Take her again and again, and yet again until the fight was completely gone from her. Tomorrow, when she was installed in his harem, she would be completely and unequivocally his. That she would recover quickly from this night, he had no doubt. She was strong, as Incili had been strong. She would continue to resist him later on, but that resistance would be only a sham, an attempt to keep his interest. Women were always so sweetly predictable.

Slowly, he stripped his clothes away and laid them neatly aside. Then, nude, he stretched himself in a leisurely fashion, not in the least self-conscious. He did not need a harem of adoring women to tell him he was handsome. His mirror told him that. He had his height from his Turkish mother. His fair skin and light eyes came from a Norman ancestor who had gone to live in Naples. The vizier was very hirsute: his broad chest and shoulders were matted with dark hair, his long, hard legs covered with it. Beneath his elegant, straight nose and above his large, sensual mouth was a beautifully clipped and tailored mustache. Cicalazade Pasha did not wear a beard. Indeed, it would have been a crime to hide his marvelous high cheekbones beneath a beard.

His gaze was fixed on the woman on the bed. She was beginning to stir, and he glanced about to ascertain that all was in readiness. A low table on the right side of the bed contained a crystal decanter of pale gold Cyprian wine, well laced with aphrodisiacs, and two crystal goblets. Although wine was forbidden by Islamic law, the sultan drank. That, according to the mufti, made it acceptable. Cicalazade Pasha did not, as a rule, indulge in spirits, but occasionally wine was useful.

He lowered himself onto the bed next to her, his hand stroking her perfumed flesh. She made a small sound of pleasure and stretched. Unable to resist, the vizier bent over Valentina and pressed his mouth to hers. With a deep sigh, she wrapped her arms about him and returned his kiss, her lips parting beneath his, her little tongue darting about to find and tease his. She was so meltingly sweet that when he pulled away from her a moment later, he groaned.

She stiffened, and her violet eyes flew open. "*You!* Must you invade my dreams as well as my life with your distasteful presence?" Her voice was harsh and angry.

"It was not a dream you yielded to, Naksh. It was me, and I will admit to liking you more docile," he shot back mockingly.

"Where are the others?" she demanded, then said, "I remember. They have returned to your palace."

"Where you will go with me tomorrow," he said.

"Why did I not go today with Gülfem, Säh, and Hazade?" she asked boldly. "I hate this place!"

"You did not go with the others because I do not intend to introduce a wildcat into my harem to sow dissent and discord among my women. Tonight I shall tame you, Naksh. Come morning, you will be a purring cat instead of a wild one." He watched closely the effect his words had on her.

Valentina said scornfully, "All summer, my lord vizier, you have attempted that feat, but you have failed. I have been pampered, massaged, fed exotic foods and liquids, caressed and tortured without cessation. All this has not made me yield. What else can you do?"

"I can fuck you," he said quietly.

"What?" She was astounded by the calm response.

He smiled, pleased to have caught her off guard. "There are times," he said, amused, "when your innocence amazes me, Naksh. It is true that I have spent the summer attempting to coax you into yielding yourself to me, and it is also true that you have stubbornly resisted me. But did you actually think that, having failed to cajole you, I would give up? No. There are some women who prefer being taken with harshness rather than gentleness. Perhaps you are one of those women. We are about to find that out, my beautiful one. Your sweet kisses of just a minute ago have quite aroused me."

Her eyes flew to the appropriate place; he did not lie. His enormous male parts were awakened, his excitement more than evident. Valentina rolled onto her hands and knees, preparing to spring off the bed. But the vizier was ready. One hand grasped

the back of her neck, forcing her head and shoulders down onto
the bed, facedown. Her body was coerced into a position that
arched her back while pushing her hips and bottom up into prominent display.

"Now, that, my exquisite beauty, is the perfect gesture of female submission, and it pleases me that you have been able to
attain it so easily," the vizier purred. He fondled the twin moons
of her buttocks possessively.

"Let me go, you beast!" Valentina shrieked when he loosened
his grip on her neck just a little. "You are vile beyond anything
I have ever known, and I despise you! I cannot believe that a
man of your legendary prowess would force himself on a helpless
and resistant woman! You are no real man to do so!"

Cicalazade Pasha laughed, delighted. Her anger was surprisingly stimulating. He could scarcely wait to get into her, and with
his free hand, he guided his huge maleness carefully to the entry
of her female passage. That other sweet entry to her body, so
temptingly visible to him now, he would save for another time.
Tonight, he simply wanted to fuck her until she begged him to
stop. Quickly releasing his hold on her neck, he grasped her hips
with both hands and drove himself into her without hesitation.

Valentina screamed furiously with his successful assault, desperately trying to buck him off her. Treated more gently these
last months, she had actually come to believe that he would not
attack her, and her cries were more of outrage and surprise than
of fear.

His fingers dug into the soft flesh of her hips, bruising her, for
his grip was strong as he held her firm, pillaging her body with
his great lance.

Allah! Allah! he groaned silently to himself. She was as tight
as a virgin, and he almost lost control of himself in his excitement.
Incili had been like this. Warm and moist, tight and inviting. A
noise, something between a moan and a sob, escaped him. He
began slowly to pump her, withdrawing himself to the tip of his
shaft, then plunging deeply back into her softness.

The reality of what was happening had now fully communicated itself to her mind. Valentina could feel the enormous manhood actually stretching her passage. It delved deeply into her;
it probed skillfully within her depths until her mind could no
longer control her body, and her body answered his call, her hips
pushing themselves up to meet the powerful thrust of his loins.

"Ah, yes, my beauty," he groaned through gritted teeth. "Come onto my cock! Yes! Yes!" The fingers dug painfully into her flesh as he ground himself into her sweetness.

For the briefest moment, her mind cleared. She thought how unfair it was that her body should give this man pleasure when she did not wish to give him pleasure. Then he loosened his iron grip on her hips and, leaning forward over her back, reached around to cup her breasts with his hands. He crushed them hard within his palms. Finding her nipples, he began to pinch and pull at them, causing her to move her hips more quickly.

"That's it, my beauty," he whispered hotly in her ear. "I have waited months to have you like this, and you have been more than worth the wait!" He gripped her hips again and increased his tempo, carefully gauging her desire. "Tell me you want me, my adorable Naksh! Tell me you want me to fuck you!" It mattered not to him that his victory was but the result of the aphrodisiacs she was being fed daily. What mattered was that she was his at last!

"Nooo!" she sobbed, frantic to prove that she could still defeat him, but her needs were screaming within her for blissful release.

"Say to me 'Fuck me, my lord Cica!' *Say it!*" he demanded.

"Never!" she gasped.

"Say 'Fuck me, my lord Cica,' or I shall withdraw from you, Naksh!" And he immediately began to make good on his threat.

"*No!* Please, no!" she begged, shamed by her words but past the point where she could stop herself.

"Say the words to me, Naksh," he murmured in a gentler tone. "Say them, and I will give you paradise. You know that I can."

Valentina was weeping openly now with desperate need. "F . . ." she sobbed. "Fuck me, my lord Cica! Oh, God! Fuck me! *Please!*"

He slammed himself into her over and over again, brutally, feeling her immediate response as her softness was racked with spasms of pleasure and her love juices drowned his manhood.

She was still gasping with the shock of it all, when, still imbedded within her, he lifted her and turned her onto her back. Pinioning her arms on either side of her head, he commanded her, "Open your eyes, Naksh," and locked his steely gaze with hers as she obeyed.

Her violet eyes were like rain-washed jewels, and so glazed with passion that he felt a wave of deep excitement sweep over him. He had not yet taken his own release, and his manhood was rock-hard and throbbing. "Tell me again, my perfect houri! Tell me what you would have me do to you!"

"Please," she whispered, and he covered her mouth with his, his tongue sliding past her teeth to her tongue.

When he lifted his head, the demand, a silent one now, was still there in his eyes. As firm and implacable as the hugeness pulsing within her. There would be no quick and easy end to this battle, Valentina realized, but he might be easier on her if she cooperated.

What did the words really mean without honest feeling behind them? She had to consider that tomorrow he would take her to his palace in the city. Once there, she might be able to escape to the Kiras' house, where Padraic surely still awaited her.

Padraic! Padraic! she silently called to him, as she had called to him in nearly every waking hour of her captivity. In Istanbul, she reminded herself, escape might be possible. On this island, it was not.

"Naksh!" His voice cut into her thoughts.

Valentina focused her amethyst eyes on Cicalazade Pasha. "Fuck me, my lord Cica!" she said fiercely. "Oh, fuck me!" And with a shout of pure triumph, he plundered her sweetness again.

The night was a long one, by far the longest night of her life. Her greatest fear was that he might give her a child, for she did not, of course, have her potion.

She would never have believed that a man could be so un-flaggingly potent. He took her there on the bed any number of times during that night, and twice within the bath, where he backed her against the tiles and, lifting her, impaled her on his mighty shaft.

He forced her to kneel before him and revive his manhood with her mouth. Then he tongued her tiny jewel until she was scream-ing for release. After each bout with passion, he poured them goblets of the pale gold wine, and they drank them down. She realized that the wine had been laced with restoratives, for his lust was unbridled and inexhaustible. When the vizier finally fell asleep, sated at last and triumphant, Valentina wept with relief.

Shakir and Halim woke them at midmorning. Shakir had pre-pared a meal of grilled fish, caught only moments before, warm, flat bread, green figs, and yogurt. There was a bowl of perfect, round oranges, dusky purple grapes, and sweet, brown-gold pears. The eunuch poured the remaining wine into the goblets for them, then, he and Halim discreetly withdrew.

Valentina could not look Cicalazade Pasha in the eye, but the vizier, triumphant, was gracious in conquest.

"How so passionate a woman can be so innately modest puzzles me, Naksh," he teased her. "I bear upon my back the marks of your sharp nails, and may be scarred forever with the evidence of your sweet, hot desire."

"A desire, my lord, wrung from me forcibly, and a desire of the flesh only. You shall never possess my heart," she told him quietly.

Reaching across the low table where they sat, he cupped her face in his hand and said in a soft, husky voice, "I shall eventually possess all of you, Naksh. Your heart, your mind, your very soul. In the end, you will deny me nothing, my beauty. Indeed, you will be eager to give me anything I desire of you." His blue-gray eyes smoldered at her, then he released her.

Her face was burning with shame. It was all she could do not to hit him. He was the most appallingly arrogant man she had ever known. She, who had always been praised for her cool, logical behavior, was quite tempted to violent, reckless actions against this man. Wisely, she held her tongue. She was not off this damned island and out of his gilded cage yet.

They bathed again after their meal, but this time Shakir and Halim were there to serve them. Afterward, Valentina was dressed in rich violet silk pantaloons studded with tiny gold stars woven into the cloth. Her ankle bands were gold, edged in purple quartz. Her gauze blouse was a deep rose color, her little sleeveless jacket striped in violet, rose, and gold and edged in the same purple quartz as her ankle bands. Shakir knelt to slip gold slippers on her feet and to tie about her a hip sash of cloth of gold.

The eunuch then seated her so that he might do her hair. He brushed Valentina's long, dark brown hair until its red and gold lights were gleaming. Then, with quick, skillful fingers, he plaited the hair into a single braid, weaving into it a pearl-studded golden ribbon.

When he had finished, he opened a small ebony box and began to adorn her with jewelry. Huge pink diamonds dangled from her earlobes. A rope of creamy pearls was placed over her head and gold bangles, some plain, some studded with pearls, and others with gemstones, were pushed onto her arms. Rings were set upon two fingers of her left hand, one amethyst and one diamond. For her right hand, there was an enormous pearl set in gold and surrounded by diamonds.

"These are now yours, Naksh," Shakir said, low. "A gift from the master. You will enter his harem as a queen. If you continue to please him, you will remain a queen."

Valentina fixed the eunuch with a disdainful look that left him feeling extremely uncomfortable. She remained silent.

The vizier was now fully dressed as well. She had to admit that he was an extremely handsome man. His pantaloons were of white silk, the ankle bands embroidered in stripes of gold and silver. His shirt was of white silk. About his waist was a tightly wrapped sash of cloth of gold, much bejeweled. His long, sleeveless robe was also of cloth of gold, but it was brocaded with black velvet tulips and its edges and hem were trimmed in rich, dark sable. His boots were of dark leather. An elegantly wrapped cloth-of-gold turban with two white plumes fitted in a bejeweled aigrette was the last item of clothing to be placed on the vizier. When he was satisfied with its fit, he held out his hand to her.

"Come, Naksh! It is time for us to go home," he said.

She put her hand in his, feeling the strong fingers closing about hers. There was no need to antagonize the man. He must be made to believe that she was accepting, albeit reluctantly, her place in life. His ego was so great that it would not take long to lull him into a sense of false security, thereby allowing her the opportunity to plan her escape. She silently cursed her own stupidity and stubbornness. Why hadn't she realized before this that pretending to yield to him was her only escape? What a fool she had been! Once back in Istanbul, it would be so easy. From this island, it was impossible.

Together they departed from the Starlight Kiosk and walked down the cliffside steps to the quay, where the vizier's caïque awaited them. Her eyes widened appreciatively at her first sight of the caïque, an absolutely beautiful boat. It was totally gilded with gold leaf, and there were red lacquer designs on its sides. The oars were painted in alternating colors of pale blue and silver. The silk awning was striped in red, gold, blue, and silver and was suspended from four gilded posts carved with leaves and flowers. The deck was of polished rosewood; the curtain in the seating area, scarlet silk shot through with gold; the double divan beneath the awning, cloth of silver, and piled high with multicolored silk pillows.

The eight slaves chosen to row the vessel, four on each side, were perfectly matched. They were coal-black, and each stood exactly six feet tall. The slaves wore about their necks wide silver dog collars studded with aquamarines. Those pulling the silver oars wore pale blue pantaloons sashed in silver, while those with light blue oars wore blue sashes and silver pantaloons. Their feet were bare, but each man wore about his right ankle an engraved bracelet.

"What does the writing on their anklets say, my lord?" Valentina asked him through her violet gauze veil.

"It gives each man's name and states that he is the property of Cicalazade Pasha, the sultan's grand vizier."

"But why the anklets? They could tell you who they are," she responded.

"No, my exquisite Naksh, they could not. You see, my rowers have no tongues, their tongues having been removed so that they cannot gossip about what is said upon this vessel," he explained.

"That is horrible!" she exclaimed.

"Perhaps, but it is also practical, for should something said on this caïque be repeated, it is far easier to find and punish the culprit knowing that my eight rowers are completely innocent. My little pleasure boat holds but a dozen people, including the rowers. Should gossip be repeated, I know neither I nor my eight rowers are guilty of indiscretion. At most, then, my hunt for the guilty party is limited to three people."

Shakir spoke up. "Halim and I shall close the kiosk, my lord, and then return to the palace."

"You have arranged transportation?"

"Yes, my lord."

"Very good," said the vizier, and waved to his rowers to begin the voyage.

As the vessel moved swiftly across the water, Valentina fully realized the wisdom of not attempting to swim her way to freedom. Anxiously, she scanned the ships moored in and along the Golden Horn and was almost giddy with relief when she saw the flags of her own little convoy flying high atop their masts. They had not left her! She had felt all along that they would not.

"There is more color in your cheeks than I have ever seen before," Cicalazade Pasha noted observantly.

"It is the excitement of being off the island," she said quickly. "It is a beautiful place, my lord, but after a while it becomes boring."

"You may find my harem even more boring, Naksh."

"With the whole city outside your gates, my lord?"

"You will not be allowed outside my gates, beautiful one" came the daunting reply.

"Never?" she cried. How could she escape if she could not get into the city?

He put a possessive arm about her and drew her close to him. His other hand slid into her blouse and fondled her breasts. "Perhaps, eventually, when I am certain of your loyalty and your love for me, I will allow you the privilege of visiting the bazaars, suitably chaperoned. You must continue to please me, however, as you pleased me last night, Naksh. And, of course, I must have good reports from Shakir, who is to be your personal eunuch, and Hammid, my grand eunuch." Gently drawing the fabric of her blouse aside, he lifted one of her breasts and lowered his head to suckle. He loosened her hip sash and slipped a hand beneath the silk of her pantaloons.

Valentina gritted her teeth and played the part she knew she had to play. "Oh, my lord!" she whispered. "What if the rowers should see us? Or a passing boat?" She sounded breathless and excited, and the truth was that his teasing fingers were beginning to have a certain effect on her.

He lifted his head and, looking directly at her, said, "The rowers have their backs to us and will not dare turn around no matter what they hear. The curtains offer us enough privacy. You, my Naksh"—his fingers thrust into her—"are more than ready now to pleasure me before we reach our destination. Lower your pantaloons for me!" He relaxed his hold on her long enough to fumble with his own baggy trousers, releasing his already hard and swollen manhood.

"Oh, my lord!" Valentina blushed, the blush having been brought on quite naturally by the situation. The rowers would hear everything!

Taking her about the waist, the vizier lifted her up and impaled her on his great shaft. She gasped as he entered her, stretching and filling her.

"Lean forward," he commanded, "that I may have your breasts," and she obeyed as his mouth closed over a nipple. His big hands cupped her buttocks. "Now, Naksh," he said, "you will fuck me."

She quickly found the rhythm and began to move upon him, her face hidden against his shoulder. She hated him! She hated his lustfulness and she hated his body, but she would endure anything to reach Istanbul again. She would suffer his lascivious attentions in order to be in a place where she might finally escape.

Suddenly he released her breast from his mouth and commanded her to put her lips near his. "No! Do not close your eyes, my beauty. I would have our souls meet at passion's peak. Ah, how your sweet sheath tightens about me! Can you feel me throbbing a message of love within your honeyed passage?" His fingers dug into her buttocks. "Faster, my beauty! Faster! Ah, what a hot little piece you are, Naksh."

Damn him, Valentina thought, feeling her crisis approaching, why must my body respond? I don't want to give him pleasure, and it seems wrong that I should feel pleasure. Damn him for the rutting boar he is! But she felt her body beginning to shudder, even as the vizier's passion burst within her, and she fell forward, exhausted, into his embrace.

"Hmm." He sighed, satisfied. "By Allah, my beauty, you have pleased me well!" His hand stroked her head possessively. "Your hair is like fine strands of silk, Naksh. I am gladdened to see you learning to be more amenable." He reached up to caress her lovely breasts.

"It does not please me at all that my body responds to yours, my lord," she said, the words escaping from her before she could stop them, but, to her surprise, he only laughed.

"I am delighted to learn that I have not broken your spirit, Naksh. You would bore me if you became too complacent." His fingers tweaked her tingling nipples.

"I shall never bore you, my lord," she promised him. "I am yet quite capable of surprising you, I assure you."

"And I, my beauty, am equally capable of surprising you," he growled softly in her ear. He lifted her off him and settled her into her place by his side. "Correct your dress," he said. "We are about to land."

When they left the caïque, he took her directly to his grand eunuch and left her there without a word. Valentina stood silently before the ebony mountain of flesh who was called Hammid, a creature, she had learned during the summer months, who was both respected and greatly feared by all of the inhabitants of the vizier's household. Sitting on a divan, dressed flamboyantly in bright orange and gold robes, the grand eunuch's height was increased by a huge cloth-of-gold turban that had a great black pearl in its center.

The fathomless black eyes stared at her from an impassive face. He did not stand up.

"Disrobe," he commanded finally in a high-pitched voice that was incongruous in so enormous a creature.

Valentina, used to these ways, peeled her clothing off gracefully, leaving only her jewelry to adorn her. She stared as boldly at Hammid as he was staring at her.

The faintest shadow of a smile passed over his face, and he said, "You are proud, Naksh. Overproud, I suspect. But women with your extraordinary beauty always are, particularly women from the West." His eyes moved slowly over her, assessing her carefully. "Put your hands behind your head, Naksh," he ordered. "Magnificent! Absolutely magnificent!" he murmured as her round breasts with their delicate pink nipples jutted forward. "Only once before have I seen breasts to rival yours, Naksh. Turn now."

Her body icy with anger, Valentina slowly pirouetted as Hammid made humming noises of approval. When she had completed a full turn, he said, "Come and kneel before me so that I may feel your skin. I am, as you can see, too large to rise without aid and I wanted our first meeting to be private, knowing that you would be uncomfortable in the presence of others."

Valentina knelt before Hammid. "You are too kind, my lord Hammid," she said acidly.

"Heh! Heh!" the grand eunuch cackled. "A sharp tongue. A quick mind. That is good! My lord has grown quite bored with the docile beauties of this harem. You will be a breath of cold, icy air in his summer garden." As he talked, his hands performed a businesslike exploration of her body. "Excellent! Excellent!" he said. "Your skin is perfection, soft as satin and firm as a young peach. Turn," he ordered, and when she obeyed, he ran his hands over her back. "Your posture is flawless," he approved. Then his fingers, suddenly talonlike, pulled apart the two halves of her bottom. "Your portal of Sodom," he asked her. "Has it ever been tampered with, Naksh?"

"What?" She forced herself not to shudder at this new and most unpleasant inspection.

"Did your husband ever put his cock into your bottom?" the grand eunuch said bluntly.

"*Never!* Are you mad?" she exclaimed. "What man would do such a thing?"

"It is a pleasure very much enjoyed by many men, particularly the men of our world." He pushed his finger into Valentina to its first joint.

"*Don't!*" she gasped, flinching, her face flaming.

He withdrew the offending finger immediately. "Good! You are a virgin there. I will give orders that you be prepared to receive our master in that fashion, for he enjoys such sport."

"Never! I will never permit it!" Valentina said furiously.

"The choice, Naksh, is not yours to make. You will be primed slowly over the next few weeks to accept our lord in such a manner, whenever he desires it. I shall tell him you are being readied. Get up now and put on your garments! I will call a eunuch to take you to your apartments, for Shakir has not yet returned from the island.

"The vizier gave orders to have a beautiful bower prepared for you. Besides Shakir, you will have six slave girls to serve you. You are a most fortunate woman."

"As fortunate as Incili, my lord Hammid?" she asked as she drew her clothing on again.

"What do you know of Incili?" he demanded.

"You would be wise to remember her, my lord Hammid," Valentina said mockingly, then caught herself. She must not trumpet her intention!

The grand eunuch nodded assessingly at Valentina. "Be warned, Naksh," he said. "It is rare that I err in my judgment of a woman, but when I make a mistake, I make it only once. You would be wise to remember that, my beauty."

Valentina bit her lower lip to stifle the quick reply that rose to her lips.

Hammid smiled. "Good," he said. "You know how to hold your tongue." He reached out and struck a small brass gong with his heavy gold ring. Instantly a young eunuch appeared. "Escort the lady Naksh to her apartments, Yussef, and see that her maidens welcome her into our midst."

Chapter Fourteen

LATEEFA SULTAN SAW her husband's latest concubine, an outrageously beautiful woman with silky dark hair and eyes like the finest amethysts. She saw her in the baths and immediately regretted her own slowly aging body, so unlike this exquisite girl's. The young one had not yet faced the rigors of childbearing.

They had named her well. *Naksh, the Beautiful One.* Lateefa Sultan found herself uncomfortable with the proud Naksh and her very direct gaze. Naksh, who scorned all companionship, even that of Gülfem, Hazad, and Säh, who had spent the summer with her. Naksh, who barely tolerated her six fluttering handmaidens or the ambitious Shakir, her personal eunuch. Discomfitted though she was, Lateefa Sultan admired Naksh's obvious strength of character.

Still, it was necessary to ascertain whether Naksh was indeed the Englishwoman, Lady Barrows. If Cica had been so foolish as to have kidnapped the sultan's half-sister, the woman *must* be returned to her people before the vizier found himself in more difficulty than even he could have anticipated.

With that in mind, two afternoons after Naksh appeared in her husband's palace, Lateefa Sultan strode across the crowded baths. The knots of gossiping and bathing women instantly gave way before her. She was the sultan's cousin, an Ottoman princess, their master's wife. She was also the mistress of the harem.

Suddenly, as if by chance, she stopped directly before the beauteous Naksh and her entourage. Shakir hissed frantically at Naksh as her slave girls prostrated themselves on the marble floor. Naksh bowed politely from the waist. Not having been properly introduced to the vizier's wife, she did not speak.

"I am Lateefa Sultan," the princess said. "You are Naksh, my husband's new woman?"

"Yes, my lady." The voice was elegant, cultivated.

"What is your nationality, Naksh?"

"I am English, my lady," Valentina replied.

"Be careful," came the sudden whisper—in English—from Lateefa Sultan's mouth. "I . . . will help . . . you."

As startled as she was, Valentina gave no indication of her surprise.

"What did the princess say?" squeaked Shakir as Lateefa Sultan moved away and left the baths.

"She was merely greeting me in my own tongue, toad," Valentina said acidly. "I am flattered by her kindness. It is the first I have received since my kidnapping." She stared after the princess in a suitably impressed fashion, which seemed to soothe Shakir's fears.

Lateefa Sultan returned with her entourage to her lavishly furnished apartments. "The afternoon is particularly beautiful and I think I shall visit with my younger daughter and her new baby," she announced. "See that my litter is ready." The servants scurried to obey her.

In the courtyard she met her husband, who asked, "Where are you going, my dove?"

"It is such a fine day that I am off to visit with our daughter, Hale, and our new grandson," she told him.

"Give them both my love," Cicalazade Pasha replied, "and tell Hale that I am particularly pleased with her. Four sons in three years of marriage is no small feat. Were our sons' wives as dutiful!"

"And what will you do this beautiful afternoon, my lord?" she asked him.

"I have not seen Naksh since I brought her to the palace. The sultan has had my entire attention these last few days. I know it is Friday, my dove, but do you mind?"

Friday was the day set aside by the Koran for a first wife's time with her husband, but Lateefa and her husband had not been intimate in so many years. Indeed, the princess Lateefa Sultan found far more pleasure in her favorite slave girl than in her husband, who usually visited her bed on Friday nights merely to sleep away the excesses of his previous six nights.

"Of course not, my lord," she answered him. "It pleases me to see you once again truly diverted by a woman. Of late, your harem has bored you."

He took her hands and, raising them to his lips, kissed them. "You are the best wife any man could have, my dove," he told her.

"No, Cica," she said quietly, "it is I who am fortunate in having such a wonderful husband, one who has given me five fine children, who now give us grandchildren that I may go and visit on such a lovely autumn afternoon." She laughed as he helped her into her litter.

She visited with Hale for two hours, admiring baby Ali and parceling out sweetmeats and small toys to his jealous older brothers, who were yet babies themselves. Mamud and Murad, the twins, were just slightly over two years old and Orkhan was a year. All were, praise Allah, sturdy and healthy, though she thought her daughter looked a bit drawn.

"No more babies for a while," she cautioned her youngest child. "You are losing your looks. Ferhad will take another, prettier wife."

"Let him," Hale replied carelessly with her father's bravado. "I shall still always be his first wife and the mother of his four eldest sons. I would welcome another woman so that I might have time for myself. Ferhad ruts on me like a boar."

Lateefa Sultan shuddered delicately. "Remember that you are an Ottoman princess," she said. "He must ask your permission to take another wife. Be careful, lest you find yourself facing a serious rival."

"Any woman can be a rival, Mother, even some unimportant concubine. At least as his wife I have not only rank but legal means of protection," Hale said.

"Is everything all right?" Lateefa asked worried.

"Gracious"—her daughter laughed—"yes. I am simply tired."

Reassured, Lateefa Sultan left her daughter's house and directed her litter bearers to return to her palace. Suddenly, as if on a whim, as they passed the street that led up the hill to the ghetto of Balata, the princess called to her bearers to stop.

"It is early yet," she said thoughtfully. "I will visit Esther Kira."

When Sarai Kira learned of the arrival, she hurried into the courtyard of the Kira house to greet the princess. Her surprise and pleasure were evident as she warmly welcomed their guest.

"Why did you not send a messenger with word of your coming, my princess?" Sarai said.

"I was visiting my daughter, Hale Sultan," Lateefa said by way of explanation, "and as the afternoon was yet young, I decided to come see my old friend, Esther Kira. I hope I have not inconvenienced you, Sarai Kira."

"No, no, madam, not at all. It is always an honor to have you enter our house. Come, I will take you to Esther, who will be delighted by your arrival, although I suspect she already knows of it. Esther knows everything first in this house," she said with a laugh.

The princess's bearers sat on their haunches in a shady part of the courtyard as their mistress disappeared into the Kira house. Betel nut was passed around, and they crouched, chewing contentedly. Lateefa Sultan was an easy woman to serve, and she had a kind heart.

Sarai Kira led the guest to the matriarch of the house and, having duties of her own, excused herself. The princess was settled comfortably, refreshments were passed around, and then, as was her custom, Esther Kira sent her servants away so that they might gossip in private. She was not long in coming to the point.

"You have news for me, my child?" Her dark eyes were curious.

"You were correct, Esther Kira. Cica does indeed have the Englishwoman in his possession," the princess said quietly.

"Ah, he is bold, your husband!" Esther Kira replied, her black eyes glowing with admiration. Then she focused her attention on the princess. "You are absolutely certain?"

"I met her in the baths and asked her nationality. She told me she was English. She is very elegant, very cool in her manner, Esther Kira. You will remember that my cousin, Incili, taught me some English. My meeting with the Englishwoman, whom Cica calls Naksh, was but a moment, but I remembered enough English to say to Naksh, 'Be careful, I will help you.' Then I left with my attendants. But I heard the eunuch Shakir demand nervously to know what I had said. Naksh never turned a hair. She calmly informed the eunuch that I had merely greeted her in her own language, as though what I had said was meaningless."

"Good! Good!" Esther Kira said approvingly. "She has not been broken, then, despite her bondage. I was afraid that after a summer of serving his desires she would be destroyed."

"No, Esther! She is strong, even as my cousin Incili was strong. I see the same steel in her. Besides, the maidens who spent the summer on the island with her have told me that Cica chose not to possess her until she came willingly to him, and she would not! He broke his vow the day before he brought her to our palace, sending the others away and forcing Naksh to his will. But even that has not destroyed her pride."

"Tomorrow," the old woman suddenly declared as if she were speaking to herself.

"Tomorrow?" Lateefa Sultan asked, puzzled.

"She must be rescued tomorrow."

"Esther Kira! Such a thing is impossible!" the princess cried.

"Nothing is impossible, my child, particularly if it has not been attempted. If one fails, one tries again," the matriarch said firmly. "Lady Barrows has been in your husband's palace for three days now, correct?" Her friend nodded. "The vizier feels safe now that she is in his home and her whereabouts are secure. Therefore, now is the time to strike, while all are unsuspecting."

"Hammid is not unsuspecting," Lateefa Sultan said quietly. "He remembers Incili and is very distrustful of Naksh, for she neither respects nor fears him. He has given orders that she is not to leave the haremlik for any other section of the palace. She is allowed to go to the walled harem gardens once a day, but only in the company of Shakir and the six handmaidens assigned to her, all of whom are in Hammid's debt. They report her every move to him."

The old lady chuckled. "Tomorrow the dutiful and cautious Hammid will find himself torn, my princess, for tomorrow is his usual day to attend the slave market. You know he will allow no one else to choose the women for your husband's harem. In that matter he trusts only his own judgment."

"But he has not visited the women's slave market all summer long, Esther Kira. Why do you think he will go tomorrow?" Lateefa Sultan said.

"Until three days ago, my princess, Hammid knew nothing firsthand about your husband's love captive. What he knows now has surely not pleased him. The Englishwoman is a proud creature who will never be his ally—and if she is not his ally, then she is his enemy. Hammid will, therefore, seek to ruin her influence with the vizier, using other, equally beautiful and certainly more amenable women.

"Tomorrow in the women's slave market, Kara Ali, our most prestigious slave merchant, a man who deals only in the finest and rarest beauty, will hold a very special auction of women. Ali Ziya, the sultan's Aga Kisler, has been invited to this auction. So has Hammid. And he will go, my princess, for the word in the marketplace is that there has never been such a group of women gathered together beneath one roof.

"I can personally assure you that the gossip is correct. Why? Because for weeks, agents of the Kira family have been seeking beautiful virgins for just this purpose. Our Tatar friends in Kaffa have culled the best of their captives for us, and received a premium price for doing so. The slave farms in Circassia and the markets of Georgia have been stripped of their best women. In Algiers, our people have purchased the most exquisite of the girls brought in by Barbary captains. All of these females have been brought to Istanbul and housed with Kara Ali, who, by chance, is in our debt.

"His silence about this matter, and the auction he holds tomorrow, will erase his debt to our bank. The excellent commission he receives from all of the merchandise sold should provide him with a fortune for his old age.

"Hammid and Ali Ziya will make magnificent purchases for their masters' harems, and they will enjoy bidding against each other. All in all, it should be quite a satisfying afternoon for Hammid until, of course, he returns to the vizier's palace to discover that Naksh has escaped."

"But how, Esther Kira? How can she escape when she is under such strict supervision?" Lateefa Sultan was worried.

"Female peddlers are permitted into your harem, my princess. Even as we speak, permission is being requested for a group to visit you tomorrow afternoon. That permission will be granted, for Hammid knows it will keep the women amused while he is away. Besides, he makes a tidy sum in bribes each time the women peddlers come.

"A group of eight or more peddlers will arrive. No one ever thinks to take a head count of such arrivals, and the peddlers will leave in two groups so as to confuse any observers.

"My great-grandson Lev's wife, Sabra, will be among the peddlers. She is expecting a child, and her bulk will attract no special attention, but part of that bulk will be an extra black yashmak and veil, the same as she and the others will be wearing.

"A distraction must be created so that Lady Barrows can don those garments and make her escape in the first group of women peddlers, who will include Sabra. Sabra will bring Lady Barrows directly here to us in Balata. As soon as night falls, Lady Barrows will be taken to her ship, which will sail immediately.

"Your husband will not be at your palace tomorrow afternoon, for he has a meeting with the sultan at the Yeni Serai. There has been great dissatisfaction recently among the general population over the currency crisis. The vizier is apt to be late returning home, and when he does arrive, there will be little he can do to regain his captive, for he can hardly admit, publicly, to having kidnapped Lady Barrows in the first place. This will work to our advantage, for by the time he has decided on a course of action, Lady Barrows will be long gone from Istanbul."

"Esther Kira, you amaze me," Lateefa Sultan said admiringly. "How do you manage to know everything? My husband's meeting with the sultan tomorrow and . . . a currency crisis? What crisis? What is wrong with the currency?"

"Why should you know of the currency crisis?" the old woman said. "Your husband is not harmed by it and he sees to all your needs, but the general population is not as fortunate. The sultan's avarice, and his mother's, is no secret, my princess. Their greed has reached devastating heights.

"For months now, all gold, silver, and copper coins passing through the treasury have been clipped by a group of mute slaves brought in for that purpose. Most of the coins now in circulation do not weigh what they should. Consequently, merchants are weighing the coins used for each purchase made. An item costing a dinar may cost two or three dinars if the first coin is short-weighted. People are very angry. There have been several small riots outside the Yeni Serai this past week. I suspect that is why the vizier was summoned to the palace for a meeting tomorrow."

"Gracious!" Lateefa Sultan exclaimed. "My cousin and his mother are shameful to do such a thing! I do not blame the people for their anger. If bread normally cost a single coin, and that is all you have to spend, it must be awful to watch your children go hungry so that the sultan may have more gold. Can nothing be done, Esther Kira?"

"The debased coinage must be made good, my princess, and it must be done soon. I expect now that the people have begun to complain, it will. The sultan cannot afford anarchy in his own capital. Knowing Mehmed, however, I expect he will find a way that does not involve his losing a penny." The old lady chuckled. "Now I wish to point out Lev's wife to you, that you will know her tomorrow when she comes. I do not want her making any show that would attract attention within your palace. The peddler women must all be as alike as peas in a pod, with no distinctions to be recalled by sharp-eyed women seeking to curry favor with Hammid or your husband, or ambitious eunuchs seeking Hammid's position."

Esther Kira clapped her hands. Her signal was answered by an older serving woman. The matriarch nodded to the woman, who bowed and left the room, returning a moment later with a young girl. The girl said nothing, but bowed politely to the princess. "You will remember her, Lateefa Sultan?" Esther Kira said as the girl and the servant left the room.

"I will remember her" was the firm reply.

"Good! Now you must go, lest your visit be thought overlong," the old woman said. "I thank you for your help in this matter, Lateefa Sultan. We have always been friends. I should not like to see the vizier lose everything merely because of his lust."

"In that we are in agreement, Esther Kira," the princess replied. "The Englishwoman is like a blade of the finest, forged Toledo steel. Cica would never really have from her what he wanted, and eventually he would realize that. I shudder to think what he would do to that poor woman in his anger and disappointment. I should not want an innocent life on my conscience, and her life would be on my conscience if I did not help you." Lateefa Sultan arose from the divan. "Farewell, dear Esther Kira," she said. "I shall come and see you again very soon." Smiling, she bent and kissed her.

Esther Kira watched Lateefa Sultan leave. Then she called to her eunuch, "Yakob! Where are you, you useless creature? We have much work to do!"

As the princess's litter was being carried down the hill into the city toward the vizier's palace, the vizier was enjoying the afternoon in the bedchamber of his new favorite.

He had learned that she performed far better without the companionship of other women, and since her preferences led to his supreme pleasure, he allowed her this little idiosyncrasy. A tiny bathing room directly off her bedchamber allowed them a proper place to make their ablutions after each bout with love. He had had her several times in the last few hours, and each time was even more satisfying than the last, for she did not yield easily.

He adored her proud spirit, for it added a piquant zest to their encounters. She was fierce. She was hard. He realized that no woman he had ever possessed, even his adored Incili, stimulated him as Naksh did. Since he had lost Incili, he had found women boring and he did not perform as well with them as he once had. He was tired. Bored. Distracted.

With Naksh, his lust soared again, finding new heights. Naksh had the tongue of a poisonous snake, a tongue that he put to better use than scalding him with her venom.

She knelt submissively before him, his great shaft in her mouth, her wicked tongue pleasuring him as he had instructed her. He stood watching her through half-closed eyes, his hand fondling her silky dark hair as he waited for the precise moment to bid her to cease her delightful work. When that moment came, he ordered her to the bed, where she lay, her legs wide and dangling over the edge of the bed, while he satisfied the longings of his own tongue.

Valentina could feel each of his fingers as they dug into the soft flesh of her round buttocks. His tongue flicked back and forth against her little jewel, and she bit her lips until they bled to stifle her cries, but here, as elsewhere, she failed. The insistent tongue slithered along the pink inner walls of her nether lips, moving ever downward until it thrust itself into her passage. His mouth pressed against her, and he sucked on the little pearl of flesh, causing her to spasm with passion. As she shuddered, he pulled himself up and ground his manhood into her, ramming himself fiercely back and forth within her until Valentina began to scream with mindless passion. The unholy pleasure swept over her, drowning her with desire while scalding her with shame. Cicalazade Pasha roared triumphantly with his own climax and fell forward upon her supine body.

He stayed with her until past moonrise. Only when he had left her and she had convinced Shakir and her maidens that she was asleep, did Valentina give in to tears. She sobbed for over an hour, muffling the sounds of her weeping with pillows. She would never allow them to know the depth of her pain! *Never!*

Valentina knew that she had to escape from Cicalazade Pasha, and his lust. She could not bear to be the object of his attentions much longer. What had the vizier's lovely wife meant by her words this afternoon? Would she really help her? How on earth had she learned the English tongue, Valentina wondered, and did she even comprehend the words that she had spoken?

Valentina drew a deep and calming breath. Her exhaustion had made everything seem dire, and insurmountable. She needed sleep if she was to think clearly. She must find a way to approach the vizier's wife tomorrow. Only then would she know what the princess had really meant by the words she had uttered.

Knowing how Naksh's afternoon and evening had been occupied the previous day, Shakir instructed her attendants not to awaken her until late morning. They stood around her bed and uttered fluttering little cries, and Valentina was able to make out from the babble that the peddler women were coming to the harem that afternoon with their wonderful goods. The lady Naksh had been invited by the princess, Lafeeta Sultan, to join her and the vizier's other favorites.

"The vizier has left a particularly large bag of gold dinars for you, my lady," Shakir said proudly. He knew that his words would be repeated, gossiped about the baths by the handmaidens, thereby making him and his lady the envy of all. He held up a large red silk bag and shook it. To the slave girls' delight, it jingled noisily.

"Where is my lord Cica?" Valentina demanded. She had decided to accept the princess's invitation and did not want her afternoon spoiled by the vizier's lust.

"The master has gone to the Yeni Serai, my lady. The sultan values the advice of his first vizier. It is unlikely that the master will return much before midnight."

Relief washed over her. Freed of the vizier's unwelcome attentions, she could enjoy the day. The fluttering handmaidens brought her freshly squeezed fruit juice and peeled sweet green grapes, piled on a bed of tangy yogurt. There was also freshly baked bread with a honeycomb. Valentina ate it all. She was ravenous. Lord, she hoped she was not with child!

She was hurried off to the baths, where the women of the vizier's harem were all gossiping in small groups. Most of them had been excluded from the princess's festive gathering, for they were not important enough to be included. The peddler women would visit them, of course, but it would not be the same as being with the vizier's wife and favorites. Still, it was better than nothing.

Their eyes turned enviously toward the new favorite as she entered with her puffed-up eunuch and her six handmaidens. As yet no one had been able to get close to Naksh, but they supposed that eventually someone would, and then they would know more about her. Her eunuch said little and her women did not themselves know her well. Only Gülfem, Hazade, and Säh, who had spent the summer on the island with Naksh, could tell them anything, but all they would say was that Naksh was stubborn and overproud. Well, who had a better right to be proud? Was she not very high in their master's favor? Several smiled and nodded to Naksh as she passed by, but she ignored them.

After she was bathed, Valentina was hurried once more through the women's quarters and back to her own apartments, where her clothing was laid out. She would wear bright scarlet pantaloons with gold thread and garnet-glass ankle bands. Her blouse was of pale gold gauze. Over that she wore a bolero of scarlet and gold silk, edged in gold fringe. Her house slippers with their funny little turned-up toes were of scarlet silk.

Shakir braided Valentina's dark hair into a single braid into which he wove gold ribbons. The braid was then pushed through an open, round gold dome affixed atop her head. The braid flowed from the dome straight and long down her back. A cloth-of-gold sash was tied artistically about her waist. It, too, was fringed, and at the end of each piece of fringe was a tiny piece of garnet glass.

As Shakir decked her with her jewelry, Valentina protested, "It is a ladies' afternoon, toad! Why must I wear all this jewelry?"

"Are you mad, my lady Naksh?" he demanded, not in the least disturbed by her temper. "The more elegant and bedecked you are, the more proof there is of the vizier's love for you. The others will be bejeweled, but none save Lateefa Sultan herself own diamonds like yours. You will be the envy of all!"

Valentina let him have his way. She put her foot down, however, at taking along her giggling handmaidens, but she soothed their disappointment by giving each a gold dinar.

Shakir clucked disapprovingly. "They will spend it foolishly," he carped. "None has ever before held so much coin," he complained in a high-pitched voice.

"Why should you care how my maids spend their dinars, toad?" she said coldly. "Are they not entitled to an afternoon in the harem with the peddler women and their friends? I shall be enjoying myself with Lateefa Sultan, and you, toad, will be sitting in Hammid's chamber on the grand eunuch's silk divan dreaming of the day when you can slip your ugly feet into his slippers." Her words hit their mark squarely. As her maids swallowed their giggles behind their hands, Shakir looked distinctly uncomfortable. "I do not deny you, toad," Valentina continued. "We are all entitled to our little dreams."

Her maidens were dismissed. Valentina followed Shakir through the cool, dim corridors of the harem to the magnificent apartments of Lateefa Sultan. He left her there, for Hammid had put him in charge of the vizier's harem for the duration of Hammid's absence, and Shakir would, indeed, spend his afternoon contemplating his future glory.

Lateefa Sultan's salon was a beautiful room with paneled fruitwood walls whose moldings glowed with a heavy coat of gilt. In the center was a large, three-tiered fountain tiled in pure, rich turquoise and a clear eggshell white. Faintly perfumed water dripped slowly from the top basin of the fountain down into the octagon-shaped pool, the wide rim of which was also a seat where one might contemplate the creamy-yellow water lilies.

Placed about the room were yellow and white porcelain *jardinières* planted with Gold of Ophir rose trees and winter-blooming white jasmine. Two corner fireplaces with decorative hoods of beaten gold helped to take the chill from the air. The fireplaces burned cypress wood, which gave off a lovely scent. Several longhaired cats, some white, some black, some multicolored, but all with marvelous round eyes, sprawled gracefully on thick green and gold rugs. There were cages of brightly colored singing birds everywhere. The cats were too fat and contented to bother with them.

The many divans and stools were covered in jewel-toned silks and patterned brocades. There were great piles of satin and velvet pillows set about. Ruby-glass lamps hung from gold chains. Tables of precious woods artistically inlaid with mother-of-pearl and glittering gemstones were placed about the salon. In a corner, a group of pretty female musicians played softly.

Seeing Valentina enter, Lateefa Sultan called to her, "Come, my lady Naksh, and join us." As Valentina approached the princess, the older woman said, "You have not yet met my husband's other favorites." She drew forward a woman in rose pink. "This is the lady Hatijeh."

The sulky-mouthed Hatijeh, with her pale ivory skin and blueblack hair, faintly acknowledged Valentina. Her look plainly said that she did not think Valentina worthy of her time.

"And this is the lady Esmahan, my dear," Lateefa Sultan said.

The sweet-faced creature with dark blond hair and lovely bright blue eyes smiled a friendly welcome. "May you be as happy here as we all are," she said in a singsong voice.

"Of course," the princess continued, "you already know Gülfem, Säh, and Hazade. Did you not bring your attendants with you, Naksh? They were welcome, you know."

"Those silly butterflies irritate me," Valentina said bluntly. "I gave them each a dinar and permission to join the rest of the harem this afternoon."

"You are overgenerous with your gold, I think," remarked Hatijeh, who was noted for her parsimony.

"My lord Cica is most generous with me," Valentina gibed wickedly. "Was he never generous with you?"

"The rumors are true, I see," Hatijeh shot back. "You have the tongue of a pit viper!"

"A tongue which also knows well how to please our master," Valentina mocked the woman who, to her delight, flushed dark red.

"I wonder what the peddler women will bring this afternoon," Esmahan quickly interjected. She was the peacemaker among the women.

The vizier had long ago become bored with her. She was the mother of his two youngest daughters, however, and he felt a loyalty toward her, for Esmahan was wholly without guile and the sweetest-natured creature he had ever known. Never had she ever scolded him, berated him, or raised her voice to him. It was impossible to be unkind to Esmahan, so she remained in his favor, beaming benignly on everyone with her gently fading beauty.

"Whatever it is the peddler women are bringing, we are about to find out," the princess said as the double doors of her salon were flung open and a troop of black-clad women entered bearing with them brightly colored bundles. The peddler women set their bundles down, then opened them to display their merchandise. The concubines, manners and protocol forgotten, all rushed forward in order to have the best choices.

Lateefa Sultan put a restraining hand on Valentina's arm. "Wait," she said softly. When she was satisfied that the others were all too busy to notice them, she spoke softly and hurriedly. "Do you recognize Sabra, the wife of Lev Kira?"

Valentina stared at the peddler women for a moment, then nodded slowly. "I see her." Her heart was beginning to hammer with excitement.

"This entire afternoon has been arranged in order to facilitate your escape, Naksh. You must do *exactly* as you are told to do, without questions. Do you understand?"

"Yes, my lady." Valentina's beautiful face was suffused with fresh, excited color.

"You are to go immediately behind the commode screen at the far end of the salon. Attract no attention. Sabra will bring you a

black yashmak and a veil. Put them on and then obey her instructions without question. If, Allah forbid it, you are caught, I
will deny any knowledge of this. It will be I who will wield the
rod of chastisement on your helpless flesh, as is my duty as mistress of the harem. If you are caught, there will be no further
opportunities for escape. I will not help you again. I do so now
only in order to protect my husband. Your very presence in his
house is a danger to us all."

"A danger I did not encourage, my lady," Valentina reminded
the princess sharply. "I would be home in England and married
to my betrothed, if not for your husband."

Lateefa Sultan smiled. "I will not argue with you, my dear.
Men are weak creatures, as all wise women know. They find it
exceedingly difficult to deny themselves anything and must occasionally be treated as the very naughty boys they are. Like
moths, men find it hard to resist a beautiful flame. It is our duty
to see that they do not get too badly burned.

"I wish you good fortune, Lady Barrows." The princess spoke
those final words in English, and then Lateefa Sultan moved with
her customary grace across the room to join the others.

The women were all occupied with the peddlers. Valentina
looked about carefully for the ever-present eunuchs, but there
were none. Lateefa Sultan had surely seen to that.

Valentina hurried down the length of the room and slipped
behind the commode screen to wait. It seemed an eternity. What
if one of the other women needed to use the commode? What
would she do? Then suddenly a black garment was tossed over
the screen and she heard young Sabra's voice whispering urgently, "Hurry, my lady! There is not much time!"

Valentina pulled the rough woolen yashmak over her body and
drew it down. The hood fell to just beneath her eyebrows. She
fastened the black veil across the bridge of her nose and quickly
stepped from behind the screen.

Sabra took her by the hand, speaking swiftly as they moved
down the room toward the women. "The vizier's wife and favorites have had the pick of our merchandise, so several of us will
leave for the main salon of the harem, where the other peddlers
await us. One of our band, however, will open yet another packet
she has brought with her. It is filled with exquisite jewelry that
the favorites will not be able to resist. Our quiet departure will
hardly be noticed." Sabra dug into her robe and pulled out an
orange silk, which she gave to Valentina. "Here! This is your

empty pack. You have sold all of your merchandise." Her eyes twinkled mischievously.

When they reached the gathering of women, Sabra gently pulled on the robes of three of her companions. Those three wordlessly packed up and detached themselves from the chattering, bargaining women. "My lady princess," Sabra said softly, "may we have your permission to enter the main harem now to offer our goods? Reba? Have you shown the ladies your special pieces yet?"

A plump little woman with a smiling face opened a violet silk to display some of the most magnificent gems Valentina had ever seen. So extraordinary were they that she was almost tempted to remain! The vizier's concubines gasped. Gems of this quality usually went only to the sultan's women. They fingered the pieces greedily, Gülfem and Hatijeh immediately fighting over some yellow diamonds.

"Yes, go along," Lateefa Sultan said quietly to Sabra without even looking up.

Sabra fixed her veil across her face and, still holding Valentina's hand, led her from the salon. The three other women peddlers with them turned without a word and moved off down the corridor to the main salon of the harem, leaving Sabra and Valentina to move quickly through the twisting hallways alone.

"We must stop at the apartment of the grand eunuch to leave him his fee before we may leave the palace," Sabra whispered.

"My eunuch, Shakir, is there in Hammid's place this afternoon!" Valentina gasped. "He will surely recognize me!"

"It is unlikely, my lady. We are unrecognizable, shapeless lumps beneath these robes. But remember to keep your eyes lowered. Your eyes are hard to forget."

Sabra knocked on the door of the grand eunuch's apartment and then the two women entered.

The room was dimly lit, the air heavy with musk and ambergris. The incense burned in footed silver burners about the chamber. Shakir was lounging on Hammid's divan, smoking a waterpipe. A young blond boy, naked but for a gold chain about his waist, was curled next to him on the divan. Shakir waved the two heavily veiled women forward. The boy stared at them with large, dovelike brown eyes.

"You have the grand eunuch's fee?" Shakir demanded in his high, piping voice.

"Indeed, my lord," wheezed Sabra, her body suddenly twisted, her voice surprisingly old. "And a little something for you, my lord, as well! Heh! Heh! Heh!" she cackled, and was immediately caught by a fit of coughing that doubled her over.

Shakir peered myopically through the cloud of blue smoke that hovered over the room. He peered at the two old peddler women, for Valentina, quickly following Sabra's lead, was now hunched over and looking crippled herself. Sabra slipped something into her hand, and when the blond boy, with the agility of a feline, leaped from the divan, his hand outstretched, the two women moved forward, bobbing and servile, to press their little bags of baksheesh into the boy's hand. They began to bow themselves from the room, backing as they went.

"You have disposed of all your merchandise?" Shakir demanded blearily, his arm going possessively about the boy, who had returned to his place.

"Aye, my lord eunuch! How the vizier's ladies love fine jewels! Reba and I were quickly sold out," cackled Sabra. "Blessings upon you, good sir! May Yahweh protect you always."

"Get you gone, old hags!" Shakir waved them out. "I do not need your god's blessings. I am a true son of Allah!"

The two women exited from the grand eunuch's apartments and, Sabra leading the way, moved into the main section of the vizier's palace and finally out onto the vizier's private road.

Sabra allowed herself the luxury of quiet laughter. "Did you see that boy's eyes?" She giggled. "He had more kohl on them than a concubine, and his lips were painted, too!"

Valentina could scarcely contain her excitement. She was free! *Free!* She wanted to shout with joy. Silent, she walked swiftly with Sabra as they hurried away from Cicalazade Pasha's palace.

"I hope you do not mind the walk, my lady," Sabra said, "but we are less conspicuous this way. Two faceless women going about their business. It is not far."

"You mean the palace is near the Kira house? I didn't know that." Valentina's voice was tense with excitement and terror. *She was out of the palace.*

"Not *that* near." Sabra chuckled understandingly. "The vizier's palace is along the sea. At the end of this little private road are the teeming streets of the city. Several streets over is the street leading to Balata. Near yet far, my lady."

"I will not feel safe until we reach your house," Valentina said passionately. She clamped her lips shut tightly, for they were passing through the main gates of the vizier's palace, past the guardboxes that flanked the entry. In a few moments they reached a public street and were lost in the crowds. "I am free!" Valentina whispered triumphantly.

"You will not really be safe until you have left Istanbul, my lady," Sabra said wisely. "The vizier is a bold man."

"Has my departure been arranged, Sabra?" Valentina asked, while wondering, *Will Padraic be there waiting for me?*

"Tonight, my lady. It was considered too dangerous to take you to the ship in daylight. Two women, even garbed anonymously as we are, would attract attention mounting the gangway of a foreign vessel. You will be transported under cover of darkness to your ship. The gentlemen of your party are there now, eagerly awaiting your arrival. Old Esther did not think it wise for them to come to the house or to be seen escorting a litter to the waterfront, even at night."

"Surely I will be missed before nightfall, Sabra. I cannot go back! I *will not* go back!" Valentina declared passionately, a note of hysteria in her voice.

"It is almost sunset now. Remember, it is mid-autumn. Your foolish Shakir is far too involved at the moment to think clearly. The women of the harem will not concern themselves with your whereabouts. They will assume you are somewhere they are not. Grand Eunuch Hammid, having spent a stimulating afternoon battling his good friend and rival, Ali Ziya, for the pick of the especially beautiful slave girls sold today at Kara Ali's slave market, will accept the invitation of the slave merchant to take supper with him. Like the vizier, who is now at the Yeni Serai, Hammid will not return to the vizier's palace until late. By then it will be long past dark and you will be safely at sea. Your ship is prepared to sail the moment you arrive.

"The vizier," Sabra reminded Valentina, "cannot make a public outcry about your disappearance, or he will be punished for kidnapping you in the first place—*and* for lying to the sultan about it. When Cicalazade Pasha does finally learn that the English ships have sailed, he will know for certain that you are gone. He will be forced to accept the situation."

"I worry that I have placed your family in jeopardy, Sabra," Valentina said feelingly. "The vizier is no fool. He will realize that I have been aided by someone here in Istanbul. The suspicion will fall on the Kiras, particularly in light of the fact that the peddler women who came to the harem were Jews."

"The vizier will not dare complain to anyone, not with his own crimes in mind," Sabra said. "Besides, the Kiras have been in favor with the Ottoman sultans too long to lose it now, particularly over such a matter as this. Indeed, your kidnapping might have caused trouble between our ruler and your queen."

Sabra, the wife of Lev Kira, spoke with the assurance of youth. Life had not taught Sabra that what is today, may not necessarily be tomorrow.

Even as Sabra was speaking, decisions were being made in the council chamber of the sultan that would change the smooth course of her young life forever.

"Then it is agreed," Sultan Mehmed said to his council. "The Jews are to be our scapegoats. But will the people believe it? Will it make them cease rioting?"

"If I may speak, my lord sultan." An elderly mullah who had been on the council in the sultan's father's time rose to his feet.

"Speak!" the sultan said.

"The people will believe the Jews are to blame for the debasement of the coinage because it is just the sort of thing that one might expect from Jews. They are a greedy, venal, and avaricious people, as their history has shown. Even the Christian West, with its teachings by the prophet Jesus that advises man to turn the other cheek and to love his neighbors, has not made its people love the Jews any more than we love the Jews."

"Nonetheless," a third vizier spoke up hastily, forgetting to obtain permission, "the Jews are very good citizens. They pay their taxes without question and contribute much of value to the economy of the empire. If this action you contemplate, my lord sultan, should spread to our other cities, there would be more harm done us than good."

"We must have *someone* to blame for clipping the coinage," the sultan insisted. "They say that my mother and I are responsible for it, and I will not have such rumors spread!"

"Blame only the Jews of Istanbul for the crime, my lord," suggested the elderly mullah.

"The Jews of Istanbul, led in their perfidy by the Kiras!" the second vizier suggested excitedly. "The Kiras, with all their power and wealth, are greatly envied by other Jews. If we claim that the Kiras are responsible for the debasement of the coinage, the people will seek to bring them to justice. They will not blame all the Jews, only the Kira family. It will take their minds off their own problems and they will cease blaming you and our gracious Valide for the currency problem. It will also allow you to confiscate the Kiras' wealth for yourself, my lord! And their wealth is legendary, as you know."

The speaker knew that the great debt he owed the Kiras was not a matter of public knowledge. Of late they had begun to press him, his loan now being two years overdue. If the sultan accepted his suggestion, his own large debt need never be paid! The sultan might even reward him for his advice, so he would profit doubly by his suggestion.

"To blame the Jews as a whole is one thing," the third vizier said, "but to single out the Kira family is not honorable, my lord sultan. For almost one hundred years they have loyally, and without reservation, served the Ottomans. They have always been this empire's most loyal subjects."

"They have served my family to their own profit," Mehmed said irritably. He liked the second vizier's suggestion very much, particularly the part about confiscating the Kiras' wealth for himself. "They claim to be exempted from taxes for all eternity by virtue of some favor they did my great-great-grandmother, the Valide Cyra Hafise, of loving memory. Who, however, can verify such a claim? For years they have been cheating our coffers of legal taxes on this pretext."

"Their claim is a valid one, my lord." The Grand Vizier Cicalazade Pasha spoke up. "The great Valide Cyra Hafise saw that it was put into the official records of the time. I have seen it myself."

"Perhaps," the sultan said, "but I still believe the Kira family presumes too much on their connection with my family. And we must have a believable scapegoat to appease the populace."

He turned to the second vizier. "See to it that the rumors are properly spread, Hassan Bey. Then, when the riots are well under way, probably by tonight, I shall send you, Cica, with several troops of my finest janissaries, to stop the carnage. In that way the riots against the Jews will not spread beyond Balata, the people will be sated of their bloodlust, and the Kira wealth will be mine—a public punishment for their crime. This will show the people that I am a fair ruler who metes out justice even to those in my special favor.

"The coinage will be called in and struck to its proper weight . . . and if the same number of coins are not released back into circulation as were taken out, who will know? The people, believing I have listened to their complaints, will be happy. Is that

not the function of good government? To make the people think
they are happy?" He chuckled richly, then said, "Leave me now,
all but Grand Vizier Cicalazade Pasha."

The sultan's ministers and advisers filed slowly from the room
arguing the merits of their master's decision. The third vizier,
his days obviously numbered, was silent.

A page hurried forward to fill the goblets of the sultan and
Cicalazade Pasha, then withdrew.

For close to an hour the sultan spoke with Cicalazade Pasha
regarding the destruction of the ghetto and the Kira family's fate.
The sultan drained his cup twice, the vizier filling it for him. The
royal goblet was filled a third time.

Mehmed drank deeply, but the vizier had merely touched his
lips with the strong wine. Slamming his cup upon a low table,
the sultan asked, "You have had her?"

"A few days ago, after I realized that gentle persuasion was
not the answer to gaining the pleasures of Naksh's lovely body,"
replied his friend.

"And was she worth all your trouble, Cica?" The sultan's look
was avid.

The vizier smiled slowly. "She was the ripest and sweetest
melon, which I split slowly with my lance. She dripped with
honey, my lord. Her cries were music, and my back is scored
with her sharp claws."

"Allah! If only she was not my sister! I should have taken her
for myself then, Cica! I envy you this delightful conquest."

"I have not conquered her, my lord," Cicalazade Pasha said.
"She has given me nothing I have not taken by force. There is
no tenderness in her, only defiance. I find it more stimulating
than anything I have ever encountered. One thing, however. I
should like her to truly understand the power of life and death
that I hold over her. Here, perhaps, my lord, I might beg your
help."

"I will help you in whatever way you desire, Cica. Are you not
my best friend?"

"If you will remember, my lord, the day you gave me permission
to take Naksh from her English companions, I promised you that
you might view me schooling my slave."

"Aye," the sultan said softly, his eyes glittering. "I remember."

"You denied yourself the pleasure of her body because she is
your sister and you would not commit incest, my lord. Yet there
is a way you may take your pleasure of her without actually com-

mitting incest. By sharing Naksh's favors with you, my lord, I demonstrate to her the great and terrible power I hold over her. *My* will, not hers! She is intelligent and will quickly see that I may do whatever I choose to do with her—even share her with another man!

"Her second maidenhead is intact, my lord sultan. Hammid will shortly begin to prepare her to receive a manhood there. Would it not give you pleasure to take that second maidenhead of Naksh's, my lord? Would you not enjoy delving into her dark channel, to be the very first man to do so? Would you not enjoy her cries of anguish as she is forced to submit to the pillaging of her bottom, even, my lord, as I fill her sheath with my burning shaft?" The vizier's voice was satiny soft.

The sultan's eyes rolled back in his head, and the vizier could see that he was having difficulty breathing. In a moment, however, the dark eyes focused on Cicalazade again and Mehmed said in a hopeful yet disbelieving voice, "You would give me your favorite's second virginity, Cica? We would take her together?"

"Were it not for you, my lord sultan, I should not have her at all" was the smooth reply.

"Am I to understand that for a night you and I will share the woman's favors?"

"As long as I do not drive you to incest, my lord," the vizier answered smoothly. "For your deeper longings, I shall set aside virgins to amuse you that night."

A grin of delight split Sultan Mehmed's face. "Excellent! Excellent!" he approved. "Never has a man had a better friend than you, my dear Cica! I am delighted to see you back in your old form again. It is Naksh who has done this for you. I shall see that she is suitably rewarded—after I have tasted of her favors. Do you remember the time we had the contest to see who could deflower the most virgins in one day?"

The vizier nodded. "I remember that you won, my lord," he said with a chuckle.

The sultan stood up. "Come. Have the evening meal with me while we reminisce. Tell me more of Naksh. Does she have beautiful breasts, Cica?"

"They are like perfect marble fruits, my lord, and sweeter than any I have had before, even my adored Incili's. Her skin is so fair that the slightest touch marks her. I find it thrilling to see in my fingermarks the evidence of my possession of her body."

"You will be eager for her by this night's end, but first you must see to your duties, Cica," the sultan said in a bantering tone.

"I always do my duty, my lord, in or out of your service" came the retort, and the sultan laughed.

They were passing through a garden that offered a view of the city and suddenly the sultan pointed. "Look, Cica! Is that a fire in the city?"

The vizier peered into the darkness and saw the reddish glow. "Hassan Bey has done his work quickly," he said. "That fire is in Balata. Perhaps I should go now."

"No," the sultan said. "I will give orders that two troops of janissaries be ready to leave within the hour, but the fire in Balata is a small one. The riots have just begun, my friend. Let the ghetto show a bit more flame before you go. There is time for something light to eat, Cica."

Mehmed smiled. "I shall be a far richer man by morning, and the Kiras poorer. Kill them all, Cica! I do not want them haunting my dreams as my brothers have haunted my dreams all these years. I can still see their trusting little faces, although the eldest, Mamud, looked at me with knowledgeable eyes. *He knew!* I still see those eyes in my dreams! *Kill them all! Destroy them!*"

"This is the end," Esther Kira said. Even within her apartment the smell of smoke was strong. "Somehow, nonetheless, we must get Lady Barrows to the docks. We are honor-bound to do so."

"Grandmother! There is no chance of getting Lady Barrows safely away," Eli Kira said excitedly. "She will die here with the rest of us!"

"Why do you assume you must die?" Valentina demanded, made furious by their fatalistic attitude. "You are the Kira family, in great favor with the royal family. The mob will not dare attack *your* home!"

Esther Kira held up her hand for silence, and the room quieted. "Listen to me, my child," the old woman said patiently. "For months, the sultan and his mother have had slaves locked in the treasury clipping bits of metal from every coin that passed through. This devalued the currency to such an extent that a poor man could no longer afford to buy a loaf of bread or a bowl of tripe for his family. Such a thing is unheard of in Istanbul. What is worse is that no one had the power to stop it. Now the

people have revolted, so a sacrificial scapegoat must be offered
to them. The sultan has obviously decided that the Jews are a
good scapegoat."

"But you are the sultan's friends," Valentina protested.

"Aye," Ester Kira said dryly, "and we are also the richest Jews
in Balata—as evidenced by our great house, perched a top Balata's greatest height. We might have survived this, as we have
survived other such incidents in our history, had we been more
discreet. But nothing would do but that my son, Solomon build
a house at the very pinnacle of this great hill. Our neighbors and
friends below will have hidden their wealth, and perhaps even
themselves, in their cellars to wait out the mobs. Perhaps some
of them will escape this attack, for there are always some who
do. To think I escaped Adrianople over a hundred years ago, to
end like this!" She shook her head sadly. In a moment, she continued. "The mobs will seek the richest and the easiest pickings,
and we are perched like a glittering crown upon a fool's head!
We cannot hide. They will tear this house apart stone by stone
in search of our legendary wealth." She laughed sharply. "All
they will find, however, is what you see, for the bulk of our wealth
is spread throughout various countries to the west in our many
banking houses. We Jews have never been safe in any land, and
we have learned through necessity to be clever with our wealth,
spreading it about so that our enemies can never take everything
or completely destroy us."

As she finished, there came a tremendous knocking at the door
and the other women in the room began to scream.

"Be silent!" Esther Kira shouted over their shrieks in a surprisingly strong voice. "Answer the door, you fools! Mobs do not
knock politely!"

With an amused look at his great-grandmother, Simon Kira
hurried out to answer the knocking, and then Padraic Burke was
striding into Esther Kira's salon, followed by Murrough O'Flaherty and the Earl of Kempe.

"Padraic!" Valentina flew across the room and into his arms,
which closed tightly around her. Their lips fused in a torrid kiss,
then they broke apart, acutely aware that a passionate reunion
was unseemly at that moment.

Lord Burke looked Valentina over carefully. She appeared unharmed. "Your costume, madam, is most revealing," he
murmured.

"In the harem of Cicalazade Pasha," Valentina replied, her amythest eyes twinkling, "my costume is considered sedate, my lord."

"What a world we find ourselves in," said Tom Ashburne, his gaze admiring. "Divinity, you have once more devastated me. Alas! I believed myself reconciled to your decision."

"We have no time for chatter," Murrough O'Flaherty said grimly after he kissed Valentina in greeting. "The mob is hard on our heels and there is murder in their hearts. Why have you not blockaded your doors and windows, Eli Kira? Do you welcome violent death?"

"There is no escape, Captain O'Flaherty," Eli Kira said softly. "We can but await our fate."

"A man's fate is what he himself makes of it, Eli Kira," came the sharp reply. "If you sit meekly by waiting for death, then you shall surely find death. But if you fight, man, there is a chance you may outwit death!"

"Captain O'Flaherty, you do not understand," Eli Kira said quietly. "We may fight, but we are outnumbered. If one or two of us should manage to survive, how do you suggest we live with the memories of the others who were slaughtered? My sons, their wives, and children are all in this house. If they are gone, what is left? It is better we all die together."

"We are trapped in this monument to our pride," Esther Kira said sadly. "We could run, but there is only one way out, and that is through the mob itself."

"Could you not escape through the gardens?" Murrough asked her.

"The gardens end in a sheer drop over the cliff," Valentina told her cousin. "Esther is right. There is but one way out."

"There is a chance that you and Lady Barrows may be spared our fate," Esther Kira said, "if only we had her English clothes. If we could but hold off the mobs until the janissaries arrive— and they will arrive, I assure you—then perhaps we might convince them that you three men and Lady Barrows were in the house on business and were accidentally caught in the disturbance. There is a chance."

"We brought Valentina's clothing with us," Murrough said. "Nelda packed what she thought her mistress would need."

"God's foot, Murrough!" Valentina snatched the package from her cousin. "Give it to me at once. I will not feel right until I am in my own clothing again."

"A pity," said the earl.

"If you are very good I shall wear these garments for you once we have returned to England, Tom," she teased him.

"You will burn them at once, madame!" ordered Lord Burke darkly.

"Secret the jewelry upon your person, child," Esther Kira said.

"No! I want nothing to remind me of the vizier," Lady Barrows replied.

"You have earned your bounty," Esther Kira said wisely. "Do not leave them for the mob. When you return to England, give the vizier's gems to the poor if you will, but take them with you!"

Valentina hurried away to change into her own clothing. She felt immediately better at seeing herself familiar once again, in a midnight-blue silk gown with lace cuffs and a starched neck ruff. She pulled her hair free of its exotic trappings and brushed Shakir's work away, parting it in the center and twisting the thick hair into a French knot at the nape of her neck. The silk stockings felt comfortable, but her elegantly heeled shoes felt a bit tight. Her face scrubbed free of kohl and red lip balm, her own natural color glowed softly.

"I will need something in which to place these jewels," she told Sabra when her friend came to ask if she needed help.

"Give me the gems," Sabra said. "I will find a bag for them." Then she began to weep. "I do not want to die, Valentina!" she sobbed piteously. "What of the child I carry? He will die, too! It is not fair! *It is not fair!*"

Valentina could only hug the girl. She had never felt more helpless. There was a very good chance that they were all going to die. At least Sabra knew what it was like to carry a child inside her. Valentina did not. She knew that more than anything she wanted Padraic's children.

The two young women returned to Esther Kira's salon to find that the men of the house had finally, under Murrough's stern direction, marshaled themselves to barricade the doors and the other entries to the house. Outside they heard a dull roaring as the mob drew nearer, working its way to the top of Balata and leaving destruction and death in its wake.

"The garden is your weak spot," Lord Burke said. "You must station manservants there to prevent the mob from climbing your walls. Tom, can you oversee that?"

"Immediately!" the earl called enthusiastically. Tom had always loved a good battle.

"My lord earl!"

The earl turned toward Esther Kira. "Yes, madam?"

"My servant, Yakob, will take you to the cellars. There you will find several excellent rifles and the gunpowder necessary for them. If you do not know how to use a gun, my servants do."

"I'm a better shot with a pistol, madam," said Tom, grinning at her. What a resourceful old woman she was!

"There are pistols, too, my lord," she replied calmly.

"Madam"—the earl bowed to Esther Kira—"you should have been a warrior queen."

"It seems that, in my old age, I am, my lord," Esther answered with a rueful smile.

The great wooden gates to the inner courtyard of the house had already been barricaded, a heavy oak beam set across the usually-open entry. Behind the gates were arranged all of the carts and vehicles belonging to the Kira family. It would take the mob some time to break through. When they did, they would find the iron-bound double doors to the house locked, barred, and equally formidable.

On the two sides of the gardens, which were surrounded by a high wall, Kira servants stood at the ready with guns. Having been so successfully marshaled to defend themselves, the family was beginning to believe that they just might survive until the janissaries arrived to rescue them. That the sultan would protect them they had no doubt.

Behind the walls and doors they could hear the heavy, rhythmic thud of feet and the drone of angry voices, hundreds of voices that became an eerie howling sound as the raging mob approached the Kira house. A great pounding began as the mob struggled to beat down the gates. The gates held. From the gardens came the occasional sound of shots as those foolish enough to attempt to scale the walls met with failure.

"Take me to the main entry hall of our house," Esther Kira suddenly ordered her family.

"Grandmother!" Eli Kira exclaimed, horrified. "Has fear addled your wits?"

"Do I look fearful, Eli?" she demanded.

He shook his head, sighing.

"Listen to me, my ever-cautious grandson. If the mob breaks through, I do not wish to be found cowering in my apartment. I would meet my death head-on, without fear. Now do as I bid you. Take me into the main entrance of the house where I may await my persecutors with dignity and honor."

Even as his father began to protest, Simon Kira stepped forward and picked up the frail old woman, carefully wrapping her in her delicate gossamer shawls.

He carried her from her salon to the main entry. Padraic and Valentina and two servants followed, bringing Esther's divan and pillows so that she might be comfortable.

Esther's three eldest great-grandsons, Simon, Asher, and Cain, and their wives, Sarai, Ruth, and Shohannah, gathered protectively about the matriarch.

David and Lev Kira patrolled the gardens with Tom Ashburne. David's wife, Haghar, had chosen this moment to go into labor with her first child. Sabra was sent to oversee the little children in the nursery, in the hope that in calming their fears, she would be able to control her own, for Sabra was the most visibly terrified of them all.

"You realize, Esther Kira, that by placing yourself here," Murrough O'Flaherty told her, "you make it impossible for us to defend your house and family once the mob breaks through the front door."

"If, Captain, the mob breaks through before the sultan's men arrive to rescue us, then we are doomed no matter where we are," she answered him. "I would not give those beasts the pleasure of chasing us through our own home in order to kill us. If they mean to kill us, then let them do it here—immediately. Perhaps with some of their bloodlust satisfied, they will spare the children. It is the best I can hope for. But you and your people would be wise to remain in my salon. By the time the mob reaches there, their first passion to kill will be assuaged. You may be able to explain who you are and save yourselves."

"It is not our way, Esther Kira, either to flee danger or to leave our friends to face danger alone," Valentina said before her cousin could reply.

"You face death by being available to the first assault," the old lady fretted.

"We English are not afraid to face death, Esther Kira. Our history is filled with instances of valor. Never have we fled before the face of the Dark Angel," Valentina answered. She took the old woman's hand in hers while Padraic placed a gentle hand on Esther's shoulder.

"You have your mother's sense of what is right, daughter of Marjallah," came the matriarch's voice, and she squeezed the young hand in hers. "May Yahweh protect us all and have mercy on us in this hour of danger."

A serving woman came into the room, crying loudly and wringing her hands, and knelt before Esther Kira. "Forgive me, gracious mistress, for the evil news I bring this family," she sobbed.

"You are forgiven," said Esther Kira solemnly.

"Haghar has perished in her travail, and her child, a boy, was born dead, the cord wrapped about his little neck."

Sarai, Ruth, and Shohannah wept, clinging to their husbands. They had all led such charmed lives. It seemed impossible that one of them should die this way.

Sighing, Esther Kira shook her head. "This is a very bad omen," she said softly. "Yahweh has spoken most clearly. We are surely doomed."

There came the awful sound of splintering wood as the great gates began to give way before the fury of the attackers. And then the mob poured into the courtyard, pushing aside everything in its way, clambering over the carts and litters placed to deter them, howling murderous intent with one shrieking voice as they began to pound on the thick double doors at the front of the house. In the gardens, the guns fired again and again, and Tom Ashburne ran into the entry, saying, "It's hopeless! They're almost out of gunpowder now. When it's gone, there'll be nothing to keep the bastards from coming over the walls."

"They've broken through into the courtyard," Murrough said grimly. "Where the *hell* are the sultan's men, I should like to know!"

Lord Burke put his arm around Valentina as she stood holding Esther's frail hand. "Whatever happens, Val, remember that I love you," he said quietly. "I have always loved you, and I will regret to my dying day that I was not man enough to say it when I should have."

"This may very well *be* our dying day, Padraic," she whispered to him with gallows humor.

"What a woman you are, Val, that you can laugh in the very face of death!" he said admiringly.

"We are not going to die, Padraic!" Valentina said insistently. "I did not escape from the vizier's harem only to die at the hands of a mob! We will survive this, as we have survived so much else.

But I would have you know something before anything else happens here. I had intended to tell you when we were safely aboard *Archangel*.

"I resisted Cicalazade Pasha's advances for most of my captivity, but in the end, he forced his will on me. I hate and detest him. I swear to you that though he forced himself on my body, he had nothing else of me. Not my heart, which I gave to you long ago, or my soul, which is mine alone. I love you, Padraic, and I know that I always have. Would that I had been woman enough to admit it to myself and tell you before giving my hand in marriage to poor Ned Barrows. How different our lives would have been!"

"But not half as exciting, Val," he said wryly. "There is much O'Malley in you. You will never bore me, sweetheart!"

"Then you still want me to wife despite what has happened?" she asked him plainly.

Lord Burke laughed. "Like my mother, you are sometimes very foolish! Aye, I want you to wife! 'Tis true that you have a most delicious and provocative form that I much enjoy, but your heart means even more to me. Do I care that Cicalazade Pasha used you? Aye, I care. Would that I could kill the man, for the pain he inflicted upon you, but 'twas not your fault, Val, and I do not blame you."

"I am so fearful that he may have impregnated me, Padraic," she whispered.

"He cannot, my child," Esther Kira's reedy voice stated clearly. "Cicalazade Pasha has not impregnated a woman in over ten years. The last children born to him were a daughter by Esmahan and a little son by Hatijeh. It was that son's birth that caused Lateefa Sultan to resort to an old remedy used by the great valide Cyra Hafise and her three sister kadins to prevent Sultan Selim from having additional sons.

"Hatijeh attempted to use her little boy to gain supremacy over Lateefa Sultan. The infant was not strong, however, and died before his first birthday. Lateefa Sultan had resolved by then that such a threat could not occur again as long as her husband no longer fathered children. Consequently, any woman who enjoys the vizier's passions is given the old valide's potion in her food or drink. None has ever conceived a child."

"Thank you, Esther Kira," Valentina and Lord Burke breathed in unison.

The old lady looked up at Padraic and said quietly, "Take good care of her, my lord. Like her mother, she is a brave and very loving woman. You are most fortunate."

With a loud crack, the hinges on the main doors began pulling away from the lintel moldings. The entry chamber was suddenly deathly quiet. Padraic, Murrough, and Tom surrounded Valentina, protectively encircling her, their weapons at the ready.

The double doors were torn from their hinges, bursting open to admit the mob which poured, howling, into the entry.

Raising his pistol, Tom took careful aim and fired at the leader of the wolfpack. A hole blossomed scarlet in the man's forehead and he fell forward, dead. The mob halted, stunned.

"By what right do you dare invade my household?" Esther Kira demanded. "You have frightened my family and servants, and my English guests will return to England saying that Istanbul is a savage, barbaric city!" Her voice was amazingly powerful now, carrying all the way to the stragglers, who were in the courtyard.

They looked at her, mouths agape. This was Esther Kira! The Esther Kira of legend! She who was born in the reign of the conqueror's son and had lived for over a hundred years. *Esther Kira!*

Suddenly, a man shouted, "You have stolen from the people, Esther Kira! You Jews could not be satisfied having all the freedom the empire gives you! You Jews could not be satisfied amassing great wealth! No, you Jews could not be happy unless you were stealing from the people! For that you must die!"

"And just what is it we have stolen from the people?" demanded the matriarch. "You do not frighten me with your talk of death, for I have lived so long now that death is merely another adventure. But if you would slaughter me in a dishonorable fashion, I wish to know why."

The crowd shuffled its feet. The Jews in the ghetto below had hidden or tried to flee the mob. When caught, they had bargained for their lives, and when the mob had wrung from its frightened, babbling victims all the treasures it could, it had pitilessly, and with much laughter, murdered them and put their homes to the torch. The Kiras, however, stood facing them, and were demanding to know the charge against them.

"It is your fault that the currency has been debased!" the spokesman cried out.

"*Our* fault?" The old lady was incredulous. "Why is it our fault?

Everyone knows that the sultan and his mother have been clipping the coinage in the treasury before releasing it back into circulation. The fact that no one dared speak the truth aloud does not make it any less a truth! We merchants, too, have suffered because of this. Our fault, indeed!" Esther Kira looked righteously indignant.

"Treason! Treason!" shouted the mob. "The old woman speaks treason!"

"I speak the truth!" Esther Kira declared vehemently.

"Jews do not speak the truth!" a voice in the crowd cried out. "Everyone knows that Jews are dirty and that they lie!"

"I speak the truth!" Esther Kira repeated. "My family's good reputation has been built upon truth! I do not doubt that some of you here tonight have profited by doing business with my family. Were we dishonest, you would not have profited and neither would we."

Suddenly stones were thrown. They were targeted at Esther Kira and all found their mark, one large, sharp-edged stone embedding itself in the center of the old woman's forehead. The matriarch fell backward, blood streaming down her face. Valentina caught her, cradling her protectively, trying deperately to stanch the flow of blood.

"It is over," Esther Kira whispered weakly. "Yahweh!" The light began to fade from her lively black eyes. Her lips moved again, and Valentina bent low and heard Esther Kira say softly, *"My lady Cyra! I knew you would come!"* Then her head fell to the side, her eyes glazed and sightless.

"She is dead," Valentina said quietly. Tears began to run down her face. She looked up at the crowd. "You have killed a good woman," she said loudly enough so that they could all hear. The Kira family began to wail softly.

"We have killed a thieving Jew," shouted someone, "and this is only the beginning of our revenge on them!" The crowd began to move forward menacingly.

Suddenly from outside the courtyard came the sound of many horses, and the crowd shouted as it scattered to make way, "The janissaries! The janissaries!"

"It took them long enough," muttered Murrough. "If they'd come a few moments sooner Esther might still be alive."

The crowd within the great entrance hall opened a path to allow the sultan's men to get through.

Valentina gasped, clutching wildly at Padraic.

"The rider in white! The leader! It is Cicalazade Pasha!" Valentina whispered desperately, watching as he dismounted and
strode inside.

The vizier was too involved to notice her. Fixing his gaze on
Eli Kira, he declared, "Your family has been accused of master-
minding the plot to debase our currency. That is treason. The
penalty is death!" He turned to the captain of the janissaries.
"Carry out the sentence."

Soldiers leaped forward to drag Eli Kira and his three sons to
their knees. Their necks were forced down and before any could
protest, they were quickly decapitated. Their heads, surprised
expressions on all of their faces, rolled across the floor to stop at
the feet of the three young Kira wives, who stared in mute horror.
Blood gushed forth from the lifeless trunks, staining the marble
floors crimson.

Sarai, Ruth, and Shohannah were not given a moment to
mourn before they, too, were forced to their knees. In shock, half
fainting, they swiftly joined their husbands in death.

David and Lev Kira, retreating from the gardens to their homes,
entered to see their family's heads held high for all to see. They
ran forward, their swords brandished, and were cut down by the
janissaries. When they lay dead and bloodied on the marble
floors, their heads were severed from their bodies, to be displayed
before the cheering crowds.

Ottoman justice was done. In only a few minutes, almost the
entire adult Kira family in Istanbul had been ruthlessly
murdered.

The vizier turned to the four Europeans and asked, "Your
names and your business here?"

"Captain Murrough O'Flaherty of the *Archangel*, out of London," said Murrough coolly. "The Earl of Kempe. My younger
brother, Lord Burke, and his betrothed wife, Lady Barrows. I
think you know the esteem in which the Sultan Valide holds
Lady Barrows, my lord vizier. We would appreciate an escort from
this house to our ship." Murrough's voice never wavered. Indeed,
it was quite stern.

But Cicalazade Pasha ignored Murrough as his burning blue-
gray gaze fastened on Valentina. "Naksh!"

Valentina said nothing, but she refused to lower her gaze from
his. In her own clothing, with Padraic by her side, she felt strong.

"How did you get here?" he demanded. "*How?*"

"How is of no consequence, my lord vizier," she said quietly. "I am here and I am leaving Istanbul tonight."

"Is something amiss, my lord?" asked the janissary captain.

"Captain Hussein, I want—" the vizier began, but Valentina called out, "Captain Hussein! I am the English lady for whom the sultan and his mother have been searching these past months. I was kidnapped. Today I was rescued by the Kira family, through their final loyalty to the sultan. I came to Balata to make my farewells to my friends before sailing for England, and I was trapped here with my party when the mob attacked."

Cicalazade Pasha's eyes blazed furiously at Valentina, for her quick speech had destroyed forever any chance he might have had of taking possession of her again. Her voice had carried far enough that half the mob now knew who she was.

"Our lord, the sultan, will be relieved to learn of your safety, my lady," said the captain of the janissaries. "It is unfortunate that you were exposed to this unpleasantness after your ordeal."

"You have the tongue of a courtier, Captain Hussein," Valentina said sweetly. "I see a great future for you in the sultan's service."

"The children! We found the Jews' children!" shouted a group of women as they herded forward Sabra, who was carrying Sarai's infant son, Ruben, and the other children.

"Dispose of them!" ordered Cicalazade Pasha.

"No!" Valentina's voice rang out clear into the courtyard. The authority in it was so powerful that for a moment no one moved. Then she spoke so softly that only the vizier heard her. "I hold your life in my hands, my lord Cica. You owe me something for your abuse of me. Is your self-importance so enormous that you actually deceived yourself into thinking I enjoyed your rape of me? I detest you and all you did to me, but I will have this one thing of you or else I shall expose you to the sultan *and* his mother."

"The sultan is my best friend." The vizier mocked her. "He was to share your favors with me shortly, Naksh. He has known all along where you were, although I will tell you that the Valide did not share our secret."

Valentina felt sick at this revelation, but she showed no emotion. "I would remind you, my lord vizier, that the sultan *and* his family were the Kiras' friends. You see about you the result of *that* friendship. Would you risk all that you have, and endanger your wife and children, simply to continue your possession of me? I think not, my lord Cica."

"What do you want?" he asked. Though he was defeated, his handsome visage showed nothing.

"This girl," she said, nodding toward Sabra, "and the children."

"The sultan has ordered that the Kira family be disposed of entirely," he said implacably.

"I will dispose of them for you, my lord," Valentina replied. "They will sail for England with me tonight. There are Kiras in England who will shelter them, and they are innocents in this affair. You are a father and a grandfather, my lord Cica. Is there no mercy in your heart?"

"So you believe I have a heart, Naksh?" He bandied words with her.

"Please, my lord," she said. "The mob grows restless while we waste time."

"I could order your English friends killed where they stand and take you back to my palace, Naksh," he threatened her softly.

"The scandal would be too great even for you to survive, my lord vizier," she replied quickly. "The sultan would be forced to punish you. He would do so by confiscating all you have, possibly including your life.

"The sultan is a greedy man. I don't doubt he has been told that he can confiscate the wealth of the Kira family, but when this mob finishes looting the house, my lord Cica, there will be no wealth for the sultan to take. You see, my lord, the Kira family long ago disposed of their wealth, spreading it among their various family branches throughout *many* countries in the West. It cannot be confiscated.

"The sultan is going to be very disappointed, I am afraid, and he will look for some way to ease his disappointment. Do not put yourself in a position of vulnerability. If you are quick, you may find another scapegoat, my lord, upon whom you may heap the blame for this disaster," Valentina finished.

There was genuine admiration in his appraising gaze. He sighed deeply. "You are only the second thing in my life that I have regretted losing, Naksh, but I think I am wise to concede defeat. You are too intelligent a woman for me to cope with."

"You cannot lose what you never really possessed, my lord," she answered quietly.

"Take the girl and the children and go," he said. "Go before I allow the heart you will not admit I have to overrule the clever mind that has kept me alive *and* in favor all these years."

He turned to Captain Hussein. "You and a party of your men are to escort the English and these children to the harbor. See them safely aboard their ship. Return to me after that. The sultan will want to discuss this evening's work with the second vizier, Hassan Bey, and we must fetch him."

Captain Hussein made a respectful obeisance to the vizier. Calling out two dozen of his men, he began to clear a path through the murmuring mob for the Kira children and their guardians.

"Farewell, my lord Cica," Valentina said, and turned away from him.

"Farewell, Naksh," he called. She did not acknowledge him. She had never accepted the name, and now, safe again in her own identity, she would not do so. She was Valentina St. Michael. She was the daughter of Aidan St. Michael, and her father, *her true and only father*, was Conn O'Malley!

Valentina put a comforting arm around the terrified Sabra. "Do not be afraid, Sabra," she reassured her. "We are going home now. We are going home to England!"

PART V

A Beginning, An Ending

WINTER 1603

Chapter Fifteen

AND SO THEY CAME HOME TO ENGLAND, *Archangel, Royal Bess,* and *Homeward Bound* plowing their way up the Thames toward London in a blinding snowstorm, Christmas Day, 1602. The voyage had been relatively uneventful until, crossing the Bay of Biscay, the weather turned particularly foul and remained so.

In other ways, the trip was hard. It had been necessary to crowd a pregnant woman and ten small children aboard *Archangel,* for the terrified group could not be separated.

Lord Burke's cabin was taken over by the five oldest surviving Kira boys. Only eight-and-a-half-year-old Dov, Simon and Sarai's eldest son, and his seven-year-old cousin, Jacob, eldest child of Asher and Ruth, completely understood the truth that but for Sabra and the other children, their family was dead and their home was gone. Dov's five-year-old brother, Aaron, and Cain and Shohannah's two-year-old twin sons, Zadok and Zuriyel, did not understand. They cried for their mothers, to the deep anguish of Sabra, who tried to mother all of her nieces and nephews while coping with their terrible loss.

Nelda, with an amazingly powerful maternal instinct for a childless young girl, took Ruben, the infant son of Simon and Sarai, into her keeping. The servant adored the baby.

In the chaos of leaving the Kira home, Valentina had pleaded for two goats so that the babies might have milk. The goats were brought aboard, and Nelda took over the earl's cabin, Ruth's three little daughters, five-year-old Mattithyah, three-year-old Hannah, and Tema, who was but a year and a half; as well as Sarai and Simon's three-year-old Tamar, and baby Ruben.

Lord Burke and the earl fitted themselves into the captain's sleeping cabin with Murrough. Valentina took Sabra into her bed.

The fact that she, so afraid of facing death, had escaped it while the rest of her family was slaughtered weighed heavily on Sabra's conscience. In her mind's eye she could still see the decapitated bodies of her family scattered in grotesque positions of death about the marble entry chamber. The jannessaries had forced her to look at the reeking, bodiless heads of all whom she loved. Their faces had all looked so surprised at the suddenness of their deaths—all but her husband, Lev, upon whose visage was anger and outrage. Seeing his sightless, staring eyes, eyes that had never looked at her with anything other than love, Sabra felt suddenly intimidated by the terrible accusatory look she believed was directed at her. She had fainted and did not recover until they reached the harbor.

It was better, Valentina thought, better that Sabra was not aware of their passage through the screaming mob who believed themselves cheated by the survival of even one Kira. Better that Sabra did not know the smell of burning buildings and burning flesh.

Safely aboard *Archangel,* Sabra wept. She continued weeping for three days. She wept for them all. For Lev, who would never see the child she was carrying. For Esther, shrunken and sprawled amid her brightly colored pillows, a stone protruding from her forehead. Sabra wept for herself and for her fatherless child. It was that child, however, who saved Sabra's sanity. "It is not right that I have survived when the others have died so horribly!" she wailed self-pityingly to Valentina. "Why has God cursed me so to separate me from all those that I love?"

"Simon, Asher, and Cain live on in their children, Sabra," Valentina said quietly. "Sadly, the line of David Kira is extinct because of your sister Haghar's death and the death of her child. But you, Sabra! You carry the living seed of Lev Kira within you! Birth that child in safety, and Lev Kira cannot die! Neither of you will ever lack for anything, for it was you who aided me to escape from the palace of Cicalazade Pasha!"

Sabra shook her head wonderingly. "You would care for me and my child, Valentina? We Kiras owe you a greater debt, for your bravery saved our children and kept the line of Esther Kira intact."

Sabra Kira put her public mourning aside, forcing herself to concentrate on the future. If she wept in private, no one saw her. Weakened by her terrible ordeal, she kept to her bed, but Valentina's cabin was filled daily with children to keep her company. Valentina began a class to teach the Kiras English. Sabra was greatly encouraged to find that she could learn, and the children were so quick that they amazed the adults.

Food was a problem at first, for the Jews' strict dietary laws were not to be abandoned, Sabra told Murrough. The young expectant mother took her duties to her family most seriously. Restrictions were explained to the ship's cook, a family man with a large heart, who did his best to comply.

Each Friday evening Sabra gathered the Kira children about her in the cabin she shared with Valentina and lit candles in the solemn Sabbath ceremony. Their family had been cruelly slaughtered. They had been driven from their home and from their land, but Sabra Kira would not allow the surviving Kiras of Istanbul to forget that they were Jews with proud tradition, and a great history. When the child within her became active, Sabra knew that Valentina's words were true. Lev lived on in his child, and Lev's brothers and Esther Kira lived on in the other children.

On Christmas Day, 1602, as *Archangel* anchored in the London Pool, Sabra looked out the rear window of the cabin and asked Valentina, "Is it always so gray in England?"

Valentina laughed. "I suppose after living in Istanbul it does seem gray, but it is winter, Sabra. It's snowing. You have snow in Istanbul."

"Not like this." Sabra shook her head. "I will have to take your word, Valentina, that we are anchored in a river surrounded by a great city, for I can see nothing outside but gray and white."

"Murrough says it will stop by nightfall. Then you will see London," Valentina replied. "Murrough will shortly go ashore to visit the London Kiras and tell them what has happened."

"Will they welcome us?" Sabra fretted. "The English Kiras came to England almost one hundred years ago, and their only contact with the Istanbul Kiras has been through our banking business."

"Did they not send their sons to Istanbul, as Simon and his brothers spent time in London and Paris and other cities?"

"Sometimes a Kira cousin came for a brief stay, but it was more important that the Istanbul Kiras learn about the other cities than that the others learn about Istanbul." She sighed.

"Now who will be head of the Kira family? Dov is the eldest surviving male of the Istanbul family, and he is much too young."

Murrough returned an hour later, bringing with him Daniyel Kira, the patriarch of the English Kiras, and his wife, Tirzah, a small, plump woman who came dressed in her best black silk gown, a fine starched ruff about her neck, and her plump fingers well-beringed.

Murrough and the English Kiras entered the cabin where
Sabra and the children were waiting. The little Kira girls, in their
shabby, now well-worn robes, looked up at the visitors shyly. The
large-eyed twin boys were playing on the floor with little Jacob
and Aaron. Young Dov, so serious, weighed down by the burden
of being eldest, rose politely to greet them. Tirzah Kira's eyes
filled with tears.

"This is Daniyel and Tirzah Kira, my lady Sabra," said Murrough formally.

Daniyel Kira bowed politely, not quite knowing what to do.
Murrough's tale of the Istanbul slaughter was more than he could
comprehend, and he thanked Yahweh that he lived in a civilized
land like England.

Tirzah Kira, however, knew just what to do. She followed her
heart. Pushing her husband aside, she held out her arms to Sabra.
Looking into the motherly face, Sabra burst into tears and flung
herself into Tirzah's embrace. "There, there, my child," soothed
Tirzah, who, with four daughters of her own, was in her element.
"You are safe now, and the little ones, too. You are Lev's wife?"

"Yes, madam" was the weepy reply.

"Madam?" Tirzah sounded slightly offended. "I am your Aunt
Tirzah, child, and you will address me as Aunt. Now tell me who
these little ones are, then let us get you all home! You will need
baths and respectable clothing. I see you are with child. When
is Lev Kira's son to be born?"

"At the end of next month, perhaps the beginning of the month
to follow, A-Aunt," Sabra replied.

"My daughter, Anna, is expecting her third child then!" Tirzah
Kira exclaimed gleefully. "We will help you, dear girl! You need
have no fears! You have a family here in England, and although
of course it is far too soon to consider it, there are many fine
unmarried men in our community who would welcome such a
pretty wife."

"I am a Kira," Sabra said proudly, "both by marriage and on
my mother's side. I could not think of marrying anyone but a
Kira."

"Did I suggest such a thing?" asked the elder woman. She and
Daniyel had an unmarried son of eighteen who would be just
right for the pretty widow.

As for the ten small children, Tirzah's eldest married son would
take Simon Kira's children; her second married son would take
Asher Kira's son and three daughters; and her eldest married

daughter, married to a Kira cousin, would raise those adorable twin boys.

Praise God that these few Istanbul Kiras had survived, thought Tirzah Kira. Praise God that they had been brought to England in safety. Messages must be dispatched soon to all of the other branches of the family so that everyone understood that the Kira family was not leaderless. The English branch of the Kira family would now head the family.

"Look, Sabra," Valentina said, entering the cabin. She had been on deck with Padraic. "The snow has stopped."

Sabra peered out through the great rear window. "There *is* a city out there!" she said.

"A wonderful city!" said Tirzah Kira enthusiastically. "A wonderful city in a wonderful country ruled by a great old queen! You will not be unhappy here, dear child."

"Then the queen still lives, Mistress Kira?" Valentina said.

"Somehow. By what miracle, only God knows" was the dry answer.

The Kiras had brought warm cloaks for Sabra and the children. They departed in a great flurry, lowered carefully into the boats below. Nelda reluctantly parted with baby Ruben, a few tears escaping from her soft brown eyes.

"He likes to sleep with this, madam," she said to Tirzah Kira, handing her a small soft doll she had sewn from one of her stockings.

Mistress Kira took the small toy and looked carefully at the cheerful, tired young girl. "He shall not be denied it, child," she said, gently touching Nelda's pink cheek. Tucking the doll into her cloak, she reached beneath the cape, fumbled for a moment, and then brought forth a strand of pearls, which she clasped about the girl's neck. "A small token, child, for all your loving care to this infant." Then turning she was gone over the side of the vessel to be swung down in the bosun's chair to her waiting boat.

Nelda gasped, feeling the pearls gingerly.

"You are a woman of property now, Nelda," Valentina said with a smile.

"I ain't *never* had *nothing* like *this* before, m'lady. My ma will be so jealous!" Nelda said.

"She will not be jealous," said Lord Burke, "until you get home, Nelda. And we will not get home until we take the first step toward home, which is departing from this ship."

"Surely we are not going to begin the trip home now," Valentina said.

"We are going to Greenwood, Val. You're invited, too, Tom," Lord Burke said. "Tomorrow Murrough is off for Devon and his Joan—and we are bound for Worcestershire and home! Our barge awaits us even now, madam, and we have precious little time before the tide turns and makes rowing difficult."

Valentina snatched up her cloak. "Then let us go, my lord!" she said. "As grateful as I am to *Archangel* for bringing us home safely, I am anxious to be back on dry land once more! I do not think I shall ever go to sea again."

"At least you do not have my uncle's fussy belly," said Padraic, laughing.

"My father is O'Malley born," Valentina said with great pride. "O'Malleys are seafarers!"

"Not Uncle Conn." Lord Burke chuckled as he seated his betrothed in the bosun's chair and eased it over the side. Of all the O'Malleys of Innisfana, poor Conn was the only one who, to the disgust of his siblings, suffered from *mal de mer*. Poor Lord Bliss's affliction was a family joke.

With several hours' notice of their coming, the staff at Greenwood had been able to remove the dustcovers from the furniture, make the beds with fresh linens, and decorate the hall with some Christmas greenery. Greenwood belonged to Skye, Lady de Marisco, though it would one day go to her youngest daughter. It served as the family residence in London. Most of the staff from earlier days had long ago been pensioned off. A butler, a housekeeper, a cook, and a head groom were the only permanent staff, for maidservants and stableboys were easily recruited from the nearby village of Chiswick-on-Strand.

The small staff were used to short notice, and the house was warm and inviting, with log fires burning in every room and fragrant smells emanating from the kitchen. They each desired one thing above all else—a hot bath—and the young manservants were kept busy for two hours running with hot water up the stairs to the bedrooms. It was nearly seven o'clock in the evening when Lady Barrows, Lords Burke and Ashburne, and Captain Murrough O'Flaherty met in the small family dining room for Christmas dinner. Murrough, the eldest, sat at the head of the table, facing his lovely cousin who sat at the foot. Valentina was festively gowned in sapphire-blue velvet. The earl and Lord Burke sat on either side of the long, beautifully polished table.

The cook, sweating from the hot kitchen and beaming with triumph at having produced a respectable feast on little notice, led the servants in from the kitchen herself carrying an enormous silver charger upon which rested a side of beef. Behind her, servants bore platters and plates and bowls filled with delicacies. There were roasted capons and ducks with a sauce of cherries. There were pigeon and rabbit pies and thin slices of salmon poached in wine. There was a small ham and a platter of lamb chops. There were bowls of hard-boiled eggs, green peas, carrots, and braised lettuce. The breads were still hot from the oven and the sweet butter, the wildflower honey, and the cheeses were perfection.

"If I'd had a bit more notice, m'lady," the cook apologized, "there would be more variety, but 'tis Christmas Day and the markets all be closed." She bobbed a curtsy.

"It all looks delicious, Mrs. Evans," Valentina told her, noting that the men were already heaping their plates with the kinds of food they hadn't seen in months. "Thank you."

They ate until they thought they could eat no more, stuffing themselves with the meats, the breads, and the cheeses.

Then Mrs. Evans appeared with a Christmas pudding, and they found there was room for that traditional, tasty sweet. They did not drink wine, favoring instead the brown October ale that everyone had missed so very much. When they had finished, they sat back in their chairs, replete with satisfaction and grateful to be home.

Carollers coming to Greenwood's door were invited in to receive cakes and ale and a silver penny apiece. They sang their Christmas songs, then went away happy, praising the bounty of Greenwood's inhabitants.

"Well, I'm off to bed," Murrough said. "Tomorrow Geoff and I are for home. I've missed my Joan, and 'twill be good to see the children again."

"And your new grandchild," said Lord Burke.

"Aye," said Murrough, pure satisfaction in his voice. He pushed his chair from the table and rose, then kissed Valentina's cheek. "A most successful voyage, coz, and profitable, too. I think, once the shares are properly divided, you will find that it has cost you nothing. *Homeward Bound*'s captain tells me your horses all survived their journey quite well."

"Everything, Murrough, has its price," Valentina said quietly, "though I am glad about the horses."

"There is a price to everything," Murrough agreed, "but now it is all behind us. We are home safe, Val!" Then he was gone.

Murrough's words echoed in her mind as they departed for Pearroc Royal the following day. They were home safe, and for that she was everlastingly grateful, but the memories would remain with her forever.

It took them several days to reach Oxford, for while the first day of their journey was bright and they made good progress, they awakened on their second day to a cold, driving rain that continued, on and off for three days, as they traveled homeward.

Valentina wondered if Murrough's journey with his son, Geoff, was as wet and uncomfortable as theirs was. At Oxford they put up at the Glorious Elizabeth and had a final supper with the earl, who would leave them in the morning and travel north to Swan Court in Warwickshire.

The inn's name brought to everyone's mind the subject of the queen herself. After their dinner at Greenwood on Christmas night, both Padraic and Tom had gone to Whitehall, where the queen had kept her Christmas. Both men returned extremely disheartened by what they observed. They had seen the queen but not made their presence known to her, for fear of being commanded to join the court.

"She is not well at all," the earl told Valentina sadly. "I have never seen her so frail. What's worse, a friend told me, is that she is getting forgetful, and who dares to say, 'Has Your Majesty forgotten?' None are that brave, nor would I be."

- "Her joints are all swollen," Lord Burke put in, "and it was necessary to file the coronation ring off her finger for the finger had grown into the ring. In forty-four years she has not had that ring off her finger! I find that a bad omen."

"You should have let me see her." Valentina was very distressed. "If she is ill, she needs people who love her about her, not the damned vultures who live on the royal largess and wait for the poor woman to die!"

"We stayed at court only long enough to ascertain the state of Her Majesty's health," Padraic answered her.

"And to hoist a few tankards with your friends." Valentina chuckled. "I heard you both come rollicking in long after the clock struck two." She grew serious again. "After I have seen my family and assured them of my good health, I shall return to court."

"When is your wedding to be?" the earl asked.

"In the spring," said Valentina sweetly.

"Before Twelfth Night!" said Lord Burke firmly. "If you think, Val, that I'm letting you go up to court before we wed, even with the queen poorly, you are sadly mistaken, madam."

"Spring is such a lovely time for a wedding," said the earl mischievously.

"Any time is *lovely* for a wedding when you are marrying the right woman," Lord Burke growled. "I warn you, Tom, you are treading on thin ice!"

"Impatient, isn't he?" The earl chuckled. "But then, divinity, I should be impatient, too, if you had chosen to wed me. You are certain about your decision, are you not?" He cocked his head to one side and smiled at her winningly.

"Tom!" Lord Burke warned.

"Very certain," Valentina said softly, looking up at Padraic.

"And am I invited to the wedding, divinity?"

"No!" shouted Padraic.

"Yes," said Valentina, "if you truly wish to come, Tom."

"I must see you commit this supreme folly with my own eyes before I will believe it, divinity," he answered her. "Send a messenger to Swan Court when the date has been set, and I will come."

"I don't know why you insist on having him at our wedding," grumbled Padraic the following morning as they waved farewell to the earl.

"Because he is a good and true friend. Because he has shared great adventures with us. And because I feel, somehow, that his life will continue to be entwined with ours," Valentina told him as she and Nelda climbed into their carriage. "Will you join me, my lord, or do you prefer to ride?"

"I'll ride," Lord Burke said grumpily, slamming the door to the coach.

"As you will, my lord," she called to him from the lowered window, then raised it up with equal force.

Padraic grinned to himself. Val was Irish in temperament for all her English mother and her English upbringing. She had the O'Malley temper, drive, and determination. He was beginning to appreciate what all of his mother's husbands, including his own father, had seen in his mother. Valentina was surprisingly like her Aunt Skye.

The sun decided to show itself momentarily as they finally reached Pearroc Royal. The carriage horses, sensing their final destination, warm, dry stalls, and extra measures of oats, galloped down the road in the late-afternoon sunlight. The door to the manor house was flung open as the coach careened to a stop, and Valentina sprang from the vehicle directly into Lord Bliss's outstretched arms.

"Oh, Papa! Papa! 'Tis so good to be home!"

Conn's arms tightened about his eldest child and he said quietly, "Have you found the answers you sought, Valentina?"

She looked up into his face, her amethyst eyes shining brightly. "There is no doubt that you are my father. I will tell you of our entire adventures if you will take me inside! 'Tis freezing out here!"

His arm about his daughter, Lord Bliss brought her into the house where her mother and several of Valentina's siblings were excitedly waiting. Colin, Payton, and Jemmie were on her at once, kissing her and grinning with delight. Aidan flew forward to hug her daughter, her lovely eyes wet with tears.

"You are safe!" she said. "Thank God! You have no idea how much I have worried, Valentina."

"Oh, Mama, I know you have worried, but now I am home again, quite safe . . . and planning to wed my cousin, Padraic."

"Wed Padraic?" Aidan's glance flew to her nephew, then back to her daughter. "Oh, my!" she gasped. "Oh, my!"

"Now, Mama," Valentina gently teased her, "haven't you wanted me to marry again? And who better than Padraic, who, it seems, has loved me since I was a child *but* felt I should wed a greater name than he had to offer. Have you ever heard anything so ridiculous?"

"God's nightshirt!" swore Colin St. Michael. "Ned Barrows was no great name or fortune."

"Precisely!" Valentina agreed. "This man, who claims to love me, let me go to another. But for the grace of God we should have spent the rest of our lives living a lie! Now, however," she said with a wicked grin, "I plan to spend the rest of my life making him pay for his foolishness!"

"Spoken like a true O'Malley." Conn chuckled, winking at his nephew. "I hope you have all the other charms and talents belonging to O'Malley women." Seeing Padraic blush, Conn whooped with laughter. "So she does, eh, my lord!"

"We are not O'Malleys," said an elegant little voice. "We are St. Michaels."

All eyes turned to the slender, copper-haired girl with the startling green eyes who was standing beside Aidan.

"Your father is an O'Malley, child, and had he not agreed to take my name so that the St. Michael name might not die out, you would be called O'Malley," Aidan explained to her youngest daughter.

"Maggie?" Valentina was astounded. What a difference these months had made! The gangling girl they had left behind was shortly to be fifteen and had bloomed into exquisite loveliness. "Maggie, you are beautiful!" Valentina said warmly.

"Did you think I would remain a child, Val? I am very much a woman, I assure you." Maggie tossed her head proudly.

"You had best not have attained womanhood yet, my girl!" growled Conn. "Now, come. Let us all sit down while Valentina tells us of her adventures—and of how she decided to accept this nephew of ours for her husband!"

The family adjourned to the Great Hall, where they gathered about the large fireplace, pulling chairs and stools and benches around the warmth. Goblets of wine and platters of cakes were passed, and when finally everyone was settled, all looked to Valentina.

She sat regally in a high-backed tapestried chair in their midst, Padraic standing by her side. She began slowly, choosing her words carefully, making them see the very things she had seen. San Lorenzo's charming little capital city with its rainbow-colored houses; the exquisite temple on the little Greek island; the exotic beauty of Istanbul; the savage splendor of the Crimean steppes. She told them of the Duc di San Lorenzo, who had wished to marry her, telling the story lightly in order to ease her mother's anxiety and avoid shocking her younger sister. She had them in fits of laughter explaining how the duc had arranged for the Gypsy dancers to entice Murrough, Padraic, and Tom Ashburne and how the three gentlemen fell willingly into the trap.

She told them of her capture by the wicked Temur Khan, but she told them just enough to indicate the danger she had faced while avoiding the truth.

Aidan was stunned by the mention of Temur Khan. "But I was

told he had been killed," she said. "What other lies were told me?"

Valentina reached out and patted her mother's hand comfortingly. "The sultan's soldiers were careless, for they feared Temur Khan. But believe me, Mama, he is dead, for I saw his head upon a lance."

"Good!" said Aidan in a hard voice. Her face softened once more and she said gently, "Go on with your tale, Valentina." Aidan did not want to say more than she should.

Lord Burke wondered how she was going to explain the vizier to them. To his surprise, Valentina did not tell them anything about Cicalazade Pasha at all. She said that their lateness in returning home had been due to delays in obtaining an audience with the Sultan Valide Safiye. Then she went on to tell them of the currency riots in Istanbul in which Esther Kira and her family were killed.

"We managed to rescue Esther's ten great-great-grandchildren, Mama. Six little boys, the youngest of whom is only four and a half months, and four little girls. And Lev Kira's wife, Sabra, a young girl, was allowed to come with us. She is expecting her first child this winter. Lev was the youngest of Esther's great-grandsons."

" 'We'?" Lord Burke looked at Valentina proudly. "Val saved the Kiras, Uncle. When she was in the harem visiting with the sultan's mother, the sultan cast lustful eyes on Val."

Aidan made a small pitiful sound, but Lord Burke quickly reassured his aunt, whose memories had never died.

"The Sultan Valide had only just finished explaining to Val why her late husband could not be Val's father, reassuring her that her real father had to be Uncle Conn. But when she saw which way the wind was blowing with her son, she introduced Val as his sister. Val used that lie to help the Kira children, telling the grand vizier, who led the janissary troops into the riot, that she was the sultan's sister and that she would not allow the little ones or Sabra to be slaughtered. She was so firm that the vizier ordered his captain and some of the janissaries to escort us safely to the harbor. And that is how the Kira children were saved."

"You might have been killed," Aidan fussed at her daughter.

"But I was not killed, Mama. I am back home safely, and I am at the end of my story." Valentina laughed.

"And now, we must plan a wedding," Aidan said, brightening.

"You are long out of mourning for Lord Barrows, so we need not wait past the Lenten season."

"We will marry before Twelfth Night, Aunt," Lord Burke said firmly. "Val is *long* past her mourning period, and I am not of a mind to spend a cold and lonely winter. Besides, the wench is closer to twenty-three than twenty-two, and long in the tooth." He bent and kissed her ear.

" 'Long in the tooth,' my lord?" She aimed a blow at his head, which he skillfully ducked.

"My mother had four children by the time she was twenty-three," he teased her. "You're a veritable hag, and have not borne your first babe."

"Hag?" Valentina leaped to her feet and began to pummel his chest. "My mother was almost twenty-six when I was born, and she bore six children after me!"

Laughing, Padraic Burke pinioned her arms behind her back and kissed her soundly. "*My* hag," he amended, and kissed her again.

"You beast," she scolded him breathlessly, but her eyes were bright with love.

Lord Bliss saw that his wife was laughing softly. Her eyes met her husband's in complete understanding. Why, she wondered, had they not seen Padraic's love for Valentina? Why had they not realized that Valentina's reluctance to choose a suitor stemmed not from overfastidiousness, but rather from a lack of understanding of her own feelings?

"If you intend a wedding before Twelfth Night," Lady Bliss said, "then it must, of necessity, be a small wedding."

"The family," Padraic and Valentina said in unison.

"I must go back up to court immediately afterward," Valentina said quietly. "I promised the queen I should when I returned. I cannot break that promise, particularly now that she is so poorly."

"How poorly?" demanded Conn.

"Tom and I went to court Christmas night," Padraic told him. "From a distance, she looked feeble. The doctors claim she will live another few years, but those close to her fear she will not see the spring. I am afraid I must agree with them. The queen is in her seventieth year, and her health has deteriorated terribly."

"Poor Bess," Conn said softly. "I shall not see her again in this life. God bless her."

"You could come to court with us, Papa," Valentina said.

"No, my dear," said Lord Bliss. "Bess would not like it if I saw her at less than her best. Remember, I served her when she was at her zenith, and there are few left who did. Only Ralegh and myself. I shall not visit that pain upon her. I shall remember her in all her glory, which is how she would like it."

"You have not lost your understanding of women, my lord," his wife said quietly.

"May I never lose it, Aidan," he told her. "Now, what date shall we set for this wedding?"

"I do not think we have a great choice in the matter, Papa," Valentina said. "Today is the next to the last day of December."

"So we shall be wed January first," Lord Burke said. "I can think of no better way to begin the new year than by taking you for my wife, Val." He drew her back into arms, his aquamarine-blue eyes loving her openly.

"Padraic! 'Tis impossible!" declared his aunt. "I cannot arrange a wedding in two days!"

"Why not, Mama?" Valentina said. Her eyes were fastened on Padraic's. "The weather will not allow us to send for many relatives anyway. There is time to make a bride's cake. Why should we not be wed in two days? I would have a little time with my husband before I travel to court."

"But Anne is near to delivering another child, and Bevin is in Ireland, and—"

"Maggie shall stand up for me, Mama! I can think of no one better, though she will eclipse me with her beauty," Valentina said, smiling at her youngest sister.

"Colin, Payton, and Jemmie are here." Conn continued with his daughter's positive train of thought. "When Padraic rides home to Queen's Malvern, he will find that Robin and his family, Willow and her family, and his sister Deirdre and her family are quite near."

"You are sending me out into the cold to ride *home*?" Lord Burke demanded of his uncle, soon to be his father-in-law.

"Aye, I am." Conn grinned. "If you don't get home soon, my lad, your mother will be knocking at my door, demanding to know where you are. I can assure you that she already knows you're here. There is nothing that happens in this part of the country that your mother does not know about first. I would prefer that she learn of your impending nuptials from you, not through some mysterious method known only to Skye.

"Your wedding will begin at half after four o'clock in the afternoon, on January the first, my lord. I do not want to see you before then, sir! Is that understood?"

"Perfectly, my lord," Padraic answered. He bent to kiss Valentina. "In two days you will be mine for all time, Val," he murmured against her mouth.

"And you *mine*, my lord," she answered him.

"You are certain?"

"I am certain," she said.

"Wear a red gown," he said. "The color suits you." He kissed her hand.

"If it pleases you, my lord," she answered, sweeping him a deep curtsy.

Lord Burke kissed his fingertips and then touched her lips with his fingers.

"Why, Cousin Padraic is most romantic," Maggie noted when Lord Burke had departed. "I have never before realized it. He always seemed quiet, almost dull."

Valentina laughed. "If there is one thing Padraic is not, Maggie, 'tis dull. No, never dull!"

Dawn had scarcely broken the following morning when there came a great knocking on the door. The sleepy servant girl laying the fires hurried to answer the pounding and admitted Lady de Marisco. Skye swept into her brother's house, flinging her heavy fur-lined cloak at the startled maidservant, and demanded, "Is no one in this house up yet, with my son's wedding to be celebrated tomorrow?"

The poor servant's mouth fell open, for she had no knowledge of the family, being on the lowest rung of Pearroc Royal's hierarchy. Lady de Marisco swept past the dumbfounded girl and up the staircase. She seemed to know exactly where she was going, and it wasn't the poor maidservant's business, so she went back to the fires, which was her job.

Skye moved upstairs into the hallway leading to the family bedchambers. She passed her brother and sister-in-law's spacious apartment, which had been built in the new wing of the house just before the twins were born, hurrying to the bedchamber of her brother's eldest child. She opened the door and entered. "Good morning, Valentina," she said. "I knew you would be awake, even if no one else was."

"I could not sleep," Valentina admitted, staring out her window into the winter's dawn. "Bridal nerves, I suspect."

"Or memories of a less-than-pleasant nature," Skye said quietly. "We will speak of them now, Valentina, and then you will put them from you, as I put similar memories from me over thirty years ago." Lady de Marisco bent and stirred the fire in the grate to new life, adding bits of coal and wood. The flame, born anew, began to take the chill from the room. Then, her niece watching her, Skye sat down in the single chair by the fireplace, smoothing her dark green velvet skirt with her long graceful fingers.

"Padraic told you, didn't he?" Valentina sighed. She came and sat on a small tapestried stool at her aunt's side.

"Padraic told me what he knows, which, I suspect, is very little. I can guess the rest," Skye answered.

"I cannot tell Mama," Valentina said. "She will only wring her hands and say that she warned me not to go. I *had* to, Aunt Skye! I needed to learn that Javid Khan was not my father! I needed to know that Sultan Murad was not my father! I had to be certain that Papa was really my father! I cannot explain it any further. I simply had to learn the truth."

"Was it worth the cost, Valentina?" Skye asked her.

Valentina became lost in thought for a long moment, then she said, "I have learned, Aunt, that everything in this world has its price, even knowledge. I do not think I could have lived in peace the rest of my life with Mag's words in my heart. I had to learn the truth, and if I paid a dreadful price for that truth, yes, it was worth it. Yes! I know it was right for me to go. Yet one thing puzzles me, and I cannot reason it out in my mind."

"What puzzles you, my dear?" Skye stroked her niece's dark head. Valentina was going to make Padraic the most perfect wife. She would no longer have to worry about her youngest son.

"How can a woman hate and despise a man, yet still react to his lovemaking? How can a woman give a man pleasure when she does not want to give him pleasure? I do not understand it at all."

"There are two forms of rape, Valentina," Skye began. "There is violent rape where a man forces a woman to his will. Then there is seductive rape. Perhaps that is worse, for seduction is difficult to deal with, my dear. After all, the surroundings are pleasant and comfortable. The man is persistent but loving. He will have his way with you whether you will or no, but he will have it in a kindly, rather than violent, fashion. He seduces your body while he seduces your mind. Your emotions are rejecting him, but it is your body he wants first, so he ignores the rest— for a time. Later, he attempts to gain more than just your body.

"A woman's body is sensitive. It is very much like a fine musical instrument. It responds even when you do not want it to respond, particularly if the touch is skilled. The rational part of you is saying *no*, but your body is saying *yes*. It seems to be the way in which women are fashioned, and I cannot explain it beyond that. Your body's reaction to Cicalazade Pasha was a normal one. I know, for I, too, was forced to yield myself to a man I hated."

Valentina stared hard as her aunt's revelation sank in.

"When Padraic was a new-born infant, his father found himself in a strange difficulty for a man. Niall was a slave in the harem of an Ottoman princess in the city of Fez in Algiers. I had been led to believe that he was dead. I had accepted a political marriage arranged by the queen so that I could protect the Burke lands in Ireland. Fortunately, when I learned that Niall was still alive, I was newly widowed.

"I believed that I could rescue Niall, and so with the help of my friend, Osman the Astrologer, I became a slave girl named Muna. I was presented to Osman's nephew, Kedar, who was a resident of Fez, a city closed to foreigners. As a member of lord Kedar's household, I was able to enter Fez. There was no other way for me to get to Niall.

"Since Kedar knew me as a slave and nothing else, I was forced to accept his loving attentions. He became obsessed with me. The more I seemed to yield myself, the more he desired of me. I have never in my entire lifetime felt more used or abused by a man, Valentina, and by the time I was subjected to this, my experience with love and lovemaking was far broader than yours has been, dear child.

"I was fed aphrodisiacs, massaged with aphrodisiacs, made to please my master's perverse passion with an ivory dildo that had been fashioned to the exact size and shape of his manhood, which was extraordinarily large. It amused him to arouse me to a frenzy with hands and tongue and then force me to use that damned ivory obscenity on myself while he watched. He enjoyed having several women together, taking them in turn or watching while they used each other. I believe there is nothing, Valentina, that you could possibly tell me that I have not experienced.

"I finally rescued Niall. But then he died, immediately after he was rescued. I wondered if what I had done was foolish, for it had all been for nothing. Then my beloved Adam insisted that we wed. He would simply not accept a refusal. I realized that if I was ever to be happy again, I must put all the terrible memories behind me. I must never again dwell on what had happened in Algiers. "She paused for a moment.

"Tell me what you would not tell Padraic, my dear Valentina. Tell me, then put those terrible memories aside. Tell me!" Skye caught Valentina's hands in hers and held them tightly.

Valentina looked up at Skye, her eyes haunted, filled with pain. Suddenly she began to speak, sobbing. "At least your sacrifice had some meaning, Aunt. I was kidnapped off the streets of Istanbul to be the vizier's love slave! What you did, you did for love of Padraic's father. I have no such excuse! It was an accident, not a mission.

"I tried! Oh, Aunt, I tried not to yield to him, but in the end I could not stop myself!" Her words poured out, tumbling one after the other as she told Skye the entire story of her nearly four-month captivity.

Skye did not interrupt. When Valentina had finally finished, Lady de Marisco said quietly, "It was not your fault that you were kidnapped, Valentina. And you did exactly what I would have done in that situation. You struggled to survive, and you did survive. No person, my dear, has the right to destroy another person's spirit so entirely that his victim finds death preferable to an unendurable life! It is over, Valentina. It is a part of your life that is now in the past. There is no shame attached to your tragic time in Istanbul. Indeed, Padraic tells me you are responsible for saving the lives of ten small children and a young girl. Osman the Astrologer, my old friend, believes that our lives follow chosen paths and have specific purposes. Perhaps it was your fate, to be in Istanbul when you were and to have the vizier in your debt, so you might save those lives.

"Now, dry your eyes, Valentina. My son's bride must be beautiful."

Valentina flung her arms about Skye's neck and hugged her. "Aunt, I love you so very much!" she said. "I am so glad Padraic is your son!"

Skye hugged her back, chuckling. "The devil took his time declaring himself, didn't he?" she said. "To think that my son would be such a shy fellow! God knows that was not the case with his father! Demanded the *droit de seigneur* of me on my wedding night to another man and had my virginity of me while my first husband fumed and raged in my father's hall. But that's another story for another time." She laughed.

"Padraic was indeed slow to declare himself, Aunt," Valentina defended her betrothed, "but he would not be bested by the persistent Tom Ashburne!"

"He's made love to you again?" asked Skye. "I hope he is proving to be a satisfying lover, my dear."

Valentina blushed furiously. "Aunt! What a question!" Then she laughed. "Beneath furs, in the Tatar encampment, and it was wonderful!"

"Not since?" Lady de Marisco was scandalized. She looked as if she might take her son to task.

"We were kept separated in the Kira house and then we were separated by Cicalazade Pasha. Aboard ship we were crowded with all of the extra passengers. There was simply no time or place," Valentina explained.

"I hope my son will not prove so laggard after your marriage, but if he does, speak to me. I will see the situation corrected!" Skye declared firmly.

"Are forty-two grandchildren not enough for you, Aunt?" Valentina teased.

"Certainly not!" Lady de Marisco said emphatically. "I must have at least fifty!" But I have another granddaughter, Skye thought silently. I have a grandchild I have never seen, nor will I ever. A momentary sadness overwhelmed her, but she hid it well.

At that very moment Aidan St. Michael entered her daughter's bedchamber. "Skye! What on earth are you doing here so early?" she asked her beautiful sister-in-law.

"Good morrow to you also, Aidan," Skye returned. "I came to have a talk with my daughter-in-law before the marriage takes place."

"You are not pleased with the match?" Aidan looked worried.

"Not pleased? God's foot, Aidan, I am delighted! I am ecstatic! Relieved! It fretted me to think that Niall's son would never marry and have children. Valentina is the perfect wife for Padraic. It is a shame none of us realized it, else that fiasco with poor Ned Barrows would not have taken place!"

Aidan smiled suddenly. "Aye," she agreed, "Valentina is the perfect match for Padraic, isn't she? And we shall have grandchildren in common, Skye!"

"My aunt tells me that she desires fifty grandchildren, and since she has only forty-two, Padraic and I will certainly have to be responsible for the others, won't we, Mama?"

"I'm going to help you with the preparations," Skye told her sister-in-law. "We've notified everyone that we could, and either they'll come or they won't, but come what may, at half after four tomorrow afternoon, my son and your daughter will be joined in holy matrimony!"

Aidan suddenly paled. "Skye! The banns! We've forgotten the banns!"

"They can be waived," Skye said airily.

"Aye, they can be waived," Aidan agreed, "Oh, my! 'Tis seven o'clock already, and there is so much to do if we are to have a wedding tomorrow!"

"We'll get it done, Aidan," Skye reassured her brother's wife. "We'll get it all done."

"What shall *I* do?" Valentina asked.

"Gracious, child," exclaimed her mother, "there is scarcely time for you to be prepared properly! What of your wedding gown?" She opened the door and called into the hallway, "Nan! Nelda! Hurry! We have so little time!"

Chapter Sixteen

VALENTINA ST. MICHAEL BARROWS, Lady Barrows, a widow, was joined in holy matrimony with her cousin, Padraic, Lord Burke, a bachelor, on the first day of January in the year of our Lord 1603. The small, intimate affair was attended by the bride's parents, three brothers, and younger sister; and the bridegroom's mother, stepfather, elder brother, his wife and children, and two elder sisters, their husbands and children. Also in attendance was Thomas Ashburne, the Earl of Kempe.

The bride, considered an outstanding beauty in a family of beauties, was resplendent. Her gown had a bell-shaped overskirt of rich burgundy velvet and an underskirt of burgundy silk, decorated with velvet and pearls. The dress was fashioned with a long wasp waist and a very, *very* low neckline. This, considered extremely fashionable, was cheered by the ladies. The bridegroom, however, complained that it bordered on the indecent. He was shouted down by his male relations.

The burgundy velvet sleeves were leg-of-mutton, banded by many little ivory-colored silk ribbons embroidered with seed pearls. The sleeves narrowed toward the wrists, the fabric turning back to form an elegant cuff with an ivory lace ruffle decorated with small seed pearls. The cuff matched the bride's ivory-and-gold lace neck whisk.

Narrow, pointed ivory kid shoes ornamented with pearls peeped from beneath Valentina's bell-shaped skirts. Her dark hair was parted in the center and dressed in a chignon low on the back of her neck. The chignon was decorated with ivory silk roses, each of which had gold leaves and a pearl center. The bride had chosen to wear only pearls. Pearls were sewn to her bodice, fell from her ears, and were draped around her neck, falling over her fair bosom.

She carried a small winter bouquet of dried lavender, rosemary, and holly, tied with pearl-encrusted ivory silk ribbons. Lord Burke had carried the little bouquet from his mother's home, in his doublet, passing it to Aidan to give to her daughter. Like his bride, Padraic was dressed in burgundy velvet and ivory lace. The colors suited his dark hair and fair skin as well as they suited Valentina.

The previous day Lord Burke had asked his stepfather, Lord de Marisco, to stand with him as his best man. "I have called you Adam all my life, to please Mama," Padraic said, "but although a man named Niall Burke fathered me, you are the only father I have ever known, Adam. You have been a good father to me, and I love you, though I know those are not words that one man normally says to another. Still, I would have you know it, and it would please me greatly if you would stand with me when I wed my Val."

Adam de Marisco was seventy-two years of age, and there had been few times in his life when he had wept openly. Tears of happiness sprang to his eyes. He loved Padraic Burke as he might have loved a son of his own flesh. There had been no sons, only his beloved daughter, Velvet. And while he had never voiced it, Skye's youngest son Padraic was most dear to him of all her children, excepting their own daughter.

"No," he said slowly, "I did not father you, to my regret, but you have been my son since the day I wed your mother. I could not have fathered a better son! Aye, Padraic, I'll stand with you, and proud I am that you asked me!" The big man hugged Lord Burke hard.

While waiting for the ceremony to begin, Lady de Marisco looked fondly at her husband and her Burke son, thinking how very fortunate they all were to have one another, how blessed they were to love one another.

Not all of the family were there for the wedding. Skye's eldest two sons, Ewan and Murrough O'Flaherty, and their families had not been able to attend. Her youngest daughter, Velvet, the Countess of BrocCairn, and her family lived in Scotland. Of course, dear Dame Cecily and her brother, Sir Robert Small, were both dead. Skye felt tears pricking the back of her eyelids. God, how she missed Robbie and his wonderful sister! Dame Cecily had loved and mothered Skye for more years than her own mother had, God assoil both their good souls!

"What is it, little girl?" Adam, ever-watchful, was sensitive to his wife's mercurial moods.

"I was thinking of Robbie and Dame Cecily," she answered softly. "It seems so strange to have an important family event without them. They have always been with us. *Always*."

He nodded understanding.

Sir Robert Small, Skye's business partner for over forty years, had died the previous winter, having caught a chill while ice-skating on the lake at Queen's Malvern with some of Skye's many grandchildren. Robbie had turned eighty-two just before he died. It was a difficult loss for them all, but especially for his sister.

Dame Cecily had taken care of her brother for most of their lives, and the separation was simply too much for the old lady to bear. "He'll not be able to get on without me," she fretted in the days following her brother's passing. Then several weeks later she began to insist to all who would listen, "Robbie says I must come and join him, for he is lonely without me." She died a few days later, two days past her eighty-fourth birthday. They buried her next to her beloved younger brother.

"Robbie and Dame Cecily are here in their own way," Adam said to his wife. "Do you think they would miss a family wedding?" He put a comforting arm around her.

Skye looked up into her husband's face. "I do not like this business of growing old," she said irritably.

"*You? Old?* Hah!" he scoffed. "You will never be old, little girl, nor will I!"

"Make me believe it, Adam," she pleaded softly.

"Come home with me, Skye," he said, smiling at her. "I shall, indeed, make you believe it." His smoky-blue eyes smoldered at her. They were still lovers.

He always made her feel better. She chuckled. "You, my lord, are a randy old man, but I should have it no other way! We will go home across the winter fields tonight and play a game of bride and groom," she teased him with a twinkle.

"As ever, my love, your inventiveness is astounding," he replied with a grin. Somehow he managed to lovingly pinch her bottom through the layers of velvet encasing it. "I still do my duty by you very well, do I not, my little girl?"

Valentina's lovely amethyst-colored eyes misted as she reached the altar of the family chapel on her father's arm. She honestly thought Padraic Burke the handsomest man she had ever seen, and it suddenly occurred to her how amazing it was that he should love her above all women. The vows were sworn, the blessing given, and then everyone toasted the bride and groom.

Lord and Lady de Marisco, with a silent promise to each other, raised their goblets to toast their children, their hearts overflowing with their love not only for each other, but for their family as well.

"To our son, Padraic," Adam de Marisco said, his deep voice filling the hall. "And to a lost love, finally found, his wife, Valentina. Long life, many children, and happiness always!"

"To Padraic and Valentina!" cried the guests, raising their goblets.

The Earl of Kempe stood. Raising his goblet to the happy couple, he said, "To my friend, Padraic Burke, and to his bride, Valentina, who, in finding her heart's desire, was forced to relinquish the better man. Long life and happiness!"

Much laughter greeted Tom Ashburne's toast as the guests again raised their goblets to the bridal couple.

Skye rose to her feet. "To my fifty grandchildren!" she said wryly.

Padraic leaped to his feet. "To the pleasure of attaining my mother's goal!" he responded, raising his own goblet to his new wife, who blushed charmingly.

"Mama!" Willow exclaimed, pretending to be shocked. "Fifty grandchildren?"

"At least," said Skye, and the family all laughed.

"Madam," said the Earl of Kempe, "you are not only beautiful, but even more fascinating than all the old court gossip would imply. Were I but ten years older! I salute you!" He raised his goblet to her with a twinkle.

"You, Tom Ashburne, are a rogue!" Skye told him bluntly. "Who gossips about me at court? All those I knew are long dead except for Bess herself."

"You are a legend, madam," he replied.

"Hah!" Skye laughed, and her Kerry-blue eyes sparkled at his charming and outrageous flattery. "What a pity I do not have a daughter left to match with you, my lord. Rogues have a tendency to breed strong children. But perhaps I might find a granddaughter in my brood who would suit you. I am told you seek a wife. Is it so?"

"It is, madam. Having, alas, lost my divinity, I shall have to content myself with another woman," he answered mournfully.

"Since you have lost Val," Payton St. Michael offered helpfully, "why not offer for our Maggie? She will be fifteen in February and she is ready for a husband."

Another girl might have been mortified by her brother's casual offer, but Maggie St. Michael tossed her copper-colored hair and said boldly, "I seek higher than an earl. Please take no offense, my lord. But the queen will soon be dead. Then we will have a king and a brand-new court. My cousin, the Countess of BrocCairn, will come south with King James. Surely with my wealth and beauty I can capture a greater name than yours."

"Margaret Cecily St. Michael!" gasped Aidan, horrified. "Apologize to Lord Ashburne immediately! I am mortified that a daughter of mine should speak in so forward, unkind, and immodest a manner."

Tom Ashburne laughed. "She has nothing to apologize for, Lady Bliss," he said kindly. "She is absolutely right, and what is more, she is not the only young lady to think what she does. Many are considering the new opportunities King James will bring. Besides, I am not a man for carrot-colored hair," he mocked, gently gibing at Maggie, who flushed a color that did not complement her hair. She hated being teased about it, but having brought this upon herself, Maggie wisely held her tongue.

"I'll find you a wife, my lord," Skye promised him softly.

"Make certain she's a fiery vixen like you, madam," he said quietly. "Now *that* would be an interesting match, wouldn't it? Have you a granddaughter like yourself?"

"Several, my lord. I promise that I shall think on it" was Skye's reply.

The wedding feast was a happy one and exactly as Valentina and Padraic had wanted. There was an abundance of food, plenty of good wines and ales, and a lovely bride's cake. They had many of their family members about them. They danced the spritely country dances, growing flushed with the exertion. About them, the children played games, scampering in and out of the Great Hall, a pack of lively small dogs always at their heels. They ate, they drank, and they talked until at last the logs in the fireplaces, huge when the day began, disintegrated into glowing, red-orange embers.

Finally the de Mariscos gathered up their large brood and departed for Queen's Malvern beneath a clear starry sky and an almost full moon that silvered the snowy winter landscape. Lord and Lady Burke remained at Pearroc Royal that night, planning to leave for Clearfields in a day or two. Valentina was anxious to return to court and see the queen, so their plans were not firm.

They returned to the hall to discover that everyone had mysteriously disappeared.

Padraic laughed. "You made such a fuss about not having a bedding ceremony that you frightened everyone away," he teased her.

"Beddings are for first marriages," Valentina said primly.

"Nonsense, Val! Besides, this *is* my first marriage," he told her, his arms about her waist drawing her against him. "My only marriage." His lips moved softly along her bare neck, sending tiny shivers down her spine.

"My lord!" She pushed his arms away.

"I shall need an hour," she said, moving toward the door.

"Half an hour," he bargained.

"Padraic, I need time to bathe, to get out of all this finery. Nan and Nelda have to get everything put away and then—"

"I surrender, madam!" he cried, laughing. "But be warned that with each passing minute my desire for you will grow and grow, and 'tis you who must quench my fires, Val."

For an instant her eyes looked troubled. Then she curtsied and hurried away up the staircase.

Lord Burke remained in the hall for a final goblet of wine, sending a servant to tell his own body servant, Plumgut, to prepare a bath for him as soon as possible.

Nan and her daughter were waiting patiently for their mistress. Neither was unhappy about making her home at Clearfields. They chatted excitedly as they undressed Valentina, putting her clothing neatly away and settling her in a scented tub that perfumed the entire room with lily of the valley.

"A new house, a new start," said the practical Nan.

"And new men to flirt with, Ma!" teased Nelda. "Ain't you in the market for a new husband yet?"

"And what do I need another husband for, girl? Yer pa was more than enough husband for me! Besides, I'm too old to break another stallion to my harness now." She swatted the giggling Nelda, then went to put Valentina's jewelry away.

"I know that my lord has only a few permanent servants at Clearfields, Nan," Valentina said thoughtfully when Nan returned. "There's the bailiff and two elderly house servants who will no doubt welcome a secure retirement to snug cottages. Do you think you would like to be the housekeeper at Clearfields, Nan?"

Nan almost dropped her mistress's night rail in her surprise and excitement. "Me?" she gasped. "The housekeeper at Clearfields? Oh, m'lady! Aye! I should indeed like it!"

"Can you do it? My husband will want to be certain that you are competent before he gives me his permission. It is unlikely that we will ever entertain royalty, Nan, but I do intend offering hospitality whenever I can, and I want Clearfields to become a great house in every sense."

Nan drew herself up, her most dignified self. "I've been in this house since yer mother, bless her, brought us both back from Ireland all those years ago, m'lady. I was yer wet nurse, then as you grew I learned how to be a proper tiring woman from your mother's Mag, God rest her. I learn real quick, I do! I've always kept my eyes and ears open, as yer well aware, m'lady. I know how to do things proper, and I know I can be a good housekeeper for you, if you'll just give me the chance," Nan said enthusiastically. The tiring woman was taking a giant step upward in the hierarchy of her class.

"Then, with my lord's permission, Nan, 'tis settled. You will be the housekeeper at Clearfields, and Nelda will become my chief tiring woman." Having decided that, the new Lady Burke rose and stepped from her tub.

Nan and Nelda hurried forward with large warmed towels to dry her, then Nelda lightly dusted her mistress with scented powder. Nan stood ready with her mistress's silken night rail, the same amethyst color of Valentina's eyes. Slipping the garment over her lady's head, she loosened Valentina's long dark hair, which had been pinned before Valentina entered her tub. Nan brushed the glorious hair vigorously with a boar's-bristle brush that had been dipped in lily-of-the-valley fragrance.

"Will you be getting into bed, m'lady?" Nan inquired politely.

"Not quite yet" came the reply.

Nan and her daughter bustled about the chamber tending to last-minute chores. The fire was banked carefully, the wine carafe checked to be certain it was full, the coverlet on the bed prettily drawn back so that the bed looked inviting. When the two women finished their tasks, they curtsied politely, wished their mistress great happiness, then departed.

Valentina was alone. She had not allowed them to draw the heavy velvet draperies, for she liked to see moonlight in the room. Clouds were beginning to drift across the sky, and Valentina turned from the window to look about the room. This was her bedchamber. It had been all her life. She had grown up in this room. It seemed so strange that she would spend her first night as Padraic's wife in this room. How different a night it would be from that first night with poor Edward Barrows.

Valentina shivered, surprised to realize that she was afraid. It was strange, for she was no virgin and Padraic had made love to her before. Of course it had been months since their last sweet bout with Eros, and since then there had been Cicalazade Pasha. The new Lady Burke desperately wanted to take her mother-in-law's advice. She wanted to consign the vizier to the past, but suddenly she was afraid she could not. In a flash, she perceived that she might not be ready to consummate her marriage. But if not now on her wedding night, then when?

"Damn him! *Oh, damn him!*" she whispered brokenly. The vizier had done this to her. He had stolen her wedding-night joy.

"Damn who?" Lord Burke had silently entered his wife's bedchamber, dressed in a dark blue quilted velvet robe that came to his ankles. He moved across the room to take her into his arms.

"No one," Valentine lied. " 'Tis of no importance, my lord."

"Good!" he told her. "I would have nothing distracting you from your wifely duties, madam."

"What duties, my lord? As your wife, I have many duties," she told him sweetly.

"Your loving duties, hinny love," he murmured, his eyes warm.

His dark head bent and he nuzzled her. "Oh, Val, you are so sweet!" His lips buried themselves in her neck, and her arms slipped up about him. He began impatiently to unfasten the tiny pearl buttons that held her gown together, and when he had bared her to the waist, he covered her beautiful breasts with hot kisses. A moment later he pushed the gown over her hips, letting it slide to the floor with a delicate hiss of silk.

"Padraic!" Her voice sounded ragged in her ears, like a sob.

He scooped her up and carried her to the bed, laying her down gently. Silently he stood above her, gazing down. Then he removed his dressing gown and the firelight played over his great nude body, turning it molten in the dimly lit room. He bent down toward her and in that moment Valentina was overcome by sudden, unreasonable fear. Whimpering, she scrambled across the bed, away from him.

There was an instant of shocked silence. Then Padraic grasped her shoulder to draw her back to him. "Hinny love, what is it?" The frightened eyes she turned on him nearly broke his heart. "Val! What is it?" Gently he drew her into his warm embrace.

"I cannot!" she whispered so faintly that he almost didn't hear it. "I cannot be your wife in the full sense, Padraic. Oh, God! I am so sorry! I am so sorry! I should never have married you, Padraic, but oh, I love you so much!" She began to weep in great sobbing gasps.

"Hinny love, hinny love! If you truly love me, there is nothing we cannot overcome together," he told her quietly. His large hand smoothed her hair. "Whatever Cicalazade Pasha did to you, Val, he did in a frenzy of pure lust."

He let her cry for a while, then went on. "There are many ways in which a man may make love to a woman. I suspect that the vizier attempted all those ways with you. I will seek to love you in many ways, too, but sweetheart, I will *love* you, not *abuse* you. Can you trust me, Val, to give you sweet pleasure?"

She shuddered. "I am so afraid, Padraic, and I know I should not be. I am no green maid to come weeping and wailing to her marriage bed."

"I have made love to you only twice before," he reminded her softly. "The first time was here in this house. Do you remember?"

"I certainly do! You could have caused the most dreadful scandal if we had been caught." She laughed weakly.

"The second time I made love to you was in the yurt of Borte Khatun. You had been through a terrible ordeal."

"Aye," she said, low, "but this is different, Padraic."

"Tell me how it is different, hinny love," he coaxed her.

She sighed deeply. "When Temur Khan and his men hurt me, it was horrible. Frightening! Yet you rescued me within a few hours. I fought Temur Khan and his men with all of my being, and although what they did to me hurt me, I was not truly violated.

"It was not the same with Cicalazade Pasha. Your mother says that a woman's body, skillfully cajoled, can be made to respond even to a man she despises. I understand that now, but I have been left with a terrible fear of being subjugated by a man. Even a man I love. Oh," she wailed helplessly, "how can *you* possibly understand?"

"Make love to me," he said quietly.

"What?" she gasped. Had he heard nothing of what she had said? Was he truly that insensitive?

"You fear being overcome," he said matter-of-factly. "I understand that. I do understand. I wish to ease your fears until we may banish them together. I desire you, Val, but I will not make love to you unless first you make love to me. You will be the one to initiate passion between us, not I. You will be the one who dictates the course our passion takes, not I. You will be the one in control, not I." He swung his legs onto the bed and lay back, drawing her on top of him.

She was puzzled. Then suddenly she understood his strategy. Part of a man's conquest of a woman involved the woman being pinned beneath the man, being overcome, overpowered, by his strength. That was precisely how it had been with Cicalazade Pasha. He had crushed her, forced her to his supreme will.

Valentina struggled into a sitting position, blushing as she straddled her handsome husband. She looked down at Padraic, her gaze intent.

He struggled with himself not to grin. Sitting there on top of him, a slightly bemused expression on her rosy face, she had no idea of the absolutely maddening effect she was having on him. She was utterly adorable. Outrageously beautiful. He longed to take matters into his own hands, but with admirable restraint he refrained. It was not easy, for her magnificent breasts soared above him like tempting fruits, ripe for plucking.

"Wh-what shall I do?" Valentina wondered aloud, her teeth worrying her lower lip.

The grin overcame him. "What would you like to do?"

"Oh, you great oaf!" she said furiously, her round bottom bouncing lightly. A mischievous light came into her eyes. Placing her hands on either side of him, she leaned forward to lightly brush just the nipples of her breasts back and forth against his chest. Leaning forward just a trifle more, she ran the tip of her tongue slowly over his lips. "Perhaps this?" she considered. "Or this?" She leaned back, carefully rotating her lower anatomy against his. Sitting straight again, her hands began to stroke his chest in small, slow circles. Then, leaning forward once more, she began to lick sensually at his nipples with a warm, teasing tongue.

Padraic groaned, a sound of pure, aching desire, but she warned him sternly, "You are my slave, Padraic! You will not touch me, no matter how desperate your desire, without my express permission. When I have satisfied my longing to master you, then and only then will I allow you to make love to me. Disobey me, and I will punish you! Do you understand me?"

Without waiting for an answer, she swung away from him. Kneeling on the bed by his side, she began to caress him again, her hands sliding over his body to find sensitive touch points he had not even known he had. She coupled her caresses with passionate kisses until he was so afire with yearning that only his deep love for her made it possible for him to restrain himself.

She growled softly like some feral animal against his throat and then began once more to stroke him, this time using her tongue, nipping at his nipples, arousing him so greatly that his manhood was hard with desire for her. Still, he reined in his passions.

Valentina sat back on her haunches and took his manhood in her hand. Skillfully she fondled his rigid length in a manner that he knew she had learned neither from Edward Barrows nor from him. Leaning over him, she placed a kiss on the burning tip, rubbing her cheek against it, crooning softly.

"Aye, and here's a big, fine fellow! Does he long to bury himself within me?" She cupped his pouch, and looking directly into his eyes, she took him into her mouth, that she might suckle upon him.

For the briefest moment he was shocked by the look of open lust, by the overbearing power in her gaze. It was as if Valentina were an entirely different person than his sweet hinny love. But then he realized that, were their positions reversed, his look of conquest would be no different from hers!

She had forbidden him to touch her, but she had not forbidden him speech. Struggling to retain control of his body, he whispered hoarsely, "Aye, my beautiful wife, I want to fill you full of me!"

With a mocking little look, she released him from the delightful prison of her mouth and climbed back atop him. This time she sat high upon his chest and, leaning forward so that a pert nipple touched his lips, she ordered, "Part your lips! You may hold me within your mouth, but you may neither tongue me nor suckle upon me. Do you understand my orders, Padraic?"

"Aye, my sweet mistress," he answered, and his lips closed around her tender nipple.

Carefully Valentina reached behind her. Grasping his great manhood, she began to work him, her hand sliding up and down the throbbing shaft of hard flesh as her hard little nipple nestled against his soft tongue.

She had gone too far. He could feel himself boiling to a crisis, unable to stop it! Unable to stop her! To force her beneath him where she belonged; to thrust himself into her sweetness again and again until they were both satisfied! There was no time! His passion burst forth, spewing itself into the air to fall like hot dew on his helpless body, on her clutching hand.

He groaned with relief and shame as her nipple fell from between his lips. He felt completely ravaged by her lust.

"*That* is what it was like, Padraic!" Her bitter voice burned him. "Do you understand? That is what it was like to be forced against my will to yield to Cicalazade Pasha! I hated it! I hated him!" she cried brokenly, bursting into wild sobbing.

He felt almost as devastated as she must have felt. He did indeed understand—now. Padraic pulled his wife into his arms and comforted her as best he could. "It will never be like that with us, my hinny love," he assured her. "It will never be like that because we love each other, Val, and people in love share their passions. Ah, sweetheart, do you not remember our time together when I soothed away the terrors of your brief adventure with Temur Khan?"

"It . . . it all seems so . . . long ago," she sobbed into his neck.

"You are much too young, my love, to have so faulty a memory," he teased her gently. "Let me refresh your memory. But first, my darling, I suggest we cleanse the evidence of this incident from our persons. Would you release me, sweetheart?" His voice was quiet, but there was a hint of laughter in it, for Padraic was quickly regaining his equilibrium.

Aware of what she had done, Valentina rolled off him, curling into a ball on the other side of the bed so that she might avoid looking at him. But Padraic would have none of that. He pulled her up and led her across the room to the fireplace, near which a silver basin rested on a table. In the hot ashes in the corner of the fireplace was a large earthenware pitcher of water. Filling the silver basin with the warm water, he took her hand and dipped it into the basin.

Valentina was beginning to regain her composure. " 'Tis I who should be maiding you, my lord," she scolded him.

"We will maid each other, hinny love," he replied, kissing the tip of her nose.

Valentina took a soft cloth that was folded neatly beside the basin. She soaked it, then wrung it out and began to wash him. He stood perfectly still as she wiped away the evidence of his passion. When she had finished, she carefully washed her hands in the fragrant water.

As she laid the wet cloth aside, he drew her into his arms, saying softly, "I love you, Val. Never forget that." Then he led her back to the bed where they cuddled beneath the plump down coverlet. "Now, my wife, we will *share* our passions with each other, as people who love are meant to do. If I conquer you, my beautiful Valentina, then so will you conquer me."

She was trembling slightly as his hands tangled themselves in the dark mane of her hair. His mouth gently brushed against hers, and she touched his face with her fingertips. He smiled at her, his aquamarine-blue eyes warm, filled with tenderness. As she pulled his head down to kiss him, his warmth enveloped her and she began to feel safe at last.

"I want to make love to you," he said softly.

"I want to make love to you," she answered breathlessly.

His smoldering gaze made her feel weak with longing. He cradled her tenderly and began to stroke her breasts. She drew his head down again and kissed him, her fingers sensually kneading the back of his neck as her mouth worked against his. Valentina could feel her breasts tightening, her nipples tingling as he fondled her. She sighed deeply and suddenly found herself turned gently onto her belly so that he could kiss her back. Shivers of pleasure rippled up and down her spine.

"Ah, sweetheart," he murmured, "you are so wonderfully soft." His lips brushed over the hillock of a buttock, and Valentina closed her eyes, sighing into the pillows, letting the warmth of his adoration envelop her, feeling his lips against the back of her knee, against her calf, on the sole of her foot.

She turned upon her back again, and he kissed both of her feet, one at a time, his lips moving up her legs, nuzzling her knees, kissing both of her silky thighs.

"Love me *there*," she said quietly, crying out sharply as he complied, his face burying itself for a long, sweet moment against her mont as he inhaled the wonderful, exciting fragrance of her. His fingers gently exposed her hidden secret, her little jewel, already wet, swollen, and throbbing with the pleasure of his touch.

He reached out with the pointed tip of his tongue and flicked it gently around and over her pearl. Valentina shuddered deeply, silently urging him in his reacquaintance of her most hidden treasure. It was almost as if her mind had separated from her body, and she watched him through half-closed eyes as he caressed her with his tongue and mouth until she was bursting with a tender pleasure that she knew now only Padraic could give her. This was a sweetness that came when a woman made love with a man she loved and who loved her in return.

"Padraic!" she whispered urgently. "Put yourself within me, my darling! I can no longer wait! I love you to distraction!"

Her direct and wildly erotic words excited him as nothing had ever excited him. He pulled himself up until his face was level with hers. His big body covered her slender one. His voice ragged with desire, he begged her, "Take me in your hand, my hinny love, and then guide me yourself through the portals of paradise!" Feeling her fingers close about him, he groaned aloud. She led him forward, and he felt the welcoming warmth of her as he pushed himself slowly into her, her sweet sheath tightening about him in an ardent embrace.

As their eyes met, it was as if time had stopped, and Valentina whispered, "Love me, my Padraic! Love me, my dearest husband!"

He began to move within her, trying desperately to be gentle but unable to move slowly, for she had aroused him far more than he believed possible. Fiercely he thrust in her, moving himself back and forth, and she met his blazing desire with her own, pushing herself up against him hard, her nails raking a trail of passion down his broad back as her head thrashed back and forth on the pillows. There was no turning back for either of them now. White-hot desire had hold of them, and where it would end, neither of them cared. They were together. Nothing else mattered.

She soared with him as she had soared those many months ago in a felt-covered yurt upon the Crimean steppes. Her heart was so filled with love for this man who was her husband that the horror of Cicalazade Pasha faded away. Aunt Skye had been right! Valentina was one with Padraic. Together they were whole as neither had ever been alone.

"Padraic! Padraic! Padraic!" she sobbed his name, a sweet litany.

"Ahhhhh, lovey!" he groaned. "Ahhhhh, you have stolen my very soul! How I love you, Val! How I love you!" His passion burst within her, filling her with exquisite sweetness.

Throughout the night they loved each other, desperate for the other's kiss or for a caress. At last they fell into an exhausted slumber, their bodies entwined, content for the moment.

They awakened in the hour past dawn to find that it was snowing.

"Damnation!" Padraic grumbled as they sat in the Great Hall of Pearroc Royal breaking their fasts. "I had hoped to leave for Clearfields this morning."

His wife shook her head. "We must go first to court, my lord. I promised the queen that I should come directly to her upon my return and instead I hurried home so that we could be wed. Besides, you have said that Clearfields has been closed up forever. With your permission, I should like to retire your two elderly house servants and appoint Nan housekeeper. When the storm has stopped, she will have the loan of some maidservants from my mother and she can go to Clearfields to put the house in order. She can hire girls and young men from your village and train them."

"An excellent idea," approved Aidan. "By the time you have made your courtesy call upon the poor queen and returned, Clearfields will be ready to receive you. It pleases me to see you show such common sense, Valentina," her mother finished, smiling at her.

"I have run my own home before, Mama," Valentina reminded her. She turned to Padraic. "Is my plan all right with you, my lord?" she asked sweetly.

Lord Burke looked somewhat befuddled, much to his uncle's amusement. He nodded helplessly, and Conn could not refrain from laughing.

"Why," he teased his nephew, now his son-in-law, "are you so surprised to find yourself outflanked, my lad? Having grown up in this family, you should be aware of how the ladies handle matters—the most important matters being their poor, helpless husbands!"

"For shame, my lord," Aidan scolded him, but her eyes were filled with laughter.

" 'Tis true, Aunt," Padraic agreed, finally finding his tongue.

"Why, my lord husband," Valentina said, "surely you are not feeling unloved?"

Padraic's gaze locked with hers, and he smiled a slow, intimate smile. "Never unloved, madam," he assured her. "A trifle over-whelmed by your tactics, perhaps, but not unloved."

"What a pity," Valentina continued innocently, "that it is snowing, else we might ride, my lord."

Lord Burke bent low and whispered so that only she could hear him, "I would ride you, my hinny love. I can think of no better way to pass a snowy day than riding on your snow-white thighs."

Valentina laughed softly. "You are bold, my lord," she murmured.

"Come." He pulled her from the table and, hand in hand, they hurried from the hall.

"If we do not have a grandchild from those two before this year is ended," said Conn, chuckling, "it certainly won't be from lack of effort. He can scarcely keep his hands from her."

Aidan smiled at her husband. "Remember when we were first wed?" she reminded him. "You could scarcely keep your hands from me."

"Not only my hands, sweetheart," he teased her.

"Conn!" She was actually blushing.

"Aidan," Lord Bliss told his wife—"I am not so old that I have forgotten the most pleasant way to spend a snowy day." He caught her by the hand. "Come, wife! Why should our daughter and her new husband be the only ones to enjoy a delightful dalliance?"

"Conn! What if the children need us?" she protested.

"If I know our sons, sweetheart, and I do, Colin and Payton will spend their day sowing wild oats among the prettier of our housemaids. Jemmie will be in the kennels with the new litter of pups. Mistress Maggie will spend her time preening before her mirror and dreaming of the day we allow her to return to court. They do not need you, Aidan, but I do!" he declared passionately.

"Why, my lord," she said, dimpling at him across the table, "have I not always been your good and most obedient wife?"

"Not always." He laughed.

Aidan aimed a mock blow at her husband. "Villain! I have been the most perfect of wives to you," she declared.

"Then how can you consider denying me now?" he demanded of her with a mournful look.

Lady Bliss got up from the table and sat down on her husband's lap. "Why, my lord," she murmured seductively, "who said anything of denial?" Her quick fingers undid the laces at his neck and she bent to kiss the pulse in his throat.

Conn growled low. Wrapping his arms about his wife, he stood up, cradling her. "Madam, you toy with me! I intend making love to you with every bit of the vigor our new son-in-law possesses!"

Aidan smiled up at him from the sanctuary of his arms. "Why should you not play the bridegroom, Conn, my love?" she said softly. "For all of our lives together, you have made me feel like a bride." She brushed her lips over his, her soft gray eyes bright with love for him.

In a twinkling the Great Hall of Pearroc Royal was empty, the room's deep silence broken only by the sharp crackle of logs in the fireplace, the icy wind that blew about the house, and the soft brushing of snow against the windows as it fell, piling up on the stone sills.

A serving wench entered from the scullery to collect the dishes and goblets from the high board. Surprised, she looked about. The Great Hall was always the center of activity, particularly on stormy days, and she wondered where everyone had disappeared to on such a bleak morning, but then she shrugged, remembering herself and her place. It was not her business to question what the gentry did. She gathered up the plates, goblets, and cutlery, anxious to get to the kitchen where Cook, in an excellent mood, was passing out the leftover wedding marzipan to those in her favor. The serving wench had heard a rumor that Lady Burke's Nan was to be the new housekeeper at Clearfields and that Nelda had been appointed her ladyship's chief tiring woman. Some folks had all the luck, the serving girl told herself as she hurried from the hall and down the stone stairs into the warm kitchen.

Chapter Seventeen

PADRAIC BURKE GAVE IN to his wife's pleas. He suggested first that they go home to Clearfields and then, in the spring, when traveling would be easier, go up to court. But Valentina would have none of it.

"Spring will be too late!" she declared. When he asked her what she meant, Valentina looked puzzled and replied, "I cannot explain it, Padraic. 'Tis just a feeling. I must go now!"

"All right, hinny love, then we shall go now," he told her, for Valentina was not a spoilt creature who must always have her own way. It was a reasonable request.

Lord Burke's half brother, the Earl of Lynmouth, and his family, would be traveling south to their Devon home. They had come up for Christmas and stayed for Padraic and Valentina's wedding. The brothers decided to travel together.

The third of Lady de Marisco's sons, Lord Robert Southwood held the greatest and oldest title of any of them. He was a charming man with a youthful countenance despite the fact that he was entering his fortieth year. He had fathered eight children, the eldest three with his first wife, who had died giving birth to her third daughter in less than three years. The two elder girls, Elsbeth and Catherine, had married recently and were happily settled. The third daughter, Anne, sixteen, would be married in the summer.

The earl's five younger children were the offspring of his second marriage, a great love match. The lovely Countess of Lynmouth had been a poor orphan under the queen's protection when Robin Southwood spied her. Having met her, nothing would do but that he marry her, which he did, with the queen's blessing. Neither had ever regretted the hasty match, and many envied them their happiness. Their children were Geoffrey, age 13; John, age 11; Charles, age 8; Thomas, age 6; and Laura, age 3.

"We can travel in my coach," the earl said. " 'Tis larger and better-sprung than yours. The children can have yours."

"Thank you, no, brother," Lord Burke replied. "I've just had my coach refurbished, inside and out, and I do not intend having your sicky-fingered offspring destroying my new red velvet seats. The children may have your coach. You and Angel can ride with us."

Robin Southwood laughed. "I shall have to have my coach refurbished after those savages of mine complete the trip to London without supervision."

"Papa!" Pretty Anne Southwood wore a look of outrage. "You do not expect me to ride alone in the coach with my four brothers, do you?"

"Perhaps you would prefer riding atop the coach?" teased her father.

" 'Twould be far preferable, my lord, I do assure you!" Anne replied pertly.

The Countess of Lynmouth intervened on her stepdaughter's behalf. "I have arranged to borrow a small coach from your grandmother, Anne. If you do not object to sharing your carriage with your little sister and her nursemaid, then perhaps you would be happier riding with them. Be warned, my girl, that the coach is small."

"No, Mama, I should be far happier with Laura and Judith than surrounded by my rough, shouting brothers," Anne told her gratefully.

On the fourth of January the newlyweds, in the company of the Earl and Countess of Lynmouth and their family, departed for London. They were accompanied by eight baggage carts, many servants, extra horses, and the warm wishes of their family.

Watching them go, Lord Bliss remarked to his wife, "Well, my love, we have just the boys and Maggie to worry about now."

"I do not think we shall have to worry long about Maggie," Aidan said with a smile. "The boys, however, are a different matter. Jemmie, of course, is too young. Payton will ask Mistress de Bohun to be his wife, I have not a doubt, as soon as she is free of the queen's service.

"We must do something for them, Conn. Mistress de Bohun has no fortune to offer Payton, and he is a younger son with no rights of inheritance or property of his own. A wife was to have brought him that, but Payton's heart did not take practical considerations into account."

"Waterside is for sale," Conn told his wife. "The last of the family has just died. There's the manor house and just over a hundred acres. That should do nicely for Payton and his wife. But what of Colin? He seems to be content to play the field when his duty as my heir is to find a wife and settle down," Lord Bliss fretted.

"He is you all over again." Aidan laughed. "Do you not remember your days at court? 'The Handsomest Man at Court,' they called you, and all of the women made fools of themselves over you. The queen adored you, and you even bedded her cousin, Lettice Knollys, if memory serves me. Colin is only twenty-one. Let him sow his share of wild oats, my love, as you did."

"Yet Payton will just be twenty, and he has already found a wife," Lord Bliss complained.

"Payton is fortunate. We must not rush Colin. Remember what we wrought by fussing at Valentina to make a match because she was the eldest girl. Colin will find his love, but he will find her only in his own time.

"Soon there will be a new king and a new court. An unattached young gentleman will undoubtedly find high adventure there."

"Do you think Bess will die soon?" Lord Bliss asked his wife.

"I have not seen the queen in years, Conn, but the gossip is not promising, and you must remember that she is in her seventieth year. She has never enjoyed robust health, and her health has been taxed over and over again throughout her life. I don't think there's ever been a time when she was really free to rest. Almost everyone she loves is gone, so she must be very lonely. I do not see how she can last much longer," Aidan said sadly, for like her husband, she loved the queen, and they both owed her a great debt for having arranged their happy marriage.

Indeed, the queen was not well. She had a terrible cold and her joints were stiffer than they had ever been. For many years she had avoided mirrors, but now she often peered into her glass wondering at the old face looking back at her. She no longer recognized herself. In her mind, she was young. What had happened to her appearance? She had not enjoyed Christmas, which, besides May Day, was her favorite holiday. The winter had begun early and was particularly nasty.

Her ladies-in-waiting watched over her with increasing vigilance. The rest of the court waited for the first sure sign of her

impending death, eager for the new era to begin. The vultures
did not fool her, and her tolerance level, never very great, even
in her youth, disappeared entirely.

On her good days the queen wished the Lord would give her
ten more years, if for no other reason than simply to foil the
vultures who waited so ghoulishly for her death. She had heard
the rumor that James of Scotland had already packed his bags
in anticipation of her demise. How she wished she might keep
him penned up in his northern realm for another few years! Her
spirits were raised briefly when her astrologer, Dr. Dee, returned
from his travels to Poland. But Dr. Dee looked at Elizabeth, looked
at her courtiers, looked out of the palace windows at the pouring
rain, and told the queen bluntly to 'beware' of Whitehall with its
gloamings and its damps. Elizabeth, more restless than ever, gave
orders for the court to remove to Richmond Palace across the
river in Surrey.

Richmond was built on the ruins of the old palace of Sheen.
It had been most beloved by King Edward III, who had enlarged
it and added rooms of great magnificence. Richard II and his
wife, Anne of Bohemia, had used it as their summer residence,
but when the lovely Anne died of plague there, her grieving husband ordered Sheen destroyed. Henry V had repaired, restored,
and enlarged it. His son, Henry VI, and Margaret of Anjou had
held court at Sheen, as did Edward IV and his queen, Elizabeth
Woodville, who loved to hold tourneys on the palace green.

Elizabeth's grandfather, Henry VII, loved Sheen above all his
other residences, and his sons, Henry VIII and Arthur, were
raised there. In 1499 the palace was destroyed by fire at Christmas, but by 1510 it had been built again and christened Richmond in honor of the king's earldom of Richmond.

Although Elizabeth had stayed at Richmond often in her youth,
she had not used it very much during her reign, for her sister,
Mary, and Mary's husband, Philip of Spain, had spent their hon-
eymoon there.

The most modern of all the queen's residences, Richmond was
better insulated than the others and had the advantage of not
being directly on the river, but set within a great park filled with
ancient oaks and herds of deer. Elizabeth referred to Richmond
as her "warm winter box."

The date of the court's departure was set for January twenty-
first. Lord and Lady Burke and their party arrived in London on

the twelfth, having spent eight days traversing the winter roads from Worcester.

"Will you go on directly to Lynmouth?" Padraic asked his brother.

"No. Angel and I intend to go to Whitehall with you, to see the queen. The children, however, will go home tomorrow."

"You feel it, too," Valentina said to Robin.

Their eyes met, and he said, "Aye, Val, I do. I served her as her personal page my entire youth, and although it is twenty-five years since I was in her service, there are times when I awaken in the night, certain that I hear her calling me. There are times when I feel what she feels, though we are miles apart and our lives have taken different directions. Today I feel her sadness and her impatience. I think that if I do not take the time to see her now, I shall not see her again in this life."

Valentina nodded. "I served her only briefly, but I came to love her when most about her, save her dear old faithfuls, were complaining and carping about her. She is Gloriana, as my papa named her, but she is also an old lady. She needs the loving attention and care of people about her. It cannot be easy to always be on guard, Robin."

The Earl of Lynmouth smiled warmly at his new sister-in-law. "I wonder," he said, "if my brother knows the treasure he has in you, Val."

"Of course I know!" snapped Padraic.

"Hah!" Robin Southwood chuckled. "What you know right now, little brother, is that she is beautiful, has a delicious body, and kisses sweeter than wine. But the many years you have together will reveal to you Valentina's many other virtues. And even if you live to a very ripe old age, Padraic, you will never know all there is to know of her, for no man ever knows all there is to know of any woman."

"Why, Robin, my love, how very astute of you," said his wife, Angel.

"'Tis not my thought, Angel, but rather our mother's husband Adam who is very wise," responded the earl.

"And who has lived with Mother for over thirty years now, a singular accomplishment in itself." Padraic laughed. "All of her other five husbands combined did not live with her so long."

"I wonder if your mother would find such a remark amusing," pondered Valentina.

"I never knew Mother to look back but once in her life," said Padraic, "but although I know she regretted it, I also know that even knowing the outcome, she would follow the same path again. Aye, I think Mother would find my remark amusing, Val, for she above all people appreciates the humor in life."

The following day they made preparations to go to Whitehall, taking pains with their appearance so as to do honor to the queen. The men were garbed in black velvet, styled in the latest fashion. Their pantaloons came to the knee, and a buttoned slit replaced the old-fashioned codpiece. Below the knee the men each wore several pairs of silk stockings to protect their legs from the cold. The outer pair was embroidered with metallic clocks and other designs.

Robin's doublet was of silver and blue brocade, and his long jerkin was trimmed in fur. Padraic's doublet was of a gold-and-black design and the sleeves on his jerkin were slashed to show gold fabric beneath. Their stockings were cross-gartered, and each wore heelless thick-soled shoes of dark leather.

The somber tone of the gentlemen's garb allowed the ladies to shine like beautiful birds of paradise. The young countess wore a velvet gown of the same vibrant shade as her turquoise eyes. The overgown had a bodice trimmed with pearls and pink diamonds. Her underskirt was embroidered with silver thread and pink diamonds. Angel's jewelry was magnificent, and she wore rings set with gemstones on every finger. If any at court remembered Angel as a poor orphan and a royal ward, none said so.

The radiant Lady Burke wore a gown of crimson velvet, for Padraic loved seeing her in red better than any other color. Red made her skin seem like white rose petals. The red bodice and underskirt were trimmed with jet beads and black silk embroidery. Valentina wore rubies and diamonds about her neck and matching earbobs, a wedding present from her doting husband.

Although the weather was bitterly cold, they traveled the Thames to Whitehall Palace, for the damp winds of the past few days had abated. Wrapped snugly in their heavy velvet-and-fur capes, tucked beneath fur rugs, with heated bricks at their feet, they found the journey from Greenwood bearable.

Valentina had sent word to Lady Scrope that they were coming, and as they climbed the water stairs from the river, they were greeted by Mistress Honoria de Bohun, who had come to escort them to the queen.

"How are you, Honoria?" Valentina asked.

"I am well, Lady Barrows, thank you," the girl replied, curtsying, but there was a pinched and worried look about her.

"It is Lady Burke now, Honoria," Valentina said, with a smile at her husband.

"Then may I wish you happy, Lord and Lady Burke," the girl said, then she blurted out, "Is Payton with you?"

"No," said Valentina, studying her anxious face, "but why do you ask, Honoria?"

Honoria de Bohun looked desperate. Lowering her voice, she said, "Please help me, Lady Burke! The queen is dying! I don't care that her physicians say she will live another few years, *she is dying!* My parents have written me that since I have been unable to make a match here at court, they are planning to arrange a marriage for me with a wealthy old merchant. The man is without heirs and he desires to wed me. Lady Burke, I love Payton, and he has said he loves me! What shall I do?" Tears spilled from her soft blue eyes.

"God's foot!" swore Lord Burke.

Both his wife and his sister-in-law sent him quelling looks, to his brother's amusement.

"I know Payton means to ask you to wed him, Honoria," Valentina said quietly. "He did not feel he should approach your family until after your service to the queen was concluded."

"But that will be too late, my lady!" wailed Honoria. "My father speaks of formally announcing my betrothal to Master Tanner after Easter! I shall die if I am forced to wed that awful old man!"

"Then Payton must deal with your family before then," said Valentina decisively. "I shall write to my father tonight, Honoria, and tell him of this. He will certainly communicate with your father almost at once."

"Oh, thank you, Lady Burke!" Honoria cried. Remembering herself, she quickly escorted them into the queen's apartments.

Lady Scrope hurried forward to welcome them. "My dear Lady Barrows! Welcome! Welcome! Your coming is a blessing, my dear, for she has been very low of late. The news of your return has cheered her greatly, believe me."

"A moment, Lady Scrope," Valentina interrupted.

"Yes, my dear?"

"I am no longer Lady Barrows. I am now Lady Burke, having married my cousin Padraic on the first day of this year. How shall I broach this with Her Majesty?" The queen could be very difficult about the marriages of her ladies.

"You have been gone from her service for a year now, my dear," said Lady Scrope. "The news is more likely to please her than fret her. She loves you, and she wanted you to marry again. I think you may tell her without fearing her anger."

"Tell her what?" demanded Lady Howard, the Countess of Nottingham. She was queen's cousin and also her closest friend. Born Kate Carey, she possessed great loyalty and a kind heart.

"Lady Barrows is now Lady Burke, having married her cousin, my dear Catherine," said Lady Scrope. "I think Her Majesty will take the news well."

"Indeed, yes," Lady Howard agreed. "When news of your return came, the queen said she hoped you had chosen to wed one of your two suitors. She wants you to give England strong sons and daughters."

"We shall strive very hard to obey Her Majesty," replied Lord Burke with a grin as his wife looked mortified.

The queen's two ladies chuckled indulgently. Then Lady Howard espied the Earl of Lynmouth. "Robin? Robin Southwood? Is it indeed you?"

"Indeed, Lady Catherine, it is I. Will it cause her too much excitement that my wife and I have come to see her?"

"No, my lord, it will gladden her heart. Only yesterday she spoke about the fine Twelfth Night fêtes that first your father, and then later you, hosted. We all remember them fondly."

The door to the queen's privy chamber opened then and pretty Mistress Joanna Edwardes hurried toward them. "My lords and my ladies! The queen is anxiously awaiting you, and 'tis not right for you to keep the queen waiting!" Her young voice was tinged with disapproval.

"She sounds just like Willow," Lord Southwood said under his breath.

"All of Willow's daughters sound like their mother," Padraic whispered. "She trains them."

With the queen's two ladies and the young maid of honor in attendance, the two couples entered the queen's privy chamber.

"Oh, dear, Lady Scrope, she is dozing again. What shall I do?" fretted young Joanna.

"Wake her gently, child, as if you never suspected that she was asleep," Lady Scrope instructed the girl in a quiet voice.

Valentina looked hard at the sleeping queen. She had grown old in a year, and she did not look well. Lady Burke's heart went out to Elizabeth Tudor, and she determined that even if it displeased her new husband, she would remain with the queen through the winter months. Neither in the outer chamber nor in here did Valentina see any new faces excepting one, a young girl she assumed to be a new maid of honor. The queen did not, in her old age, like changes.

Joanna Edwardes succeeded in awakening the queen gently. As Elizabeth's dark gray eyes began to focus on the people about her, Lady Scrope whispered to Valentina, "She has suffered dreadful insomnia these past weeks, so we let her sleep when she can."

"Who is here?" demanded the queen, squinting at the group.

Lady Howard replied, "It is Valentina St. Michael, dear cousin, come home to England and returned to court to tell you of her adventures, just as she promised you she would."

"Valentina! Come here, my child," called Elizabeth Tudor. "The light is poor in this room, and my sight not what it once was."

Valentina stepped forward and knelt gracefully before the queen, her scarlet velvet skirts belling out around her. She took the queen's hands in hers and kissed them. "Dearest madam, I am so grateful to see you once again," she said fervently.

The queen's face softened, for she knew Valentina's words came from the young woman's heart and were not some artful flattery meant to influence her. "And have you made a choice between your two suitors, my child?" she asked.

"I arrived home on Christmas Day, dearest madam, and on the first day of January I wed my cousin, Lord Burke. He came to court with me to see Your Majesty. We left Pearroc Royal three days after our marriage, and arrived in London only yesterday. We hope you will give our marriage your blessing, dearest madam," Valentina said.

"So," the queen said, "you have married *that* woman's son, have you? Good! If that is what your heart dictated, then that is what you should have done. I am old now, Valentina, and I know only too well what I have given up to be queen of this fair land. I have given up all the things *that* woman has had in abundance. Love. Marriage. Children and grandchildren."

"But you would have had it no other way, madam," said the Earl of Lynmouth, stepping from the shadows to kiss Elizabeth's hand. "Confess it, madam, for 'tis so!"

"Robin Southwood! You have come to see me, too? What plot is this?" demanded the queen.

"No plot at all." Valentina laughed, then rose to her feet. "Robin and Angel were at Queen's Malvern with their children for Christmas. We decided to travel south together to London. It was a most enjoyable journey, dearest madam."

"Humph!" snorted the queen.

The earl grew serious. "Madam, you do not look well," he said bluntly. The others all held their breath at this dangerous honesty.

"I am _not_ well, Robin," the queen replied just as bluntly. "The doctors say I shall live another few years, but doctors say what they think you want to hear. In truth, they know little more than the rest of us mortals." She eyed him critically as if seeking some flaw, then said, "You, my lord, have changed little that I can see."

Robin Southwood smiled, answering, "I am in danger of a paunch, madam. My wife frets me for my love of good food and wine, but as for change, we all change. How kind that you remember the boy who once served you, when that boy faces a fortieth birthday this year. Why, madam, my two eldest daughters are married, and I shall, no doubt, be a grandfather before Christmas next."

"_That_ woman has more descendants than is decent," the queen said. "Seven living children and how many grandchildren, Robin?"

"Forty-two at last count, madam, and seventeen great-grandchildren, although most of them are my elder brother's, Ewan O'Flaherty's, get. Ewan has eight children, and the eldest three are sons who are now married."

"More Irish rebels to give England trouble! But I shall not be here to be bothered by them. Let the king handle it—if he can! Well," she continued, her gaze turning to Lord Burke, "here's one Irishman I've made into an Englishman."

Padraic took the queen's hand and kissed it. "Even had I been raised in Ireland, dear Majesty, I should have been your loyal liegeman," he declared.

"Hah! You are like your mother," the queen accused him. "_That_ woman, like all the Irish, has a silver tongue and a love for her own independence. So do you, my lord! When I took the ancient Burke lands from you and gave you Clearfields Priory in exchange, I saved you from a traitor's noose, Padraic Burke, even though you were an infant at the time. I remember telling your mother that I should make you a good Englishman, thereby assuring me of one less Irish rebel! Ha! Ha! Ha! I was right!"

"You did me a far greater kindness, madam," Lord Burke said with deft charm. "Had I not been raised here in England, I should never have found the greatest love of my life."

"You're a romantic like your mother as well," the queen remarked. "I never knew such a woman for love as Skye O'Malley!"

"Our mother," said Lord Southwood, "has lived an extraordinary life, madam."

"I remember when she was married to your father," the queen reminisced. "What fêtes and parties they gave! There were few who could match them for style and elegance. You would not remember, of course, being just a baby, but bless me, if I am not rambling like some ancient crone! Sit down, my dears, all of you. You, my dear Valentina, must tell me of your adventures."

As they seated themselves, Angel having greeted the queen and been received warmly, Valentina told Her Majesty, "My adventures, dearest madam, have consumed a full year of my life and cannot be told in a little space of time."

"Then, dear child," said the queen, "you must enter my service again, if only for the winter months. Then I may learn of all your wanderings. Your husband will not mind being at court, will you, my Lord Burke?"

"Madam, I am honored that you ask my wife and me to remain. It is many years since I was part of the court," Padraic replied, heeding Valentina's pleading look and being as gracious as he could. He wanted to go home to Clearfields, to have Val to himself this winter, but he understood her desire to remain and his heart went out to the sickly old queen. Yes, Elizabeth needed her friends.

"And with your kind permission, my wife and I shall stay the winter months with you also," announced Lord Southwood, surprising them all. "It is many years since I was at court."

Angel was stunned by her husband's statement. The queen saw it and hid her smile.

"I will enjoy having gay young people about me again," Elizabeth said brightly. "It is too much like a death watch at court now, and the strangers who come to court these days have neither manners nor elegance. You four will show them, my dears! Show them what my court should be like! Aye, you may stay, all of you, and welcome, say I!"

Elizabeth had appointed no new mistress of the maids since Valentina's departure, so Lady Burke was welcomed again to that position. The maids of honor were now a group of charming, well-behaved girls. They were Honoria de Bohun, at nineteen, the eldest; pretty Beth Stanley, now sixteen, who, to her family's annoyance, had insisted on remaining with the queen; Valentina's three cousins, Gabrielle and Joanna Edwardes, seventeen and thirteen, and Anne Blakeley, fifteen, who was also Padraic's niece. The one newcomer was Susanna Winters, thirteen, a distant cousin of both Sir Walter Ralegh and Kat Ashley. These girls, unlike many of their predecessors in the recent past, considered their chastity paramount.

January 21 dawned dark, a rainy and windy day that did not promise to improve. The queen wished to travel by the river and she would not change her mind. Her ladies all fussed at her about the filthy weather, for if she went by the river, then so must they. All envisioned catching colds, which, of course, would not excuse them from the queen's service, and that would make their illness twice as hard to bear.

"You are not dressed warmly enough, cousin," the Countess of Nottingham scolded Elizabeth. "You would do better to wear a gown with a high neckline rather than exposing your chest to the elements. You will catch your death!"

"I will have a fur-lined cape about me, Kate. God's foot, you fret too much. What is worse, you sound like an old lady!"

"I *am* an old lady, and so are you," the countess muttered under her breath, out of patience with the queen for the first time in her entire life.

Unfortunately, the maids of honor had overheard the Countess of Nottingham and they fell into a fit of the giggles.

"Maidens!" Valentina cautioned them sharply. "Have you finished your packing? Remember, there will be no returning until spring."

The Countess of Nottingham appealed to her husband, who was also a blood relation of the queen. "Madam," he told Elizabeth bluntly, "you are old and should have more care of yourself. If you would travel the river in this sharpest season, at least dress yourself warmly."

"Charles," the queen replied scathingly, "I may be an old woman, but you are an old fool, which I judge to be far worse! Leave me be. I shall dress as I please."

The Earl of Nottingham told his wife privately, "There is no contentment to a young mind in an old body, Kate, and that, I regret, is Bess's greatest problem."

The queen was irritated by her relations, and except that the earl insisted, she would not have had him on her barge. Indeed, she banned Lady Howard, Lady Scrope, and Lady Dudley to the barge that would follow hers, instructing Lady Burke and the youngest maids, Joanna Edwardes and Susanna Winters, to accompany her in her vessel. "I would have merry company," she said pointedly.

The weather was foul. Valentina was glad she had instructed her young charges to dress warmly. She herself wore several pairs of plain silk stockings topped by a pair of knitted ones and three flannel petticoats. Her silk chemise was lined in soft rabbit's fur, but even those garments and her fur-lined velvet cloak and hood could not keep the damp chill from insinuating itself into her bones. The maids, too, shivered in their capes. But if the queen felt the bitter cold, she did not betray herself. She sat easily beneath the fur rugs in her barge and never complained.

Valentina had begun, during the few days they spent at Whitehall, to tell the tale of her adventures. As their barge made its way along the winter-roughened river, Lady Burke asked, "Shall I continue with my story, dearest madam?"

"Not now, dear child. Instead, tell me of your family. How is your cousin, the Countess of BrocCairn? It is several years since I saw Velvet. They used to come to court in the summertime, but no more."

"I should think not, not with five little boys and Alex's daughter to look after." Valentina laughed. "Velvet adores her children. She is a wonderful mother. She leaves her brood only rarely. The boys are young yet, and her stepdaughter, Sybilla, will be thirteen on February first. Sibby is becoming quite a young lady, dearest madam, and is such a joy to Velvet, who has no other daughter."

"They will come south one day soon," the queen said quietly.

"Next summer for certain," Valentina agreed.

"I do not mean then," the queen replied. She turned to the earl. "I told you my seat has been the seat of kings and I will have no rascal to succeed me; *and* who should succeed me but a king?"

Valentina felt a prickle go down her spine. The queen had steadfastly refused to name her successor officially, though most assumed she would designate Scotland's King James VI, son of her mortal enemy, the late Mary, Queen of Scots. Elizabeth Tudor's aunt, Margaret Tudor, her father's sister, had been married to James IV of Scotland, who was the current James' great-grandfather. With both Tudor and Royal Stewart blood running in his veins he was the most logical choice to succeed Elizabeth, although there were several other claimants.

The queen always enjoyed being obtuse when referring to the succession. Was this her way of telling the Earl of Nottingham that her choice was James? Valentina dared not pursue the subject, which was a forbidden one, for to speak of the queen's death was considered treason.

Lord and Lady Burke were given a small apartment at Richmond Palace. It consisted of a small anteroom and a small bedchamber. Lord Burke's manservant Plumgut and Nelda were forced to sleep on pallets by the fire in the antechamber. Despite their cramped quarters, Richmond was a comfortable place. Lord and Lady Burke spent a great deal of time apart, however, since Valentina's duties kept her in almost continual attendance on the queen.

"I miss you, damn it!" Padraic murmured to his wife as they dressed for a royal reception being given the Venetian ambassador that evening. His wife was attired most fetchingly, he decided, in black silk stockings embroidered with gold clocks and held up by tight garters decorated with gold rosettes. Padraic cupped her bare breasts, nuzzled her neck.

"Padraic!" She sighed softly. "You will make us late."

"Not if you will cease your foolish protests, and I can get these damned buttons undone," he growled, nipping at her ear, while he fumbled with his buttoned slit.

"We've not made love in almost two weeks," he murmured, "and I've barely seen you since we got to Richmond. We are newly wed, Val! We should be spending our time in the pleasures of Venus, not dancing attendance upon the queen. Oh, I do understand, hinny love, but damn, sweetheart, I need you as much as Her Majesty does!"

Valentina understood his need for her. She needed him as well. Her glance went to the little clock on the mantel. If they hurried—could such a thing be hurried?—there might just be time. She was as eager for him as he was for her. She began to draw him across the room as she kissed him. As she felt the bed against the back of her thighs, she fell backward, wrapping her legs about his waist as she pulled him atop her. With a groan, slipped into her waiting body, delighted by her actions. "Ah, sweetheart!" he whispered hotly against her ear, catching the passionate rhythm she had initiated and plunging forward eagerly.

"Oh, Padraic!" she encouraged him onward. "Oh! 'Tis sweet!"

He bent over her, kissing her breasts with great ardor while he thrust harder and faster into her burning sheath.

The swiftness of their passion was sharp and sweet. Valentina felt herself quickly soaring upward as her husband's hardness pierced her to her soul. She stuffed her fingers into her mouth to keep from shrieking her pleasure, for their servants were close by, but she could not muffle her moan of sheer delight as her crisis overtook her and she shuddered with complete pleasure.

A little later, coming to herself, she stroked his dark head, which lay against her breasts. "I will ask the queen for some time with you," she told him, "for I have had no time for myself or for us since we arrived. I shall ask to be excused from serving her tonight, for this is not enough, Padraic! I must have more of you!"

"And I, you, hinny love," he said with a happy laugh. "Swear to me, my love, that whatever happens, we will go home this spring!"

"I swear!" she vowed. "But now get up off me, you great oaf! I must call Nelda, and get dressed, or we shall be late. If I displease Her Majesty, she may not give me the night to be with you, my darling lord."

In defiance of those who worried about her, the queen wore a gown suited to summer weather. It was of silver and white taffeta, trimmed with gold and encrusted with a vast quantity of bright gemstones. Her jewels were pearls, most of which were the size of pears, and she wore the imperial crown. She had resorted to an old trick. The ladies of the court had been instructed to wear dark colors so that the magnificence of the queen would appear even greater.

Valentina's gown was of gold and burgundy velvet, trimmed with small pearls, garnets, and jet beads. If the queen was the most magnificent woman there, then Lady Burke was the most radiant, for the queen had acceded to her request. After the gala Valentina would be free of her duties for two whole days.

The Venetian ambassador, Giovanni Scaramelli, was the guest of honor. He was deeply impressed by Elizabeth, who chided him in flawless Italian because the Venetians had waited until the forty-fifth year of her reign before sending her an ambassador. Did Venice not think England worthy? Or perhaps they had not thought a mere queen worthy? She apologized prettily for her Italian, saying that she had learned it in childhood but had not spoken it in years. She hoped he had understood her. The ambassador, of course, understood her perfectly, for her command of his language was perfect. She was, he reported in dispatches to his masters, everything her reputation proported, even though she was elderly and her hair "was of a light color never made by nature."

The excitement of the Venetian ambassador's visit over with, the court settled into a dull winter routine. The Countess of Nottingham had been battling a bad cold ever since their arrival at Richmond, and she begged Elizabeth's leave to retire from court and go home in order to recuperate from her illness, which seemed to be growing worse instead of better. The queen assented, but was much saddened at the departure of her favorite cousin.

For weeks the court was penned in because of foul weather. As February spent itself, the English spring began to show signs of its arrival. Walking in the garden for the first time all winter, the queen and Lady Scrope saw brightly colored yellow and purple crocuses dotting the lawns and small, early golden daffodils blooming in the shelter of the garden wall. Her Majesty was greatly cheered. The bitter winter was nearly over. She and Lady Scrope strolled together, joking, as the queen's page came running, bringing his mistress a dispatch just arrived. Elizabeth opened it eagerly, for it was from the Earl of Nottingham. The queen read it, screamed, and fell into a faint.

Lady Scrope knelt by Elizabeth while the young page ran to get help for the queen.

When Her Majesty had been put to bed, Lady Scrope and Valentina quickly read the message. Lady Howard was dead. "May God have mercy on her good soul," said Valentina.

"Amen," whispered Lady Scrope, sobbing. "Oh, dear Lady Burke, I do not know how she will survive this! Kate was with her almost her entire life."

The queen took to her bed for several days, refusing to see anyone except her ladies. The French ambassador, Monsieur Beaumont, was told that Her Majesty was in mourning.

In fact, Elizabeth Tudor was beside herself with grief, and as her melancholy deepened, her cold symptoms returned with a vengeance. She refused to take the medicines her physicians prescribed, shaking her head and pushing them away. She sat on cushions on the floor, oblivious to the cold floor or her surroundings. She neither ate nor changed her garments. A great swelling in her throat prevented speech, and persistent fever sapped her strength, as did her constant weeping.

The abscess in her throat broke. It nearly choked her, and the ordeal left her exhausted, but the doctors dried the abscess, and Elizabeth began to feel a little better.

For a few days it appeared as if the queen would recover. Some of her appetite returned and she was cajoled once more to walk in the garden, one of the few things she still enjoyed. But as soon as she appeared to be recovered, Elizabeth Tudor fell once again into a state of deep sadness.

"Dearest madam, is there some secret cause for your grief? Something we might assuage?" Valentina asked the queen who had again taken to sitting on cushions on the floor of her privy chamber.

Elizabeth looked at the young woman for a long while. Finally, with a deep, mournful sigh, she said, "Nay, my child, there is nothing in this world worthy of troubling me now." She grew silent again and appeared to go into a sort of trance, a single finger in her mouth.

The queen's ladies turned away, tears in their eyes. No one but a fool could doubt that the end was near. Word came from London that the plague had broken out in the city and the suburbs. It was much too early for plague. Such an early onset of plague portended a worse epidemic than had been seen in years.

"Our presence here does no good," the Earl of Lymnouth finally said to his cousins. "The queen has forgotten that we are here. I think it best that Angel and I go home to Devon. With plague raging nearby, it is dangerous for us to stay. Do not risk yourselves once you are no longer needed, I beg you."

"I must stay until the end," Valentina said firmly.

"Of course," replied Robert Southwood, as though he had expected her to say just that. "It is your duty, Val, and like all the women of our family, you know your duty well."

The Earl of Nottingham arrived in his mourning garb to try to cheer the queen, but when she saw him, she burst into piteous tears.

"She will not eat or take her medicine or go to bed," Robert Cecil told the earl.

Charles Howard knelt before the queen, who was sitting on her cushions on the floor. Kissing his cousin's still beautiful but feverish hands, he begged her to take some broth.

"Oh, Charles, do I not know my own constitution?" she said irritably. "I am not in such peril as you all imagine me to be."

"Nonetheless, Bess, you must take some nourishment," he said gently. "Your ladies and poor little Pygmy have not your stamina. You are frightening them to death with your melancholy. Kate would be most furious with you, and you know it. You are their queen and you must be as courageous now as you have ever been!"

Elizabeth Tudor looked directly at her cousin and said passionately, "All my life I have been forced to be brave, Charles, and I have been brave! From the moment of my birth I needed to be brave, for I had dared to disappoint Great Harry himself by being born a mere female instead of his greatly desired son. My gender is what caused my poor mother's death when I was not even three, but I was brave then, too! Even as a child I realized the danger that surrounded me. I saw poor Queen Jane die in childbed giving my father his son. Their servants were so anxious for poor Edward's safety that they neglected the queen, thereby causing her death. I saw Anne of Cleves divorced for not being as young and as pretty as Holbein had painted her. I saw poor Kat Howard beheaded on Tower Green even as my mother was, and then Queen Catherine Parr almost fell victim to the politics of my father's court, *and I was brave,* Charles! Brave when Tom Seymour tried to seduce me in order to gain my throne. He almost broke Catherine Parr's heart, for he was the one man she loved. Brave when those about my sister Mary would have had me killed.

"Then I became England's queen. But even then I was not safe! I could not marry the only man I ever loved, and I realized that to marry at all would only endanger me and my position— *yet I was brave,* Charles!

"I am tied, my lord! I am tied with a chain of iron about my neck, and so I have been from the moment of my birth. I am tied, I am tied, and nothing can alter the case with me now!"

Her words pained him, for he knew the truth of them, and he realized for the first time in his life how terribly lonely his cousin, Elizabeth Tudor, had always been. The Earl of Nottingham blinked back tears. "Will you not take just a little beef broth, Bess?" he pleaded with her.

She saw his distress and all her queenly instincts surfaced. She patted his face. "Very well, Charles, I shall take a little broth," she told him.

As Robert Cecil sighed with relief, Lady Burke hurried to the sideboard and ladled some steaming soup into a small porcelain bowl that she set within a silver filigreed holder. Joanna Edwardes brought Valentina a spoon and draped a linen napkin over her cousin's arm.

Valentina brought the soup to Lord Howard, handing him the bowl in its holder and the spoon. Gently she tucked the napkin beneath the queen's chin, receiving a faint smile from her mistress in return.

Outside Richmond Palace quiet groups of people from the nearby villages had gathered to watch the comings and goings of the great and the near-great. There had been no official mention of the queen's condition, yet the people knew in some mysterious way that all was not well with the queen who had reigned over them for so long. Elizabeth Tudor was dear to them, and they showed their concern by gathering outside her home to wait, to watch, and to pray.

"There!" the queen said. "I have finished your damned broth, Charles. Now, leave me be!"

"You must get some rest," the earl chided her. "You need to go to your bed, Bess. Cecil tells me you have not slept in your bed for many days now."

"If you saw in your bed that which I see in mine, Charles, you would not persuade me to go there," Elizabeth answered him firmly.

"Does Your Majesty see spirits?" Robert Cecil dared to ask her. The queen glowered at him and refused to be baited.

"My lord," hissed Lady Scrope, "you go too far, I think!"

"Please, Bess, seek your bed," Charles Howard pleaded. "After a good night's sleep everything will look so much better."

"Aye," agreed Robert Cecil. "Your Majesty must go to bed if for no other reason than to content your people who worry over you."

"Little man, little man—if your father had lived, ye durst not have said so much! But ye know I must die and that makes ye so presumptuous. The word *must* is not one to be used to Princes!" the queen told poor Cecil scathingly.

Robert Cecil withered beneath the royal rebuke. He said nothing more.

Eventually, Lord Howard prevailed upon his cousin and Elizabeth agreed to seek her bed. Her ladies took her soiled garments from her and gently bathed her emaciated and withered body, putting a fresh white silk night rail on her that smelled of fragrant lavender. The queen's thinning hair, once gloriously red, now lank and dull white, was brushed, braided, and tied with a pink ribbon, which seemed to amuse Elizabeth. Finally, wrapped in a crimson velvet quilted gown, she was helped to her bed. But she refused to lie back and rest.

Her voice failed her once again and she communicated with them by means of signs. She would eat no more, taking only occasional sips of wine. Then, for four days, she sat on her bed surrounded by pillows, staring straight ahead, saying nothing at all and refusing food and drink. Her body was alternately hot and racked by cold sweat. Her finger went into her mouth again.

She was attended by only four of her ladies and the two eldest maids of honor, for Lady Burke had advised Lady Scrope that the younger girls should be spared the queen's travail. Lady Scrope concurred.

"We do not need hysterical, fainting misses about us during this crisis. Dare we send the others home?" she asked Valentina.

"I think not," Valentina replied. "It would be considered presumptuous of us to do so. And I believe the girls should all be here to attend the final rites for the queen. Her Majesty would not want her final pomp to be lacking in spirit, would she?"

Lady Scrope smiled. "You are so young, my dear, to be so wise. She has never been one for the ladies. You touched her as no other did. I will tell you now, for she cannot scold me for my loose tongue, that she prayed daily for your safe return, often telling me when we were in private that she wondered if you were safe and when you would return. The queen had a special feeling for you from the beginning because she was so deeply fond of your father, and she matched your parents. She came to love you for yourself, however."

Lady Scrope paused for a moment and patted Valentina's hand. "You have served her well, my dear. You have served her with kindness in a time when she was not the easiest of mistresses. You know we have had few new people about us, for as she has grown older the queen has not liked change, yet you fit yourself into our little group with great ease despite your youth and our age. You have been a ray of bright sunlight in our dark winter, Lady Burke. Thank you."

"You must not thank me for doing my duty, Lady Scrope," Valentina protested. "I have always wanted to serve the queen, and had my mother not been so insistent on a marriage for me I should have been to court long since. No, no, Lady Scrope! Do not thank me for doing a duty that has been a joy for me. I love the queen even as I love my mother and my husband's mother!"

A day later, a second abscess burst within the queen's throat. Once again her speech was restored. She asked for a little bit of meat broth. The doctors came to examine her, shaking their heads and making mournful faces. One of the physicians dared to inquire, "How spend you your time in so much silence, Your Majesty?"

The queen fixed the speaker with an irritated stare and said, "I meditate."

The doctors departed. The queen's ladies changed her bed and garments again, and helped her back into her great wooden, ornate bed.

The queen lay back on her satin-covered pillows, beneath her embroidered linen sheets and down coverlet. Gathering her ladies about her, she told them with her characteristic bluntness, "I wish not to live any longer, but desire to die."

The council was sent for, for it now became imperative that the queen name her successor. They gathered about her bedside. The men were shocked by her appearance, having never seen her in her bedchamber or without all the trappings of her great office. Suddenly Elizabeth was just an ordinary old woman.

The queen's dark eyes were scornful as she looked them over, for she could easily read their thoughts. She had always read their thoughts. The council shuffled uncomfortably as she glared at them, for even on the brink of death Elizabeth Tudor was stronger than everyone about her.

Robert Cecil spoke. "We realized that Your Majesty's throat is greatly troubling her, and we would not intrude, but that we very much wish to remain Your Majesty's loyal servants and do only Your Majesty's bidding in all things. I would name all the claimants to Your Majesty's throne, and if you would just make some sign to us—perhaps hold up a finger—when we name your choice, then it shall be done as Your Majesty instructs us."

The queen made a small impatient noise of irritation and Robert Cecil quickly began naming the legitimate claimants to the English throne. At the name of Arabella Stuart, who was the granddaughter of the queen's great rival, Bess of Hardwick, the Countess Shrewsberry, Elizabeth Tudor made a disapproving face.

Cecil continued. "Do you then remain in your former resolution to have the king of Scotland, James Stewart, for your heir?"

For a moment everyone in the room ceased breathing. Understanding that this was her last and perhaps her most important public moment, Elizabeth Tudor, with much effort, clasped her hands around her sweating forehead in imitation of a kingly crown and rasped a single word. *"Aye!"* Then she closed her eyes and fell into the first sleep she had slept in days.

The council stumbled away from the queen's bed, more exhausted than the dying old queen herself. It was done! England was to have a king again! In a few days, James of Scotland would reign, uniting the two ancient kingdoms that had so long warred with each other.

"See that everything is prepared for the inevitable," Robert Cecil told his secretary as they all filed from the room. "And no one is to leave the palace without my written permission. Where is Sir Robert Carey?"

"Here, Cecil!" The queen's nephew stepped toward Cecil.

"You are prepared to ride for Scotland, sir?"

"Aye, my lord. I have horses posted all along the route for me," replied Carey.

The door closed behind the men, and once again the queen's bedchamber was silent but for the gentle activity of her women and the crackle of the fire. Outside it had begun to rain and the wind was beginning to rise.

"So it is settled at last," Lady Scrope said in a low voice.

"Was there ever any doubt?" replied Lady Dudley.

"I wonder what King James's court will be like?" Lady Southwell ventured.

"What does it matter?" Lady Scrope said. "We will not be here. We are the old regime. Off with the old and on with the new."

"Perhaps Lady Burke will visit the new court," Lady Dudley said. "She is young. If I remember correctly, she has a sister-in-law who is wed to the Earl of BrocCairn, a cousin of King James."

"Aye," Valentina told her, "my husband's little sister, Velvet Gordon. I do not know, however, if Padraic and I will join the new court. We are country people by preference and, being newly married, wish to have a family."

"Coming to court is a great expense," noted Lady Southwell.

At a knock on the door, Honoria de Bohun opened it to reveal the archbishop of Canterbury, John Whitgift, and a group of his priests. Entering the room, the five men knelt about the queen's bed and began to pray.

The queen awoke and whispered angrily at them. "Be gone, all of you! I am no atheist, and I know full well ye be but hedge priests! Get you gone from my chamber!"

The clerics scuttled from the room. Valentina held a cup of warmed wine and herbs to the queen's lips to ease the soreness in her throat. The queen swallowed some of the mixture with difficulty, then lay back. Valentina turned away, but the queen's bony fingers clutched at her sleeve and she turned back again, leaning down to catch the queen's whispered words.

"Do not forget me, my child," Elizabeth said. "Go home when this is done, and name your eldest daughter for me."

"I will, dearest madam," Valentina replied hoarsely, unable to restrain her tears now, and kissing the queen's hand.

Elizabeth Tudor weakly squeezed Valentina's fingers. She said, "Tell *that* woman I shall be waiting for her." Then she closed her eyes and slept again.

When the clock struck six o'clock that evening, Elizabeth awoke again and weakly asked that John Whitgift be sent for, as she wished to pray with him. He came with his chaplains and knelt by her side. The queen lay on her back, one hand on the bed, the other outside it. The archbishop took the frail hand, and by the opening and closing of her eyes, the queen answered his questions regarding her beliefs.

Then John Whitgift told her, "You have been a great and glorious queen, Elizabeth Tudor, but now you have reached the hour of your death and must yield an account of your stewardship to the greater King of Kings."

A faint smile touched the queen's lips, then she closed her eyes. After a moment the archbishop attempted to rise, thinking the queen had gone to sleep, but Elizabeth's eyes flew open and she gestured to him to continue his prayers. She clutched his fingers with hers in the same gesture her father had made to Archbishop Cranmer so many years before.

"O most heavenly Father and God of all mercy," prayed John Whitgift, "we most humbly beseech Thee to behold Thy servant our queen with the eyes of pity and compassion. Give unto her the comfort of Thy Holy Spirit. . . . O Lord punish her not for her offenses, neither punish us in her. . . ." The archbishop continued with his intercessions on behalf of Elizabeth Tudor until at last, several hours later, she fell into a deep sleep. The archbishop was helped to his feet, and he and his chaplains walked slowly from the room. Dr. Parry, who was Elizabeth's favorite chaplain, remained behind to watch over the queen.

There was nothing to do but wait. Honoria de Bohun and Gabrielle Edwardes sat together on a settle by the fireplace, their young heads nodding with exhaustion. Lady Southwell was quite openly asleep in a chair, her head to one side, snoring. Lady Dudley and Lady Scrope were praying while Lady Burke sat next to the queen's bed, Dr. Parry opposite her.

The rain and the wind stopped as midnight came and March 23 became March 24. Outside Richmond Palace there was an unearthly quiet that extended as far as London, Elizabeth's own city, itself. The candles burned low and soon only firelight lit the great chamber. Exhaustion had claimed them all, and they slept.

The clock striking three awakened Valentina, with a start, and turning she glanced at the queen with a certainty that was more instinct that anything else. Taking the little mirror that hung from a gold chain about her waist, she held it over the queen's face. The mirror remained pristine clear.

With tears sliding down her face, Lady Burke rose and walked across the chamber to awaken Lady Scrope. "The queen is dead," she whispered to that good lady. "Just, I think, for I only fell asleep briefly."

"We all did," Lady Scrope said gently. "How like the queen to slip away when we weren't looking. Her final little jest on us." Arising, she went to examine her mistress herself. Finally, with a deep sigh, she said, "Aye. Bess is gone." She lifted the queen's still-warm hand and removed from the longest finger a blue sapphire ring that had been given to Elizabeth by the Earl of Essex. This would be proof to James Stewart that his cousin was truly dead. Alive, Elizabeth would never have been parted from this most precious love token.

She hurried to the door of the chamber with the ring and, opening it, called softly for her brother, Sir Robert Carey, to be brought. Silently she handed him the ring, then the weeping pair hugged each other.

"I'll tell Cecil," Sir Robert said, "and then I'm for Scotland. The queen is dead. Long live the king!" He turned and departed, while behind him, in the queen's bedchamber, rose the sounds of bitter weeping.

Valentina could not remember ever having been so tired, but she could not yet leave the royal service. She and the others accompanied the queen's body by water to Whitehall, where it was watched over by Elizabeth's ladies as it remained in state for five weeks.

April 28 dawned fair. The sky was a bright, cloudless blue from which the sun shone on the sparkling River Thames. The trees were green with new growth and the flowers were all in bloom as Elizabeth Tudor made her last progress through her city of London, the city that had loved her so well and been so unflaggingly loyal.

All the trappings of royal mourning had been prepared to honor Elizabeth Tudor as she passed through the streets of the city to her final resting place in Westminster Abbey, next to her unfortunate sister, Mary. The streets were so crowded that it became difficult for the royal procession to make its way. People hung from windows, from rooftops, even from house gutters.

Elizabeth's effigy was set on top of her coffin, fully robed and crowned, the ball and scepter of her office in her hands. The head of the effigy had been painted by Master Maximilian Colte and was so lifelike that seeing it caused general weeping and sighing among the citizens of London, most of whom could remember no ruler other than Elizabeth Tudor. She had reigned over England for 44 years and 127 days, longer than any English ruler since Edward III.

Valentina, dressed in deepest mourning, her final act of homage to the queen, managed to obtain from a balladmonger a parchment on which was written a poem lamenting the queen's passing. She read it once and showed it to Padraic before tucking it into her pocket to take home.

> *She rul'd this nation by herself*
> *And was beholden to no man,*
> *O she bore the sway and of all affairs*
> *And yet she was but a woman.*

Valentina laughed aloud at the last line, and Padraic said, chuckling, "No one having a personal acquaintance with Elizabeth Tudor could dismiss her with the epitaph 'And yet she was but a woman'! Still, it was meant to be complimentary, and I know the queen would have appreciated it."

"Perhaps," Valentina considered with a small smile. Then she tucked her hand in her husband's arm and announced, "I am ready to go home, my lord."

"To Clearfields, my hinny love? And what shall we do there once we have arrived?" he teased lovingly, smiling. Their eyes reflected their love of each other.

"I do not know what you will do, my lord," Valentina told him matter-of-factly, "but *I* intend preparing for the arrival of our child."

"Our *child?*" He was absolutely stunned. "Our *child?*" he repeated.

"My lord, is that not what you want?" she demanded, a mischievous smile on her pretty lips.

"You are with child?" His face was a picture of perfect delight.

"Aye," she said calmly, her hand smoothing her gown over her flat belly. "I am with child, Padraic."

"When?" His heart soared with happiness.

"November, midmonth probably," she said softly.

"*A son!*" he crowed, as if he alone were responsible for this wonderful turn of events.

"*A daughter,* my lord," she corrected him. "*And her name shall be Elizabeth!*"

EPILOGUE

Queen's Malvern

CHRISTMAS 1605

ON CHRISTMAS DAY, 1605, there was an enormous gathering in the family chapel of Queen's Malvern, the home of Lord and Lady de Marisco, the Earl and Countess of Lundy. On this day, Lord and Lady Burke's second child and first son was to be christened.

Attending the gathering were the proud father's three older brothers: Ewan O'Flaherty, the Master of Ballyhennessey, who had traveled from Ireland with his wife across a winter sea to attend the event; Captain Murrough O'Flaherty; and Robert Southwood, the Earl of Lynmouth. Two of Lord Burke's three sisters, along with their respective mates, were there: Lady Willow Edwardes, the Countess of Alcester, and Deirdre Blakeley, Lady Blackthorn. There was also a huge variety of assorted nieces and nephews. Lord Burke's youngest sister, Velvet, the Countess of BrocCairn, was still in Scotland. She and her husband and family would finally be coming south in the spring to join King James's court.

On his maternal side, the guest of honor was represented by two of his mother Valentina's three sisters and their husbands; and Valentina's three brothers and their wives. Payton's wife, the Lady Honoria, was due to present Payton with a child in the early spring. Present, too, was the guest of honor's elder sister, Elizabeth. It was a most festive celebration that had been planned in his honor, and the baby, at six weeks, was alert enough to look about him a bit, even if he did sleep a great deal.

"He looks *exactly* like Padraic did at that age," Skye said, her beautiful Kerry-blue eyes misty. "He is just the sweetest little baby!"

"You only say that because you are a most doting grandmother," said Valentina to her aunt, cradling her son discreetly to her breast. "He is actually a shamelessly greedy, gluttonous little piglet, aren't you, my angel?" she cooed at him as he nursed vigorously at her breast.

"What do you think of your baby brother, Bess?" demanded Lord de Marisco, who was holding his two-year-old granddaughter in his arms.

Elizabeth Burke stared with violet-blue eyes at this intruder who had taken all the attention away from her and ruined her life. "Hate him, Grandy! Bess wants him go 'way!"

"Bess, my sweeting, you must not say such wicked things about your baby brother," chided her other grandmother, Lady Bliss. "You and your brother must love each other, for that is the first rule of a family, to love one another."

Elizabeth Burke stuck out her lower lip in a distinct pout. All this fuss over a creature who cried and smelled funny. She didn't understand it.

"Perhaps it would help if I took her home to Pearroc Royal with me after the festivities," Aidan suggested. "Just for a little while, to help her come to terms with the baby."

"No, thank you, Mama," Valentina replied. "You will only spoil her even more than Padraic has already spoiled her, and then what will I do? No! She must learn to accept her brother with good grace, and as quickly as possible, for with God's blessing this baby will be only the first of many siblings for Bess."

"You were just as hostile to the twins when they were babies," said Conn, laughing, to his eldest child's mortification.

"I most certainly was not," Valentina declared vehemently. "I couldn't have been!"

"I distinctly remember a summer's day when you took Anne and Colin from their cradles where they had been set on the lawns and tucked them into Leoma's willow laundry basket. You set them adrift on the estate lake," her father replied, laughing all the harder at his daughter's horrified look.

"Papa! I didn't! *Did I?*" Valentina cried.

"You did, my daughter, but fortunately the basket was watertight. The twins were sleeping soundly, and we caught you before the basket had drifted more than ten feet from shore," her father told her. "It was the only time your mother ever spanked you, Valentina. My wee granddaughter's nose is only slightly out of joint, isn't it, Bessie?" Conn teased the little girl, taking her from Adam and tickling her until she was overcome with giggles.

"It is time!" Lady de Marisco announced to her family. They all trooped into the chapel, which was not really large enough to hold them all, so they spilled out into the hallway.

Padraic and Valentina's son, with Payton and Honoria St. Michael standing as his godparents, was christened Adam Niall Burke.

"For both of my fathers," Padraic had told his mother and step-father. "For the father who gave me life, but whom I never knew. And for the father who raised me and loved me—and whom I love most dearly."

Adam de Marisco's smoky-blue eyes filled with tears at Pad-raic's tribute. I am becoming a sentimental old fool, he scolded himself. Both his stepdaughter, Willow, and his daughter, Velvet, had named sons after him, but Padraic and Valentina's decision to give their first son his name was a different kind of honor. It was almost as if his own family line was continuing. He was moved more than he could express.

Adam Burke, having been properly baptized and duly admired, was removed to the nursery while a great party was conducted in his honor in the hall below him.

The Great Hall at Queen's Malvern was decorated for the twelve days of Christmas with pine, laurel, holly, and bay leaves. Great beeswax candles burned everywhere, and in the main fire-place of the hall were gigantic Yule logs. At the high board, and at the tables just below it, Skye and Adam, Conn and Aidan, and all of their children watched contentedly as their descendants scampered happily about the hall. A fine feast was served, and many cups of wine were drunk to the baby's good health.

"Well, little girl," Adam de Marisco said affectionately to his wife, who had been unusually quiet. "Forty-five grandchildren. So we have but five to go, eh?"

"*Forty-six* grandchildren, Adam," Skye said softly.

"I have not forgotten," he replied, "but our little princess is the one we may never talk about."

"We are going to have to talk about her sooner than later, my lord," Skye informed her husband. "I received a message this very day from India. A servant of the emperor himself brought it. Even now, the messenger warms himself in our kitchen."

Adam looked puzzled. "The birthday pearl?" he said. "It is that time of year again, is it not, my love? Has the birthday pearl arrived? She is fifteen now, is she not?"

"Aye," Skye said. "She is fifteen, *and* she will be in London by the end of January, Adam."

"*What?*" Lord de Marisco nearly choked on his wine.

"The granddaughter we have never been able to acknowledge, this child whose existence has always been a secret from our whole family, this little princess of ours will be in London by the end of next month," Skye repeated. "Her father has sent her to live with us, Adam. She is to remain in England."

"But *why*? Why now, after all these years?" Adam asked his wife, forcing his voice lower in case those about them were curious enough to listen in.

"That, Adam, you may read for yourself in the emperor's letter. As you will see, he really had no other choice. Now we must prepare ourselves and prepare our family to accept the existence of this child and welcome her into our family—a family that will find itself in an uproar over her very existence. She is, after all, Velvet's firstborn. And she is our granddaughter." Skye put her hand on her husband's arm, and when she looked into his face, he saw that her eyes were filled with tears. "We cannot turn Jasmine away, my darling! We simply cannot! She has no one but us, poor child."

Lord de Marisco began to laugh softly. "Madam," he said to his wife, "I thank God every day of my life that you are mine! I might have been old years ago, but living with you has always been one adventure after another."

"Then you will welcome her?" Skye was relieved.

"Aye, little girl, I will most certainly welcome her! Surely you did not think I would not? She is my granddaughter, my own flesh and blood, my first grandchild," Adam de Marisco said. Then his full laughter burst forth, rumbling up from his big chest to fill the hall.

"What, I should like to inquire, is so amusing?" Willow Edwardes demanded of her parents. She had always hoped that age would finally mellow them, that they would learn to contain their exuberance and curb their penchant for attracting difficulties. In this hope she was doomed to disappointment.

Lord de Marisco gasped, then said, "Your mother and I were discussing our forty-sixth grandchild, Willow, my dear."

The others stopped talking and listened to the conversation taking place between Adam and Willow.

"Your *forty-sixth* grandchild, Papa? There are but forty-*five*, including, of course, Alex's daughter, Sybilla." Willow glared suspiciously around the hall at all of her female relations, but each shook her head in denial. "When is this forty-sixth due, Papa?"

"A great deal sooner than you can imagine, Willow, my dear," Lord de Marisco murmured, then burst into fresh laughter.

Skye began laughing, too, and Willow looked askance at her

mother and stepfather. Might they be drunk? If there was a jest, she did not understand it. Her stepfather was talking nonsense. Was Adam becoming dotty in his old age? No, not Adam! which made the mystery even greater, and certainly more intriguing.

"Papa," she said as patiently as she could, "I do not comprehend your meaning."

"You will very shortly, Willow, my dear," Lord de Marisco told her, laughing. "Indeed, very shortly, you will all understand." Then catching his wife's eye, Adam de Marisco began to chuckle once again.

Author's Note

Lost Love Found is the fifth book in the O'Malley Saga. I hope that those of you who have followed the series faithfully will forgive me my little joke in the epilogue. Of course there will be another book in this series. If you are a fan of the O'Malley family, I suggest you spend some time rereading the books in the series in preparation for Book 6 which should, God willing, be coming to you in 1991. For those of you who are new readers, and have chosen to read Lost Love Found at random, the O'Malley Saga books are as follows:

Book 1   Skye O'Malley
Book 2   All the Sweet Tomorrows
Book 3   A Love for All Time
Book 4   This Heart of Mine
Book 5   Lost Love Found

If you have not read the previous O'Malley books, I hope you have enjoyed this one enough that you will want to read the others.

For those of you who love history as much as I do, I wanted you to know that Elizabeth Tudor's death is portrayed here as accurately as I could describe it. In fact as I wrote it, I had several histories open on my desk from which I drew my account of her last days. Many of the words spoken by her real contemporaries (as opposed to my fictitious characters) are given in this novel exactly as history has recorded their words.*

As always readers, new and old, are always welcome to write to me at P.O. Box 765, Southold, New York 11971. You must allow us plenty of time to respond, however, because although my secretary, Donna Tumolo, is Supersecretary, she is still one very overworked lady. George, Tom, Donna, Checquers and Deuteronomy, Nicholas the Cockatiel, and I send you our very best. Good reading to you all!

* I would also mention that Esther Kira was indeed stoned to death in the Istanbul Currency riots of 1602.